JOSHUA: THE ODYSSEY OF AN ORDINARY MAN

Theckedath M. Mathew, M.D.

Printed in the U.S.A.

For information address:
Odyssey Press, Inc.
P.O. Box 741623
Dallas, TX 75374

Library of Congress Cataloging-in-Publication Data
Theckedath M. Mathew, M.D.

Joshua: The Odyssey of an Ordinary Man/ by Theckedath M. Mathew, M.D.

Library of Congress Catalog Card Number: 2012955661

p. cm.

ISBN 978-0-9887130-0-0

First Edition

10 9 8 7 6 5 4 3 2

Visit our Website at:
http://www.joshuatheodyssey.com

Book design by Theckedath M. Mathew, M.D.

More Praise for *Joshua: The Odyssey of an Ordinary Man*

Finalist for ForeWord First' Winter 2013 competition include *Joshua: The Odyssey of an Ordinary Man*, by Dr. Theckedath Mathew. The award contest recognizes the brightest self-published and independently published works of debut fiction.

Five Star Reviews on Amazon:

"In his historical novel, *Joshua: The Odyssey of an Ordinary Man*, Dr. Theckedath Mathew, M.D. writes like a seasoned writer. Characters are carefully drawn, pulling the reader in and not letting them go until the final page is turned. This is one read you don't want to miss."

J Hamilton

"Whether you are Christian or not, this historical journey will captivate your soul with intense details and wonderful narration. I would recommend this book to any reader wishing to learn and expand their knowledge of one of the greatest journeys in history. This novel truly is a great piece of literature to add to your collection."

B. Allison

"A must have in your personal library if you like historical or biblical novels. This is a richly detailed story of a young man as he discovers life among philosophers, peasants, and many people from different walks of life. The writer pays very vivid attention to detail and as a reader, you become very engrossed in the everyday life of the characters. The main character, Joshua, stands up for women's rights in a time when women were stoned to death for "crimes" against men. I highly recommend this book to book clubs looking for a book that is sure to please all readers and engage in conversation about the book."

Kathy2526

"If you want to become absorbed in a brilliantly written historical novel set in first Century Nazareth, you should pick up a copy of the book *Joshua: The Odyssey of an Ordinary Man*. It is an account of a few years in the life of an adolescent boy called Joshua. The novel opens up the life of Jesus during the years when there is no mention of him in the New Testament.

Joshua: The Odyssey of an Ordinary Man is a unique story. It is certain to be interesting to eaders. The author's viewpoint is skillfully presented in a way that will challenge thinking of anyone who reads the work."

Mona Moody

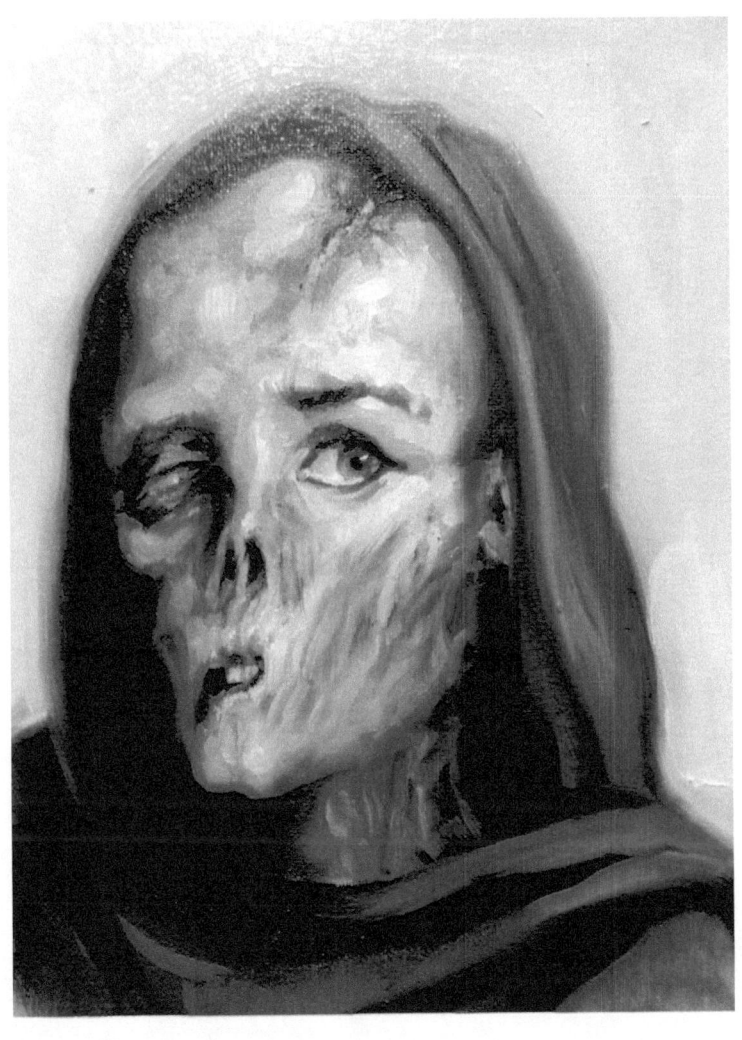

This book is dedicated to the many millions of women worldwide who are cut, mutilated, stoned, burned, and buried alive in the name of Gods and Prophets.

Acknowledgements

I gratefully acknowledge the hard, diligent work by Ms. Kathy Saunier in preparation of this manuscript and Mr. Suresh Kumar for the illustrations. I am indebted to Ms. Karen Venable, my editor and publicist, for her most impeccable and tireless efforts that led to the publication of JOSHUA: The Odyssey of an Ordinary Man.

I have had the privilege to learn about good literature and have gained inspiration from many brilliant authors. Fyodr Dostoevsky of Russia, Mr. M.T. Vasudevan Nair of India and Earnest Hemingway of the world are the most notable of all.

Prologue

Joshua at the Temple

The boy prayed, with a sense of foreboding. He vividly remembered his previous encounter with Thaddeus.

"Adonai, get me there in time, Adonai . . ."

A thick fog hung in the air as the boy walked along the much-traveled country road from Nazareth to Sepphoris. Joshua began the four-mile, uphill trek at the early cock crow, some two hours before the first light. Shrouded in thick layers of raiment of home-spun lamb's wool, the boy climbed the pebbled route slowly, struggling, and at times stumbling in the dark.

The side door of the temple on the hilltop was open. A cold wind whistled through the room as the boy appeared at the threshold. The sixty-man congregations' gazes turned towards the door.

Joshua closed the door and moved noiselessly to the rear aisle.

Incensed by the interruption, the rabbi, Thaddeus, stood frozen mid-sentence in his recitation of Ezra's admonitions. He was a large man in his early forties, with a large hawk-shaped nose. Thaddeus gave the boy a hard look, then turned to the congregation of men wailing in the main hall and the five or six hoary women muttering in the rear corridor separated by a black curtain.

"Thus, from the smoking ashes of the Babylonian devastation," the rabbi said. "A new temple was to be built under the leadership of Zerubbabel, and Joshua, son of Jozada."

"Nevertheless, the enemies of Joshua and Benjamin hear that the Israelites are building a great temple at Jerusalem. Then what did they say?" Thaddeus asked. "The remains of the Assyrian scum! The Samaritans!" Thaddeus puckered his lips, and mimicked the Samaritans with imbecilic talk. The crowd began laughing, ridiculing the ridicule.

"You, children of Israel, the Samaritans say, we are also seeds of Abraham. We also seek your God too. We have made sacrifices to Him. Let us worship Him with you. Let us help you to make this temple." Thaddeus stared at the crowd, his face scarlet like his sacred vestments. "And what did Zerubbabel say to them? No, no. Yahweh is our God. This is the land promised to us. This is our temple, only ours. You are no part of it."

The crowd applauded, chanting, "Jehovah, our God, Jehovah our God. Our Promised Land it is."

Thaddeus glanced at the boy standing in the rear aisle. He stroked his beard with the back of his hand. All eyes turned to the boy. The crowd recognized Joshua, the thirteen-year-old carpenter boy from Nazareth, with his honey-brown curls tumbling down to his shoulders.

2

He had a large, shiny forehead, a patrician nose, and sharp blue eyes. Joshua stood tall with his chin up and hands folded across his chest.

Thaddeus nodded at Joshua.

"Rabbi, are the Samaritans not our neighbors? What's wrong for them in seeking our god?

Thaddeus' eyes narrowed as he stared at Joshua. "What kind of talk is this? The Samaritans, our neighbors? They worship Yahweh? Gibberish."

"Who is a neighbor?" Joshua asked.

Thaddeus took a step towards Joshua, pointing at the door. "Get out! Out! I told you not to interrupt our services. This is the House of God."

The boy left the room by the same door through which he had entered. As he exited, he heard the rabbi's voice from behind. "See me after the services."

**** **** ****

Thaddeus hastily reprised the sermon, emphasizing the purity of the Jewish people and the absolute need to eliminate those of all other nations and tribes from the Promised Land. Then he transitioned to the burnt offerings of the day.

It was a modest altar fashioned in the traditional way, as specified in the Law of Moses. Apart from Jerusalem in Judea, it was the only altar in the whole of Galilee where sacrifices were permitted, and only with special permissions gained through the efforts of Rabi Tannaim, the previous head of the Sanhedrin.

Against the backdrop of a purple curtain embroidered in gold, stood the table made of shittim wood and trimmed with gold moldings. Atop the altar were two large bronze cherubins, a seven-branched lamp stand, utensils and vessels for offerings, and a large fire pit for burning incense, topped with an iron grate.

Alcimus, the sacristan assistant, brought the sixteen doves over, one by one. Their legs were tied, and their broken wings hung loose by their sides. He lifted each bird high to the altar, holding tightly to its legs with one hand, while smothering its head with the other and bending its neck into an arch. Thaddeus sliced the bird's neck with a single stroke and spilled the blood into the burning pit. Clouds of smoke drifted up, and the aroma of burning blood carried the blessing to the congregation.

After all the doves had been sacrificed, a lamb was brought over, its legs bound with one rope. The struggling animal was laid on the altar. Alcimus extended its neck backwards. It struggled, unable to make a sound. Thaddeus sliced the neck of the lamb, and blood spewed into the sacrificial fire. Nine other lambs were also sacrificed in a similar manner.

By the time the bloody service was over, the roof of the house of God was filled with thick smoke.

Joshua stood outside in the cold, against a frieze cut into the stone wall. The scene of fruit-laden palm trees, clusters of grapes and the procession of the Holy Torah reverently wheeled on a pull cart were carved into the wall. The depiction was reminiscent of the ancient Passover celebrations held in Jerusalem before the Babylonian captivity. The thick fog on the hilltop slowly dissipated as the city slowly came to life.

Sepphoris, the city on the hilltop that housed observation posts, army barracks, government quarters and administrative buildings, housed a large detachment of Roman soldiers. Sepphoris was the crown city of Roman Galilee. The present temple built from the ruins of a six-hundred-year-old Jewish synagogue once stood at the crossroads of the Roman-built cobblestone highways that stretched from the port city of Accra in the west to Tiberius in the east, Babylon in the south and Damascus in the north. In addition, minor pebbled country roads leading to Cana in the north and Nazareth in the south also traversed through the hilltop city near the temple.

Joshua glanced around looking at the views of Galilee. The vineyards and olive gardens would soon be ripe with fruit. The air held scents of the orchards of pomegranates, figs, and pistachio. Thousands of acres of wheat and corn fields, the breadbasket of Palestine, stretched before him.

Joshua stood in the cold, humiliated and shivering. It was hard for him to believe that he had been cast out of the very temple that he had helped build with his carpenter father.

He thought that a group of a thousand patriotic Jews who, led by zealots twenty years ago, had revolted against the Romans and laid siege to the city in an attempt to liberate Galilee from the Roman yoke. But within seven days the ferocious Roman army, more than five thousand men of size and strength, with brass helmets, iron swords and heavy leather boots, under the direction of the Roman general Verus, surrounded the hill and marched to the top, slaying every Jew on sight and finally burning down the temple to ashes. Once the rebellion was quelled, the Romans permitted the remaining Jews to build a new place to worship on the same site. The building changed, but the services didn't. It will never change, Joshua thought.

After the temple services, Joshua approached the door to the priest's quarters and was let in by Alcimus. At the far end of the room facing the rear wall, Thaddeus sat on the hearth, his feet and arms spread in front of a charcoal grate. To the right of the fireplace, facing the entrance door, the eighty-year-old Rabbi Zephaniah lounged on a heavy sofa, directing Alcimus how to cut the meat of the burnt offerings as stipulated in the holy writings.

Zephaniah was the rabbi of the temple during the Jewish revolt, in which he lost his left eye. The hollow socket was covered with a black pad. Now, bound to his chair, he was unable to walk, as his legs could not carry his pendulous belly weight.

Joshua took a few steps across the room to the hearth, made a little coughing sound to announce his arrival, and stood calmly behind Thaddeus with his arms across his chest.

"You have been told not to come here anymore with your questions," Thaddeus said.

"Yes, rabbi," Joshua said.

"Why did you?" Thaddeus asked.

"The temple is my father's house, too," Joshua said.

"Who is that?" Zephaniah asked.

"He's that meek Mary's son from Nazareth," Alcimus said.

"I'm Joshua, son of Joseph of Nazareth," affirmed Joshua.

"Ha! Son of Joseph," Thaddeus said. "Hum, the carpenter."

"What are his questions?" Zephaniah asked. "What does he want?"

"Rabbi, his questions are many," Thaddeus said impatiently. He stood, stroking his beard with the back of his hand.

"Let him speak," Zephaniah said. The rabbi sank deep in the chair, his gaze focused on Joshua.

"What are your complaints today?' Thaddeus asked. He took a step towards Joshua.

"Please tell me, Rabbi, why we need to be eternally hostile to our neighbors, the Canaanites, the Philistines and the Samaritans?" Joshua held Thaddeus's gaze.

Thaddeus glanced at Zephaniah.

"This bad blood and vitriol will only lead to war and more blood to be shed," Joshua said.

"Haven't you read our holy scriptures?" Thaddeus took another step towards Joshua. "The revelations at Mount Sinai?"

"Let the boy speak," Zephaniah said.

"I too have read the Torah, Rabbi, but I don't understand this eternal hostility," Joshua said. "Did not the Amorites offer abode to Abraham in Hebron, while the patriarch was a stranger in their land without a home or land? Were not the Hittites, his neighbors, helpful and non-hostile? Did they not sell land to Abraham to bury Sarah, lest her body rot in the streets? Was not Uriah, the first general of King David, a Hittite? Uriah trusted David, but how was the favor returned?"

Thaddeus glared at Joshua.

"This land belonged to the original tribes of Palestine and their thirty-one kings," Joshua said. "Did we not exterminate the city of Jericho to its last seed? Also, did we not chase and slaughter all the tribes, apparently on a divine order?"

"Apparently?" Thaddeus' face turned crimson. He pointed a finger at Joshua's face and took another step forward.

Zephaniah took a deep breath. "Let him continue."

"What did Prophet Ezekiel say about Jerusalem?" Joshua asked. "It's ancestry?"

The two rabbis exchanged a look.

"By origin and birth, you are of the land of Canaan, your father an Amorite, and mother a Hittite." Joshua's gaze moved from one rabbi to the other. "Violence will only lead to more violence. Let me ask you once again, Rabbi, what is wrong about the Samaritans offering a hand to rebuild our temple in Jerusalem? Are we not charged with the commandment to love thy neighbor?"

Another tense silence followed.

Thaddeus tried to say something but nothing came out except a guttural noise.

"Who is a neighbor?" Joshua asked. "What has become of our people as a nation, the people chosen by Yahweh? The tribe God destined to rule over all the nations of the world? We, the chosen people, have become the slaves of the world. We were evicted from our own land, enslaved and taken away, and returned at the mercy of the Persians. Who knows that it won't happen again? A permanent eviction, with the children of Israel wandering in the wilderness of the world again, without a home, without a land. What went wrong with the promises given to Abraham, Isaac and Jacob?"

Thaddeus scoffed with disgust.

"It's time for introspection," Joshua said. "A sword against a sword will keep the heads rolling; an eye for an eye will turn the world blind. A tooth for a tooth . . ."

Thaddeus leapt at Joshua, and pulled him up by the hair. "You insolent bastard; how dare you."

Joshua struggled like a fettered animal, trying to escape the rabbi's grip. Yet, despite the pain, he made no sound.

"You bastard . . . maggot, never again should I see your face in Sepphoris." Thaddeus spit on Joshua's face and slapped him.

Still, Joshua did not scream or cry. Suddenly, with a mighty shove, he pushed Thaddeus back and dropped to the floor. He bit Thaddeus on the forearm, sinking his teeth to the bone. Joshua's mouth filled with blood.

Thaddeus fell to the floor and groaned.

Joshua kicked the rabbi in the shin. Then he spit the mouthful of blood in Thaddeus' face, before running out of the temple.

BOOK I
Roman-Occupied Galilee

The reign of Tiberius Caesar

Joshua witnessing Rachel's trial

Noah was hard at work pulling the weeds and checking the kernels of the barley. He looked up and saw Joseph running his way. "Papa, please hurry home, now," the boy yelled, before turning around and racing back home.

Something's the matter with Judith, Noah thought. *At first light, when I left for the fields, she had only mild abdominal discomfort, no different from her previous pregnancies. But come to think of it, last night she was restless, twining and turning on the bed. Did I miss the signs in the morning?*

Noah, a hardworking farmer, was a tall man with a sunbaked face, strong shoulders and long, muscular hands. A receding hairline and a small, forked beard surrounded a strong nose and bushy eyebrows. He rushed home, reaching the side of his wife moments later.

Judith's fingers were knitted against her belly. Sweat dripped from her face.

Noah stood frozen, staring at her pale, death-like face. *What a difference the last two hours have inflicted on my wife,* he thought. His heart pounded, heavy with guilt.

Judith's breathing was shallow, her eyes sunken, and her lips cracked and dry. Rachel cradled her mother's head in her lap and gently wiped the sweat off her brow with a linen towel.

She glanced at her father.

Noah sat cross-legged by Judith's side, relieving Rachel. He lifted his wife up to his chest to rest her head in the cradle of his elbow.

Judith's eyes opened and rolled up. "My husband, it all came suddenly. The pain is unbearable. I'm sorry, but I think I'm about to lose our baby." Tears rolled down her cheeks.

Noah touched her lips as a few tears fell from his own eyes. "My dear, you will be fine. We're all here for you. Nothing will happen to you, my dear. Nothing will happen to our baby. Don't worry, everything will work out." He swallowed heavily. Noah noted Judith's underclothes and garments heavy with blood and turned his gaze to Rachel.

"Father, I've sent for Hannah," Rachel said. "Rubin has gone to fetch her."

Noah nodded, his eyes still fixed on Judith. Hannah, their closest neighbor, was also a midwife.

Rachel made some barley water, sprinkled a pinch of sea salt over it, and sat down beside Judith, feeding her a few drops at a time. Noah gently blew air over her face and slowly rubbed her belly, saying words of comfort in Judith's ears. A few minutes later, Hannah arrived and put down her bag with a clink. A heavyset woman in her late fifties, Hannah had a round, pleasant face, with generous gray and white hair. She was married to Serug, and was an extremely kind and helpful neighbor. Over the years, she had assisted Judith with the births of all four of their children. She always carried a leather purse with several pouches, some containing powder and linen, some ointments. In other larger pouches she carried a knife, a few blunt brass rods, and a small, sharp sickle for her work.

Hannah sat beside Judith. She examined her eyes, tongue, and stomach. She gently opened Judith's lips and placed her index finger in her mouth for over a minute. Hannah's face turned somber, but she attempted a little smile. She took Noah and Rachel aside and whispered, "The baby is dead. I fear it's been dead for a while. She has a fever. More fever inside than outside. I don't understand why she is bleeding so much, particularly before the birth of a dead baby, but her womb is very soft, and this is not a good sign. I can give her some powder to harden the womb – that will help her to push the baby out – but I don't know about the fever. Whenever I have seen this type of fever, the mother has always been in danger. I pray this is not so in Judith's case."

"My mother was shaking earlier on," Rachel said. "I had covered her with a blanket, but after a while she removed it, saying it was too hot. Actually, she felt cold and sweaty."

"Yes, Hannah, I want you to give her the powder," Noah said. "I know of a Greek physician on the coast of the Great Sea in the city of Bucolonpolis, Aristophanes. He is known to be a great healer. I will travel immediately to seek his help. It is a journey for a day and night, and I hope I will return in time, but I must risk it. Please do whatever you can for my wife."

Noah soon started packing his bag for the journey. Amos stood on the porch with a bleak face, his arms folded across his chest, searching Noah's face, ready for any orders from the family to help Judith. "Noah, I will go to Bucolonpolis and talk to the physician, so you may stay here with Judith."

"Thank you for the offer, Amos, but you might not present the problems to the physician properly."

Amos managed a rueful smile.

Noah collected the bag, mounted his favorite mule, and set off to see Aristophanes. The sun was sinking beyond the mountain. The route required an arduous and often dangerous climb up Mount Carmel, a thousand cubits high. Amidst the trees, bushes and boulders, Noah's mighty mule ran like a horse carrying the not-so-light farmer as if the beast itself had realized the urgency of the mater.

When Noah reached the top of the mountain, he could see the plains of Sharon opening up before him. The descent was steep and treacherous, with loose soil and sand. He started down the mountain's slope. Soon the crescent of the cherry-red sun descended behind the mountains. Visibility became poor. It appeared the whole sky was soon filled with thick, low-hanging clouds.

A strong south wind started blowing, whistling on the tree tops. Before long, the wind turned heavy, bending and uprooting trees, and the air was quickly filled with leaves, dust and debris. Noah had expected at least one hour more of sunlight. He decided to stop and wait out the night in a small cave, while his mule rested under a large oak tree nearby. In the shadowy darkness, Noah opened his package, which contained four silver shekels, a large loaf of bread, honey, dates and an omer of wine in a skin. He shared the meal of bread with his mule, planning to proceed at daybreak. For a time he could see a faint red hue on the western horizon, but very soon it became black. A cold, heavier wind beat down from the south as thunder and streaks of lightning cleaved across the sky. A barrage of thunder shook the earth, and water poured down from the heavens, drenching him and his mule. The rain lasted less than an hour, but water gushed down from the top of the hill, turning the ground to a flash flood. Noah clung to a bough for his life and held on as tightly as he could, but his feet drifted away and his legs floated in the torrent like a reed in a waterfall. He frantically glanced around to find his mule, but she had already vanished. The swirling water tore him from the tree and he was swept down the mountain along with the boulders, the brushes, the mud, and the soot.

He was buried in mud chest deep, down in the valleys. It was pitch dark. He was unable to move, unable to see. *Judith is gravely ill. Many works unfinished. Is this my end, too*, he pondered. In the Jewish calendar, it was the year 3774. The farmers of Galilee were busy getting ready, sharpening their sickles, emptying the silos and yoking their donkeys, all preparing for a great harvest. The dark-green, bustling growth of the wheat and barley in the lowlands, the loaded clusters of pinkish-green tender pomegranates, and the heavy cluster of pale-green almonds in the shades and slopes declared the vengeance of the land as it was laid to rest the previous sabbatical year.

For generations, Noah's family had found solace in the fertile valley, sheltered under the umbrage of Mount Carmel and nurtured by the waters of the Kishon River. There were seven other families, too. They were all part of the town of Gabe, although they preferred to say, "We are from Carmel." In the summer months of Tammuz, Av, Elul and sometimes even in Tishrei, the river shrank into a few channels of brooks separated by deltas of sand and stone. Throughout the year, one could walk through the river, except in late Tishrei, and the whole month of Heshvan, when the river crests with heavy rains. From the river banks, Mount Carmel rose steeply and stretched all the way west towards the Great Sea. The people revered the mountain, because it was here that the Prophet Elijah slew the false prophets of Baal.

Noah had been born in Carmel, thirty-six years ago, in the same house built by his father Pekaliah. His house was perched on a bluff, on the mountain slope overlooking the river. It was a humble house, with just one large room – the only living area of the house – and an enclosed front porch, which housed all the domestic animals. A descending walkway stretched from the front porch about a furlong to the threshold of the riverbed. The family cooked, ate, played, prayed and slept in the living area. At the back of the room, set against the wall, was a full-length wooden bench – a long box with a lid – where all the family valuables were stored. Most of the cooking was done on the saagh, set on three stones. Judith always kept a fire going in the little fireplace, even when she and Rachel were not cooking.

On top of a cedar shelf was kept a decorated box made of shittim wood that Noah had brought from Jerusalem. The box was modeled after the Tabernacle in Herod's Temple, but the decorative work and inlays were made of brass instead of gold. It even had winged angels and a replica of the mercy seat. In this box Noah kept his most precious possession, a copy of the holy Torah, a beautifully appointed book bound in red leather with pages of vellum, created in Alexandria, Egypt.

Every evening as dusk set in, Rachel would pull out the lamp from under the bushel, light all seven wicks and place it on top of the bushel. After a humble dinner, Noah would read aloud a passage or two from the Holy Torah, mostly from the Prophets.

Noah was twenty when he married Judith, a soft-spoken, thin girl with a round face, sparkling eyes and enchanting warmth. The following year they begot Rachel, then Joseph, Rubin and Judah, all at about eighteen-month intervals. Judah's birth left Judith feeling sick with joint pains, frequent coughs and colds. Later she suffered shortness of breath when climbing up the hill or even going down to the river to draw the water.

For the past twenty years, Noah had worked intensely on his land from the time the skies turned yellow in the east until they turned dark red in the west. Every morning Noah would get up long before the eastern horizon turned golden yellow. He would look at his family as they slept, then go for a walk through his grain fields, pulling weeds and checking on his barley and wheat.

Six years ago, when Rachel was eight years old, Noah hired a young man named Amos from the town of Gabe, across the river, to help him with all the work in the house and fields. Amos was now twenty-one years old, a sincere and hardworking lad of great muscular build, tanned skin and strong jaws. He was considered more like a member of the family.

Noah and Amos leveled the uneven riverbank into three plateaus, all bordered with stone hedges – his wheat and barley fields. Higher up by the mountain slope, Noah tended two hundred heads of olive trees and about a thousand roots of grape vines. There wasn't a day that he didn't see every one of those plants. He knew exactly when the kernels of the wheat were milky, when they hardened and when they were ripe to be harvested.

In between the major harvests, Noah nursed a vegetable garden with lentils, chick peas, onions, and garlic – short crops that needed irrigation. When Judith was healthy, she would draw all the needed waters from the Kishon, carrying two jarfuls, one on each hip as if carrying two babies, and water the plants. That was the reason why Noah decided to build the shaduf. When he needed water, Noah would stand wide on a wooden platform over the well and lower the bucket to the bottom of the well. With a wide swing and dip, the bucket was filled with water, and then he would slowly release his grip and observe with a glowing grin, the bucket rising by itself like magic. The water emptied into the channels, then flowed to the plants. His vegetable garden was so robust that his neighbors both admired and envied it at the same time. The great crops of wheat, barley and wine that Noah produced each year were a testimony to his hard work.

The farmer's mind was filled with thoughts about his wife and children. He was always a very happy and contented man, except for Judith's health. She was becoming more and more sickly, looked pale and had stopped having the monthly bleeding the previous year. Though he did not suspect pregnancy at first, when she began to vomit nearly every morning, it became known that Judith was having the fifth child after a gap of nearly eight years. Luckily, she gained some weight, the joint pain and swelling resolved, and she felt great relief as the pregnancy advanced. Judith was told to rest, and she was even relieved of her kitchen duties, all of which were taken over by Rachel.

Noah's beloved first born, Rachel, was the stalwart of his house. Now fourteen years old, she had transformed into a comely young lady with a smooth, shapely body, full breasts, large shining brow, robust lips and the strong buttocks of a farmer girl. She liked to watch Amos drawing the water using the shaduf with great interest. She also wanted to do the same, but Noah discouraged it. *Rachel is made for finer things, and I will make sure she has them,* Noah thought. But Noah did not hesitate to give the job to his eldest son, Joseph, reasoning that he would soon have to learn this job anyway.

At the age of seven, Rachel began planting flowers on either side of the walkway in front of the house. In time, her garden went all the way down to the river, with several rows of flowers on either side – white daisies, scarlet anemones, yellow cyclamens, hula lilies and a few varieties of flax. By mid-spring, the walkway became a gorgeous carpet embroidered with the parade of flowers.

Noah had seen that Rachel was drawn to Amos, particularly since last year. She found a reason to talk to him about one thing or the other. Noah noticed she beamed at Amos with a sparkle in her eyes. She appeared to have a concealed smile on her lips, and her brisk gait and long dark curls reminded Noah of Judith when she came to Carmel for the first time. So, it came as no surprise to Noah when Amos requested Rachel's hand in marriage.

Noah didn't say yes or no to Amos, but just smiled and changed the subject to another project on the farm.

"I'm not a rich man, Noah," Amos said. "But I love Rachel and will be a good husband for her."

"Enough of this kind of talk," Noah said. "Rachel is but fourteen years old."

Amos lowered his gaze, biting his lower lip. He walked away. Noah watched Amos leave, his shoulders slumped.

Noah knew he had become dependent on Rachel for everything in the house. She had become both the big sister and mother for her siblings. She did all the cooking, cleaning, knitting, and even fed the animals. Noah secretly knew he had become dependent on her for everything in the house.

**** **** ****

Noah felt the heat of the rising sun on his face. He woke up sore and groggy. He opened his eyes and squinted against the bright sun. Unable to move his arms, he looked up and saw his mule walking towards him like a guardian angel.

A miracle, Noah thought, as his mule pulled him slowly to his feet. His body and clothing were caked with mud. *Perhaps this is a fortunate sign that Judith will be well,* he prayed. He still had his leather bag with all of his provisions, tied across his shoulder to his waist. "I love you miracle. You rescued me," he said to the beast, and patted on her brow. There were large puddles of clear water on the low-lying areas. He washed himself and his mule in the clear puddle and resumed the journey towards the city.

Before noon Noah reached the city of Bucolonpolis on the west coast, a community mainly occupied by people from Greece, seamen sailing on merchant ships to the far west. Everybody in Bucolonpolis knew the Greek physician, Aristophanes, and his villa perched on a rocky hill overlooking the wharf. Noah was graciously received into his office on the second floor.

Aristophanes, though well into his eighties, was well groomed with long white hair and a flowing beard, prominent creases of age and experience on his face, a long nose, sharp eyes and an entrancing gaze. His room was decorated in a busy fashion with busts of famous people, two of whom Noah could easily identify: one of Alexander the Great and another, the Greek physician Hippocrates. A large, elegantly framed parchment of the Hippocratic Oath hung on the wall. There were at least fifty large books of parchment and several scrolls on papyrus stacked unevenly on a wall shelf.

Perched on the high chair, leaning forward with his chin resting on his clenched first, Aristophanes carefully listened to the history of Judith's illness and her current trouble in childbirth. He asked many questions.

"When did the swelling in her limbs begin?"

"Five years before my marriage," Noah said. "When Judith was ten years old, I'm told she had fever and throat pain that lasted for a month. The swelling in the joints started a month after that. But she was well for many years after that."

There were many more questions. Which joints were first afflicted. How often had she got a fever? Was there any evidence of stiffness in the neck, limitations of the girdle movement, intolerance to walking or climbing? And many other questions that Noah answered as best he could.

"When do you think Judith started the fever?" Aristophanes asked, the physician leaning forward.

"Probably yesterday," Noah said, his voice turning husky. "I don't know, maybe I didn't pay enough attention to my Judith. I am so sorry." He sobbed.

"Noah, I hope your wife will be all right," Aristophanes said. "Don't be afraid." But after hearing about the fever and the softness of her womb, the physician frowned. He made some notes with a filled quill on a papyrus. After listening to the entire story, he leaned back in silence, and then reached for one of his old tattered papyrus scrolls. He read the scroll left to right, noting the information and shaking his head. He took a brown medicine bottle and poured about one-eighth of a log of thick brown liquid into a small glass bottle and corked it. Then he spread a palm-sized dry leaf across the table and added a spoonful of dry powder to it. He then carefully folded it into a packet and tied it with a flax thread.

"The liquid is to be divided into six parts. One part is to be mixed with half a cab of fresh goat's milk. Mix it thoroughly and have Judith drink this medicine three times a day for two days."

Noah received the little bottle in the cup of his hands, reciting the instructions to him.

"The powder must be carefully handled," Aristophanes said. "First, you will need a fist-sized, soft cotton cloth that has been soaked in warm mustard oil. The cotton cloth is to be rolled into a ball and then covered with this powder. You must carefully clean the birth canal, remove all the blood clots and pack the medicine ball high up to the womb, pushing gently. In addition, you should tightly wrap her waist with a linen roll, directly over the womb so that the womb should feel tight."

Noah listened to those instructions reverently, like Moses at the Sinai in front of the burning bush.

Finally, Aristophanes said, "If she is to survive, you will see an improvement in three days." Then he stood for a long moment.

Noah could hear the faint distant noises that filtered in from the fishermen's wharf. He collected the medicine from the physician with great gratitude and reverence and carefully put it in his pouch. He bowed before Aristophanes and placed four shekels of silver on the table. "Sire, I am thankful to you forever, for my Judith, for my family. Shalom."

Noah raced home, his mule practically running up the hill as if she, too, sensed the urgency. Fortunately, the heavens were clear, and they arrived home well before sunset.

**** **** ****

Since morning, Amos had sat crouched against the almond tree, his face buried between his knees, without food or drink. At the first sight of Noah descending the hill in the distance, he stood up with a hopeful smile. Noah dismounted the mule in haste and threw the reins in the air for Amos without acknowledging his presence and rushed to Judith

Judith burned with fever, her breathing even shallower than when he'd left. All color had drained from her face. He touched her face and saw her breathing. "She's still alive," Noah whispered. He took a breath and looked to the Heavens. "Adonai, I thank you. Your humble servant, I thank you," he said.

Rachel and Hannah had never left Judith's side, holding her hands, sponging her face and feeding her sips of barley water. The younger children, Joseph, Rubin and Judah, were hovering over their mother with red weepy eyes. Noah hugged and kissed Judith, warmly embraced Rachel and sent the younger kids out with Amos.

Noah shared with Hannah and Rachel everything Aristophanes had told him. Soon Rachel went out and milked the goat to get the required amount of milk and prepared the medicine as instructed by the physician. Hannah collected a basin with warm water.

"It will be difficult for her to swallow the medicine, the musty smell, she is too weak," said Hannah. "Wait a minute," she said, "Pat on her back". Hannah slowly lifted Judith up, opened her mouth and placed a spoonful of the medicine deep in her throat, gently pinching her nose and rubbing her back. Judith swallowed the medicine with a gurgling noise, despite coughing few times.

"This is the first sound she has made since the previous night," Rachel said. Gently, she fed her mother the full dose of medicine, one spoonful at a time.

Hannah and Rachel prepared the warm mustard oil and soaked the clean linen ball in it, coating it with the powder from the leaf and being very careful not to lose one bit. Noah sat down and pillowed Judith's head in his lap, while Hannah removed the bloody loin cloths, lifted and separated her legs, and meticulously cleaned her birth canal of the blood clots. Then she packed the medicine ball deep in Judith's birth canal, gently pushing upwards.

Rachel trembled as she watched Hannah work.

Noah noticed her pale color and softly patted her back.

Then they applied the linen waistband, as directed by the physician, and laid Judith to rest.

"Tonight, you should sleep with the other kids," Noah said to Rachel.

"No," Rachel replied. "I wouldn't be able to sleep. I'll stay here with you through the night."

Late in the night, after Amos and Hannah had left for the evening and Judith was dozing quietly, a calm silence embraced the little house by the mountainside. A cool north wind washed in the musty animal smell from the porch to the family room, but it was pleasant and normal for the dwellers, as it was part of their daily life.

Noah woke when the first cock crowed, and looked at Rachel, who was still holding her mother's hand. Noah looked at her for a long moment in deep thought and said, "Rachel, you are now fourteen," he paused. "Someday soon I will find a good man to take care of you."

Rachel turned to her father, *how tired he had looked over the last two days,* she thought. The lines under his eyes had turned into swollen bags, his hair almost full gray at the temples, and a few more silver hairs glinting in his beard.

"Life is a long journey, my dear child," Noah said. "As a young girl, you did everything in this house, much more than should have been expected of you. Your mother's illness has required you to become a woman while you are still a girl, but I look forward to that day when you will dress up as a bride coming home with your husband. I will certainly find a very good man for you. I want you to be a very happy bride and then soon a mother, and then later a grandmother, and you shall age in grace, I pray."

"Father, I understand the responsibilities of a Jewish woman. Mother taught me all about it, and I am prepared." Her voice quivered as she sobbed, head bowed. "I will oblige to whatever you decide."

"Rachel, I know all about Amos," Noah said. "He's a good boy, a good worker, but he is poor. He has no house or a piece of land of his own, and still lives as a tenant in Gabe. I want you to be much better off in life. Maybe it's a selfish dream of a father who loves his daughter the most. I believe you deserve it and I hope that ultimately you'll be happier, even if you doubt me at this moment."

Rachel smiled ruefully, about to say something, when Judith whispered, "Rachel, Rachel, Rachel."

Writhed in fever, wet with sweating, Judith made an attempt to rise on her elbows, but collapsed back, fatigued, retching and spitting bitter slimy mucous and some yellow fluid that drained through the corner of her mouth.

Noah tapped her shoulder. "My dear, I see you are not feeling any better."

Judith squeezed her tummy with both hands, her eyes tightly shut, and her face wrinkled with pain. "It's happening now . . . I have . . . a different feeling now . . . I think it's finally coming out."

"Don't worry dear, we will help you." Noah sat down cross-legged and placed Judith's head on his lap.

Rachel began assisting her mother to complete the process.

She works like an experienced midwife, Noah thought.

Noah and Rachel removed and disposed of the dead fetus.

A constrained moment followed. Noah struggled for words. "I am glad we got Judith back." His eyes welled up. "But I am so sad . . ." He chocked.

" . . . I lost a little sister," Rachel completed.

21

Rachel stepped outside and boiled some more barley water, added a pinch of sea salt and gave it to her mother.

Judith sipped from her alabaster cup and drank about half a log's worth of fluid. They bathed her, changed her clothes and put her back to bed. Shortly after the bath, Judith stopped sweating as the fever subsided, and some color returned to her face.

"The family knew they had their 'pass over.' They smiled at each other, praising the Lord.

The house became peacefully quiet.

Noah stood and saw Rachel sleeping by her mother's side, still holding her hand.

He walked out onto the front porch and sat on the floor, his legs dangling over the edge. Noah gazed at the sky, the fore waters of the night had just broken on the eastern horizon, turning the firmaments painted in blood red; another day was just unfolding, and Noah breathed a deep sigh of relief.

**** **** ****

On a dull December day, when the sky was gray and the north wind blowing colder, Judith started shivering again, her breath broken with loud wheezing since daybreak. She felt a bit better as the sun rose. Amos heated some red wine and gave it to her with a pinch of cassia as a remedy for her cold.

"Amos, come sit with me." Noah motioned for the boy to sit by his side. He handed Amos the flagon of warm wine he was drinking. "Amos, I am thinking of making some additions to this house."

Amos nodded.

Noah pointed to the roof and the back wall. "We need to strengthen the roof and make an additional room behind it."

"By digging through the back wall?" Amos asked.

"Exactly," Noah said. "I don't think it presents too big a problem."

"We can hire John and Nehume from the town," Amos said. "They are good workers."

Work began on the new room during the winter weather. The four men dug through the rear wall of the house for nearly two weeks, removing about two hundred homers of dirt, rock and soil. The room to be was about six yards long and five yards deep, with a sloping roof, three sides set against the mountain and a door connecting to the main living area.

"The design of the roof is the most important element of the construction." Noah gestured at the roof. "For the new room, the roof will be sloped, while the roof over the main living room would remain flat as it is now."

Mount Carmel had an abundance of woods of various qualities. At the top of the mountain, mostly fir, tidhar, terebinth and large clusters of evergreens grew. At the descent of the mountain, ash, cypress, pines, cedars, gofer, oak and shittim trees grew in abundance. They chose cypress, and collected enough wood to build the full span of the roof. The wood was measured, cut, chipped, chiseled, shaped straight and placed on the roof from beam to beam as the first layer. They left little space between the sections, filling the tiny crevices with smaller branches of the same wood. A mortar mixture made of sand from the river and sticky clay was mulched to a paste then spread across the roof about a palm thick and thumped with foot-shaped timber. After the roof was left for a week to set and dry, the second layer, a thick mixture of bitumen and acacia resins mulched into a smooth, thick paste, was spread on top of the roof with a spatula. In ten days, this layer hardened to the consistency of stone and even repelled water.

"This looks perfect," Noah said to the three men. He looked at Amos. "Congratulations. Well done."

"Over time, molds and tiny grasses will grow to cover the roof and render it indistinguishable from the surface of the mountain," Amos said. "It will be so strong that mules or horses could walk over it with no problems."

The room they built looked beautiful, quite cool and comfortable as they covered the floor with tiles and the walls with tapestries.

Noah looked with pride at the finished room. *This is my ark,* he thought. *It is here that Rachel shall sleep with her husband when they come home for the first time.*

**** **** ****

After the barley harvest in the first week of Iyar, Noah made a trip to Nazareth where his elder brother, Joseph, lived as a carpenter.

Early in the morning, Noah started on his small, open carriage coach, pulled by Miracle. The mule kept a steady pace through the narrow, pebbled country road framed with rows of sycamore, the branches of which had overgrown and met in the middle kissing in the sky like an arbor. The countryside had more varieties of plants than Mount Carmel, boasting palm trees, hollies, pistachios, mustard and several varieties of willow.

There were a few wayfarers tramping the road silently with burdens on their shoulders, but one man riding a donkey a few yards ahead of Noah was loudly singing an old Jewish song, flailing his hands and making figures in the air.

"Next year in Jerusalem, I will see you, dear,

Over there in the city of David,

Over there in the city of Zion,

In Jerusalem, I will see you, my love."

Nearing Nazareth, the landscape transformed like a painting with many varieties of anemones in blue, yellow and gold; hula lilies standing tall created waves of white, orange and crimson-red revelers of nature. The fields were resplendent tapestries of chrysanthemums, marigold, amaryllis and pink poppies. An endearing smile rippled on Noah's face as he looked at the beauty of the landscape and the joyous play of a family with three young children frolicking in the fields at the threshold of the city of Nazareth.

Nazareth, on its southern crescent boulder, is at a high elevation. Noah entered the town through the stone gate located on the eastern wall. Seen from a distance, Joseph's house was a small, flat-topped house shaded by three tall sycamores on the right and a very large, aged cypress that stood over the house in the front yard. The footpath to the house was fenced on either side by a series of yellow-leafed poplars that grew over and cascaded above.

Mary came out, running to greet him with a jug of water and a piece of linen for washing his feet. She was a thin lady in her early thirties with an angelic face. Joseph, crouched on his work bench under the cypress, was working on a project involving plows and yokes. At the visitor, he stood shading his eyes. Joseph nearly laughed when he recognized his brother. "Noah," he cried. "My brother, I last saw you . . . how many . . . three years back. Welcome to my house."

The two men embraced and kissed each other on their cheeks. Noah was taken aback by the change in Joseph's appearance. During the past three years, he appeared much older than sixty-four years, his posture stooped and hunched as if he carried something heavy on his back.

"Where's Joshua?" Noah asked.

Joseph glanced at Mary, and then turned to Noah. "Joshua goes to Japha three days a week."

"Hasn't he started working with you?" Noah asked.

"Sometimes, but he's busy learning Greek and studying philosophy with an old Greek teacher, Zilinos," Joseph said.

"Really." Noah scratched his beard. "Who is this Zilinos?"

"He is said to be a great scholar amongst his people. He held high offices in the palace of the Seleucids in Damascus. He moved to Jerusalem to learn more about Judaism. He married a widow from Crocodilopolis and settled in Japha."

"Joshua is only fifteen, is he not?" Noah asked. "Shouldn't he be spending his time studying the holy scriptures of Torah and the writings of the great prophets?"

"He has studied them all in great depth," Joseph said. "He seems to have more knowledge about our holy books than the high priest of Jerusalem; at least that's what he says. He knows all of them, almost by heart, but . . ." Joseph paused. His face clouded and the crow's feet on his face deepened.

"But what, Joseph," Noah said. "Is there something wrong with the boy?"

"Nothing is wrong with him, except that he has questions, a lot of questions – maybe too many," Joseph said. "He wants answers that I can't provide. He's even talked about going to Jerusalem and having a 'discussion' with the high priest there; can you imagine? He had one experience in Sepphoris, but that wasn't enough for him."

Noah looked at Mary, who stood silently, leaning against the back wall. "What is your opinion about all of this?" he asked.

"Joshua is a great boy," she said. "He has learned the scriptures extremely well, but he does not seem very happy with many of our beliefs and traditions. In fact, he is bitter about quite a few of them."

"It's the Greeks," Noah said. "The Greek influence can lead to no good for a nice Jewish boy."

"How is Judith?" Mary asked. "I trust she is in good health? The last time I saw her, she had joint pains and difficulty walking for more than short periods of time. And your children – Rachel, Joseph, Rubin and Judah – how are they?"

"Judith still has problems," Noah said. "She nearly died during child birth, two months back. The baby was dead, and she developed a fever and lost a great deal of blood. Had it not been for the help of Aristophanes, I fear we would have lost her. Judith has recovered some, but she is not traveling much anymore. Rachel is now fourteen and became a woman last year. My other children are all doing very well."

"Are you looking for a match for Rachel?" Joseph asked.

"That's the reason I'm here," Noah said. "You remember the family of Hannaniahs in Tiberius? I believe we met them in Jerusalem three years back. The father, Senior Hannaniahs, is a rich businessman – very generous. His eldest son, Hannaniahs Junior, lost his wife last year. He is also a very rich man, fully engaged in his family businesses. He has a great contract to provide cut stones for the palaces that are being built by King Herod in Tiberius. He even has a quarry in Amathus where hundreds of people work, and is known to be a very generous man, too."

"But he's thirty-four years old and has three children, all of them boys," Mary said.

Joseph shook his head. "Rachel is only fourteen, still practically a child, although we are aware that some girls are married as young an age of nine or ten. However, I don't approve of such child marriages, unless there are . . ." He looked at Mary, her gaze fixed on the floor.

"Yes, Joseph, I agree," Noah said. "Rachel turned a woman last year. She's quite proficient at all the skills of running a home. Since Judith's illness, she has been taking care of all of the affairs of my family."

"The Hannaniahs live so far away from your family," Joseph said. "Are you sure this is the right thing, Noah?"

"She will be a great wife. In Hannaniahs' house she will be very well off and live like a queen. Maybe it's my selfish desire too, I admit. An envoy from the Hannaniahs came to my house with a proposal last Shevat. I thought it was a God-given opportunity."

"So what's next?" Joseph asked.

"Tomorrow, if you can, we will travel to Tiberius and discuss the matter with the family of the Hannaniahs."

"What did Rachel say?" Mary asked.

"She's a good, obedient daughter. I believe she is quite lucky," Noah said.

Noah noticed a young man approaching the house through the poplar-lined walkway who was thin and a lot taller than the average Nazarene – at least six feet, a heavy leather bag slung across his chest held in place with his left arm while the right freely swung to the rhythm of his gait, his face framed by flowing, curly brown hair tumbling over his shoulders.

Joshua recognized Noah and quickened his pace towards him, a big smile on his face.

Noah embraced Joshua and kissed him on both cheeks. He held him by his shoulders and searched the face of his nephew. *What a comely boy*, Noah thought. *His features are more like the handsome Romans.* "I hear you go to Japha where you have a Greek teacher? "Noah asked.

"Yes, uncle," Joshua said. "Zilinos, my teacher, has studied all of our holy books and has great knowledge about our Torah. But he is an authority on Greek civilization, literature and philosophy. He lived and taught in Alexandria for four years."

"What are these, books? Quite heavy, aren't they? Can you read and write Greek?" Noah asked.

"I can read most of it, but I still need some help," Joshua said. "But reading is the easy part. To understand the Greeks and their philosophy of life and society is an entirely different matter."

"Can I see a book, Joshua," Noah asked. "I have never seen a Greek book."

Joshua pulled out two large books of parchment, bound in leather and decorated with golden inlays.

"This is really the first time the master has ever allowed anybody to take books from his library." Joshua lifted one of the books. "This book called *The Republic* is written by Plato. This is the first of the five volumes of his book."

"What's the book all about?" Noah asked.

"It's about Plato's philosophy of a society and his own thoughts about an ideal republic, Gods and beliefs." Joshua paused and thought before continuing. "Uncle, did you know there were several Greek cities that were ruled by their own citizens in a system called democracy?"

"Are you saying that the people are both kings, as well as subjects? And the people rule by themselves? Like the time when Moses went to the mountain?"

"No uncle. When Moses went to the mountains, it was chaos. This is different. The Greeks created a system of government where they elected their own rulers and submitted themselves to be ruled by the people they elected – a system called democracy. But Plato himself was not much of a democrat. He envisioned a state ruled by philosophers – philosopher kings, so to speak – the Republic."

"Noah, this discussion could go on for days. Joshua could engage you for the whole night and more if you had the time. But you have to eat and rest before your journey tomorrow."

"Yes Joseph, interesting, interesting." Noah turned his gaze to Joshua. "I would like to hear from you a bit more after dinner. I'm a poor farmer from Carmel; the only book I have read is our Torah. But what is this thing called philosophy? How can there be a rule in a land without a king and a high priest?"

Joshua, brimming with energy, continued: "The philosopher continually seeks the eternal truth, wisdom and enlightenment, a perpetual search for the innermost reality of life and virtually everything else."

Noah's face clouded. "I don't understand any of these things, Joshua."

Joseph came to the rescue, "Noah, you won't get away from here if you keep on talking to him. For us, all our beliefs and convictions are written in our holy scriptures. They are the words of our Lord, given to us through our man of God, Holy Moses. That is our life. That is our philosophy," Joseph said.

Noah was impressed with his young nephew's energy and enthusiasm, though he could understand little of what he spoke of Plato or Sophocles. However, Noah understood the Torah well and asked Joshua several questions to check the depth of his knowledge and was amazed by his answers. *Joshua will make a great rabbi, someday*, he thought.

Joshua lit all seven wicks on the oil lamp and placed it on top of the bushel in preparation for dinner. The air in the house smelled of freshly baked bread, steamed vegetables and spiced goat meat.

Joseph spread a mat on the floor. Mary then brought in the bread, meat and vegetables. Joshua read a few passages from Prophet Jeremiah as they sat cross-legged for dinner.

When dinner was finished, Joshua helped Mary clean the floor and dishes. Noah and Joseph made plans for the next day, before retiring. The two men left for Tiberius long before sunrise.

By the time they returned, it was again dinnertime in Joseph's house. Mary and Joshua were waiting for them to hear the news from Tiberius.

As it was the first journey Noah had taken to Tiberius since the construction of the new city by King Herod, the spectacular Kings Palace, the amphitheater and the gymnasium were all new to both of them.

As a carpenter, Joseph was impressed by the exquisite works on the marble capitals of the Corinthian columns that made it look like a Greek temple. Even the figures were all naked and Greek.

"The house of Hannaniahs is a palace itself," Noah said. "It had a stone arch gate, flagstone-paved front yard, marble columns, mosaic floor, colored tiles, spiral stairways, and very many rooms on two floors. Rachel and Hannaniahs will have their own room, servants and maids."

"How is the groom?" Joshua asked. "Is he a nice man? Will Rachel like him?"

"He's a very wealthy man . . . nice . . . beautiful house," Noah said.

"Yes, but will Rachel like him?" Joshua stared at Noah. "What did she say?"

"What is there for her say?" Noah said. "Our liking is hers, too."

Joshua sensed the tension. "Did you see the grounds where the games were held?" he asked.

Noah looked at Joseph. "No, what games?"

"Last year in celebration of the coronation of Tiberius Caesar," Joshua said. "King Herod organized a month-long games and entertainment in Caesarea, Tiberius and Sabatti. Like the Olympics in Greece. The athletes played all of their sports and games in the nude."

"Naked?" Noah said.

"Is it the type of Greek culture you now study, Joshua?" Noah asked.

"No uncle. But let me tell you, our own Sadducees were the patrons of the games, and there were very many scribes as invited guests for such occasions. Did you know that?"

When nobody replied, that conversation ended.

"Did you set up a date for the betrothal?"

Noah nodded. "Yes, the fifth day of Sivan," he said. "And the twentieth of Sivan shall be the wedding day, immediately after the wheat harvest."

There was not much conversation after the dinner. Before the sunrise the next morning, Noah left for Carmel.

**** **** ****

The evening Noah left for Nazareth, Rachel met with Amos in the vineyard behind their house. Hesitating to broach the subject of the marriage, the two of them sat there for a while with their gazes locked. Amos noticed Rachel's eyes were moist with tears. He lifted his hand to wipe the tears from her face, but Rachel grasped his arms and hugged him, burrowing her face in his muscular chest. Many a moment passed as Rachel rested in Amos's arms.

"I never wanted to go away from this land of ours, Amos." Rachel's voice quivered. "I had hoped that my father would give me to you in marriage. But now . . ."

"I understand, Rachel. He has other plans. Maybe we are not meant for each other. Maybe it is Yahweh's will."

"I don't want to go to a new city and new surroundings."

"That is what Jewish women do, Rachel. Her house is away from her father's house."

Rachel held his arms tightly. "No, Amos, my house is right here. I'm sure of that. I have a fear that something horrible is waiting for me."

"Say no more, Rachel. Nothing bad will happen to you. Be bold. Cast these doubts from your mind. Remember, I will always be here between this mountain and the river. Should a situation arise, I will be there for you. You can trust that I will always cherish these delicious moments in our life. Now, I have to move on, and you must do the same."

Amos started to unlock her grip.

"No, Amos, don't go away now, please," Rachel said. "Sit down here with me for a little while more."

"Rachel, my heart bleeds for you." Amos said. "Nothing has happened so far, we are just friends. It is getting dark now, and we must go. I will definitely talk to you another time.

Two days later Noah returned home, beaming with joy. Judith, Joseph, Rubin and Judah all eagerly gathered around him, as he told them all about Hannaniahs' elegant family, the tiled floors, and the four great Ionic columns at the entrance, the many rooms, the servants and all. The children were all happy about the big event. It was the first wedding in their family, and Rachel tried her best not to show her sadness.

"Noah, are you convinced that this is the best for Rachel and our family?" Judith asked. "She's only fourteen. Hannaniahs' children are older than she is."

"Certainly, Judith. Would I plan a wedding for our daughter if I were not convinced? Our Rachel will be like a queen in the family. They even have maid servants for her."

Rachel sat down, her head resting on her knees. *I never wanted the palaces, servants, or ornate bed chambers. I'm perfectly happy sleeping on my reed pallet spread on this floor.*

'Don't worry, it will all turn out to be good for our family," Noah said.

As the next day dawned, Amos and the two other workers had already arrived, and the barley harvest was in progress as Noah remained upbeat and enthusiastic. It was a great harvest, yielding four donkey loads of barley, and the wheat harvest was even more promising, expecting at least six donkey loads.

Some fifty people were expected for the betrothal feast, nine from Hannaniahs' home and about forty from the bride's side, including important relatives and elders of the town.

Rachel resolved herself to go along with her father's wishes and proceeded with the preparations.

Noah emptied the front porch of the animals and housed them in a new stable he had built up in the hills behind the house. The manger was emptied, and the floor was mucked out, resurfaced, stomped smooth with heavy, flat wood, and layered with a paste made of cow dung, pine resin, and sticky clay. The floor dried up with a smooth shine, onto which he added three area rugs made of flax to make the home even more attractive.

The family from Nazareth arrived a day earlier, at Joshua's insistence, to be with cousins for one more day. He also wanted to explore the ranges of Mount Carmel, looking for the Elijah Cave and the places where Elijah slew the false prophets of Baal.

It was the morning of the sixth day of Sivan, the day of betrothal. Amos, with his great culinary skills, was the appointed cook for the occasion. For the previous two days and most of the nights, he had been working on the preparations for the feast with his assistants Pecka and Eglon.

Before the cock crowed, two lambs with no blemishes were slaughtered, skinned, chopped and marinated with sea salt, coriander, and crushed balsam seeds. Then the meat was wrapped in linen soaked with virgin olive oil. Fresh bread and cakes were baked, and sixty small chickens – one for each guest – were stuffed with anise, coriander, dill and tansy and rotated on the slow-burning charcoal spit fire.

Judith laid out Rachel's betrothal clothes and ornaments, including a Chinese silk scarf in shining gold, a rare treasure she had saved to give her daughter. Aunt Mary had brought a small bottle of dye made from kopher leaves mixed with cinnamon oil, with which she polished Rachel's toes, fingernails, the palms of her hands and soles of her feet. The reddish-orange shine made Rachel's toes and nails glow like rubies.

"Now, it is time for you to rest and pray," Judith said. "You shall not engage in any other work."

Rachel sat silently on the bench in the inside room, made up and gowned. Inside, she cried with a broken heart. "Whatever Yahweh plans for me will happen to me," she told herself. "Amos, please stop working, take me as your bride," she whispered to herself. "Let us go away to the mountain top and make a small hut for ourselves. Put me to sleep in the folds of your strong arms, wake me up whenever you want. I will do whatever you like, any way you want. I am yours, all for you, you alone."

Noticing how quiet her niece had become, Aunt Mary came and sat by her side, holding her hands and telling her a little of the folklore pertaining to weddings. The children, Joseph, Rubin and Judah, were all in a festive mood, even more playful than usual, particularly with Joshua, whom they chased around with great fits of laughter.

By late morning the bride's family and friends started arriving. Most of the guests gathered in the front yard and the walkway to the riverbed. Many marveled at the exquisite flower garden that Rachel had created.

A group of elders lounged under the shades of the almond trees on benches specially reserved for them, while they waited on the group from Tiberius.

Joshua came down to the porch and sat. He gazed at the stream, idly listening to the heated conversations of the older folks.

One of the men said loudly. "Hmm . . . the day after Sabbath there had been a procession of Roman soldiers in Sepphoris . . . did you hear . . . with great reverence and worship, the soldiers held up a life-size bust of Tiberius Caesar . . . on their shoulder . . . on a litter."

"Yes, yes, I heard about it," said a one-eyed old man walking with a cane. "They even demanded respect and reverence from the crowd as if this was a procession of the Holy Torah," cried another Jew resentfully. "They want to consecrate the statue of Tiberius Caesar in the Jerusalem Temple, I hear, trying to turn us all into idolaters," Ahazia, the oldest man of the lot, "Now directives of Herod are enforced by Roman soldiers," a young man said. "The high priest is now dancing to Roman tunes."

"They collect their tithes and double the tithes without fail," one of the elder men said. "Herod is not even a Jew. What does he know about our ways?"

Suddenly, the boisterous conversations settled. The group noticed three horse-drawn carriages arriving on the opposite bank of the river. Noah came out, shading his eyes with the palm of his hand.

"The party of the bridegroom has arrived." Noah walked down to greet them.

The group began crossing the river. Some tiptoed from one rock to another. Others joyfully walked through the water.

Noah welcomed the party of the bridegroom. He hugged and kissed the men, then guided them up to his house.

Mary was busy teaching Rachel about various ceremonies and proceedings of the betrothal and the events to come.

Rachel sat on a stool, barely listening, fighting the unpleasant emotions in her mind.

At the rear of the main living area, the bridegroom sat on a quilted cushion reserved at the seat of honor. The elder Hannaniahs and the other seven men from the bridegroom's party sat on the left.

Noah sat down, along with four elders from the town, on the right side facing the group of the bridegroom. Wine and pomegranate juice, along with varieties of fruits, nuts and snacks, were served.

Hannaniahs Senior raised his flagon and shouted, "To life," and swallowed half of the wine in one gulp. Everyone began to clap, and soon the crowd erupted in raucous celebration. Hannaniahs again raised his flagon and said, "We from the house of Hannaniahs have come here to the house of Noah for the betrothal of my son Hannaniahs to your daughter Rachel, the firstborn from the house of Noah." The flagon slipped in his hand, and he poured wine on Noah's gown.

Noah paid no attention to the spill. Everyone lifted their cups and cheered. "To life and the glory of marriage."

"In accordance with the customs and traditions of the children of Israel, the next step is the bedekin. My son will officially lift the veil of the bride and confirm her countenance."

Hannaniahs Senior took the hands of his son and stood, as did Noah. Then, they walked to the rear room for the bedekin.

Outside under the broiling sun, Amos was preparing the main item for the dinner, the lamb chops. The cauldron on the fire, half-filled with olive oil, started bubbling. Amos threw a handful of mustard seeds that popped like fire crackers. The rings of chopped red onions sprinkled over, sweltered, hissing, and turned golden crisp. Finally, Amos dropped the meat pieces, one after the other, into the boiling cauldron, creating music of hissing and sizzling, until the pieces were fried fully. The golden lamb chops were quickly transferred to large silver salvers sprinkled over with goat's cheese and freshly picked coriander leaves. The meal was ready to be served with garlic and horse radish condiments.

Amos and the group carried in the celebration dinner, one tray after the other, and arranged it in an orderly fashion; the exquisitely prepared betrothal dinner covered the entire floor. As soon as Hannaniahs and Noah returned to their respective seats, the dinner started, with eating, drinking and merrymaking that continued until mid-afternoon.

Towards the end of the dinner, the elder Hannaniahs glanced at Noah. "Have you had the opportunity to prepare the contract?"

"Yes, I have," Noah said. He took out a one-page contract written in Aramaic on vellum, looked at it and began to read – a standard Ketubah. It outlined the obligations of the husband to his wife; food, clothing, sexual satisfaction to the wife, and such other items that are important to a marriage agreement. It contained a clause placing a lien on the bridegroom's property, promising to pay Rachel a sum of one thousand silver shekels and other compensation should he decide to divorce her or if he should die before her. The contract was agreeable to both parties. The contract was to be signed in Tiberius on the wedding day.

Amos stood there listening to the contract, head down and arms crossed across his chest for a short minute. He forced himself to recover from the shock after the reading was finished and went to wash the dishes.

There were some debates concerning the wedding date. The Hannaniahs wanted the wedding to take place within a week, but Noah wanted at least three more weeks to complete the wheat harvest. The date, settled in Noah's favor, was to be on the twentieth of Sivan in Tiberius at the Hannaniahs house. The bride's and bridegroom's groups hugged and kissed in friendship. The Hannaniahs praised the exquisite quality of the wine and food, commended Amos for his culinary skills and soon departed, making their way down to the river and on towards Tiberius. The bridal group watched the Hannaniahs leaving until they disappeared from view, and then the party continued with added vigor, noise and exuberance. Rachel was brought out unveiled and seated on the honor seat, and participated in the dinner festivities with the immediate family. Towards the evening Joseph, Mary and Joshua all left for Nazareth.

**** **** ****

The day after the Sabbath, on the nineteenth day of Sivan, the women of the hamlet of Carmel had assembled at Noah's house from noon onwards for an early dinner and preparations for the wedding procession to Tiberius. Dusk arrived. The sun sank below the mountain, turning the sky gray.

Noah became restless and was unable to sit or rest, and began pacing back and forth in the front yard. He watched the heavenly crescent dip behind Carmel into the great sea. Noah stood motionless beside the almond tree, head tossed back and chin up, reading the sky east to west and north to south, over and over again.

An hour passed before he saw some bright, twinkling spots in the sky. "I can see not three, but three hundred. Yes, there are stars in the sky. A new day is born, the twentieth of Sivan, a blessed day for our family."

Noah stood with his legs apart at the threshold of the family room. All eyes were on him. "We will leave from here an hour before midnight," he said. "We will reach Joseph's house in Nazareth way before sunrise. There, we will rest, refresh and then proceed to Tiberius in full procession."

The response was a prolonged silence that Noah took as agreement.

Amos, a fine singer as well as a harp player, prepared the music for the wedding procession along with Josiah and Samuel. Josiah played the shakers and Samuel the drums. Aapphia, wife of Jonathan; Eunice, wife of Nahor; and Hannah, wife of Serug, were the rest of the musical team. Drusilla, a thin girl with wry hair, a narrow face, thin lips and smooth, straight nose, was the most talented singer and dancer in the group.

The preparations for the bridal procession were already underway in the foyer. Drusilla assumed her usual leadership role for the bridal preparations in the family room. She focused her gaze on Judith. "Go now and take a rest. Sit down and stop running around doing this and that. You need to save your strength for the journey. You must tell us what to do, and it will be done."

Then she turned to Rachel. "Now it's time for you to start the bathing." She took Rachel by the hand and led her into her new bedroom, where a basin of warm water and perfumes of myrrh, aloe and balsam were all brought in. She closed the curtains and instructed Rachel to remove her clothing, and made her sit on a stool in front of a small looking mirror. With a soft moist cloth, she started washing Rachel's curly hair and face. Then she began telling her the traditional bridal advice, step by step, in a pleasant, musical voice, while continuing to sponge and clean her.

"Rachel, you have lived your life for this day, to become a bride and a wife, the next phase of your life. You will become a proud wife and soon a mother. Someday, you will be a happy grandmother and gracefully age as you fulfill the obligations of a woman of Israel."

Rachel sat quietly, her eyes closed. *Amos,* she thought, *you are the man whom I want to hold tight. I don't want to be a queen in any king's palace. I just want to spend my life as a humble farmer's wife with you beside this mountain.*

Drusilla rubbed between Rachel's thighs. The young bride pressed her lips together, closing her eyes. "The gateway to your garden, like the lilies of Sharon," Drusilla sang, "Its petals moist with the morning dew. He will come with might and right to enter the gate with his dagger of love. Let him show his might; you hold him tight until the dagger is in; the first blood is shed."

Wiped dry, oiled and perfumed, Rachel was ready when Judith, Hannah and Aapphia brought the clothes and jewelry. Mary painted her fingers and nails with henna, her palms and soles with the reddish-orange Kopher and cinnamon dye. Hannah with her artistic skills in bridal preparations, highlighted Rachel's eyebrows with fine, black powder moistened with oil that added to the sparkle to her lovely gaze. Rachel's bridal dressing began with Hannah, first slipping a soft white ankle-length linen inner garment on her and the outer full-sleeved wedding gown made of glistening white silk with a golden waist girdle and blue fringes.

Is this right? Rachel thought. *Or maybe this is my destiny. I have only one road to travel, and travel I must, with full faith. Today is my wedding day, tonight is my first night.* Rachel got up wearing a smile.

As the final step, Drusilla styled Rachel's hair into a tapestry of braids and curls, perfumed her armpits, and then the bride was all ready for the travel to the groom's house. Noah arranged for a carriage for the wedding procession, which was to be pulled by his own mule, Miracle.

It was midnight and the procession was about to start. The four torches were lit, Rachel with her gleaming silk dress dawned like a full moon amidst the stars, and the bright light that reflected on the happy faces permeated all around the house in endless ripples.

The torch bearers walked in front of the group in rows of two followed by the bridal group, all dressed in white, slowly descending down the walkway; a gorgeous sight, as if the belly of Mount Carmel had broken open into a gleaming, milky brook, now gliding down the steps towards the Kishon. Noah carefully lifted Rachel and seated her on the honor seat, and helped Judith into the carriage, and the procession started with the torch bearers leading the group. The musicians marched immediately behind, followed by the carriage and the rest of the bridal group.

Noah walked in front of the carriage alongside his mule. Amos blew a few notes on the bugle, signaling the beginning of a cherished traditional bridal procession in the heart of Galilee. Nahor played a tune on the harp, the drummers followed, and the girls began singing. The bridal procession moved slowly towards Nazareth through the Megiddo Plains like a slowly moving milky way amidst the vast ocean of darkness. The drums, rhythm and the strings blended in, and the band repeated the chorus.

The chorus sang:

"Forget my daughter; forget thy father's home,

Forget the Mount of Carmel and the flowers of the valley,

Forget my daughter; forget the music of the Kishon,

The king is waiting for you, hungry for your soul and self."

Soon the whole group started singing and dancing as the bridal group moved on to Nazareth. The group had one destination, one soul, one prayer: all should happen for Rachel's good.

In Nazareth, in the house of Joseph, the morning lamp had been lit at the first cock crow. Mary had baked a special honey almond cake for Rachel. Joshua spread the thick leather table on the floor and set out the breakfast with warm milk, pomegranate juice, waffles and honey. From Joseph's house – near the city wall – they saw the wedding procession with its bright torches at a distance.

Joshua went to the city gate and greeted the group. "Uncle, welcome home," he said. Then he hugged Noah.

Mary walked up to the carriage. "Rachel you look beautiful," she said, and put an arm around Rachel and guided her to the house. After breakfast, Mary took Rachel aside. "Go with courage, my daughter. This is your destiny," she said. "Love and serve your husband well. Good things will happen to you."

Drusilla checked and adjusted Rachel's dress, freshened her makeup, veiled her again and took her to the carriage seat. Rachel napped for an hour, before Drusilla awakened her. "We're ready to move east towards Tiberius," she said.

The road was wider than Rachel could have imagined. It was busy with people – masons, carpenters and handymen – traveling towards the city of Tiberius. Several horse-drawn coaches trotted by them towards Tiberius.

Drusilla sang:

"Let him kiss me with kisses of love, my love,

His mouth will taste better than the best of wines,

His fragrance better than myrrh and the roses of Sharon,"

Hannah sang. The men followed:

"Behold thou art fair, my love. Thine eyes twinkle like the doves.

Thy hair a flock of goats from the Mount of Gilead."

As they neared the city, there were a lot more travelers on the road, who moved aside to allow the procession to pass. Some sang with them, others danced with them, but all wished well to them.

The reality of Rachel leaving his side hit Noah hard. *She was there every day of my life for the last fourteen years; my help and support. Tomorrow, when the sun rises in the east, Rachel won't be there with me.* Noah bit his lip, and then willed himself to smile. *It's her life. I cannot be selfish anymore.*

A few children brought bouquets of wild flowers to the bride, smiling and giggling as they approached. "She's so beautiful," a boy of no more than four years said.

"I want to be a bride like her," a little girl said.

Rachel smiled at the children and bowed as she took the bouquets, and the procession continued with grace and elegance to the groom's house in Tiberius.

Rachel watched as the giant edifices of the city of Tiberius came into view. The two men leaned against the bastions, wearing shining helmets with flowing red plumes, brass breast plates and high leather boots: *Roman soldiers,* she concluded.

This new land suddenly felt frightening. *How different from the hills, valleys, ravines and flowers of my tranquil village,* she thought.

She had imagined a life with Amos. He would build her a home. There would be an orchard filled with her favorite fruit trees, a bountiful vegetable garden and, of course, children. It would be a quiet humble life that would be theirs, a life filled with love. But it was not to be. Her father wanted bigger and better for her. She knew Noah loved her, but she realized he didn't understand her.

"We've arrived," Josiah yelled.

"Look at the house. It's like a palace," Hannah said.

The procession stopped in front of a stone gate. Two men from the house walked towards them. They hugged Noah. "Welcome to the house of Hannaniahs."

A group of four women came out. Noah helped Rachel out of the carriage. He took her arm and escorted her, along with the four women, into the house.

The Hannaniahs house, designed like a Greek temple, had four imposing Corinthian columns at the entrance. Heavy doors of cedar opened to a gaily decorated house with marble floors. A regal purple wedding canopy adorned with golden fringes stood in the center of the grand hall.

The elder Hannaniahs lounged on a chair high and ornate like a throne, set at the far end of the hall. To his left was an empty seat of honor, along with a series of chairs for the bridal group. To his right were some thirty elders and priests, and another fifty people crowded around.

When the bridal group entered the hall, the elder Hannaniahs stood and walked towards Noah and hugged him. "Welcome to my house, welcome," he said.

Hannaniahs gestured Noah to the first seat on his left side. Out of the corner of his eye, Noah noticed the drooling of Hannaniahs mouth and the tremors on his hands.

All heads turned towards the bride as Rachel crossed the hall, escorted by the women to a room in the right wing of the house. The men from Carmel were seated. But Amos stood respectfully by the canopy, his hands folded, observing the reaction of the crowd. Joshua also stood behind the bridal group, searching the faces of the men studying the demeanor and the grandiose.

Rachel entered the bridal room, the room decorated with lush carpets, curtains, wall paintings, and several large sofas and chairs.

In the center stood an imposing bed, covered with sheets of white silk and pillow covers made in blue linen surrounded by fringes. The bed was set under a large canopy with a silk curtain that reached from ceiling to floor; the curtain was tied back with blue ribbons at the foot end. Seated on a high stool by the corner, a Greek woman in a flowing blue robe and a blue headband played lovely, but unfamiliar tunes on a lyre.

Rachel was seated on a regal cedar chair with silk cushions. A group of women gathered around, gazing at her with admiration. She greeted each of the women one by one, while they could hear laughter and applause emanating from the men's hall. The Kabbalat Panim was in progress.

Up in the great hall, the bridegroom moved slowly down the stairs, making an official entrance. He was a man in his mid-thirties, overweight, with a receding hairline. He wore a white, ankle-length silk robe with long loose sleeves and a leather girdle buckled a bit below the waist to flatten his jiggling belly. A bright scarlet-colored purse was hooked on the left of the girdle, the purse flopping up and down with a metallic clink with each step down. Eight men in pairs, dressed in white, closely followed the groom as he descended the stairs to the hall and was respectfully ushered to the honor seat on the left side of his father.

Exotic wines in elegantly carved flagons and silver goblets floated across the room, changing hands from one guest to the other. Freshly squeezed juices of many fruits, filled in carved glass chalices, along with cakes, biscuits and a large variety of fruits and nuts were all liberally distributed. Similar beverages and drinks were also served in the bridal room, but no drinks were served to the bride or the groom as per tradition. Joshua took a chalice of pomegranate juice and sipped; his face looked heavy and sulky.

Mahalalel sounded the first note; the musicians joined, playing melodies with the lyrics borrowed from the Song of Songs, until the bugle sounded a long, high note, and everyone became silent.

Eliphah, the high priest, and most respected amongst the three priests present, a thin man with fire in his eyes, stood to make an announcement. Turning towards the father of the bride, he bowed his head. "The next item is the reading of the *Ketuvah.*" He bowed again towards Noah, extending his arm for him to start the item.

Noah stood. He rolled out a scroll and read the *Ketuvah.* The reading was agreeable to both parties. It was signed by the groom and witnessed by two elders.

Wine glasses were raised. "L'chaims, to life," the men toasted.

"Respected guests," Eliphah said, "the next item in our proceedings is the bedekin. As you know, this custom was practiced right from the time of Abraham, our grand patriarch. As we read in our holy scriptures, Laban tricked Jacob into marrying his elder daughter, Leah, instead of the younger, more beautiful Rachel, whom was promised. As the bride was veiled, this deception was not discovered until it was too late. We, the children of Israel, shall not make that mistake again. The tradition of bedekin shall continue." Eliphah sat down as the bridegroom, flanked by his father and Noah, walked towards the bridal room.

The groom entered the room, doors closing behind him. After a few minutes, he came out smiling and raised his hand, confirming everything was in order.

Eliphah stood and proclaimed. "The next step is the chuppa."

The groom's mother, Keturah, a heavyset woman in her fifties, walked to the great hall followed by a group of women. She walked up to the groom, stood on his left side and held his hand. Both elder Hannaniahs and Keturah escorted him to the canopy and seated him on the chair.

The musicians began to sing again from the Songs of Solomon: *"Come with me from Lebanon, my spouse. From the top of Shenir and Hermon . . ."*

All eyes turned towards the bride coming out to the great hall, accompanied on either side by Mary and Judith. Everybody in the great hall stood up. Rachel was conducted to the canopy and seated by the left side of the groom.

Amidst loud applause and cheers, the music sang at high note:

Thou have ravaged my heart, my spouse,

Thou have ravaged my heart with thine eyes,

Thine smell better than myrrh and frankincense . . .

"Children of Israel, like the pure white blemishless kittle worn by the groom, today a new life is starting here, pure and fresh," Eliphah continued with the high notes of the ceremonies.

"The bride shall now circle the groom seven times," Eliphah said. "The bride is the light that surrounds and illuminates the house and protects from harm from outside."

Rachel, flanked by Mary and Judith, circled the bridegroom.

Hannaniahs stood quietly, still in meditation, as the crowd watched the ceremonies.

"The seven circles represent the seven days of creation of the world," Eliphah said. After the seven circles were completed, the bride and groom sat on their respective chairs under the canopy.

Mary and Judith lifted the hem of Rachel's gown and spread it like a flower around the chair. The bride and groom were given a glass of wine each.

The junior rabbi, Jeduthun, recited a wedding blessing over the wine. He emphasized the morality and the sanctity of marriage and the family traditions of the Jewish people. "The wine is the symbol of the marriage," he said. "Like the juice of grapes, it begins sweet at first, but as it goes through fermentation and maturity, the wine finally becomes a great drink that brings joy and satisfaction."

"Now is the time for kiddushin," Eliphah said.

The bride and groom stood face to face. The groom took a gold ring from his purse and placed it on the ring finger of the bride, who stood with her head bowed.

"Behold," the groom said. "With this ring you are now sanctified to me as my wife according to the Law of Moses."

The groom sat and the crowd clapped and cheered.

"This ring has no beginning or end," Eliphah said. "It goes on endlessly. For every end there is an immediate beginning. Likewise, the husband will encircle, protect and provide for his wife forever. Now,

I shall read the Ketubah one last time." After the reading, the priest handed the document to the groom, who presented it to Rachel.

After much applause, Jeduthun proceeded with a speech of blessing, the *Sheva Brachos.* One by one, he recited all seven blessings and gave his own interpretations.

Then the groom slowly rose to his feet for a long minute, looking to the ceilings, his glass of wine raised high up in the air. A soft solemn tune was played on the bugle. The bride swiftly swung the glass – as if possessed – and smashed it to the hard, marble floor. The wine glass shattered, the wine sprayed, and the crowd was arrested in a solemn silence.

Rabbi Eliphah jumped up, his face beet red: "Amidst all this celebration, the children of Israel shall never, never forget the destruction of our Temple in Jerusalem by the barbarians of Babylon"

The crowd replied, "Amen."

Joshua sat calm, with his lips pursed and chin resting on his fist. He glanced at Amos, who stood still, arms folded across his chest and eyes fixed on the floor.

"God prevailed upon the enemies of Zion to test our love for Him: our loyalty, and steadfastness," Eliphah said. "The House of God is now built in Jerusalem again, as a testimony that the children of Israel shall never be defeated again, and that they shall flourish and multiply like the stars of the heavens and the grains of sand on the shores."

The subtle grimace on Joshua's face was not perceptible. *The temple was built by a Roman stooge and the children of Zion still in bondage,* he mused.

The grand wedding feast had begun. The dinner tables were all set and the servants set out the meal. Jars of wine began flowing to the hall, until every hand held a flagon full. The Senior Hannaniahs and his immediate family sat around one table with the priests and spoke casually over a glass of wine.

Noah lifted his chin and smiled. Judith and Mary did not show any emotions of overt happiness. They all watched Rachel for what emotions she was showing.

The grand dinner that followed was an exceptional experience for the group from Carmel.

Joshua moved around, occasionally sipping from a glass of wine. A lot of his time was spent talking to Amos. He knew that Amos was grieving the occasion, although he confided to Joshua quite soberly, "I only want to see good things happen to Rachel."

"Will you be working in Noah's home from now on?" Joshua asked.

"Of course," Amos said. "Noah is like a father to me" He swallowed heavily. "You may not know this, Joshua, but I'm an orphan; I know not my parents. Noah's house is home to me." Amos struggled for a smile, but Joshua slapped on his shoulders consolingly and made a little smile for him.

The celebration continued well past midnight, even after the musicians and dancers had escorted the bride and groom to their bedroom and closed the door.

The bridal group from Carmel was given three rooms for the night on the second floor, left wing of the mansion. Noah lay awake all night. The bitter feeling of separation from his daughter stuck like a lance in this throat. He got up and paced the room, ruminating over the day's events.

Joshua could not sleep either. He and Noah sat up talking, mostly about Noah's irrigation of his land and the various types of plants, flowers and animals on Mount Carmel.

Joshua soon dozed off on the window sill.

Noah remained awake, feeling if he was suffocating. He missed the birds singing and the pleasant sounds of water flowing in the Kishon, and even the stench of animal droppings that sometimes carried into the family room. Above all he missed Rachel. From the first day of her life, he was with her. He had become dependent on Rachel for everything. It was with her that he conversed most often, and now she would be gone – no longer part of his daily life – no longer living in his home. Now she belonged to somebody else in a faraway land because of him. Tears rolled down Noah's cheeks. In his heart, he knew Rachel did not want to leave Carmel.

A few morning birds sang. Noah opened the windows. The eastern horizon had turned yellow and blood stained, the fore waters of a long, painful night had broken, and an infant day was popping up its radiant head.

Suddenly, he heard a tumult of urgent footsteps, sandals scratching on the marble, noise of people colliding, screaming, yelling and guffawing; sounds that resonated louder and louder heading towards his wing. Joshua suddenly sprang up with a pang of anxiety and grasped Noah's arms, asking huskily, "Uncle, what is the matter?" as Noah stood numb with a vacant face. Presently, the door rattled with loud kicks and blows. Before Joshua could reach the threshold, the door flung wide open. There stood an ancient bent lady, with one foot inside the room, shivering, with fire in her cavernous eyes, yapping incoherently, her toothless mouth rhythmically moving like a blacksmith's bellows. Behind her stood Keturah and three other elderly women with similar attitudes. Noah was arrested at that moment of uncertainty with a feeling of impending danger. He had expected them as tradition had taught. But he was baffled by the expressions of anger on the ladies' faces. Keturah attempted a smile.

"Come and see," the old lady shouted.

Noah gestured to Judith and Mary, who nervously followed the four ladies to the room where Hannaniahs and Rachel had consummated their marriage.

What possibly could have gone wrong, Joshua wondered. Then he recalled several statutes and commandments and sank to the floor.

When they entered the bedroom, they found the groom lying face down against a pillow. He looked at them sideways without turning his head, his face dark purple with rage.

"Rachel," Judith called. Then they heard muffled weeping sounds from behind the headboard.

Mary and Judith rushed behind the headboard, where they heard Rachel's voice.

Hannaniahs got out of bed, glared at Rachel's parents, then walked out of the room.

The three ladies with Keturah opened the curtain around the bed, and all of the windows. They carefully inspected the white bedspread, and then turned it over.

The old lady with cavernous eyes lifted a corner of the bed sheet with two fingers, holding her head back. Then she looked around, her gaze moving from person to person. "Do you see anything?" she screamed. She scanned the people in the room again. "I ask do you see anything?"

Nobody answered.

"I ask you one last time," the old woman screamed. "Do you see a sign?"

Noah joined Judith and Mary behind the bed and found Rachel crouching down, her head buried between her knees. Noah took her in his arms and lifted his daughter's chin until he saw her face. Tears streaked her face, her voice incoherent. "It will be all right, dear, it will be all right," Noah said.

Rachel buried her face in her father's chest, sobbing and grasping his robe.

The old lady folded the sheet and threw it to Judith. "Keep it," the lady shouted. "This is a sign of shame." The old lady turned her gaze towards Rachel. "Harlot, harlot, you have brought shame to the house of Hannaniahs."

Noah put his arms around the three ladies. The noises of stampeding footsteps neared towards the bridal room.

"Out, get her out," a tall male yelled at Rachel. "You have no place here."

Joshua ran into the room, elbowing through the crowd gathered at the door. He stood facing the crowd with his arms spread wide.

Noah and Mary shelled Rachel from either side and escorted her to the front hall. Everyone who had been staying in the mansion had assembled there, except for elder Hannaniahs, who was slowly making his way down the stairs.

Joshua's face turned dark as the clouds of Heshvan. He conducted the shamed and disgraced bridal group through the large cedar doors to the front yard. Amos was seen prowling the ground like a caged lion, angry and ready to fight.

A short while later, Judith and Noah were summoned to the room. Noah's face was white and ghostly like a dead man when he came out, Judith slumping on to his shoulders.

"What's next, uncle," Joshua asked. The bridal group from Carmel surrounded him, as the large oak door behind was shut loud.

"We must get to the temple and present our case," Noah said. "I know my daughter is innocent."

"What can I do, sire?" Amos asked.

"Not a thing, my son; the proceedings must take place in accordance with our law."

Amos pulled at Joshua, the two of them moving to a nook. "Joshua, I know Rachel is an angel," he whispered. "This should not happen to her. I am an orphan. Is the Law of Moses applicable to orphans . . .?"

"Let us go to the temple and finish the proceedings first," Joshua said. "I will talk to Rachel and ask my uncle. We will talk to you later."

Later that morning, the two groups assembled at the synagogue in Tiberius, a small building that could seat a hundred people. Five elderly men, the judges, were seated in front of an altar. The High Priest, Eliphah, sat on a higher level, flagged by Jeduthun and three other elders of the temple. They were all dressed in ceremonial garments, with robes, breast plates and tall hats. The group from Carmel was seated on the floor. Some fifty men from the groom's side stood around in no orderly fashion. The judges recognized the arrival of father Hannaniahs by bowing their heads and offered him a seat at their level.

There, stood one empty chair facing the judges.

Eliphah sat glancing at a large scroll, his face dark and calm. He signaled. Rachel was brought to the chair.

"Based on our traditions and in accordance with the Holy Scriptures," Eliphah said. "If any man from Israel taketh his wife and goes into her and hates her, as has happened in this case, then the father and mother of the bride have the right . . ."

The Hannaniahs crowd made a group noise of approval.

"I call Noah and Judith to spread the cloth of the first night for all of us to see."

Noah and Judith did as ordered. The judges inspected the sheet, raised their eyebrows, and stared at Rachel.

Joshua sat behind Rachel. *They will never believe Rachel*, he thought. *They will never humiliate Hannaniahs. They respect and admire his family and his wealth.*

Eliphah then turned to his right and left, and asked the judges, "Do you see the token? The token, do you see it?"

They shook their heads, no. The high priest stood, stretching his back. "The evidence clearly proves that Hannaniahs hates her. His jealousy is justified. Rachel, daughter of Noah, is not a virgin, but a harlot." He delivered the verdict.

A combined voice of exhaustion and dismay rose from the group from Carmel. But the much boisterous cries of approval that erupted from the Hannaniahs' buried it.

"This girl has brought shame to the house of Hannaniahs, the house of Noah, and the village of Carmel," Eliphah said.

Rachel slumped to the chair, her head hanging to one side.

Noah and Judith hugged each other, burying their faces on each other's shoulders.

"This is not true." Joshua rose to his feet with a defiant look and determined voice. All eyes turned towards the young man. "Rachel is not a whore. She is an innocent young woman who never brought anything but kindness and love to her family and neighbors."

The high priest cried, "Blasphemy! Blasphemy!"

"She is an innocent girl who would never hurt anyone," Joshua said.

"Blasphemy, you infidel," the high priest yelled. "Get out of this house of God."

Joshua took a step forward. "Rabbi, this bed is not her own making. Ask her what happened on her wedding night, and you will see she's innocent."

The judges shook their heads.

"Who are you to question the writings of the Holy Torah?" Eliphah asked.

"I am Joshua, son of Joseph of Nazareth. Rachel is my cousin. She is like an angel. She would never . . ."

"Say no more," Eliphah yelled. "You are a blasphemer. Let me remind you what would be for you in the *Book of Moses*. Should you shout any more, you will be taken out of this temple to the city gate. All men who heard the blasphemy you uttered now shall be obligated to put their hands on your head, and in the name of our Lord, you shall be put to death by stoning."

Joshua said nothing, but stared at the High Priest with his piercing blue eyes.

"Hannaniahs is an honorable man," Eliphah said. "In normal circumstances, no further proof would be needed, but the benevolent Hannaniahs has agreed to administer the jealousy test as a gesture of his compassion and magnanimity."

Joshua sat and buried his face in his hands.

As the priests prepared the jealousy offering in an earthen vessel, Eliphah started reading from the scroll. "Then shall the man bring his wife to the priest, and he shall bring offerings for her, the tenth part of an ephah of barley meal. He shall pour no oil on it, nor frankincense thereon, for it is an offering of jealousy, an offering for an appeal in question of guilt."

The priest placed the cereal offering on the altar. In another earthen pot, he collected water from the ablution basin, which was filled with mud and dirty oil floating. Then he scraped some hardened animal blood from the filthy floor. The priest mixed the dried animal blood with the ablution water, stirred, and handed the mixture to Rachel.

"If no man has lain with you, and if you have not lain with another instead of thy husband . . ."

Joshua stood with arms across his chest: the men from the bridal group pulled him to sit.

"If you are innocent," Jeduthun said, "then you will be free from this bitter water that cause the curse." The priest looked around. "But if you have gone to one other than your husband, and if you have been defiled, and some man has lain with you besides your husband, then the Lord curses you, causing your thighs to waste away and your belly to swell, when you consume this holy water."

The priest stood over Rachel. "Drink," he commanded.

Hannah stood, her hands held high. "Yahweh, God of Abraham, Isaac and Jacob give courage to Rachel, and reveal the truth." She prayed in high notes. The group chorused.

Rachel placed her lips against the pot, but her head pulled back in revulsion. *Almighty father of the Heavens, what have I done for this?* She wondered. She forced her mouth to the bowl and took a sip. Her cheeks swelled, and her throat closed. Rachel gagged on the vile liquid, convulsed and spewed the dark fluid on to Jeduthun' face. She tried to breathe with a guttural noise, but choked on her own saliva, followed by paroxysms of coughing, ending in convulsions, and collapsed to the floor and began to writhe in agony.

Joshua rushed to her side, lifted her up and started to pat on her back while cleaning her mouth. There erupted a chorus from the bridegroom's side. "Praise the Lord, for revealing the truth. Praise the Lord for revealing the truth."

"Cursed. Cursed art thou, disgraced woman! Take her to her father's house and let the scriptures be fulfilled," Jeduthun screamed.

**** **** ****

The return journey to Carmel was about to start. Nehume and Jonathan had already left for Carmel; they were to inform the villagers to prepare for the ceremonies.

Joshua looked a different man. His face bleak, confidence drained and movements brisk, swirling in a space of helplessness. He wheeled in the temple courtyard, searching faces one after the other for the immediate next step. His attention quickly turned to Amos, and their eyes met in the middle. Joshua took him by the side and they talked for some brief time. Joshua was visibly upset, speaking rapidly while arms flailing and pointing to the priest and at times to Rachel, while Amos was seen nodding his head. At a certain point, Joshua folded his hands in salutation and appeared to be imploring to Amos.

Noah appeared aged by another twenty years overnight, bearing the face of a dead man. Though he could barely stand, he carried Rachel to the carriage, assisted by Joshua. Rachel was half-conscious with froth in the corners of her mouth. Joshua pulled Noah to a corner and spoke with him, pointing to Amos. Noah shook his head undecidedly and signaled to the carriage.

In the meantime, Amos brought another carriage rented from the town.

"Where is Joseph," somebody asked. Old Joseph was found inside the temple sitting in a corner with an empty face: it appeared that he didn't grasp what was going on. Joshua carried his father in the cradle of his arms and laid him in the carriage, as if a sleeping baby is put to bed. Mary and three other elders from Carmel were also helped to the carriage.

The procession started to move towards Carmel. For a while, Joshua walked immediately behind Rachel's carriage, at times pushing and supporting Carmel. After a while, he climbed into the carriage. Rachel was still semiconscious, lying cradled in her mother's lap. She was going in and out of a trance. Joshua spoke tenderly to her, whispering kind words in her ears. Rachel at times opened her eyes and looked at Joshua, and appeared to have understood what he was saying. At other times she was incoherent and barely recognized her cousin. Joshua continued speaking into her ears, at times wiping her face and gently blowing on her face to cool. He then got out of the carriage and started walking along with the others.

After some time Rachel woke up and asked for Joshua to be near to her. She looked at Joshua closely, managing a weak smile. There was a deep respect and intimacy in her gaze. At first he could barely hear her, but later she regained strength and spoke with Joshua for a few long minutes. There was a feeling of determination on her face. She grasped Joshua's hands, kissed his palms, and gave them back to him with a grimace of confidence and resolve. She pursed her lips and nodded her head several times, confirming her resolve. When Joshua got out of the carriage, his eyes were red and teary. He stayed at pace with the procession initially, but soon he quickened his pace in long strides ahead of others towards Carmel.

There was no singing or celebration on the return journey to Carmel.

**** **** ****

In Carmel, it was late in the evening, and the blood-red sun was about to hide behind the mountain. On the northern banks of the Kishon, opposite Noah's home, some fifty men in white clothes and skull caps had assembled under a large poplar tree. To kill the time, some were playing cards and others, dice. A local rabbi awaited the arrival of the wedding group impatiently.

They parted ways for Joshua as he walked past them quickly. The children saw Joshua as he approached Noah's house and dashed out to greet him. They danced around him and wanted to hear all about the wedding celebrations. Joshua took the children to the hillside behind the house. He sat down under a tree and explained to them what had happened, in a manner that children would understand. "Your sister is like an angel," Joshua said. "She has done nothing wrong, as we all know, but we are all children of Israel. There are some statutes and commandments, which you may not understand well."

But the children were nothing, if not confused. They just couldn't understand what had happened or what was about to happen, but they understood that there was something wrong. The children's questions were very many, and there were no plausible answers for any of them from Joshua. "So, what is going to happen to my sister? So, she is not married anymore? We all like Amos. Can he take her as a wife? Can she go away with Amos to some faraway place? Joshua, can you take her away to some faraway places."

Joshua further tried to explain, saying that there are many things far beyond man's control, and that everything is determined by Yahweh and all. Staring into Joshua's eyes, Joseph, the eldest of the three demanded, "Joshua, are you sure all these things are told by God to Moses?"

"Yes, I believe so," Joshua said. "It all happened a long time ago in the mountains of Sinai."

Then the children spotted the group with two carriages arriving on the other side of the river, and they ran down to see their sister. By the time the group reached Carmel, the sun had already gone down, leaving a grayish reflection in the sky, and the men had moved up to the front yard of Noah's home. Noah and Amos carried Rachel across the river, but halfway through, Rachel signaled them to stop. She sat down in the middle of the river on a rock and dipped her feet in the waters of the Kishon. Rachel looked at her undulating reflection. She took some water in the cup of her arms, drank from it and splashed the rest over her face. Then she reached for her father's extended arms. Amos moved as if to lift her up again, but she signaled no. She appeared to have recovered her energy, as if she were removed from all that was happening. She ran towards the sobbing siblings with arms wide open, but slipped into a freshly dug pit that had not been there when she had left the previous night. She immediately recovered from her fall and stepped out of the pit, embraced her brothers, hugging and kissing, as if she would never let them go.

Joshua managed to usher the children back into the house again and beyond to the mountain valley.

Silence and darkness fell, and the four torches were lit again. A small sitting stool was brought over. Rachel was asked to sit on it. She obliged. The chief priest from Gabe, dressed in ceremonial clothes with a hat and breast plates, came to the forefront and positioned himself, legs apart, to the left of Rachel, holding a thick book covered in red leather with a page finder dangling from it like the tongue of a dead dog.

Upon entering the courtyard, Judith had collapsed and was carried to the family room by Amos and another man dressed in white. Noah moved towards Rachel as if in a trance. He embraced Rachel. Two elders came forward. They detached Noah from that deep embrace and led him to the family room. Noah crawled towards Judith, cradled her head in his arms and slumped to her chest, "My Rachel is innocent, my Rachel is innocent," he kept on saying.

Joshua returned to the front yard. He looked like a smoking mountain ready to explode. He saw one of the elders cover Rachel's head with a dark, thick cap that hung beyond the threshold of her shoulders. The other man, also an elder, gently pulled Rachel's arms behind her back and bound her wrists tightly with a flax rope. "No," he cried. But the voice didn't come out. A strong arm smothered his face and dragged him back.

The priest made a cough with a manufactured smile and brought back the attention of the crowd to the ceremony. "Children of Israel, I know it's already late in the evening; I know dinner is waiting for all of you. I suggest you all please come around the sacrifice. We will quickly consummate the ceremonies . . . yes?" The men did so. They made a circle.

The priest turned his eyes wide around with satisfaction.

"The Lord of Abraham, Isaac and Jacob, as it is written in the holy scriptures . . ." The crowd remained silent as the Rabi continued reading from the book. "If any man takes a wife and goes into her and hates her . . . the token of her virginity?"

Some of the elders raised their eyebrows and shook their heads.

"Therefore, Hannaniahs' hate and jealousy are justified, true to God and to the scriptures. Rachel, daughter of Noah, has shamed the house of Hannaniahs, defiled this house and this town." The priest nodded. "Now, it is the solemn duty of the men of this town to wash away the defilement as prescribed in the Holy Torah."

A heart-wrenching shriek came from the house, "Have mercy on Rachel, have mercy on Rachel. Brethren, I beseech you to have mercy on Rachel." Noah was beating his head against the floor.

Two mounds of stones were already gathered under the almond tree. Some stones were the size of a man's fist, others were smaller. The elders instructed the men to arm themselves with stones; each man took two stones each. Amos wheeled around, clenching his fist and at times quenching his anger by grinding his teeth. His face darkened. He collected two large stones and stood directly in front of Rachel, a step closer to her with his leg forward. He was turning the stones in his hand, around and round. An elder from the crowd noticed the size of the stone in Amos's hands. It was a giant among those stones, with sharp edges.

The priest angrily approached Amos, grabbed the stone from his hand and threw it towards the Kishon. "Take stones no more than the size of your fist," he admonished. He gave him two stones as specified in the scriptures and pushed him back in the line with the others. The priest then examined the stones in everyone's hands to make sure that the size of the stones fit the tradition according to the Law of Moses. "Because she has brought abomination to the land of Israel to play the whore in her father's house, so that you may put away evil from among you," the priest continued reading.

Several of the elders lowered Rachel into the pit and covered her in soil up to her shoulders. The head covered in the black turned to the right and left, and the cloth fluttered and puckered as she breathed heavily.

Rachel made a meek cry like a ram tangled in a thorny bush.

Seconds felt like hours to Amos. He sighed, and then moved from one foot to the other. He turned the stone in his hand, round and round.

"Children of Israel," the priest said. "This is the moment of our duty to celebrate the sacrifice."

"Oh, God of Abraham, Isaac and Jacob," Amos screamed like a war cry. He took a step forward, then leaned back with his arm fully stretched, still the stone rolling and rolling in his hand and violently charged forward, striking Rachel with a mighty blow right between her eyes. The stone sank into her forehead.

By the time they were finished, the two piles of stones all became one single bloody heap.

BOOK II

Joshua in Galilee

Joshua at the Temple in Jerusalem

When the ceremony had finally ended, Joshua was let out of the dark room. He walked down towards the Kishon, dizzy and sweating. He dipped his feet in the cold water, cupped his hands, splashed water on his face, drank a few mouthfuls and descended into the darkness. Almost involuntarily, he looked back towards the carnage. The frightening dark backdrop of Mount Carmel was a weeping wound that was surrounded by flesh-eating ants. He felt nauseated.

His pace quickened. Joshua squeezed his throbbing temple with both hands as he tramped the country road alone in the dark night.

What could I have done differently, he wondered . . . *six hundred and thirteen written commandments, six thousand three hundred oral commandments, statutes and traditions. For what nation is there so great who hath God so nigh unto them as the Lord our God is?* Joshua struggled hard to steady his head. A thousand scenes and thoughts flashed through his mind. His thoughts settled on the Exodus.

Thousands huddled together, ready to flee in the middle of the night – the Exodus. "You, neighbor, please let me borrow your gold and silver ornaments for tonight."   🌸

"Now, it is time to move," the thunderous voice came down from the firmaments. "I'll show you the land where milk and honey flows, flowing freely. Remember, you must. I am the one who took you out of the bondage. I am the one, the angry one, the stiff-necked one."

The yearning crowd marched through the scorching sun. Then there were pillars of clouds and blinding darkness? No, there were pillars of light. Hungry? No, quails dropped down from the heavens, flapping and gasping, and manna poured down like snowflakes. Thirsty? No, streams broke open from the desert rocks. The waters of the sea parted like magic . . . remember I am the one . . . the only one.

In Pharaoh's court, the shepherd's staff wriggled with life, Nile turned blood. The land of Egypt was ravaged with dead frogs, hailstorms, death and plague. The revenge. The wrath of God . . . "remember there shall not be another; I am the only God!"

With his road to Nazareth barely visible, Joshua walked even faster. His vision was clear and his mind was full. "What's going to happen to my sister? Joshua, what's going to happen to my sister? Where is the sign . . . the token . . . can you see it? Take her to thy father's house. Oh! Daughters of Israel, what's going to happen to any one of you?"

The Promised Land, he thought. "Yes, the one I promised for you and your children as an inheritance," the Lord said. "I brought you out of your bondage. Now you wait and wander, not one, but forty years; suffer hunger; suffer thirst; let your bile rise up to the head in rage and anger. The fire of revenge shall burn in you and then you are ready to slaughter, to conquer. I will deliver them to you. Slaughter everyone in your sight . . . until the very last seed is slain."

A thousand scenes and events rolled one over the other and crashed on the shores of his mind like the waves of Galilee tormented by a hurricane. Green bushes burned. The fingernails scratched on the tablets. "I command you, all ten of them. I give it you for an inheritance. Never forget – thou shall not have another God like me. That's the command. Go you, all of you, all sixty thousand of you men."

The children of Israel roared a mighty shout. The city walls crumbled like powder. Jericho fell. Cities fell, one after the other. All thirty and one of their kings, their subjects and all their cities, all run over, all conquered. Streams of milk flowing side by side with streams of honey, mixed with the blood of slaughter.

That is your land. Wherever you put your feet shall be yours for an inheritance. I give it you, all the land, from the Red Sea to the Sea of the Philistines, from the great river to the desert. I will deliver all the inhabitants to your hands. You drive them out. Don't look right or left. You shall be a stiff-necked people. I will teach you all the offerings, all the statutes, all the commandments. If she conceives a male child, she should be unclean for seven days and continue to purify for thirty-three days. If she bears a female child, she should remain unclean for fourteen days and continue to purify for sixty-six days. And what nation is there so great that has statutes and righteous judgments as this law which is set before you, for every situation attended to; a man sleeps with a beast, father entering into daughter, son entering into mother, brother entering into sister, sister going harlot, man going into a beast . . . You shall go to their cities, overthrow their altars, break their pillars, hew down their graven images, burn their groves and utterly smite them with no mercy; remember, you are a stiff-necked people and I am your angry God . . . You shall inherit all: the houses that you did not build, the wells you did not dig, you shall pluck grapes from the vineyards and fruits from the orchards which thou planted not. All of them, you shall eat and enjoy and be full. Never marry a damsel from them. Never give a son to them.

The lone traveler trampled through the pebbled road, drained and exhausted, at times stumbling down, ruminating, how strange, *never marry a damsel from them, never give a son to them.* He remembered the old man who had descended down to Jerusalem, all the way from Babylon, just released from captivity. As he flew through the firmaments, he surveyed the land, all the houses, all the wives and their ways of life. He sat on a stone in front of the temple, motionless until the sun set, until the evening sacrifices. As the people were coming to the temple to pray, the man got up in anger, tore off his cloak and mantle, smeared ashes on his body, plucked his hair in bunches and sat down there stupefied. Men gathered around. Then he rose up in his wretchedness and fell on his knees, stretching out his hands in front of the Lord and bellowed:

> My Lord, I am ashamed. Our wicked deeds are heaped up above our heads and our guilt reaches up to heaven. The people of Israel and even the priests have not separated themselves from other beings of the land, doing all deeds according to their abominations. The Canaanites, the Hittites, the Jebusites, the Moabites, the Egyptians and the Amorites, all have taken the daughters of Israel to wife, and they accepted daughters of the unclean beings to be their wives and produced offspring from their wombs and defiled. I am ashamed. Lord, thou hast commanded through the prophets that the land, onto which you go to possess, is an unclean land . . .

The assembled people were horrified and trembled at these words because of their transgressions. The sage stood up in front of the congregation, wept and cried. "Go. Go to your villages and cast them out. Cleanse yourselves." The congregation wept and screamed, fled to their homes, threw out the foreign wives, plucked their hairs, beat them and their children, and cast them out of the city walls. The High Priest went from house to house and made sure that no contamination remained. He turned to God and said, "Thus, I cleansed them of all foreign contamination."

The cleansing . . . the cleansing . . . when will this all come to an end, he asked himself. Many a word echoed in his mind endlessly.

"So what is going to happen to my sister?"

"Joshua, I am an orphan, I am ready to go away with her tonight. Nobody will hurt her."

"Take her to her father's village . . ."

Joshua remembered Rachel's words on the way back from the wedding.

"No Joshua, I will never do a thing like that. Let the scriptures be fulfilled. Let me retain the honor to my family. My mother has taught me the duties of a Jewish woman."

"Rachel, tell me. What really happened?"

In the darkness of the night, he came upon me. He held me tight. I couldn't breathe, but I knew the duties of a wife. I was ready to cleave. He was cold, sweating heavily and breathing heavily, cold and moist. He sat on me, rubbed over me, laid upon me. I just couldn't breathe. He pressed onto me, all over my thighs. No dagger came, I am sure; no dagger came. He slapped me on my face, on my bosom, kicked on my vagina. He shouted angrily, got up and sat on the chair for a while. Then he flung himself upon me quickly. I tried to hold him. I wept, but only I knew it. He came over me again, angry and shivering, and slapped me on my cheeks. He again pressed onto me, on my tummy, in between my thighs on my vagina. No dagger came, I swear; no dagger came. He came over me again for a third time. I didn't know what to do. I closed my eyes. I wept. He stood over me on the bed, straddling over me. He kicked me on my belly and on my groin. He stooped over me, on four legs like a goat, like an animal, and spit on my face. Then I knew it was all over.

Joshua felt dizzy; his legs felt heavy; it felt that he was walking, but not moving forward. Yet he kept on walking. Then he sensed a crowd approaching him from behind. He thought he was running and running away from them, but could not distance himself from the mob closing in. The crowd was building up in numbers shouting, "False prophet . . . false prophet . . . bastard, thou shall not enter God's temple, and neither shall your children nor children's children, false prophet!"

The crowd swelled. They threw stones at him. Many voices followed him. "If there arises among you a prophet or a dreamer of dreams, then giveth a sign or a wonder; thou shall not hearken unto the words of that false prophet. Thou shall put him to death because he has spoken to turn you away from the Lord, our God." The boy ran and ran, but the crowd was faster. They were closing in on him. "Prophet! Bastard! Prophet! Bastard! Your mother should have been stoned. Stone him and all Israel shall hear and fear, and shall cease to do such wickedness as this among you."

He ran as fast as he could, but the crowd had already overtaken and encircled him. A dark cloud came out, covering him.

"Get up. Get up, son. Get up. Why are you lying down here on this road? What are you mumbling?"

Joshua opened his eyes. There was morning light. He was soaking wet and trembling. He pleaded with clasped hands. "No. I am not a prophet. I am not a prophet."

"Son, what are you talking about? What is your name? Where are you going? Why are you here lying down by this roadside?"

Joshua looked up. He saw an old man with a beard above his head standing upside down.

The man shook his shoulders. "Young man, get up. Are you troubled? What is your name? Where are you going?"

"My name is Joshua; I am on my way to Nazareth."

A man in his sixties with a gray beard, a farmer by attire, helped him to his feet with arms around his shoulders.

"But you are on the way to Japha, less than a mile from here."

Joshua looked around, a bit confused.

"Young man, for you to go to Nazareth, you must turn around and go north about three miles. You will reach Nazareth if you are going that way."

"Well, I will go to Japha. My teacher is there," said Joshua soberly.

"Who is your teacher in Japha?"

"Zilinos, the Greek teacher."

The old man nodded signaling that he knew of Zilinos.

"But you look so tired. All your garments are soiled. Come to my home, take a rest, wash up and eat some food, and then you can proceed to Japha," the man said. And he took Joshua to his house. After a brief recess of rest, cleansing and refreshments, off Joshua went towards Japha.

**** **** ****

Joshua was glad; it so happened that he was going to see Zilinos after all. *At least I can talk to him for a while,* he thought. *Cassandra had always asked me to stay on for a day or two, but I never did. But today, if she asks, I will say yes.*

Cassandra recognized Joshua walking towards their house from a distance. The robe with the blue borders, the drooping left shoulder from the weight of the bag, the right arm swinging to the rhythm of his strides and the bouncing of his curls were all familiar. But today Joshua looked pained, his head down, and was brushing back his hair distractedly. As he came close, she couldn't escape noticing his bleak face.

Zilinos got up from his wicker sofa and greeted him. "Joshua, welcome! Such a pleasant surprise. What made you come here today? I was not expecting you." Zilinos came forward and embraced Joshua with fatherly affection.

"Come in, Joshua. Sit down," Cassandra showed him to the chair with motherly affection. "What shall I get you for a drink – pomegranates or grape juice?" She left for the kitchen in a hurry, with youthful exuberance.

Zilinos and Cassandra listened to his entire story of the wedding in Carmel without interrupting as Joshua recalled every detail. Cassandra was visibly saddened and looked into the eyes of Zilinos frequently. Zilinos asked neither questions nor for clarifications. He showed no changes in his countenance that would betray his emotions.

"We are very sorry for your cousin, Joshua," said Zilinos. "This story comes so close to you Joshua; therefore, you are a bit shaken, I see. But, it was like this always for your people. It will always be like this. You can't or won't change. You are a stiff-necked people, as it is written in your books."

Joshua rubbed the back of his neck. "Yes, Master, I too have a stiff neck."

"How did that happen?" asked Cassandra.

"I couldn't wait to get away from Carmel!" He resumed, squeezing his neck. "I was walking towards Nazareth. The road was dark, but I was always sure that I could find my way. Obviously, I was very tired."

Cassandra came over to Joshua and began massaging his neck. Joshua glanced up and gave her a gentle smile. "I had neither food nor drink for the whole day. I rested for a while by the roadside. I was awakened this morning by a kind man who dwelled by the roadside." Joshua paused, then said, "I am quite upset, teacher. I feel I betrayed myself. I didn't have enough courage to stop anything. I didn't know what to do or where to go. I was not planning to come here today, but somehow I found myself heading towards you."

Zilinos leaned forward. "This is a very difficult situation, Joshua, but don't punish yourself. Neither you – nor anybody for that matter – could have done anything differently. Everything will continue the same as long as your people exist. Because, in your case, your God created you, protects you, and has given specific, irrevocable statutes and commandments to you for all matters of your daily life. Your deeds are destined. Any words spoken against it would be blasphemy. Any attempt to change it, is an act against Israel and against your God. It's all written in stone."

Joshua nodded. He looked at the lines of his outstretched palms as if he understood it all.

"Would you like to stay over tonight, Joshua? I am making preparations for dinner. Maybe you should consider staying here for a couple of days. You look very tired," she said, as she patted Joshua's shoulders.

"Yes I would like to stay with you for a day or two. I have a few questions to ask the master."

Leaning forward on the sofa, Zilinos grasped his student's palms. "Joshua, you have been shaken by the events of yesterday. I think you may need a cup of nice wine." He went to the kitchen and brought three cups of wine, and shared them with his pupil and Cassandra. He downed a mouthful of it, savoring the essence of the drink and turned to Joshua.

Joshua also gulped a mouthful and started conversationally, "Teacher, I wonder would such a situation as that of Rachel have happened anywhere else . . . in Greece?"

"Hmm," guffawed Zilinos, "Joshua, such a thing would never have happened in a Greek community. Therefore, there is no need to think about handling such a situation." For the Greeks," Zilinos continued, "they have no creation stories such as yours. Instead, they found God in the wonders of nature. They saw the bright light of the sun and said, 'Well, this is God.' They saw the wonders of the nature and said, 'Well, this is God.' They saw the magic of fire, thunderstorms, air, water, sky, and stars, and in amazement they said, 'Well, these are all gods.' . . . The Greeks were not believers, they were thinkers. In fact, I cannot imagine of a single facet of human thought that has not been touched by a Greek thinker," stated Zilinos.

"Master, I agree. But coming to women, I haven't heard of a Greek woman who was a philosopher, a playwright, an architect, a sculptor . . ."

"Yes," said Zilinos thoughtfully. "In general, the Greek culture has been built around the virtues of men. However, a Greek is not going to peep into the bedroom of a newly married woman, searching for tokens of virginity. In general, the Greek philosophy always seeks the virtues of wisdom, courage and morality. As far as the relationship between a man and a woman goes, it has always been considered to be a private matter. Fundamentally, it is a relationship and a covenant between a man and a woman. However, women in general have been considered vassals for procreation, and relegated mainly to housekeeping and raising of the children. They were never allowed to appear too frequently in public. They were not part of the great political system or Greek legacy.

"Joshua, even in art, painting and sculpture there is great emphasis on the male physique and its majestic beauty, power and agility. You know, the Greeks always appreciated the perfect majesty of male nakedness a lot more than that of women. There are some people who believe that any garment that covers the body is a cataract that dims the radiance of your natural beauty."

Cassandra, while cooking, was listening to her husband's dialogues with cocked ears and at times shaking her head with a sideward smile. She brought a plate full of toasted almonds, dried figs, dates and cubes of goat cheese, and came into the conversation, scolding. "Joshua, you ask for a drop, he will give you an ocean. I can already see that this is going to be a long night." They all broke out into a spontaneous laughter.

"That's all right, Cassandra, the day is too young," Zilinos turned to Joshua with an eliciting gaze.

Joshua took a small refill of the vine, took a sip and asked curiously, "Teacher, you had mentioned about the great theater and stage shows in Athens. Why were women not allowed . . .?"

"Joshua, the theater activities were exclusively for men, even the female characters were played by men with masks," Zilinos said. "Then again, there were some major activities such as the Panathenian festivals and temple ceremonies where women participated side by side with men."

"Teacher, when I was going through *The Republic* . . ."

"Ha! *The Republic*, interesting . . . yes, go on."

"Master, in the making of the ideal republic, did Plato expect women to sleep with several men – like harlots?"

Zilinos took a deep breath, "Plato envisioned the grooming of philosophers to rule the state, the philosopher kings, so to speak. These guardians were to be selected, trained and groomed, step by step, to be the rulers of the country. Women played no role in the ruling of the Republic, except for selective breeding."

Joshua nodded. He lifted the wine cup, swirling and enjoying its circling purple waves. "So, extending that thought process, the women are also the property of the community, which the men can share."

"Of course, but by sharing, they don't become harlots; instead, the concept of possession and selfishness is taken out of the equation.

Joshua, they believed that men outclass women in all aspects of human life and are superior in just about every sphere. The women were termed as the weaker sex."

Cassandra didn't like the progression of the dialogues. She started to say something, but the teacher spoke in advance: "At the same time, they accepted that women could excel in several other aspects of life, such as medicine or music."

"Zilinos," protested Cassandra, "I have never heard you saying such things as selective breeding. What is this all about?"

"Cass, there are very many things that I have not told you about the Greeks." He smiled sideways and then continued professorially. "Plato believed in selecting handsome, strong, intelligent men and beautiful women for breeding to create a very healthy, intelligent breed of population that would be raised as governors."

"What happens if a child is born with some deformity?" asked Cassandra.

"Sadly, children born with defects should be disposed of at birth."

Joshua was in disbelief. Many a line of the Torah flashed in his mind, "Impossible," he said to himself. " . . . with blemishes . . . and everybody like him, the lepers . . . throw them all out of the camp."

Zilinos continued stoically. "They are of no use to the community and will eventually turn out to be a burden, they believed."

"That is disgusting, teacher," Joshua protested. "Using women as breeding machines and disposing of disabled children is simply sickening. Didn't God create all humans equal?"

"Creation! Well Joshua, as of today I'm not quite convinced who created whom. Man created God, or the other way round. That would be your work. Tell me the answer when you find out."

"Maybe someday, I hope, teacher."

"Well, come on. Let us take a walk in my orchard." Zilinos rose to his feet and pulled Joshua up by his hand. A warm southern evening breeze blew over them, fluttering the foliage and waving the boughs. It was a small, well watered and robust orchard that Zilinos had nurtured. The heavy bunches of pomegranates had turned from yellowish-green to orange-red, now gently dancing in the breeze. The silver leaves of the olives gleamed against the strong rays of the summer sun. The robust vines that cascaded over the meshwork of fences bore heavy bunches of grapes that hung low, kissing the ground.

"See, I have just a hundred roots of grape vines, enough for my needs for the whole year. We have plenty of vegetables, a lot more than we both need," He turned to Joshua as if sharing an important secret, "Joshua, do you know why the Greeks live longer and healthier than most others?"

"No master, tell me."

"Because, I think, we eat lots of vegetables, little meat, just enough wine and do exercise most every day, maybe."

Interesting, Joshua thought. *This is a very interesting man – exercise every day; his body strong, lean and slim; extremely bright with a wealth of knowledge and a wonderful memory. I am fortunate I got him as a teacher and friend. I can ask him any question; he will have an answer. Let me try.*

"Master, I am not so sure about the various classes that Plato was talking about in his republic. Is it all practical?"

"It's a bit complicated, Joshua. I don't think it is practical or morally right. In his republic, the society is divided into three classes. The Gold Class are the governors – the philosopher kings; the Silver Class are the supervisors and soldiers; and the Iron Class are the common laborers. If you compare the society to a human body, the governors are the head. They determine the direction of the entire community. The supervisors and the soldiers are called the auxiliaries – taking orders from the governors – they are the heart, the executive power of the society. The workers represent the limbs. Plato believed that by sharing wives, children and property, the unity of the state would be enhanced, since possessiveness tends to cause greed and dissension amongst the people."

"Teacher, this is absurd, thoroughly disgusting," Joshua said. "Is there any role for a high priest in the governance of the state?"

"None. Religion has always been a part of Greek culture, as you know, but it does not really dictate how people were supposed to live," Zilinos said. "Greeks believe that it's important to keep the gods happy, or at least appeased, lest curses, plagues and punishments. Keeping the gods happy is the obligation of the state. Zeus did not write any statutes or commandments. Religion primarily consisted of celebrations and ceremonies, more or less, but the common man has more faith in 'oracles' than in gods."

Joshua nodded.

"Master, when you told me about democracy the other day, I thought it was an excellent system. The citizens participate in election, and they rotate the responsibility of ruling such that one governing today will be governed by the others at another time. Why were Plato and even Aristotle not enthusiastic about democracy?"

"The experiment with democracy in Athens died four hundred years back. Plato postulated the Republic as an answer to the pitfalls and the eventual failure of democracy. He believed in a benevolent king."

"Endorsing a dictator as the guardian of the society?"

"Yes, that is correct, a benevolent dictator," Zilinos said.

"In such a case, who is guarding the guardians? It seems they are supremely powerful," Joshua added.

"In Plato's thinking, the successful making of the Republic is rooted in the wisdom of the guardian, the philosopher king. But Joshua, as we know now, Plato's ideal republic never came to be. Just fifty years after Plato wrote *The Republic*, the country was taken over by Alexander."

When they returned home, Cassandra had prepared the dinner. The dining table was set tastefully, with a porcelain amphora filled with wine at the center of the table. The amphora had an engraving of an elderly Greek man courting an adolescent boy with sexual gestures. Cassandra had prepared a special item for Joshua, a selected piece of lamb flayed and filled with goat's cheese, garlic, coriander, dried grapes and herbs, wrapped around and roasted to golden brown and seasoned with pickled onions, olives, parsley and herbs.

"See, Cassandra has made a feast fit for a king, especially for you, Joshua." He poured three flagons of wine, then raised his cup and said, "To your health, Joshua," and took the first swig, squished in the mouth and savored with closed eyes and said, "Joshua, tell me. How do you like this wine?"

Joshua took a sip and said, "The very best I ever had. Then again," he chuckled, "this is only the third time I've ever had a cup of wine."

Cassandra smiled and said, "Joshua, please eat. Zilinos will talk throughout dinner and well into the night, as long as you are there to listen to him. These days he is lonely, more or less, and looks forward to your arrival. I believe you are a victim of his lectures today."

"Joshua," Zilinos pointed to the jug on the table, "I make two types of wines. This one is my favorite. Although the quality of the wine depends on the soil, the grapes and the brewing barrel and all, some years the wine will come out just right. This wine is from two years back, and this is the last bottle, and I'm delighted to share it with you."

"Thank you, Master."

Cassandra cut a piece of the meat carefully and laid it on Joshua's plate. "Joshua, I hope you will like it. This is not traditional Greek cooking. Now that Zilinos doesn't eat meat that often, I make this only when we have guests, and I hope you will savor it."

"Joshua is no guest, Cassandra, he is our son not born to us," said Zilinos gaily.

"Son he is, Zilinos," said Cassandra, still keeping the smile on her face. There was a brief period of silence when they began to eat. Cassandra enjoyed looking at Joshua eating with pleasure and satisfaction like that of a mother feeding her baby.

After dinner, Joshua and Zilinos helped clean the table and the dishes, and they all came to sit on the porch. Cassandra burned some incense in the censer, and the fragrance filled the room. "Zilinos likes this fragrance, and we burn it nearly every day," Cassandra said.

Zilinos leaned back on the sofa and raised his legs to a cushioned foot stool. "Joshua, I can see that you are at a difficult place in your life now; nowhere to go, yet you need to move on. Tell me what your thoughts are."

"I'm not sure, but one thing I know: I must leave Israel. I need to go away to see and learn more about the world."

"Forever?"

"No, I will come back some time, but for the time being, I need to go away."

"Where are you planning to go, Joshua?"

"I don't know, but I'm hoping you can provide me with guidance."

"Joshua, I have traveled extensively in Greece and also have visited Rome, Syria, Egypt and Morocco. Beyond that, I have not ventured. I have always wanted to go to Babylon and Persia, but I never got there. When I was a young man, I also wanted to go to the Hindu land way up in the east. The Greeks call it India. Actually, Alexander had planned to go back to India for a second time to conquer and found an eastern capital at Taxila . . ."

"Joshua, you have talked to us about a certain girl, Mary, whom you liked," Cassandra said. "If you travel, are you planning to leave her here or to get married and take her with you?"

"Mary is a beautiful girl. She always likes to see me and to be with me. I like her too, and if ever I plan to marry, then I will marry her. But I am not ready for marriage, and I don't expect her to wait for me indefinitely. I am preoccupied with the future of this land, and also I want to study more about other religions and their concepts of social justice. I believe that is my calling. Marriage is not in my mind."

"How old is this girl Mary you are talking about?" Zilinos asked.

"She is almost my age – fifteen. But she already looks like a grown up woman," said Joshua.

"You also have grown quite a bit." Cassandra gave him a long look. "You have become much taller, and your shoulders have become broad in the last year. You even have a few whiskers. Certainly you look older than a fifteen-year-old boy," she said with an endearing smile, pinching on his cheeks gently.

"Joshua, the things you said about social justice and righteousness were the preoccupation of Greek philosophers even before the time of Socrates." Zilinos leaned forward. "I know you have read some of their works. It is not possible for a man to travel to all the different civilizations of the world. However, you must go to Egypt and spend as much time as you can in Alexandria. Remember, we talked about the great library in Alexandria?"

"Yes, Master. Ever since our discussions, I've wanted to visit Alexandria, but I don't know how much of the library is still left there."

"When Julius Caesar invaded Alexandria . . ." Zilinos looked at the empty wine glass and turned to Joshua. "Do you need another glass of wine?"

"No, teacher; I am fine." Joshua said. "Please continue."

"When Julius Caesar attacked Alexandria, a portion of the library was burned down, but they were able to save most of the books and scrolls." He took a few more swigs. After a conscious, noiseless burp, he resumed. "There is this temple of Serapis in Alexandria built by Ptolemy. I have been there. They have a library at Serapium – the sister library – with an excellent collection of very well-preserved documents, not affected by Caesar's attack."

"Zilinos, how long ago were you there in Alexandria? Is it a safe place to go?" asked Cassandra.

"Of course it's a safe place. Alexandria is a world by itself, quite amazing. You will find all kinds of people there from all across the Mediterranean coasts; Greeks, Romans, Syrians, Persians, Babylonians, Egyptians, Nubians, Libyans, and even some traders from the Orient."

"From the Orient?" Joshua raised an eyebrow.

"Yes. For over four hundred years, or even more, there was a trading route extending from China and India, via the Parthian countries to Damascus and all the way to Alexandria through the Phoenician highways here in Israel," Zilinos said. "Most of the caravans you find here are part of that. From Alexandria, their commodities were traded and exported to other Mediterranean countries via ships".

"Joshua, it appears that you are very serious about leaving this country and going to all these places. We will certainly miss you," Cassandra gave him a sad look. "These days, we fondly look forward to your coming here to spend time with Zilinos. In fact, Zilinos talks about you all the time."

"That's quite true, Joshua," Zilinos said. "I never had a student as bright and inquisitive as you are. You have a great future. You could be a teacher in a big institution, or maybe an advisor to a king or some very high officials in the government here or elsewhere."

"Master," Joshua said, "I have no such ambitions. Israel is the preoccupation in my mind, that's all."

"Joshua, the next place you must visit is Rome. Rome has collected all the spoils of Greek civilization, and they have built upon it. During the reign of Augustus, the fortunes of Rome have grown beyond comprehension. You must certainly go to Athens, Delphi, Damascus and, if possible, to Babylon as well. Getting to India and China is quite cumbersome, but maybe you could consider giving it a try. Your proficiency in Greek will take you a long way."

The conversation lasted long into the middle of the night, but Joshua could not stop asking questions, while Zilinos could not stop explaining things. He talked about some people in Alexandria for Joshua to meet and begin his studies.

They all slept very late in the night. Zilinos woke up before sunrise and was getting ready for his morning walk. Without waking up Joshua, who was sleeping on the couch, on tiptoes he got out to the front yard.

"Master, can I go with you?" asked Joshua from behind.

The old teacher's face lit with a fresh sparkle in his eyes, and there was a new energy in his voice. Of course, son. You young people need more sleep. I thought I would sneak out without you. Well, come along. It's always good to have company for a morning walk."

Japha, a small township in the fertile Megiddo planes, had a population of about six hundred. It was a clear morning. They could see the rise of Mount Tabor in the east, beyond which the rising sun had just come up.

"Joshua, what you want to talk about in this pleasant morning? Alexandria is by far the most exciting place I have been to."

"Master, if you don't mind, I need to ask some more about the creation of the world . . . I know you have read a lot. In your opinion, how did the world came about?"

"Ha-ha, the creation story, again! Joshua, this is the most debated question of all. A question that all civilizations and philosophers have tried to answer, and many of them have even given explanations about it, as well. The creation story of the Hebrews, though, is unique – interesting to read. What the Greeks did was to try to reason out the origin of the universe. Agreed, they had ridiculous stories in their mythology that the entire universe came about through a colossal sexual intercourse between heaven and earth and all."

"I remember reading about Thales of Miletus, who argued that in the beginning, the universe was a formless mass of moisture, Joshua said. "But my question is: how did that formless mass, come about without somebody creating it. Did they explain?"

"No, not exactly. It's all postulation. It was about six hundred years ago that a younger Greek thinker, Anaximander, who knew the works of Thales, postulated that the origin of the universe started from a mass of boundless moisture – apeiron – in which the elements existed in a dormant form.

"Is it the same boundless mass that Aristotle wrote about?"

"Correct. He also said that the apeiron was in everlasting motion," Zilinos said. "At some point, portions of this mass just broke off, like a piece of clay from a potter's wheel, and became the original seed or germ of the world, a form of fertile nucleus. Then, the cold and hot elements condensed into a wet mass of earth at the center, surrounded by firmaments or mist. The combination of dryness and heat that developed from this everlasting motion ignited into flames, which burst out into rings or wheels of fire evolving into the sun, the moon and the stars."

"So, they were saying that the sun and the moon came into being after the earth was formed, right Master?"

"Yes. With the fire and heat from the sun, portions of the earth dried up, the waters receded and the land masses started to appear. Then, listen to this carefully. Between the dry land and the water masses, there was mud or slime from which the first particles of life were formed. These initial life forms were like tiny fish," Zilinos wriggled his fingers. "From which larger fish, and then animals with scales and feathers, and eventually man evolved. That is to say that man evolved from some tiny fish over a period of time."

They sat on a stone bench by the wayside. Zilinos looked into the distance.

"So, our earth is the center of the universe, surrounded by the sun, moon and stars revolving around as rings of fire. The earth, as we see it, stays quite at the very center of this universe, motionless. Does that make sense Joshua?"

"I have never questioned that God had created man, although not exactly as stated in the Torah," Joshua said. "What I would like to know is who then created that initial 'mass of moisture and confusion', and how did the very first particles get started?"

"Most people believe that the beginning was some type of void or confusion, or a formless mass," Zilinos said. "Nobody is certain. Whatever the case may be, Anaximander postulated, for the first time, an account of the origin of the universe in purely natural terms."

"Are they talking about some kind of evolution from a finite particle, all the way to the formation of man?" Joshua asked.

"That is not an unreasonable way to put it," agreed Zilinos.

Then, at the old cemetery on the east end of Japha, they turned around to go back.

"A bit later in history, another Greek philosopher, Anaximenes," Zilinos said, "claimed the origin of the universe came from a primal substance called air. He believed air is life itself, distributed all across the universe. At some point the air condensed into mist and water, but the air contained all of the elements. Moreover, he maintained that air is the ultimate substance of life in the world. Air is God, and it is life itself. We are alive when breathing air, and without it we are dead. When we breathe air, we imprison a piece of God within us. Interestingly, Joshua, in your books after your God had created Adam, he breathed air into him as well."

"Yes," Joshua said, "I agree the concept of air as life itself is quite interesting."

"It is seen in many other civilizations as well, probably the very first time in Babylonia, and later in the Isis and Osiris stories from Egypt."

Joshua glanced at Zilinos. "Is there anything more specific with reference to the creation of man as such?"

"There are some, for example Empedocles, who lived approximately five hundred years back, who said that the universe is composed of four fundamental elements – air, fire, water and earth – and that various proportions and combinations of these resulted in the formation of anything and everything that we see in this universe today, including man. He denied the idea that human beings were created by a certain god. 'Love,' he said, is the force which harmoniously integrates one element with another. Strife, on the other hand, is the dissociation of elements leading into disintegration."

"Master, is he trying to say that it is the difference in combinations of these elements that separate plants from animals and man."

"Yes. For example, there would be cows with ears of tree leaves and humans with arms like the branches."

"That sounds a little ridiculous. What do you think, Master?"

"I agree, but his strongest contribution was that knowledge is the key to understanding; with knowledge, he said, one can arrest the wind, bring rain to the earth, halt thunderstorms, and bring water from Hades. He also said that the soul is a piece of God that migrates from one person to the other: transmigration of soul."

"He certainly is a very interesting man; in fact, all those philosophers are interesting, and their discoveries are enlightening."

"Wait a minute Joshua," Zilinos said. "Empedocles insisted that there is nothing called inventions: they are simply discoveries of that which was already there."

"Teacher, these are all profound stories, but are these stories truly any better than the creation stories?" Joshua asked. "This universe, with its immense glory, cannot have originated from nothing. There has to be a divine source for this universe and I believe that source and power is God. Would you agree?"

"I agree, Zilinos said. "There is a divine power about which we know nothing. We gave him names. We defined his likes and dislikes and what he wants and does not want, and created his images in papyrus, stones, bones, wood and mud, in shapes and forms of our imagination. In your book, God himself created a fully formed man and breathed life into him. The Greek philosophers assert that there is a tremendous, time-consuming process of evolution from which primordial substances develop all the way to their present state. But the man who tried to explain all of these things in a more concise fashion was Aristotle, who got the clues from Plato. His teachings will address your concerns more clearly."

"I have read a bit about him," Joshua said. "I am glad you brought Aristotle here."

"I know you like Aristotle. Aristotle believed that this universe is entirely real and constantly evolving and moving, and that there is no illusion about it. He said, 'Beneath all the turmoil and confusion of this universe, there is permanence, stability, rhythm and order.' He contends that for every effect there is a cause. For this universe that is always in a state of motion and change to come about, there must be a cause. That cause must be infinite beyond motion and change, which can start only from a point of immobile perfection, which is God. That's what he stated," Zilinos smiled. "As you can see, I'm an Aristotelian at heart."

"So, the eternal force that initiates all the other movements is static, permanent and divine?" Joshua asked.

"Aristotle held to the dictum that the universe is eternal. He had learned from his predecessor Parmenides that '*ex nihilo nihil*,' meaning 'nothing comes from nothing.' Therefore, the concept of anything beginning by itself is absurd."

"Absurd, indeed. God is the prime mover of all moving things. It's beyond contest. But, Master, did Aristotle believe in an omniscient God?"

"No. He did not define God. He did not believe in a God who became involved in controlling the activity of beings on this earth. God does not speak to the world, nor can the world go to him seeking help. For Aristotle, time is eternal, perfect and immutable. For every second, there is a second before and one after. However, he went further to explain his concept about the universe. He said that the universe is spherical in shape with a motionless earth at the very center, and all the stars and celestial bodies are revolving around the earth on their own axes at varying speeds. And all those celestial bodies are composed primarily of earth, water, fire and air, except at the very periphery, where the fifth component or the quintessence is ether, an invisible substance, purer, divine and more perfect than fire. When he spoke of the creation of beings in this universe, Aristotle to a great extent submitted to the earlier philosophers such as Empedocles."

After a long moment Joshua said, "I'm disappointed. Aristotle is a great philosopher, all right, but his views on some of these issues are flawed. I am fully resolved, teacher, that man is a special creation of God for a purpose."

"What would be that purpose, Joshua, in your view," Zilinos asked.

"I believe man is created to spread peace on earth. He is the representative of God on earth, to help and love fellow human beings and to make this world a better place."

"Very profound, Joshua, I am really impressed. I am just sharing with you a short introduction to some of the Greek thoughts regarding the origin of the universe and God, for that matter. You will need to study for many years to learn and understand them on a deeper level. Honestly, as far as I know, you are the very first Jewish boy even interested in learning anything about other civilizations. When you study them, you will develop your own thoughts about them: some you may like, and some you may not."

Joshua stayed with Zilinos and Cassandra for two more days. On the third day he returned to Nazareth.

**** **** ****

The house felt somber and lifeless when Joshua reached home. He saw Mary, red-eyed and subdued, sitting beside a sleeping Joseph. Mary wiped her tears and welcomed Joshua with a hug. "My son, I know how hurt you are. We all are," Mary said.

Joseph opened his eyes and sat up. He looked weak and frail: the color had drained from his face, and the bags under his eyes had swollen. Over the last few days he had grown progressively weaker, particularly after the events at Carmel. He was never hungry and seemed to have forgotten everything that had happened recently. He even grew uninterested in his carpentry work and spoke only when it was necessary.

"Son, Mary was here twice yesterday, looking for you," the mother reminded the son. "She is quite upset, as you can imagine. She was here today early in the morning, and left only about an hour ago. She was eager to see you and worried that you hadn't yet returned. Did you tell her that you might take her with you to Jerusalem? Is Naomi going with you?"

"Yes, mother. I'm planning on going to Jerusalem, but the more I think about it, the more unsure I become," Joshua said.

"Are you planning to see Mary today? That child will not sleep tonight unless she sees you." Mother searched Joshua's eyes.

"No, mother, not today; I will go tomorrow." Joshua sat down by his father's side and held his hand.

Joseph looked up with glassy eyes. "Son, I didn't know you had come in. I probably slept a bit. I am so glad to see you. Did you go from Carmel to Japha? That's what we guessed, or that you may have even gone to Jerusalem. Son, please don't go to Jerusalem. You'll get nothing by arguing with those rabbis. You didn't forget Sepphoris, did you?"

"I understand father, let me think about it."

The family had a quiet dinner. Nobody spoke much, and everyone went to sleep early that night. The next morning, Joshua went off to visit Mary.

Mary and her mother, Naomi, were originally from Magdella. Naomi became pregnant out of wedlock. She escaped stoning owing to the timely interference of a priest by the name of Meddad, who had concern for the unborn child. She was taken out of Magdella in the night and resettled amongst a small gypsy community about two miles north of Nazareth on the way to Garis.

Joseph's family met Naomi, at their local synagogue in Nazareth. Mary was compassionate towards Naomi, understanding how it felt to be pregnant without the traditional protections of the community. She began to visit Naomi, and soon the families became friends.

Naomi was a beautiful woman with a round smooth face; a long, slender nose; flowery, full lips; and dark, curly hair. Her parents were of Babylonian descent. Meddad had visited her frequently until about four years earlier, but when Mary was around eleven years old, Naomi ended the relationship after noticing the priest cuddling with Mary on the hearth. She supported herself and Mary by working in the fields for a daily wage.

**** **** ****

Joshua could not remember when he had begun to like Mary. As very young children, they had played together, making up games, such as hiding and trying to find each other, games that children liked to play. Although they were the same age, Mary had showed the indications of adolescence much faster. Soon Joshua found himself thinking about her and wanting to spend more time with her.

He remembered it was about a year ago; Mary began speaking to Joshua in more intimate terms. One evening in Naomi's house while they were sitting on the hearth, Mary said to Joshua, "Joshua, Look at me. Look at me carefully," she said with a secretive smile. Joshua looked at her but did not notice anything new.

"Don't you see anything new?" she demanded.

Joshua shook his head.

"Well, close your eyes," she said.

Joshua closed his eyes. Mary pulled down the neckline of her gown and pushed her chest forward.

"Look, I am starting to get breasts," she said with a smile.

"Mary, what are you doing?" Joshua shouted.

"I'm growing a bosom," she explained. "My mother says these are for feeding babies."

Joshua looked at her small, budding breasts. He blushed again and stammered, "Mary, pull up your gown. A young girl should not behave in this way."

"Joshua," Mary confessed, "you are the only one who will ever see me like this. To whom else am I going to tell the feelings and secrets of my bosom? Tell me, young carpenter."

Although the scene of showing her bare chest had happened one year ago, those images stuck in his mind and frequented his thoughts more often than not. Joshua spotted Mary from a distance. Her features had changed markedly within the last year: she had gotten taller, her opulent dark curly hair was parted in the middle and her red lips had become full and smooth like rose petals. Even her smile had a glittering radiance with two beautiful dimples formed on either side of her cheeks.

He didn't have to wait much longer, to see those dimples again. Mary came running to Joshua and hugged him as he approached her house. Then she began to hit him on his shoulders and chest, and then grabbed his hand and playfully bit him on his arms. Joshua smiled and held her hands to control her. "Joshua, I hate you. You didn't tell me you weren't coming home from Carmel. I came to your house four times in two days. Your parents were also very upset. I thought you were gone forever, that you had gone far away and were never coming back."

"Mary, please calm down. I'm here now. I came to see you. Going away; I wouldn't do it without telling you."

Naomi was getting ready to go to the fields. She came out of the house, knotting her scarf tight over her hair and with a wide smile.

"Where are you working now, Naomi?" asked Joshua.

"The plowings have started in Obadiah's wheat fields, and I began working there last week. I will work there for another three weeks. He has plenty of fields. He needs more workers. He wants Mary to work for him, too, but I don't like the way he looks at her – like a hungry fox," Naomi said with disgust.

"I will never go and work for him," Mary said. "I prefer to starve. He looks at me as if I am wearing nothing and smiles, showing his dirty teeth. Huck! Disgusting, like rotten almonds."

"Mary," cried Naomi, "watch your tongue. You are not supposed to talk like that." Mary made a playful face at her mother and smiled at Joshua.

"Are you going to stay for dinner?" Naomi asked.

"Yes, he is." Mary said.

"Mary, you start preparing for dinner; I will be back in the evening," Naomi called as she packed a few pieces of bread and some nuts for lunch and left for work.

"Joshua, come and sit down." Mary pulled him by the arms to the front porch of the single-room house. Mary and Joshua sat down on the floor, cross-legged. She brought a flagon full of pomegranate juice, fresh waffles and toasted almonds and sat by his side without wasting a second, not looking at his face. "Joshua, I feel deeply saddened about Rachel. Let me ask you this. Why didn't Amos save her? They could have escaped to some place where nobody knew them and lived there forever."

"Amos could have — it was possible — but Rachel didn't want such an escape. It would have branded her family as outcasts forever, destroyed the honor of her family."

Her face suddenly clouded. She spent a long minute gently biting her nails and in deep contemplation.

"What are you thinking, Mary; tell me?"

"It's sad, Joshua. I pray such a thing will never happen to another Jewish woman." She looked into his eyes with her lips parted, but words did not come out.

"Come on tell me, Mary."

"Joshua, I want to tell you a few things now that nobody else is here. I rarely get to see you alone these days, particularly since you are always going to Japha. I don't know whether you are trying to avoid me or not." She folded her hands and sat, silent and somber, for some time. She grasped Joshua's hands in the cup of her hands and, staring straight into his eyes, began softly.

"Joshua I am getting scared and very restless. I think about you all the time. I fear that someday you will go away from here and never come back to me again. Sometimes my heart races, other times it is heavy like a millstone and sinks inside my chest. I don't sleep well at all. I don't know how to say it. Look at me, I am growing and changing every day. There is this inexplicable feeling of throbbing or tickling in my bosom. When I see you, my breasts swell and throb with pain, and my desire is beyond anything I can imagine. I don't know what." She beamed at him, face down, with the upper corner of her eyes.

"Girl! Are you not bashful at all? Have you no shame to tell me this?" Joshua asked.

"None at all, Joshua" Mary replied steadily. "I have no one else to share these feelings with. You are my best friend. I think of you all the time. When I go to sleep, you are there. When I get up, you are there. You are with me always. I have no secrets to myself, none. I don't want to have any either. In fact, I feel comforted when I tell you all that is in my mind, and I feel guilty when I don't. But you are different. You never tell me anything about yourself. You always talk about going away from here, that's all. My mother tells me that girls grow much faster than boys. I have had monthly signals for the last year. Mother tells me that a girl should get married within about a year after the bleeding starts." Her face suddenly lost the light, her eyes filled up and drops suddenly grew larger, ready to fall as she gazed at the yellow-leafed poplars in the front yard.

"Mary," Joshua said. "I like you. I like spending time with you, but I am not thinking about you all the time."

"Then what are you thinking about, Joshua? Tell me. Tell me exactly what were you thinking on the way to my home?" She moved closer to him, touching his knees.

"Really," Joshua hesitated, "You want to know that?"

"Yes, I want to know that," she said. "What were you thinking on your way to my house?"

"Mary, it will be such a boring story for you."

"No, Joshua. Please tell me," she pleaded. "I like to look at your eyes and listen to you when you are speaking. Your voice has changed, and it sounds solid, deep and tranquil. Please, Joshua."

"All right," Joshua began, "Mary, do you know what the soul is?"

"Yes, it is in everybody. Somewhere around here." Mary took Joshua's hand and pressed it to her left breast.

Joshua tried to pull his hand away, but Mary held him tightly. "Yes, you are touching on my soul, right now. Press on it and feel it. Let my soul rejoice," Mary said, closing her eyes.

"Mary," Joshua continued, with his hand still on her breast. "Long, long ago, about six hundred years ago, there lived a sage, a philosopher and a mathematician called Pythagoras." Joshua tried again to release his hand from her breast, but Mary tightened her grip with her chin covering the folded hands.

"No," Mary cried, "This is not the story I want to hear, but I will listen if you stay on my soul while you tell it."

Joshua continued, "Pythagoras, he believed in the equality of men and women. He didn't think that women were inferior to men and should be subordinate to them."

Mary laughed gaily, "Good story. I like him. Tell me more." She kissed Joshua's hand, held it in the cups of her hands and pressed it against her breasts.

Joshua could not have resisted any more.

"Pythagoras thought the universe was a living object surrounded by air. The air inside of us is the soul, which is part of God. When we die, the soul departs and migrates into other beings."

Mary looked confused. "I don't quite understand Joshua," she said.

"This is called the reincarnation of the soul."

"Reincarnation? Why would this happen? I have never heard of anything like this in our teachings."

"Pythagoras believed that if your deeds were bad, then you would reincarnate into an animal. Then, as you lived better lives, you would progress into another being, and so on, until your soul has been fully purified. When the soul is devoid of all blemishes, then it will join with God as its final destination."

"But my soul has already reached the final destination, Joshua. This is my last abode. I don't want to go anywhere else. You are my God."

"Mary, listen to me."

She smiled. "I'm listening, Joshua."

"Our soul, this life, this air, is all part of God," Joshua said. "We are the abode, the temple where God is situated as the soul. Therefore, we must keep ourselves pure and clean. The Pythagoreans do not eat any meat. They do not kill animals either."

Mary said, "Are there no sacrifices in their temples?"

"No, they have no temples or sacrifices."

Mary said, "Good, I like that. I want to be a Pythagorean. Do they think the lamb they sacrifice may have the soul of their grandmother?"

"Probably, yes. Probably they believed like that," said Joshua.

"What else did he say?"

"Mary, Pythagoras said many, many things. I do not know all of them. Some of them are very deep and very complex. He was a mathematician, too."

"Like what? Tell me a thing he said, please?"

After a moment of hesitation, Joshua started. "He said that in a right-angle triangle, the square of the hypotenuse is . . ."

"Joshua!" cried Mary interrupting, "Stop! Such things are all for you. What did he say about me?"

"He would have said that you are a girl with a soul." Joshua gave her an endearing smile. He loved her wit and often laughed in delight.

"Mary, I do understand your feelings towards me, but you are not in my mind at all times," Joshua said. "I'm always restless myself. I believe I have a different calling. I have no intention of marrying now, but if I were ever to marry a woman, Mary, it would be you. But . . ." he said seriously, "but . . . you must not wait for me. It may never happen."

"It will never happen?" Her face clouded again and her voice quivered. She moved even closer to him almost hugging. "Joshua, then I will never marry. But my mind says that I will marry you someday, and I pray that . . . that day will be soon. I will go wherever you go and do whatever you say, except don't tell me to go away from you. I know the call of my soul and my body. I am so incomplete, and only you can make me full. Then only will I fulfill the meaning of my creation."

Mary sank to Joshua's chest, and he clasped her and caressed her tenderly on her back for a long minute.

Mary unfolded Joshua's hands and got up saying, "Joshua, drink your juice. I'll make some bread and meat for you. Tell me about your plans of going to Jerusalem. When are you planning to go? What are you restless about? Ever since you started going to Japha, I have seen the changes in you."

She kindled a little fire under the saagh and Joshua sat on the hearth facing the fire.

Mary's voice turned somber and husky, "Joshua, there are so many things happening to me that I don't even know how to explain." She paused for a while, looking into his eyes, looking for an answer.

"Tell me, whatever it is, I would like to hear," he said.

"There are some days in a month, particularly after my monthly signals, that I have this burning compulsion to be with you. It is so intense, that my heart beats so fast, and sometimes I even blush and sweat and feel like running to you, to be with you. I have such blazing desire to be with you. My mother understands it. She tells me to pray to God and fast, but when I pray to God, He tells me that my yearning for you is right."

"Joshua," Mary touched his ribs. "I came from here. God created me from your rib. I am part of you. I am you. I feel we are one. How can you say no to me? I have no more secrets to tell you. You must understand me." Mary stayed close to his chest. He embraced her and held her for quite a while, looking at the fire under the saagh.

"Joshua, I can hear your heart. When I keep my ears pressed against your chest, I can hear your heart saying, lov-it, lov-it, lov-it. Really, I can hear the music of your heart. Joshua, what are you thinking now, right now? Tell me."

"I was thinking of going to Alexandria."

"Do you see me going with you?" she asked.

"No," Joshua said.

Mary's eyes welled up, and she began to cry. Joshua kissed off her tears and held her tight.

"Joshua, if you must go, you must go. If you don't want to take me with you, so be it. But please give me something to hold on to. In my days and my nights and in my solitude, give me something to hope for, something to hold on. Tell me that you will come and marry me and be with me someday. That's all I ask of you."

"That's not fair to you, Mary. My future is so uncertain. I don't know when I will come back. It will be many years before I come back, if at all," Joshua whispered.

Mary ran her fingers across his lips, "I want to hear from here, from your mouth, that you will come back for me someday. I will wait and pray for the day when you return, and we will be together as husband and wife. You will certainly see the token of my virginity. I promise you." She pressed her lips tightly on his chest.

A long minute passed.

Joshua sighed deeply, "Mary, I can't say no to you. Yes, someday I will come. It will be a long ways out." Mary held him tightly and kissed him all over, on his hair, brows, eyes, lips and chin. She was smiling and crying at the same time.

"Mary, what were you talking about; this token of virginity," Joshua asked.

"Yes, what about it?"

"It's a primitive, irrational custom. Both Zilinos and Cassandra tell me that there are many, many girls who are virgins who will not get any bleeding at all after a sexual union with a man for the first time."

"My mother told me the same as well, but I don't care. I will have it. I will wait for you. I shall not be defiled."

**** **** ****

In Nazareth, Joseph grew weaker each day, at times withdrawn and sleeping more than usual. Sometimes he could not even remember names that had been familiar to him. Yet he always had a wide smile for Joshua, showing all of his thin alabaster-like teeth, three on the upper gum and two below.

Joshua stayed back in Galilee for the arid months. Each morning and evening he walked over one mile with his mother to the village well to draw water for them and the animals. When rain and thunderstorms announced the arrival of another Tishrei, the Galileans were overjoyed. There was an abundance of work for carpenters in particular. Joshua helped Joseph with the carpentry works – Joseph had set up his trestle and work bench under the shades of the poplar trees. They worked hard together, making plows and yokes, boxes and chairs, and any others required of a carpenter. For many weeks Joshua and Joseph earned more than two shekels of silver a day. Joshua put away his money in preparation for his travels.

One day, after a noon rain while the descending sun was scorching the earth, Joshua took Joseph for a walk outside the city gate where the poplars grew around the tall, old cypress trees. Even though Joseph was weak, he was thrilled to spend time with his son. Joshua locked the old man's hand in the nook of his elbow and walked slowly, holding on to his waist, talking about their family and family history.

They stopped and sat on large stone beneath a thickly foliated fig tree. Joshua looked straight into Joseph's eyes and said, "Father, you are the most pious man I have ever known. You are kind and loving. I have never seen anything but love and compassion on your face."

The old man smiled gently, "I know you are planning to go away from here, Joshua." Joseph looked sad and tearful but no tears came out. His eyes were dry and dusky.

"Yes, father. I plan to leave here soon. I'm not sure when I will return. I don't know when I will see you again. Maybe I won't. I am eternally thankful to you for my being in this world. But for you, my mother carrying me in her womb could have been just another story of a stoning in Galilee, another harlot cleansed from the village, a routine in our traditions. I am not asking why you did it, but God bless you. You will have a special place in heaven." Joshua kissed Joseph on his brow.

Joseph finally wept, his face tightened as his lower lip trembled. He held Joshua very close, squinting. He stared into his son's eyes with a rhythmic slow tremor of his head and started very slowly.

"Joshua, I've yearned to tell you the true story of your parents someday." Joseph paused for a while and continued very slowly and tenderly. "Son, I was never a marrying type of man. I had never been with a woman in my life. My love was always with trees and woods. Trees are the most wonderful creations of God. Each one is different in size, shape and countenance. I used to study the trees from my childhood days, the wonder that stems from a small seed or a twig, the trunks, brushes, leaves, flowers and fruits. I marvel at the food and shelter the trees provide for us, but the wood . . . that is something entirely different." He wetted his dry lips by swirling his moist tongue around. "Each type of wood is different in color, consistency and design. I always felt sad when I cut down a tree. In my mind I used to say a prayer to God to forgive me for cutting down this wonderful creation of His. Yet when a piece of wood is cut into a shape, chiseled and polished, each one looks like a sculpture. You can see the whole world in the meat of the wood, in those grains, the twists, the turns, the curls and curves, the flow of the countless designs. If you look carefully, you can see the designs of the whole world in a piece of wood, the firmaments of the sky, ravines and rivers, the landscapes, the waves of the ocean, the parting of the sea, the mountains of Sinai and everything – everything is there in the wood, as if in a painting. I enjoy looking at the perfection of wood. When I finish a piece of furniture, I feel that my sin of cutting down the tree is now forgiven. Some wood even has its own oil within it to protect and polish. I love the smell of freshly cut wood, even the taste of it. I can work on the wood for days on end without food or drink. It doesn't bother me."

He paused for a while and shook his head a few times as if he was determined to say something but was turning inarticulate. Joseph turned to Joshua passively and stumbled saying, "Your mother . . . your mother . . ."

A long minute of silence elapsed.

"I was forty years old when Mary was born. I knew her parents very well. Mary's father was an excellent craftsman. Mary grew up as a lovely and pious Jewish girl. When she was nearly fifteen, every young man in Nazareth was fascinated by her. I'm sure she would have had many offers of marriage." He choked a bit and grasped his son's hand, looking at the writings on his palm and stroking his finger over the lines. He continued.

"Roman soldiers," he scoffed. "A few of them are good people, but most of them . . . scoundrels . . . believe and behave as if they have the right to the first night of every Jewish virgin." Looking at the far distance, he continued. "He was a handsome man, of course. But like a ferocious vulture he descended on the poor little dove. He was a centurion." Joseph paused.

Joshua looked into Joseph's eyes with surprise.

"A centurion?"

"Yes, son. A centurion. I don't know his name. I have never seen him since. Son, in our society, even if a woman is totally innocent, even if she did nothing to provoke her attacker, she is always judged to be at fault. What could that young child do, in front of that raging lion? Yet some elders immediately pointed the finger of blame at her. 'Maybe she walked in a way that made him look . . . maybe she dressed without modesty . . .' They were getting ready to take her to the elders in Sepphoris. That was when I came to stop them. I have helped to preserve the purity of that woman ever since. My marriage was a salvation. I have never known your mother as a woman. My only goal was to save you both from the wrath of the Law of Moses . . ."

Joshua and Joseph spoke late, even after the dusk turned dark, and then headed home. Mary was praying, and dinner had been prepared. "My goal was to save you and your mother from the wrath of the Law of Moses . . . the wrath of the Law of Moses . . ." reflected Joshua all the way walking home.

Over the following months, Joshua spent a great deal of time with his parents and visited with Zilinos at least once a week.

In the meantime, as suggested by Zilinos, Joshua traveled to the port city of Caesarea to meet with a man called Abhi Faroosh, a Parthian trader now settled down in Damascus. Faroosh was a leading business man who traveled between Alexandria and Damascus and spent several months in Ptolemais with one of his wives Sophiar.

At Caesarea, Joshua met Sophiar and her only daughter, Layeela, in their house. Abhi Faroosh was not in town. Sophiar was a very soft-mannered, heavyset woman of Greek descent. Her original name was Lydia, but after marrying Abhi, she had changed her name at his insistence. After speaking with Joshua, Sophiar agreed to recommend him to Abhi. But she cautioned, "Abhi goes to Alexandria only twice a year these days. He is expected to arrive with his caravan sometimes in the middle of Sivan, not sooner."

**** **** ****

In Galilee, the almonds bloomed again and people were preparing for the Passover celebrations. Joshua made plans to go to Jerusalem, and counted his savings – forty-three shekels of silver and twenty bekah. Mother Mary was afraid for her son's safety in Jerusalem. The priests could charge him with blasphemy and take action against him, she feared. "You won't gain anything by arguing with those priests in Jerusalem." Joshua remembered Zilinos' cautions. Still, he was determined to go to Jerusalem first and then to Alexandria. However, young Mary held him tight, and just wouldn't let him go without her.

The night before Joshua planned to leave, Naomi and Mary came to Nazareth. Mother Mary, Joseph and Naomi conferred and finally agreed that they would permit little Mary to accompany Joshua to Jerusalem.

Mary and Joshua packed their bags and started off to Jerusalem early on the morning of the sixth of Nisan. The Passover celebration would begin on the fourteenth night. It was typically a seven-day journey by foot from Nazareth to Jerusalem. Mary was like a bird let out of the cage for the first time. She was walking, talking, pushing and pulling Joshua, and leading the way on the road.

"Joshua, I have money with me," said Mary. "My mother gave me ten shekels of silver and thirteen bekah. How much do you have?"

"I have nothing, Mary," Joshua said.

Mary laughed. "Don't you worry, Joshua. So long as you are with me, I will take care of all your needs? I will buy you food, I will find water for you, I will find a wayside inn and finally we will go to the great temple and see everything there together."

"The wayside inn demands too much money, Mary," Joshua said. "In this festival season, the inns are all usually full. If I were alone, I would have slept by the roadside, under a tree or on the porter's rest."

"Is that true, Joshua? Then I will do the same. I will sit up and sleep. You shall rest your head on my bosom. That's all," she said in a low loving tone.

Joshua pulled a purse of money from his bag and gave it to Mary. "I have been working hard for the last seven months. I made some money. I will not let you sleep by the roadside. We will find food and stay at an inn by the roadside every day."

"I'm not worried about that at all, Joshua. But if the innkeeper asks me who I am to you, what should I say?"

"What would you say?" Joshua asked.

"I will say we are betrothed. My mother told me to say that. If you remember, we are betrothed. Just the other day you promised me that you would someday marry me? That is a betrothal, and God is our witness."

"Yes, my dear. You are right, someday." Joshua smiled and took her hand. "Mary, have you ever walked this much in your life?"

"Never. The farthest I have ever walked is from my home to yours. This is the first time in my life that I have walked with you freely, that too, to the temple of Jerusalem. Tonight is the first night I will have spent with you in the same room on the same sheet.""On the same sheet?"

"Yes, Joshua. We shall sleep on the same bed, holding each other. Remember, we are betrothed. But you and I both know where we must stop."

Joshua was quiet. *How does this village girl have this level of wit and wisdom*, he thought.

That evening they stayed in a wayside inn about a mile past the city of Nain. The inn was located on the foot of Mount Tabor, which stood high over five hundred yards into the sky overlooking the Jezreel valley. The innkeeper, an old crimpled man greeted them, "Welcome you young couple. You must be newly married?"

"Yes," Mary exclaimed, rolling a ring on her finger.

Joshua noticed a ring on Mary's finger for the first time.

"This is the year following the jubilee, the festival must be very full," said the innkeeper as he took the couple to a room at the back of the inn. "People have been heading to Jerusalem for a week now – so many people."

It was a small room, with no windows or furniture. A long-necked earthenware water pot and an oil lamp with one wick were kept in one corner of the room.

"If you want any food, you can tell me, and I will arrange it," the innkeeper said.

"Thank you, but we have enough," Mary said.

"Thank you for your help," Joshua went on as he handed him a silver bekah. The man looked at it carefully and put it in his purse. He returned to Joshua with a few copper coins as the balance.

Joshua and Mary sat quietly on the floor for a few minutes. It felt strange, different. Joshua had fixed his eyes on the signet ring with surprise.

"Joshua, the ring was my mother's idea," Mary started explaining. "She said it would be safer for us if I wore the ring, so that there wouldn't be any questions from strangers, and that it would prevent men from approaching me. Mother said there are many harlots around the temple during the festival season." Mary took off the ring and handed it to Joshua.

"Joshua, you are the one who should put this ring on my finger. I want you to do it," she said.

Joshua stood up and helped Mary to stand. They walked out hand in hand, behind the inn and into the mountain range. Dusk neared. The setting sun was orange on the western horizon, and the firmaments crimson red and glowing golden. The moon was visible, rising above Mount Tabor in the east. A few stars glittered. A pair of low-flying partridges with berries in their beaks descended and perched on a stone cliff beside their nest. The baby birds cried meekly with open beaks. Looking at the parent birds feeding the babies, Joshua and Mary clasped each other intuitively.

Joshua grasped Mary's left hand, looked into her eyes passionately, looked high up into the heavens, and said in a tranquil voice, "Mary. In witness of the descending sun in the west, the rising moon in the east, the glittering stars in the sky above, and as we stand here on the bosom of Mount Tabor, I promise you this: I so dearly love you. But no man should marry a woman and go away indefinitely. I certainly am going away, you must know that."

So saying, Joshua slipped the ring onto her finger, held her close and they both stood motionless, their eyes closed and lips locked. When Joshua finally opened his eyes, the sun had already gone down to the great seas, leaving the remnants of a deep-reddish glow on the horizon. The moon blessed them with a shower of silver rays. When they returned to their room, the oil lamp was already lit, and the pot was filled with cold water.

Naomi had packed a few parcels of food for the road. Mary took one of them, opened it and set out for dinner some bread, cheese, nuts, dried figs and a few dates. After the dinner, they spread the sheet on the floor and put out the lamp. That night they slept together in each other's arms.

Sometime after midnight, Joshua was awakened by a tumult of sounds: cocks crowing, dogs barking, birds chirping, and the chaotic sounds of many animals at once. "What do you think is happening," Mary asked. "Perhaps a fox violated the chicken coop?"

"You may be right. There are a lot of wild animals in these mountains. I don't know how many hours to sunrise from now; let me see." Joshua went outside and looked at the sky. There was no sign of a morning aurora in the eastern horizon. The moon had moved further to the south, showing more of her blemishes. He returned to the room.

Mary asked, "What do you think?"

"I am not quite sure. Maybe we can start now; we have a lot of distance to cover today."

**** **** ****

The couple started off to Ginae. Joshua carried both backpacks on his left shoulder, wrapped his right arm around Mary's waist, and together they walked into the moonlight.

Under the moonlight, the landscape glowed. They saw the gorgeous Mount Tabor illuminated and then, after a long while, in the distance mount Gilboa appeared on their left with the Jezreel plains on the right. It was very late in the night, but the wild was wide awake with foxes chasing quails and rabbits, wild goats roaming and deer still watching their predators with their heads up and ears cocked. Nothing bothered the young couple, and they continued on their way to David's City.

"Joshua, you say you have been reading a lot of stories from many writers. Could you please tell me a story? If I listen to you telling me stories, I won't get tired of walking," Mary said.

"Which story would you like, Mary?" asked Joshua.

"I don't know any of them, so pick one of your favorites."

Joshua thought for a while and then started. "There is a story about a girl named Antigone, written by a great playwright, Sophocles. The story is very complex – a conflict between the rule of the law and the wishes of the Gods. Maybe it is too complicated . . ."

"That's fine, Joshua, keep talking."

"To start with, there was a king called Oedipus, the king of Thebes, who unknowingly murdered his father and married his mother."

"That is disgusting," Mary said.

"Mary, the Greek stories are all like that, but listen. Later, when the king came to know the truth, he blinded himself, and his wife and mother, Jocasta, killed herself."

"Oedipus and Jocasta had two sons, Polynices and Eteocles; and two daughters, Antigone and Ismene. Literally, Antigone means

97

opposite to everything." Joshua explained the characters in detail. "In every man there is an ego or a subconscious desire to outdo his father and gain all of his possessions, which may even include his mother."

"The two sons of Oedipus were thoroughly disobedient to their father. Oedipus cast a curse on them, prophesying that they would destroy themselves fighting each other."

"Like Kane and Able in our book," added Mary.

"More or less. Later on Oedipus died. The sons fought each other for the throne. They finally reached an agreement that they would draw lots to rule the city in alternate years. Eteocles, the younger brother, used trickery and he drew the winning lot for the first year. The subjects who loved Polynices were heartbroken when Eteocles stole the throne. Polynices, knowing how cunning his younger brother could be, feared for his life and fled to the city of Argos in refuge. He settled there and married the daughter of the king."

"Polynices then sought out all the present and past enemies of Thebes and, in concert, mounted a huge invasion on Thebes in an attempt to remove his brother from the throne."

"So, Polynices is warring against his own country?" Her face furrowed into a frown.

"Well, yes and no," said Joshua, "he wanted to defeat and destroy the bad king to save the people from his brother's tyranny."

"I understand," Mary said, "Please continue, Joshua. Do not stop. Tell me the rest of the story, every bit of it. I like it."

"The army, under the leadership of Polynices, invaded Thebes through all seven gates of the city simultaneously. In that war, however, both brothers died, bringing Oedipus's curse to pass. The next in line for the throne was Jocasta's brother Creon, who became the new ruler of Thebes. Creon declared Polynices to be a traitor to the city, denied him a proper burial, and decreed that his body should rot in the street in shame and disgrace for all to see."

"It's absurd," Mary said.

"Absurd it is," Joshua agreed. "Absurdity is part of Greek plays, too. But listen. The story becomes even more complicated. Creon's son,

Haemon, is already betrothed to Antigone. Antigone, overcome with grief and rage, decided to defy the king and give her brother a proper burial. Giving an honorable burial to the dead is fundamental to Greek society," Joshua explained. "A determined and valiant Antigone walked to the city center and sprinkled earth over her brother's body, declaring that God's law is more important than the city laws."

"That's great. She is brave," Mary exclaimed. "Now I am getting the story."

"Creon, being a selfish and erratic tyrant, did not heed the elders of the city. He ordered the arrest of Antigone and sentenced her to death by starvation in a cave, despite the pleading of his son Haemon.

"King Creon was admonished by the prophet Tiresias, as well as the elders of the city, that his decision was wrong and that the citizens were opposed to his decree. Further, he was cautioned that the gods were deeply offended and angered by his actions. Bad things happened in Thebes. At the end, Creon realized that he had made a terrible mistake. Creon unsealed the cave only to find that Antigone had hung herself. When Haemon heard of this, he was infuriated and crossed his sword against his father. He was unsuccessful in avenging his father, but accidentally stabbed himself to death. Upon hearing of her son's death, Creon's heartbroken wife, Eurydice, also killed herself.

"By the end of the play, Creon had lost everything: his wife, his two sons, the goodwill of the people and the blessings of the gods, all because of his foolish act of tyranny," Joshua said.

"Joshua, I like Antigone. She was a very brave woman. She had the courage to challenge even the king. But the end of the story is very sad. Why did she kill herself?" Mary asked.

"Good question. Maybe she despised Creon enough, and was determined not to give him the satisfaction that he had killed her. Mary, it's up to us to arrive at our own conclusions. Antigone lived by the strength of her morality. In Greek society, moral strength is considered the greatest strength of all."

It was a very long story that Joshua narrated to Mary. They had walked a great way in the meantime. A yellow hue was suffusing on the eastern horizon. The cocks had started crowing, the wild animals had settled and the silhouettes of a few people walking ahead of them were in view.

"Joshua, here in our land, a girl cannot even claim her own innocence, even when she is accused unjustly – like Rachel," Mary said. "Men rule everything, and everything is done according to the written laws and traditions."

Joshua nodded. "Mary, it's not just men; it's considered a divine intervention, which I don't believe. Someday this will all change – it must. Without such, as a nation, we have no future. A house divided against it will not survive forever."

Early in the morning the couple reached the town of Esdraelon. The town had already come to life. There were a lot more travelers on the roads, and the shops were open for business. After a brief rest and refreshments, they started south towards Samaria.

The lush greeneries of Galilee gradually disappeared. The land became more barren and hilly, with numerous mounts, fissures, valleys and dry ravines. The rocky red soil was sparsely covered with wild, thorny shrubs, occasional fig trees and namesake olives here and there. The road that ran through the western belly of Mount Gilboa was filled with rolling stones, gutters and fissures – difficult to tread.

That evening, they lounged under an old poplar tree, braised against a porter's rest. The Samaritans who passed by, climbing the winding country roads and hills, were friendly and even offered abode in their house for the two young travelers.

"You won't see synagogues like in Galilee here in Samaria. They have no temples; they go to the hilltops to pray to their God," Joshua whispered.

"Who is their God, Joshua?" Mary asked.

"There is only one Father in the Heavens, Mary."

Mary cradled Joshua's head in her lap and murmured gently, "I don't know anything Joshua; you have to tell me everything."

On the third day noon they arrived in the holy city of Sychar. Around Joseph's well there were always pilgrims, tourists and lots of Samarian vendors and hackers.

"That place looks like a dirty market rather than a Holy place," Mary said.

"That is only a small example of what our lands have come to." Joshua breathed a heavy sigh.

"There are many holy sites here in Samaria," Joshua explained. "It is here in Shechem, a bit more south and west from here," pointing in that direction, he continued, "that Abraham and Jacob built altars for Yahweh, and later on our forefathers buried Joseph's bones brought over from Egypt."

On the fifth day evening, they crossed over to the rough mountainous terrains of Judea and arrived at the city of Ephrain. The roads were full of people, most returning from the city of Jerusalem to their homes or inns.

"Tonight we will rest in an inn. Before sunrise we can start, and we will reach Jerusalem by sunset," Joshua said.

Way before sunrise the next morning, the couple started off to the city of David. There was an added energy and enthusiasm for Mary as she walked in front of Joshua, carrying her own bags. The road – constructed by the Romans – was wide and paved with cobblestones. On either side of the road, all along the way, hundreds of pilgrims had set up their tents. Joshua had only vague memories of the temple as he had seen it once, many years ago as a child.

Presently, they heard a tumult of heavy noises from behind, noises of screaming and metal hoofs of a dozen or so horses stomping on the cobblestones and people fast parting ways for the helmeted Roman mounted police to pass. Mary was thrilled to see for the first time the galloping horses of such size and strength. She stood frozen for a moment with her palm covering her open mouth.

"Really, they are Roman soldiers, aren't they, Joshua?" Mary asked.

"Indeed they are, Mary,"

"Will we see more of them? I like those horses."

"Of course, you will see many more in Jerusalem"

"I can't wait, Joshua," Mary quickened her pace.

After a few hours of walking and as the evening fell, they reached the apex of a hill on the northern border of the city of Jerusalem. Reflexively, both of them stood still for a moment holding hands, gasping in awe, catching the first glimpse of the Temple of Jerusalem shimmering in the golden rays of the setting sun. The silhouette of the of the Antonio tower, Herod's palaces and the whole city of Jerusalem slowly unfolded in front of them as a dream come true.

Mary stood frozen in excitement with her lips half parted and eyes widening. Joshua folded his arms around her waist and she nestled into his chest. After a while they slowly descended to the temple grounds towards the Bethesda pool, still staring at the wondrous porticos, columns and towers. They drank cold water from the taps, performed the ablutions in the Bethesda pool, and sat on the pedestal resting their heads against the cool, shiny surface of a Corinthian marble column.

Mary studied the exquisitely crafted aqueducts that brought over water to the pool from distant places, but Joshua was saddened by the unkempt premises of the temple that were heavily littered with leaves, debris, food crumbs, and bones and discarded wrappings.

A priest in a white linen robe and a tubular hat came towards the young couple and said shortly, "Today's services are finished. Nobody will be permitted to stay on the temple premises overnight."

Mary and Joshua soon got up and walked around to the western quarters where they were approached by several vendors offering to sell them lodging and food. Not far away from the temple, near the Damascus Gate, opposite the Hasmonean Palace, they found a place to stay that cost three silver shekel for four nights. The 'inn' that they rented was merely an annex to the front porch of a house. It had a roof overhead and a wall at the back, with two wooden enclosures on the right and left, but the front entrance was open except for a very small balustrade. There was an oil lamp and an earthen pot for water. The lack of privacy was somewhat compensated by the great view; they could see the western quarter of the temple from the porch.

The innkeeper offered them food for an additional charge, but Mary and Joshua were so tired that they declined. Presently the sun had set, but a thousand lights were lit on the temple walls and porticos, and Herod's temple glittered like a house on fire. Soon a sudden chill brought on by an eastern wind made them shiver, and the drizzle that followed blew heavily into their makeshift room. The spray of water on the skin made goose bumps on their skin. They spread their sheet on the floor and lay down to sleep.

The moonlight faded, and soon it was dark. Mary snuggled closer to Joshua, grasped his hand and made him feel the sole of her feet. There were a few tender blisters from her new shoes.

"Do you feel pain, dear?" he whispered.

"No," she murmured, shivering.

"Hold on to me," he said. "These blisters will heal very soon." A deep sleep soon embraced them.

**** **** ****

They woke early in the morning to the tumult of the bustling city. It was the first day of the Passover festivities. From their bed, they saw the silhouette of the temple glowing against the golden rays of the rising sun. A cacophony of voices from a number of nations filtered into their room. They both sat up, covered under the same shawl, watching the people pass by: Greeks, Egyptians, Babylonians, Romans and people of other cultures.

The innkeeper showed them the way to the daily rituals and ablutions. After breakfast, they rested before going to the temple.

The temple premises had come to life already, with voices rising by the minute. There were already hundreds of people waiting for entry at the southern gate of the temple. Merchants selling sacrificial animals, doves, lambs and oxen crowded the place like an animal market. Musicians playing pipes, jugglers throwing rings and balls into the air, magicians showing their tricks, hackers barking for their wears and vendors selling food and drinks all gave the atmosphere of a vile carnival in the holy temple grounds. Hawkers crisscrossed the crowd, selling handheld fans, flowers, capes, hats and clothes of all kinds and colors. Some sat like a statue without even blinking in front of portrait painters, surrounded by rings of spectators shouting invective comments. Shops selling trinkets, figurines and miniature models of the temple were all arranged against the wall near the Hulda Gate. There were a series of food stalls in makeshift tents selling burnt meat, bread and wine. The sizzling and crackling noise of meat burnt on open fires and the smoke coming out of those braziers filled the whole atmosphere.

A few Roman soldiers roamed, observing, not interfering with the activities of the temple or the pilgrims, but looking for cheap bargains and girls for a commission. Vendors had already begun to approach the tourists for lodging and inn facilities, and bargaining for nightly rates. Harlots strolled around with seductive looks.

Mary was aghast, but Joshua was not surprised at the sounds and sights of the Holy Temple. They patiently joined the crowd at the end of the line. There were several Jewish tour guides with their sales pitches. One of them approached the young couple.

"Just four bekah for a tour of the whole temple and overview of the city. You do not have to stand in the line. I can give you privileged entry to the Court of Gentiles through the Golden Gate," he cried.

Normally, all public entry to the temple was controlled via the Hulda Gate in the southern quarter of the temple. First, the pilgrims buy an animal for sacrifice and check them in with the guards. Then they visit the Micah – special baths – for ritual cleansing, collect the animals and climb fifty-six steps in all, and finally enter the Court of Gentiles.

"Joshua, are you buying an animal?"

"No, Mary," said Joshua.

"I thought not," Mary whispered in Joshua's ear. "Look at them. These birds; they are so beautiful," she said.

The doves with their characteristic jerking of the neck and tilting of their heads to either side appeared to be asking the pilgrims precisely what they were planning to do with them. The lambs had tears running down from their eyes, and the oxen majestically swayed their heads with a stately posture and at intervals wildly shook off the blood-sucking flies from their rump, hump or limbs.

Mary whispered in Joshua's ear again. "Joshua, Adonai was very happy when he created and gave life to all these beautiful animals, right?"

Joshua nodded.

"Then, why would he be pleased when we kill all of them in the temple as sacrifices?"

"Mary, in our holy writings this spilling of the blood is a way to wash away our sins . . . but it's a lot more complex than that," said Joshua.

The line was barely moving, but it continued to grow longer. Another man in a white robe and long beard approached the young couple.

"Would you like to have a private tour of the temple?" he asked.

Mary quickly asked, "If I give you one bekah of silver, would you take us?"

The man looked at the girl with an innocent smile. Obviously, he was amused and said, "Yes, I will take you. Come with me."

Another seven people joined the tour guide, and they all gathered around him as he separated his small group from the main crowd.

"Have any of you been here before?" he asked. Nobody answered. Then he waved his hand high up towards the wall and said, "This is the southern wall of the Temple of Jerusalem." Then, pointing towards the tower on the southeast pinnacle of the wall, he continued, "That is the tallest part of temple, about two hundred and thirty feet in height from here."

"No," shouted a man, clutching the outstretched arm of the tour guide. The tour guide forcefully untwisted his arm and pushed him to the ground.

"I . . . tell ya . . . all . . . you wanna . . . hea . . ." The man, heavy with wine, unsteady on his feet, was ranting, "I will tell ya . . ." Another one, equally drunk, chewing a barely cooked piece of meat, dribbling bloody juice through the corners of his mouth, came to his rescue, and the both staggered away into the crowd.

Mary, frightened of the unruly men, held on to Joshua.

The tour guide ignored the men and moved on. Pointing towards the gate, he continued, "This is the Hulda Gate, the main entrance to the temple for the public . . ."

He slowly walked towards the western wall of the temple with his group. "What you see here is the nearly completed second temple of Jerusalem, begun by Emperor Herod." The guide turned and asked, "Does anybody know when the first temple was constructed?"

Nobody opened their mouth for a while, but Mary pinched on Joshua's hands as she knew the man who knew the answers.

"About nine hundred and thirty years back, by King Solomon," Joshua said.

"Very good." The guide continued to describe the various events that had happened up till that day in great detail, answering the questions the group had.

"This temple stands on Mount Moriah. It is on this mount that Yahweh tested the faith of Abraham by asking him to sacrifice his son Isaac. The first temple was comparatively very small, facing east, looking over an elaborate peristile and courtyard. Behind the altar in a sacred room was where The Torah, The Word of God, was secured. Only the High Priest could enter in this room. The temple contained an immeasurable wealth of gold, silver and bronze utensils. The entire building was adorned with inlaid gold and silver, which would shine under the moonlight with all its glitter."

"Tell me; who destroyed the first temple?" The Guide turned around, quizzing his group.

"King Nebuchadnezzar of Babylon, some six hundred years ago," replied an old man from Elephantine Island.

"Very good," the guide resumed. "They plundered all the valuables from the temple and stole or destroyed the Holy Torah." The guide placed his palm against his brow and remained silent for a moment. "The Babylonian soldiers razed the temple to the ground, took the entire population of Jerusalem captive, and transported them to Babylon, where they lived as slaves."

The tour guide explained in detail the very many sufferings the Jews had endured and how the kind Persian king had brought them back to

Jerusalem. "Under the leadership of Zerubbabel, the construction of the second temple was completed. When compared to this temple built by Herod, the second temple was also of modest scale. The temple services that began back then continues as of today, unabated."

The group slowly moved closer to the western wall of the temple. "I want you to know that this is still the second temple of Jerusalem, because Herod never discontinued the services while the building was in progress. The construction of this temple is part of the legacy of the Roman occupation of Israel." Within about a second after the tour guide had said the phrase, "Roman occupation," two soldiers, faces blank, passively joined the group.

"You may know, about nineteen years before the assassination of Julius Caesar, the Roman general Pompey invaded Palestine, and the people of Israel once again lost their freedom. Some fifty-two years back, the Roman Senate named Herod came to oversee the eastern territories and appointed him as the king of Judea." Then he lowered his voice and, under his breath, "Jews didn't trust him at all. To show his might and splendor and to appease the Jewish people, Herod decided to construct the most magnificent temple ever built on the face of the earth here on Mount Moriah." The guide gestured at the grand structure.

"Herod had traveled the world, had witnessed the great architecture of Egypt, Greece and Rome, and, in fact, was a great builder himself," the guide said. "The Jewish people demanded that the temple must be constructed by priests only, and Herod agreed. But for the foundation work, all kinds of workers were employed, of course."

"In the splendid plan of Herod, Mount Moriah did not have enough foundation space to contain the massive structure of the temple. Therefore, as a first step, he flattened the top of Mount Moriah and built up enormous walls surrounding, with gigantic stones, each side one furlong in length, and the space in between was filled up with earth. On the western side, the mount itself was rocky, which was vertically cut into shape with columns, arches and friezes carved into shapes simulating the other three sides. It was on this colossal foundation square that the temple and the various courtyards were built."

The guide pointed to the tower to the north.

"Look over here: this is the Antonio Fortress on the northern wall. King Herod built that tower to honor Mark Antony. When the foundation square was expanded, the fortress had to be incorporated into the grounds." The tour guide looked around. "Is there anybody here from Egypt?"

Elaizer, a soft-spoken, thin, old man with sparse white hair, identified himself as an Egyptian Jew from the Elephantine Island.

"Well, there is something here that is very similar in its style of construction to the temple in Abu Simbel," the guide said. "Now we can go up to the temple grounds and the courtyards, but first we go to the pools."

After a ritual cleansing at the Israel pool, the group followed the guide to Solomon's porch on the eastern wall. The majestic Golden Gate built with cedar wood from Lebanon, adorned with inlays of gold, ivory and intricate art works, opened to Solomon's portico. The portico, housing banks and expensive shops selling ornaments, jewels, perfumes and precious clothes, was bustling with people talking different tongues of the world.

They climbed some thirty steps to get to the level of the temple ground. It was a phenomenal square, two hundred yards in length on each side. At the very center of the grounds, on an elevated plateau occupying a third of the space, stood Herod's temple, in all its elegance, surrounded by ornate balustrades made of stone, iron and brass.

The tour guide continued in a low tone. "People, you get an idea of the elegance of the cloistered Court of Gentiles. Here, entry is permitted for all visitors and tourists who are not even Hebrews. Beware of your bags and other possessions. You all go for a stroll and meet me right there at the Royal Stoa." He stood holding high his folded umbrella pointing to the Royal Stoa on the south end of the squire. Mary held on to Joshua. She was amazed by the opulence of the place, as if transcended to a place only seen in dreams; one hundred and sixty-four Corinthian columns, each separated by an aisle cloistered by cedar and cypress wood, with lifelike artwork of carved vines, grapes, palm trees, pomegranates and the like, inlaid with gold, silver and precious stones. The most elegant, much wider and taller, two-storied Royal Stoa was where most of the banks and most expensive shops selling Egyptian perfumes, exotic spices, Chinese silk and precious stones were located. Momentarily, Mary stopped in front of a shop selling Egyptian gold ornaments

Joshua immediately knew where her eyes were fixed. The young carpenter had enough money to buy that bangle with tinklets. The smile on her face was priceless.

The open ground surrounding the holy temple – the Court of Gentiles – was the most noisy and unruly place in the whole temple complex. It was like a flea market bustling with business, bargaining with vituperative arguments, yelling invectives, screaming, guffawing, and yet others scrambling around, joking and merrymaking. Flaming revilement between money changes and customers for excess commissions, at times went to yelling of the conduct of banker's wife in the dark and his daughter's rate for a day. Cries for an immediate money-back settlement at times lead to scuffles and fisticuffs in the traditional manner of an eye for an eye. Cheap figurine imitations of the temple, in white soft stone, were at times smashed to the ground for high prizes and poor craftsmanship by drunk and vile customers.

Harlots plastered with power and soaked in perfumes, wriggled through the crowd, swaying their rumps and bouncing their bosoms. Temple ladies and gypsy girls were in abundance on the grounds, enticing clients with bargain prizes and sweetening deals, all in broad daylight while the holy temple services were going on so nearby. Joshua's face turned purple, and his brow knitted in anger. "This is disgusting," he said.

Mary locked her hands with Joshua's, her head hanging.

Roman soldiers, roaming tall in shining brass and helmets adorned with flowing red plumes, enjoyed the show with delight and at times settled a case or two receiving, bribes from both.

A few old men clad in black shaggy robes sauntered in the corridors, wailing and squealing for the lost days of Solomon and the valor of David. An old man with frizzy, dirty hair clad in torn flax burlap, with his hands spread high up into the sky, was barking at the clouds for the instant return of the Messiah. People watching around cast tiny copper coins and pieces of bread on to a rag spread about his feet.

Here and there on the temple grounds, people gathered around enjoying the tricks of magicians and jugglers. Some gypsy girls were doing their belly dance accompanied by playing drums and stringed instruments for which the reveling spectators were liberally throwing coins into their hats while making dirty comments.

"I can't believe this; Caiaphas permitting these hoodlums on the holy grounds," he whispered to Mary." If I had the power . . ."

Mary nodded.

The group moved to the anteroom of the temple proper. "Entry to the temple is permitted only for Jews," the guide said, pointing to a notice at the entrance of the temple:

"UNCIRCUMSISED ENTERING THE HOLY TEMPLE SHALL SUFFER THE PAIN OF DEATH."

The group climbed the nine steps leading to the Court of Women, a spacious hall with several niches built around for the women to rest and relax. Many Jewish women were singing, praying and dancing in this hall. Another fifteen steps led to the Court of Israelites via the Nicanor Gate, where only Jewish men were permitted to enter. Another nine steps up was the Court of the Priests where the sacrifices were going on in front of the great alter. "Only priests are permitted to enter this area," the guide said.

Joshua watched the ceremonies in the Court of Priests. Sacrificial animals were brought to the altar one after the other through a side gate. Four priests were continuously chanting lines from the Torah and slicing the throats of those animals, spilling a torrent of blood before the altar into the huge grate of burning charcoal with a great sizzling noise. With each slice on the animal's throat, the trumpets, bugles and symbols rang with deafening noise. The room was filled with thick, heavy smoke and a strong stench of burnt meat. The carcasses of the sacrificed animals, the rites of the temple priests thrown out through the opposite door, were readily sold for a profit to the tavern merchants for their spit fires.

Joshua saw the magnificent gold-laden, incense-burning altar, the menorah, the famous vessels of the temple, and various other implements, some of which at times were purified with blood, as well. Behind the altar was the enormously ornate large purple curtain on which the world map was embroidered, embellished with glittering stones, and gold and silver.

"Behind the curtain, the chamber is now empty. It was where the Holy Torah was kept," the guide said. "We believe that this is the sacred spot where Yahweh asked Abraham to sacrifice his only son, Isaac. Only the High Priest is permitted to enter this holy area, and even then only once a year on Yom Kippur." The tour guide then turned around, facing the group. "It is here, the Roman Counsel Pompey . . . breached the threshold of the Hollies with his Roman boots."

An uncomfortable silence hung in the air for some minutes.

The group reassembled in the Royal Stoa. The guide concluded, "Here you can spend time, walk around and buy your souvenirs, and I thank you for taking this tour with me," and he left to find new customers.

Joshua and Mary took the steps of the Hulda Gate to the lower grounds. "Joshua, I know that you are upset. What can we do?" Mary said.

Joshua sighed, but did not reply.

The sun had peaked to the heights. It was warm and humid. The temple grounds were bustling with a multitude of visitors. The taverns, makeshift tents of wine shops and beer stalls were thronged with merrymaking people drinking and eating burnt meat and frolicking skin to skin.

Joshua and Mary walked away from the madding crowd towards the southern quarters and sat on the stone steps of the Council House facing the temple. Smoke from all the burnt meats billowed up into the sky like clouds of Heshvan. Vultures and hawks circled above the temple through the smoke for their turn to descend to the carcasses. Joshua gazed at the temple, heavy in thought. His heart sunk in heavy pain. "The House of God has been defiled," he said disdainfully, "robbed by vendors, prostitutes and profiteers."

Mary was thirsty and fatigued. She rested her head in his laps and fell asleep. Joshua sat there gently stroking Mary's hair and caressing her shoulders. "Jerusalem, how far away are you from Sodom and Gomorrah?" He asked himself.

In the distance he could still hear the vendors crying. "Blemishless doves, one for two bekah, and three for five . . . Souvenirs of all kinds . . . pieces of bricks from Solomon's temple, one shekel a piece . . ."

After a while Mary woke up with a question, as if she had been sleeping on it. "Joshua, why do they kill this many animals?"

"The laws demand sacrifices . . . many sacrifices."

After a long minute of silence, Mary gently pulled on the baby beard appearing under his chin. "Joshua, what is the matter with you? I saw you talking to yourself. You didn't say a thing about the temple the whole day. You promised me that you would show and tell everything about Jerusalem and the temple on the way."

"What is there to say, Mary? You heard it all from the tour guide. The rest, even a blind man can see . . . this is not the House of God. These are all Pagan activities."

"What do you mean, Joshua?"

"I guess the Romans like it the way it is. Caiaphas will keep it the way it is. The Levites and the scribes are all well employed. The rich Sadducees find it convenient for the Jewish holy temple with Pagan activities for their business."

"I understand, Joshua. I am surprised by the noise and the disorderly . . ."

"I believe that God's House must be open to all His creations to come, pray and pay their tribute. There must not be the threat of death to enter the House of God. Open to all; the sinners, the defiled, the lepers, and the meek. This is no place for those ruthless traders and hackers or harlots."

"I understand all that, Joshua," Mary said. "But I never expected the temple to be this huge and magnificent, all seen and done."

"Magnificent. Yes, it is. This is business in the name of Adonai. I shall not be disappointed if this Temple of Herod crumbles down to the ground into rubbles." he said, pounding his fist on his palms.

"I'm sad that you are so disappointed, Joshua, but when we started, you were planning to meet with the High Priest and ask him some questions. Are you still planning to do it?"

"Mary, I have no more questions to ask. I came, I saw, and I got all the answers to my questions. Tomorrow, the fifteenth of Nisan, the temple will swell up with visitors and business as usual; more sacrifices, more bargains more drinking and eating more harlots; the peak of the Passover celebrations."

"So, we will come here in the morning?" Mary asked.

"No, Mary. We will be returning to Nazareth early in the morning."

"Then we will go in the morning. Are you hungry, Joshua?"

"Well, we will eat something." He got up and pulled her up the feet sauntering to the vendors of the southern Hulda Gate compound. After a piece of burnt meat and a cup of red wine, color rose to her cheeks, and she turned perky and bubbly again. Joshua also had a piece of meat and some wine. The heat of the day was settling, and a breeze from the west gently cooled them.

The rest of the evening they strolled the city all the way up to the Siloam pool on the southwest end of the city wall. They washed up in the pool, and sauntered further down and west to the imposing edifices of Herod's palaces.

"These are the famous towers of Herod's palace, the Miriamne, Phaseal and the Hippicus towers," Joshua explained to Mary, as he pointed out the structures.

A mounted Roman soldier quickly approached them and admonished him not to point towards the king's palace. "No. No strolling here. Go. Go away," he pocked Joshua with the blunt baton with a push. Soon they left the palace grounds to the inn for the evening.

On the way to the inn and for several hours thereafter, the couple didn't talk much. Deep in thought, Joshua kept looking at the Temple late into the night, long after Mary had gone to sleep. Storm clouds moved in, lightning flashed and thunder boomed. The wind gushed, whistling over the roof and rattling the shingles. The noises from the temple grounds soon died out. The down pouring flooded the streets. *Even this rain will not cleanse the defile of this harlot,* Joshua thought.

Mary was still sleeping. Joshua came back to her side, kissed her brow and gently uncovered the sheet from her legs and felt her feet. The blisters were softer, and one of them had burst.

"I have no pain, Joshua. Come, come and sleep with me. We have a long way to go tomorrow," Mary murmured.

She held his head close to her chest. There was a cold breeze in the air.

**** **** ****

Up in Nazareth, the parents were preoccupied with the safety of the two youngsters gone to Jerusalem. Mary was worried about the safety of the children, and Naomi was deeply concerned about the possibilities of Mary coming home pregnant and the jeopardy that would create for her daughter.

But after Joshua and Mary returned home safe, their anxiety was all alleviated. Within the next few days they decided on the wedding of Joshua and Mary. It was the celebration of a humble wedding with no elaborate feast. Joseph's Brother Nathan – who lived about six miles west of Nazareth in the city of Besara – his wife Rebecca, and children James and Miriam were the people present other than the immediate family.

It was about a year after the wedding in Carmel, on the twentieth day of Sivan, that Joseph, Mother Mary, Naomi, Joshua and Mary sat around the dinner table in Nazareth. Joshua, now fifteen, had finalized his plans to go to Alexandria. None of them spoke much during dinner. The decision was made that Naomi would move to Nazareth near Joseph's house and live in a small rented house with Mary.

That night Joshua and Mary talked late into the night.

"Mary, I know that it's not right that I go away to farther lands indefinitely." Mary crossed her fingers across his lips. "No Joshua.

Don't say one more word. I know that your going away is beyond your control. It is the passion of your heart and the calling of your life. I have come to learn that you are far more that I can possess only to myself. You go and learn as much as you want. I am not alone here." She gripped his hand and pressed it against her chest and continued sobbing. "You are here . . . here in my heart . . . always . . . come back safe."

Joshua fell asleep, but Mary stayed awake by his side, stroking his hair and sobbing. The next day they all awoke long before daybreak. They filled Joshua's backpack with two sets of undergarments, robes, a head cover, and a pair of new shoes. Mary and Joshua counted all their money. They had saved sixty-one silver shekels. Joshua took forty shekels and put them in a purse. The remainder, he handed to Mary. Everyone except for Joshua had teary eyes. First, Joshua hugged his mother, Mary, and then Naomi. He drew close to Joseph, hugged him for a long time, and kissed him on both his cheeks, three times each. Then, for the first time, his eyes welled up. Tears rolled down his cheeks.

Then Joshua brought all four of them together, spread out his arms around them, and offered a silent prayer. He took his backpack and placed it on his right shoulder across his chest. Tilting his shoulder to the right for a little balance, he swung his arm and walked with long steps towards the southern route, at a rapid pace. Mary followed him for a short distance. Then she froze and began to cry.

BOOK III
Joshua in Egypt

Joshua at the light house of Alexandria

Abhi Faroosh's caravan, with four riders and thirty camels, had already arrived in Caesarea when Joshua reached Sophiar's house. Two tents had been set up for the safekeeping of Abhi's merchandise and provisions. The riders, all in their thirties, bantering amongst themselves in the Parthian language, were busy feeding the camels, storing water in the skins and making preparations for the next day's journey.

Joshua quickly recognized Abhi Faroosh, a thickset man in his fifties with a large beaked nose, and a strong bull neck. He was perched deep on a wicker sofa relaxing on the front porch and sipping a cup of wine. Layeela, a seductive girl of about sixteen, sat in his lap facing him with her legs around his waist, playfully braiding his beard. "This is the young man from Nazareth I talked to you about," Sophiar said to Layeela.

"Nice to have you, Joshua," Abhi replied, his voice boomed with a heavy Syrian accent. Layeela didn't pay any attention to the newcomer and was engrossed in her braiding. Abhi gently caressed his pet and at times kissed her on the mouth while talking to Joshua. Sophiar smiled approvingly.

After a while, Layeela slipped off Abhi's lap, sauntering towards Joshua with a swing of her hips and offered him a drink of wine. She was a well-built woman with dark curly hair braided to the sides, a large smooth forehead, long thin nose and full lips. She gave him the cup and a wicked wink, and then went back to her hot seat.

Abhi talked to Joshua mostly about himself, emphasizing some of the adventures and other heroic incidents he had encountered. It was soon apparent that he had excellent ideas about the routes, the various inns along the way, places to see, as well as great knowledge of the history of Egypt.

Abhi outlined the responsibilities and role of Joshua in the caravan group. "I don't need any money from you, but you will help the men load and unload the burden from the camels, collect water in the various skins, feed the camels and work as my personal assistant. You can sleep in my tent, unless, of course you prefer otherwise. These Parthian men like delicious boys like you ever so much." Layeela looked at Joshua through the corner of her eyes with a smile. Joshua bowed his head in acceptance.

During the dinner, Abhi talked incessantly. He spoke with such exaggeration and confidence, as if he had dined with Alexander the Great and seduced Cleopatra. Soon after dinner, Abhi retired to bed with the two ladies on his arms. Joshua tried to get some sleep on the front porch. There was light and laughter in the camel riders' tents, though nothing to compare with the screams and squeaks from Abhi's bedroom.

The half-crescent moon in the northern sky had just finished that night's duty. After a while the frolicking noises subsided, soon to be replaced by a loud, gargling snore. At times the snoring would stop for a minute or two with a frightening silence as if he had already taken his last breath, followed by a violent hack, a terrible snort, and a fit of coughs. Then the heavy breathing and snoring resumed in cycles. Joshua lay on the porch listening to the cycles until he drifted off to sleep.

Joshua was startled awake by the feeling of something crawling between his thighs. He grasped at it in haste and heard the jingling sounds of bangles. Layeela quickly cupped his mouth, snuggled closer to him, rubbing the curls of her groin against his thigh and whispering in his ear, "I am sorry I couldn't come earlier. The old man doesn't like me engaging with anybody else." Joshua lay frozen. A cold sweat poured over him. With her face nuzzling on his waist she hissed, "He wants mother and me to sleep with him and for everything else. We are afraid of him, but now it's all right. He is dead asleep. He won't wake up, and even if he does, mother is with him now. She will handle it." Layeela groped her way from his chest, down to the tenderness of his groin and up again.

Joshua couldn't utter a sound. Layeela buried her face into his chest and, she playfully kissed and licked his nipples. For a brief moment the wildly wicked young woman drove him to the threshold of the pleasures of the flesh. He felt warm, and his heart pounded hard. His body swelled, but his mind betrayed. He gently grasped her hands, untwisted her and politely pushed her away. Her voice quivered. In a tone of apology she said, "You didn't like me coming to you now? Don't worry. Mother knows everything about it. I don't need any money from you. I just want to make you happy, that's all. You are a handsome man away from home. I can make you happy. I don't need any money from you," she sobbed.

"I am very happy, Layeela. You be happy in your own ways. Let me catch some sleep. We have a long way to go tomorrow."

Layeela quietly left to go to her bedroom, while the snoring continued from next door.

Early in the morning, the caravan moved south across the Philistine Highway. Abhi was dressed like an army general with high boots, a leather belt with a large sword buckled to the waist belt, an elaborate glistening feathered head cover, and a leather bottle filled with wine slung across the shoulders. Joshua rode with Abhi on a double-humped, strong, tall beast. There were twenty-nine camels altogether, but only four of them had riders. Twenty-five camels carried fairly large loads of merchandise in two large pouches balanced on either side of their backs.

Abhi said, "From here on we have to cover over five hundred Roman miles to reach Alexandria. People from many nations have gone to Egypt through this road to Egypt for livelihood or protection from tyranny. I have taken a few people to Memphis and Alexandria, but they were all looking for work; you are the first who is going there to learn. Isn't that what you said?" he wondered.

"Yes, Abhi," Joshua screamed from behind him. "Our history as a people originates from there. I want to learn more about other religions and civilizations."

"No doubt Egypt is an excellent choice," he confirmed. "It's a great land of wealth and prosperity. They seldom went to other countries to conquer and rule, with a few exceptions in Canaan, Nubia and Libya. Whatever they wanted – wheat, vegetables, fish, beer, wine or gold – they had it there. Egypt was heaven for the Egyptians. People from other nations; they all wanted to go to Egypt."

"Thank you. Abhi, how many trips you have taken in route to Egypt?"

"Eighteen in fifteen years. I have been attacked by highway robbers twice, on the desert stretch from Gaza to Pelusium. You saw the four men with me? They are not just camel riders; they are superb sword fighters. They can swing a sword with such great speed, as if they are encircled in a space of fast moving blades. They can butcher a man before he has a chance to respond. Even an arrow cannot penetrate them. For this protection, I provide them with whatever they need; money, wine, women, boys, or whatever."

Abhi took a few more gulps from the skin, burped heavily and continued incessantly. "Aha! In Caesarea, you saw the two women. Hum . . . I wouldn't let anybody touch them. That girl, Layeela, she is really something else. She will be my fifth and last wife. When I am all done with my business, I will pick her up and go to Damascus. I will make a few more children with her. I have enough seeds left, Ha, Ha, Ha!" He guffawed so gaily, fluttering his thighs against the camel.

No matter what subject Joshua inquired about, Abhi shifted the subject back to his own achievements, visions and concerns of the world. Often Joshua had to politely interrupt him and change the subject back.

Abhi continued, "Yes, it will take about thirty-five days for us to reach Alexandria. We will stay one or two nights each at my relations or at an inn in Apollonia, Joppa, Azotus, Ascalon, Gaza, Raphia, and then finally Pelusium on the Egyptian Delta. The route is quite different and exciting."

The caravan moved carefully through the highways into the Plains of Sharon. The blazing sun had beaten on the ground and made it red, but the gentle breeze from the Great Seas pleasantly cooled the heat of the summer sun. The cattle grazing in the harvested fields, the tiny farmer's markets, the young boys selling water melons, a thousand different varieties of roses swinging in the breeze and the full-bloomed lilies in endless rows shimmering in the sun all added to the mystic mosaic life in the Sharon Plains.

"Abhi, do you know why this road is named the Highway of the Philistines?"

"I don't know. Maybe it was cut through the land of the Phoenicians. But I know it was through these roads that the Egyptian Pharaoh Seitho I led his army to quell the Megiddo uprising thirteen hundred years ago. His son, Ramses II — you should know him well — led his army twice through these roads". He paused for a while, turned his neck and glanced at Joshua to make sure that the young man was paying proper attention to all these pearls of information. "One reason is that Egypt wanted the safety of Lebanon. They loved the cedars of Lebanon. All the major wood constructions in Pharaoh's temples, palaces, barges, and funeral boats were all made with the cedar woods from Lebanon." Abhi breathed heavily. He appeared tired with his loud nonstop bellowing.

"Abhi, I am very interested. Tell me about Ramses II."

"Why, Joshua?" Abhi questioned.

"It was around his time that the Exodus happened," Joshua explained.

"Oh, the Exodus. The Exodus, if it happened!" Abhi laughed sarcastically. "Of course, Ramses is an interesting Pharaoh," Abhi appraised, "one of the very few Pharaohs who traveled outside Egypt. In pursuit of the Hittites, Ramses once marched through Gaza to Quedesh, felling cities one after the other. Finally, they reached the southern skirts of Quedesh. The astute Hittites king, Muwatallis, had planted two Bedouin spies in that area. The Bedouin spies were captured by Ramses' army. When they were questioned, they told the Egyptians that the cowardly King Muwatallis had fled the city, afraid of them. In reality, they were hiding in the bushes with forty thousand foot soldiers and two thousand five hundred charioteers for a surprise attack. In that attack, Ramses had a setback."

"Really, the Pharaoh retreated?

"Yes. He couldn't finish the job, but saved the day with some minor victories here and there. A fatigued Ramses, far away from the comforts of Egypt with scarcity of water and provisions, returned to Egypt. Ramses, tired of fighting, at the end established a treaty with the Hittites."

Abhi pulled out a leather bottle, drank some wine and offered some to Joshua, as well. Unable to wait for his momentary break, he gulped down the wine and continued, "It's funny, and eventually the Egyptians and the Hittites reconciled and Ramses took two of the daughters of King Hattusili III as his wives. Ha, ha!" Abhi's great belly shook as he laughed.

"Abhi, what kind of a king was he, Ramses?"

"Joshua, this Ramses was a great soldier and a builder. I think he was the greatest of all Pharaohs. He liked women so very much. Ha, ha, ha!" Wine spewed out of the corners of his mouth, spraying all over Joshua's face as he laughed. "He had over forty wives and about one hundred children. After his famous wife Nefertiti's death, he married three of his own daughters."

"Such things were . . ."

"Of course, Ramses could marry anybody he wanted, daughters or granddaughters. He was the Pharaoh," Abhi guffawed, nodding his head up and down.

Abhi told Joshua a lot of Egyptian stories, but of all the Pharaohs, Ramses II was his hero. "Nearly half of the great constructions you see in Egypt today, except the pyramids, are his constructions," he continued with appreciation.

The camels plodded, Abhi talked, Joshua listened and the caravan continued.

Each evening they set up two tents, one for Abhi and Joshua, and another for the men. The men carried their swords at all times and routinely scouted the area for any invaders or robbers. They were extremely cautious and seemed even paranoid at times. On the third night while they were unloading the camels, Faizal abruptly stopped his work, cocking his ears and gazing to the bushy knolls to the east. He suddenly dashed onto his heels and out into the hills with his bow and arrows. Just a few minutes later, he came back dragging a mountain goat. The meat was seasoned with sea salt and some other exotic condiments from the east and cooked in an open-pit fire with thorny burnet.

During the dinner Abhi commented, "There is nothing like goat meat burned with thorny burnet." He took mouthfuls of large pieces of goat; half chewed it and washed it down with several gulps of wine. He burped loudly and growled, "This is excellent meat. This is the best. What do you think, young boy?" Joshua agreed. The flavor of the thorny burnt had permeated into the burnt meat: it was a wonderful dinner by the side of the Philistine Highway.

At night Joshua found it very difficult to sleep in Abhi's tent, as the heavy snoring pierced his ears and even shook the tent. For quite some time he used to sit outside the tent looking at the stars, musing at the stories Abhi had told and the journeys of many of his ancestors who had taken the route of the Philistine Highway, including Abraham, Sarah, Joseph, and numerous other invaders.

Early next morning the caravan started moving south. "Tonight we are sleeping in Apollonia," Abhi announced to Joshua. "If you like fun, you will enjoy it. I stay there one or two nights every time I travel." After a while riding, Abhi tapped on Joshua's thighs somewhat forcefully with his strong heavy left hand and suggested gently, "Young man, you appear very uptight and serious beyond your youth. You should loosen up a bit. You are alone. Life is to enjoy," he laughed gaily.

That evening they arrived at a house close to the seashore in Apollonia. The inhabitants of the house were seven ladies of the night: Rhoda, the mother, her three daughters and another three women who worked for her. The eldest daughter, Julia, was in her early thirties, a somewhat plump woman with curly hair and womanly curves. As soon as she spotted the caravan, she came running to Abhi as if she had known him for a lifetime. She hugged and kissed him and quickly escorted him to her room.

Before he left the room, Abhi whispered something to Rhoda, pointing towards Joshua. The other men were immediately surrounded by the five younger women, and they also disappeared into the house.

While Joshua was unloading his burdens, Rhoda came to him with a motherly smile. "Do you want anything to drink now? Abhi told me all about you. Whenever you are ready, I will serve you dinner. I will also find a place for you to sleep quietly."

"Thank you. I will be there in a while," Joshua replied. He looked at the blue waves crashing onto the sandy shores.

While the other men cuddled in the bosoms of Rhoda's girls, Joshua embraced the gentle waves that reached out for him at the Apollonian shore. The seawater was pleasantly warm, and he could smell the overtones of the salt as he soaked in the waves. After three long days of travel and labor, Joshua was tired, sweaty and sticky. The waters of the Great Sea refreshed him, and he felt exhilarated.

"Do you want me to jump into the water?" Joshua imagined Mary asking, as she slipped off her clothes, joining him. He felt the pain of separation from her for the first time. *If only she could be here*, he mused. Joshua was not quite sure if the salt in his mouth was from the seawater or from his tears.

"Come out, young man," Rhoda called out to Joshua. "It's getting dark. You have been in the water for over an hour now . . ." Joshua came out of the sea. "Sometimes the undertow can take you down to the womb of the sea. I was worried," She came to him and covered him with a towel for drying and led him back to the house.

Rhoda had prepared a great supper for Joshua. She served him corn bread, conch stew, fresh fried fish, green olives, and beer. While eating, she sat by his side with a smile on her lips and arms folded across her knees. At times, she refilled items, one after the other, onto his plate. Then her face clouded, voice fluttered and started as if talking to herself. "I have given birth to seven children. Three girls died, but then I got a beautiful son. He was only seven. While playing on the sand, the waves swallowed him. It was my mistake, my mistake." Tears grew in her eyes, ready to fall.

"I am sorry Rhonda," said Joshua, but she didn't hear that.

" . . . From the moment you went to the waves, I was watching you from here." Her lips pursed slowly. "I am sorry I didn't mean to interrupt your dinner . . ."

After the dinner she made a bed for Joshua and put him to bed. The men and women were partying wildly inside the rooms. All the *ooh*s and hollering didn't bother him. He was full of thoughts of Mary. He imagined her in his arms as he drifted off to sleep quickly.

For the next nine days and nights, the caravan moved through the Plain of Philistia to reach the arid city of Gaza. They stayed one night each in Joppa, Jamnia, Azotus, Ascalon, and finally in Gaza, where they stayed for two nights. In each of these places, Abhi had receptions with wine, women and food. Abhi was very kind to Joshua; he provided Joshua with a safe place to sleep and protected him from the wild sexual revelries.

The following morning Abhi reminded the group, "For the next few days our ride will be tough until we reach Pelusium at the Egyptian border. We will be staying in tents in the desert for seven nights. One night, we will stay at my house in Raphia, and two nights at Rhinocolura. Remember, all animals must be fed very well. Don't forget to keep extra water in all the leather bottles." So saying, Abhi mounted his beast with Joshua behind him and kicked the animal to move.

"Joshua, the dry heat of the desert can be intense," Abhi cautioned, "particularly at this time of the year in Sivan. I take good care of my men and animals. So far, I have lost not a single man or beast."

The landscape changed rapidly as predicted. Lush vegetation transformed to stubby bushes, sand dunes and miles of dirty brown sand. The direction of the wind blowing also changed: it was a dry, hot wind from east to west. On the third day of the journey, the wind became intense. Sand swirled into the sky and swept the caravan with wave after wave. It was impossible to proceed. Joshua completely covered his head and face, yet sandy dust still blew through his head cover, irritating his nose, eyes, and ears. Even his hair was filled with sand. Breathing was difficult, and his mouth felt like mud.

Abhi's skill in desert navigation was commendable. He knew all the valleys, hills, knolls, dunes and wadies well. He found a cave in an old wadi where they rested for the night.

On the eighteenth day, on the way from Rhinocolura to Pelusium, the air turned intensely arid. The dry heat seared their skin.

"You must drink extra water, as I told you," Abhi implored.

By midday, Joshua was both exhausted and dizzy. He sipped weakly from his leather saddlebag. The water didn't taste right. It was warm and he felt nauseated. He held onto the camel's hump, hoping the day would be over soon. By early afternoon, he was totally exhausted. The east wind was intense as an inferno. Joshua started belching and was trying to vomit, but nothing except a bit of dark bile came out. Abhi held Joshua with his left arm around his waist, but he couldn't hold him up straight. Abhi felt the heat of Joshua's skin and knew what the problem was right away. Joshua felt sluggish, his eyes rolled backwards, and he slumped to the saddle and slipped to the sand, unable to hold onto Abhi or to the saddle.

"Faizal." Abhi shouted to the other riders and the caravan came to a halt. Faizal immediately dismounted and came to help Abhi. "There is no point in waiting. Let us pack him in a sack," Abhi ordered. They spread a sheet on the sand and placed Joshua in the middle of the sheet, his arms and knees folded and bent over. They picked him up like a baby in a cradle, balanced him on the right side of the camel and hung a counterweight on the left. They soaked him with a bottle of water and quickly proceeded towards Pelusium as fast as they could.

Abhi checked on the young man several times to make sure he was still alive. He felt very hot. At least this meant that he was not dead. Abhi splashed Joshua with water to cool him down and poured a bottle of wine on him as well.

The caravan reached Abhi's wayside inn in Pelusium a bit after sunset. The wind and heat had subsided. Some eight women, all in their twenties and some in their thirties, came flocking around the arriving men. Faizal carried Joshua to the veranda as a backpack and cried with haste, "Fill the tub with water."

"Oh, this is another one of those desert deaths," muttered one lady casually.

"He hasn't gone yet," cried Abhi. Faizal pulled Joshua out of the cradle and splashed more water on him. They immediately took off Joshua's clothes and put him in a stone bathtub, which looked more like a sarcophagus, and poured water on him and filled up the bathtub. One woman continuously poured water on his head like a stream, as if she were anointing a king.

"Take care of him; he is like a son to me," cautioned the big man. After a while, Abhi and the other riders went on their way with drinking, eating and frolicking, but two women stayed with Joshua, obeying the orders.

One woman washed his head and daubed his face with wet clothes, while another fanned his face with a pretty Egyptian fan made out of palm leaves.

"What a nice looking young man. Look at his brows and those beautiful lips," drooled the lady with long hair and salacious eyes. The other woman rubbed his cheeks and chest. "What a gorgeous body. Maybe he's a prince. I hope he survives," she wished sincerely. "He must survive. I have never known a prince in my life," she giggled capriciously.

"Dirty bitch! Let the boy survive first, then you can have him anyway you like," admonished the other lady.

Abhi came back to the bathroom on several occasions to check on the young man. Each time he felt Joshua's body and stuck his little finger in his mouth for at least a minute with a little grin. On the third occasion he did this, he also screwed his knuckles into Joshua's forehead forcefully. Joshua grimaced, extending his neck backwards, and flexing his elbows and stretching his legs. Abhi's face glowed. His booming voice rang, "Hay, Faizal, Manju, Joshua is awake, almost. He will be all right by tomorrow." He thanked the two women profusely and grasped each of them by their hands and walked to his room saying, "You are very good at what you do. Let us go. We have worked to do." They disappeared and two other women, Jasmine and Shakira, took over tending to Joshua for the rest of the night. They continued pouring cold water on his forehead. Shakira, the younger of the two with a rosebud-like mouth and dark curly hair, tenderly wiped Joshua's forehead and ran her fingers over his lips and chest.

By midnight, Joshua showed some spontaneous movements on his lips and broke out into a paroxysm of coughing, bringing up sputum like mud. By early morning, color filled his face and he opened his eyes, looking around vaguely. They took him out of the tub, wiped him dry and put him on a bed. Shakira sat by his side crouched, holding his hand. Joshua's lips parted with a vacant smile, "Where am . . ." The words got stuck in his throat. Shakira's face dawned. She pecked on Joshua's cheeks with her rosebud lips and said consolingly, "Joshua you are fine. You had a heat sickness."

"Where is Abhi? How is he?" he murmured.

"He is fine. They are all used to the desert winds. You are tender." She gave him sips of pomegranate juice. She patted on his thighs as he rested and went to sleep again.

By the next day, Joshua was up on his feet eating and drinking well.

The mild weather in Pelusium was a pleasant relief from the desert winds. "From here we will go to Memphis. It's about a hundred and forty miles going through the cities of Bubastis and Heliopolis. The weather is good, and the sceneries are excellent. We can reach there in about nine days," Abhi observed correctly. Joshua, fully recovered, was thrilled to be in Egypt on the highway to Bubastis.

**** **** ****

The caravan stopped at the check post on the Egyptian border. A tax collector with a friendly grin came over to Abhi, flanked by two Roman soldiers with hard faces. The tax collector soon recognized Abhi and hugged him, welcoming him back again to Egypt. It appeared Abhi knew them all. They paid the tax, and the caravan proceeded on the road to Memphis that nearly paralleled the Pelusiac branch of the Nile. Joshua was enthralled to be in Egypt as a free man, unlike his forefather slaves.

With the reins gathered in the left hand, Abhi swept his hand behind, tapping on Joshua's knees and said, "Joshua, Egypt is the gift of the Nile. It is the life and blood of the land. Right now you see and enjoy the strength and fertility of this land."

Very soon the landscape had changed. The reeds by the threshold of the waters with leaves like fans and the date palms in the wet lands were all blue and robust and yielding heavy bunches.

"Abhi, where about is the land of Goshen?" Joshua wondered.

"I don't know exactly, Joshua. There is no province in Egypt with that name now. Are you wondering about the Exodus story again?"

"Yes."

"I don't know much about it either, Joshua," a rare submission from the big man. Pointing a bit to the left and west, Abhi rejoined, "Probably somewhere about there was the land of Goshen. In about four days we will ride through the ancient city of Pi-Ramses. The city is in ruins now," Abhi described, acting as a travel guide for Joshua. "All that remains there now are broken pieces of great statues and columns, the remnants of the palaces of this once glorious city."

Joshua's curiosity rose, "Abhi, it is written that the Jewish slaves were put to work in the construction of the cities of Pi and Ramses. Have you heard any Egyptian stories in that context?"

Abhi shook his head sideways, "No, Joshua, I haven't heard of any Jewish stone workers or sculptors in Egypt making palaces. There must have been so many slaves and other foreigners working in different capacities, but nothing that stood out," Abhi concluded.

Maybe Abhi doesn't know it all. The life in bondage in Egypt is the beginning of the history of my people. How could it be not known to all? Maybe he doesn't know it, Joshua ruminated.

In another four days the caravan entered the ancient twin city of Pi-Ramses. Joshua anxiously looked around to see some of the monuments constructed by his ancestors while in captivity. None at all. No buildings standing. The remains of the city laid waste, spread over several miles. "Nobody lives here anymore," Abhi reminded. The old buildings were all covered by wild growth and ant hills. There were some clusters of hovels where the poor, dark-skinned Egyptians lived and worked in the farms, but no sign of a previous Jewish life there. Is this the place where my forefathers worked and lived? How many of them were there? Were they slaves? What were they building? Is it the city that Moses built for the Pharaohs? Were they brutally treated by the Pharaohs? How did they escape? Numerous questions, so few answers, but he was determined to find his answers.

Upon entering the city of Bubastis, Abhi called Joshua's attention to an old stone-walled canal in bad repair with stagnant waters covered with green weeds. "Look. This canal will take you all the way to the Red Sea connecting the Pelusiac branch of the Nile, through what used to be the land of Goshen," declared Abhi. "Ships from India used to come through this canal on the way to Alexandria and to Rome."

This city was very rich and busy with people of many nations, Joshua observed; Egyptians, Nubians, Libyans, and Greeks, but no Jews. The grain and vegetable farms were most impressive. The heavy yield of pomegranates just turning red bent the tree branches kissing the ground. One bunch of a palm yielded a donkey-load of dates, and a cluster of bananas gave forth several head loads of succulent reddish-orange bananas. Joshua's eyes widened and glowed with excitement.

How so different, he thought, *even the most fertile plains of Sharon cannot match the abundance and fertility of the Egyptian soil, let alone the arid, brown rocky terrain of Judea.*

As they traveled west, the weather changed again. The sun was blazing the land to toast, and the sandy winds started blowing once again. The strong and tireless camels waddled through the loose sand with a rhythmic rocking of the riders. Vision at a distance was hazy, with the dazzling undulations of the hot air as if the sand was sizzling with the heat.

In another six days the caravan reached Memphis via the city of Heliopolis. They stayed by the river for two days in the guest house of one of Abhi's merchant connections. The camels were left at the stable for safekeeping, and the merchandise was transferred to the awaiting barge. The next day they boarded the barge that would transport them to Alexandria.

The barge was about one hundred and fifty feet long, and forty feet wide, constructed with cedar wood from Lebanon and contained three cabins, a full kitchen and other facilities. The moment they entered the barge, the deck stewards served cold beer in wide-mouth, Egyptian glass flagons. Abhi assembled all the four riders and Joshua around him with the flagon full of reddish-brown beer with a full head. He raised the flagon to the sky and shouted, "To a pleasant ride to Alexandria." He raised the cup to his lips and drank the whole flagon of beer in one draggy gulp, slowly tilting his head backwards as the bottle was emptied, followed by a noisy storm of a burp. "No matter where you go, you won't get this stuff anywhere. This is the best part of my trip. I want all of you to drink. Drink well, eat and rest." Then he turned to Joshua, "Before the sunset you will see the pyramids. It will be a fine sight against the setting sun . . . I will see you all tomorrow." Talking out loud to himself, Abhi drifted to one corner with the next flagon of beer. The barge started sailing with the tide, north towards Alexandria.

Joshua was drinking beer for the first time. It was so different from the fresh sweet Galilean vine. The reddish-brown beer tasted pleasantly cold and bitter in the mouth, easier in the throat and full in the stomach. He slowly drank the whole flagon. The mild north wind swept over his face, blowing and fluttering his curls. Soon he felt at ease and calm sitting by the deck looking at the setting sun. That evening Joshua saw the great pyramids.

**** **** ****

Abhi and the group slept much of the time, and when they were awake, drank large amounts of Egyptian beer and lavishly dined on bread and fish from the Nile. For the next five days, the barge sailed slowly through the Canopic branch of the Nile towards Alexandria. Joshua was rested and well fed. At times he felt overwhelmed by the thought of sailing through the water of the great Nile River, the same waters that Yahweh turned into blood several hundred years ago.

Hector, the captain of the barge, was a man in his forties, thin, muscular with short hair and prominent cheek bones. With a firm and commanding voice, Hector distinguished himself as the leader of the ship. He spoke fluent Greek and Latin, and was happy to learn that Joshua spoke Greek as well. He owned the barge and ran it as a business.

Hector was very curious about Joshua and asked many questions about Israel and, in particular, about Jerusalem and the temple. Many times, Hector had made it a point to detain Joshua with a question or two of no consequence. He invited Joshua to the captain's cabin to dine with him the very first evening. While talking with him affectionately, Hector addressed Joshua as "adorable" and lovingly smoothened Joshua's shiny curls and threw his arm around his shoulders, and all. But Joshua respectfully and carefully avoided his advances and declined Hector's invitation to sleep with him in the captain's cabin.

In the meantime, Abhi sniffed at the dressed-up news that the captain had tried to violate Joshua on the bridge. His face turned purple. "Bastard," he guffawed, and rose to his feet as a smoking mountain ready to erupt. With one hand gripped firmly on the hilt of the double-edged Bedouin dagger, he grasped Joshua and extended his indomitable presence to the captain's room. In vain, Joshua pleaded with him not to fight, but he was unable to be stopped. Abhi kicked the door to close it behind him. Only one man's boisterous shouting was heard for the next several minutes. Faizal and his group were alert and on their toes, ready to move, just in case. After a while, the noise from the captain's room died out. They both came out friendly, as if nothing had happened.

Thereafter, Hector was overtly helpful and friendly to Joshua, like an elder brother. And, after learning of the reason for Joshua's journey, Hector was more than happy to share his exceptional knowledge with the young scholar, particularly about the Nile and navigating the river tactfully. "Navigation on the Nile is made easier by the ever present north winds which carry the sailboats and barges from Lower to Upper Egypt with little effort," Hector revealed. "The natural downstream currents of the Nile carry the vessels from Upper to Lower Egypt effortlessly. Even during the great inundations, navigation is possible," he stated confidently. "Joshua, whenever possible, I will sail the boat closer to the shore so that you can see the life up close in the Delta," Hector added caringly.

Close to the shore, Joshua observed several fishermen catching fish with nets, hooks and spears. Small boats and canoes were common both in the main water of the Nile and the numerous canals that carried water to the inlands. The farmer's houses were on raised platforms to escape the heavy soaking rains and inundations. However, the supreme fertility of the land was reflected in the strong, lush, and robust vegetation that lined the shores. "This land is naturally blessed," Joshua said to himself. "No wonder that for generations, foreigners flocked to Egypt for protection and livelihood. Is it from here that Joseph amassed grains that were stored in the granaries, foreseeing the great famine for the next seven years? Is it not the land where milk and honey really flows," he mused.

Watching the sunset from the deck was a memorable sight as the deep red skies almost merged with the blue waters of the Nile at the threshold of the western horizon. After a full day of work, the tired Sun God of Egypt gradually descended for a cool dip and rest. Joshua stayed awake late into the night contemplating the splendor of this gigantic river and the great civilization that had sprung up on its shores. Sailing the Nile under the moonlight was a soothing, as well as exhilarating experience, as the waters of the Nile bounced and scintillated against the rays of the rising full moon. Each day Joshua woke up way before the first light filled the east to watch the birth of a new sun, the most thrilling moment on sailing the Nile. The golden yellow rays of the rising sun were intensely bright as they reflected and scintillated on the silver white waves of the Nile, creating the illusion that both heaven and earth melted together into one place here in Egypt on the waters of the Nile.

Joshua was pretty much confined to himself, and he had plenty of time to reflect on his mission. *Why are my people so harsh and brutal on women? Why do we not freely mix with other nations of the world? "Love thy neighbor" is a commandment so long as the neighbor is a Jew. All nations come to Egypt for a good life and prosperity. Why did they enslave the Israelites, if they did?*

The barge sailed gently down the Nile, and the next day they reached Letopolis. The sun had barely been up for an hour when Abhi approached Joshua holding a jar of beer in one hand and his mouth stuffed with bread, growling, "Joshua, I see you are awake early in the morning. Isn't it great, relaxing, sailing the Nile? We eat, drink, rest and enjoy. No responsibilities or bothers. Most of the things I know about Egypt, I learned in my travels from the captains and guides while sailing the Nile. But you will learn a lot more from the farmers when you get a chance to get to know them," Abhi growled.

"Joshua, do you know how the Greeks became Pharaohs of Egypt?"

"It probably started with Alexander," said Joshua.

"That's my boy," guffawed Abhi with delight.

Abhi put a heavy hand on Joshua's shoulder, shaking him with fatherly affection and demanding, "Son, it's a bright morning today. Tell me what you want to hear first. There are thousands of Egyptian stories that might interest you, but don't ask me about the Jews and their stories," he said as he knit his brows. Hearing Abhi's booming pronouncements, Captain Hector strolled into the group, joining the conversation.

"At Bubastis you started telling me something about the origin of the Nile." Joshua threw a log into the fire.

"Correct, the Nile, the Nile." He poured the rest of the beer down his throat by bending his head backwards until the last drop. He let out another loud burp and started bellowing, "Joshua, Egypt is the Nile. Nobody knows where it begins. The belief is that way beyond the

Upper Egypt in the land of Nubia in a cave there sits the God Hapi with a gigantic amphora filled with water. As a blessing for Egypt, he pours the water down the river in the form of great inundations every year." Joshua stared at his face eagerly and interestingly. "Hapi is both a man and a woman God." Abhi erupted into a loud rattling laugh. "Can you imagine a phallus and a vagina all in one person?"

"That's quite correct." said Hector with a friendly pat on Abhi's back. "I am impressed with your knowledge of Egyptian history, Abhi. But really, do you know how Alexander became a Pharaoh?"

There was no answer. A rare moment when Abhi did not have an answer.

"Well. I will tell you," said Hector. "After defeating the Persian king Darius III at Issus, he marched into Egypt with the dream of becoming a Pharaoh, a God. As the very first step, with some Egyptian priests, Alexander went to the Oracle of Ammon at the oasis of Siwah across the desert on the Libyan border. As coached by his tutors, including Aristotle, he demanded the oracle, "Who is my father?"

A clairvoyant oracle obligingly answered, "The Sun. You are the son of Sun."

"Was the oracle bribed?" Asked Abhi.

"We don't know. But that's all that Alexander wanted to hear: the lineage has been established. The jubilant young king marched to the capital city of Memphis, and there the Priests of Ptah crowned him as the new Pharaoh of Egypt, the son of Ra, the ultimate Egyptian God. Soon Alexander won the hearts of the Egyptian priests by undertaking the restoration of sacred sites and construction of glorious new structures. The new Pharaoh restored the chapel of the sacred boat at the temple of Ammon in Karnack and restored the run down sanctuary as well."

Abhi was silent for a moment, as if humiliated, but soon he turned to Hector. "Hector, did you know that Alexander's father was a Pharaoh?"

Hector was puzzled for a moment. "No," he said.

"Ha . . . ha . . ." Abhi laughed gutturally. "Then I will teach you something. You know boys, the last native Egyptian Pharaoh,

Nectanebo II, was defeated by the Syrians some twenty years before Alexander was born. Nectanebo disappeared from Egypt, went to Nubia and finally reappeared in the court of King Phillip in Macedonia. Nectanebo, with his physique, charm, magic and knowledge in astrology, enchanted and enticed Queen Olympias. He prophesized to her that God Ammon, the upholder of justice and creation, would appear to the queen and bless her womb in dreams. To fulfill this prophesy, Nectanebo disguised himself as Ammon, appeared to the queen in her chamber and blessed her with his skills. The queen conceived a child that night, and Alexander was born," concluded Abhi laughing with delight.

When they started narrating the phallic skills of Nectanebo, Joshua slowly drifted out to the oarsmen fishing. They had anchored a couple of fishnets about the side of the boat. Every hour or so they would raise the net, and Joshua never saw them disappointed, each time the net was filled, teeming with writhing and fluttering silvery fish. The lunch and dinner on the boat always had an abundance of fried fish, bread, beer and sun-dried dates. The leftover fish were salted and sun dried on the rear end of the deck.

They reached the port of Canopus that noon, and in the evening the captain invited Joshua and Abhi for dinner in his cabin. "Tomorrow morning we will reach Alexandria," Hector reminded them. Fixing his eyes on Joshua, the captain resumed. "Joshua, you can learn all that you desire in Alexandria, but first, you must try for a job at the library or at the Serapium. You have a big advantage because of your skills in Greek," Hector observed.

After dinner, he pulled out a sheet of papyrus and made a note, rolled it up and handed it over to Joshua, saying caringly, "I know this man Epimenidis. Although his name sounds Greek, he is actually a Jew, a rich Jew. His son Elon is a close friend of mine. I have done business with him. He is a nice man. He has a house in the Delta section in the city. You find him and give him this note. He will certainly help you. In case you become stranded, come over to the port and look for my office. I will leave word with my staff."

The next morning Joshua stepped down from the barge to the port of Alexandria. His bag slung across his shoulders, Joshua walked towards the eastern gate of the city recollecting the many stories he had heard about Alexander from Abhi and Hector.

Joshua missed Mary and longed for the feel of her arms around him. Questions that he couldn't answer danced in his head. How is she doing? Am I doing the right thing in undertaking this expedition? But, I need to know the places where my forefather's toiled as slaves. Where are the temples and the palaces they built with their sweat and labor? Or is it all a long story told by a man called Moses to enforce discipline to a disorderly crowd?

The walled city of Alexandria readily came into view, where the Roman standards with the double-headed eagle fluttered on the turrets of Alexander's fort. By noon Joshua had reached the Canopic Gate at the eastern wall of the city of Alexandria. The Roman soldiers stopped him at the gate and questioned him about his intentions. Joshua explained that he was planning to visit Epimenidis, living in the Jewish quarters. The soldiers allowed him in and were kind enough to give him some travel directions as well.

**** **** ****

It was not difficult to locate the house of Epimenidis. He had a gated house with a colorful garden at the front yard with marble statues of naked Greek women watering the flower plants and Priapus tending the shrubs. Joshua was warmly welcomed by Epimenidis and his wife, Lydia. Epimenidis was a well-groomed, clean-shaven man in his early fifties. Lydia was obviously a Greek woman with brown hair, blue eyes, a straight nose and comely face, and in her forties.

"Where is Elon?" Joshua asked, as if he knew Elon from before.

His parents were equally surprised. "How do you know Elon? They both countered excitedly. "Hector from the barge," clarified Joshua.

"Oh, Oh, Hector, from the barge," Lydia's face clouded momentarily, but soon she regained her composure and joined in casually. "He usually comes late," she paused with a vacant gaze on to the garden. Soon Joshua would realize that both Epimenidis and

Lydia were upset with his loose lifestyle and habits. He worked as a supervisor in the underground cisterns of Alexandria.

In the dining room, a prominently displayed painting of an elderly Jewish man caught Joshua's attention, and he wondered who it was. "That's my great-grandfather, Elijah," Epimenidis explained as he noticed Joshua studying the painting. "He came to Alexandria from Joppa nearly two hundred years ago. He was a bit rebel of a person. Lydia painted this portrait, copying it from a small older painting. Elijah worked with Aristobulus in writing and publishing the book, *The Explanation of the Book of Moses.*" When Joshua heard the name *Book of Moses*, his eyes lit up. He couldn't contain his enthusiasm. "Do you have a copy of that book here?" Joshua probed.

"No, but there is one copy in Serapium," Epimenidis said.

In the meantime, Elon showed up at the threshold of the anteroom. He briefly surveyed the room and people, and crossed the hall to his bedroom in total disinterest in their conversations. As soon as he entered the room, the sounds of his harp filtered into the living room. All conversations stopped. The music he played was different than the music of Nazareth, but Joshua found it pleasant to his ears, and soon Elon's presence was felt in the whole house.

It didn't take much time for Joshua to get to know Elon. He was a very pleasant man a few years older than Joshua, tall, thin, very handsome with blue eyes. His voice was soft and sweet like a girl, and his gestures, with smooth flowing hand motions and the dancing of his eyes, were all just different.

For the next several days, Elon took Joshua to familiarize him to the city; first to the Paneium, the sanctuary of the God Pan, located almost at the center of the city. They climbed the man-made, rocky hill over two hundred feet in height in the shape of a pinecone with a spiral road winding round to the sanctuary at the apex.

"From here you can study the city in clear view in all directions," said Elon

He was correct. The entire city lay around them as if it was large a painting.

Alexandria was a fortified city, hemmed on a narrow strip of land between the Mediterranean Sea and Lake Mareotis. The city wall enclosed a rectangular area about four miles long, and two and a half miles wide. From the vantage point on the top of the Paneium, the Pharaoh's Island appeared to be shaped like an airborne antelope frozen in mid-air, two miles in length, leaping over the city from west to east. The foreleg of this antelope was connected to the mainland by a mile-long land bridge, the Heptastadion. On one "horn" of the island, stood the lighthouse of Alexandria overlooking the bay and the port.

Elon explained: "Alexander himself chose this site to be his future capital. The lighthouse and the library were also his idea. It all evolved as an Aristotelian combination of power and intelligence. But, as you know, immediately after Alexander was crowned as the Pharaoh of Egypt, he left Egypt and traveled to the east to conquer the nations all the way to the Hindu land of India." His explanations were precise and clear.

The city was divided into several squares and rectangles by crisscrossing streets and avenues. The grand Canopic Way, stretched from the Canopic Gate to the western city wall, was more than one hundred feet wide and adorned by magnificent villas and shops on either side. It was the main thoroughfare for ceremonial parades and processions. At right angles to the Canopic Way was the broad street, starting from Serapium in the south, continuing north through the Heptastadion all the way to the island of Pharaohs and to the lighthouse.

The Great Harbor and the bay of Alexandria were east of the Heptastadion. All the royal palaces, painted in bright colors, were built closer to the shore overlooking The Great Harbor. In between the Paneium and the harbor were located the Great Gymnasium, with its giant colonnaded porticos, arenas, playgrounds, baths, public and other sacred structures. The streets were busy with business tourists and Roman soldiers patrolling. Adjacent to the gymnasium were the enormous low courts and the Agora, all elegant constructions finished in white marble.

"Elon, where was The Great Library located?" I heard the library lost most of its possessions by a fire," Joshua wondered.

"The library was located in the palace complex itself adjacent to the Caesarium," Elon explained. "When Julius Caesar attacked the harbor some eighty years ago, he set fire to the library. In spite of the fire, only a few of the scrolls were lost. The majority of the books and scrolls were saved and are now kept in the Serapium, the sister library."

"Thank you." Joshua nodded

The next day they took an elaborate tour to all the five designated sections of the city in a horse-drawn carriage. "The royal palaces and the residences of the high officials – the Alpha section – are on the beach overlooking the harbor," Elon explained. "Then the Beta section is occupied by the Roman generals, army officials and dignitaries. The Gamma section around the Serapium is occupied by the Romans, the Greeks and the Macedonians. The southeastern quarter, the Delta, is where we live. To the west, outside the city wall, is the Necropolis – the Epsilon section – occupied by the native Egyptians and other low-grade workers in the city. Joshua was concerned to learn that the native Egyptians were committed to live outside the city wall in the Necropolis, although he understood the genius in the construction of the planned city of Alexandria.

They concluded the tour with a visit to the Island of the Pharaohs and the lighthouse. The enormous lighthouse was built in stone and marble and looked like an ostentatiously carved wedding cake, 423 feet tall, completely decorated with numerous frescoes columns and statues depicting figures from Greek mythology. It was built as a three-stage tower with a colonnaded cupola and a rostrum at the top, on which stood a statue of Poseidon. It had a central hollow core and an elevator pulley that manually lifted fire wood to the top level where the light was located.

"Joshua, you should go up to the lighthouse and take a look at the Harbor and the city. It will be a great sight," Elon encouraged. Joshua nodded without changing his squinted gaze fixed at the pinnacle of the building.

"Are you not coming?"

"No. I have been there before. I will arrange for you to go all the way to the lights."

Climbing some three hundred steps, Joshua reached the visitor's terrace. From there, he saw the amazing Harbor and the city of Alexandria as if looking from the sky. "Alexandria – Inspired by Alexander the Great! All the power and all the knowledge of the world assembled in one place, one city, Alexandria!" Joshua was ecstatic.

"Are you the man with Elon?"

Joshua heard a scream from above, from about the third level of the building. While searching for the person behind the voice, another scream came down through the central core.

"Are you the Jewish boy with Elon? Come up by the ladder"

Joshua climbed the narrow ladder to the top level. There were two heavy black men with stiff faces arranging the fire wood for the Great Lantern and the silver reflectors. They nodded when he arrived. The reflectors were engineered to focus the light as parallel beams that would travel as far as thirty miles out to sea, and were manually rotated by the workers at 180 degrees east to west and west to east. At night, the lighthouse would appear to be a rotating full moon, a beacon of hope for the sailors riding the waves, eluding crashing onto the rocks or coral reefs.

**** **** ****

A few days later, Joshua was interviewed for a job at the library of Serapium with Antonio Caprilius, the librarian there for thirty years. He was a tall, clean-shaven man in his seventies with a thin slit-like mouth. His noticeable frowning look with squinted eyes, with his palm shading the eyes, were all due to poor eyesight.

"What made you come to Alexandria all the way from Galilee, Joshua," asked Antonio. "The job is to manage the air and heating system of the library. Do you have any experience in such jobs?"

"No sir. I am a carpenter by profession of my father. But I can learn things quickly."

"I have no doubt about that. I have yet to see a lazy Jew. But you are no ordinary Jew; I can tell you that right away. You speak reasonably good Greek. Tell me what is your ulterior motive?" demanded Antonio.

"I promise you, I will work to your satisfaction. I beg you to let me read some of the books you have at this library." His voice was solid, and he seemed sincere and believable.

Antonio paused for a few moments. "I have been here all these years and have never heard such a request," he recollected. He leaned forward, resting his chin on the clenched fists, searching the face of the new applicant.

"Well the job is here for you. I will instruct Marcellus to train you for the job. Well, regarding the scrolls, let me think about it. Tomorrow morning I will see you and take you around to show you the various rooms, and all."

Joshua was elated at this turnaround. He thought, *I can make a living and study as well.*

**** **** ****

Joshua would soon learn that the Serapium, the greatest Greek temple in Egypt, was constructed by Ptolemy the III about sixty years after Alexander's death. It had become the educational and religious center of Alexandria, containing temples for Isis and Osiris, but primarily dedicated to Serapis, the bearded Greek god of fertility and prosperity. The legend was that Isis became the wife of Serapis in due course. Joshua was curious to learn that the giant column in the central courtyard of the Serapis contained the severed head of Pompey buried in its granite capital.

The next morning Joshua appeared at the office well before Antonio Caprilius came to work. Marcellus came a few minutes later. Antonio, dressed in a white toga, walked in soon saying, "Oh, you came early in the morning. That's the first quality I like in the staff."

Before getting into his office, he instructed Marcellus to show the new employee the air and heating system of the library.

The temple of Serapis had two large fireplaces. From those fireplaces, terracotta pipes channeled dry, hot air through the marbled walls into the various rooms where the scrolls were kept to keep the papyri dry from Alexandria's humid air. Periodically, the papyri were physically examined by the temple curators to make sure that they were in good condition. By accepting this job in the original air conditioning system of the world, Joshua had direct access to the scrolls of the library.

Joshua was ecstatic and overwhelmed at the same time, looking at the wealth of information available to him at his fingertips. I will learn and research whatever I can, even if it takes several years. Joshua fondly thought about his teacher Zilinos who taught him to read and write Greek.

Monday the next week, early in the morning, the young man from Galilee walked behind Antonio Caprilius getting introduced to the layout and treasures of the library. First, they entered the great hall of the library dedicated to the works of the Greeks.

"The works of the great writers and philosophers of Greece are all housed in this room and the next. We call this room the Lyceum of Alexandria," Antonio explained. "Homer, Hesiod, Aeschylus, Sophocles, Euripides, Herodotus and Pythagoras are all here."

Joshua's eyes widened and his breathing tightened at the site of all those books and scrolls. Over a million lines from Zoroastrians, the writings of the law giver Khammurabi, and the voluminous Babylonian writings, filling over two thousand Egyptian papyri – all translated into Greek.

"My father, Julius Caprilius, was the first Roman librarian here at the Serapium," said Antonio. "Altogether we have twenty-eight rooms here for the classified documents, starting with this room, the great hall. Room 2 contains all the works and allied writings of Plato and Aristotle. Room 3 might interest you particularly," he continued to the next room with a pleasant grin. "This is the Babylonian room, which contains more than ten thousand classified documents. You will find many similar ideas and adaptations of Babylonian thoughts in your own Torah."

"Do we have a room dedicated to the Hebrews?"

"Yes, of course. All the documents about the Hebrews, as well as the writings of the Septuagint, are housed in Room 16. We will get there soon.

"This is the Roman room, Room 17," said Antonio proudly. Upon entering the room Antonio stretched his back and turned, making sure that all the scrolls were in place. He pointed to a section marked "Cicero" and proceeded to the next rooms. "Rooms 18 and 19, all the mathematical thinking and scientific inventions of mankind, Pythagoras, Strato, Archimedes, Eratosthenes, and Zenodotus." Room 23 had the travel logs and works of historians Herodotus, Strabo and others. Antonio continued as Joshua felt dizzy trying to digest it all.

"Antonio, how did the Ptolemies managed to collect all of these documents here in one place?" queried Joshua, wide-eyed.

"Joshua, it is the impact of the Aristotelian vision on Alexander and the resolve and resources of his dynasty that made this impossible mission possible," he confirmed.

"Antonio, do you know how many scrolls were lost in the fire?" asked Joshua.

"Joshua, it is estimated that fifteen hundred of the seventy thousand scrolls were destroyed. Most were from the Far East, the works of the great sages of India. Those had not been translated. Sadly, they are all gone," Antonio recollected somberly.

Joshua's face momentarily saddened, but he soon regained his composure. Antonio continued from room to room as Joshua shadowed him obediently.

"Julius Caesar had a vision to found the greatest library of all in Rome," Antonio continued his lecture. "With Varro as the chief librarian, he had plans to translate all these works into Latin, but his assassination put an end to those ambitions." He pursed his lips and glanced at Joshua.

Antonio took Joshua to all twenty-eight rooms. Each room had life-sized busts of several of the authors and philosophers contained in that section, creating a magnificent sense of their presence, but the Hebrew room didn't have any busts at all.

Joshua was simply overwhelmed and barely able to speak. He stared at the busts and scrolls with reverence and amazement. He wanted to read them all.

"Joshua," Antonio nodded his head sideways, "it would take more than three lifetimes to read all of these great writings," the old man put his hand on Joshua's shoulders and affirmed. "I will certainly help select a few very important documents for you to read.

It was past high noon when they took the rounds of the buildings so far. It was time for a break. They sat on a stone bench in front of Room 19. The cup bearers had brought ale and bread for lunch. It was sour bread made like a cone, filled with thin layers of smoked meat seasoned with pickled olives, garlic and oleander, with added sea salt. After a quick meal, their tour resumed.

Come here, Joshua; I'll show you something very interesting." Antonio's pace quickened as he walked towards Room 19. Joshua kept a slower pace, closely shadowing.

"Joshua, do you know how big the earth is?" looking squarely into Joshua's eyes, the old man questioned with pouted lips.

"It's very large. Very, very large," Joshua said, but he struggled to find the correct words for its enormity.

"You know that the earth is a globe, right?" Antonio continued shaking his head vertically.

"Yes," Joshua murmured apologetically, as he was unsure.

"In Greek mythology, the earth is held in place by Atlas," Antonio declared. His voice rose, "But Aristotle had an entirely different belief about this and made the first scientific postulation that the earth is suspended in space at the center of the universe . . ."

Joshua knew that lecture very well from Zilinos. Joshua asked Antonio about Zilinos, who taught somewhere in Alexandria, but he had no recollections.

"However, I brought you here to show you something entirely different." Antonio took a scroll. "This is the scroll of Euclid's elements, written just about three hundred years ago, representing the most important first work of the study of calculus."

Pointing to another set of scrolls, he continued. "This is a landmark work by Aristareus of Samos, on 'Size and Distance of Sun and Moon.' The next one, 'Conics by Apollonius of Perg,' and the following one, 'The Method of Mathematical Problems,' by Archimedes of Syracuse, and, of course, the whole stalk of books on the top shelf belongs to Pythagoras." Antonio paused for a while. He reverently lifted another scroll and carefully unrolled it against Joshua's face and said in hushed voice, "Joshua, this scroll here contains the work of Eratosthenes calculating the circumference of the earth."

Joshua gasped in astonishment. He carefully held the scroll along with Antonio and, staring into Antonio's eyes, asked, "Eratosthenes was able to calculate the circumference of the earth? Did he travel the entire world around?"

"No," answered Antonio with a strong grin. "He did all of his work from right here in Egypt by applying the general principles of calculus and geometry." Antonio spread the scroll on a table and started explaining the diagrams to Joshua who stood over the table with his hands folded across his chest.

"This is the obelisk at the entrance of the Caesarium, here in Alexandria . . . or rather it was. Emperor Augustus removed that obelisk and took it to Rome, but that is beside the point. On midday at the summer solstice, the sun is directly above Syene in Upper Egypt, which is on the same meridian as Alexandria, some 547 miles north. In Syene at midday, the sun's rays shone directly at the bottom of the well, but it did cast a shadow on the obelisk at the Caesarium in Alexandria. Eratosthenes measured the angle of the shadow cast by the obelisk. He hypothesized that the rays of the sun strike the earth as parallel beams, and that the oblique shadow cast by the obelisk is due to the curvature of the earth's circumference. Based on the angle of the shadow cast by the obelisk in Alexandria and the direct rays of the sun in Syene, Eratosthenes calculated that the value of the angle at the center of the globe, which separates these two points on the meridian, was one-fiftieth of a circle. The distance between Alexandria and Syene is calculated to be 547 miles (five thousand stadia) and, therefore, the circumference of the earth would be 27,350 miles, or two hundred and fifty thousand stadia," Antonio explained.

Joshua stood transfixed at the genius of Eratosthenes that had allowed him to think in such an advanced way – a way that was unfathomable to most people.

**** **** ****

Joshua enjoyed his long stay at the Epimenidis' house. With Antonio's help, he was able to study many books and scrolls, but for the past year he had focused mainly on Hebrew scrolls trying to understand how they related to Babylonian writings, still searching the truth about the Exodus.

At times he went out with Elon in the city. Joshua wished to see a theater show, which was held every year at the Roman theater for three days in the month of June or July. Though it was difficult for the average man to procure a ticket, it was not a problem for Caprilius. Joshua saw his first ever Greek theater show – *Oedipus the King*. The show made a strong impression on Joshua, and the dialogue stuck in his memory.

Of mortal race, we must call no one happy

Until he has crossed life's borders, free from pain.

**** **** ****

But Joshua's preoccupation was to understand the truth about his ancestry in Egypt. Once, he went to the synagogue in Alexandria wanting to talk to the rabbi. The old Rabbi Nathaniel, a thin and frail man, received Joshua cordially. He said, "To the best of my knowledge, the Jews in Alexandria and Egypt dated back to the period following Nebuchadnezzar's siege of Jerusalem. Most of our ancestors had settled here in the Delta area, but some of them had migrated to Upper Egypt and settled on the Elephantine Island." The more Joshua talked to people and the more he read the Egyptian history, the clearer it became that the so-called Exodus did not happen in any form as noted in the Torah.

One day, about six months after his arrival at the Library, while Joshua was working in the Hebrew room cleaning and arranging the old scrolls, Antonio stepped in scratching the back of his head. He said: "Joshua, I was thinking about your questions the other day. Did you know that your Torah was corrected and edited here in Alexandria?"

"What?"

Antonio was a bit puzzled. He didn't want to offend the Jewish boy. "I thought you might be interested to know," he said apologetically.

"Did you say our holy book was corrected and edited in Alexandria?"

"Exactly, the official edition . . . the *Septuagint*." Antonio pulled out six cataloged scrolls of papyri and told Joshua to go over them carefully.

The Galilean started the new assignment.

Joshua would soon learn that there had been a colossal attempt by the Ptolemies to ensemble the entirety of human knowledge in one city, in one museum, in one library, in Alexandria. The descendants of Alexander became the caretakers of the intellectual heritage of humanity. Scholars from near and far brought manuscripts to Alexandria, copied and translated them into Greek and, at times, edited, commented and summarized them, and all of these were made accessible to the scholars of the world by opening up the bibliographies of the library. Multiple variations of texts were edited into one single Alexandrian edition that included Homer, Hesiod, Sophocles, Euripides, Aeschylus, Plato, Aristotle, and other known authors of the world.

But how could that include the Torah? It's the word of the Lord, he wondered.

"No offence, but your Torah is also a story told by a man, Joshua. You keep on researching," concluded the librarian amiably.

A week later, Epimenidis and Lydia invited Antonio Cornelius to their house for dinner. The family was thankful to Antonio for his fatherly affection and guidance to Joshua for the last two or so years. Elon also agreed to sit at the dinner table. Lydia had prepared a sumptuous dinner for the occasion. The table was filled with the very best Alexandria could offer, including roast beef, butter-fried fish, corn cakes, steamed vegetables and flagons filled with exquisite wines.

148

Antonio, being a man living alone, was not usually accustomed to such get-togethers or elaborates dinners. After two goblets of wine, color rose high on his cheeks, and he became gaily animated, talking incessantly and became difficult to interrupt. He profusely commended Lydia for the portrait of old man Elijah that hung above overlooking the dinner table.

Elon sat on one corner, just as an interested onlooker, without saying one word in those lively discussions.

Antonio sat deep on his chair at the head of the table. Staring at Joshua, he said, "This young man from Galilee is a very bright boy. He has the wisdom and the inquisitiveness of a Greek philosopher. He has asked me many questions of great interest that even encouraged me to refer to some of the scrolls again." He paused, looked around, and then fixed his eyes on Joshua again. "So, I guess, now you are well read up on the evolution of the Alexandrian Torah?"

"Yes."

"So, you can tell us now. Let me see how for you have progressed. I am losing my memories too fast. It took six months for me to recollect the Septuagint story."

"Well." Antonio took a deep drink of wine and leaned back. "Come on, young man."

Elon stared at Joshua with a sarcastic grin. *They are all treating Joshua like a baby*, he thought.

Joshua started, "Yes. At least for about six hundred years there were Jews in the Delta area. By the time the city of Alexandria was built up, the Jewish population grew larger and became a Jewish community of some significance. It is my understanding, mostly from *The Letters of Aristeas to Philocrates*, that it was Demetrius of Phalon, a legal expert and an influential advisor to Pharaoh, Ptolemy II Philadelphus, who initiated the compilation, translation and editing of the Torah."

"Very well said, young man; Demetrius was an Aristotelian philosopher. Very close to the Pharaoh. Continue," said Antonio.

"At that time, a few copies of the Torah in Hebrew existed; however, under the powerful shadow of the oral Torah. Ptolemy II was intending to set up an all-inclusive and fair judicial system for all of Egypt. His

149

plan was to include appropriate segments from the Law of Moses for the Greek-speaking Jews into a comprehensive legislative code."

The room was silent except the voice of Joshua and Antonio. All the others ate and drank noiselessly, paying attention not to make even any clatter of their wares. All eyes were focused on the new apprentice at the Serapium.

After a polite burp, Antonio leaned forward, reflexively turning the stem of his wine goblet and watching the small purple waves of the wine rising and falling. "So, Demetrius was planning to translate the Torah to Greek, right?"

"Yes," said Joshua. "At that time in Palestine, it was the oral tradition that was the Word. King Ptolemy sent an envoy to Jerusalem to meet with the high priest Eleazar, requesting him to send competent experts in the Law of Moses to Alexandria to assist in the matter."

"It is said that the king rewarded the High Priest with several talents of gold in return for the services," added Antonio.

"So, the High Priest was corrupt, even in those days?" asked Elon.

Nobody replied.

"If the Jewish belief was that the Lord's Words must not be written in any other languages, how could the high priest assist in such an endeavor? Would that not be blasphemy?" said Elon.

There was a strained moment of silence.

"You are correct, Elon," said Joshua, and he continued. "Eleazar selected seventy-two experts in the Torah – the Septuagint – six each from the twelve tribes of Israel, to go to Alexandria. The king interviewed the delegates and clarified several questions pertaining to the judicial aspects of the Law of Moses. They compiled and created the Alexandrian Torah, after seventy-two days and nights of work. The Jewish community then took a solemn oath that this translated text would be established as the final, immutable Word of the Lord."

"Joshua, you are fresh from Palestine. What did the Pharisee in Israel do with this Greek edition of Torah? Did they accept it?" asked Antonio.

"No. In Israel the oral tradition still rules," said Joshua with a deep sigh.

The next day – a holiday – the library was closed. The previous night he was restless and couldn't get to sleep until the first light of the day. It was in the latter part of autumn, and Alexandria was chilly. He walked the compounds of the great Serapium and settled on the pedestal of Pompey's column. He sat cowered, with his hands around his knees and head covered with a Jewish clock. *How could the words of Yahweh could be altered*, he thought. *Why did the High Priest send seventy-two experts to Alexandria? Why had he accepted the bribe from the Ptolemies?* He realized for the first time that the Torah that he had studied was the Alexandrian edition.

**** **** ****

Joshua continued working for several more months at the Serapium. The work required him to meet with Antonio every week with a status report on the working order of the air conditioning system. He needed to ensure that the vents were all working well, and that the rooms were kept at the correct temperature to preserve the scrolls. However, Antonio enjoyed quizzing Joshua about the topics he had been studying at the library and would always begin by asking, "Joshua, are you getting any answers to the questions you are looking for?"

And, Joshua's usual answer was, "I'm still working on it."

One day, Antonio sat down with Joshua in his work room. "Joshua, you have been here with me for about three years now. I need to ask you a couple of things. You are pleasant enough, yet you always seem so serious and preoccupied. Tell me what is bothering you and what exactly it is that you are searching for?"

"Antonio, as I have told you before, I am still working on my project."

"Joshua, are you avoiding my question? I think you are reading too much Cicero. Are you still researching on Judaism, the Exodus story and the revelations of Moses?" Antonio demanded.

"Yes, that is correct." In a guarded tone he continued, "Antonio, there are very many statutes and commandments in the Torah pertaining to women and dealings with peoples of other nations, words of anger, vengeance, retaliations and brutal violence. I know that God is love, it cannot be anything else. I need to know who wrote these words in God's name."

"I believe you have already read Aristobulus', *The Explanation of the Book of Moses*," Antonio said.

"Yes, I have. But it is not much more than a reaffirmation of what is already known. Antonio, tell me, did the Egyptians have a system of slavery? How were all these great temples, pyramids and the canal systems completed? Did my ancestors, as slaves of Egypt, build them? Tell me what you know."

"Joshua, in the ancient Egypt, there was no slavery," Antonio apprised. "Even though the people of Upper Egypt and Lower Egypt fought and conquered each other several times, the Egyptians did not enslave other Egyptians. However, when they fought wars with their neighbors, such as the Nubians or the Libyans, some of the enemy was enslaved, but the captives in general were killed. The great buildings here in Egypt were built by the hands of free Egyptians, before the Jews ever lived in Egypt."

Joshua nodded, requesting him to continue.

Antonio continued with a firm grin. "As you have learned, Egypt is a country with three seasons. From July to October is the flooding season. From November to February, the land is prepared with plowing, seeding and agriculture. From March to June it is the season of harvesting and festivals. During the season of inundations, when the land was under water, all able-bodied men were drafted by Pharaoh into a massive army and workforce. This workforce created the great structures such as the pyramids, the great temples, and all; it was not slavery, and it was not the Jews."

Do you have any information about the presence of Hebrews in Egypt before the Babylonian invasion?"

"No, certainly not," Antonio countered. "The Jews were not even in Egypt when all of this construction took place."

"It is disturbing, Antonio." Joshua resumed, as if talking to himself in a monotonous tone. "The whole history of my nation originates from the story of the Exodus. If it is so, then all our beliefs are flawed. No, it cannot be. We are missing something, somewhere."

"Maybe. In any case, I understand that you are planning to sail to Upper Egypt, aren't you?"

"Yes, Antonio. Thank you for permitting me to take some time off from my job and for giving me the references and the connections. It will certainly help me."

When they started taking about the Upper Egypt, Antonio's face filled with light, and he became animated like a child. "You have to see them with your own eyes to appreciate such magnificence. It's beyond capacity to understand how the ancient man created all those great cities, temples and obelisks, but most of all, how they conquered the inundations. Any number of words will not explain it."

A faint smile dawned on Joshua's face. His eyes opened wide with interest.

"Homer has described the Temple of Karnack as the city of a thousand gates with immeasurable wealth. Well, when you return, we must sit down and speak more." Antonio said as he stood to leave.

In the meantime, Elon, too, became interested in Joshua's research. One day, he came to the library of Serapium to see what Joshua was studying. As the discussion of religion and traditions came about, Joshua asked him about Elon's religious beliefs.

"I am a Jew by birth, uncircumcised. I never practiced the faith. I have never been to a synagogue, nor have I read a page of the Torah," Elon said.

"That would mean your parents never bothered to raise you in the traditions."

"Correct, Joshua. My father was more interested in educating me in mathematics and music. It's the reason I got the job that I have now."

"So, what makes the trip today, friend?"

"Joshua," Elon said tersely, "I have been wondering about you. You have spent over three years here in Alexandria, lonely most of the time. You have a family at home . . ." Elon threw his hands over Joshua's shoulders. "What are you still doing here? Why don't you go home to be with your family or bring them here to be with you? You already have a good job here, and it would be very easy for you to care for your family here."

Joshua was happy that Elon had some concerns and thought about him. "Elon, what a coincidence. Antonio also told me more or less the same things. I trust you both didn't have a conspiracy. However, I am at the end of my time here in Alexandria. One more project left. I am planning to sail up the Nile to Syene and to the Elephantine Island. Then I will leave Egypt."

"I see. Tell me what are you going to do with all the information you have gathered so far?" Elon persisted.

Looking out at a distance, the Galilean took a deep sigh. Then he looked straight at Elon.

"Elon, I am not sure yet." His face was pale, and his voice, somber. "More often than not, I think about the poor people of my land. They are ill-treated equally, both by our occupants and by our own high Pharisee."

"You are a very bright man. Brace yourself; go back to your land; form an army; fight the evil and become a . . ."

"Stop, Elon, stop!" Joshua cried. "None of that kind. We will resume the subject at some other time."

"Yes, some other time. But tell me what your plans to travel to Upper Egypt are?"

"Why you ask? Are you interested to go south?"

"Maybe." His face lit up. "I have never traveled beyond the Oasis of Fayoum. That too when I was a child, many years ago."

"That's a great idea, Elon," Joshua exclaimed. The two of them hatched out a plan to travel together. They agreed the best way would be to combine the travel with some government officials who traveled to the cities of Upper Egypt. Elon agreed to talk to some people in his office regarding the matter.

**** **** ****

In the first week of June, Joshua and Elon set sail to Middle Egypt on a government boat accompanying Kufone, a Toparch from the Nome of Fayoum, as he returned home from government business in Alexandria.

Kufone, a strong, muscular man in his forties with dark curly hair and an intense countenance, who seldom smiled, was a native Egyptian. Kufone appeared to be a man of serious disposition who was pleasant, but spoke very little. He recognized the two young guests with a casual nod. He was dressed in short sleeves, a skirt and vest. The most prominent item he wore was a belt buckle fashioned like a Roman eagle. Most of the time Kufone stayed in the stateroom reading and writing notes on papyri.

**** **** ****

Kufone sailed on an expertly crafted, modern sailboat made of cedar wood. The boat contained one stateroom, two guest rooms and carried a crew of sixteen. Two helmsmen navigated a large rudder post mounted securely on a strong trestle in the rear of the deck. The prow of the boat had a cedar wood carving of a raging lion embellished with brass and silver. On the fore bridge, on the prow, was an ornate royal box where people could relax.

One late morning in June, Kufone's boat started sailing south from Alexandria to Fayoum. The large rectangular sail that was emblazoned with the double-headed Roman eagle in red and yellow was fluffed up well with the northern breeze that pulled the boat with a good speed, requiring only occasional help from the oarsmen. From midday onwards there was strong, dependable north wind that would bloom the sail and set the boat traveling at a much higher speed.

Joshua and Elon had settled near about the prow of the boat, dangling their feet, watching the sceneries by the land. They talked very little. Late in the afternoon, a lady dressed in a soft, flowing, white silk robe appeared on the royal box with her gown fluttering in the wind that fell on the young traveler's face. It was the first time they had even realized that there was a woman on the boat. After a few minutes she turned around, strolling towards the state room at the rear. Joshua looked back; he couldn't catch her face, but the wind had pasted the flowing gown on her body revealing every curve and contour visible through the translucent robe.

"Did you know there was a woman on the boat." asked Elon.

"No. Maybe we are not supposed to sit here." They moved from the prow to the side bench near the oarsmen on the hull. From the oarsmen, they realized that the lady was Leyandra, Kufone's secretary, also his wife in travel, a woman of mixed blood, her mother Egyptian and father Roman.

A few minutes later she came out of the stateroom, her gaze locked Joshua's in passing, and she swept a little imperceptible nod of recognition and crossed the floor to the bridge on the prow. She then pulled out the ribbon from her hair, tossing her head, and her hair rippled down fluttering in the evening breeze. Joshua's head turned towards her reflexively, while Elon looked to the other side with a contained smile.

It was obvious that she wore no undergarments. Even her pubic darkness was explicit in her Egyptian cotton gown. She took another stroll from the state room to the bridge, casually, flauntingly. She had an attractive olive complexion with long, dark curly hair, a shining forehead and full everted lips. The oarsmen frequently turned their heads to look at her, though they pretended not to notice.

By evening both Kufone and Leyandra came out to the deck; they did not pay much attention to the two young sailors, but made certain that the staff took care of all their needs. The boat had an ample supply of food and drinks, bread, fish, wine, ale and a large variety of fruits, but the ripe, sticky, sweet dates from the Delta were Joshua's favorite.

The boat sailed nonstop, day and night. On the third day, on either side of the canal, endless stretches of wheat fields came into view. The wheat harvest had just started. Rows and rows of reapers were cutting the wheat as if in a synchronized line dance, singing harvest songs in good tune and rhythm. Fifty or so men and women, all leaned forward in perfect timing, grabbed a bunch of wheat stems, cut them with a sickle, seemingly as one unison action. The severed bunches were placed on the ground. Over and over again they repeated this dance, the rhythm of it pulsating through the group.

"This is amazing; the song sounds great," Elon exclaimed. "It reminds me of the grape festival of the Greeks."

"How come; are they not singing about Isis and Osiris?"

Elon nodded, drumming the rhythm on the hull of the boat. "Yes they are. But the music is more or less the same, in tune and rhythm."

"Tell me what they are singing about?"

"Something like Isis protecting the land and Osiris giving the flesh and blood for the soil of Egypt . . . sort of a thanksgiving song . . . I don't get it all."

"I have an idea what the song is all about."

"Good, I don't know much about the Egyptian history. You are the one who knows it all. Is it the same Isis–Osiris story you were mentioning about."

"Yes. The legend is that Osiris was born to earth, here in Egypt, to civilize the men on earth. He taught the farmers how to tame the Nile, arrest the flood, cultivate the land and live in prosperity. After successfully completing his mission in Egypt, he left for Babylon to teach to the rest of the world. He placed Isis, his wife, in charge of Egypt and also cautioned her to keep an eye on her evil brother Seth from plotting against them."

"Obviously, Osiris came to earth from heaven, right?"

"Right. When he had finished civilizing the rest of the world, Osiris returned to Egypt to be with Isis, unaware that Seth had created a plan. Seth tricked Osiris, luring him into a small box. Osiris entered the box, unaware that it would be his coffin. As soon as Osiris was completely in the box, Seth closed and nailed it shut. He poured molten lead on top of Osiris and threw the box into the Nile. Osiris died inside the coffin, but the box floated down the Nile to the Great Seas all the away to Byblos in Lebanon. A great cyclone slammed the box into the branch of a large Cyprus tree."

Leyandra had come out again from the stateroom, tarrying to the prow, and each time she had made it a point to dart a glance at Joshua with a teasing smile. She stood on the royal box at a hearing distance from the young travelers. Elon grasped the idea quickly, and he whispered in Joshua's ear, "Joshua, the Isis is here already. She is looking for her Osiris. If I were you, I wouldn't waste . . ."

"Never mind, Elon; I can tell you the rest if you like," Joshua said.

"Of course, Joshua, please. It is ironic though . . . is it a story or a belief?"

"All the same," Joshua resumed. "The tree grew out of proportion and engulfed the coffin into its trunk. The king of Lebanon cut down the tree trunk and used it as a column in his palace. A devastated Isis traveled the world and finally reached Lebanon and discovered that her beloved husband was buried within a column in the palace of the Lebanese king. She pleaded with the queen and the king. They permitted the column to be dismantled and Isis recovered the coffin and brought it to Egypt for a proper burial. However, her evil brother Seth discovered that Isis had recovered Osiris's body. Seth confiscated the coffin. He hacked Osiris's body into thirteen pieces and scattered them into different parts of the Nile. A devastated Isis once again sailed the Nile. She recovered twelve pieces, all but his phallus, which had been engulfed by a fish. She pieced together Osiris's body, fashioned an artificial phallus and fit it onto his body. Isis blew her breath into his mouth and Osiris was resurrected."

"Interesting," exploded Elon, "So, the son of God descended from heaven to save the world. He was tortured, killed, dismembered and scattered. Finally, he was reassembled and resurrected to life, right? Wonderful story. I am impressed," commented Elon with a sideward smile.

It appeared that Leyandra had listened to the latter half of the story. She returned to the state room.

"Well, a good piece of Egyptian myth, or is it their religion. What do you think?"

"Elon, religion takes place in historical times, but mythology seems to take place out of time."

"Joshua, I am not trying to tease you. Your beliefs of Judaism; is it a myth, religion, or what?"

After a long moment of thought, Joshua said, "In philosophy, beliefs and convictions are supported by reasoning and logic, proof that is derived from critical study. Religion is beliefs based on faith, on believing what you have been taught or told by the religious leaders, your parents, elders and your community."

"I see you didn't waste any time in Alexandria," Elon observed judiciously. "You have learned a great deal. I am glad I took the trip with you."

Another night they spent telling stories and engaged in friendly arguments.

**** **** ****

It was the fourth day of their sail on the Nile. The morning was windless and sultry. By early afternoon, the wind caught up strongly on the sail, ballooning it up. Though the waves were gentle, the boat was gliding fast up south. While the young men were involved in their usual discussions about mythology or philosophy, Leyandra strolled out and stood on the fore bridge for a while, enjoying the breeze, looking at the distant harvest fields. Elon pinched on Joshua's thighs with a grim.

She spread out her arms as if embracing the wind. Her silk gown was stuck to her body, and she appeared to be flying naked with her long hair fluttering like a flag. The sailors in the ship, including Joshua, captured a piece of that scene. Pleasantly and graciously she smiled at the ship's crew and passengers as she walked back to the state room.

The next evening, Joshua and Elon were invited to dine with the captain. Kufone introduced Leyandra to the two guests, his personal assistant, educated in Alexandria, who had a special interest in the last Pharaoh, Cleopatra. Kufone asked the young men a few questions about their backgrounds and intentions for the trip. He was quite intrigued to learn that Joshua had come all the way from Galilee to study his ancestry, that too at a very young age. He filled wine in all four goblets. Leyandra downed a couple of goblets in a short while, but said nothing. After a few long, dull minutes, Kufone leaned back and started talking in a slow, somber tone, looking to nobody particularly. "The glorious days of the pharaohs are all gone now," he lamented. Then the dialogue stopped.

"Why did you say that Kufone?" Leyandra asked.

After a long moment. "You have come at a wrong time to see Egypt. The country has been robbed. The Romans have picked Egypt bare, leaving not much more than a skeleton of the old splendor." Kufone sighed, almost as if talking to himself. He then searched everyone's eyes and finally settled on Joshua, "The Ptolemaic pharaohs lived here in Egypt. Egypt was their home." Kufone scowled disdainfully. "Emperor Octavian visited here just once, chasing Mark Antony. But after he became Emperor Augustus, he never again stepped foot on this land. So also it is with Tiberius. We are being taxed into starvation. The canals are deteriorating. As long as their shiploads of wheat keep sailing to Rome, they will do nothing," Kufone said as his nostrils flared in contempt. A constrained silence followed. Leyandra refilled her goblet a few more times: food seemed of little interest to her.

"But, you are here to learn, not to hear our troubles," Kufone observed grandly. Gesturing towards Leyandra, he resumed. "Leyandra will be glad to share her knowledge with you if you so please. Administration and agriculture are my fields of expertise . . . let's go to the fore bridge," he stood up. He appeared restless.

Kufone sat on a stool on the fore bridge and Leyandra stood behind him. Joshua and Elon silently sat on the deck. The gentle breeze from the north continued. In the cloudless sky, the stars appeared brighter than ever as the pink of the sky gave way to gray. They returned to the state room and the boat continued sailing.

"Did you sleep last night, Joshua.? When I went to sleep, you were here gazing the skies, and when I woke up, you were still here. What's the matter, Joshua; you miss your woman?" asked Elon.

"Of course, I did sleep some last night. But I got up early."

"Did she come looking for you?"

"Who?"

"Cleopatra. She is the only *she* on this boat . . . if she hasn't, she will soon."

"Elon, be serious."

"Well, I can be serious. Tell me what exactly you have found to be the connection between the Jews and Egypt? I must admit, I have neither read the Torah, nor been to a synagogue," stated Elon politely.

"Elon, it's a long story. There was a righteous man named Abraham who was born in Ur, in the land of the Chaldeans in Babylon some eighteen hundred years ago. He had a vision from God: to leave the city of his birth and travel to the land of Canaan. God promised him prosperity and protection there."

Elon looked perplexed. "What was so special about Abraham that God would choose him?"

Joshua stopped.

"Sorry for the interruptions, but please continue, Joshua."

"Abraham was seventy-five years old, childless. He left for Canaan with his wife Sarah, his nephew Lot, with all of his family and belongings. A few years after they reached Canaan, there was a famine in the land. Abraham and Sarah left for Egypt to escape the famine."

"Joshua, tell me, why did God take Abraham from Ur, making him all kinds of promises, only to put him in the middle of a famine?" Elon grinned.

"Maybe he was testing Abraham's resolve and faith," Joshua countered companionably. "So, continuing on, when they arrived at the Egyptian border, Abraham feared that Pharaoh might desire

Sarah and kill Abraham if he knew that they were husband and wife. Abraham asked Sarah to pretend to be his sister, and just as Abraham feared, the Egyptians took Sarah to the house of Pharaoh."

"How old was Sarah at that time?" Elon asked with a contorted smile.

Joshua didn't return the smile, but continued after a brief pause.

"Close to seventy years. Still, she was lovely, and the Pharaoh desired her and took her to his bed chamber."

"This is getting ridiculous," Elon guffawed violently. "It seems that the Pharaoh had a deep Oedipus complex."

"However," Joshua continued respectfully, "God protected Sarah and struck Pharaoh with sicknesses that would not permit him to lie with Sarah. When Pharaoh discovered that Sarah was really Abraham's wife, he was dismayed and sent them away with all kinds of gifts and presents, and they continued on to Canaan when the drought was all over. They dwelled in Canaan for many years and grieved that Sarah had been unable to conceive the child that God had promised to them. By the age of seventy-six, Sarah was despairing and lost faith that she would ever bear a child. In an attempt to bring God's promise about another way, she presented her young and beautiful Egyptian maid Hagar to Abraham, suggesting that he father a child with her. But as soon as Hagar conceived, Sarah grew jealous and began to despise Hagar. She grew so unhappy that she finally insisted that her husband throw the pregnant Hagar out into the wilderness."

"That's horrible. They cast the woman bearing Abraham's child out into the desert?" Elon asked with disbelief.

"Yes, they did. While Hagar was wandering in the desert, frightened and thirsty, an angel of the Lord appeared to her and led her to a fountain. Once Hagar had refreshed herself, the angel advised her to go back to her mistress Sarah, and submit to her. Hagar did what she was told, and a short while later her baby, a boy whom Abraham named Ishmael, was born. Many years passed, and Sarah still had not conceived the child she had been promised. Then, when Abraham was ninety-nine, and Sarah nearly ninety, Sarah conceived and gave birth to a male child, Isaac. Though Sarah was delighted at the birth

162

of Isaac, her old jealousy returned. Hagar and Ishmael were banished, and they wandered in the wilderness."

"You are saying that Abraham was a man with no backbone?" Elon held his laugh with efforts.

Joshua didn't answer, he continued. "Hagar, devastated and hopeless, placed Ishmael under a bush to die, and then she sat under a tree and wept. Once again God intervened on her behalf, and an angel of God called out to her and led her to a spring of water that saved the mother and child."

"What happened to them?"

"The boy would grow up to be a strong warrior. Ishmael later took a wife from Egypt and dwelled in the wilderness of Parana."

"Did Ishmael go to Egypt?" Elon asked, still in wonder at the story.

"Yes, he did." Joshua said. "Ishmael had twelve sons, and they all had children. Soon Ishmael's clan grew very large, and their land extended from Havalah as far as Shur in the eastern Delta of Egypt."

"This is amazing. So, tell me, what happened to Isaac?" asked Elon with genuine interest.

"Isaac, the chosen son, grew up as a righteous young man. God made a covenant with Isaac that from his seeds a great nation of people would be born, a 'chosen people' that would rule over other nations and God promised them all of the land between the Nile in Egypt and the Euphrates in Babylon."

"What about Ishmael? After all, he is the first born to Abraham. Will he get a piece?" asked Elon, drumming his left fingers over the closed right fist.

"No. The land is only for Sarah's children. She is the mother of the king of all nations," said Joshua, looking down at the waves lapping on the hull of the boat.

The two young men continued the ride with the many bible stories of Genesis and Exodus.

The boat sailed beyond Letopolis to the old city of Memphis. They could clearly see the gigantic pyramids of Giza on the west bank of the Nile. On the ninth day of their sail, the boat made a turn into another branch of the Nile, flowing west into the Oasis of Fayoum.

**** **** ****

It was another day off sailing the Nile. As usual, the two of them assembled on the fore bridge of the boat, immersed in conversations, at times argumentatively.

"So, the Jews borrowed gold and valuables from their Egyptian neighbors and fled the city at night . . . that's where you left off yesterday," reminded Elon. "But I was wondering, Joshua; if the Jews were slaves, they must have lived in a slum with fellow slaves. Why would the rich Egyptians allow their valuables to be borrowed by the slaves?" said Elon with a grin.

Amidst all those pocks and sarcastic comments, Joshua would patiently narrate the very many stories of the Bible, the ten plagues, the parting of the waters of the Red Sea, the wandering in the deserts and the final invasion of the Promised Land.

"You certainly can't be saying that you believe these stories, right?"

"Elon these are stories of our ancestry, our beliefs."

"Joshua, honestly, is there any truth to these stories? Any documents?"

"I understand, Elon. I am only sharing the stories that have been written in the books of Moses, but, of course, history is written by the victors in their own way. Don't you think so?" asked Joshua reticently.

"Agreed. But the horrible ten plagues would have devastated the nation of Egypt forever," stated Elon argumentatively. "But, as you know, the golden age of Egypt was yet to come after your stories of the so-called Exodus and your God's attempt to annihilate the Egyptians," hammered Elon. "Do you really think that the Egyptians would not have been able to chase and kill some five thousand or so Jews fleeing through the deserts of Sinai?" he asked, with a twist of his lips to one side.

"That is why it was called a miracle, Elon," Joshua reminded him. "There is no possible way that the Jews, unarmed and weakened by years in slavery, could ever have escaped from the Egyptians without God's intervention. He was their armor, their protection, and the light that guided them through the desert."

"If it's a belief, let it be so. Then what are you researching for? Now you are bringing God into history to explain the unexplainable. Isn't that what you call mythology? Isn't that what you told me mythology was all about: stories before time; stories passed on in the oral tradition with no authorship? In any case, what happened to your people in the Sinai Desert is certainly mysterious, if not simply mythology," Elon finished, looking at Joshua as if he thought him foolish.

"Elon, I have heard all your questions and arguments, and it is clear that you don't have much regard for the beliefs of our people. But God appeared to Moses at Sinai, declared them as His chosen people, and gave Moses the commandments and statutes for their guidance. But because the people were disobedient and cowardly, God punished them to wander in the desert for forty years before he allowed them to enter the land of Canaan under the leadership of Joshua. They fought the Canaanites and many other tribes along the way, and established the nation that God had promised to Abraham, Isaac and Jacob, and it is believed that all the five books of the Torah are God's words directly given to Moses. It was subsequently written down by Aaron and others."

Once again there was a needed silence, and both of then exchanged blank smiles reflectively.

"I, too, have questions, but finding answers for them is more difficult." Joshua shrugged and continued, "As I have told you before, I am here for the purpose of researching the history of the Israelites in Egypt."

"So," Elon asked skeptically, "your God is just a God for your tribe only, and He will fight a war for you and with you whenever needed? Yet in your books, is there any mention of the gods for the whole universe, including the Egyptians, Babylonians, Persians and all the other people of the world?"

"Good question, Elon. In our creation story, there is only one God, who is the creator of the whole universe. He is the same as Yahweh of the testament, except that he chose the tribe of Israel over the others as His chosen people with a land promised to build their nation to be an example to all other nations of the world."

Elon noticed Leyandra slowly approaching them from the stateroom behind Joshua.

"But Joshua, if I was your God and I had to choose a land for your people to develop a nation, it would have been right here in Egypt, in the Delta of the Nile and the Oasis of Fayoum, don't you think?"

"Elon, I haven't seen the whole world, but I can imagine that it would be difficult for any place to match this land of Egypt in nature and prosperity." Joshua agreed.

"Let me ask you one last question, then," Elon continued.

"Let me hear the question, too," Leyandra interrupted with a seductive smile. The two men immediately stood up. She smoothly ran her fingers through Joshua's locks, gently squeezed the back of his neck and motioned for them to sit down.

"I have been watching the two of you for the past week," she said in a silky voice with her mouth like a blooming rose. "You are continuously in conversation to and forth, arguing about one thing or the other. It looks intense and interesting from a distance. If I am not a bother for you, let me join you for a while without interrupting your discussions," said Leyandra freely, and sat between them.

The conversations ceased. Elon and Joshua looked at each other knowing not what to say.

Leyandra felt uncomfortable in the silence and the smile on her face buckled into a frown. "Maybe I should leave the both of you," she said, standing to leave, but Joshua intuitively took her hand and pulled her back to the seat. "Go on, Elon, ask your question," said Joshua in a frolicking tone.

"Joshua, I was wondering whether at some point your God withdrew the blanket of protection he promised for you. As you told me, Palestine was invaded and occupied by virtually every nation in the world, and your temple was destroyed, and your people enslaved and exiled. Did your God change sides?"

A half smile sprouted about Leyandra's lips, and her eyes danced between the two young men.

"Elon, I have no explanation that would appease you," Joshua assured, "but the scriptures indicate that God told the Israelites He would allow these things to happen to them as punishment for their disobedience. However, He also made it clear that He would never abandon them for good. We'll just leave it there. Agreed?"

Elon shrugged his shoulders as a servant approached and informed Leyandra that Kufone needed her in the stateroom. "Well, it's lunchtime. I will see you at the table," she said, and rose to leave.

The sun had risen high in the sky. The scenery had changed. The boat was now sailing northwest against the winds to the Oasis of Fayoum, and the oarsmen were sweating with the effort of rowing against the gusts. The golden ripe wheat was ready to be harvested alongside the canal leading to the Fayoum, and in some of the fields the harvest was already in progress.

This time, Elon and Joshua had a better view and could hear the music of the reapers more clearly. Elon became hypnotized by the songs and began to whistle the melody of the field workers on his lips, tapping out the rhythm with his toes and fingertips. He talked to himself. "This is gorgeous. This trip is worth the trouble."

Joshua said, "Elon, how do you know the harvest song of the Egyptian agricultural fields?"

"Music is the same no matter where you go," Elon said. "All music is created using the same eight notes in different ways, making all different kinds of melodies and rhythms. The harvest song they sing here in Egypt sounds almost the same as the Greek."

"Did the Egyptians copy these tunes and songs from the others?" Joshua wondered.

"No. I don't think so," Elon said confidently, leaning forward to explain. "There is a certain universal order to the sounds that make up music as described by Pythagoras − the octaves in music."

"Really?" Joshua exclaimed. "I have read about his work in philosophy and mathematics."

"In his time, he became popular because of his work in music," declared Elon authentically. "The millions of sounds that seemed to exist in chaos, he abridged into eight simple notes, all arranged in a ratio between the numbers one, two, three and four. The harmony of the notes is perfectly consistent. Joshua, Pythagoras firmly believed in the organized harmony of the universe; the days and nights; the cycles of the moon; the mornings and evenings; the regularity of the seasons." Joshua shook his head, as he also knew it.

The music of the harvesting fields wove a thread through their conversation. The melody was easy and simple. As they listened, they noticed a pattern in their performance. The lead singer would sing the first two lines of the song, and then the group would echo it as a chorus. As the boat moved farther away, the music from the fields faded to be replaced by the lapping noise of the wakes splashing against the hull of the boat. Joshua mirthfully enjoyed watching the flying fish as they glided up and down, playing with the wakes of the boat.

On the tenth night of their journey, they sat down for dinner with Kufone in the stateroom.

"Within two days we shall reach the city of Arisone in Fayoum," Kufone announced. Kufone barely spoke much, but was apologetic that he didn't spend any time with the youngsters, and offered, "As soon as I reach Arisone, I will start the field trips. If you two would like to go with me, I would be delighted to have you." He gestured towards Leyandra and suggested, "Why don't you spend some time with our young guests? I know you have much to teach them." Leyandra searched the eyes of the two prospective students, and she nodded.

"Leyandra has studied in Alexandria and has a great deal of knowledge about the civil administration of Egypt, but the stories of Cleopatra are her favorite," Kufone exclaimed.

That evening, after the dinner, Joshua and Elon relaxed as usual on the prow's bridge with their legs dangling. The moon had risen high and bright in the cloudless skies of Egypt. The heat and sweat of the high day had changed to a pleasant breeze. A servant appeared from behind with two flagons of wine on a tray and presented it to them, as specially ordered by Leyandra. Soon Leyandra came out with a glass of wine in her hand and sat between them.

She was dressed in a soft Egyptian cotton gown that elegantly revealed the contours of her shapely curves. Her half-exposed, bulbous breasts bounced to the rhythm of the rocking of the boat. She sat closer to Joshua. Taking a sip of wine, she inquired, "How is the wine, Joshua? This is the best Egypt has to offer. Special." She completed the gulp. Joshua took another sip and replied gaily, "Excellent, thank you." Leyandra had a mischievous grin, and then she laughed. Her laughter ran out over the waves like a basketful of pearls sprayed over a marble floor. Elon had already gulped the whole flagon and whistled a little song to himself. He didn't pay much attention to Leyandra's chats, yawned loud, and laid back on the bridge disinterestedly with his hands folded behind his head, gazing at the stars.

Leyandra cupped Joshua's hand, pulling him towards her, and he threw his hand around her shoulder reflexively. She ran her fingers through his curly hair caressingly." You have beautiful hair," she murmured. "You have beautiful lips," she continued. Joshua responded with an imperceptible grin. His face, turning red, was not visible in the moonlight. Her companionship, silky words, sensuous touch and the penetrating scent of jasmine drew him to the threshold of the pleasures of flesh.

"How old are you, Joshua?" she asked.

"Nineteen," he replied.

"An adorable, full nineteen," she purred. His heart pounded and groin swelled with a sudden rush of blood. Leyandra grasped his left hand and cupped it against her breast. His palm tingled. His mind resisted but his body succumbed. She bent backwards with a gentle spasm. She kissed into his yielding mouth for a very long minute in a delicious lassitude. She hunched on to him closely. He was unable to resist and folded her in his arms tenderly. Leyandra slipped her hand through his side pocket, groping and feeling the throb. Intuitively, he slipped his hand through the gown and felt her succulent breasts throbbing. She hissed into his ears, "I can stay longer. Do you mind?" He responded with a nod. "Life is to be enjoyed," she murmured passively. Unable to resist the itching on his palm, Joshua ran his fingers through her hair again. "When we reach Fayoum, Kufone won't need me anymore. I'd love to know you then, I hope."

They stayed on the prow's bridge until after midnight.

The next day after the morning meal, Leyandra came out to the deck flaunting, with her hair tumbled down, clad in a bright red silk gown with a golden waist band embedded with rubies and emeralds. Joshua searched her eyes with a certain intimacy in his gaze. On the prow's bridge, she sat interposed between Joshua and Elon. "Kufone says the temperature will be very high today. Well, I am ready for whatever you want to talk about," she said.

"We know nothing much Leyandra. You may tell us whatever you know about the Hebrews of ancient Egypt, if you please," said Joshua.

"I don't know anything about the Hebrews, sorry."

"Do you know where Cleopatra is buried? There is a saying that she is in a pyramid somewhere," asked Elon.

"I have no idea. I don't think anybody knows about it."

"Leyandra, would you please share more about Cleopatra," Joshua implored. "I've always been curious about her."

"Why, I wonder, Joshua." She concealed her smile with pursed lips.

Joshua laughed gaily. "A woman Pharaoh, a ruler of a nation like Egypt, is no ordinary matter."

"For that matter, we had a woman Pharaoh over fifteen hundred years back for your information," she countered with a proud grin.

"Over fifteen hundred years back!" Joshua wondered. "That is even before the time of Moses." His forehead knitted.

"Joshua, it is difficult to understand Cleopatra without knowing how the Roman Empire was operating at the time. Rome was focused on conquering other lands and expanding its power around the world. The earlier Ptolemies respected the Egyptian beliefs and cultures, but later on, the Ptolemaic Pharaohs became disinterested in the state affairs. They allowed the canals to deteriorate, but still raised the taxes on the people. They fought and killed each other and ignored the needs of the people. While Egypt was in decline, the Roman Empire was on the rise, and, finally, Rome invaded and conquered Egypt, ending in the story of the last Pharaoh, Cleopatra."

"Well, Leyandra, the Roman connection will be most helpful to Joshua," interposed Elon. "Did you know he is planning to go to Rome later this year?"

"Really?" exclaimed Leyandra, "Rome is everything now. The whole world is ruled by the Romans." Her face clouded momentarily.

The sun had risen high in the blue sky and it was turning warmer and humid. The breeze had ceased and the rowers were in full swing on their oars. Leyandra beckoned a servant for beers, while blowing air for relief in between her breasts, lifting the neck line of her red gown. Soon three flagons of cold beer arrived.

"Young men, see the story of Cleopatra is interwoven with the decline of Egypt and the rise of Rome." Leyandra explained with occasional breaks for a gulp of beer.

"I thought Rome was always the greatest power after Alexander," said Elon.

"But they had all sorts of internal fights and divisions. You may have heard about the First Triumvirate that came into power some eighty years ago – Julius Caesar, Pompey and Crassus. At this stage, the Roman Republic effectively came to an end. It was a three-headed beast that ate away the ethics of the Roman Republic."

"Strange. You think Julius Caesar was also a ruthless man?"

"He too, Joshua. To strengthen this new alliance, Caesar forced his beautiful daughter Julia to marry Pompey," she added wincing at Joshua.

Sweat beads grew large on Leyandra's face that started to drip down. She looked for a handkerchief to wipe off her face. Reflexively, Joshua wiped her face with the large wide sleeve of his cotton gown. She nodded and resumed. "Pompey and Crassus were suspicious of Julius Caesar's intentions: they suspected that he would eventually try to take all of the power for himself."

"Like a king?'

"Yes, like a tyrant, Joshua,"

**** **** ****

"In due course, Pompey and Caesar crossed swords, and their followers began to riot in the streets of Rome – once again civil was in Rome. Caesar's army marched on and fought Pompey in every village, on every highway, even in the Forum. In every one of these confrontations, his army was victorious. Pompey fled to Greece, but Caesar pursued him to Pharsalus. Pompey, however, escaped and came to Alexandria."

Leyandra paused for a long moment, stared squarely into Joshua's eyes, and declared, "Remember that was the first time a Roman general had put his boot on Egyptian soil, although he was a fugitive. Julius Caesar followed him to Alexandria," Leyandra emphasized. "There was a confrontation at the harbor. Caesar's army attacked the harbor with fire cannons starting a huge fire that destroyed a portion of the great Library of Alexandria, destroying some of the finest scrolls. But by that time, Cleopatra's brother, Pontius, had murdered the fugitive Pompey and dumped his body in the fields to rot, and his head was buried in the capital of a column that stands in front of the Serapium. Joshua, you have seen that column. Haven't you?"

"Yes, Leyandra."

"And the Alexandrians besieged Caesar's army for over a month, cutting off food, water and provisions, but they survived because of the fresh water cisterns of Alexandria," said Elon.

"How correct, Elon! I'm impressed. How did you learn of these finite details?"

"Elon is a supervisor for the underground cisterns in Alexandria," Joshua explained. Leyandra took a brief break. She finished her beer and rose to her feet, stretching her legs and back. A very timely breeze swept the boat, and her hair flew back, fluttering, and lifted her red gown high above her waist, which she didn't mind. A servant came and refilled the flagons and brought over a tray full of snacks, including pickled olives, toasted nuts and fried fish eggs. He informed Leyandra that Kufone was looking for her in the stateroom.

"Well, we'll continue this story after the dinner. Let me see if I can convince Kufone to join us. He would have much to add to these interesting discussions."

Kufone had ordered a feast for the final dinner of the trip. They had prepared several varieties of meat, which was a delicacy in Egypt. The smoked rabbit seasoned with rock salt, coriander, garlic and peppers deep fried in olive oil, smelled and tasted ravishingly delicious. They all ate and drank well. Even the normally reticent Kufone appeared relaxed and more talkative.

Leaning back, seated deep in his chair, Kufone asked Leyandra relaxingly, "How far have you come with the Cleopatra story?"

"We haven't started it yet. I know that you are the best at telling the Cleopatra story," Leyandra said, smiling at Kufone. "I have given them the background story, up to Caesar invading Alexandria."

"Well, that was nearly seventy years ago, at the tail end of the reign of Ptolemy XII, Cleopatra's father; his name was Neos Dionysus," stated Kufone in a deep resonant guttural voice. "He was a flute player. He never paid much attention in state matters, but he loved music almost as much as he loved sailing the Nile," Kufone scowled sarcastically. "He had six children whom he often took on long vacations to Middle and Upper Egypt to teach them about the history of their country. He had four daughters: Bernice, Cleopatra the Elder, Cleopatra the Younger – who would later become the Pharaoh – and the youngest, Arisone. He also had two sons." As the wine rose to his temple, his voice rose, and his speech picked up speed. He leaned forward, searching the eyes of his listeners with each pause. "It is said that the younger Cleopatra was fascinated by the great past and legendary traditions of Egypt and became a scholar of Egyptian history. She was the only Ptolemy who ever spoke the Egyptian language and spent a substantial time of her youth at the Library of Alexandria reading the great tomes. She also knew how to read and write both Latin and Greek, and was very well trained in humanities and the politics of the Greco-Roman civilizations. Her father, afraid of the expansion of Roman power in Egypt, bribed the Romans with shiploads of grain. To pay for this, he levied very heavy taxes on us, and eventually the farmers revolted against him and forced him into exile in Rome, and his daughter, Arisone, became the Pharaoh."

"So, the people of Egypt revolted against the Pharaoh, and the king had to flee?" asked Joshua.

"Yes, but he came back to reclaim his throne accompanied by Roman troops led by Mark Antony." Intoxicated by money and power, Bernice refused to relinquish the throne. In the brief war that ensued, Bernice's husband was killed in the battle and she herself was murdered by her father."

Kufone paused for a needed silence, shook his head and talked to himself. "He was a totally incompetent Pharaoh . . . totally." His face turned pale. Leyandra nodded acceptingly. Joshua listened to every word he said with cocked ears.

"When Ptolemy XII resumed power, it became clear that he was very much under the power of the Romans." His tone turned sad as he said, "after his death, the eighteen-year-old Cleopatra should rule the country along with her younger brother Pontius as her husband. However, within three years, Pontius, who became Ptolemy XIII, plotted to kill Cleopatra, and the great Queen escaped to Syria where she raised an army and planned to come back."

"Interesting," murmured Joshua, as color rose high on his cheeks. He leaned forward with his elbows on the table and rested his chin on his interlocked fingers.

"Cleopatra understood that Julius Caesar was truly in control of Egypt and sought a meeting with him in Alexandria. The meeting was denied. Cleopatra, unwilling to accept rejection, sent him a large carpet as a gift. In Caesar's court where the carpet was unrolled, a stunning, voluptuous and glowing Cleopatra was revealed to the Roman Counsel. The fifty-one-year-old Caesar was utterly captivated by the beauty and charisma in the intensely desirous eighteen-year-old Cleopatra. There began the love story of Julius Caesar and Cleopatra. Of course, Julius Caesar banished Ptolemy XIII and restored Cleopatra to the throne with her youngest brother Ptolemy XIV as her ornamental husband." Kufone stopped telling the story and turned towards Leyandra to ask if she had anything more to add.

174

"Well," Leyandra responded smiling, "Cleopatra was not quite as beautiful as you might think," Leyandra countered. "Perhaps her jewels and golden dresses glittered. It is said that her voice was lilting and melodious like a harp. She had a way of speaking that was most enticing, but her looks were somewhat less than perfect, with a large beaked nose. But she had long curly hair, full lips, a thin waist, and alluring hips."

"Is there any statue of Cleo in Egypt anywhere," asked Elon.

"No. She never posed for a portrait or allowed a bust to be made of her likeness, because she never liked her nose. But . . ."

"People used to call you Cleopatra," Kufone snapped teasingly.

Everyone except Leyandra laughed mirthfully. "I don't have a large nose," she protested feeling her nose impetuously and beamed with delight, showing her pearly, shining teeth.

"How did you know all these intricate details about Cleopatra?" Joshua wondered, gazing at Leyandra.

"From the writings of Julius Caesar's scribes," she filled in.

"She had incredible self-confidence," added Leyandra. "She perfected the art of seduction, and with little delay had Julius Caesar at her feet or more literally, at her bosom."

For that, you yourself are not behind Cleopatra, Joshua contemplated.

"You may not know this," Kufone interposed with a pleasant grin, "but Leyandra is a distant blood line to Queen Cleopatra." While the youngsters searched her eyes in delight, she reflected with a half smile.

"Cleopatra took Caesar for a honeymoon trip sailing the Nile," Leyandra resumed. "They visited the great pyramids, the city of Thebes, and all the wonders that are built in stone and painted in detail on the shores of the Nile. Caesar was treated as a consort, a Pharaoh, a God. It is said that Caesar spent an enormous amount of time with Cleopatra on the bed, frolicking and making love. On that trip, Cleopatra became pregnant and in time gave birth to the boy, Caesarian. Caesar was besotted with Cleopatra. He had never imagined he'd find such a bright, intelligent and educated woman in Egypt, or anywhere in the world for that matter. He wanted to bring the mother and son home to Rome, as trophies. Cleopatra, as brilliant and manipulative as she was, refused to go to Rome as Caesar's concubine. She insisted that Caesar declare her Queen of the Roman Empire and make Caesarian, the heir to the throne."

"Did Caesar accept her demands and make any . . ." intercepted Joshua.

"Yes and no," snarled Leyandra, "but he took Cleopatra to Rome. Though the citizens of Rome had grown accustomed to witnessing ceremonial victory parades and exotic pageants, there was nothing that could compare to the magnificence of Cleopatra's entourage entering the Roman Forum. Naturally, Caesar's wife, Calpurnia, was outraged, as were the Roman people. But Caesar was blind with bliss. He didn't care about Rome or their opinions. He situated Cleopatra and Caesarian in a palatial Roman villa and treated them as his wife and son. He even built a gold statue for Cleopatra in the style of Isis, which implied that she, too, was divine, and declared Caesarian his legitimate heir. Cleopatra won the game. But there was another Roman general liking her with his lustful eyes. Who was he?" Leyandra searched the eyes of the two young men.

"Mark Antony," answered Elon.

Leyandra grinned delightfully and continued with the story. "But Caesar's exaltation was short-lived. His dictatorial style of rule cultivated a lot of enemies among the pro-Republican senators, and they were plotting to assassinate him. The Roman senate truly believed that Caesar was behaving like a dictator. Even Mark Antony had mixed feelings about him. He hated Caesar as a dictator, but admired him as a bold Roman."

Joshua leaned further forward, shaking his head as if now he understood the story well. Elon sat passively, drumming his right fingers on the knuckles of his closed left fist.

Leyandra's face turned red and in a more serious tone she rejoined. "A special meeting of the Roman Senate was convened on the fifteenth of March at the theater of Pompey. The Senate feared that it may not be possible to accomplish the task with the mighty gladiator-like Antony present. They tricked Mark Antony with an inconsequential dialogue on the marble steps of the building, and by the time he arrived at the Senate meeting, Caesar was bloodstained and mortally wounded. Julius Caesar had been assassinated on the Senate floor at the pedestal of the statue of his former archenemy, Pompey," Leyandra concluded.

Kufone noticed Joshua's face color drained, and chin down.

"What are you thinking, Joshua? You seem uncomfortable with this story," Kufone inquired.

"Well," Joshua said slowly, "in Galilee we have heard the story of Julius Caesar. We were told that Julius Caesar was a righteous king. We believe that Pompey, who most disrespectfully defiled the sanctum sanctorum of the temple in Jerusalem, was a despicable man and deserved what Caesar did to him. We all thought it was most abominable to murder the Counsel on the Senate floor, the very place where truth and justice is supposed to be defined."

"Well, Joshua, your sense of justice is commendable, but things are more complicated than you might think," Kufone said. "I believe you are ready for a good drink now." Kufone noticed two servants bringing four tall flagons of amber Egyptian beer along with an assortment of snacks. It was once again a very warm day with little wind.

The high sun had started to descend to the west. The two servants brought out their handheld palm leaf fans and started waving from behind them for a cool breeze. Joshua was interested to know how Leyandra was related to Cleopatra. He leaned towards her, asking privately. She was amused by the question. She opened up the answer to the benefit of all with a large giggle. "No, Joshua, not at all." She slapped his shoulders forcefully and rollickingly. "I am no relative of Cleopatra. In fact, all her blood relatives were chased and assassinated to make sure that nobody in her blood line survived. Kufone thinks I have the looks of Cleopatra; I don't know why," she rolled up her eyes flirtatiously.

"For this warm weather beer is the best drink," insisted Kufone, and he asked for more refills for everyone.

This is a nice sail, Joshua mused. *The discussions, the people, the drink and the food are all great. Maybe this is the Promised Land,* memories flashed momentarily through his mind.

"There were many events that led to the decision to assassinate Julius Caesar," Kufone resumed on a serious note. "In any case, soon after Caesar's assassination, civil war broke out in Rome and its waves rippled all over the Roman Empire. The second Triumvirate came into effect, and the Empire was divided. Mark Antony got the Eastern Roman Empire – that includes Egypt, too. Octavian inherited most parts of the Western Roman Empire. In the wake of these events, Cleopatra returned to Egypt with Caesarian. In Alexandria, Cleopatra poisoned her younger brother, Ptolemy XIV, assumed the throne and ruled Egypt with her son, Caesarian, as her husband."

"Here," Leyandra added with a contained grin, "Cleopatra paralleled the life of the God Isis; a grieving widow, protecting her divine infant, Horus. She even had paintings of herself with Caesarian as divine Isis and Horus created on the walls of the Temple of Dendera."

Even amidst these serious discussions, at times Leyandra would beam at Joshua with her teasing secret smiles and winces. Her intensely desirable looks, her soothing musical voice, the confidence of her words and the inviting movements of her lips, and all, churned his stomach.

"During these years, Mark Antony had thought about making a conquest of Egypt, the most prosperous and richest land in the whole world" Leyandra rejoined passionately. "Fueling this idea was his desire for Cleopatra, which had been growing inside him ever since he first set eyes on her with Caesar in Rome."

"Antony," Leyandra continued, "looking for some excuse to see her, invited Cleopatra to Tarsus in Asia Minor to discuss some charges that had been made against her regarding her aid to the anti-Caesarian forces in the civil war. Cleopatra, seeking a powerful ally to help her defend her throne in Egypt, very much desired to meet Antony, as well."

"She was not afraid of Antony at all?" Joshua posed logically.

"Ha-ha . . . ha-ha," Leyandra bellowed cheerfully. "Cleopatra! For her, no antagonist was undefeatable. She was confident to win him in the folds of her hands. I believe she was the most self-assured woman who ever lived."

"Her goal was to save Egypt from foreign powers and, if at all possible, to win over Rome with her charm and skills," Elon commented after a long silence, leaning back with his fingers knitted behind his neck.

"How correct again, Elon," Leyandra recognized. "So, Cleopatra's entourage set sail for Tarsus to meet Antony. The Queen's boat was the most extravagant floating palace that had ever been built, filled with exquisitely decorated furniture made out of precious woods and adorned with gold and silver. Antony met Cleopatra in her boat and was immediately distracted by his desire for the elegant Queen, who had dressed herself as the goddess Venus. During their first formal encounter, the elegant and eloquent Cleopatra successfully exonerated herself of the charges against her in no time," said Leyandra passionately.

"It is said," Leyandra said with emphasis, "that when Cleopatra began to speak, it felt like music to Antony's ears, and he was immediately spellbound."

"Correct, Leyandra," Kufone affirmed. "You know a lot about what happened later on. Very interesting story. It is always fresh whenever I hear it again. Please continue."

"The banquet that followed in Cleo's boat probably has no equal in all of human history. The food and drink were the very best Egypt could offer, and were served on plates and cups of pure gold. An exuberant Antony, at a certain point, dropped a rare pearl from Cleopatra's earring into his wine cup, and drank it and danced like as if he was possessed."

Leyandra leaned forward as if to whisper a great secret. "Antony was mesmerized by Cleopatra. There he was, the great Roman General, helpless in the bosom of the Egyptian Queen, a slave to all of her wishes. For the next three days, the couple stayed busy frolicking in the royal chamber of Cleopatra's barge. Antony followed Cleopatra to Alexandria like a tamed dog, wagging his sword. Just as she had with Julius Caesar, Cleopatra and Mark Antony went for a romantic honeymoon trip in the great waters of the Nile to Middle and Upper Egypt. Antony promised Cleopatra the world, and their dalliance was public. Cleopatra became pregnant with twins, Alexander Helios and Cleopatra Selene. She believed the relationship would become permanent." Leyandra's face turned purple, her voice became shrill, and she screamed, "for Antony, the ruthless, selfish brute that he was, this relationship was temporary, a royal vacation with the most beautiful woman in the world."

"But wait a minute," Joshua snarled, "Cleopatra asked for it, didn't she?"

There was a constrained silence. It was clear to all that Leyandra was emotionally attached to the memories of the last Queen, who had tried to save the Egyptian cultures and traditions at any cost. Leyandra appeared sad and sat for a while transfixed, looking at the distant skies.

In an apologetic tone Joshua said, "I was just asking."

"I understand you, Joshua," she said meekly. "Cleopatra was desperate. Yet a man must not promise the world to a woman, make children with her and walk away from her as if nothing happened."

Joshua stared at her for a long minute. She was transparent. He saw the other side of the seemingly flamboyant Egyptian girl. He swallowed a deep sigh. *A man must not promise a world to a woman,* he thought. *What did I do? Did I promise a world to Mary? Did she expect a world from me? Probably not. But my mind is faltering. I must remain true to her. I will.*

"But this is only the beginning of the Antony–Cleopatra story," Kufone said, as he regained the balance of the conversation. "But when Antony returned to Rome, Octavian arranged for his sister Octavia to marry Antony to keep things harmonious between them. Thereafter, Antony went to Athens in command of the whole Eastern Roman Empire, and Cleopatra was abandoned for the next three years in Egypt. Antony placed Herod in Jerusalem as his vassal."

The very name Herod knitted Joshua's forehead involuntarily. "The reason why Herod built Antonio's tower on the temple grounds in Jerusalem."

"Antony's desire was to win over Parthia, and he requested that Cleopatra help him with money and an army, which she did. In the meantime, relations between Octavian and Antony turned sour. Antony spurned Octavia and sent her back to Rome, while Cleopatra joined him in Syria."

Joshua asked, "Leyandra, why did Cleopatra once again go back to Antony after their previous fallouts?"

"Both were desperate. Antony needed Cleo for money and support to win over Octavian, and Cleo wanted a strong bull by her side to protect her throne, to put it simply. Certainly it was an unholy alliance," she said somberly.

"This time Cleopatra was not that gullible," Kufone continued. "She demanded a prenuptial agreement with Antony. Antony agreed to marry Cleopatra. In addition, he promised Cleopatra that he would expand the Egyptian Empire to include Sinai, Judea, Cyprus and Arabia as part of the Egyptian Empire."

"Are you saying that Cleopatra ruled over Jerusalem?" Joshua wondered.

"No," Leyandra came back. "Even though there was a prenuptial agreement, it never materialized. Cleopatra never got possession of Judea. However, Cleopatra insisted that Caesarian and not Antony's son should become the next Pharaoh of Egypt, to which again Antony agreed. Antony's war with the Parthians went poorly, but he was victorious over the Armenians and returned to Alexandria jubilant. The pageantry that followed in Alexandria is unparalleled in the history of Alexandria."

"Is it the celebration where Antony declared the donation of Alexandria?" Joshua recalled.

"Exactly" Leyandra exclaimed. "For the celebrations, first a large silver platform was constructed in the gymnasium at Caesarium. The floor was covered with flowers mimicking a large flowering meadow. The ceremony started with the sacrifice of a thousand oxen. Numerous chariots and floats depicting scenes from Egyptian and Greek mythology were exhibited. A very large statue of Cleopatra dressed as Isis that mechanically turned sideways, waving and blessing the crowd, was a special attraction. It was a combination of the Ptolemaic and Roman victory celebrations. Antony, Cleopatra, and the whole family were seated in golden chairs. Cleopatra was dressed like Isis. Antony made a great speech, declared Cleopatra the Queen of Kings, and promised to give a very large portion of the Eastern Roman Empire as a donation to Alexandria. Moreover, Antony declared that Caesarian was the true son of Julius Caesar and, therefore, the legitimate heir to the Roman Empire. Cleopatra's barge sailed the Nile again with the Roman General. She conceived again and gave birth to baby Ptolemy Philadelphus."

"The crowd erupted in cheers."

"So, Cleopatra won. Egypt was safe," Joshua remarked.

"Yes, at least for the time being," replied Leyandra. "But Antony's speech in Alexandria was the most dangerous statement he ever made. News of the giveaway of Egypt and the Eastern Roman Empire to Cleopatra ignited all patriotic Romans with extreme anger. Octavian was infuriated. Antony still had some supporters in the Roman Senate, but not enough to quell the gale of Roman wrath."

"To make it even worse, Octavian published a document in Antony's name stating that Antony desired to be buried in Alexandria," added Kufone.

"Yes, a war – the final episode of Antony and Cleopatra – was imminent." Leyandra stated. "The Roman navy, under the leadership of Agrippa, moved east, felling coastal cities one after the other. Antony with his forces and Cleopatra with the Egyptian Army established their war capitals in Ephesus and Athens. The armies of the two great Roman Generals met for a final episode in Actium. Antony was a mighty general when he had to fight a land war, but he was no match for Agrippa's armada and naval skills." Leyandra's face clouded, and she paused for a long moment. Kufone read that Leyandra was turning emotional to describe the final scene.

"Fifty-one years ago," stated Kufone, as if making a declaration, "on September the second at Actium in the Gulf of Ambracia, Antony was decisively defeated, his forces devastated. Cleopatra, however, with her fifty ships carrying all of Antony's treasures, miraculously escaped to Egypt. Antony followed. Ten months later, the entire naval force of Rome and Octavian was fast converging on Alexandria, creating terrible fear and panic in the hearts of the Egyptian people. When Mark Antony with his troops was guarding the Great Harbor on the lighthouse, somebody told him that Cleopatra had committed suicide. On the distant horizon, Antony saw the vast armada of Octavian fast approaching the harbor. Antony was heartbroken. He didn't find any vigor in facing the enemy without Cleopatra. Antony wailed for Cleo and sank his sword through his heart to join her."

Leyandra's face turned languorous; her eyes welled up and her voice grew husky. "The news about Cleopatra was false," she said. "As of today, nobody knows how such news erupted. In the meantime, Cleopatra had lost her nerve to fight the gigantic navy of Octavian. She tried for a deal with the Roman emperor, but Octavian with his sword drawn, was busy marching towards Caesarium. Cleopatra was stunned upon hearing the news of Antony. The dying Antony was brought to Cleopatra, with the sword still in place. Antony was drained pale and looked like death. The gasping Roman general was laid in Cleo's bosom, slouched like a wet cloth. A new breath of life swept over Antony's face. He attempted to lift his arm towards Cleo. His hands didn't move but his lips trembled "Cleo," a meek, guttural sound, "you are the only one I ever loved," he managed to say. Cleo slumped to his chest, her face aghast. After a long minute, Cleo woke up bold as if from a bad dream. She herself pulled out the sword from her husband's heart."

The conversations stopped with a minute of needed silence. Leyandra appeared sad and exhausted as if she had lost her own sister. "They had a chance to say a few words finally," she talked to herself. "Octavian's army had surrounded the Caesarium, forcing on the doors. He permitted Cleopatra to bury her husband. Cleopatra had already prepared for her escape."

Very well said Leyandra, Kufone stated. "So, the last Pharaoh of Egypt, who wore an asp on her crown for protection, resorted to the bite of an asp to end her life and spare herself from the humiliation of Octavian marching her into the Roman forum as a slave. Caesarian was quickly and clandestinely sent to India to begin a dynasty. However, he was tricked into returning to Alexandria, where he was killed. His death eliminated the last of the bloodline of Cleopatra and Caesar," Leyandra concluded somberly.

By evening, Leyandra had regained her normal gay composure. Joshua was preoccupied, but Elon could care less, as he had heard the stories many times over.

After the dinner, Joshua sat alone on the prow's bridge. It was the last night on the boat, a night before the new moon. The first lights of the evening had started shimmering vaguely from the distant houses. Presently, somebody had covered his eyes from behind. It wasn't difficult to discern who it was. The tenderness of that palm and the ravishing scent of jasmine were not unfamiliar to him. He grasped the hands firmly and pulled her towards him, and she rested her chin on his curls. "I came to cheer you up," whispered Leyandra softly in his ears, and came about and sat by his side.

"I thought you yourself needed cheering up. Your descriptions were vivid and lifelike. You really have a talent for teaching and telling stories," he said.

"Thank you, Joshua. It also depends upon who the listener is. Kufone has already teased me, saying that I was flirtatious with you."

"Were you?"

Leyandra pinched his cheeks and hunched her shoulders against his chest.

"You appeared emotional on describing Cleopatra's last days."

"Who wouldn't be, Joshua?" countered Leyandra. "People have described her as a whore, but she was the most sincere person, yet a desperate queen who struggled to save Egypt," persisted Leyandra.

"I couldn't agree with you more."

"Leyandra," Joshua hesitated in mid-sentence.

She ran her fingers across his lips. "Come on, don't be bashful. Ask me whatever you want; talk to me," she encouraged.

"Leyandra, at any point in your history, did you have stoning in Egypt?" asked Joshua.

"What? Stoning whom?" She sharpened her tone.

"Well, stoning a woman, for example . . . for any which reason," he drawled.

"Be clearer, Joshua," Leyandra insisted.

Joshua couldn't find the right words. A strained silence followed.

"I don't know what exactly your question is," Leyandra observed. "But in Egypt, a woman is revered. This is the God's own land of Isis. There is no crime in this world or in the afterworld that will amount to stoning a woman. In Egypt a woman is a daughter, wife, mother and an equal partner in life with a man."

Joshua was speechless at that answer, but he acknowledged the answer by pecking on her cheeks.

"Joshua," she called him, "I was very surprised by your question. How could a man like you even think about such a heinous act? One thing is clear: Your mind is unsettled. You are constantly bothered by something, but I don't know what." She snuggled close to him, rubbing her cheeks against his beard. He found her presence, words and touch intensely desirous. He hesitated, but his hands impetuously cupped her in his arms for a long time.

The following morning, Kufone's barge reached Lake Moeris in Fayoum. The barge was docked and moored. Kufone's small cedar boat took them to the port city of Arisone. A mile-long private canal led to the front yard of Kufone's princely villa – a house built around a central pedestal courtyard. At the very center, there was a fish pond with water lilies and varieties of silver and gold fish. Surrounding the pond were several varieties of flowers and fruit trees. Facing the pond against the approach road and canal one could see the colonnaded portico of the villa. To the right of the portico was a canopied wooden platform with sofas and several ornate chairs.

Kufone's wife, Ahmose, a woman of size with a thin neck, dressed in a gown that graced the floor and an elaborate head cover, greeted them. Leyandra had her baggage carried to her room. Joshua and Elon were escorted to a guest room adjacent to the front portico.

That evening Kufone and Ahmose ate alone in their private chambers while the young scholars ate with the villa officials, including Leyandra, at the portico.

Ahmose and Kufone joined the group after the dinner, and sat together on the sofa overlooking the pool and the gardens. Kufone had two wives and eight children: four boys and four girls. The eldest of them was a thirteen-year-old girl. All of the children were naked, mingling freely with the guests. Joshua was a bit puzzled at first, watching the children with bangles, chains, earrings and waist tinkles, but otherwise naked. Four musicians entertained the group with lovely melodies accompanied by flute, lutes, string instruments and drums while the maids served wine and finger foods.

Eight dancers entered the poolside arena, moving to the rhythm of the music. The men, in thin loin cloths, were unusually tall, muscular and handsome. The dances were choreographed with many intricate and contorting yet fluid body movements and gymnastics. After the first dance, eight female dancers joined the men. The girls, too, were shapely, with smooth long legs, strong butts, narrow waists and comely faces. They wore great hair-dresses with plumes and shining beads, gold chains, glittering waist strings and anklets. Like the children, they were mostly naked, with bare breasts and groins. Then two girls came forward for the final act. They stood side by side with a somewhat wide gait and frozen smiles. They simultaneously flexed their torsos all the way back and, finally, brought their faces between their bare thighs and waved their hands to the cheers and applause of the whole crowd. After the poolside show, Kufone's family went to sleep, but Leyandra stayed with the young men late into the night.

She told Joshua and Elon, "Every tenth day of the week, Kufone holds a pool party."

"Why on the tenth day of the week?" asked Elon.

"Didn't know that? In Egypt it's still the ten–day week, not like the calendar established by Julius Caesar; ten days for a week, three weeks for a month, and twelve months for a year," Leyandra explained.

"But that doesn't add up to 365 days," Elon commented.

"Elon," Leyandra clarified, "I know, it adds up to only 360 days. The remaining five days were added as harvest festival days. By the way, the festival days will begin in just a week from now. If you are going stay here for a few more days, you will see and hear the harvest dance and music in the ancient Egyptian style."

"Certainly. We will be here for a few more days," said Elon. He yawned with a sulky face, almost collapsing with sleep. "I will see you tomorrow," he went away to his room.

"Maybe you should also go to sleep," Leyandra said. "I will see you before long," she hissed in his ears, and quickly left.

Joshua lay down on his bed, face buried in the pillow. His heart raised, and his body trembled. He suddenly sprung up and swept the room. "I will see you before long." Those soft words started a hurricane in his mind. He returned to the bed, lying down, and then sat raised up on his elbows. *I am weak*, he murmured to himself. *Like all men created by God, I am feeble.* He felt helpless, lonely and momentarily scared. *I wish she never comes. But she will, surely, very soon.* He gazed at the half-closed door anxiously. He went up to the door. His arms felt moist. A long anxious moment passed. Then there appeared the silhouette of Leyandra at the threshold of the door, vaguely seen against the dark-gray reflected lights of the corridor. The irresistible aroma of the Egyptian perfume permeated through his blood to his soul. A sudden rush of blood harried through his veins. He was near to fainting with desire. He was crushed with guilt. He sprung back to the bed, weak and exhausted.

Three gentle knocks on the door. Then another three. Then it was silent.

Joshua felt calm and relieved. His mind traveled to the little flat-roofed house guarded by the tall cypress. Joshua felt Mary's presence in the room. He saw her waiting for him, the voluptuous girl with curly hair and full lips. Joshua waved her in, and she flung onto the bed, and in no time she sealed his mouth with her luscious, irresistible lips. Her flowing hair covered over his head like a veil. She grasped his shivering hand and gently guided it around her shapely waist, back to her buttocks, her blooming breast into the warmth of his mouth. He clung to the feather-filled Egyptian pillow with pain and pleasure.

The next morning, Joshua, Kufone, Leyandra and Elon boarded the barge, along with two scribes and eight staff, to begin the field trips in Fayoum; the harvest season was at its peak. The Oasis of Fayoum formed a distinct basin in the desert west of the Nile. Lake Moeris collects all its water not from natural springs, but from a branch of the Nile. The two Alexandrians followed Kufone to the numerous fields and cities around Lake Moeris. Joshua had longed to see the canal system of Egypt up close and could barely contain his excitement.

Joshua would soon learn that the Egyptians had been digging canals from the Nile for over two thousand years. The canals – hefty stone-walled constructions, thirty feet deep and forty to fifty feet wide, built to resist the force of heavy floods – were dug on either side of the Nile, mostly on the west. They extended to the rise of the desert, as much as thirteen miles in some areas. Numerous subsidiary canals cut sideways from the main canal diverted water to the farming fields that were more inland. In most other years, the flood waters rose, anywhere from twelve to twenty-eight feet, filling up the canals and overflowing to the farmlands. In some places, dikes had been built to divert the water sideways, depending on the elevation of the land. The floods began in July and continued through October. Then the fields became soaked with rich, dark silt brought down by the Nile. During this time, the entire fertile area of Egypt looked like a large ocean of water, all the way from the river to the threshold of the sandy desert. The cities and towns appeared to float like islands above the immense swamp. In September, when the flood waters began to recede, the mouth of the canal was shut off from the river with large wooden planks to maintain a water level of eighteen to twenty feet above the level in the river.

Wow, what an ingenious mechanism, the ancient Egyptians . . . Joshua thought. "The glory of Egypt is not only the blessing of the Nile, but also the vision of the ancient Egyptians. They tamed the Nile and conquered the floods." Abhi's words reverberated in Joshua's mind, "while other civilizations were building the ark and washed away by flood waters."

The next day, Kufone's team visited one of the harvest fields on the bank of Lake Moeris. The golden, ripe corn fields of Fayoum stretched to farther distances that the eye couldn't catch. The air was already filled with the harvest songs from men and women shaving the sheaves in the distance. Men and donkeys carried the sheaves to the threshing square. Grain that had been threshed, winnowed and packed in sacks of flax were heaped one above the other like knolls.

"These bags will soon be shipped to Rome," Leyandra murmured with disgust. "This season, you could see flotillas of wheat bags heading north to Rome."

"What are those for?" Asked Joshua, pointing to a row of whitewashed giant towers – silos – where men were seen climbing up the ladder with basketfuls of grains and depositing them through a small window at the very top. "For us, at times of famine," she said.

Plenty of workers and an abundance of harvest, Joshua pondered.

"Leyandra, I don't see landlords here, on these harvest fields. Why?"

"What do you mean, 'landlords'?"

"Landlords – men who own the land. In Israel, for example, during the grape harvest season, the landlords visit the fields carried on a litter, commanding . . . yelling . . ."

"I see. Well, here in Egypt, it used to be that the land belonged to the Pharaoh. Now, of course, everything belongs to the Romans. The Pharaoh was responsible for the maintenance of the canals and the farmlands. In fact, when the Pharaoh was dead, he was tried before entering the underworld. That's totally another story. The farming in Egypt is done collectively. It was always like that. An agent of the Pharaoh will oversee the work. But he is not the landlord. Osiris is the landlord. Well, I will ask Kufone to explain. He knows a lot more."

Kufone was busy with the scribes measuring the grains and taking accounts.

"Well, we will ask him later, but for now, what is collectively farming?" Joshua was intrigued.

"The land is cultivated collectively. All able-bodied men of Egypt will work in the fields during this season. The land belongs to Egypt. No one owns any particular piece of the land. The agricultural season is quite hard on the workers." She said in a tone of compassion. "They labor from the first light in the east through the scorching sun, until the sun sets. As you see, there are no trees to provide shade and no covers for their heads. They stop only for an occasional drink. The wheat harvest season lasts for two weeks, and tomorrow is the last day. All the wheat the laborer reaps tomorrow he can take home. It will be quite a lot, and will last for the whole year.

Joshua enjoyed the thought of the whole family going home carrying head loads of their share, singing songs merrily. *Nobody owns the land; but, everybody owns it. Everybody works, no sloth, nobody with a whip on their tails, nobody on litters on the embankments. Even Kufone is working under the scorching sun, alongside the laborers. Egypt is built by the sweat and blood of*

Egyptians and not by any men in bondage. Joshua felt heavy with thoughts and breathed a deep rueful sigh. Where were my ancestors?

Elon felt fatigued and thirsty, but nobody offered him a beer. Even Kufone and Leyandra had had nothing to eat or drink since early morning.

Elon asked, "Leya, where can get some water or beer?"

Leyandra tried a smile. Her lips were dry. "Did you see anybody drinking anything in the harvest fields?"

"No."

It was the last day of the harvest – the day the harvest belonged to the harvesters. Until sunset, until all the workers had finished their work, until all workers had collected their harvest and gone home, Kufone did not rest. In the evening they rested, drinking beer and eating farmer's bread, and stayed in a temporary tent that was set up on one of the embankments. Kufone appeared unusually relaxed. He was smiling to himself as if a big load was off his shoulders. Leyandra refilled his beer mug many a times, rubbing his shoulders, then she whispered something in his ears.

"Well, that's no problem. Joshua, Leyandra says you wanted to know why the Pharaoh is tried at the gate of the underworld."

"Yes, Kufone," Joshua entreated.

"Yes. The Pharaoh is Ra on earth. The Pharaoh's most important duty on earth is to maintain the canals, keep the crops well watered and keep peace in Egypt. At the trial, his heart will be weighed by Anubis and Toth. If it is found that the Pharaoh did not maintain the canals and the harvest was poor, he will not be allowed to meet Osiris or be with Ra. He will be sent back to Earth."

"What if he maintained the canals well and fulfilled everything asked of him."

"Well then, the Pharaoh will be admitted to the Elysian Fields – like your paradise, where there is plenty of water – can grow corn as tall as a man, eat bread and drink beer that would never perish, and live forever."

Joshua nodded in thoughts. "Thank you," he said.

**** **** ****

Now that the harvest had ended, the five days of the harvest festival were about to begin, thanking the snake God Ratuna. Kufone's celebration was to take place at the harvest field in front of the nomarch's Palace in Arisone. The workers had erected a canopied platform in the front yard facing the harvest fields. The high officials and Kufone were to be seated there.

However, on the morning of the first day of the festivities, Joshua and others were woken up by the tumult of a wailing procession approaching the tent through the levee. At the head end of the procession were men carrying two people on wooden planks followed by a tail of some twenty people wailing loud and beating on their chests. Kufone came out, flanked by the rest of the group.

"This is snake bite," Leyandra whispered in Joshua's ears. They downed the litters in front of Kufone. By that time the nomarch with his retinue had also come to the scene. Troubled by the unexpected sight, Joshua was frozen still. Leyandra came to his rescue. She held his hands, consoling.

One man was still, and his skin had turned a bruised blue color with serous blood draining from his mouth, nostrils and eyes. The other was still breathing shallow.

"The one on the right is already dead. I know the snake bit him first," said Leyandra in a hushed tone.

As if he was expecting these visitors, the palace physician came out with three of his assistants. All of them had ceremonial dresses with colorful kilts and headdresses, but the chief also had a fearsome mask of an angry beast with three eyes. He had bells, whistles, and tinklets on his dress and was shaking a knife violently with his right hand. His assistants were also shaking and chanting. One of them swung a censor of burning incense. They danced around the bodies, chanting and shouting for some time, and then the chief priest made some crisscross cuts on the leg of each victim to mark where the snake had bitten. No blood came from the first man. Little came from the second, but he also was dead soon, and their bodies were lifted shortly thereafter.

The families left the scene through the same levee carrying the victims. Their chanting changed tune, and the flailing and thumping on their chests heightened. Soon the procession disappeared into the distance. Joshua's grip on Leyandra's hand tightened. "Why did you say that the blue man was bitten first," he asked.

"The venom from the first bite is so strong that he could not have taken more than twenty-one steps before he fell down dead. The same snake also bit the second man, but because it had less venom, it took longer for the second man to die." She paused for a minute and continued on in a husky whisper, "This is the story every year. On the very first day of the festival some people will die of snake bites." She pursed her lips in disbelief. "The people are grateful to God Ratuna that only a few people died, and all the others were spared. The festival is a thanksgiving for that generosity of the gods." *Amazing,* Joshua mused, *these people are grateful to God even in their misfortunes.*

The evening fell; the festivities started. Kufone and the other officials sat on chairs on a higher platform in front of the tent, while Joshua, Leyandra and Kufone walked around and settled in one corner with the other few thousand spectators. At sunset, about two hundred torches were lit, as a ring of fire around the showground.

"Watch carefully; the show is self-explanatory. I will add something as and when needed," she said.

In the opening scene, the stage, the large squire area, was empty. The musicians sang and prayed to God, invoking Isis and Osiris, thanking them for the harvest and asking them to bless the land once more. Following this, some two hundred dancers cascaded down to the arena, waving white glittering cloths cut in the form of butterfly wings. As they rushed towards the stage, they bent down and stretched up, waving the fluttering rags. As the singing continued, the dancers kept on waving their wings gently, but higher, above their heads.

"This is to create the illusion of the flood gushing to the fields."

"Fascinating. It really looks like flood waters," said Joshua again in a low tone.

Slowly the waving settled down and they all sank to the floor. In what seemed to be one single unison motion, they covered themselves with the dark clothes and lay down on the floor. "The flood had has now settled and the land now covered with dark, rich fertile soil."

The next scene began with thirty new dancers entering the scene in groups of three. There were two men dressed as yoked oxen, and one woman behind them holding a plow. All three dancers moved in unison, the men's heads down, bending forward, the woman leaning on the plow. These dancers stepped over the other dancers, who were lying on the floor covered with the black cloths.

"You know what it is; it doesn't need any explanation."

Immediately behind them was a large group of children carrying hoes made out of papyri stems. They pretended to be loosening and raking the soil, preparing the ground for the seeds. The next set of dancers in this pageant-like performance were all female, carrying leather bags slung across their shoulders and scattering seeds over the prepared land. The graceful movement of their heads, necks, and arms, and the swinging of the whole body was choreographed exquisitely. Once the sowers were just exiting the scene, music was played loudly for a minute.

At this time the dancers, still on the ground, switched their dark clothes for green. They all rose up gradually.

"Beautiful. The corn has now grown," said Joshua. Leyandra pinched on his cheeks.

The crowd erupted in cheers and began to dance vigorously to the music. Joshua had goose bumps all over his body. His face glowed in joy. He sang with the crowd, locked hands with Elon and Leyandra, and danced like the Egyptians, like never before. Presently, they saw some scribes inspecting the crops and making notations in their books. Then there were two dancers, slim tall men, dressed up as snakes, wiggling around the field, who slowly disappeared at the other end of the field.

"Now watch," said Leyandra.

The dancers presently covered in green began swinging gently to the left and right. Swiftly, they all wore tall golden crowns with fringes on their heads to simulate the ripe wheat dancing gently in the breeze.

At that point Kufone stood up with a golden sickle in his hand, the ripe corns still dancing in the breeze. Kufone came down to the field and reaped the golden crown from one of the dancers. He raised the crown above his head and waved, singing the beginning of the invocation song to the harvest god, Min. The crowd responded to this invocation by wildly dancing and beating their chests, all the time calling upon Goddess Isis. The final scene of the harvest ceremony commenced with the men and women, standing in line, moving step by step, reaping the sheaves with a motion that Joshua saw enacted earlier in the real harvest fields.

It was now the first week of July. Joshua still had some unfinished businesses in Egypt: to learn more about the philosopher Pharaoh Akhenaton and to visit the Elephantine Island in Upper Egypt. Kufone assisted, "Traveling up the Nile is easy. There are boats traveling frequently to the various Nomes for administrative purposes. I will be happy to assist you," he said. Leyandra was unhappy. That evening she asked, "Joshua, will we meet again? On the way back, could you please come back to Arisone and look for me?"

Joshua was not sure. He nodded sideways ruefully thinking.

Later on Elon said, "Joshua, if I were you, I would have certainly married that girl. After all you have only one wife."

"Why don't you, then?" asked Joshua jokingly.

"She never loved me. Maybe I can look for her brother."

Joshua didn't smile.

The next morning, the two youngsters set sail up to Upper Egypt.

**** **** ****

It was the height of summer; the air was still and humid, and felt like steam. Joshua and Elon arrived in the old and mostly abandoned city of Amarna, where they stayed as guests in Seitho's house – Seitho was a farmer and fisherman. Seitho lived with his wife Nuferi and their four children. There was laughter, songs and lots of conversation in that house.

Situated between the land of the pyramids in Lower Egypt and the great citadel of Thebes in Upper Egypt, the small city of Amarna was located on the east bank of the Nile, where some fourteen hundred years previously, the great Pharaoh Akhenaton had ruled Egypt for a short twenty years.

Elon questioned Joshua about why he was pursuing the issue of the Jews with such cunningness in such a remote place, and what was so special about Amarna. "So far as I could see, there is nothing here, not even remains of stone buildings; it's all overgrowth over mud walls and bricks. Is it that your people worked on mud and bricks; is that it?" he protested.

"Elon. Please be patient. There could be something here that might interest, too. First of all, Akhenaton was no ordinary Pharaoh. He insisted that he was not a Pharaoh God, but simply a prophet of the almighty Sun God Aten. He emphasized the sanctity of the family and the spirituality of mortal human life. Yes, unlike the other great cities of Egypt, Akhenaton's palace was built with brick and woods in a simple but elegant way by a dignified class of artisans who dwelled and worked near the palaces of the king."

"Were there Hebrews here?"

"Oh no. It was well before the times of Moses. But there is something unique here. The palace of the king was fashioned to accommodate an ideal Egyptian family with quarters for husband and wife, rooms for children, and a large common family room. There was also a visitor's hall where any citizen could come and visit with the king and seek resolution of a problem – like our King Solomon. The king wrote poems like Solomon, painted pictures, and even made sculptures."

Elon grew some interest in this ancient king. He didn't protest anymore. The two of them walked the whole length of the ruins of the ancient palace. "Akhenaton himself was a very tall man with a prominent jaw, enormous palms and feet, a huge drooping belly and obese thighs. In contrast, his wife was the most beautiful Egyptian Queen who ever lived – the glorious Nefertiti."

"I am surprised. How do you know all these things, Joshua? Then again, how do you know all these things are true? I have heard that Nefertari, Ramses' wife, was the most beautiful of all."

"Maybe, but listen. Akhenaton was truly the first philosopher king, about a thousand years before Plato even dreamt of it."

"Well, how long before Moses was Akhenaton?"

"About a hundred and fifty years. There are several similarities. Akhenaton was a bold king. He cast away all the graven images of Gods from the temples: he forbade the people to worship the other gods of Egypt, declaring that there was no God other than Aten, the eternal disk who shines upon the people, giving them life. He believed that Aten was not only the creator of Egypt, but also creator of the entire universe. He taught them a new system of worship. The people offered their prayers in the open air, directly looking at the Sun God, bathed in his rays, like the Samaritans of Israel. Akhenaton never assembled an army. He did not believe in violence or war.

"Appears to be a noble philosopher. Joshua, I admire your determination in pursuing your search. From your passion, I take it that you liked this Akhenaton and learned about him a lot more than your Moses." Elon Commented.

"Elon, Akhenaton was an admirable philosopher, a prophet, but listen. What happened to him . . . like all philosophers?" Joshua face clouded.

"Somebody murdered him?"

"Don't know. There is no evidence that he had ever been mummified. As you see now, the city of Amarna was demolished and abandoned. Egypt returned to the old divine order and resumed the worship of many gods."

"Interesting. You said he wrote poems. Recite one for me. No, sing; sing one for me."

I can't sing, Elon, but I will recite a few lines:

"Oh God, the creator of the universe, thou who knows all,

I beseech you. Grant me wisdom, Holy Omnipotent, most ineffable father.

Bless me with the virtues of thy wisdom so that I may become,

Worthy of knowing you, for my people and my country."

Elon clapped his hands, which echoed in that lonely place. *"Hymns of Aten* – very good lines, Joshua. I will put some music to those lines, and I will sing it for you before we depart."

"Thank you. Interestingly, some of his writings are reflected in the *Book of Solomon.*"

They saw Seitho approaching. "Sire, please don't sit in those bushes. There could be snakes. It's time for prayer and dinner," he said. They followed Seitho to his home.

"Seitho, how many villagers are here now?" asked Elon.

"We are twenty-two families, all farmers."

"Do you have any temples here; to whom do you pray?"

"Like Pharaoh Akhenaton, we all believe in one almighty God, the powerful Aten. He gave us life. He provides for us the riches of the Nile."

As they were walking home, Seitho was seen frequently searching the sky over the setting sun, shading his squinted eyes. There were numerous flocks of birds – ibises – like white clouds, flying low to the north. Near sunset, thousands of them had landed and settled on the harvest fields of Amarna. The birds were white in color with long legs and pointed, bent beaks. They waddled through the waters and fed on small fish.

Seitho's face glared, and he cried, "Yes, see? The birds have arrived, flying north. The floods will be coming in two or three days. This is a good sign. When there are many birds in the sky shortly after the harvest, the flood will be great."

Dinner was ready in the house. The very pleasant Nuferi treated the young travelers fondly, like an elder sister. She had prepared the best food that they could afford – plenty of toasted dried fish and wheat bread, and some condiments. She gave them beer in earthen pots and asked them to sit down and relax until sundown.

Then, the family of six all went out to the yard and stood in a row looking west. As the crimson red crescent of the setting sun sank behind the horizon, they all raised their hands, bowed their heads, and prayed loudly, "Almighty Aten, you are the one and only creator of this universe. Thank you for all your blessings today. Give us a great rise this year and shine your golden rays on us tomorrow." Then they sang a song, which so happened to be the same one Joshua had recited for Elon an hour ago.

Joshua was moved by this prayer and, in fact, he joined them for their daily routine. *This is Akhenaton living through the ages,* Joshua mulled. *What a pleasant family with amazing clarity, peace and satisfaction.*

After the dinner, Seitho went out to the water's edge and mounted a few fishnets on poles and tightened them with ropes. "The birds come first, then the fish. Tomorrow you will see all these nets filled with fish," he explained.

The next day, just as Seitho had promised, when the nets were raised, there were baskets full of fish in each one of them. The birds were all gone, and the water didn't rise. The next day, Seitho and the other farmers were busy removing all the dikes from the canal mouth and the subsidiary canals while the family was busy salting and drying the fish in the intensely hot rays of the sun. Later on that day, more flocks of birds arrived and perched on the fields. There were so many of them, the fields appeared to be painted white.

Late into that night, Joshua and Elon were awoken by a cacophony of frog crocking and the noises of small animals running, cooing or sneezing. Seitho was already out in the fields near the canals waving a torch made from dried papyri leaves and rinds. Many such waving torches were seen in the adjacent properties as well. Joshua and Elon followed him to the canal mouth. As they neared, the cries of the frogs became more frantic and louder, but the whistling and sneezing of snakes was frightening.

"Seitho, what is happening?" Joshua asked with excitement as he neared the river.

Seitho cried, "The rise has started! I am sure this is a good one," he observed confidently.

The frogs' croaking further intensified and became continuous. Frogs, snakes and all the ground creatures were fleeing the canals as the water gushed onto them.

"You must watch out for the snakes – they can kill you," warned Seitho again.

"Then why are you walking on the canal side, Seitho? Are you not worried about the snakes?" Joshua queried.

"I have been bitten by the snakes several times. The first time I was very sick and nearly died, but Aten saved me. Since then I never had any problems." A few minutes later, Seitho noted a fast shiny movement about his feet moving towards Elon. He quickly caught the snake by the tail, spun it like a wheel, and just cast it away.

All through the night Joshua stayed awake, staring at the sky and observing the rising waters under the moonlight. Morning arrived. The waters of the Nile rose by the hour. The sky was bright, clear and blue. No speck of any clouds, white or dark. No winds, rains or thunderstorms. The waters of the Nile rose by the hour like a miracle. The sun shone bright, strong and hot. The water still rose. By the fourth day, the color of the water changed to brown, and then a strange shade of dark red. The following days, the water looked like deep, red wine and still the levels continued to rise. After two weeks, the canals were filled to the top and began to overflow onto the fields. The water rose all the way to the front yard of Seitho's house. The Nile had become a large red ocean spanning all the way to the far west up to the threshold of the deserts.

This is a miracle indeed, Joshua thought. The Nile has turned red. Just like Jehovah's miracle, the Nile had turned red. He pursed his lips in deep contemplation, gazing at the far distant horizon where the red waters swept the dry desert dunes.

People took out small canoes made of papyri stem and paddled them down the Nile, jubilant in celebration. The youngsters rode skiffs, racing each other for fun. They shouted, "The rise is great; the water is thick and rich." Seitho also went out on his skiff. But each time he brought home a head load of papyri stems. Papyrus plants were plentiful in the wetlands on the Nile banks. The children selected good stems, which were as thick as a man's wrist, cut them into pieces nearly a cubit in length and stacked them in the foyer.

It appeared that the family had more time for relaxation and storytelling after the water had fully risen. The evening meal in Seitho's house was a lot more than a simple dinner; it was a happy occasion for the family, with food, beer and a lot of conversations. They all sat around cross-legged and leisurely ate the food that Nuferi and the children had cooked.

After the dinner, they started with the papyri works. Seitho's family was quite industrious and had a family business making papyrus rolls, which were in great demand in the Roman world. "Now the water is up, we have more than three months without any farm works. We make papyrus during these days," he Seitho said. "In ancient times during the season of flood, men were recruited by the pharaohs to construct pyramids, temples, or palaces. But now there are no more temples built."

Elon had not been feeling well since morning, and he went to sleep as soon as the dinner was over. He didn't eat much either. Joshua stayed awake with the family to see how they made paper from the papyri stems. Seitho showed him how to remove the rind from the stem. The children collected the rinds and put them away. "We use the rinds to make bags, baskets, foot wear or whatever."

Joshua was captivated by the way they made the paper by simple steps. First, papyri stems were sliced lengthwise into thin strips using a very sharp blade. With each slice coming out, the children placed them lengthwise on a flat wooden board, leaving no space in between. The next layer of strips was arranged breadthwise on top of it. While the strips were still moist, Nuferi beat them gently with a wooden mallet. The thick, sticky juice from the papyri hardens like a gum and fuses these layers together to form the paper. These sheets were then pressed between two wooden boards for several days to dry. The paper was further smoothed and polished with smooth diorite stones. Joshua helped the family to make the paper on all the nights.

In the meantime, Elon had not been feeling well. It started as a headache. In three days the headache worsened, and he developed fever and chills. At times the chills were so bad that his teeth chattered, and he crouched. After about six hours with the fever, he broke out into a cold sweat and felt better temporarily. After three days the symptoms recurred and became worse, with vomiting.

Seitho noticed the yellow color on Elon's face, and the young man curling up, shivering under a pile of clothes and making incoherent noises. He knew instantly what the matter was. He reassured the youngsters and began to prepare some medications. He had a cupboard full of medications; dried leaves, barks, roots; nuts, seeds and dark liquids in many little glass bottles.

"I am very sorry for your friend," Seitho said. "Be assured, I know what the problem is. Let us make the medicine right away." Seitho was very patient in explaining to Joshua what he was preparing. He took a balance, a brass rod suspended on a flax thread, stout on one end and thin on the other, where a wooden saucer was suspended – the balance. He carefully weighed a certain measure of dried willow leaf and put it in an earthen pot with a measure of water. He then covered it with a lid and boiled the leaves for an hour.

In the meantime, Elon's condition had noticeably deteriorated. He was semiconscious and uttering words meaninglessly. He passed urine unknowingly which looked like dark blood. Anxiety rose high in the family. What Joshua saw at this point was poignant and heartwarming. Nuferi and the four children were on their knees with their hands raised up to heavens praying to God Aten for a speedy recovery for their guest in the house.

To the mixture Seitho had prepared, he added a few drops of a thick medicine from another bottle. Elon was able to hold it down. He gave him a second dose after a two-hour interval. After the second dose, Elon shivered violently, followed by a profuse, soaking sweat. He was deeply fatigued, weak and thirsty. Color drained from his face, and his eyes looked cavernous. Joshua feared that he might die. The only drink he was permitted was barley water with salt that had been cooked for a long time.

About an hour after the third dose, Elon's breath became short and labored, and he wheezed every time he breathed out. This became worse as the moments passed. Seitho returned to his medicine cupboard, collected some dried datura flowers, put them in an earthen pot with a very narrow neck and heated them over wood fire. After a short time, a thick smoke curled out of the bottle mouth, which he had covered tightly with a papyrus stem pierced by a reed straw. Seitho held the reed to Elon's nose and encouraged him to breathe in the smoke as it came out of the reed. After a few minutes his breathing eased. Seitho repeated this treatment several times over the next few days until Elon recovered and was back on his feet.

Joshua and Elon stayed with Seitho until a week after the floods had peaked. Then they left for their final destination – the Elephantine Islands – on a small boat that sold spices during the time of inundations, sailing from one village to the other. The journey was somewhat arduous and very slow due to increasing southward currents and weak north winds.

They stopped to visit Thebes for a week. The two travelers learned that the glorious days of Thebes were over, but that the temples, sanctuaries, great palaces and avenues still remained, unkempt. The three-mile-long temple complex was the largest and the most magnificent temple ever built by man. The complex was a conglomerate of four different temples, including the Temple of Amon at Luxor at the north end, the Temples for the Gods of Mentu and Amon Ra at the south end, and the temple for Mut in the center. The most magnificent Egyptian constructions are in this temple, the royal pylons of Ramses depicting victory scenes from his war of Quedesh with the Hittites, the Avenue of the Sphinxes and the Great Hypostyle Hall with 134 granite columns.

Joshua was well read about Egypt at the times of Ramses the Great, but Elon, an Egyptian, was not. "Thebes was the capital of Egypt," Joshua explained to Elon. "This was a very busy place in those days. In addition to the twenty-thousand standing army, the temple complex had nine thousand daily employees working to maintain the buildings, canals, water systems, security, food services, and the flower gardens." The Luxor Temple on the Nile waterfront had three canals cut to the front of temple, each of them terminating in pools in front of the temples. Both Joshua and Elon were stunned, feeling the ingenuity, vision, and abundance of wealth of the ancient Egyptians.

"This palace can hold one hundred temples of Jerusalem," an awestruck Joshua told Elon. Once again Joshua searched for any element of Jewish contribution or mention in any of the inscriptions, which were all in vain.

Next, the young scholars journeyed on to Elephantine Island and Syene. The arduous 150-mile sail took two weeks and involved traversing several rapids so steep that the boat had to be physically lifted over the cataract to the upper waters to continue the sail.

At this juncture, the nature and appearance of the great river changed remarkably. There were vast expanses of placid waters and numerous small islands that looked like giant hippopotamuses bathing in the muddy waters, the Elephantine Island one amongst them, bordered with giant elephant-like stones, which turned red against the rising sun in the morning and black in the evening.

It was not difficult to find the villa of Eleazar, the owner of the jeweler shop. The old man was very excited to see Joshua seven years after they had briefly met at the Temple of Jerusalem. He had turned thinner, but was healthy and soft spoken as before. "I remember you very well, Joshua," the old man recollected fondly. "How could anyone forget you once anyone has seen you once? You have grown into a full man. Welcome. Welcome to the island." He was exited with joy.

The two young men received a warm welcome in Eleazar's home, a palatial home with eleven bedrooms. Eleazar's extended family of thirty-eight, including his two wives, their four sons, their children and grandchildren, all lived together in his home. There were six girls in the family ranging in age from thirteen to twenty-four. The girls in Eleazar's abode could not hide their excitement when they saw Joshua from their ancestral home of Israel and his friend Elon. The girls brought water to wash Joshua's and Elon's feet, along with wine, dates, nuts and cakes for refreshment. The girls, all with high colors on their cheeks, hung around the two young men, giggling and asking very many questions, most of which of no consequence. It was easy to observe that the Jewish girls in Elephantine Island were very liberal compared to their sisters in Israel. They wore no head covers and mingled very freely, even with strangers.

Joshua would soon learn that there was no synagogue on the island and that nearly all of the religious functions were held on the front porch of Eleazar's home. He had become the grand patriarch for the Island. The whole island had only one copy of the Alexandrian edition of the Torah. It was written in Greek, and was never read by the people who lived on the island. There remained an Elephantine version of the oral Torah, but that too was rarely used.

Eleazar was the only one in the group who could speak a little bit of Hebrew, and the girls put him to work helping them to communicate with Joshua and Elon. The girls knew how to communicate with the young men in ways that did not require words, using gestures, facial expressions, making signs in the air, and a little bit of mimicry. They were so enchanted by the visitors that Elon told Joshua it might be difficult for them to leave the island. Joshua laughed, as Elon's comment reminded him of a famous Homeric story where Ulysses got stuck on an island inhabited only by women.

The girls vied for the opportunity to spend time with Joshua and Elon. They escorted them around the island, showing them the old ruins, tombs, caves, gardens and other sites. The island had large palm groves not only yielding enormous quantities of dates, but also adding to the beauty of the Upper Nile Island. An ancient Nilometers stood in pristine condition as a testimony to the skill of the architecture of the ancient Egyptians. The girls shared with them the wonders of Ramses' statues, the Temple of Nefertiti, and the inner sanctorum where Ramses was portrayed as a god sitting side by side with Amon Ra, Harmakhis, and Ptah. Everywhere Joshua looked for any sign of an ancient Jewish presence, but there was none to be found.

Mabel, Eleazar's sixteen-year-old daughter, looked very much like Mary. One morning, flaunting around in a blue silk gown, she darted an entrancing gaze at Joshua, and he noticed that she had the same dimples as Mary, the same curves and curly brown hair. He beamed back graciously, but not encouragingly while he felt a strong yearning to be back at home, stronger than ever before.

Eleazar had the time to talk with Joshua, but he had to steal away the time from the girls late in the evening. "Joshua, I am not a scholar," he said. "But I believe that all of the Israelites living here in Upper Egypt were exiled from Jerusalem during the Babylonian invasion. Most of them remained in the Delta, primarily in Alexandria, but you will find a few in Memphis, Thebes, and all over Upper Egypt. Here on the island, we are separated from the rest of the world pretty much. I am the first from this island ever to visit Jerusalem, and I am sure you are the very first to visit us from Israel," he admitted soberly. "Ours is a small community, just two hundred in all. We always had more girls than boys." His face clouded. He abruptly stopped the conversation.

"What's the matter Eleazar," asked Joshua. The man didn't talk.

Did I offend him by words or . . . thought Joshua. He grasped the old man's hand and shook him to talk.

"We have a curse," he said in a very low tone. His face twitched.

"What curse, Eleazar? If it's anything you can tell us . . . sorry . . . sorry that I . . ."

"Nothing for you to worry about Joshua. We do have a curse. It's a long story. A lot of our boys died with circumcision. Died with bleeding. Somehow, if they survived the ceremony, they died with bleeding in the nose, mouth, in the bowels or somewhere else. Many years ago, our elders met. There was a fear that the tribe may become extinct. We adopted men from other tribes – Egyptians, circumscribed, of course – but, as you know, it's not the same. That's why we have no synagogues. Not ,many traditions anymore. We find it very difficult to match grooms for our girls." The man paused for a long moment with closed eyes. With a pale smile, he said, "I was weeping inside; I know Mabel likes you." The old man closed his eyes again.

Joshua was speechless. Elon had something to say, but he didn't.

"In earlier times, many of our men had three or four wives, but now a man does not take more than two wives, the first wife and a sister-wife. The first wife is the elder sister, and the sister-wife, the younger. A few of our girls were coerced into marrying Greeks and Romans by their fathers, and the girls left this island with teary eyes."

"So, nobody escaped to Upper Egypt during the time of the Exodus?" asked Joshua dryly.

Eleazar's forehead knitted and he shook his head sideways. Breathing a rueful sigh, he growled, "No, no."

"Do you believe that the Exodus happened," persisted Joshua icily.

Eleazar drooled in a low tone, "Not in the manner as written in the Torah." His voice became stronger and more confident as he added, "Certainly there was a small Jewish community in the Delta area at that time. They went away for whatever reason; I don't know why.

Maybe some Egyptians had ill-treated them and, as the book says, Moses may have killed one or two Egyptians, and the tension escalated so that they had to leave for safety." He paused for a while and his lines of wisdom on his brow deepened, and he resumed unwillingly, "We will never know what happened, but certainly the writings are all greatly exaggerated. Surely here in Upper Egypt we are treated well and respectfully by the local officials. All of them are Egyptians, although Egypt is now under the Roman rules." He pursed his creased lips and nodded concludingly.

Eleazar took the two young men for a leisurely sail on the lake and to some of the smaller islands on his special cypress skiff. The blue, placid waters of the Nile reflected the many little small islands crowned with temples, palaces, gardens, peristiles, porticos and other monuments, as if a floating city was built over the waters. The tall white sails of the feluccas were special to this place. Sunset in particular was a breathtakingly beautiful scene where the reflections changed colors from yellow to crimson-red as the day aged. "Most of these buildings were constructed during the Ptolemaic and Roman periods," Eleazar revealed. At the Isis Temple of Philae Island they noted numerous inscriptions in Greek, all exaggerated glories of the Greek and Roman rulers of the past. But nothing about the Hebrews in Egypt, Joshua observed.

In the afternoon, the skiff sailed near the island that housed the Biga Temple. "We are not allowed to set our feet there, as it is a holy place for the Egyptians," Eleazar cautioned. "You have heard the story of Osiris, I believe. The legend says that when Seth cut him into pieces and scattered him throughout Egypt, one of his legs was put here on this island."

"Before you leave," Eleazar said emphatically, "you must see the quarries. In my opinion, the construction, transport, and installation of the obelisk are undoubtedly the most complex and laborious project the Egyptians have ever undertaken,"

"Not the great pyramids, Eleazar?" asked Joshua.

"Certainly not. It is the obelisk."

The next day they made preparations to go the quarries of Syene. Although the girls were not invited on the trip, all six had risen early, dressed up, and had prepared food and drinks for the day. They slipped onto the boat before anybody arrived and sat there gaily as if going for a great wedding celebration. Eleazar smiled when he saw them sitting, looking at him expectantly. "Joshua, Elon, it looks like we have some company today," Eleazar chuckled.

It was a memorable sail on the Nile. The girls, hoping to get the attention of Joshua and Elon, sang songs in solo and in chorus. Some of them even danced on the deck of the small boat. They all hovered around the young men like honeybees around poppies.

After two hours of sailing, they reached the granite quarries. Joshua and Elon got off the boat first and helped the others get off by extending their hand, stabilizing them. Mabel got off last and kept holding on to Joshua's hands as if she needed more help to climb the steep slope to the quarries. "Joshua, get ready to hear a long story from Papa. He likes telling stories," Mabel said into his ears, chuckling." We have heard it many times."

They walked up to the unfinished obelisks that Queen Hatshepsut had begun to build some fifteen hundred years back. "Queen Hatshepsut ruled Egypt as the one and only Egyptian Queen Pharaoh, other than Cleopatra, who was originally from Greece. Her construction plans were quite ambitious." Eleazar flailed both his hands up into the sky. "This is the fifth obelisk she started after erecting four in Thebes. All of them were built with pink granite, right from this quarry." Pointing to the unfinished obelisk Eleazar rejoined. "This obelisk weighs thirty thousand talents, equal to the weight of two hundred and twenty-five elephants."

The youngsters climbed the obelisk, and they all sat on the tail end and Eleazar started: "The construction of an obelisk begins with the chief engineer who is able to visualize this giant structure while it is nothing more than a piece of rock inside the belly of the mountain. They would then mark the parts of the rock where they wanted to begin to dig. Remember," Eleazar emphasized, "they didn't have iron tools or the metallic chisels we have today. It was during the old times, but still they found some ingenuous ways to cut through the rocks." Eleazar stopped for a second for a good breath and resumed. "They did this by setting an enormous bonfire within the perimeter of the surface markings. When the stone became so hot that it was about to turn red, they doused the fire with water. The sudden cooling of the stones caused the rock to crack, and then the men would strike the cracked stones with very hard, iron-like diorite stones." Mabel quickly disappeared from the group and came back with a diorite stone, a dark ball double the size of a man's fist, and she simply gave it to Joshua to hold as if it was her duty to do so. Eleazar smiled to himself, showing his two thin, translucent upper teeth as he caressed his bald head. Joshua also couldn't hide an innocent little smile while he was assessing the weight of the stone.

After a moment Eleazar resumed. "The first fire enabled them to reach a depth of one or two fingerbreadths. They continued the process, setting fires, dousing, and smashing the stone until the upper plane of the obelisk began to form." Slapping his palm on the obelisk Eleazar continued, "The bottom of this obelisk is a ten foot square. After the surface was formed, they burned, doused, and dug laterally on either side of the stone until the desired depth was reached." Eleazar supplemented his description by drawing pictures in the air as well.

"When they had dug down on the lateral aspects of the obelisk, the remaining work was done with the diorite stone and man's hand."

"They made a series of caverns under the obelisks and filled them with wooden beams, and then the wooden beams were soaked in cold water. The water caused the wooden beams to swell and exerted pressure from underneath the rock to split off from the remaining stones in between the caverns. The process was repeated until the obelisk was separated from the mother rock." Eleazar got up and gradually walked down to the waters. He quickly turned back and grasped Joshua by his shoulders and asked dryly, pointing to the unfinished obelisk, "Joshua, tell me why this obelisk was not finished or erected." He quickly raised his voice, pointing to Mabel, and cried, "You are not supposed to answer." She closed her parted lips ruefully with a frozen smile.

Joshua searched the obelisk with squinted eyes thoughtfully.

"Why was this obelisk unfinished? Look carefully at the stone," Eleazar pursued.

"There is a crack on the . . ."

"Heee . . . " shrieked Mabel, clapping her hands and jumping up and down. The other girls also laughed hilariously, congratulating Joshua for answering correctly.

"Yes." The old man shook his head with joy. "There is a natural crack in the rock veins," he declared proudly. "The Egyptians were perfectionists in their work and proud of their architectural marvels. There are no blemishes in any of their constructions, let alone the obelisk," he said as he kept on walking to the river.

At the threshold of the water, all the girls waited until either Joshua or Elon helped them into the boat. Mabel made it a point to sit close to Joshua.

"This is a great piece of information you told us Eleazar," Joshua acknowledged with gratitude. "And I can tell you this," he continued. "The Egyptian civilization is long gone now. In the future, people will build all kinds of palaces, some perhaps greater than the palaces in Thebes, but I doubt anybody will ever again make an obelisk as gigantic and perfect as the Egyptians."

That evening Joshua tarried along the rocky boulders of the island, pensive and ruminating. He sat against a rock by about sunset, watching the large red disc "Aten" retiring to his chamber. In Egypt Joshua had four long years, all the way from Pelusium to the Elephantine Island, read whatever he could and saw whatever he possibly could. *Did Yahweh really appear to Moses at the Mount Sinai? Who wrote down all these statutes and commandments? At one point He commands to love thy neighbor, at other times the command is to destroy their abodes and possess their properties. Who is a neighbor?* Joshua felt dizzy and confused. *A stiff-necked tribal God. An angry God*, he thought to himself.

The next day Joshua and Elon packed their belongings, getting ready to leave. The girls were visibly sad and gloomy and did not sing or dance.

****   ****   ****

The young scholars sailed down the Nile the next day. On their way back, they stopped at Seitho's home in Amarna. The family was grieving the death of their eleven-year-old daughter, Kami, who had been bitten by a poisonous snake a few days after Joshua and Elon had left their home. Though they were filled with grief, they didn't slacken in their work and kept making paper.

Elon profusely thanked the family for saving his life with medications and care. As they got ready to depart, Joshua fondly hugged Seitho, saying, "I will always remember the love and hospitality you offered to us. Yours certainly is an ideal family." He then pulled out two gold coins from his purse and presented them to Seitho as a gift. Seitho was pleasantly surprised and his eyes welled up. "No please don't give me any presents," he begged waving his palms. "You found comfort in my abode, and you came back to see my family again. What other present do I need?" His lips contorted with pain and gratitude. After much cajoling, Seitho accepted the coins, but only after he had presented Joshua with a roll of paper he had made. Then Seitho raised both his hands to the rising sun, praying to Aton to see the two young men safely back to their destination.

Two months later, in the second week of November, they reached Alexandria. Antonio Caprilius was delighted to see Joshua, whom he had come to think of as a son. He threw a party in his house to celebrate Joshua and Elon's return.

Joshua told Antonio of his plans to continue on to Rome as early as he could. "You may not learn as much as you think by traveling to Rome," Antonio cautioned dryly. "Rome is the center of the universe now and, of course, Palestine is under direct Roman rule, so a visit is worthwhile. Did you accomplish what you came here to learn in Egypt?" Antonio asked.

"I believe, yes," Joshua said confidently. "I was able to read and learn so much with your help, and I thank you for all your help."

"Joshua, as I had told you, our collections from Babylon will definitely help you in your research," Antonio declared. "A good many of the stories in your Torah have a comparable story in the Babylonian writings, and you may want to explore these connections some more," he advised thoughtfully.

"It is true. I have taken a lot of notes from the Babylonian archives," Joshua appraised.

"Well, I don't claim to be an expert on anything, particularly when it comes to religion, but do you have compelling questions before you leave."

"Yes, Antonio. Tell me, who were the Hyksos? Do you think they were the Israelites?" demanded Joshua explicitly.

"They certainly were not Jews," stated Antonio firmly. "They were a group of sea people. They invaded the Delta and established a kingdom with Avaris as the capital. Nobody knows where they came from. They certainly were not slaves. In fact, the Pharaoh fought and virtually destroyed them here in Egypt, and the remainder fled to the east, never to come back again." Antonio paused for a while, searching Joshua's eyes, "Are you thinking about the Joseph story?"

"I cannot make a definite connection, but I thought I would l ask . . ."

"There is a story in the Egyptian Book of Dreams that is similar to your Joseph story in the Torah," Antonio remembered. "But I don't believe they are speaking of your Joseph in that story. What do you think? You have been studying these stories for a long time." He motioned towards Joshua.

"I didn't think so."

"Correct. That's my impression too. What else is in your mind?" Antonio continued teasingly. "Honestly, Joshua I will miss you when you are gone from here"

"Moses. Moses is the man I was looking for, Antonio," Joshua persisted in a serious tone. "He is the most important person in the Exodus story. In fact, he is the central figure in our beliefs." Joshua gently bit on his lower lip, waiting for a reply.

"Moses," echoed Antonio. "Moses is an Egyptian word meaning birth," stated Antonio staunchly. "I have never seen or heard that name connected to any of the papyri or Stella in Egypt. The closest sounding name is Kamose and his brother, Ahmose, who finally expelled Hyksos, in fact. But there is something you should know. You are familiar with Pharaoh Merneptah?"

"No," said Joshua abruptly, as if he had missed a central point.

"I thought not. I had no idea about that either, until brought to my attention recently by the assistant curator, Akashi."

"Tell me what about Merneptah?"

"He was the grandson of the Ramses. You know, when the Torah was edited here, with the Septuagint from Israel; Ptolemy's palace historians had conducted a lot of research to the veracity of the Exodus story. They came across the draft of a certain stele that was buried in the chamber of Merneptah. Would you like to see that?"

"Of course."

Antonio took Joshua to the museum wing of the Serapium, where a large collection of old, unclassified scrolls, statues, and fallen apart pieces of freezes were collected, and men were working on them.

Akashi explained: "Merneptah was the thirteenth son of Ramses the Great. He fought a war with the Israelites, it says, about twelve hundred years ago. This piece documents the story of that war." He spread out the old Papyrus scroll and read, translating: "The nine princes fell prostrate and begged for mercy. The cities of Ashkelon and Gezer had been overcome. Israel is laid to waste. It's seeds no more."

Joshua stood transfixed.

"Joshua, is it possible that these are related to your Exodus story?" asked Antonio.

"Not really. But I am glad that there is a mention about Israel." He was silent in thought. They walked back to Antonio's office.

"Tell me what you make out of it?" insisted Antonio.

"I am a bit confused Antonio . . . twelve hundred years ago . . . no, it's not time for the survivors of the Exodus crowd to build up a nation of such significance, that the Pharaoh wrote it on the stele . . . until otherwise there was already a substantial crowd of Israelites in Canaan at that time. No, it doesn't make any sense either . . . see, his father Pharaoh Ramses made two foreign expeditions to pacify the Hittites in northern Syria. He did not succeed completely. But he did control all of the major coastal cities by the Philistines highways, as their vassal cities. But no mention of Israelites. There must have been some skirmishes between those vassal communities and Israelites. To protect his vassals, Pharaoh Merneptah sent an army to Palestine to quell the Israelites. The Stella is probably highly exaggerated, too."

"Interesting. Your guess is as good as anybody else's. One thing I will say, the scribes could have . . . must have exaggerated the Egyptian victories, but they would never scribe a war that never happened. Let me ask you this. In your story, the Jews had no army and no weapons. They were fleeing from the Pharaoh with borrowed properties. Do you ever think that the Egyptian army would have found it difficult to annihilate the Jews?"

"Until, of course, Yehovah . . ."

"Well, that is possible. For which I have no arguments . . . mythology."

"That's what you think; it's a mythology?"

"I am afraid so," said Antonio. "I didn't want to hurt your feelings. The Exodus story as it is written in your Torah never happened. Yes, it's very possible that there was a Jewish community in the Delta area. It is likely that they were looked upon as foreigners without political power, even if some of them held significant positions in the Pharaoh's administration like your Joseph."

"Is it possible that they weren't citizens at all, but slaves?"

"Yes," Antonio agreed. "You might say that they were slaves and had been put into hard labor. But the Jewish population still would have been relatively small, and they would never, ever have posed a threat to the Pharaohs. How can a small immigrant community without any power, army, weapons, or a fortified city of their own be a threat to the mighty Pharaohs in their own land? What does your Torah say was the total population of the Jews in Egypt at the time of the Exodus?"

"Six hundred thousand men alone," Joshua remembered.

"Six hundred thousand men alone?" Antonio said, astonished. "That would imply a Jewish population of over two million. Never." Antonio cried and resumed in a strong husky voice. "It's not possible; twelve-hundred years ago the entire population of Egypt, all the way from Nubia to The Great Sea, was not much more than two million. There could not have been a Jewish population of that magnitude anywhere in the world, let alone in the Delta."

"The Torah says the children of Israel multiplied abundantly and filled the land," parried Joshua. "The Pharaoh was worried about the size of their population and the possibility of the Israelites uniting in force to fight against them. Therefore, the Pharaoh enslaved them and put them into very hard labor in the construction of the cities of Pithom and Ramses and ordered the deaths of their firstborn male children."

"Joshua, the story may have some truth. But by any stretch of the imagination, the group could not have been anything more than five thousand in total," Antonio argued emphatically.

"Antonio," Joshua leaned forward demanding, "Have you seen any references to or mention of a series of major, natural or unexplained calamities that happened in the land of Egypt around the same time of construction of Pi-Ramses?

"No," Antonio affirmed, "there is no reference to any such calamities in Egypt at that time. The Nile flooded each year, in some years very heavily such that the flood water turned red due to the mud; some people call it blood red."

Joshua couldn't find words to counter the argument. A few moments dragged aimlessly. "But Joshua," Antonio rejoined, "why do you look to the writing of the Egyptians to prove the stories in the Torah? Your people believe that the contents of the Torah are what your God revealed to Moses at Mount Sinai. Fundamentally, it is a belief. A belief need not have any proof or any rationality. It is a state of mind. That's what you and your people believe, that's all. Does it matter if it's true?" Antonio asked dryly.

"It does mater Antonio. It certainly does. It is the crux of the matter." His face froze with a pale, lifeless smile. Joshua slowly rose to his feet unsteadily. *It appears the earth under my feet is moving loose, like my beliefs. I am glad I came to Egypt. I confirmed my suspicions.* He sauntered home, as it was getting late in the night.

In Alexandria, the cold north wind was blowing harder. It was the beginning of another December. Joshua, now twenty, began his journey to Rome in his search for the writings of Cicero the philosopher.

BOOK IV
Joshua in Rome

Joshua at the Roman Forum

On an early spring morning, in the seventh year of the reign of Tiberius Caesar, the heavy Roman barge from Alexandria carrying more than two hundred tons of Egyptian wheat, pulled by sixty slave oarsmen fatigued to fainting, sailed slowly up the river Tiber. The barge was docked and moored on the eastern embankment close to the stone arches of the Amilian bridge at the very hem of the Imperial City of Rome. The city, presently the center of the universe, was just waking up for another day under an overcast sky.

215

After being huddled in a lower deck – a slave cabin – of the Roman barge, sleeping crouched between heavy wheat bags, in the companionship of slaves, cooks and oarsmen, without seeing sunlight for eight days – days and nights impossible to distinguish – a fatigued Joshua, with his back aching and head spinning, took his first step on land to the threshold of the imperial city. He shouldered his bags and walked along the cobblestone-paved Viscus Tuscus towards the Roman Forum. He sat on the marble steps of the temple of Castor with his head against a tall marble column, preoccupied with his uncertain next step. A foreigner in the land of his occupiers, with limited means, no connections and no job, his first call was to find a roof to rest his head.

He glanced at the many majestic edifices and the vast esplanade of the open forum – Imperial Rome, he recollected. Fifty-two years after the historical end of the Roman Republic and the glorious reign of Emperor Augustus, peace, prosperity, and tranquility abounded in Rome; all nations surrounding the Great Sea were under the hegemony of the Roman Empire; wealth was flowing to Rome from all over the world; and civil wars, riots, food shortages and slave revolts were things of the past.

Soon the rising sun broke through the gray clouds; more sandals scratched the cobblestones. As people crossed the streets in masses, venders began spreading their wares on the roadsides and magistrates set up their courts on the flagstone-paved Forum. The lone traveler from Galilee crossed the Forum to the Parliament house and stood near the Speaker's Forum and gained his first glimpse of the grand vista. The air was clean and crisp, the city luminous in the bright sunlight.

Rome, the city ringed by seven hills, the throbbing center of political, spiritual, and commercial life of the Empire; and the stupendous Roman Forum, at the very center – a grand vista, surrounded by magnificent structures – Hymettan marble columns, white stone mansions, shining monuments in pink stone, vine-clad peristyles, porticos and frescos, marble benches, little wayside baths, whore houses, lively theaters, and shopping centers, all abuzz with life and activity. Most of the buildings were designed to resemble Greek temples with ornate Corinthian, Doric and Ionic columns; and lintels, freezes and frescos depicting the stories of Greek and Roman mythology, as well as monuments celebrating the victories of the Roman army. Massive domes, arches and obelisks created a sense of awe, an aura of invincibility – seven hundred years of building and rebuilding, a continuum of majestic buildings arrayed shoulder to shoulder, each one appearing to compete for the crown of the most splendorous.

Rome is rich, Rome is power, and Rome is the center of the universe, Joshua thought. *The most fearsome tyrant the world has ever seen. My people! What's to become of them in this world under their hegemony? The Roman yolk on the shoulders of Israel is made of iron, welded to the bones, and any attempt to pull it out, will pry out flesh, blood and bones with it – impossible! Nothing is permanent. Even you! A more powerful people may yet come, conquer, destroy and build over again.*

Joshua quenched his thirst with a cup of cheap red wine and settled his stomach with a serving of pottage. Sated, he began walking about the Forum, six hundred yards long from the Capitoline Hill in the west to the old Kings Palace in the east, hoping to find a place to stay.

There were a few people resting, eating and chatting, lounging on the stone steps of the palace. Joshua unloaded his bags and rested at one nook of the esplanade, sitting crouched with his hands holding his knees and his head resting on his arms.

Three friendly young Roman men, all chewing something in an imperceptible manner, came and sat beside him. "Are you lost, young man?" asked a tall man with full facial hair – Marcus – in a compassionate manner.

"You look like a Jew, from your dress only," commented another one, a thin man with long hair – Lucius. The handsome third one – Marcus – attempted a friendly smile. The men appeared pleasant, loquacious and gaily, without any tension or worries.

"Yes, I am Joshua, a Jew from Galilee . . ."

Having realized that Joshua was a single man, honest at the first look, and having noted that he was weak, fatigued and in need of some help, the men invited him to stay with them in a shared room at the Aventine Hill apartments for a nominal fee. Joshua accepted the invite with gratitude. They strode the deep-rutted cobblestone, uphill through side alleys, and reached the Aventine Hills.

A few women without veils, dressed up showing their knees, peeped through the doors without shutters as they approached their shared room on the second floor of the three-storied apartment.

"You may keep your belongings anywhere you like; there is some bread and cheese in the cupboards; rest or sleep or do whatever you like; make yourself comfortable," said Marcus, and they left the room.

Joshua sat on the bricks of the fireless hearth for a long minute. The shared room: A large crack spreading out like a spider web covered most of the ceiling of the room. Brown drops of water that dripped from the roof in a regular rhythm were caught in a stinking pot in one corner of the room, which was overflowing. A long moving line, an army of ants, marched in single formation towards the miasmic leftover food in unkempt dishes. Joshua kept his bags on the hearth and made an attempt to clean the room. He sat on a stool leaning against the wall, and soon he dozed off, but not for long; cockroaches and rats that foraged the room startled him to awake.

Joshua would soon realize that The Aventine Hill, one amongst the seven hills that constituted the Roman metropolis and whose patron god was Minerva, the goddess of arts and sciences, was considered a haven for artists, musicians, painters, writers, actors and free thinkers. Also, the cheap rents had attracted a large number of foreigners, widows and prostitutes to the hill.

**** **** ****

For the next several weeks Joshua tarried the streets of Rome with his bag containing the rolls of papyrus from Amarna across his shoulders. He spent most of his time at the library of Augustus, which contained almost all the works of Cicero.

The foggy figure of Cicero was becoming clearer in his mind, but all under the shadow of the greatest Emperor of all – Augustus. The history of the two, so were closely intertwined. Emperor Augustus, made out of the boy named Octavian and handpicked by his great uncle, Julius Caesar, was trained in philosophy, politics, and the tricks and tactics of governance by none other than the philosopher king, Cicero, himself. But it was about Cicero – the man who achieved what Plato could only envision in Athens – that Joshua wanted to explore the most; his rhetorical skills, style of governing the nation, diplomacy, philosophy and, above all, what kind of a man he was.

Once Lucius realized that The Galilean was researching Cicero, he started mingling closer with Joshua. Lucius was a playwright for their Little Theater group at the Aventine Hill; a group that wrote and produced plays in many small theaters in Rome. Through him, Joshua came to know that the three young men – his roommates – were not just carefree pleasure seekers, but indeed were young philosophers in their own right.

"Forever, I worshiped Sophocles as a writer," Lucius said, "and Aristotle as a philosopher. But I should say that I have turned a Ciceronian myself."

"Why would you say that?"

"Cicero was a class by himself, a rhetorician, writer, philosopher, attorney, Roman counsel . . . I learn from him every day – a philosopher of all ages."

"Which is the most important aspect of his life or works that influenced you the most?" Joshua asked.

"Joshua, when a person excels in many aspects of human thought, it's difficult to separate the excellence of one aspect from the other. They become interlinked and become one; they become a part of the person, his personality. See, people say that Cicero was the greatest orator of all times. What does that mean? He thought about the substance to speak – new, timely and provoking. Then he formulated it in his mind, like a baby is evolved in the womb. Then he selected his words so well that they fitted like the chipped and chiseled stones on a Roman arch. His delivery was impeccable; starting with a smoking evocation, and then picking up speed with thunder and exploding at the end with a glare. The words he wrote are for generations to remember. Having said that, tell me; why you are interested in Cicero?"

"I had a teacher in Galilee, Zilinos his name. He had taught me that 'words are the most powerful weapons that can heal or kill, and make peace or war; the arrows that cannot be recalled once launched; the reason why wise men speak only very little.'"

"Very well," Lucius said. "What else did he tell you? It appears that he is a very wise man."

Joshua was timid to answer.

"That . . . man is defined not by what goes into his mouth, but by what comes out of the mouth."

Lucius laughed gaily, "Wonderful man, wonderful. Let me talk to Marcus and Rocco about this . . . this hidden treasure, then we will take you to the little theater."

Both Marcus and Rocco were also amazed by the interest and deep knowledge of Joshua, a simple carpenter boy from Galilee. But more than anything else, they liked him and were willing to tell him whatever they knew about Rome and Roman authors.

Not so long after that, the three roommates invited Joshua to go for an outing to dine at a wine house on the boat-shaped Tiber island. At the wine house near the temple Aesculapius, they were served thin red wine, fried fish and thick crusted breads by maids with large breasts who served the guests close by, touching and caressing. As everybody had a cup or two of wine, and as the noise level went up, the conversations started:

"So I hear, Joshua, you are a very learned man. Tell us about your Galilee and what made you come to Rome?" said Rocco. Amidst the many voices that crisscrossed their table, Joshua started to answer, but was soon cut off by Marcus saying, "this is no place to talk about such matters . . . we will talk more when we reach the Hill." Then, there came the three girls: Amelia, Decia and Fabia. Amelia, the eldest of the three, sat on the laps of Rocco. She took a sip from his cup, staring at Joshua. "This one is new. What's your name," she asked.

"Joshua."

"Decia is sleeping. I can get her," she motioned to Rocco for permission.

"No, I would rather be alone," Joshua said.

Rocco went with Amelia to the maid chamber for some brief time, but the two others gave company to Joshua.

Back at the hill, they sat on the stone steps of the Minerva temple, the place they often got together during the evenings.

"Amongst us, Lucius is the man who knows everything about Cicero. So, you two talk; we will listen," said Marcus.

"Joshua, you are here just about two weeks now. Coming Sunday, we will walk the Forum. We will show you some things. Get used to the city; come and participate in one of our theater plays, then we will talk more." They left for the room, and Joshua stayed alone longer at the temple steps, intentionally.

Initially, Joshua was not sure what his roommates did to provide for themselves, but he soon discovered that they were a bit of everything: poets, musicians, writers, critics, actors and handy men. They lived an open, hedonistic life, seeking sensual satisfaction with men, women, food, and wine. They routinely indulged in chewing the poppy gum brought over by traders from Parthia. Most nights the three men would hire a prostitute and share her services, as a matter of convenience and economics. They did not respect or believe in the state religion, gods or traditions, yet they were gentle, pleasant and well-informed men. They were all part of a theater group, staging short plays which they called "Little Theater".

Three weeks later, on a Sunday morning, Joshua's new friends invited him to walk the Forum with them on the way to Pompey's theater. The small theater was where they were holding the final rehearsal for their upcoming show, a play in three acts based on the final days of Cicero. Joshua listened with interest as his friends bantered back and forth about Cicero.

From the Aventine Hill, descending down about five hundred yards, going north through the rutted cobblestone road and beyond the hoof makers ally, the Circus Maximus was on the right, immediately before the famous Palatine Hill. "In our legends, it is believed that the original city of Rome was founded by Romulus, here at the Palatine Hill," Rocco said. He pointed to the Hill. "Most of the royal palaces were built on this Hill, including Augustus Caesar's, now occupied by the old man Tiberius. Cicero also maintained a villa there in earlier days when he was the Counsel."

As they entered the esplanade of Viscus Tuscus leading towards the Forum, the sun had risen high over the city, reflecting glares from the temple of Castor on the right and the magnificent three-storied Basilica Sempornia on the left, and the streets had come to full life with the tumult of voices of many nations, meddling, bargaining, arguing, and buying and selling in the shops and streets. Amidst money lenders, vendors, prostitutes and people of all kind and color, plodding through the Etruscan alley, they entered the east end of the Forum.

"Joshua, you are a strange visitor to the city." Marcus casually threw his hand over Joshua's shoulder. "Young people come here to have fun, but you seem to be preoccupied with your own world. You are too young to be a philosopher. You don't even speak your mind. What is really bothering you?"

Joshua responded with a half smile.

"You are wasting your youth, young man," Marcus said. "Once you are in Rome, be like a Roman – have fun, drink our wine, love our women, and take part in the baths and the games at the sports arena."

"We will be glad to take you wherever you want," Lucius said.

"Thank you, friends," Joshua said. "My mission here is limited. After all, I am also a subject of the Roman Empire by way of the occupation of our land. It's always better to know what to expect from our occupiers."

"Ha!" Marcus laughed, squeezing Joshua's shoulder. "Expectations! That's very easy to explain: taxes, more taxes than you can imagine. And obedience. Uprisings will be crushed. Peace, they say, is the objective. Peace under Roman rule. Oh, yes. Also, something more . . . strong men . . . for the army that's all. That's what old man Tiberius expects."

The men laughed heartily in agreement.

"Was Tiberius Caesar elected by the Senate or appointed by Octavian?" Joshua asked.

"A little bit of each," Marcus said. "Tiberius, a man with no skills, is Octavian's wife Livia's son from a previous marriage. Octavian didn't want any more civil wars after his reign. Therefore, he groomed Tiberius as his successor and put a senate stamp of approval on his head. However, Livia made sure that any other contenders to the throne either died in their sleep or were killed in accidents."

"Did she not attempt to poison Octavian, too?"

"Very good, Joshua!" Marcus exclaimed. "I'm impressed. You have read your Roman history well."

They walked east of the forum through the marble-stone-paved courtyard, between the Temple of Luturna on the right and the king's palace to the temple of Vesta. "You had asked about the Vestal Virgins; here it is," Lucius said.

In front of the convent of the Vestal Virgins, on a stone platform, in a marble cauldron half-filled with oil, a flame flickered on a large wicker – the eternal flames. Tending the flame, stood two pale, thin young girls of about sixteen, their heads down, faces somber, eyes transfixed on the flames, motionless, and barely breathing – the Vestal Virgins. The place was meant to be quite except the hushed 'into-the-ear' talking of a few tourists.

"This flame has been burning here for the last five hundred years," remarked Marcus. "The flame is always tended by six virgins, two at a time. Their purity and virginity keeps the city protected and blessed by the gods. At least that's the belief."

Lucius had a sarcastic grin on his face. While walking back to the Forum, he told a story about the Vestal Virgins. Pointing towards the large, gated marble building behind, he narrated. "They live there in the house of the Vestal Virgins. No men, women, or animals were permitted in their living space. The Vestal Virgins are spiritually married to Pontifex Maximus; we call him 'Pope'. He resides behind them in that elaborate palace. The virgins are chosen between the ages of six and ten years and are bound to serve for thirty years, the time at which their protective blessings ceased. If any of these virgins broke her vows and took a lover, they would be buried alive, and her lover would be whipped to death."

The Romans must have read the Torah. Joshua thought. *How strange; these Romans who are notorious for violating women by force or by fear of death, now revere their virginity in public. To please the Gods! For their blessings!*

"Joshua, you might want to hear the story, "It was during Sulla's reign that a Vestal Virgin gave birth to a baby," Rocco said. "The Pope, who was the only man who ever had access to the House of the Virgins, took stiff actions immediately. First, he cut off the mother's tongue and then buried the mother and child alive. Next, a destitute from the Aventine Hill was accused, convicted and then whipped to death at the assembly ground, all on the same day."

"Was the woman allowed to speak?" Joshua asked.

"Remember, her tongue . . . " Lucius said. "Joshua, each spot of the Forum – and for that matter, each one of these monuments – will have a story or two to tell."

They continued walking the Forum towards the Capitoline Hill, sharing myths and anecdotes of the Roman world. On their left, between the Temple of the Vestal Virgins and the Basilica Sempornia, loomed the imposing colonnaded mansion, The Temple of Castors, which contained a courtyard and another Speaker's Forum. On the ground floor were shops for money lenders and money exchangers akin to the temple of Jerusalem. Senate meetings were sometimes held at this site, but not exclusively. The senators chose other locations at which to meet, in consideration of the populace.

"Joshua," Marcus called to his attention, "you will find it of interest that Cicero has argued several of his cases right where we are standing at this Speaker's Forum. In fact, Cicero's first case, the famous one . . . his performance as an advocate, happened right here on this platform".

"Marcus," Joshua's interest peaked. "I have heard a bit about such a case. Please tell me about the case."

"It was the first case of the young Marcus Tulles Cicero, some one hundred years ago, during the dictatorship of Sulla. A rich farmer named Roscius was murdered when he visited Rome. It was known that the victim was not getting along with his son, Sextus Roscius, who in fact was minding the family estates in a hill station named Ameria. A very rich man named Chrysogonus, a freed slave, and an ally of the dictator Sulla, devised a plan to acquire the victim's properties by surreptitiously inserting the dead man's name in the proscription list."

"Marcus, please tell me what proscription is?" Joshua asked.

By that time the four of them had reached the center of the Roman Forum. There was a special attraction for the tourists. A small natural fountain was surrounded by three plants, a vine, a fig tree, and an olive tree, encircled by a metal balustrade – The Pool of Curtius.

"The proscriptions. That's a story you must know. Let's sit down for a while," said Marcus. They all sat down in a circle, cross-legged on the marble flag stones, having bought enough red wine and burnt meat for the lunch. "Before I go into the sad stories of proscription, let me tell you about the pool of Curtius. According to the legend in the Oracle Books, in ancient times, a chasm suddenly appeared here in the forum. The oracle prophesized that the gap would close only when the earth goddess received what the Romans valued most. People gathered and poured the things Romans loved: wine, perfume, precious stones, silk dresses, silver and gold coins; and, even their family pets were thrown into the chasm. In fact, the Romans threw everything of value that they could imagine, but still the hole in the earth would not close. One day, a cavalier dressed in a helmet with red plumes and a breast plate with shining brass appeared on the scene, and declared: "A soldier's courage is what the Romans value the most," and he galloped with his horse down into the cave, where he disappeared into the abyss. This small pool is a revered remembrance of this event."

Joshua smiled, "A great story to tell the children," he said.

"Now, about the proscriptions, Joshua. In the Roman Republic, dictators were appointed by the Senate to deal with special situations. But some dictators were self-appointed, and they were the worst," said Marcus.

"Is it not a bit oxymoronic – an elected dictator?" Joshua asked.

"Yes, but it's true. The dictators had unrestrained powers to maintain law and order in the country and to suppress revolts by the people. The dictator would draw up a list of people he deemed to be unlawful, and the state had the right to kill them."

Joshua raised an eyebrow. "To kill them, just like that?"

"Yes, just like that."

Marcus pointed to the Speaker's Forum. "The list of proscriptions was published at the Speaker's Forum, and any Roman citizen was legally authorized to kill the proscribed person. A reward of twelve hundred dinari was awarded to the citizen once he showed proof of death – the severed head – of the proscribed person.

"About a hundred years ago, when Sulla became dictator,' Lucius caught up with the story, "the news spread in the city that a proscription list was being drafted. Not knowing who was on the list, people fled in fear until the city was deserted, and civic life came to a standstill. When they were through with the massacre, there was not enough space in the assembly ground to display all their heads, some nine thousand of them, including forty Senators, were wasted," Lucius said.

"That's the most horrible story I have ever heard," Joshua said. "And now you say that all those killings were legal and approved by the Senate?"

"Yes, that was the way it was in the Roman dictatorship."

"Well, whatever it may be, proscriptions, statutes or commandments; they're all the same. The innocent and the meek are always persecuted in the name of God, in the name of the king, or in the name of a tribe. The weak are always exploited by the strong." Joshua turned, vacantly looking at the distant temple of the Vestal Virgins.

"In the case of Cicero's client, even though the farmer's name was included in the proscription list, by popular appeal from the people of Ameria, his name was removed," Marcus said. "However, Chrysogonus' men murdered the farmer, inherited his properties and put the murder charges on his son Sextus Roscius. That was the case Cicero had to defend, Sextus Roscius, against an array of witnesses and circumstantial evidence against his client. Cicero's arguments were well thought out, and his words were structured precisely like the construction of a perfect Roman arch where each stone fits in and complements the others, providing strength and grace. His rhetoric was *par excellence* of Demosthenes, and he delivered the words with voice modulation and expression. His words were much more powerful than the best Greek actor playing Oedipus at the Acropolis in Athens. The jury was convinced beyond a reasonable doubt. The spectators were spellbound. Cicero won the case. Sextus Roscius was acquitted, and Chrysogonus convicted. Rome cheered Cicero. That was the way the young lawyer became the uncrowned King of the Forum."

When they reached the Speaker's Forum, a court hearing was in progress with a toga-clad magistrate presiding over the proceedings. Twenty jurors listened with interest to the declamation of the prosecution. A small crowd had formed behind the defendant, as well as the prosecution, cheering for their concerned parties like in a gladiator game. Joshua listened to the arguments and watched the proceedings silently from one corner. *Rome is violent; Rome is brutal; Rome is immoral. But now, Rome has a system of jurisprudence, an accused is innocent until proved guilty by a jury of his peers,* he thought.

After watching arguments for a while, Marcus guided the group around and plodded west towards the Capitoline Hill, where the most imposing collection of buildings – the Tabularium, The Temple of Concord, the Basilica of Opimia, the Temple of Saturn, and the altar of Saturn – all came into view like the luminous glare of edifices as the bright rays of the high sun reflected from one building to the other, making even the eyes blind.

The crowd in the forum was a peculiar mix of people. Amidst the Romans were the dark-skinned and spring-haired Africans; tall, black heads of Babylon; tanned, wavy-haired traders from the Middle East; short spice dealers from India; and thin yellow-skinned Chinese; but all respectfully giving way to the occasional toga-clad Roman senator crossing the Forum.

"You have way too many temples here; too many deities. Is Jupiter the head God?" Joshua asked.

"That's correct. Did I hear that you have only one?" Rocco inquired.

"Yes, that's true, Rocco. We believe that there is only one God," Joshua replied.

With a grin, Rocco said, "For us, one God won't do the job. We have a God for virtually every natural phenomenon and its vicissitudes. We have Jupiter as god of the sky, Neptune for the sea, Mars for war, and Venus for sex. There are so many gods, and I can't even recall all of them."

"Women and gods can never be too many," Marcus added.

A chill ran down Joshua's spine, and his face turned gray. "Marcus, do you really mean what you are saying?"

Rocco immediately threw his arms around Joshua's shoulders, patting and admonishing the others, "Enough. That's enough."

Presently, they reached the Speaker's Forum in front of the senate house. The platform was adorned with the brow of an old ship – a trophy collected from the sea battle during the Latin League Revolt over three hundred years ago – several helmets, breast plates, a few skulls and other artifacts nailed to the rostrum.

"Is it at this place where Cicero's . . .?"

"Yes, Joshua," Lucius said. "It was here that the severed head and right hand of the philosopher were nailed by Octavian. This is the same place where Mark Antony made his thunderous speech after Julius Caesar's assassination that led to a citizen's revolt. This is also the same Forum where Cicero's first wife, Fulvia, vented her anger at her beheaded husband. She ripped Cicero's nailed head from the rostrum, sat down and set the head in between her knees, spat on it, pulled out his tongue and pierced it with her hair pins, laughing and screaming like a crazy woman."

"Was she insane? A wife insulting the severed head of her husband?" asked Joshua.

There was no answer.

"The greatest philosopher Rome had ever seen, like Socrates in Athens, or Akhenaton in Egypt. The Roman Counsel; tutor to Octavian! Author of over sixty books; brilliant orator; defender of the accused; supporter of the suppressed – all of that brilliance severed and nailed to this platform. Joshua's mind was a blur of flashbacks.

**** **** ****

In the afternoon, the Little Theater group assembled in the conference hall at the Pompey Theater in front of the major assembly hall. A majestic marble statue of Pompey stood in a posture of blessing to everyone. It was at the pedestal of this statue that the great Caesar was cut; it was here that Brutus cried out to Cicero, "Freedom is back," while brandishing his bloodstained knife.

The theater group presented the play, *The Fall of a Philosopher*, depicting the last twenty months of Cicero's life.

Some twenty youngsters, including six girls – actors and actresses – sat around a table. Lucius made the introductions, and he set the stage for the play with a speech:

It was the dictatorship of Julius Caesar that brought Cicero back from retirement to active politics. He could not stand by and watch as his beloved Rome drowned once again in another dictatorship. Cicero believed that Julius Caesar was a dictator, and Antony, his right-hand man, a bully, a drunkard, and a womanizer who was unworthy to be a Counsel, and that both must be deposed. But things did not work out that way. Soon Julius Caesar was assassinated. Mark Antony aspired to Caesar's crown, but Caesar had willed Octavian, his adopted son, to be the heir. The power struggle started. Cicero aligned closely with Octavian, whom he called the "God-given boy." Octavian needed Cicero with his oratorical gifts to influence the Senate and gain credibility and support for his future plans. Cicero hoped and believed that Octavian would succeed, and reestablish the traditional Roman Republic. Octavian won the game. He proclaimed himself to be Emperor Augustus. He no longer required Cicero. Let's begin the reading.

The first scene depicted a meeting between Octavian and Antony that took place on a small sandy island of river Bononia in northern Gaul, where the two tyrants and their entourages met for three days and penned a power-sharing agreement. One actor, a centurion, read the long list of proscriptions they had prepared. Antony carefully listened to the list without a blink. "This list is incomplete," he said. "The senile man Cicero is the root cause of all these troubles. The Republic will be a much better place with his head nailed at the rostrum," he insisted. Octavian's silence was a "yes" in answer to the question. He did not bargain a prize to save the head of his Guru.

In the following scene, money-hungry Roman citizens marched through the streets and byways of the city proclaiming huge rewards to the heads of the individuals, whose names they read out loud: "Felix Romanus, 34; Gaius Rufus, 53; Lazarus Serevus, 40 . . ." Men raided houses, people chased, hunted down and beheaded on the stage, even without verifying the proper names and addresses were all acted out very well by the young actors and actresses, albeit grotesque. Men's bodies without heads, strewn all over the stage surrounded by wailing women and children, showed the surrealistic pathos of the dictatorship – a very dark scene.

In the final scene, in the late hours of the night, an old, frail and confused Cicero was seen on Appian Highway escaping Rome. Wrapped in a bundle of blankets, the man was shivering and muttering incoherently. Unable to take the next step due to fatigue, he slumped on the roadside and fell asleep momentarily. Dogs barking in the distance were fast approaching. Presently, the wretched old man got up as if in a nightmare and started screaming. " . . . No! I shall not run away from Rome. I shall not run away from my home. I will go to Octavian. Let him dagger me . . . let him dagger me . . . ."

"When Cicero woke in the middle of the night, he considered going to Octavian's palace to commit suicide on his hearth," Lucius said. Instead, he returned to his villa in Astura and submitted himself to his servants. They were escaping with him to the city of Catea."

Four men carried Cicero on a litter to the stage. Horse hoofs sounded high. Four cavilers – bounty hunters – confronted them. The litter was brought to the ground. Through the small window curtain Cicero put out his head and asked, "What would you like, gentleman. Who are you?"

Cicero looked carefully at the leader of the horsemen, and smiled, "I know you. You are Philologus. Aren't you?"

"You are correct, Cicero."

"I argued your case. I liberated you from slavery, didn't I?"

"You are correct, Cicero."

"I sent you to school to educate, didn't I?"

"Correct, Cicero," said Philologus, and signaled his men.

The head cutter drew the saber from the sheath in a swift action with a "sish" noise.

From the litter, Cicero beckoned Philologus close to him, and said: "I am not going anywhere. You came to do your job, but do it right."

Then he stretched out his neck. The head cutter severed Cicero's head in one simple swing. They quickly collected the bounty and headed to Rome.

Joshua was deeply moved by the play, which he found terribly sad and unsettling. For the first time, he appreciated the powerful impact of a well-written and produced play. *There will come a time when the people of Israel would write plays of such profound impact,* he said to himself.

In the coming weeks, Joshua dwelled deep into the philosophical writings of Cicero. He pulled out a scroll of blank papyri from Amarna and made many entries from his teachings: "Life is a preparation for death. Physical sufferings can easily be met by fortitude. Through meditation, a man could separate the mind from the body and have a near-death experience that prepares him for his physical death. Death is a bridge that everybody has to cross, and of which there should be no fear. Death is not the end of life. Souls transmigrate."

What Cicero wrote about pain and pleasure was of special interest to Joshua. "No one avoids pleasure, because it is pleasure; nor desires pain, because it is pain. Endurance of pain, when it will deliver pleasure, can become a pleasurable pain. Grief is just an emotion that must be rejected with the right attitude. Pain is immaterial, minimized during the pursuit of happiness, like the marathon runner who notices a muscle tear or cut on his foot, only after crossing the finishing line. Yet in his final hours, even Cicero was frightened of pain and death and wanted to run away from the inevitable."

****　****　****

In the weeks that followed, Joshua walked the city, often accompanied by Lucius, and frequented the Library of Julius Caesar, presently relocated within the mausoleum of Augustus at the north end of city inside the city wall.

At the entrance of the mausoleum on a high altar under the frescoed ceiling stood the imposing marble statue of Augustus, adorned with royal emblems, raising his right hand with his lips slightly parted as if quieting the crowd before a speech. The museum contained countless statues, works of art, frescoes with mythological scenes and processions exemplifying the Imperium.

Among many other works of art, one in particular caught Joshua's special attention. The complex statue depicted the scene of a man and his two sons bound by two giant serpents desperately trying to escape their grip. The feelings of fear, anger, and ultimate desperation seen on their faces were beyond words to describe, even for the great poet Virgil. The creation was so lifelike that Joshua pinched the hand of the father to see whether he was alive. As he stood, puzzled, gazing at the statue, Lucius said, "This work, the *Laocoon*, was created by the Greek sculptors Hagesandrus, Athenodorus, and Polydorus about a hundred and seventy-five years ago. It portrays a famous scene from the Trojan War, and Julius Caesar brought it back from some place in Athens."

"What does it say?" asked Joshua.

"This large man, Laocoon, was the high priest of the Trojan King Poseidon, and the other two are his boys. In Homer's Iliad, the Trojans find a gigantic wooden horse stationed outside the city gates of Troy. A clairvoyant, Laocoon, the precinct priest, smelled the trouble and made a speech warning against bringing the horse inside the city gate. 'Behold,' cried Laocoon. 'Behold my poor people, the men of Troy. Are you insane? You think the enemy is gone? What is their gift without a scheme? Don't you know the way Ulysses works? When the Greeks bring a gift, suspect poison in their wrap.' Saying this, Laocoon heaved his spear into the belly of the wooden horse as a sacrifice to his god king, Poseidon. Instantaneously, two giant serpents come out of the sea and encircled the priest and his two sons, strangling and suffocating them to death."

"Brilliant work. But why should the sacrifice by a high priest to his god king end in such a violent sacrifice of the priest himself?" Joshua asked.

"Well, the serpents were sent by the god Apollo for an earlier disobeying of the priest," Lucius said. "In Greek stories, no questions are left unanswered."

The next Saturday, in the first week of June, Joshua woke to the boisterous sounds of firecrackers, bugles and trumpets rising from the streets of Aventine Hill. He looked out: early in the morning the

Palatine hill had grown to a tumult with a carnival atmosphere. Streets crowded with men and women, their faces painted blue, wearing blue headbands and scarves, cheering and screaming, some already drunk to the gutters carrying flasks of wine, spilling and at times spraying on others. His roommates were all up and ready, in a festive mood, wearing blue head bands, chewing poppy gum, and preparing to join the celebration, one helping the other paint their faces.

"Joshua, you should come, too. It will be fun; our horses are running today," Marcus said. "Joshua, you are way too serious for your age," scolded Marcus. "What do you do all day long . . . reading, writing and thinking all by yourself? I told you, you are too young to be a philosopher. Remember, yesterday is dead and gone. Tomorrow is unsure and unborn. Today is the reality. Be real, and come with us."

"What is this all about? Why you are all dressed in blue and wearing scarves?" Joshua asked, half asleep.

"Our horses are racing today," Marcus said. "We, the Aventonians, the Blue Team, our team. We all go and root for our team."

Joshua's reluctance was no match for their resolve. They brought out a blue scarf, tied it around his neck, put some blue paint on his face, popped an olive-sized poppy resin in his mouth, and dragged him out of the building to join the crowd marching to the Circus Maximus. The crowd in the streets moved slowly towards the main street, while the musicians and the dancers were pushing and elbowing each other, shouting. Joshua went along by his friends through the heavily crowded narrow streets and didn't really protest too much. The four-storied Circus Maximus was less than a mile from their apartment located in the valley between the Palatine and Aventine Hills.

It was the day of summer games of that year. All the government offices, shops and schools were closed. There were people all around, happy, jubilant, and all caught up in the moment.

Is my head getting a little lighter? Joshua thought. *Am I floating? No, it's alright. I know where I am. No war; no violence; no knives; no spears or beheadings. Blood dripping from Cicero's hands.* He felt the streets were covered in glittering gold, and the sky filled with glowing suns, one for each color – red, green, blue, yellow . . . The philosopher's hand hung from the sky, the hand that wrote all those great words. Blood flowed like a stream from the philosophers head nailed to the platform. Like the Kishon River, a river of blood . . . stream of slaughter. These images tumbled around in Joshua's head as the poppy gum began to take hold.

"I am sure I know where I am. Have I ever seen these many happy faces in Galilee, Jerusalem, or anywhere in Israel?" Joshua threw his arm around Rocco's shoulder, steadied himself and floated along with the crowd. The crowd moved really slowly; slowly like a large serpent, the serpent with many heads, heads with many colors.

Joshua shook his head, and steadied himself again. The processions of various colors joined from side streets to the main streets and merged together. Fans of the Blue, White, Red and Green teams formed a large multicolored mass. Everyone was singing, dancing, shouting, kissing and hugging. No statues. No commandments. No pain. No suffering. It's the games day in Rome. *When you are in Rome, be a Roman,* Joshua thought. *I'm in Rome.* "Hail to the Blues, hail to the Blues," he yelled.

Presently, the friends from the Aventine Hill found Joshua mixed in the crowd, wrapped tight in the arms of a big girl wearing a blue hair band – kissing, kissing him in the mouth. She had grasped him tightly, pressing her robust throbbing breasts against his face. Lucius pared them apart, and whispered Joshua's address at the Aventine Hill into her ears, and proceeded to the fair grounds. Joshua was under the influence of the poppies, they knew. From then on, Lucius and the others protected Joshua like a child, not to get lost in the vile crowd. By noon, they reached the Circus Maximus.

The chariot race was commissioned by Tiberius Caesar. Since Tiberius had assumed the throne there were more sporting events and festival activities, not only in the main cities, but also all across the Empire. Over the drums and bugles it was announced that Emperor Tiberius would be present for the races.

The men were seated in the Blue's section, specifically. Joshua stood up and took a lingering look at the enormous Circus Maximus that had been renovated by Julius Caesar – a rectangular stadium, more than two thousand feet long and three hundred feet wide, with a spine in the median surrounded by numerous four-story buildings, and stadium seats that could accommodate about two hundred and seventy thousand spectators. The glorious royal stoa for kings and higher officials was at the head end of the stadium where the riders turned around. The median spine was adorned with marble and golden statues of Roman gods, with an Egyptian obelisk at the center.

The musicians on the platform of the royal stoa had begun to play, but the tumult from the crowd drowned out the music. When the stadium seats were finally full, the royal bugles began to play the imperial anthem, and the entire crowd grew silent and stood in respect for the king. The master of ceremonies came up to the rostrum and announced the entry of the Emperor.

Accompanied by the usual standards and pageantry, a frail old man with a bend, wearing a glittering gold and emerald crown over his white hair, dressed in purple – the emperor – holding steady with his arms wrapped around two young women, appeared on the stoa. The whole crowd bowed in reverence. As he reached the throne, Tiberius raised his right hand, blessed the crowd, and signaled everybody to sit down.

The opening ceremonies of the chariot race were a series of processions, parades, floats and dancers representing the various parts of the Roman Empire. There were no representatives from Palestine, but the Egyptian floats – the harvest scene and the snake dancers – were spectacular, and the floats from Greece, depicting the Panathenian procession at Acropolis, involving nearly a hundred young men and women, were was astonishing. The processions continued for about an hour, before the races began.

For each team, the first set of races consisted of a two-horse chariot with one charioteer, and each race was seven laps, about four miles, around the stadium. The first team to gallop to the starting line was the White. To the wild cheers of their fans, the chariot came to the starting line on the inner lane. They were followed by the Red Team on the second lane, about a hundred feet ahead of the White, the Blue on the third lane another hundred feet ahead of the Red. The Blue Team's fans cheered even more loudly than the previous two, and even Joshua stood up and cheered for his team. Finally, the Green Team came and settled on the outermost lane, another hundred feet ahead of the Blue. From the rostrum, a soldier waved a white flag left and right three times, and then suddenly downed to signal, which timed perfectly with the first gallop of the horses: the race had begun. The first lap was civil and there was no violence on the track. As soon as the first lap had ended, as indicated by the nosedive of a dolphin doll set on the median, the strife and trickery of the teams began.

Aquilo, the charioteer for the Blue Team – a champion in several earlier tournaments – was a well-known rider in Rome. But this year the Green Team with Ascalaphas, a Greek rider, was considered the best bet. About halfway through the second lap, Aquilo had a very slight lead on the third lane. But Ascalaphas, on the outer lane, slapped his horses wildly and drove them as hard as he could, overtaking the Blues on his right and quickly veering to the median, virtually trying to crush the Blue horses against the ramp. But the brilliant Aquilo lashed Ascalaphas several times, which jolted him and his chariot off that attempt. Ascalaphas tried all his trickeries, always attacked at the short end of the stadium, knowing his opponents were at their most vulnerable as they lost stability taking the fast, sharp turns.

In the middle of the sixth lap, the Green Ascalaphas was comfortably on the inner track, barely in front of the Blues. He tightened the reins, allowing the Blue to overtake on the right. When the Blues leveled with him on the right, nearing the apex of the bend, he whipped his horses hard and veered them to the right, trying to catapult the Blues out of the race. The Blue horses brayed violently. But the brilliant Aquilo quickly tightened the snuffle and slowed down his horses, turned left, gracefully entered the inner lane and rode off, not only avoiding the collision, but also placing him clearly in the lead. Missing the intended collision, the Green chariot careened off the track, and horses stumbled, overturned and crashed onto the stone wall of the rostrum with a noise like a giant tree falling on top of a house. The horrible bleating of the horses ceased abruptly; the beasts were reduced to a mass of broken bones, lacerated meat and spilling blood. Ascalaphas was catapulted to the Rostrum, and he instantly died with a brief seizure. While the Green fans made the tumult of "oohs," the rest of the colors rose to their toes in cheer and celebrations, stomping their feet and clapping their hands. The emperor himself stood up and waved his hand, congratulating Aquilo.

Joshua was petrified at the site and trembled with despair. He sank to the seat with his hands crossed across his head and closed his eyes, while the rest of the crowd continued their wild jubilations. "My father in Heaven, the people don't know what they are doing . . ."

As the first round ended, the Red Team was in the lead, the Blues a close second. The Red Team's spectators cheered loudly and guffawed wildly, pointing fingers to all the others until the second round of the racing started.

In the second round each team had four horses and a new charioteer. The Blue charioteer, Pupis, was popular, and a crowd pleaser. Likewise, Visellius was a champion and a popular rider at the Circus Maximus for the Red Team. Visellius was a ruthless driver, responsible for several fatal crashes in previous races. Visellius connivingly planned his strategies, insuring that his high tactics took place right in front of the royal gallery at the short bend, receiving maximum favor and applause from the king. His techniques, while well known, were difficult to address. On the final round, on the long stretch of the ride towards the royal gallery, he would position himself on the inner lane a few feet behind the others. On approaching the bend near the rostrum, just at the moment when his opponents are negotiating the left turn, instead of negotiating the turn to the left, he pokes his preconditioned horses with a sharp needle mounted at the tip of the whip, which makes the horses bleat and leap forwards violently, riding his chariot directly into his opponents' on the right, overturning and shattering the other chariots onto the rostrum. Pupis had observed Visellius's treachery frequently and decided to beat him at his own game. He also had mounted a sharp needle at the tip of his leather whip and positioned himself on the inner lane. As he reached the tail end of the stadium, when Visellius was least expecting a problem and negotiating a left turn to the finish, Pupis charged from the inner lane and poked his opponent's horse with the sharp needle-laden whip. The animals, unable to take the left turn, bleated and leapt forward violently, cutting him off from the track, smashing onto a giant statue, reducing his chariot to rubble and assuring victory for the Blues. The charioteer was instantly killed. One beast was wounded, but the remaining horse, amazingly, to the delight of everybody in the house, ran to the finish. The horse qualified for the finish, but the team didn't.

Every one of the Blue fans, except Joshua, was jubilant and exalted, screaming and cheering loudly. Joshua painfully watched the soldiers remove the dead bodies of the charioteer and the horses. He began to sweat and his stomach was heaving. He broke out into a cold sweat, and soon the stadium blurred, and he sat down for the rest of the show. He regretted the moment when he had decided to go to the show. People cheering and entertained by watching people killed for the fun of it. "Oh Rome! Land of Cicero?"

For the third and final round, each chariot had six horses, each arrayed in pairs of two. With the Reds out of the race, the Blues were the favorite. The two remaining teams mounted a combined attack to crush the Blues.

Aquilo, the charioteer once more for the Blue Team, had a reputation for coming from behind and pulling off the last-minute victory. During most of the last race, Aquilo maintained a low profile, riding defensively in the last position behind the other two teams. The two leading charioteers were fighting as usual, whipping their horses to fatigue and trying to crash each other to the median spine or to veer off the track.

Aquilo watched the other riders patiently, riding a horse-length behind them, keeping his cool and avoiding clashes. As he reached the final turn towards the royal gallery, Aquilo signaled the horses with a gentle flick of the whip and let out a violent scream. The horses took off, racing to the finish with nostrils flared and tails raised, galloping to victory. The Blues were victorious: Aquilo was the hero. The Aventonians were jubilant.

Joshua appeared somber and exhausted, color-drained and pale.

"What did the Galilean think about our games?" asked Rocco while the crowd was dispersing.

Joshua didn't say a word.

"It appears our friend didn't enjoy the games much," Marcus said.

"If only I had known that the games were this brutal, I would not have come. It is really sad; people dying in violent crashes and the spectators are laughing in delight."

"Joshua, you are a budding philosopher. You came to Rome to see what it looks like and how people live. A real student must know both good and bad. If you want to see real bloodshed, let us take you to one of the Gladiators' games."

Joshua shook his head, saying, "Oh no, I can imagine."

That night there was a huge torch-lit victory celebration at the Aventine Hill. Everybody was euphoric, except the young philosopher from Galilee, who went to sleep early.

**** **** ****

Several weeks passed, but Joshua was mostly gloomy and heavily preoccupied. *Rome is a mixture of extremes*, he thought. *On one end, they have great philosophers like Cicero, a parliamentary system of government, elections, a trial-by-jury system, and above all a man is presumed innocent until proved guilty by a jury of his peers. On the other end, sheer violence, rampant prostitution and gladiator games, where people are killed for fun and entertainment .*

He retreated to the library and read all the books and speeches that Cicero had written. He walked the length and breadth of the city, appreciating the stupendous temples and constructions, marveling at the vision and architectural excellence of the Roman civilization, while regretting the senseless brutality and lack of ethics of an agnostic culture.

One afternoon, he visited the Pantheon, constructed by Agrippa about fifty years back. It was a large monolithic concrete dome with an oculus at the apex. As soon as Joshua entered the temple, he reflectively turned his head up towards the oculus, nearly hypnotized: the vision of the heavens, the haunting blue skies and firmaments, caused him to pause and contemplate the beauty of the universe and the splendor of creation. There were eight exquisitely carved naves and altars for the deities of the Roman Pantheon – the temple of tolerance – where the head God did not admonish: "Thou shall have no Gods other than me."

The Pantheon made him think about the engineering mind and marvel of the Romans; concrete from pulverized soil and water transformed into gigantic arches, bridges, domes, aqueducts and roads. *They are both brilliant and brutal; a gap between their accomplishments and humanity. Power and hunger for more power is all that Rome is for now. The days of Caesar and Cicero are over. Now, it is decadence, gladiators, horse racers and exotic festivals.*

"Sword fights, gladiators and chariot races are not your cup of wine," Lucius said. "Go to our lighter festivals; read Virgil or go to a bath. It will ease you up; that's what I would suggest. There are plenty of things to do here in Rome."

With Lucius, Joshua went to The Festival of Flora that took place on the nineteenth of April at the Circus Maximus. "Flora is the goddess of the spring flowers and the vines. The festival is to please her so that the flowers would blossom and the harvest would be good," said Lucius.

It was a much less crowded event at the Circus Maximus. The participants were young – almost all of them under thirty – many, lovers hand in hand, clad in brightly colored clothes. Burnt meat, oven-roasted birds, baked goods and wines were in plenty for nominal prizes. Many rich men had their stalls giving away food and drinks for their name and glory. People assembled in small groups, in many places, watching pantomimes, dances, clap songs and entertainments of many kinds. As wine got to the young Roman temples, with clothing flying and wine flowing freely, it did not take long for men and women to separate into couples and retreat to any space they could find in the hall to show their intimacy with no curtains. The festival became an orgy, with couples and groups indulging their desires, presumably to please the goddess, Flora.

Joshua waited away. *Where I am from, people would be stoned for this*, he thought as he pushed his way through the hall of naked flesh, trying to get out of the Circus Maximus. When he got outside, he needed to steady himself, and sat down on a stone bench at the exit gate.

After the festival of Flora, resolving that never again would he go to another Roman festival, Joshua determined to take time away from the decadent culture of Rome and focus on the works of Virgil and other romantic poets of Rome, although he had become so disillusioned that he wondered if there really was any point. Romans had turned like the Jews in the Sinai desert, when Moses went up the mountains to receive the commands from God. *Maybe there will come a time when this nation will be guided by a prince of peace,* he thought.

To settle a turbulent mind, Joshua turned to Virgil. It was like a badly needed cool breeze on a stifling hot day. Virgil, the son of a hardworking farmer, was born in the Cisalpine Gaul, near Mantua, on the banks of the River Po, which snaked around that picturesque village. His autobiographical notes revealed that he had lived through the worst and best of times in Roman history – Sulla's dictatorship to the rebirth of imperial Rome under Augustus – he had seen it all. Poetry was his passion, farms and farmers were his inspiration, and his idyllic poems were pictures of the farmer's humble and rustic life, written on the green canvas of his own pastoral lands. Joshua savored Virgil's writings about the simple events of pastoral life – the first rain of the season; the pleasure in tilling the land, tending the cattle, and keeping bees; the joy of watching the first flowers of the spring and the change of colors of the season; and admired the artistic skill of the Almighty, who made the leaves and bushes turn color. Such thoughts about the simple wonders of the splendid creation were close to Joshua. *Look at the lilies of the field; they neither toil nor spin, yet Solomon in all his glory was not arrayed like one of them,* he thought. Virgil wrote about the emotional attachment of the farmers to their families and to their animals – the old man sitting in the moonlight, surrounded by his children and grandchildren, telling his stories of myths and ghosts, then holding his frightened child close to his chest to comfort him; the cows wagging their ears and licking the hairy arms of their masters; lambs shedding tears when one of their own died from an illness; the heartbroken farmer saying goodbye to his beloved betrothed daughter who was soon to move to a distant town.

"Poets are people who would relate yesterday the way it was, narrate today the way it is and foretell tomorrow the way they wish to be," said Lucius. "But Virgil was such a mystic and clairvoyant poet. In his legendary work *Eclogues*, he wrote about the birth of a savior child who would rise up to power in righteousness, banishing sin, and bringing back the good old days of ancient Rome, he wrote. Most of his contemporaries interpreted this to be the child of Mark Antony and Octavia, but they now believe that the savior child was the nephew of Julius Caesar – Augustus."

Joshua took to the job on the learning about Virgil. Many months later he would tell Mary the story of Culex. "Mary, Culex is the epitaph for a mosquito. Early in the morning, the shepherd drove out his flocks to his pastures, reminiscing about what a gratifying job he had, breathing the fresh air, touching and feeling nature, listening to the music of nature, and being with his beloved and faithful herds to feed them and to nurture them.

"At noon, the shepherd took his flocks to the fountain at Diana's woods for water and rest. The man fell asleep under the shadow of a willow tree. In his sleep, a mosquito stung him on the eyelids, and he sprang up, crushing the mosquito to death, only to see a giant serpent fast approaching to attack him. Fierce predator snakes used to frequent these meadows in hot summer days to cool off by immersing themselves in the mud. Quickly, the shepherd jumped aside and grabbed a thick bough, and beat the snake to death. That night, in his dreams, the ghost of the mosquito appeared to him. 'I believed farmers were gentle and loving people, but you are full of ingratitude and brutality,' the mosquito said. 'I was only trying to wake you up to warn you of a calamity. But shame on you; you smashed me to death.' The mosquito then went on to narrate the sites, people, and events and sufferings he had witnessed. 'You, as a farmer, should preserve and protect the spring meadow and the woods of the pastures and respect the role of every being, however small and insignificant you think they are.' The gnat disappeared."

"The shepherd woke up, troubled by his dreams, and the next morning he decided to make a monument for the Culex. He made a big mound of earth and bordered it with white stones, planted the mound with flowering shrubs, made an epitaph and placed it front of the mound. 'Oh little mosquito, the guardian of the flock, for thee I erect this ceremonial tomb, the least I could do in my duty, in payment for a life I owe to you.'"

For Joshua, the simplicity of the themes and the originality of Virgil's poems were like a cool breeze in a blazing desert.

**** **** ****

In all, Joshua spent over a year in Rome, and saw everything he had wanted to see, and some things he wished he hadn't. The winter was fast closing in, and he would have to wait another four months more before catching a boat headed east. The last two weeks of the year in Rome were an easygoing time of festivities, celebrations and carnivals as a prelude to the greatest Roman festival of all – the Saturnalia. The cooler weather is ideal for enjoying a relaxing time, and for Romans to go to the hot springs or baths to spend a day of leisure.

It was December, and Joshua was about to turn twenty-two. Marcus, Lucius and Rocco had made up their minds to celebrate Joshua's birthday early, on their account of the hectic days of Saturnalia lying ahead. They decided to take the Galilean to the baths. Although Joshua didn't condone the beliefs and convictions of his Epicurean friends, he admired their honesty and appreciated their willingness to live harmoniously with other people of differing views. With much insistence from his roommates, Joshua accompanied them to the baths.

There were over twenty baths in Rome for the pleasure and entertainment of the citizens, including two new ones commissioned by Tiberius. Joshua had learned that all of the Emperors supported and funded these leisure activities, as they were integral to Roman society, an essential element of daily life and an important symbol of Roman civilization. Bathing was such an important event that the construction of the bath houses was elevated to a high level of creative Roman architecture.

There was a bath recently constructed in Galilee, Joshua knew. "I would like to see how the bath houses work," he said. They showed him the enormous maze of engineering works in the bath house. From the hills of Subiaco, some fifty miles north of Rome, large quantities of spring water were brought to the city through aqueducts, stored in the colossal cisterns, and distributed to the subsidiary chambers connected by ducts. Under the ground, wood-burning hearths made hot water, steam, and hot air that were sent through several hundred terracotta ducts to the various steam rooms, sweat rooms, and hot basins. Terracotta pipes carrying hot air ran inside the walls and the floors of the bath, reminding Joshua of his previous job at the Serapium in Alexandria. The hot springs were like small pools, where heated water mixed with air bubbled up from underneath the water.

In addition, cold water basins, steam rooms, hot sweat rooms, exercise rooms, foot stalls, bars, haircutting salons, massage parlors, reading rooms, libraries, chat rooms and temples were all part of the facility. All services were provided by slaves taken from different nations, and the overall supervision and management of a bath was a challenging task.

Joshua's good friends had paid his entrance fee to the Thermae. As Joshua stepped into the bathhouse, he was shocked at the public nudity of men and women – except the slaves who wore loin clothes. Marcus murmured in his ear, "Look at them; the soft curves and sculptured muscles; this is a free show, Joshua. Enjoy. Remember you are in Rome," he said and pulled off Joshua's gown.

Rocco murmured in Joshua's ears, "Remember, this is only a bath house, not a brothel. You are a philosopher; why should you be worried about nudity?"

Joshua sat crouched on the marble bench with his head buried on his knees, thinking. "Nude. The way God had created man and woman. Adam and Eve were not bashful until they disobeyed God. Did I disobey my God? Why am I bashful and fear nudity . . ."

Presently, a tall, dark man with round shoulders wearing a loin cloth clasped Joshua's wrist, lifting him up: "Come with me," he said.

Joshua – stark nude – followed the man's lead, entered the Unctuarium and lay down on the marble slabs. The slaves, probably Nubians, gave him an oil bath with a gentle body and facial massage, before they guided him to the exercise room. After about half an hour of bending, flexing weight lifting and floor exercises, they led him to the Caldarium for a hot-air and steam bath

The next step in the bathing experience was dipping into the warm, bubbly Caldarium. After a relaxing thirty minutes of swimming and stretching, Joshua was taken to the next room, the Frigidarium. The cool air in the room was a big relief for the Galilean. After some rest and refreshment, he was taken to the massage room where he lay face down on a leather-cushioned wooden table.

A hefty slave with shaggy hair, a large, flat nose and thick lips, rubbed perfumed massage oil in his palms and tempered it by rolling with a squishing noise, and rubbed it over Joshua's neck. "What is your name?" Joshua asked.

"Tembo from Eritrea" the slave said. Tembo ran his strong callused palms from the back of Joshua's neck all the way down to the tip of his back bone. Then his large hard palms gripped Joshua's buttocks and firmly squeezed them several times running the heel of his palm upwards to the base of Joshua's skull. Joshua flinched with pain but Tembo ignored it and kept on working. After he'd completed a series of deep massage, Tembo paused for a while. "Sire," he said in a soft, yet resonant voice.

"Your body is shaped perfectly like a Greek sculpture, but it is not firm enough. It is soft, like a girl. You should go to the gymnasium every day and come here every week." Tembo continued his intense systematic massage, which presently had started at his feet and continued upwards. At the end of the massage and total body thumping, Joshua's body was as red as a shrimp. As he rested on the table, Tembo sponged, wiped and perfumed his body. His friends also had completed the same routines by that time.

"How do you feel?' Rocco asked.

"Good," Joshua replied.

"I have heard this from greater ones," Rocco said. "Nudity is the purity of nature – nothing to worry about. For now, let's go for a walk."

Feeling clean and relaxed, the four young men went for a leisurely walk through the gardens and colonnaded walkways. The gardens were decorated with mosaics and gorgeous statues made of the finest marbles, basalt, granite, alabaster, and bronze. No public building in Rome was without a giant statue of Augustus, as was the case in the Aventine bath. Augustus was there in the garden observing and blessing them.

That evening, they ordered a gourmet dinner at the bath with a variety of meat and a great selection of wines. The burnt ox meat and the smocked sea fish made in Roman style with delicious brown and white sauce prepared with ingredients from the Far East was a real birthday dinner to savor.

The theater show was an unforgettable event. The musical, based on Virgil's *Eclogues*, was presented in Latin. It lasted only for forty-five minutes. To understand and appreciate a great musical, one doesn't have to know the language, he learned. That night he slept well.

**** **** ***

Joshua grew impatient as he waited for a boat to leave for Athens and to home. It was late in December, and the days were getting shorter and shorter. Merchant ships to the east were not scheduled to sail for another ten weeks, and Joshua had to be patient. All of Rome was preparing for the greatest festival of all, Saturnalia, the festival that honored the god Saturn, considered by many to be the patron god of Rome. Saturnalia brought forth the best that Rome had to offer, celebrating with food, drink, art and theater shows; friendship and gifts; and, above all, the temporary reversal of the social order of slavery – an idea that caught the attention of Joshua. During the celebrations, all Romans, including slaves, wore pileus, or the freeman's hat and the official toga is set aside for the week.

The celebrations started on the sixteenth of December. Joshua's friends had invited a bunch of youngsters, prostitutes, foreigners and other destitutes to their apartment on the Aventine Hill. They entertained them with drinks and dinner and even gave them gifts at the end of the evening.

At the end of the week, on the twenty-third of December, the Grand Festival of Saturnalia commenced – the longest and most luminous night in Rome. From early morning onwards, the crowd spilled into the streets of the Aventine Hill, wearing the best of their clothes, some with glittering face masks, some wearing crown with plumes and some dressed up as kings and queens. Flags fluttered on rooftops, bugles ran with marching songs, drums beat to the rhythm and people sang and cheered at the top their voices. As the evening fell, numerous candles were lit on window sills and entrance halls, and all doors are kept open for people to visit and be visited. Carnivals were held in households, street corners and public places all over the city. During this time, the slaves are treated the same as the freemen. Harlots did not charge for their services, and swapping wives and husbands for lovemaking was not uncommon

In Joshua's apartment there were very many visitors; amongst them were a mother with grace and flesh and her two daughters, both slim and pretty. One of the girls, not more than fourteen, instantly fell in love with Joshua, which she displayed with gestures, winks and at times putting out her tongue through her pouted mouth. A bit later at some point, she tweaked on his gown, pulling him to her.

Joshua responded with a disdainful grimace.

The girl didn't flinch. She clawed his hand and asked, "What's the matter with you?"

Joshua untwisted the grip and slipped out to the streets for a walk.

By the time the sun had set, the streets were lit with candle sticks, oil lamps and large torches. Wine, cheese and finger foods were arrayed at the entrance of each of the houses. Men high on wine and women high on demands were all common. The crowd had turned boisterous and stupid by the hour. Avaricious desires of the flesh were displayed everywhere. Older ladies on the second floor sat by the bay windows with their candles lit, dangling and caressing their pendulous breasts, hacking for new customers, while the young ones were all in the streets or in their chambers. As the night aged, licentious crowds in the back alleys were screaming shrill in games of flesh-orgy – Saturnalia had reached the bottom level.

Joshua, wearing a pileus, walked the streets for a while and quietly went back to the room, silently reciting his lines on *The Satire*. Staging the widely popular play *The Satire* written by Horace, a play about social justice and equality, was one among the highlights of the cultural activities of the Saturnalia. Horace himself – the author – was the son of a freed slave. The play was staged, or rather read out loud from a stage – no actor was meant to be sober on that night – by actors in different parts of the city, including the Little Theater Group's production at the Minerva Temple at Aventine Hill.

The message of the play resonated well with Joshua. He strongly agreed that all men were created equals and should be treated as equals. He even agreed to play the role of the slave, Davus, his first ever in any stage production. In the late hours of the night, on the steps of the Minerva temple, in front of some four hundred spectators, the Bohemian youngsters of the Hill staged their play. Davus, the main character – whom Joshua played – had intense dialogues with his master Horace, brutally criticizing him for self-centered arrogance and double standards. Horace, played by Marcus, argued that only wise men deserved to be free. Davus rebutted with fire in his words: 'Why, Master, wise by birth? Is it not by erudition? Why, Master, you hate and beat the slave maid one moment and put her down and penetrate her for your whimsical fancies the next moment?' So went the numerous sharp dialogues in the play. Horace's play brought the dark realities of slavery to the forefront, even if it was only for one day. The longest night of the year was not a night at all for the Romans, but an endless day of unparalleled revelry.

Another December passed, and Joshua, now twenty-two, boarded a merchant ship headed east to Athens. The skies were mostly overcast and the days were cold and windy with rough and choppy water on the ride to the east.

BOOK V
Joshua in Athens

Joshua at the Acropolis in Athens

After two weeks of a turbulent ride on the waves, a tired, homesick Joshua reached Athens on a Roman merchant ship. The ship was to be docked in the Athenian port for four weeks before proceeding to Lindros in Rhodes, and finally to the port city of Ptolemais on the coast of Israel.

The Athens Joshua stepped into, barely resembled the Athens he had learned about and envisioned. Roman boots were on the ground,

Roman orders were in the air, and democracy had been buried for over four hundred years. The "ideal" government of the city state, where every male citizen was given the opportunity to serve on the council and share in the rule of the city, was over. The participation of the Demos with public accountability, equal rights, justice through legislation, and the right to be judged by one's peers was nothing more than a memory stuck in the pages of the history books.

The Olympic Games, however, continued uninterrupted, where nude men and boys strived in the stadium of Olympia for Citius, Altius, and Fortius for the undying glory, like Homer's heroes. The Oracle at Delphi – the ashen-clad, fuzzy-haired Pythia – still meditated on a tripod, chewing laurel leaves, inhaling the inebriating fumes that the earth breathed out, uttering sibylline incantations and answering to the questions of kings and queens who waited in silence with pelanos on their shoulders.

Joshua dropped his bags on the flagstone pavement and gazed at the vast expanse of the Agora, with its numerous temples, shops, altars, porticos and stoa, including the Panathenian way leading towards the Acropolis. A thousand scenes and events that had taken place on that majestic expanse flashed through his mind. He stood on the same walkway that had graced the footprints of Socrates, Plato, Aristotle, Alexander Sophocles and many others. After a few minutes of rest and contemplation, he picked up his bag, looked for the address of Barnabas and proceeded to the Jewish enclave outside the city gate.

The Persians came here, with ambitions of honor, but disappeared in dishonor. The Spartans came here to kill, but retreated, stepping on their killed ones. Alexander came here to conquer; conquer he did, but now even the great Alexander is just a memory. The Romans are thinking they'll be here forever, but time passes, and so will they, Joshua thought.

Just outside the northwest wall of the city of Athens, in the district of Akademos and close to the majestic gate of Dipylon, was the Jewish colony of the ancient city state. Here, Joshua stayed with the family of Barnabas the shoemaker. He was a thin, frail man in his late seventies who lived with his wife, Euodias, also about the same age, in a small house facing the street, where he displayed his wares and sat on a leather cushion, and worked from morning till evening every day except on the Sabbath. They warmly and lovingly received Joshua as a guest. They had no children, and the couple reminded him of Zilinos and Cassandra.

"We are always delighted to see somebody from Palestine. Many a people have come and stayed with us from home," the old man said.

"It's a long journey from Rome," Euodias said. "You look tired. I will bake you some fresh bread."

"Papa, have you ever been to Palestine?" asked Joshua.

The moment Joshua uttered the word "Papa", the old man was arrested on a half-breath. Euodias came out of the kitchen as well. There were tears of joy in her eyes. She hugged him and kissed him on his cheeks. It was a very happy moment in the life of that old couple, the effect of a simple word from the mouth of the young philosopher.

After the dinner, Barnabas and Euodias spent time late into the evening talking about their life and being in Athens: "Some hundred families fled this way after the Babylonian invasion," Barnabas said. "Only about forty reached here; the rest of them died or were killed on the way." Pointing to an old leather-bound book kept reverently on a pedestal, Barnabas continued, "The *Book of Moses*, brought from Jerusalem."

It was an ancient copy of the Torah, written in Hebrew, tattered with several pages lost.

"There are no synagogues in Athens, no rabbi: we keep our traditions simple and within our houses. We were all slaves. We fled from one slavery to the next." The man continued in a monotone. His face was heavily creased with age and fatigue, and there was a tremor in his voice, but his memory was sharp.

"What happened to the Jews when democracy came to Athens?" Joshua asked.

"First of all, whatever happened within the walls of the Acropolis didn't affect the Jews. We were always outsiders, just menial workers like all the other immigrants and slaves. But it is an interesting question. When Alexander came, we got a promotion; from a slave to a menial worker!"

"How many Jews are here now?"

"Most of the Jews died during the great plague. That was about four hundred and fifty years back. Now, we are less than three hundred families, masons, woodworkers, stonecutters, some painters, tailors, shoemakers, and all. We all live here in this alley." Then, a sudden flash of confidence reflected on his face, and he continued with a smile. "Now, we are all getting busy for the festival preparations. You know this is the festival year?"

"No, which festival you are talking about?" Joshua asked.

"The Panathenian festival; this is the festival year – the year before the Olympics. All the dresses, crowns, shoes, decorations and ornaments are all mostly made by us, the Jews."

Barnabas was one among the elders in the Jewish alley where everybody knew him as the history teacher. The alley had one public school where the children of the immigrants were educated in reading writing, and other arts and crafts that are needed for the working class, a system that started after the Macedonian occupation, education for all, an Aristotelian idea implemented by Alexander.

The next day, after noon, Barnabas accompanied Joshua, holding onto his hands, to walk the citadel. His shop was less than one hundred yards from the Dipylon double gate, one of the main portals to the citadel.

"See the double gate, son, only the side gate is opened now. The main gate is always closed except for the festival processions and for the winners of the Olympic Games to enter the city," Barnabas said.

"I heard that the Olympic winners enter the city through a fresh breach on the city wall."

"Right. For many centuries, it was so. When the champions were given reception in the citadel, it is said that the Athenians used to shout, 'Bring down the wall. Bring down the wall. What need is there for the city to be fortified when we have such men of valor, our heroes of the Olympics to defend us?' Then they broke the wall and created a new void. The Olympic heroes entered the city, galloping on their horses. The men and woman of Athens cheered them and showered them with flowers and garlands."

Joshua's visit to the Agora was the most interesting part of his journey so far. He sat on the marble steps of the Temple of Ares, marveling at the formidable civilization that had given definition to human thoughts and shaped the Greek philosophy. The vision of Pericles and the genius of Phidias were all exemplified in the shining temples on the hill of the Acropolis. The citadel had grown much larger with the addition of several new Roman monuments, including the Temple of Rome with the giant statue of Augustus, which stood in front of the Parthenon on the east end.

"Will you be here for the festival, son? It's in July."

"No papa, I will leave in a three weeks," Joshua said.

"Well, it's a festival for a lifetime. By evening of the first day, the citadel will be filled with people. A priest will enter the esplanade through the Dipylon gate with a lit torch raised high up. The flame is then transferred to the torches in the hands of everybody, and soon the Acropolis will be filled with Athenian revelers, and finally a lamp is lit at the altar of Athena signifying the divine birth of Erichthonios – the founding king of the city."

As they walked towards the Parthenon, the old man stopped, holding his palm against the center of his chest, and said slowly, "I cannot walk long or climb too many stairs, my son. There is a catch in my chest as if something is going to burst inside. If I rest for a while, I will be fine." Joshua held his hands and they sat down. After regaining his breath, the man said, "Now I can talk."

"Papa, what is divine in a Greek birth," Joshua asked. "My understanding is that the Greeks never believed in divinity."

"Not so, my son. These stories are from way before – the time of mythology. The story is that Athena was born not from a woman's womb, but from the head of Zeus split open. Athena came out like a rising sun, the virgin patron goddess in full armor, and from her came Erichthonios, conceived not in her womb, but in her thighs, keeping her virginity intact – the Greeks call it a divine birth. The celebration of her birth is the theme of the second day of the festival. The very best of Athens will assemble here on that day with seemingly endless processions; processions with old men waving olive branches, damsels carrying sacrificial vessels, sacred baskets filled with the best of the harvest, amphora filled with new wine, and the women of Athens solemnly carrying garments for the patron god, woven with their own hands. There will be competitions of gymnastics, sports, and chariot races, followed by contests of poetry, music and drama – the ultimate celebration for the men, women, and children of Attica."

They walked slowly for some distance, at times resting for Barnabas to catch a breath, and came to the Roman Agora, which was much busier than the ancient Agora.

"On the final day, there are sacrifices, a lot of sacrifices. Whatever that may be, we, the Jewish people, had lots of business during those months."

**** **** ****

The previous night Barnabas had had difficulty in breathing. He spent the night sitting up, pacing the floor and eating some herbs. Joshua stayed in the Jewish alley, visiting their shops and talking to people. He found the community similar to the one in Elephantine island – Jewish by heritage, but Hellenistic by traditions. Barnabas was the very last man in the enclave who held strong affection for Israel.

Barnabas had kept a note book with several entries, which he had used for teaching the students in previous years. "I haven't looked at this book for very long. You can take a look at it; see if it's of any use to you. It appears to me that you are well read."

"Yes, Papa, but you have told me many things that are not found in any books. I had thought that democracy in Athens had included all the people, including the Jews . . . but . . . ."

"You like democracy, don't you? I will tell you; democracy in Athens was not a well-thought-out process or social reformation by the people; it came by deceit and accident. It worked for some brief time," Barnabas said.

"Why deceit? Was that the people . . .?"

"Not quite Joshua . . . long ago, around the time our temple in Jerusalem was sacked by Nebuchadnezzar, this land was in chaos, ruled by different tribes from the shores, planes and hills. Pisistratus belonged to a well-known aristocratic family. One day, at high noon, when the market was filled with people, he crawled to the Agora, bruised and disheveled. "Citizens of Athens," he yelled. "I have been attacked by the enemy. They are on the way to kill all of you. We need to defeat them. If you give me power and bodyguards, I will give you peace.'"

"Obviously, there was no enemy."

"Correct. The clever Athenians detected the fake and threw him out of the city. But three years later, he returned to Attica; this time, with a gorgeous, six-foot-tall Athenian girl dressed in golden armaments like Athena. 'Look Athenians, this is Athena, your goddess. Can't you see that she is with me?' he said. And through this, and many other trickeries, he took over the city of Attica.'"

"Is it that simple, Papa, for him to take over the city just like that? The Athenians certainly were very clever people?" Joshua countered.

"Who knows, son? However, he was a benevolent tyrant; he allowed elections and festivals, appointed magistrates, built temples and allowed some freedom for the people. When he died, chaos ensued. Then another man came to the scene."

The old man got up and started walking towards the Agora. "Come on, Joshua; I feel better. We will go for a slow walk. He held on to Joshua's hand and kept on talking with a passion. Occasionally, he broke sentences as his breathing was getting shorter, "His name, Cleisthenes, again from a well-known aristocratic family."

"Once again on a busy market day, he came with a few people of size and strength to the market, and climbed on the portico. "Athenians, our beloved Athens is in disgrace," Cleisthenes yelled. "We deserve better. We should have a definite say in our own government. We must rule ourselves for our well-being and stability. I say we can decide amongst ourselves what to do and what not to do. You elect the leader; every one of you vote. You will all be part of the government; you will be the government, I promise you. It will be the rule of Athens by the Athenians."

Barnabas continued like reading from a written script. "The crowd cheered, and he got very wide support for a system of government they had never tried. Clisthenes with his men traveled from one corner to the other speaking to people for the next several days. Finally, there was a consensus. The citizens of Athens assembled on an evening here in this Agora and elected a council of five hundred people to rule over their city state. Democracy came into effect in Athens."

"It's a truly intelligent design of governance, but everybody must be included," Joshua said. "Everybody getting an equal voice to be part of his government."

Likewise, the old man told several stories to Joshua: the invasion of the Spartans, the Plague of Athens, Phillip's invasion and the great speeches of Demosthenes. Joshua had known about Demosthenes; even Cicero had tried to emulate his rhetoric style.

"Papa, your memory is very sharp. You may have taught Demosthenes to students many times. Can you recite to me a few of the words from his speech?" Joshua asked.

Barnabas was amused. He stood up, "I used to know the whole lines of his speech against Phillip of Macedonia. I will tell you a few."

It appeared Barnabas traveled back to his childhood. He laughed gaily, showing his thin, full row of teeth, and started as if doing a play.

"One day, a white horse galloped onto the Agora. Demosthenes dismounted, then he ascended to the podium, and silence ensued. "Athenians, the time is now," Demosthenes said. "Shake off your indulgences and realize the ultimate danger. It was not the Spartans, it was not the Persians, and it was not even the plague or the Peloponnesians that posed the biggest danger to Athens ever: it is this Phillip of Macedonia. But no danger can assail Athens so long as we remain on our guard. We must fight Phillip on his home turf, put him on double jeopardy, and let him fight us with one hand and protect his home and properties with the other, but not with both . . . The moment they come to Athens, be assured, they will terrorize you and set fire to your prize possessions. They will kill our minds first, and then smash our heads. Fight we must, but on their turf. This enemy represents a very clear and imminent danger for the citizens of Athens and our cultural legacy. Fight we must, but on their turf. If we don't act in a timely and decisive manner, our culture will be history. Athenians, Phillip has already taken over our strong outposts. Remember, the property of the absentee belongs to the one who is in possession, and I submit to you, Athenians, if we put to rest our differences, cast off our indolence and apathy, and are willing to serve the state together, we will remain our own masters . . . Fight we must, but on his turf . . . Phillip is drunk with his triumphs; intoxicated with his plunders. I warn you, if we refuse to fight him at Thrace, we will be forced to fight him right here, at the Agora.'"

Joshua stood up and clapped for the old man. Barnabas held his hand heavily on his chest. He searched Joshua's eyes for a moment and said. "Demosthenes made a lot of great speeches. It is said that when he spoke about the enemy, people even heard the thunderous noises of thousands of footsteps fast approaching the Agora, and some even ran home to collect their arms. His speeches were powerful, moving and invigorating. He got some support. But a weak city state was no match for the army of a large kingdom. As you know, Phillip came, and then came Alexander, with Aristotle holding his coat tails closely behind."

"Papa, I am so glad that you were able to make that speech. I felt that I was in the Agora when Demosthenes was speaking."

It was late in the evening; they went back home. Barnabas went to sleep, so also Joshua.

Those were the very last words spoken by Barnabas. The next morning the old man was found dead in his sleep. Jews from the neighborhood all assembled at the house, and he was buried in a public cemetery about two miles north of the city. Euodias moved out of the house with her brother Zachariah, about ten houses west of the street. Joshua moved out of the house.

**** **** ****

One afternoon, after walking the Agora, Joshua sat on the steps of the Temple of Twelve Gods leaning against a huge marble column. His mind was filled with visions of the philosophers who thought about the world unlike any other he had studied. *How different! How different were these people,* he mused. *They strived to find an answer for every question. But are there not questions for which man just cannot deduct an answer without the light from heaven? No hair turns gray; no leaf falls from the tree; no*

257

day breaks, nor sun rise in the east without the knowledge of God. That, the Greeks failed to understand, he thought. He closed his eyes.

He woke to the voices of gypsies, who were singing as they set up their tents for the night close to the steps of the temple. The sun had set, and the full moon rose in the east. The stunning complexes of the Acropolis, the Propylaia, the lifelike Caryatides of Erechtheion, and the incomparable Parthenon shone on the hill with glorious intensity.

A breeze from the ocean chilled him. He pulled out a shawl from his bag and wrapped it around his shoulders to settle the goose bumps. Warm and comfortable, he hummed along with the gypsy melodies.

Gypsy life was the same everywhere in the world, he thought. *They are like the birds in the sky; they don't sow, reap, or gather in the barns. They have no regret of yesterday, grief for today, or worry about tomorrow. They have few possessions, and yet they are happy and content. They have no commandments to obey or statutes to fear; they don't hate their neighbors or have enemies to fight; no paradise to gain or Hades to dread. If not Adonai, who created them? Who protects them? To whom are they answerable, or are they answerable to anyone at all?*

Even though he could afford lodging, Joshua resolved to settle for the evening in a nook on the temple foyer close to the gypsy settlement.

The next day Joshua visited the Hill of the Muses and the cell where Socrates was jailed. His mind was filled with images of the jail where Socrates spent his last days; a philosopher who meant only good things to his fellow Athenians, who walked the streets and conversed with the common people, to teach them − more, to learn from them − who always argued that undertakings of the spirit can lead to happiness only when conducted with morality and wisdom. Yet they pushed hemlock against his lips. *No philosopher is respected in his own town,* Joshua thought.

He returned at twilight, exhausted, and once again settled into the foyer of the temple near the gypsy camp. They had come back to build the nest for the night. Their voices were the music of love, help and compassion. They never seemed angry. He never observed any fights or conflict amongst them.

The clouds glowed orange-red on the western horizon. The gypsies had quieted and settled in for the night. The thick smoke from their bonfire billowed and swirled under the roof where Joshua lay. A few rays of light from the setting sun slipped through the cracks on the roof, forming a narrow shaft of light through the smoke. He stared at the smoky ray of light for some time, noticing the thousands of tiny motes dancing aimlessly, up, down and sideways. The more he watched the pencil of light, the more he felt connected to the heavenly light in which millions of little motes danced endlessly. What are these dancing particles, so tiny, so numerous, so invisible? *The many that I can see, and the more that I cannot*, he wondered.

Atoms, the finite particles in all the elements. Is it all an illusion? Joshua wondered. All these temples, these magnificent marble columns, me, this smoke, all made of these minute particles . . . these atoms, moving endlessly in empty spaces, clashing, colliding into each other in endless space. Atoms, some tightly packed and hard; some loosely bound and soft; some smooth and soothing like honey, like the soul, like the Supreme; some spiked and prickly like vinegar, like the evil.

The Agora came to life in his mind – the time of philosophers, sophists, stoics and the politicians. A crowd of elderly men with flowing beards, clad in togas, converged on the Agora, to present their views, argue out the cases, to agree, to disagree, as they always did. The men, from Pythagoras to Aristotle, formed a circle around the man sleeping on the floor, some argued with a smile, others with a shout.

"Yes, of course," cried Epicurus, "atoms are finite and solid, regardless of their varying shapes. Therefore, they must fall through a vacuum at uniform speed."

"Can you prove it?" Parmenides asked.

"Time will prove it. They are all solid. At some point one atom swerved off the path, collided with others, combined and entangled, creating new substances and even newer ones – atoms are the nucleus of the world," Epicurus said.

Parmenides stepped forward, "No. There is no space. No vacuum. Reality consists of one motionless unchanging substance. Motion is an illusion: only mind can reach the real truth."

"No, there is vacuum. What is empty, after all? So, I say to you, what does not exist, no less than what is? Movement and change in time are the only realities of the universe," Aristotle said . . . "But the more important question is, what is the origin of the motion?" he questioned. "What begins the first motion that keeps all motions in motion?"

The old man Pythagoras moved to the front of the group. "God. That is the origin of everything. Life is a part of God. The real truth is the immortality of the soul, the incarnation and the reincarnation. The whole universe is a living creature – the cosmos – each one of us is a cosmos in miniature."

"I disagree," Heraclitus said. "The world is an eternal fire; everything came out of it and everything goes into it. Fire lives the death of air, and air lives the death of fire; all things live in conflict. Conflict is good; strife is justice. Motion and change are the only realities of life."

"Please unthink, the thinking," Aristotle said. "Is there not a force that is so permanent, which has been there from the beginning and is the cause of all motion?"

"Under all the turmoil in this universe, there must be a harmonious system," the Milesians said. "But there is nothing as new as you might think in your inventions! Everything you claim as new was already there, but you didn't realize it until you discovered it," Thales said.

"Maybe, there are no inventions," Anaximenes argued. "But was it not air that was first, I ask of you? The invisible atmosphere?"

"The entire universe was a primal mass of Apeiron," Anaximander said. "The boundless mass condensed into fumes and further evolved into water and earth." Anaximander stood a head above the others and explained calmly. "In the beginning, the primal mass was in perpetual motion, the motion without boundaries. Time and motion separated opposing qualities. In that unstoppable motion, the cold and wet elements condensed into a primordial seed, a germ, a wet mass, wrapped around in eternal mist that revolves around and around, and bits and pieces split off to outer rings, like pieces of clay from a potter's wheel, such that so many rings of stars started rotating around the immobile earth at the epicenter of the universe. Somewhere in the threshold of this motion, in the warm mud, in that slime, tiny beings appeared that changed gradually, atom by atom, bit by bit, to replace, to substitute, and to adapt to be motile, to swim, to crawl, to fly, and to walk, a permanent evolution, all from that primordial mass of confusion."

"But, where does the universe rest?" several of the philosophers asked.

"Nowhere! It's just suspended at the center," Aristotle said. "No need for it to be supported, just suspended, at the very center – the earth."

"But who or what controls it all?" several of the philosophers shouted.

"By the power of the soul, the soul of the living universe – the cosmos – that controls everything," Anaxagoras said. "Neither the sun nor the stars are divine. There is only one divine force – the cosmos. The world is shaped out of the chaos of matter by that powerful mind."

"I am glad that Anaxagoras echoed some of the things that I said many years ago" declared the pious Pythagoras, clasping his hands in prayer. "Listen, fellows: this universe is limited, single, orderly and in great harmony. Everything is interconnected, like the days and nights, the sunrise and sunset, the seasons of the year: first a bud, then a bloom, then a fruit, then a seed, then a sprout, then a bud – utterly organized, definite, predictable and cyclical. No confusion at all; it is the orderly cosmos; each one of you is a complete miniature cosmos, perfect like mathematics, like music, like the octaves, like life and death. Stability is born of the right proportions of heat and cold, bitter and sweet, dry and wet, good and evil; the harmony of the cosmos."

"Everything is subjective," Democritus said. "What is hot for you, may be cold for the other. What is sweet for you, may be bitter for the other's taste; it's all based on the arrangement of atoms, both in the subjects and objects."

"If heat and cold are not real, then what about right and wrong, justice and injustice?" Archelaus said.

"God is an illusion," Gorgias said. "Even if God existed, we don't know where and how, we couldn't know it nor communicate with it. The idea of God is obscure, and the human mind too small to comprehend this concept."

"That means man is the measure of all things. Virtue is knowledge, knowledge of both good and evil. The unexamined life is not worth living," came in Socrates. Behind him, a young Plato was busy writing down these dialogues verbatim.

"Truth is relative," Socrates said. "It is the way the matter appears to a man or in his perceptions at that specific point in time. Good for one may be evil for the other. Right for one may be wrong for the other; is it not so? What is wrong? What is right?" What is ethics? What is justice? What is piety?"

"Why you ask all these questions." Protagoras asked. "What is your answer?"

"I have none; do you? You think about it; think for an answer before you ask a question"

"Then why did you ask? Are you belittling the Athenians," some yelled.

Socrates never flinched; he questioned more. "What are democracy, autocracy, city gods, ethics, morality, and righteousness?"

The youngsters adored him.

The elders abhorred him.

Plato walked to the forefront, "Justice is the answer to many of those questions. Justice is happiness, an inner organization of the healthy spirit. We have suffered tyranny, its brutality; we have seen democracy, its incompetence. Therefore, for the happiness of the community, there must be rules based on the convictions of our nation, ruler rooted in the philosophy of our culture. But, of course, the naturally strong have the right to be strong, simply because they are strong and can subdue the weak. The naturally superior and intelligent will always be superior and intelligent; that is the law of nature. All these arguments of right and wrong, wisdom, justice and goodness are all but prudence based on experience."

Socrates, with Plato shadowing, was surrounded by throngs of youngsters who hovered around them. They traveled from one corner to the other, pollinating their knowledge through the process of asking questions and listening intently for the answers.

"Knowledge is virtue," Socrates reaffirmed. "The end of every endeavor should be in sight before you even begin. Knowledge is the means of understanding the end. Therefore, I ask of you, what is the function of man?"

"I know not. I am ignorant. Please tell me, Master," responded an eager student.

"Good. Understanding that you are ignorant is the first step in acquiring knowledge. For this reason, I believe awareness of ignorance is a good thing. It means that you are ready to learn," said the master.

The angry crowd shouted, "You ask too many silly questions, belittling. You are corrupting the youth, demeaning the Athenians, and disgraceful to the Gods. You are no prophet. We Athenians, don't we know what we do? Did we not chase these Parthians, defeat the Persians, and construct the Parthenon? Did you forget Homer, Hesiod, Euripides and Sophocles? Can you answer: what is truth?"

"Truth, you will never know so long as your soul is bound in your body, for the body corrupts the soul, with passion, greed and fear," Socrates said.

"You are insane. You speak in tongues. How do you acquire true knowledge?" asked one of the philosophers.

"Once you release the soul from the bondage of your body, then you will be enlightened with the real truth, the real God."

"Is Apollo not the real God, and Athena not our city God?"

"Gods, carved out of stones, without souls," Socrates replied.

The crowd turned unruly and boisterous. More and more middle-aged and senior Athenians encircled him with angry faces.

One man from the crowd called out another question.

"What is piety?"

"Piety," replied Socrates, "is what I practice now, so that you cannot define it at all, is it not so?"

"Socrates, you are blunt in questions and evasive in answers. Answer to the question. What is your vision of the future of Athens?" The old man sat on a stone bench.

"Democracy. Why do you ridicule democracy? A hefty, toga-clad man with bushy beard asked.

Socrates protested: "We had democracy for a hundred years, and Athens was in decline. How can we protect ourselves from the mighty enemies at our gates with this democracy? Why are the gods so silent? The plague decimated our city state. Why are the Gods impotent? The tyrants are at our doorsteps. Still Athena didn't move her little finger to protect us. Should we not search for permanence and stability?"

"What are you saying about the city gods? We have never heard such things before. You are corrupting the youth," someone in the crowd yelled. "What about aristocracy?"

"Aristocracy? Yes, which, of course, is entirely dependent on the good will and wisdom of the ruler," replied Socrates

"Aristocracy – phoo! An aristocracy is the beginning of autocracy! Tyranny! Old man, are you out of your mind?" someone in the crowd shouted. Then the crowd surged forward.

"Athenians. Athenians. Hear him out, please." Plato raising his hand. "But, I should say, there are benevolent aristocrats. There can be. Unfortunately, as you fear, most are tyrants" Plato said. "They do not receive the proper education or training to gain the wisdom to rule effectively. They indulge in wine, sex, and of all kinds of debauchery; they slip into timarchy."

As he spoke, the old man walked to another corner in the Agora, and Plato shadowed him, writing rapidly in his notebook.

"What do you propose then?" someone in the crowd asked.

"A Republic. An ideal Republic. Please listen to him," Plato asked.

But the old man was weak and tired. He sat hunched over on the stone steps of the Agora and strained to bring his voice above a whisper.

Plato spoke, "Athenians. Yes, a poor democracy will eventually create a tyrant who will assume power by force under the pretext that he will bring order, peace and stability. Soon they will burden you with taxes that you cannot afford, implement oppressive policies that you didn't ask for, and rob you of your rights and freedom. With armed bodyguards he will keep you from rising up while he indulges, at your expense, in all of the luxuries of life; women, wine, and whatever debauchery one can think of, including the beheading of a few citizens just for the thrill of the game and to send a warning to the rest of you.

And he will smile in public and promise you a better tomorrow, which he will never provide," Plato said angrily, and paused.

"We Athenians know all that," someone in the crowd shouted. "Show us a system that is fully protected from corruption, yet strong, stable and benevolent? Do you really have such a system?"

"Yes," said Plato, emphatically. "That system is the Republic. Let Socrates speak, please."

"A Republic. All men are not cut from the same rock. By nature and disposition, each man is different and has different strengths and abilities, as well as different weaknesses. Each man must function like different parts of a single organism."

"First, we must create a strong structure for our Republic that is built on a hierarchy of strengths," Plato said. "The structure will rank people as gold, silver and iron, and they will serve within these designations."

"Our republic will breed, then raise and train them. The most resourceful group of men will become the Guardians of the Republic."

"Did you say, breed," shouted a citizen.

"Yes, breed," Plato said. "The best of the crop, the chosen ones, will be the Gold Class – the rulers, the Guardians. They will possess extraordinary wisdom, morality, courage and resourcefulness. The next group will be the valiant auxiliaries, the warriors who will protect our Republic and guard our homes, streets and borders. They will belong to the Silver Class and take their direction from the Gold Class of Guardians. The final group will be disciplined workers, the Iron Class. Each member of this class will perform a specific function that is critical to the Republic. They will be trained to perform their tasks in such a manner that in totality they will seem to function as a single organism. The training and resourcefulness of the guardians shall provide the wisdom for our republic; the lawful bravery of our auxiliaries shall be its courage; and the obedience of the workers shall be our self-discipline. I do emphasize that the Guardians are the brain; the auxiliaries, the heart; and the workers, the body and limbs of the society. The first two groups shall represent the elite of our society, and the others, the masses."

"Ridiculous," someone shouted from the crowd. "This will create war amongst the classes. How do you propose to select the Guardians? The man is senile and insane!" shouted the crowd.

Socrates composed himself and continued passionately.

"Athenians, we know each man is innately equipped to do one job that suits him the best. Some are gifted to govern, others to fight, and still others to labor. But when all of them work in unison, there will be a perfect society, a Republic."

"What is to be the role of women?" someone asked. "Will they be permitted to become guardians based on this so-called innate nature you speak of?"

"Can you conceive of a single endeavor in which men do not far outperform women?" Socrates asked. "And it would be too distracting for women to train and exercise naked along with the men to develop combat skills. In truth, there is not a single administrative task in which a woman can match a man? No, I tell you, by nature women are not suited to be guardians or auxiliaries."

"So, tell us, Master; how we get such a society?" Someone in the crowd shouted.

"To make the best breed of the guardians and auxiliaries: first, we must select men and women of superior quality, including good height, weight, physique and intelligence, and have them live together for some time to get acquainted. During this time, we will train them with reading in politics, philosophy and classics in addition to physical training and other educational programs." Socrates then sat down and signaled Plato to continue.

"Once the training is complete we will hold what we call 'marriage ceremonies' for want of a better term," Plato said. "Selected men and women will be paired. They will be bathed, oiled, and perfumed, and brought to rooms with lovely cushion beds for breeding. They will join together for the sake of the Republic to create a special breed of citizens who will be groomed as future Guardians."

A cacophony of laughter, shouts and screams arose from the crowd, signaling a combination of approval and disapproval. Some men with round shoulders shouted, "Yes! Yes!"

Socrates once again stood in front of the crowd. "This would not be an orgy of the barbarians, but a solemn ceremony for the Republic. There would be music and lyrics composed by selected poets with words that fit the theme. Men and women with exceptional qualities will mate frequently, more than the others. Permit me to borrow from Homer, 'that men of exceptional skill will be rewarded with the honor seat, the best cuts of meat, goblets full of wine and sex as much as they want, with whomsoever women they want. And children born will not know their parents. They grow up well cared for, in a commune.

Plato managed to bring the crowd to listen,

"Those children that are born sickly, deformed, and off-color are disposed of. The remaining male children would undergo intense physical training and philosophical education, though the stories taught them would be thoroughly screened. The stories of the Homeric heroes filled with lust, violence and immorality, and the stories of the corrupt gods must be eliminated from their curriculum. They must learn in such a way that their minds remain pure. And the community of guardians will share the women and children, basically in keeping with the new order of the day – the Republic. And in such a community, each will share the others' pains and pleasures. As they will have no possessions of their own, there will be no conflicts or lawsuits. Their lives will be dedicated to the well-being of the Republic. As for the Guardians, once they have served their time, they will be released to live a life of their own. I would prefer that they would engage in additional education and teach the grooming guardians. Unless states have philosopher kings, the struggles of strife, division, money, hunger, nepotism and revolution shall ensue forever," Socrates said.

An old man shouted, "Socrates, you are against the state. You are against the gods. You are definitely corrupting the youth. Tell us how a bastard growing up without a father mother or family will grow up to be a king?"

"Yes, tell us philosopher, insane philosopher, how can this happen?" someone else in the crowd shouted.

"The child born in this manner will not be a bastard at all, but a child of the Republic," Plato said. "The Republic will be the father, mother and family of these children. They will be the most prized possessions of the society."

"What is justice?" an old man asked stepping forward. "How will you define justice in your new Republic?"

"Justice is simply the creation of human law based on punishments and rewards," Socrates explained. "Justice does not exist in nature. Its meaning changes like the colors of a chameleon. What is considered justice today may well be injustice tomorrow"

"Who will be the city God in your Republic?" asked one of the elders.

"Gods! They are no more than products of the human imagination," Socrates said. "The gods only exist because we have invented them."

The crowd grew angry, and many joined their numbers. They encircled the old man, and though he tried moving from one corner of the Agora, he was unable to escape the throngs that had surrounded him.

The crowd bellowed with anger and vengeance. "You corrupt the youngsters. You dishonor our Gods. You will bring disaster upon us!"

"To that, my fellow Athenians, I say God does not hide in wooden or marble statues. God is the creator of all emotions and manifests in all of us as our psyche, our sprit. Our psyche exists before our body and moves on after the body is dead. All of these are not accidental. Everything has been designed by a supreme intelligence – God. You won't be able to imprison him in a marble statue," Socrates declared.

"Socrates, you are corrupt. You defile the gods. You contaminate the minds of the populous," the throngs grew menacingly. They shouted. "Treason! Blasphemy!"

Presently, a group of fifty jurors surrounded him. Socrates was charged.

Socrates responded wearily, "I lived my whole life in Athens with all its freedoms. I spoke my mind with ethics and responsibility. Is it not heinous now to run away? I will abide by the law of the land, which I believe is the right thing to do at this moment; obey. For who can rightfully say that what is awaiting me is not better than what I have now? So, it is my delight. In fact, my whole life was a preparation for this moment." He paused from speaking for a moment and stretched his hands for the cup of hemlock.

Joshua woke up cold and stiff. He felt weak and tired. His throat was scratchy and voice husky, his temples throbbing with pain. It was a holiday in Athens, and all shops and offices in the Agora were deserted with the exception of Joshua and the two gypsy families who stayed near the temple. One family of eight and another family of five had pitched their tents side by side. One fully pregnant girl was seen sitting outside the tent caressing her womb.

Joshua watched the gypsies folding the tents and packing up for a new day.

"You slept for a very long time," said Sasha, the eldest of the gypsy girls in a musical voice, donned in a brightly colored skirt with great frills that floated around her waist like a fan.

"It was cold last night," Joshua said.

Folding her blanket, she said, "You were shivering. Tania covered you with her blanket."

"That's what you get for sleeping on this cold stone, a stiff neck," giggled Tania the younger one, who looked identical to Sasha with rosebud-like mouth and blue eyes. As she quickly turned around, her skirt flew around her waist in a circle and the tinklets around her ankles jingled.

Soon the girls brought some warm oil to Joshua. Tanya poured some into her palms and began massaging Joshua's neck. Sasha kneaded and massaged his hands and legs. A man with braided hair brought him a cup of warm soup. Tanya raised the warm soup close to his lips, gently holding onto his curls behind his head. The first few sips of the soup put the color back on his face.

Up above, on the ceiling of the temple, the girls noticed a fly fluttering with a humming noise, and a baby lizard hanging upside down on the lintel was constantly on the attack to catch the fly with its large tongue pulling in and out of the mouth.

Sasha giggled, looking at the scene, happy to see that the fly was out of danger. She asked Joshua, "Do you know what the lizard is thinking now."

"No, Sasha. Tell me," said Joshua.

"He thinks that he can hold the whole ceiling in place and yet cannot catch this naughty gnat." As they all laughed, the girls kept on working on Joshua's neck and arms for some time, gently flexing and extending. Joshua thanked the girls profusely for the much-needed soup, and he sat there enjoying the simple life of the gypsies.

"Now, drink some more broth." Sasha said, lifting the bowl closer to his lips again.

Joshua gulped the warm liquid and a wave of warmth washed over his body; he felt comfortable.

The girls spoke over each other, showering him with questions. "You are not one of us. What's your name? Where did you come from? What are you doing here in Athens?"

Joshua told them about his journey.

The girls brought him sunbaked fruits, and bread toasted on an open fire. They fed him smoked fish, dates and more broth. After a day of fasting, the gypsy meal seemed like a God-given banquet. Joshua felt a kinship developing with the gypsy family.

Shasha and Tania had skills in music, dance, and string instruments. But Tania also had great skills in fortune telling and reading palms.

No moments wasted – Joshua didn't have to ask any questions – they kept on talking about the places they had seen, the troubles they had faced and the interesting encounters they had experienced. They seemed to have no worries at all, but Joshua wondered if his perceptions were correct.

Tania had spoken frequently about her sister – Titly – who was pregnant and expecting the baby to come that day or the next. "Last night and the day before, she had pains," said Tanya.

"Father had given her medication to help her sleep. Still, she would awaken in pain," added Sasha. "We lost our mother in childbirth two years back."

"After our mother died, father took Titly, our big sister, as his new wife. This is her first baby," added Tanya.

Joshua's face turned cloudy. The girls sensed the change instantaneously. They stopped talking. In the tense silence that ensued, the girls repeatedly attempted to evoke smiles on their lips. Joshua had finished the soup by then.

With apologetic smiles, the two girls sat cross-legged on either side of Joshua, snuggling against him.

"Tanya wants to read your palm," Sasha said, squeezing Joshua's shoulders.

"What do you see in my palm that I cannot?" Joshua asked.

"Come, I will show you," Tanya grasped Joshua's right palm and spread it in her lap like a book. She pulled his hand closer to her eyes and said with a furtive smile, "I can read your palm and tell your future correctly. Can you give me money to do this?"

"No, I don't want you to read my palms," Joshua withdrew his palm. Tears welled in her eyes ready to fall.

"How much money?"

"Any money – gold, silver, or even copper. It doesn't matter. Give me any money you like," she said extending her palm close to his lips.

"But I'm like a brother to you. Why would you take money from me?" Joshua asked.

"Joshua," she retorted, "telling your future is my job, for which I need payment. Anything else you need – food, drink, music, dances; whatever, you ask of me – I will gladly give it to you for no money. Just give me a little money, and I will tell you everything that's going to happen to you."

Joshua, amused by Tanya's perseverance, handed her a silver coin. When she saw the coin was silver, she jumped up and down screaming with glee. Gathering herself, she bowed in obedience to Joshua, kissed the coin and, with great reverence, pressed it against each of her closed eyes before putting it into her purse.

Tanya sat down in front of Joshua with crossed legs, and grasped his right palm. Her face turned red, there was a fine tremor on her lower lips, and her eyelids fluttered. She began to gently trace her finger over the lines in his hand, seeming to study each one. She paused occasionally to look in his eyes and then returned to studying the lines of his palm. By this time, some five other members of the group, some children and some adults, came over, stood over them in a circle and watched in reverence and silence.

"I see a great storm in the sea. The waves are tall and violent. The sky is overcast with clouds, and the winds are whipping." Then she looked up at him silently for a few moments, and continued. "The calm on your face is a façade. Your mind is turbulent. The ship is going to capsize. You are trying hard to safely reach the shores."

Joshua said nothing.

Tanya continued. "You are lost, looking for the North Star, but the clouds are heavy, and it's about to rain. You can't see a thing. I see a small house, a lamp lit for days on end, not put out. I see a woman sitting in front of the lamp. She is very sad. I see her tears."

Joshua folded his palm, but she forcefully opened the clenched fist with both her hands, pulled it towards to her chest, and kept on reading.

"I see you going from one shore to the other," she continued, "but you neither anchor nor get off shore. I see people chasing you, but you're not running away. You face them and walk into them." She paused for a moment. "I see blood on your hands."

A short distance away, the gypsy elder was listening to Tanya. He rose slowly and came to stand in front of Joshua. Easing Tanya aside, he bent down and looked intently at Joshua's open palm as Tanya continued.

"I see blood on your palms." Her face was only inches from his palm. A tiny drop of tear fell to the lines of his hand. "I see blood on your feet, on your head, and on your chest. I see people whipping a man."

Joshua closed his eyes.

"And now, I see a hill," she said tensely. She turned her eyes up and looked at the grand old man above her head, as if asking for forgiveness.

"Tanya," the old man whispered. It was uttered softly, but the command felt like a thunderbolt. Tanya was arrested on a half breath, and froze for a moment.

"You give the coin back to him," the man said, and walked away.

Tanya was sweating and breathing heavily, but Joshua seemed stoic. He removed his hand from Tanya's grip and squeezed it with his other hand. He thanked the family for the hospitality, and soon gathered his bags and belongings and walked off to the port.

"Brother." A soft voice called him from behind. It was Sasha.

"Brother, we gypsies are ignorant people. We say a lot of things. Many of them never come true."

Joshua turned around and attempted a smile over a somber face.

"Here is your money, please take it."

He bowed his head. "Now, it's your money," and continued walking away.

"Sorry," she said.

A new baby's cries were heard from behind, then much laughter. The voice behind him slowly faded.

Joshua walked down the steps towards the port. It was the same route that Plato took when he had fled the city, talking to himself, "I don't like to see Athenians commit another crime against philosophy."

BOOK VI

Joshua in Babylon

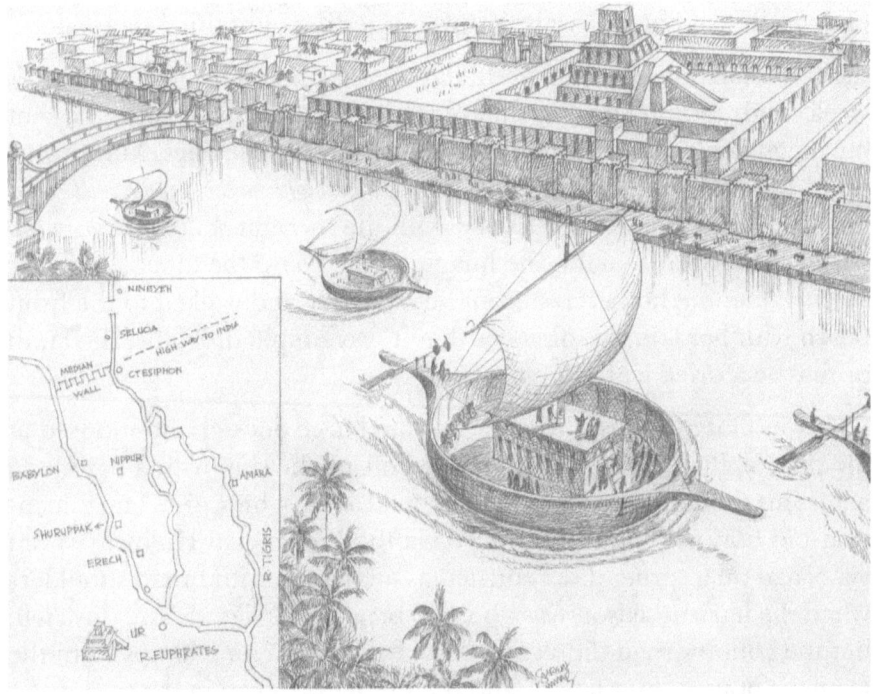

Joshua in Babylon

The spring flowers had bloomed and fallen, the wheat and barley kernels were hardening, and the land was baking under the blistering sun of Lyar; it was the beginning of a hot summer in Galilee. The tyrannical reign of Tiberius Caesar had tightened its strangle hold across the entire Eastern Roman Empire. Any sign of insurgency was ruthlessly quelled. The bodies of vocal and patriotic Jews left to hang on crosses writhed, and were devoured by vultures, as chilling reminders to others. Roman soldiers patrolled the big cities with the vigor of hound dogs, but in the villages traditional Judaic religious life, ceremonies, and traditions seemed to continue unaltered.

However, organized groups of men assembled secretly in houses and synagogues, lamenting the state and future of their Promised Land. Most agreed that they were destined to suffer oppression for a long period of time under the Roman yolk that seemed impossible to break. Others were invigorated by the stories of the Maccabeus. This group hoped for an armed uprising, and was prepared to spill blood. The elders evoked Amos and Micah and, as usual, hoped for the Messiah. "A deliverer has been promised, and he will come. Be patient. Be patient and wait. Yahweh is testing our faith," they said.

In a small house in Nazareth, days broke and nights fell, week after week; and, months on end uneventfully, the evening lamp was kept burning from dusk to dawn without fail. Each of the days, Mary woke up in the morning with the hope that, *this might be the day he will come*, and each night she retired to bed with the thought that *this is the night he will come.* Many a night, she imagined she heard the footsteps of her beloved coming home, rose from her slumber and walked to the front porch with her lamp to discover that it was simply the mule, the lamb or maybe a dried leaf falling.

It was close to sunset when a Roman barge docked and moored at the port of Ptolemies. A man stepped off of the ship with a bag slung across his shoulders and another bag held against his waist. The fifteen-year-old boy, who had left Galilee via the Phoenician Highway seven years ago on a spring day, returned as a tall man with broad shoulders when the harvest season was about to begin in Galilee. Soon, dusk fell, but the country road didn't feel desolate. The evening lamps from the farmer's houses shimmered, and the fire flies winked in the bushes.

The walk to Saab is about nine miles. *I can easily reach there by midnight,* Joshua said to himself. *I can relax a while on a wayside porter's rest and proceed to Sogane in the morning.*

With each step forward, he became more energized. The thought that he had been away seven long years, struck him like a burning charcoal. He imagined Mary, his parents, and maybe even a small young child rushing to welcome him home. All the stories he'd read in

Alexandria, all of the places he'd seen, and the lessons he had learned, he could barely wait to share them with Mary.

The next day by noon he had reached the town of Cana. The landscape and streets were familiar. Mary and Naomi had lived in Cana many years ago. He recognized their old home, now whitewashed and occupied by somebody else. The town hadn't changed. The old tavern, the little synagogue and the country road to Nazareth all remained the same. It was the day of the Sabbath; the roads were empty and the shops were all closed.

By sunset his feet were heavy. His leather bottle was empty, and he was consumed by hunger and fatigue. Soon, he saw the silhouette of a few men walking with a torch in front of him. He quickened his pace.

Nervous to see a lone traveler quickly approaching them in the dark, the group of four men turned around quickly and paused defensively with their arms fisted and heads pulled back.

"Stop," One shouted. "Who are you?"

"Brothers, be afraid not," said Joshua calmly. "I am a carpenter from Nazareth, going home late, though to catch pace with you, that's all."

Having realized that he was neither a Roman solider nor a spy, but simply a Nazarene, the group felt at ease. They revealed to him that they were all assembling in a house to discuss some important political subjects, and invited Joshua to join them.

There were some thirteen men sitting crouched in a room under one oil lamp. One of them, a very thin, frail, old man sitting on a bench with white beard and long black clocks, intensely gazed at the new arrivals. The rest of them were all young men ranging in age from about sixteen to thirty-five.

"This is Joshua from Nazareth," Cohen introduced Joshua to the group. The old man smiled. Others nodded.

There was bread and wine, which Joshua cherished more than the others. They all talked in hushed voices, at times barely above a whisper. They all carried daggers and swords. The Nazarene traveler soon realized that though the landscape remained the same, much had changed since he left, particularly after Tiberius had become the Roman Emperor.

From the meeting, Joshua soon realized that secret meetings such as this one were being held in several houses and synagogues all across Galilee, Samaria and Judea. There had even been a few attacks on the Roman administrative stations and barracks. But the hard truth was that for every Roman soldier that was attacked, at least ten Israelites had been crucified. The Sadducees in Jerusalem appeared very happy and felt safe under the Roman yolk. They all retained control of the temple, their money and privileges. Even the Pharisees and the Scribes were at ease with the Romans.

However, the rest of the people, the huge majority, did not feel this way.

"Why do we pay tax to Caesar? Yahweh promised this land to us," said one.

"When we don't have a morsel to bite, any tax to the temple is cruel," complained another.

"Tithe, even for the produces we buy from the market? That is double tithing."

"There should not be a tax when the crops fail," another said.

Although many voiced their concerns, there was no resolve as to the next step. Some young men strongly argued for an armed revolution. Whenever a voice in favor of violence was raised, the old man raised his hands.

"Remember, you are few men here and there," cautioned the man. "Caesar is mighty. His army is big. Be patient. There will be a savior for Israel. He will be born in Bethlehem. One day he will enter the temple with an army, riding on a colt. The Romans will all be destroyed. Be patient."

One of the men asked Joshua for an opinion.

"I am not in favor of any kind of violence," he said.

It was a group with lots of ideas, but without a direction or a leader. However, the air in the room was in favor of an armed revolution.

After about two hours, the group was dissolved, and Joshua resumed his journey back to Nazareth.

It was shortly after the cock crowed that a stranger, his head covered in a woolen shawl, approached the front yard of the little house in Nazareth sheltered under a large cypress tree. The fatigued man unloaded his bags on a work horse and sat hunched over, patiently waiting for the sun to rise. A lamp was still burning inside the house. He didn't have to wait long for a young lady, apparently fearless, to come out of the house. She carried a lamp, raised it high, and stood back for a while. She took a few steps forward, intently studying the figure. The man stood up. In a very calm yet loud voice, she stammered, "Joshua, is that you?" And then a bit louder, "Joshua, is that you?"

"Yes, Mary," he said, as he walked slowly towards her. She raised the oil lamp against his face, studying. A tall man with long wavy unkempt hair, assured and resolute countenance, looked a lot older than the twenty-two-year-old Joshua she was expecting, but it was him.

"Joshua," she shrieked, and ran to him. The lamp dropped from her hands to the ground and left them in the darkness. The two embraced for a long while. Mary was shivering and panting. There was sorrow and exhilaration in her voice.

"I knew, Joshua, I knew you'd come back. I thought it would happen a week ago. I waited for you every day, every minute, every second." Mary felt the salt and warmth on her lips when she kissed his eyes. She grasped, hugged and felt him all over. "Oh, my heavens. You've grown so tall. Your shoulders are so broad. Look at you. And this beard." She touched him again and again. "I have to make sure this is not a dream, that you are really here." She kissed him deeply and pressed him close to her. "I know this is real. I taste the honey on your tongue. Oh, Joshua, let's go in."

When she turned around in the dim light, they saw the silhouettes of two women hugging and sobbing. There was a reddish hue on the eastern horizon. Joshua entered the house, and hugged and kissed his mother and Naomi. There were many sobs, but very few words. Joshua searched the empty nook where his father used to rest and sat in that spot for a while in meditation while Mary brought warm water in a basin with a towel for a sponge bath for her returning husband, while his mother, Mary, made some soup.

Soon, the silver rays of the morning sun illuminated the house. Joshua was bathed and dressed in fresh clothing. Mary blew off the steamy vapor from the soup and spoon-fed him like a hungry baby. Mary sat by his side, afraid to blink, unwilling to lose sight of him even for a moment. She rubbed and massaged his tired feet.

When they woke up, it was already high noon. Mary and Joshua went to visit the burial place where Joseph was laid to rest. "Tell me, how did father die, how were his last days?," asked Joshua.

"He died about two years after you left," Mary said. "For the last month of his life, he thought everything and everyone that he came across was you, Joshua. Every person or object that came near him, any sound or movement, he thought it was you. He ate none, drank a little and slept a lot. At times he would get up saying, "Hah! You came. Finally you came. I knew you would come before I had to leave." And then he would fall back to sleep. During the last week of his life, the only sounds he uttered were, "Jo-sha-wa," and then, "Jo-Jo-Jo." That's all. At times he smiled and then pursed his lips until he took his last breath, smiling with his mouth a bit open. The undertakers closed his mouth by applying a binder over his head to keep it in place, before taking him to the burial place."

"Did he suffer any pain?"

"Certainly no," Mary said.

Mary and Naomi walked behind the young couple, watching them.

"I think it's time for me to visit my sister in Judea," said Mary. Judith nodded and said, "Yes, I think it's time for me to visit my mother in Magdella," said Naomi. They both left the next morning.

It took some time for the young couple's feelings to turn into words, but once the words started, they quickly formed a torrent. Mary had a million things to tell him, and he, so many stories to share with her, but for several days and nights they stayed together, lips locked with him inside her, staying as close together as they could.

"Before you left for Alexandria, I hoped that I would be with child," Mary said. "But a week after you left, my monthly signal returned and shattered my hopes. I wept for many days and weeks, but now my hope has been rekindled." Her face turned red. She breathed heavily.

Joshua flinched with pleasure in the warmth of her breath and the power of her grip. She held onto him tight and cried out, "Hold onto me, Joshua. Please don't let go. Let your love and life fill my heart and bless my womb. Rain your seeds into my womb. From your life, from my life, let a new life sprout from there.

Mary had even kept a journal of most of her thoughts and activities since he had left, and she imagined in her mind what he might have been doing, day after day.

"Mary, how did you know that I was coming home this week? Joshua asked. Yesterday when you called out for me in the dark, it appeared that you were already expecting me."

"Joshua, I have been seeing your images in my mind every day. For the past three days I could almost hear your footsteps. I was nearly certain that you were on your way home, but I couldn't clearly imagine the changes in you. Your voice has become so deep, and your features have changed, and . . . this beard . . ." She gently ran her fingers through his beard. "You have become a man – a very handsome man."

"What else did you see, Mary?"

"I saw you riding a boat on the great rivers. I saw you sitting somewhere in a school or a temple discussing, and at times arguing with the elders. I saw women coming after you. I saw women hugging and kissing you."

"Were you jealous?" asked Joshua mirthfully, stroking her hair and holding her face close to his chest.

"You just stood there without responding. I didn't see you being intimate with another woman, but, of course, if you did, who am I to say no? The traditions will permit you to do so."

"Mary," Joshua said. "I want you to know. I am a man created with all the inherent weakness of men. I had my share of transgressions. I beg your forgiveness."

"Joshua, I thank you for telling me that, but in my eyes you didn't do anything to offend me, but I want to listen more about all of the places you saw and the things you learned."

Joshua had created an abundance of notes over the last seven years, the majority from the Babylonian literature. While arranging and putting the papers in order, Joshua told Mary many small stories from his travels. Mary listened to them, snuggling close to him.

A few days later, Naomi and Mary returned home.

After a few weeks, Joshua and Mary made a visit to Carmel. Noah's house hadn't changed much, but the surroundings had; the walkway had no more flower beds, but was instead covered with wild grass. Joseph, now twenty, had married, and his wife was now with child. Amos had built a small house up hills in the woods, was married with one child, and continued to work with Joseph in Noah's family farm.

Joseph very quickly identified Joshua from a distance, as he walked up the steps to their house. He went out and greeted Joshua and Mary. A guttural noise coming from the left corner of the house demanded Joshua's attention to that nook, where there was lying a very old looking man, thin, covered in a gray blanket, his breathing labored, marked by the up and down movements of his bony chest, his glassy eyes vacantly gazing at the wicker ceiling, his mouth half open and dripping, was the one-time strong as a bull Noah, the farmer. Joshua and Mary sat cross-legged on either side of the paralyzed man, holding his hands.

"Uncle," Joshua said.

The man responded with a sudden twitching of his face; that pulled the right corner of his mouth towards his ear. Then he broke out into a paroxysm of labored crackling cough and started to choke. Presently, Amos, now having a beard with some gray on it, came in with a welcome smile, pleasantly surprised at seeing Joshua and Mary. While conversing with the guests, without delaying any moment, he approached Noah, lifted his waist up, tapped on the back of his chest and cleaned his mouth with a cotton towel and made Noah at ease.

Joseph gave the update. "On the first anniversary of my sister's ceremony, mother died. The Pharisees of Gabae refused the traditional burial of my mother in the Jewish cemetery."

"Refused? On what cause?" Joshua asked.

Joseph raised his palms spread upwards and said in a sad voice, "Who knows. They can say whatever they want. What they say is the law."

"Where was she buried finally?"

Pointing beyond the almond tree, Joseph said, "there, by the side of the wheat field. On that day amidst the burial, father complained of an intense headache, he was talking incoherently. He fell back on his head with a seizure. There was blood in his eyes. He has never been whole since then. It's a miracle that he is still alive – all because of the care of Amos."

"I didn't see Rubin or Judah here," Joshua said. "Where are they?"

Joseph's face turned cloudy. Amos answered, "The two boys became extremely upset and angry when their mother's burial was denied by the elders. They both threw stones at one of the Pharisee. His head broke, spilling blood.

"Catch them," he cried.

Both the boys fled the scene. We made lots of searches, but they were nowhere to be found."

After paying a visit to Judith's grave, Mary and Joshua left for Nazareth.

After a while, Joshua broke the silence, "A good many of our traditions are brutal."

Mary agreed with him with a sigh, put her head towards his shoulders, and wrapped him behind his back, tapping on him consolingly.

"But to make it even worse, the Pharisees and the Scribes interpret the laws in their own convenient ways. There must be an end to such barbaric statutes and traditions. Look at the plight of the family. What did they do wrong? What did they do to deserve this? They even sacrificed their daughter. There must be an end to it . . . must be."

"I agree," Mary said.

**** **** ****

In the first week of Elul, when the peak summer heat had settled down, and when the air was thin and crisp, and the afternoons were milder except for the occasional hot wind from the east, Joshua and Mary packed their bags and visited Japha. The old couple were overjoyed when they saw the mule carrying Joshua and Mary approaching their farm house through the narrow country road, as if a long-lost son was returning home safe with his young bride.

Zilinos, with his swollen knee, came limping out as the visitors reached their front yard. "Joshua," he cried out. "I knew you would be coming one of these days. You have grown big, but my old eyes would know you no matter how much you change. You are my unborn son." The old man almost pulled down Joshua from the mule hugging him.

"That's wonderful. Even this morning Zilinos was talking about you, Joshua,' said Cassandra. "You must be Mary. Joshua has told us everything about you. You look beautiful. Come in." Cassandra clasped Mary in the folds of her arms and kissed her on either side of her cheeks warmly, motherly. She took Mary in by her hand through the front porch of the house into the kitchen.

Zilinos had lost some weight, there were more lines of aging on his face, there was a gray hue on the blue of his eyes, and obviously a bend in the back, but still he appeared energetic and high spirited.

Situated on his lean-back wicker chair, Zilinos called out, "Cass, bring the one bottle that is kept in the alabaster jar. Bring out Mary. Let me see her, too."

Cassandra soon came out with a dark bottle of wine, and Mary with a platter full of snacks. They all sat around Zilinos.

Zilinos took the bottle of vine, turned it around within his palms and said, as if talking to the bottle, "Joshua, the year after you left for Alexandria, the vine harvest in Galilee was bountiful and of supreme quality. This is the last bottle out of the three hundred that I brewed that year. I saved it for you." So saying, he opened the one gallon bottle and poured it into the blue wine cups, raised his cup and cheered, "For your safe return, Joshua."

"Thank you, teacher. We are honored." Joshua bowed.

As color rose to his cheeks with the wine, his voice turned louder and dialogues more animated, "Now, tell me everything about your tour from the first day onwards," Zilinos said. "And please, do not plan to go back for a few days."

Joshua narrated his travel to his teacher, up till it was time for the evening lamp.

In the kitchen, Cassandra was teaching Mary how to cook the special baked lamb as she had prepared some long time ago. They both made a dinner with lamb, freshly baked bread, cheese and a vegetable soup.

After a relaxing dinner, they sat out under the moonlit sycamore tree in the front yard, as the hot eastern winds were intense, and they were sweating heavy with the high humidity.

"I plan to go to Babylon," Joshua said.

"I've long desired to go Babylon. I know there is not much left there anymore. I'm not as young as I used to be. Still, I would love to go with you. I believe I have enough life and energy left for at least one last trip. What do you think, dear?" He turned to Cassandra with a grin, needing a *yes* answer.

"It would be a dream come true to travel with these children of ours to go to Babylon," she said exuberantly as her eyes danced with joy. "But I want to tell you this, Joshua: Zilinos is weaker than you imagine. He forgets things quickly, but past memories are very good. He has to take a nap in the afternoon."

"Don't you worry, Cass, I would be fine; we will go," reassured the old man. "Joshua, you are fresh from Alexandria; you have to teach me all about Babylon. I am very forgettable these days," Zilinos said. "For a good many of the original Babylonian thinking and inventions, they are not properly credited for. For example, the calendar we use now – the months, the weeks, hours, minutes and seconds, and the eclipses – they are all Babylonian inventions. My people, the Greeks, took credit for most of that. In any case, this is an exciting proposition, and I am ready, Joshua – I am." The old man stood up and walked around in quick paces.

The next morning, with the plan to travel to Babylon, the young couple returned to Nazareth and started preparations. Mary was ebullient when they decided that she would travel with Joshua and Zilinos to Babylon.

A couple of weeks earlier, Mary had complained to her mother of a nipping pain in her right lower belly. Joshua's mother Mary and Naomi were strongly opposed to this plan of Mary traveling to Babylon. But young Mary was determined to go; she cherished the thought of spending time with Joshua and hearing stories from his lips. She was not willing to be separated from her husband for another indefinite period of time so shortly after his return.

In the beginning of autumn in Galilee, as the grape harvest was in full swing, the young couple started off to Japha on their mule Jaaba, now a beast large enough to carry two or three riders, which had been only a cub when Joshua had left for Alexandria. In Japha, Zilinos and Cassandra were packed and ready for the long journey.

"It's a very long ride. I don't want to separate you young couple; you two ride on Jaaba. Drink plenty of water; tell lots of stories; we will take sufficient brakes on the way. Let's go," said the grand old teacher enthusiastically. On two fully loaded mules, the four of them started off for Damascus. They journeyed to Damascus by way of Tiberius and Capernaum, past the plains and vineyards of Galilee and through the coastal villages where they would watch the fisherman casting their nets from their little boats into the Sea of Galilee.

Mary insisted that Joshua sit behind her on the mule, holding onto her and telling stories in her ears.

"Joshua, first tell me a short story, then tell me a long story that will last all the way to Damascus," Mary said. Joshua told her the stories from Amara, about the family of Sethos and their prayers to the sun, the making of the papyri, and the changes in the nature before the inundations, and finally the death of the little girl from the snake bite.

"Joshua, this is a sad story. I can see the whole thing in my mind the way you tell it. Now, I want to hear a very long story where little girls don't die," she insisted.

They could hear Zilinos singing a Greek harvest song loudly, flailing his hands and making signs in the air.

"Well, Mary, I will tell you a very long story. Listen carefully. Once upon a time," he started. "Some three thousand years ago in Sumer, there lived a king in the land of Erech. His name was Gilgamesh. He was two-thirds god and one-third man. He was a mighty hero and a ruthless taskmaster. He imposed free labor from his people to build all the roads, canals, palaces and city walls. The people, in desperation, cried out to god Anu, for deliverance, who in turn ordered the god Arena to create a deliverer. Arena fashioned a giant man of clay, breathed life into him and created a deliverer, Enkidu."

"Good. Did Arena breathe life into Enkidu like . . . like, Yahweh did to Adam?" She asked, pinching on his thighs.

"Yes, Mary. Enkidu was a huge man covered with thick hair and possessed invincible powers, and he ruled over all creatures of the forest. He was a friend and protector of all wild beasts. He sucked the breasts of cattle; ate herbs, fruits and roots; and lived as one with the wild animals. About this time a mighty hunter appeared in the forest. He dug pits; set up traps, nets, and ropes; and made all the necessary waggishness to capture his prey. Though a great many animals fell into his trap, to his dismay they all escaped. Then, in a secret place, the hunter spotted Enkidu – the deliverer – and realized that he had released all of the animals that had fallen into the hunter's pit. The hunter, terrified by Enkidu's size and showing, ran to King Gilgamesh for help. Gilgamesh made a plan to ensnare Enkidu. He employed a gorgeous harlot with great sexual skills to seduce him. The harlot waited near a stream where the animals came to drink and rest. The next day, Enkidu came to the stream with the other animals. The harlot cast off her clothes and enticed Enkidu into intercourse with her right away. Their sexual union lasted nonstop for six days and seven nights."

"Really, Joshua," Mary started screaming, "Six days and seven nights? Hau!"

"Yes Mary, listen. Yes, six days and seven nights, until her vagina sucked the whole juice out of his phallus like cubs feeding on its mother's bosom. On the seventh day, Enkidu woke up, dry, frail, shivering and shamed, and covered his loin with leaves in disgrace."

"It's like Adam, who became shameful after eating the apple, right?"

"Right."

"What did the harlot do?" asked Mary.

"The harlot followed him with great adoration and convinced him to go with her to Erech, where King Gilgamesh lived. The harlot brought Enkidu to the shepherd's village and fed him bread and beer. This restored most of his lost power and made him more human. He took up a bow and arrow, and began hunting wild animals, protecting the shepherd's flocks."

"So, the harlot changed the wild man into a normal man, right Joshua?" said Mary, proudly posing as if she also knew a thing or two.

"Mary, you are a good listener. Let me continue. At this time, Gilgamesh offered a great banquet for the city dwellers, and, in return, he expected the customary gifts from all newcomers to the city – their wives for the night. That night, when the king came to claim his privileges at Enkidu's hut, he resisted. In the great duel that followed, Enkidu was the victor, but in fact, the two powers shook hands and they became friends and allies. Do you like the story so far, Mary?"

"I love it, but I was thinking, how could they do it for six long . . ."

"That's only a story, my dear," said Joshua. "Anyways, Gilgamesh planned to construct a mighty mansion, for which he needed cedar woods from the forest. He invited Enkidu to accompany him, but Enkidu had known that the gods had appointed Khumbaba, a fearsome ogre, to guard the cedar forests. Khumbaba was known to roar like a lion, breathe out fire, and feed on the flesh of men, and Enkidu tried to dissuade Gilgamesh from the trip, but Gilgamesh ignored his warnings and proceeded to the forest.

"The blue bucolic Cedars Mountains were seen in the distance. But, in order to reach them, they had to circumvent six arduous barriers, including earthquakes, volcanoes and finally the dangerous fort of Khumbaba. But the Sun God, whom Gilgamesh worshipped, came to his defense and sent mighty storms in Khumbaba's direction, effectively paralyzing him. Gilgamesh cut off his head, collected all the cedars he wanted, and triumphantly returned to Erech."

"So, Gilgamesh was successful . . ."

"So far, yes. Gilgamesh returned to his palace jubilantly. He washed himself clean in the river Euphrates, dressed in splendid attire with ornaments of gold, jewels, pearls, and lapis lazuli, and glowed like a star. The vision of Gilgamesh ignited a flame of passion in Ishtar, the goddess of love and fertility. She became sexually aroused, and her womb cried out for him and her vagina wept, but Gilgamesh resisted the advances. He cited the fate of the ever-so-many of her previous lovers who had been tortured and mutilated to death after violent sex with her, and told her that his fortune would not be any different."

"So, this goddess Ishtar would torture and kill, after making love to them?"

"Yes, that's the way it is with some gods."

Joshua paused for a while as they reached a roadside village well. After a brief rest and refreshment, they continued the ride to Japha with the story of Gilgamesh.

"Mary, it's probably easier for you to understand the depth of the passion and the fire of the anger of a sexually deprived woman, but when that woman is also a goddess, the anger assumes dimensions beyond the realm of human description."

Mary didn't say a word in reply. Joshua resumed the story. "Ishtar ascended to the heavens weeping, and complained to her mother, the goddess Anu, and her father, Antu, about Gilgamesh's rejection of their daughter. Angered by the news and infuriated by the insolence of Gilgamesh, Antu decided to destroy Gilgamesh. He created an indomitable bull and sent it to Erech. The raging bull entered Erech, broke open the city walls and destroyed several hundred men, houses and properties. However, with the help of the Sun God, Enkidu and Gilgamesh were able to overpower the bull and slay the beast. The victory processions that followed were witnessed by everybody in Erech. A jubilant Gilgamesh, drinking beer from the enormous bull's horn, cried out, "Who is the most illustrious among men?"

The crowd screamed, "Gilgamesh! Gilgamesh!"

"Who is the most glorious among heroes?"

"Enkidu! Enkidu!" the crowd screamed.

"Joshua, you are a great storyteller; I love this story, but did Gilgamesh give sacrifice to the sun god for his blessings?" Mary asked.

"No." said Joshua. "In his arrogance and insolence, he forgot God, like Nebuchadnezzar of Babylon."

"After the great celebrations, Gilgamesh had a disturbing dream, in which he saw the gods in heaven, angered by his insolence, planning to destroy him. The dream slowly came into effect. Soon thereafter, Enkidu started wasting, fell sick and died. Gilgamesh was grieved and frightened by Enkidu's death. The feeling of his own death suffocated him like a rope being tightened around his neck. He walked the streets of Erech in tattered clothes, lamenting about Enkidu, the great deeds they had accomplished together and the friendship they cherished. He suffered nightmares of his death and made a plan to escape from it somehow. The rest of the story is Gilgamesh's pursuit of immortality."

On the fourth day evening, they reached the gate of the ancient city of Damascus. "Joshua, you tell me the rest of the story another time."

"Yes, dear," Joshua said.

In Damascus, about a mile east from the Damascus Gate, everybody knew the mansion of Abhi Faroosh. When Abhi realized who his visitors were, he was nothing but exuberant. He grabbed Joshua, embraced him, and kissed him on both of his cheeks. "I am honored," he exclaimed. "Come on, everybody," he shouted flailing his arms. Some fifteen servants and aides assembled on the courtyard instantaneously.

"These are my honored guests," he said. "Wash their feet. Bring them unguents. Bring them wine. Ha . . . I will celebrate today. Thank you, thank you, Joshua, for visiting me." He continued speaking as the guests were seated. Joshua introduced the members of his party one by one. Abhi most graciously greeted them by deeply bowing his head.

"Let me introduce my wife." He looked in the direction of the inner kitchen and bellowed, "Lulu." From there emerged Layeela, the girl who had been braiding Abhi's beard at the brothel in Caesarea eight years earlier. Her unmistakable blue eyes beamed at Joshua. Her face round like the moon, breasts and buttocks swelled, and her bulging belly showed that she was pregnant again. Three small children stood by her side holding on to her tunic. She appeared more gentle, dignified and grown up than Joshua had recalled.

"Do you remember her, Joshua?" Abhi asked gaily.

Layeela smiled innocently.

"Of course, Layeela." Joshua rose.

"Certainly, everybody will remember her. Once you have seen her, you will remember her forever," Abhi said.

"Abhi, you have a beautiful family," said Joshua. "When did you go to Alexandria last?"

"I am retired from my business for six years now. My only job now is making children and raising them properly." Looking at Zilinos, he continued, "Zilinos, throughout my travels I have had many men travel with me to Alexandria and other places, but I have never seen a man as smart and likeable as Joshua. I'm sure he will do amazing things in his life." And looking at Mary, he said, "You are a very lucky girl, lucky indeed." Mary smiled and looked down to the marble floor. Cassandra and Zilinos enjoyed the moment, smiling at each other.

After the dinner, Joshua and Mary strolled through the courtyard, where Abhi's camels were tethered to the palm trees. The servants were feeding and cleaning them when Joshua recognized Jumba, the double-humped animal on whom he had ridden all the way to Memphis. Jumba seemed to recognize Joshua. The camel stomped the ground a few times and swayed his head, showing his teeth, and brayed a few more times. As Joshua gently caressed Jumba's nose, the animal settled with gentle rocking of his head.

"See, Jumba realized it was Joshua," guffawed Abhi. "These animals have long memories and deep affection. Jumba also has augury senses and can see and hear things that we cannot. One day on my way from Antioch to Quedesh . . ." Abhi began one of his stories in great detail of how Jumba had saved his life by signaling a raging lion in hiding, about to attack.

Abhi had some definite opinions about Joshua's trip to Babylon. "It is nothing but foolish that you have decided to travel all the way to Babylonia with these mules," he said emphatically. "They are not travel-worthy for the kinds of conditions you will encounter on the way.

You need good-breed camels like Jumba." In an incredible gesture of generosity, he offered to lend two of his camels, including Jumba, to Joshua at no charge. With the female travelers in mind, Abhi arranged to have two camels with canopied, saddle-bucket seats. The arched seat conformed to the animal's torso in between the two humps, with the bucket seats on either side, making it well balanced and safe.

"I will not advise you to travel to Babylonia alone with two animals; it is too dangerous," Abhi told them. "You must also be accompanied by a caravan."

"You proceed from here to Palmyra and then to Dura-Europas as part of a caravan. The caravans these days do not go south from Dura-Europas anymore. They go east to Selucia, Ctesiphon and Sussa, all the way to China and India. There is a big Jewish community in Dura-Europas with a synagogue, and all. Most of them are businessmen. You must stay there a couple of days and rest. From there you can travel south all the way to the Great Seas by boat, but I won't advise you to do that. You must proceed to Ctesiphon and make arrangements to go south with a tour group."

Layeela had prepared packages filled with cakes, biscuits, dried fruits, nuts, and several skins of wine and water for the travelers. Fed and prepared, the four of them set off for Babylon, accompanying an east-going caravan.

It was a long and arduous journey. The heat of the sun at high noon was intense enough to bake bread on the sand. The air shimmered with the heat, and from a distance it looked like ripples of waves in an ocean. The camels plodded the sand with long swinging strides. As a routine, they did not ride at high noon or when the hot winds are unbearable. There were a few inns by the oases for comforts and refreshments.

It was the sixth day of their travel, and the air was filled with blinding sand storms, that they had to break the journey for two days. They had a lot of conversations to catch up, and Mary had to hear the rest of the Babylonian flood story of Gilgamesh.

After the breakfast, as they sat around chatting and trying to kill the boredom of this unexpected break in the journey, Mary was seen constantly poking Joshua and whispering in his ear, "Tell the story, tell the story."

Cassandra came to the defense of Mary and requested that Joshua tell the story, or whatever she was asking for.

"What is the story she is asking for," intervened Zilinos.

"The story of immortality . . . about, um . . ." said Mary trying to remember the name of the character.

"What's it, Joshua – is it the Gilgamesh story?" Zilinos asked.

"Yes, I told her a bit about it already."

"Well, it's a great story – in fact, the mother of all stories. Most of your writings come from that story, so go on, Joshua, I read the story many years ago . . . I don't remember much, please." insisted Zilinos.

"So, I was telling about Gilgamesh," Joshua said. "After the death of Enkidu, Gilgamesh, thinking of escaping death, remembered that his great ancestor, Uta-Napishtim, had gained immortality during the great flood of Babylon several centuries ago."

"The great flood," Mary talked to herself out loud. "Joshua, is it like the great flood in our books with Noah, and all?"

"Yes, Mary," said Joshua.

"Where Uta-Napishtim lived, Gilgamesh didn't know, yet he was determined to find him and coax the secret from him. Based on his intuition, first he set out westward to Mount Mashu, where the sun god sets to rest at night. He had to overcome several obstacles. First he crossed the bottomless abysses of death, then walked the land of eternal darkness, then had to climb the mountains that erupted continuously. Finally, he approached Mount Mashu, only to find that the mountain was protected by the most fierce scorpion men. At the very sight of these pugnacious men, the king fainted. But the psychic scorpion men soon discovered that the flesh of Gilgamesh was two-thirds God and one-third man. They took pity on him, revived him by blowing air into his nostrils, and took him to their palace for questioning. Gilgamesh told them, "I have come to find Uta-Napishtim.""

"What!" the scorpion men bellowed, ridiculing. They warned him: "It's impossible for any man to continue the journey safely. The passage is perilous, dark and with bottomless abysses. You are sure to die. You must go back immediately." But Gilgamesh would not be deterred and continued his journey. He jumped over the abysses of death, flew over the blazing mountains, and finally reached a garden with bright lights, flowers and the tree of gods with luscious fruit dripping nectar. The place where he stood was the fortress of the goddess Siduri, and he went to her palace to see her. Siduri initially refused to see him, as he appeared downtrodden, dirty, and weird, clad in animal skin with a terrible stench," Joshua paused.

Subsequently, Siduri gave an interview to Gilgamesh, and they began an argumentative dialogue for a very long day pertaining to life, death, and life after death.

"Siduri advised Gilgamesh that his quest for immortality was a vain pursuit, that death is decreed for a man at the time of his birth, and, therefore, he should enjoy all the mortal pleasures as long as life lasted, but not seek to extend it indefinitely."

Zilinos had a question: "What do you make out of that, Joshua? Definitely the Babylonians believed in life after death, I thought."

"Of course, Zilinos," Joshua said. "Siduri is only a god of mortal pleasures."

"In spite of her advice, Gilgamesh persisted with his quest and continued his journey. He overcame every obstacle and finally reached the threshold of the waters of death. He found Ur-Shabani, the boat man, and started riding the waves to the castle of Uta-Napishtim. Uta-Napishtim, who was watching from the other shore, noticed the stranger approaching. He came down to meet Gilgamesh."

There followed a great dialogue between Uta-Napishtim and Gilgamesh, which Joshua again narrated as if it were a poem.

"Gilgamesh, you must abandon this endeavor. I warn you, on this earth, there is nothing eternal. Mammitum, who holds the tablet for destinies, has determined that birth is the beginning of death. Nobody knows the hour of his death. There is no way to escape it. Immortality is a burden even for gods and must be a curse for humans. Gilgamesh did not answer.

"Seeing that he would not be deterred, Uta-Napishtim said, 'I will test your resolve to live forever. Stay awake for six days and seven nights. By that time I would gather all the Gods together to make an appeal.' Gilgamesh agreed."

"Joshua, I know that is a very nice trick, that Uta-Napishtim did. Nobody can stay awake that long. Can you?" Mary asked.

"I think not," Joshua said. "Gilgamesh was so fatigued that he was overcome by sleep the same night. He slept for the next six days and six nights. He woke up vexed with his failure and more obsessed with the thought of death. Uta-Napishtim's wife took pity on the king and counseled her husband to help him. He did. Gilgamesh was advised that there was a precious plant in the abyss of the Sea of Death, and that if he could find the plant and eat of its fruit, he would become immortal."

"Heee . . . this is the story like Adam and Eve. I know it," Mary said.

Joshua nodded. "Gilgamesh tied heavy stones to his feet and sank to the depths of the waters and resurfaced, holding *Shibu issahir amehi,* the plant of eternal life. Rather than eat immediately of the plant, Gilgamesh decided to bring his prized plant back to Erech and show it off to his people before he ate his way to eternal youthfulness. As he continued on his way home, he came to a clear lake where the water was pleasantly cold and smelled like perfume of roses. Gilgamesh dove into the water to bathe. A monstrous sea serpent, who had been trailing the plant through its scent, swam to the boat, grabbed the plant, and swallowed it whole. Gilgamesh saw what happened but was not fast enough to stop it. He sat down on the shore weeping, and cursed and lamented over the waste of his toil all the way to Erech."

"God punished him for his pride, Joshua," said Mary.

"Yes, for his arrogance and vain," Joshua said.

"Great story. Tell me then, what happened next?' Mary said.

"Now that he had lost his chance at immortality, Gilgamesh was convinced that he would go to the underworld. He wanted to meet his old friend Enkidu's ghost. The moon god, hearing his fervent prayers, opened a hole in the earth, through which the spirit of Enkidu rose like a wind. The two friends embraced, and at Gilgamesh's urging, Enkidu began to tell him stories of the underworld. He told him of how the great kings that once ruled Babylonia, Nimrod, Erech and Akkad, were now reduced to ugly beasts, crouching sadly in the pitch dark, covered with feathers and eating nothing but mud. Gilgamesh was petrified by the picture and was near to fainting in fear of death. Enkidu insisted that Gilgamesh must visit the underworld, to see it, to believe it. Like a servitor, Enkidu guided Gilgamesh to the underworld. They had traveled deep into the underworld when the opening in the ground gradually began to close. The darkness of the underworld fell upon them. Gilgamesh soon started growing feathers. He ate mud and turned into one of those beasts"

"Hau! That is some story," Mary said.

"Yes, Mary. The Babylonians answer to the pursuit of immortality."

The next morning the sand storms had settled, and they continued to Dura-Europas

**** **** ****

At the threshold of the desert, Dura-Europas had palm trees by the roadside, smoke in the sky, voices in the air and people moving – it was a bustling city. It was the main hub on the trading route from India to Alexandria. The streets in the commercial district where merchants – mostly Jews – bought and sold carpets, textiles and oriental spices were narrow enough that the traders could shake hands from across the alleys. The voices of the crowd sounded Persian, Babylonian, Hebrew, Greek and Chinese.

Zilinos' group rented two rooms at the Jericho Inns near the Jewish quarter. The man at the reception counter appeared to be Jewish, wearing the traditional skullcap, beard and payas. When Joshua wrote down the addresses of the guests from Nazareth and Japha, the receptionist looked askance at both guests, offering not even a smile of courtesy.

This strange behavior bothered Joshua for a while. *Did he not recognize me as a Jew?* Joshua wondered. *Or, has the six hundred years of separation from the land of Israel transformed their behavior to not trusting any stranger?* The owner collected four shekels for the two rooms and one shekel for attending to the camel for one night. He briefly showed them the rooms, and left.

Zilinos and Cassandra occupied the ground-level room. Mary and Joshua went to the terrace. They were all tired and famished. They found a Parthian restaurant in the alleys at the east end of the city.

The restaurant with a large dining hall after the anteroom, was a space where guests were all seated on a mattress on the floor. At the center of the dining hall was housed a large wide-mouthed oven that was buried in the ground. Charcoal burned in the oven like a smelting pot, emitting a red glow, plenty of heat and very little smoke. Guests who had not seen the Parthian way of baking the bread, stood around watching. They spread out the dough and slapped it on the inner side of the oven with a long wooden spatula. They called the bread nan, and it was best when served hot, fresh from the oven.

The words of Abhi echoed in Joshua's mind. "One can make bread from wheat a thousand different ways, but there is nothing to match the nan and paratha."

The steaming goat-meat dinner with nan tasted spicy hot in the mouth and required several gulps of wine to wash it down: *Food so different from everything else that I have eaten so far,* Joshua thought.

"Yes, I like these flavors: the oriental peppers, the ginger and the garlic," Zilinos said. "This taste makes drinking wine even more pleasant." He emptied chalices of wine, one after the other.

Towards the end of the dinner, the host brought two cups of cloudy milk he called "hashish." Zilinos' face lit up. He grabbed one cup and drank all of it, saying, "Joshua, this is what the gods drink up in heaven, wherever they are. This is the same as bang or marijuana, whatever it is called; it's one and the same. You are young; you can handle a couple of drinks. It will be exuberant tonight. Come on, drink it and go to bed, and you will have a most memorable night with your lovely bride," Zilinos said and winked. "But don't make too much noise."

Mary blushed a bit. Joshua declined the drink and told of his experience with the poppy gum in Rome.

"There is something else that goes with it," remembered Zilinos, "maybe it's not for you young people, but for folks like me – old men . . . Yohimbine."

"I am going to celebrate today." Zilinos finished the two cups of cloudy milk, and Cassandra had her share too. Zilinos purchased two sachets of the Yohimbine powder, mixed it with the ganja and drank it all in one gulp. The young couple retired to the terrace as the older couple had just begun to revel in their return to youth.

The terrace was pleasantly warm. The starry skies of Babylon looked different; the stars hung low and shimmered brighter. Joshua and Mary lay down for a while, staring up at the sky. Mary crossed her legs over his waist and snuggled. Joshua broke the silence.

"Mary, look at the stars."

"I am."

"What do you see?"

"The stars."

"What do you think?"

Mary said, "I think they are all angels. I think they are jealous, keenly watching us, winking their twinkling eyes."

"Very good, dear. I will tell you something. The ancient Babylonians saw something interesting amidst those stars. They connected the dots in the sky and saw some constellations shaped like a ram, a bull, a crab, and likewise; twelve of them in all. They described the eclipses."

"Joshua," interjected Mary, "I don't understand what you are saying. What is this thing called eclipse?"

"Yes, Mary. There are two types of eclipses. When the moon is covered by the shadow of earth – that is a lunar eclipse – and the solar eclipse is when the moon covers the sun, when we look from the earth."

Mary rolled over to Joshua, as her face blocked his view of the stars and the moon in the sky, and pulled her hair over, covering their heads like a medusa. "Tell me what eclipse is this. Is it the stellar eclipse or the Mary eclipse," she asked.

"Now, I have heard all about the stars in the sky, but there are none as sparkling as these two." She rubbed her warm lips on his closed eyes. He couldn't say a word as his tongue was already locked. She cradled his head in the cup of her arms. They didn't make much of a noise on the terrace. But even if they had, nobody would have heard it, because Cassandra was screaming, crazy like there was no end to it amidst the thumping noises.

The next morning the group from Israel took a twenty-five-mile canal ride, and crossed over from the city of Nephridia on the Euphrates to Selucia, the new city built by Alexander's followers on the banks of the Tigris, a bustling hub on the eastern trade route. The several government buildings on the banks were impressive, all made in Greek style, with grand edifices, gymnasium, libraries and temples.

The library of Selucia, a tourist attraction, contained copies of the old Babylonian writings translated into Greek for references, and some copies in vellum available for purchase. For Joshua, the library was like a dream come true, although he had taken many notes on the Babylonian writings when he was studying at the library of Alexandria.

While Zilinos and Joshua spent most of the time in the library, Mary and Cassandra leisurely strolled the gardens and shopping centers, enjoying the grandeur of the new Alexandrian city.

But ten miles south of Selucia, the city of Ctesiphon was the present capital of the Parthian empire. The new capital, where people wore tall Parthian hats, was the showpiece of the new empire, where the grand edifices were taking shapes with new architectural styles dotted with tall minarets and large ornate paisley-shaped doors and windows.

As Abhi had said, tourism to the ancient cities of Babylonia was a thriving business in Ctesiphon, and the tour companies sought to attract customers for educational tours all the time. With ten other tourists, the group from Galilee started the trip with their tour guide, who answered to the name Sam – Samsulina.

Sam looked as if he had just walked out into life from one of those Babylonian freezes, a muscular man with thick dark hair, eyebrows that met in the middle, curly beard and a pleasing countenance. He was both a historian and an astrologist, and had taught astronomy in the Greek schools in Selucia.

After helping all the sailors onboard, Sam addressed them very politely: "Ladies and gentleman, my name is Samsulina. You may call me Sam. First, let me tell you something about the boat on which you are now sitting. We run our tours using a modified version of an age-old Mesopotamian leather bucket boat . . . this boat, due to its unusual construction, is much stronger and resilient than the Egyptian or Roman wooden boats, believe it or not."

The boat was uniquely shaped like a round shield, about forty feet in diameter and ten feet deep. The circular hull and the ribs of the boat were made out of very strong Armenian willow trunks bent and shaped like a wide-mouthed basket. The outside was covered with thick camel hide that had been stretched tightly and stitched to make it watertight. The inside of the boat contained a platform, carpeted walls and cushioned seats with holding rails. There was also a small kitchen for preparing simple meals.

"We have four men with us, who will function as our oarsmen and cooks, and assist you in your whatever requirements." He spoke in an odd mixture of Aramaic and Greek, like so many others in the region. The boat started sailing south, and Sam started his commentaries.

"A couple of years back, I had a tourist from India – a learned sage. He told me that the ancient Sumerians, we call them the Blackheads, came from northern India. It may be true, or may not be. If you have a point to raise or correct me on an issue, please feel free to do so. I want to make this a pleasant experience for you. After all, for the next thirty days we will live, tour, and enjoy things together. Make sure at night that you cover yourself well, as we have many mosquitoes here. We'll have a stopover in each city for five or six hours for you to stretch your legs and visit some interesting spots. Downstream, the ride will be fast. In four days we will reach Kurnath, cross over to the great Euphrates and ride up north, visiting the cities of Tall-Al-Lahm, Ur, Erech, Shuruppak, Kissura, Marad, Borsippa, Babylon, Kish and Sippar. After that we will cross over to Ctesiphon, thereby completing the round trip. We will rest for one day in Ur and two days in Babylon".

The group introduced themselves to their fellow travelers. There were four tourists from Peshawar, two from Sussa, two from Alexandria, and four from Athens.

"I already know that some of you are very learned men, historians, so to speak," Sam began. "We have a young man from Galilee here, Joshua. He asked me a few questions earlier, comparing the Torah and our history and writings. Certainly there are some close similarities; I will tell the Babylonian stories as they are written; you make the comparisons and interpretations."

Sam continued, "As you may know, Emperor Alexander chose Babylon as the capital of his Asian empire. After his death, the empire was divided amongst his generals, and Babylon was given to the Selucas, as per Alexander's will. The beautiful city of Selucia, which looks like a miniature version of Athens, was the capital of the Hellenistic Kingdom. For the last one hundred and fifty years, Babylonia has been a Parthian territory under the Arsacid dynasty. Long live our King of Kings, Artabaenas II, the most benevolent of all. Yesterday, you saw the great city of Ctesiphon, our capital city of the empire, and how harmoniously we live together here with the Greeks, Hebrews, Sumerians, Chinese and all kinds of foreigners. Just like Khammurabi's time, a maid can walk the city alone in the middle of the night without fear of harm."

The waters of the Tigris gently flowed without any rapids, fast currents or swirls. Overhead, the sun rose, beating on the roofless boat.

"To tell you the entire story of Babylonia, would take years, so I will share only some of the most important stories and facts with you," Sam said. "I'll begin with a bit of history, and then you can ask questions about things that interest you. Our written history begins over three thousand five hundred years ago, maybe over five hundred years before the Egyptians started writing. But the Egyptians had a great advantage over us: They had an abundance of limestone and granite, with which they built their everlasting temples and etched their stories and histories that would last forever. Even the writings on the papyrus were well preserved in the dry heat on the desert, as were the paintings and writings in stone. The inundations were a big blessing for the Egyptians, but for us, the floods were devastating, and often a curse. We constructed our great buildings with baked clay, and wrote our stories on clay, as well. The yearly floods washed away a good deal of our structures, as well as our written history. For example, Khammurabi had seven Stella inscribed with his codes of law, but

301

they are all gone except for one that was saved in the library at Selucia. To my knowledge, there is another one in the city of Susa."

"Do you believe that the Egyptians borrowed the art of writing from you, the Babylonians, at a later stage, Sam," Zilinos asked.

"I don't believe so; these are two different systems of writing. We had invented a certain primitive manner of writing about four thousand years ago, but we do have written documents with a clean structure and grammar form about three thousand years back, well preserved in our libraries in Ashurbanipal at Nippur."

Georgia, a lady from Athens who looked like the statue of Athena, asked the question: "Sam, the Egyptians strongly claim that they invented the calendar first. Do you, or can you, attest to their claim."

Sam replied with a smile: "The Egyptians had a predictable annual event, the inundations. They certainly should have described an annual calendar. But the ancient Babylonians read the skies, observed the stars, and identified the constellation of stars. The Greeks called them zodiacs. We made the first calendar in the world based on the movements of the celestial planets, probably five hundred years before the Egyptian calendar, with 365 days in a year, named the twelve months, divided the days into twenty-four hours, sixty minutes and sixty seconds. The whole world now follows it with the modifications made by Julius Caesar. We had water clocks and sun clocks three thousand years back. Our mathematical system of geometry and calculus continues unchanged as of today, as well as addition, subtraction, division and fractions, including a decimal system that is currently in use."

"Is it true that the Babylonians learned the art of healing from the Indians?" asked a middle-aged man, Husani, from Arachosia.

"What made you say that, sire," Sam asked.

"In my city, Alexandria, in Arachosia, the healers practice Ayurvedic medicine. That is the only medicine we know. Everybody says that the Indians are the pioneers in the art of healing."

"Babylon and India had trade relations for a very long time," Sam said. "There must have been some exchange of ideas in medicine, and in many other areas, between the two countries. They do have a system of medicine, of course, but we have written documents that we had a system of medicine, physicians and places where patients were kept to heal, away from home, for over three thousand years. Neither the Egyptians nor the Indians can claim that, to the best of my information."

" . . . We studied the human body, diagnosed illnesses, and prescribed medicines. Our surgeons conducted complex and delicate surgery on the eyes with very fine copper blades. We used a wide array of substances in the art of healing: asafetida and belladonna for the stomach; cannabis and poppy for sedation; cassia, castor oil and cinnamon for bloating; and juniper and licorice for a burning stomach. In all, the Babylonian pharmacopeia had more than two hundred vegetable substances and twenty minerals."

An Egyptian tourist raised his hand. "In the Egyptian writings, Osiris came to Babylonia to civilize the people, to teach them how to cultivate the land and tame animals, so . . ."

"My friend, I read your question," Sam said. "You may be confusing mythology and history. If a man called Osiris came here around the time you said, he probably had learned a thing or two from the Babylonians and went back to teach the Egyptians. It's true that the Babylonians imported gold from Nubia, silver from the Taurus Mountains, rock salt from Syria, copper from Cyprus, and elephants, peacocks and sandal wood from India. But surely so, the Babylonians never imported any ideas from anywhere else. Even our stories of creation, floods, religion, and prayers have all been generously copied by many other civilizations and claimed to be their original inventions."

Zilinos whispered in Joshua's ears, "See, he did not like that question. The Blackheads are very smart people, but a bit hot tempered. But he indeed knows what he is talking about, that's sure."

"I had asked him a few questions for clarification, earlier on," Joshua whispered. "But he said that I knew too much, and that I didn't need any further clarifications. What do you suggest?"

"Wait. We came all the way from Galilee; we will ask him all the questions we need to; he will answer; let the time come."

Sam explained many inventions that originated in Babylon, quite impressively, as if he were reciting a story that he had told many times before.

In the meantime, Mary had not been feeling well for the last two days. She felt nauseated and was belching. She couldn't tolerate any food, but had a craving for an apple. This was a problem, as it was not the season for apples. Joshua held her close to his chest, and she enjoyed the warmth of his palms as he gently massaged her belly against the womb.

On the sixth day, the boat navigated west, upstream to the great Euphrates, and two days later they reached the old city of Ur – one of the main focuses of Joshua's visit to Babylon.

The ancient ziggurat was visible from a distance as a large mount covered with overgrowth of weeds and bushes. The three levels of the ziggurat, with a staircase on the northeast side and some remains of the wall, were still visible, but most of the bricks had been taken away by the farmers to build walls and kitchen floors for their houses.

The group stayed at a distance, listening to Sam. Joshua detached from the rest of the group, walked to the upper terrace of the ziggurat, and kneeled down and kissed the ground. His face had turned calm and absorbed. As he came down, he embraced Mary tenderly and whispered in her ear, "Our grand patriarch, Abraham, came from here. I am very glad that we were able to make this pilgrimage together."

"Sam, do you think Abraham knew how to read and write when he left here?" asked Zilinos soberly.

"Yes. I believe Abraham belonged to a wealthy farmer family. He most likely knew how to read and write; he probably worshiped Marduk at the Esaglia, read Khammurabi, paid the taxes and lived like a normal honest Babylonian."

"How sure are you when you say that Abraham could have read Khammurabi," Joshua asked.

"Joshua, we know clearly written down that Khammurabi ruled Babylon for forty-three years, one thousand nine hundred and fifty years back. The codes were well known to all the citizens of Babylon. The stele was not only displayed in the public, but the citizens were also instructed to refer to them. If Abraham was an average or above average citizen, there is no reason to think otherwise; he must have known not only the stele, but also a lot more of the Babylonian customs and writing. Let me ask you, Joshua. According to the stories of the Torah, what was the period of Abraham?"

"About the same time as Khammurabi," Joshua said

"Well, some say Abraham had not read the stele of the king, but the laws that are inscribed on the stele were nothing new to the Babylonians. Khammurabi did not invent any new laws; he only classified the existing laws and oral traditions and inscribed on diorite stone and exhibited them in public for everyone to read and abide by. Those are all old Sumerian laws," Sam said.

Zilinos noted Joshua had become preoccupied. *Maybe it was because Mary was not feeling well,* he thought. He wanted to kindle a dialogue. "Joshua, Mary will be fine. It's not unusual for people to get seasick, even though this is not a sea."

Joshua nodded.

"Did you learn anything new from Sam's lecture?"

"Not much; only to confirm my thoughts. He is a very good tour guide."

**** **** ****

Well before sunrise, the skies in Babylon were filled with light, and it was already warm and humid. Mary woke up fresh and well. The heat bothered her the most. She waved her hair around to cool the nape of her neck, and Cassandra was there by her side for assistance.

The next day they sailed to the old city of Erech. The south wind caught up well, and the sail of the boat ballooned. As Sam started the story of Sargon, the boat sailed past the forgotten city of Agade.

"The story of Sargon has many latter versions, like Moses of Israel and Romulus of Rome. You have all heard ancient stories where a hero child is hidden in a reed basket, secretly floated in a river, and is later miraculously recovered and then grows up as a hero to glory.

305

Yes, I believe you have. But the Sargon story is the mother of all such legends, written over three thousand years earlier." Sam pulled out an old scroll and gestured for the attention of everybody.

"Let me read portions of the story as narrated by Sargon himself." The tourists assembled closer to him, leaning forward, cocking their ears to listen to all the words without losing a syllable.

"My city is Azupirini on the shores of the Euphrates," Sam started to read. "I was born out of wedlock by my father's brother. My mother brought me forth secretly. To escape the shame, she put me in a reed basket and floated me on the river. The river carried me to Akki. A farmer who was watering the fields rescued me and raised me as a gardener and further as a warrior. I felt very happy and proud when people said that I was very strong and handsome. The goddess Ishtar fell in love with me. I grew in favors and power and became the king of Akkad. So, goes the Samarian story," Sam said.

Zilinos whispered in Joshua's ears, "The Hebrew story of Moses being floated in a reed basket in the Nile and recovered by the Egyptian queen, and so on, were written at least fifteen hundred years later, don't you think so?"

Joshua nodded. *Who was Moses?* The weight of the baggage of unresolved questions, increased by the day in his mind.

The leather boat sailed further north through the Euphrates, past the great cities of Shuruppak, Kissura, and reached Babylon ten days later for two nights of stay.

"I can't wait to hear Sam, his narration of Babylon. Look at him; his face already has turned serious," said Zilinos, gesturing to Sam.

The passengers landed on the ancient royal dock near the citadel of Khammurabi. Sam signaled all of them to sit on the stone benches. "Whenever I come here to this city, my heart bleeds with pain. Babylon indeed was once the most glorious and coveted city in the whole world. The city was at the zenith during Nebuchadnezzar's time. Everyone wanted to own Babylonia – the Egyptians, the Syrians, the Persians, the Romans . . . some came, some destroyed, some built, and some simply came and left. Now, all that remains are the ruins of Babylonia."

Joshua took Mary's hand when they climbed up the majestic seventy-foot-high city wall that surrounded the citadel.

She pulled him back, pointing to the fierce creatures that sprawled in the brown waters of the deep moat that encircled the city wall. "Crocodiles," Joshua said.

The avenue they walked through on the top of the rampart was wide enough for a four-horse chariot to turn around. "The Greek traveler Herodotus has written about these nine gates and the most glorious Ishtar Gate on the northern wall on the Processional Highway, which you are about to see," Sam said. "In Babylon at present, the most preserved structure from the olden times is this gate, the most beautiful gate ever built by a king – the Ishtar Gate. Pay attention to this decorated dragon, its shining golden scales, serpent's head carved in lapis lazuli, foreleg of a lion, and hind legs of an ostrich sculptured in gold. It was made as a tribute to the city's patron god, Marduk."

"Sam, in many of the Babylonian stories, Ishtar comes up time and again, but was she not in a habit of enticing men and later torture . . .?" Zilinos asked.

"Ishtar is a major goddess in our stories," Sam said. "She is the daughter of the moon god Sin, and is considered to be the most beautiful woman ever created, capable of seducing gods and men, including our supreme god, Anu. Ishtar actually even displaced Antu – the wife of Anu – and became concubine to the almighty God. She was the embodiment of extreme passion and lovemaking. She made love with extreme amorousness that turned to violence, torture, mutilation and the death of her partners."

"But why is that Ishtar is revered in Babylon?" asked Joshua.

"She is the goddess of love, ecstasy and supreme bliss. The Babylonians believed that the gods created men to die and go to the underworld, where, as you know, conditions are abhorrent. Therefore, live life to the fullest extent was a popular philosophy; make every moment a moment of exhilaration. Extreme bliss is considered a near-death experience by many. Ishtar is the goddess of bliss. There are others who believed or practiced sex with torture and violence for extreme pleasure. Ishtar had a big following, even among kings. Ishtar is a part of human conscience."

"Violence for extreme pleasure, a part of human conscience! Was she a demon goddess?" Joshua asked.

"Joshua, in Babylon, gods are both good and evil," Sam said. "I will certainly continue this discussion with you while we are sailing. Now, let us continue with the ziggurat."

"This is disgusting," Joshua whispered to Zilinos.

"Disgusting is also part of life," Zilinos said.

The group assembled around the old ziggurat. Sam continued with the explanations.

"This is the most famous ziggurat of Esaglia in Babylon, the largest ever built," Sam said. He pointed at the mound. "A meeting point, a link between the gods in the heavens and man on earth. It was here that the gods descended from the clouds and man ascended from the ground to the mountain top for a transcendental union between heaven and earth."

In a flash of thought, there appeared the figure of Moses in Joshua's mind, going up to the mountain top to meet with his god to receive all the statues and commandments.

"At the top of the ziggurat, there used to be a gold-paneled sanctuary," Sam said. "Every night, there waited a gorgeous virgin maid, selected from the city to commune with the gods in mind and body."

"Sam, I have read that some of those virgins were killed, and some others became pregnant. Is that true?" Zilinos asked.

"You are correct. It has happened." Sam said. "The celebrated altar of Marduk was also a celestial observation point for the Babylonians. But, Alexander the conqueror smashed down the ziggurat. His idea was to build a greater temple complex with a gymnasium and bath as a showcase for his future capital. But, as you know, destruction he did, construction he did not."

The tourists walked about the remains of Esaglia; some climbed the mount, only to see the remains of the once glorious temple, the dilapidated palaces, some empty altars, cracked floors, broken down columns, ablation pools covered with weeds surrounded by overgrowth of wild grass and infested by rats and snakes.

"There were many frescos and statues of winged lions all throughout the city. You can only imagine the splendor, seeing what remains here," Sam said.

That evening the boat docked and moored on the Euphrates near the ancient palace of Nebuchadnezzar for the night. Joshua had a plan: "Teacher, I have a desire to see the cells and dungeons where my ancestors were kept during captivity. I have the directions from Sam," said Joshua to Zilinos. In the shadowy darkness of the night, Joshua and Zilinos ventured for a small trip. They went several hundred yards into the depths of the deserted city up till the eastern wall where the Jews were kept in wretched conditions of slavery. The old slave quarters were all covered with overgrowth of wild bushes and ant hills. Joshua ventured to go deep into the bushes to take a look at one of the dilapidated huts. The mud-walled rooms were all less than ten feet long and wide, with a single opening on the wall – the door – with no windows, where up to a dozen people lived, night and day.

He knelt down, "This is where my ancestors suffered and died," he said to himself. He thanked his father in heaven and the benevolent king, Cyrus of Persia, for the ultimate release of the Jews from captivity.

**** **** ****

The next morning, they briefly visited the remains of the Hanging Gardens of Babylon, located on the north end of the city near the Ishtar Gate. "It was within this palace that the famous Hanging garden of Babylon once existed," Sam said. "They are barely recognizable now. "The hanging garden was a series of earthen terraces built one above the other, like a terraced ziggurat, that created the vision of a majestic flight of stairs about four hundred feet wide at the bottom and two hundred feet high above the ground. The gardens were planted with trees, vines, fruit and flower plants, with numerous sparkling fountains. Nebuchadnezzar built this garden as a gift to his Persian wife, who missed the flowers and plantations of her homeland. Water from the Euphrates was lifted to the top of the garden and delivered to the plants through a series of small fountains. Does anyone know how it worked," Sam asked.

Nobody answered. "Please explain, Sam," Zilinos said.

"The hydraulic system consisted of three cylinders arranged in a row, at the water level on the Euphrates," Sam explained. "The two larger ones on either side were about ten feet in diameter and thirty feet deep. The cylinder in the middle is only one foot in diameter. The three cylinders are connected at the bottom with sturdy iron tubes. An iron pipe ran from the top of the middle receptacle cylinder to the top of the garden, emptying into a man-made pond. The large cylinders had heavy pistons that could be lowered and lifted by adding or removing stone weights, and further assisted by rotating screws operated by men."

Sam guided his group to the ground on the water level and drew diagrams in the sand. "It's here abouts that the cylinders were located. Water from the river fills the two big cylinders with the piston. Then the behemoth pistons are carefully lowered into the two cylindrical wells. Because the cylinders are connected at the bottom, water rises in the middle cylinder with very high pressure, and will flow to the top of the garden via the iron pipes. The plants are watered, the fountains sprayed, and the hanging gardens come to life." Sam looked around, pleased to see his group captivated by the most accurate description of a very complicated system in so few words.

"Did the captives from Israel work here, in the irrigation system?" asked a man from Syria.

"Possible, highly possible. But before we get onboard, I would like to show you all a stele, which not many people have paid much interest to. I know our handsome young philosopher from Galilee has interest in such matters. Let me show you." He gestured the group to follow, and walked towards a stele about the size and shape of a man, covered in dust and erected on a pedestal, by the side of the processional highway. He cleaned the dust of it with the palm of his hands and said, "This is an old Babylonian prayer. Nobody knows who said it first. This is a prayer to Marduk – the city god of Babylon."

The stele read: "Oh, Lord Marduk, the God of Gods, hallowed be thy name. I adore thy lordship for creating me and committing

310

me to the sovereignty over the people. May the house that I made for you endure like thy kingdom forever. Be compassionate to me. Give sustenance to my people and bless me with children. Do not give me enemies and allow me . . ." the remaining writings were unclear. "I think Nebuchadnezzar erected this stele, but I am not sure."

Joshua took a long look at the stele and scribbled some notes in his papyrus.

"The visit of the city is now concluded. Let's get on board," said Sam.

The southward current of the Euphrates was getting stronger. The oarsmen dug deeper and stronger, and the tour boat started sailing north.

For the next two days it was all rest and relaxation for the tourists. There was much time for discussion and clarification with Sam and other co-passengers. As the day progressed, the heat and humidity grew intense. Mary appeared more tired than the rest of the tourists, at times even listless. While all the others took beer and plenty of bread, Mary kept hydrated on water and fruit juices.

Sam joined the Galilean travelers at the rear of the boat to catch up with the discussions they had left uncompleted. "Joshua, I know you were perturbed with the reverence the Babylonians give to Ishtar, but the fact is, like it or not, Ishtar is a manifestation of God and a reality of man on earth. In religious beliefs, Gods are both good and evil, the balance of the two that make the equilibrium of the universe."

"Sam," asked Zilinos, "the question was about the extreme brutality of Ishtar, after making love to a man, to kill him, or even curse him to become a scorpion or a snake or some such heinous being. Lovemaking is a pleasant and heavenly act, a blessing of God . . ."

"That is one way of looking at it," said Sam, "but, lovemaking is also a very powerful and deep interaction between two people. There is passion; there is power; there is penetration, ejaculation and forceful interaction; sometimes biting and some uncontrolled bodily activities, just to reach a blissful climax to the act. For some, at a certain point the control is lost. Some will do anything to attain that point of ultimate bliss; anything! Bad and despicable it is, I agree, but it has happened before, and it will happen again; it is a fact of life. There are cults, cults that love it and adore it, that's all. You don't have to like it; you don't have to practice it. It's a Babylonian expression of a real yet bizarre human behavior."

"To glorify such a devilish goddess and personify her by erecting such a majestic gate, that too in the heart of this city shows the decadence of the civilization," Joshua said.

"Joshua. For that matter, nobody has claimed that Babylon is the most moral or righteous city in the world," Zilinos said.

"Sam, what is the Babylonian belief about soul?" Joshua asked.

"Joshua," said Sam gaily, "I know that you are a very well read man, not only because Zilinos had hinted so, but also from listening to you. It appears to me that you already know the answer, but I will tell you what I know."

"Sam, it's no tricky question; I ask these for clarification," Joshua said.

"In Babylonian beliefs, soul is immortal; the body is the covering made of mud. At death, the body dissolves into mud again, but the soul goes to the underworld, where Anunnaki and Mammitu will sit in judgment to balance the good and evil deeds of that man. Some are condemned to eternal shame, the soul transforms into a dirty bird with feathers, sitting in wet mud in eternal darkness with no light or possibilities to get out. But there are others sitting on recliners, attended by their wives, children, friends and parents, drinking wine and eating food – the blessed souls. However, their well-being also depends upon the prayers, libations and sacrifices by their living relatives on earth."

"How interesting," commented Zilinos. "Tell us more. How does that work, Sam?"

"It is believed that the souls enter the underworld through an opening on the surface of the earth. The sacrificial libations will spill through the soil and reach the underworld to nourish the souls."

"Is there any escape for such souls from the underworld at any point?" asked Joshua.

"There is. Some are permitted to return to the earth. Some believe in the final union of the soul with its creator, the God, as well."

"Sam, permit me to ask a few more questions. Tell me, in your beliefs, how did the world come about?"

"I guess you are asking about the creation of the world, isn't it?"

"Yes."

"Well, this is a question so many people are asking. Therefore, I will tell the story tomorrow when we all assemble."

**** **** ****

The next morning they woke to a cold breeze from the south and the sky overcast. Mary was beginning to feel better as she inhaled the crisp air . . . she drank some warm barley soup. There was an air of general fatigue amongst the passengers; eleven days of continuous journey in a boat was not easy on any of them. The peculiar lapping noise of the waves hitting on the leather hull of the boat and the splashy sound of the oars digging the waters was the predominant noise in the boat.

Sam helped Joshua to discover a few additional Babylonian prayers from the book of hymns and prayers. "This one is probably the most said prayer of all. Even today, people say this prayer before their evening meal. The prayer read: "Almighty God, I know not the many sins or the transgressions that I have committed. I have angered the gods and outraged the goddesses. Here, I cry for help in vain; nobody to comfort me or take my hand. Almighty God, whoever you are, forgive me. I shall praise thee."

Joshua was caught up in the profundity of the prayer. He bowed his head. In his mind, he pictured an ancient Babylonian standing in front of the altar of Marduk addressing God as if He were his father, asking for forgiveness of sins, and petitioning for favors and blessings. Joshua meditated on these lines for quite a while, and that night he wrote down his own prayer to God on a piece of papyrus.

"Our Father who art in heaven," he wrote. "Hallowed be thy name. Thy kingdom come, thy will be done on earth as it is in heaven, give us this day our daily bread and forgive us our trespasses as we forgive those who trespass against us. Lead us not into temptation, but deliver us from evil, for thine is the kingdom and the power and the glory forever and ever. Amen."

The next day by high noon, the sun broke through the gray clouds as the tour group came to life and activities as usual.

"Ladies and gentlemen, I am glad to see that we all survived the bad weather of yesterday and last night, but we were very fortunate without a rain. Our young philosopher, Joshua from Galilee, had requested me to tell something about our creation stories in Babylon. Well, we have several versions of creation stories, but the most popular one is at the beginning of the epic story of Gilgamesh." When Sam brought up the name of Gilgamesh, Mary pinched Joshua on his thighs and gave him a pleasant smile.

"In the beginning," Sam started, "there existed a boundless mass of moisture and chaos, living and powerful – the Apsu. From this mighty mass, there evolved a series of gods, self-created, shaped like humans, that occupied the upper half of the Apsu – the heaven. Then, again there came out another series of grotesque gods – the devils – that occupied the lower half of the Apsu – the earth and the underworld. Anu is the supreme god of heaven, and Ea, the god in charge of earth; Tiamet and Mammu became the gods of the underworld."

The tourists, intrigued and engrossed by the story, remained attentive. "But," Sam said, "Apsu was dissatisfied by the arrangement, and he hatched a monster – Tiamet – the mightiest of all evils and identified her as the mother goddess of the universe and empowered her with the Tablets of Fate of all the beings of the earth. But Ea came to know of the plot and launched a fearsome fight with Tiamet and Mammu. Thus, a perpetual struggle between the good and the evil of the universe started. Between the two of them, they created a vast array of weapons such as thunder, whirlwind, fire-spitting mountains, floods and drought on earth, and, scorpion, bull, crab, ram and the like twelve Zodiacs, and placed them in the skies. Thus, the long chain of cosmic power struggle between the good and evil started that continues as of today . . ."

"What about the creation of man?" asked a man from Egypt.

"Very good. Does anybody here know the story?" Sam turned around, searching faces one by one, and fixed on Joshua. Mary was thrilled at the recognition of her husband. "Say. Say Joshua," she poked him with her fingers on his back.

"So far, what you have said is about the universe. Now, I believe, Bel-Marduk created the man," answered Joshua.

"Correct. Presently, Marduk, the son of Ea, is the appointed god of earth. He is the city god of Babylon. Marduk fashioned man from mud and breathed air into his nostrils and gave life, like that in your Torah, except that the Torah was written at least fifteen hundred years after the Babylonians etched the story in wet bricks." Sam cleared his throat. "Then, there is a more popular version of the creation of man. First, Marduk created the surface of the earth by kneading mud and spreading it on a mat of rushes, and placed the mat over the body of the water that existed. Then he created the mountains, rivers, plants, birds and beasts in it. He wanted to create man as a special being. He killed one of the gods, and from that flesh and blood, man was created. So, the Babylonian man is the son of god, totally different from all other beings on earth. The gods were rejoiced and, in favor, they created the sanctuary – the temple of Marduk – that we saw two days back in the city of Babylon."

"In shambles," Zilinos whispered.

That evening after the dinner, Sam and the Galileans discussed many of the other Babylonian stories between themselves. In Babylon, Eden was described as a pure and eternally sunlit land of bliss, inhabited by gods and humans who were given the gift of immortality. Predators did not exist, fresh water continuously nourished the fields, fruit trees always yielded, flower shrubs always bloomed, and no one ever grew old or ill. In the epic story of Gilgamesh, the hero Enkidu, like Adam, was supremely happy in the forest until the prostitute enticed him into a violent sexual intercourse. After this act, he gained knowledge, including a conscious awareness of his own nakedness, which resulted in his own downfall and banishment from the forest.

The boat sailed north to Nehardia for the final leg of the tour. Presently, the sky was covered with dark clouds, brought over by another cold whistling south wind with drizzles spraying on their faces. The men and women pulled over their long coats and covered their heads with warm shawls and hoods.

"I saved two of my most favorite discussions for the last days of the tour – the Babylonian story of the great flood, and the life and times of Khammurabi," Sam said. "There is no nation in the world that does not have a flood story. From my tour groups, I have learned something new every time. Last night our esteemed guest Huristo Zilinos, who was a philosophy teacher in Alexandria, told me a story of a flood, which I trust he will share with us." Sam gestured to Zilinos.

"Well, Plato, the Greek philosopher," Zilinos said "had concluded that some ten thousand years ago there was a huge deluge from which no nation escaped. Huge land masses were covered by sea. Several land basins and abysses were submerged into the sea, including the legendary civilization of Atlantis. Plato had even postulated that gigantic masses of ice melting about the North Pole had caused the flood . . ."

"Thank you, Zilinos. The Babylonians have several versions of the flood story," Sam said. "In one version, the Blackheads multiplied in abundance and became terribly noisy, evil, drunken and disorderly. The gods who dwelt in Shuruppak could not control the noise and disobedience, and they beseeched Anu, the God of the Highest; Enlil, the god of wind and sun; and Ea, the god of earth and wisdom to create a mighty storm to scatter the Blackheads. Enlil shouted and ordered the storm. But Ea, who was compassionate, urged Enlil to spare the righteous men and women of Babylon. In a dream, Ea appeared to Uta-Napishtim and warned him about the coming of a devastating deluge and instructed him to construct a mighty ship. Uta-Napishtim did so. He fortified the ship, plastered it with bitumen, and loaded it with food, grain, water, gold, silver and other possessions. Fulfilling Ea's instructions, he told his neighbors: 'I have incurred the wrath of Enlil, and I am leaving the city, never to come back. I am planning to sail the ocean to my God, Ea.' Then, he anointed himself in unguent, collected his family, kinsfolk and servants, entered the ship and closed the doors. As the night fell, lightning and thunderbolts lit the skies. The fountains of the great deep gushed out, the flood gates of heaven broke loose, and waters came down to earth with the force of a thousand Euphrates falling all at once from skies. Ominous black clouds covered the skies; it was dark, and the storm raged with a vengeance; but the boat was strong and safe. Waters rose at even tide, yet his boat was safe and sound. The earth shook, and the whirlwinds lifted the ship afloat.

For six days and six nights, the torrents continued, and the raging waters reached the mountains. The violent current swept away men, women and children along with their houses and belongings. Trees and humans twirled and were sucked deep into the waters. The gods themselves were terrified at the size of the flood they had created. They withdrew to the highest heights of the heavens and crouched by the wall, shivering. Ishtar bitterly lamented, looking at the bodies of men floating like dead fish. The other gods joined in her wailing. On the seventh day, the clouds cleared, and the skies grew quiet. Uta-Napishtim opened a small window to look around, but he saw only vast expanses of ocean. For the next twelve days, the ship floated on the water and finally came to rest on top of mount Nisir. After the ship had been on the mountain for seven days, Uta-Napishtim opened the window and released a dove from the ship. The bird returned, having found no land on which to perch. After a few more days, he sent out a swallow, only to see that it came back, just like the dove. After two days he sent out a raven, which did not return. Certain that the waters had subsided, Uta-Napishtim came out of the ship, and set foot on dry land. He thanked Ea and made a great sacrifice to the gods and poured a libation on the ground. The hungry gods smelled the aroma of the burnt meat and gathered around the tasty offering. A teary Ishtar, sobbing, bitterly lamented the flood that had destroyed nearly all of mankind. She pulled out her rainbow-colored lapis lazuli necklace and threw it to the skies, and swore that she would never forget the ravaging days and nights that had passed, nor permit such a thing to happen again. She invited the other gods to celebrate the sacrifice and support her vow, but Enlil, who had ordered the terrible flood, was furious to see that Uta-Napishtim had escaped the curse and sentenced him to death."

"Adonai," a voice came from somewhere. People looked around; Mary was holding her palms against her open mouth and looked around apologetically.

Sam nodded that he understood the emotion. "A great argument erupted amongst the gods. Ishtar pleaded on behalf of Uta-Napishtim. In the end, Ea and the other gods resolved to spare him. They also agreed with Ishtar that this flood that had virtually destroyed most of mankind was an abomination, and that the gods would never create devastation of this magnitude again. Then Ea appeared in person and brought forth Uta-Napishtim and his wife, and asked them to kneel on the ground facing each other. He stood between them, placed his hands on their heads, and blessed them, declaring that they would be immortal henceforth. He then assigned a place for them at the river mouth on the Sea of the Dead, in their far west where the sun goes to rest at night."

"Was Uta-Napishtim a demigod?" Zilinos asked.

"Yes."

Sam paused for a while and spoke to the group again. "This is a very brief summary of the many flood stories of Babylon. Let me ask you a question. If Enlil had promised Ea that he would send a flood to destroy all men, then why was Uta-Napishtim saved?"

Zilinos answered, "Maybe as a man, Uta-Napishtim died and lived as an immortal god."

"How correct; I am really impressed with this group. When Ea appeared to him in sleep, Uta-Napishtim was already elevated to the position of a demigod."

In the afternoon the clouds cleared, and the sun beat down again brightly, warmly. The servants had started preparing a goat for the last day's feast on the boat. New and fresh flasks of wine were brought over, and the group turned to a gaily mood.

After the dinner Sam made a request: "There must be somebody in this group knowing to sing." A few hands rose up. Mary sang an old Jewish wedding song. The crowd supported her with clapping of hands for a rhythm. It was followed by an Egyptian harvest song and a Parthian hunting song, and a few others.

**** **** ****

On the final day was the tour of Ctesiphon, the capital of the Parthian Empire. They assembled at the elaborate seven-story mansion of the King's Palace where all the treasures of the land were kept and kings were crowned. The entrance gate to the great hall of the palace had an astonishing arch made of glazed and gold-plated bricks, in front of which had been erected the resurrected Khammurabi's stele.

In the morning, Sam gave a copy of Khammurabi's code of law to everybody in the group as a souvenir. "This stele you see here was originally erected at the temple of Marduk in Esaglia, in the city of Babylon. Look at the very top of the stella. You will see a humble-looking Khammurabi receiving the laws from Shamash, the God and judge of the Heaven. If you look closely, you'll see him with his right hand raised and his left hand resting on his breast, creating the aura of a divine order to the codes. The law outlines the standards by which the population is expected to live and, interestingly, the expectations are different for different people in different walks of life, even to the degree that they are treated differently for exactly the same crime. The standard to which a priest or a physician is held accountable is significantly different than that for an illiterate worker. Women had equal rights under the law, and nobody was above the law. There is a punishment for every type of crime one can imagine, including, but not limited to, two hundred and eighty-two of these laws etched in stone here: murder, violence, dismemberment, slave sales, price control, property ownership, parental abuse, teacher abuse, divorce, and many others. If you can think of a crime or a law, it is likely covered in this stele. People accused of a crime were given a trial by a jury of elders."

"Who were those elders? Priests, king's men, or what?" asked Joshua.

"Good question. The 'elders' were not elders at all. They were men from all walks of life: barbers, physicians, farmers, and all. No. There were no religious laws in our system. The eyes of the law were blind and did not differentiate between a servant and a high priest. He strongly believed that justice would rise over his people as the sun brightened the land with its rays. But for the same crime committed, the high priest will be more intensely fined and punished, because the expectations of the state from a high priest and a servant were different.

"Sam, please make it clear," asked the woman from Athens.

Sam turned around, searching the faces of everybody. "Please look at Law N° 8. It says: If a man steals a boat from a temple, for example, he shall pay a fine ten times the worth of the boat. If the thief is a very poor man, he shall pay twice the amount, and if the thief is a physician, he shall pay thirty times the amount. In addition, his hands will be cut off. If the thief has no money, his head will be cut off."

"The fundamental principles of jurisprudence, such as swearing an oath before testimony, and hearing from the accused and the presentation of witnesses, were all practiced here in Khammurabi's court. His tremendous respect for the gods and parents were a central theme in his laws. For example, one of the laws states: If a son sayth to his father, "thou are not my father," they shall brand him, bind him in feathers and sell him for money as a slave. But compared to many other lawgivers, Khammurabi was a compassionate leader. I have learned that the same crime in Israel would carry the penalty of death by stoning."

Sam looked around and noticed Joshua holding his head in the cup of his palm, deeply absorbed and quiet.

"Thanks to Law N° 15, a woman can travel unmolested in Babylon at any hour of the night or day. He leaned over to read the words aloud: "If a man has violated a maid of the temple or the palace, a slave girl or a maid of a poor man outside the gate, he shall be killed." According to Law N° 1, the punishments were harsh for perjury, and for those who accused others falsely. It read, "A man who casts a spell on another man and cannot justify his actions shall be put to death."

"It appears extremely harsh," said Zilinos.

"Why is it that this is the first of all laws?" asked one from Parthia.

Sam smiled, "Can any one of you try an explanation?"

There were no takers.

"Joshua, can you?" requested Sam.

"Slander could be the most widespread ills of all. Most other violent crime originates from a malicious talk," Joshua said. "What comes out of the mouth can never be taken back; it's the most important expression of one's soul."

"Well said, Joshua. You are stating as if reading from our *Book of Wisdom*. Let me continue. Protections of private life and property were of the utmost priority," Sam said. "'The housebreaker shall be killed and buried in the hole he dug on the wall. Likewise, a highway robber shall be killed.' Then there is a series of laws from Law N° 195 to Law N° 206 that carry penalties requiring an eye for an eye, a tooth for a tooth, a limb for a limb, and so on." Sam's gaze moved to the group from Galilee. "I know of some laws that treat women ruthlessly." He paused for a few moments as Joshua, Zilinos, Cassandra and Mary quietly stared at him. "There are laws written several centuries later, that would permit a woman to be stoned to death by a jealous husband. The woman is not even allowed to state her case. She is permitted no jury, no witness testimony and no opportunity to save herself. Let us examine the way the same woman would be treated under Babylonian law."

"Yes! Yes!" shouted Mary excitedly.

"Let us read Law N° 141: 'If a wife spends her time out of the house and behaves foolishly, the husband may say, "I divorce her" and send her out without paying back her dowry. If the wife is found to be without fault and has been abused by her husband, she can reclaim her dowry and return to her father's house. Moreover, if a man falsely accuses his wife, he shall be branded and punished, even including death.'"

Joshua was visibly moved at this time. The many scenes of Rachel's wedding, the trial at the synagogue, and the helplessness of the girl all traveled through his mind. He cursed the writers of the Jewish laws. "Oh, elders what have you done to us? Why did you go to the mountain tops? You should have taken this stele to the Promised Land." He grasped Mary, resting his brow on her shoulders.

Sam looked around. "Look at the next law – quite interesting. If a man and a woman were both caught committing adultery, they are both sentenced to drown in the river. The man cannot swim to the shore. He must die in the water. However, if the husband of the woman felt pity on her, he can intervene to save his wife, by jumping into the river, and save her from drowning. But only the king may intervene to spare the man's life."

Zilinos raised his hand. "Why is this so, Sam?"

"Why do you think it is so, Zilinos?"

"Maybe woman is the weaker sex, not trained in swimming and sure to die," said Zilinos.

"Probably so, probably so. In any case, there is an element of compassion in favor of the woman, is there not? Don't you think? But look at some of the interesting laws to maintain social law and order: Law N° 109 and Law N° 110," Sam implored. "'If a wine merchant allows riotous men to assemble in his shop and doesn't expel them, he shall be killed.' Why is that?"

"Is it corruption of the society, Sam?" asked Zilinos.

"Of course, it is. Corruption of the society is considered an unforgiveable crime. Holding a license for a wine shop is a very responsible privilege. Likewise, when you read through the laws, you will find that judges, priests, physicians and those in elevated positions in the society are held to much higher standards than the average person. As a result, they receive much harsher punishments for relatively minor crimes." Sam looked around at the tourists. "Ladies and gentleman, we haven't got enough time to discuss all of the laws and their interpretations. Before you all leave, I have a few points to discuss. As you may know by now, many nations so far have learned and adopted from Khammurabi's codes; however, in my opinion, the most profound Babylonian writings are in our *Book of Wisdom*. While most tourists are not that much interested in those, I did not dwell much in that area. But, I am delighted to see that our young man from Galilee already has a copy in his hand, and I even saw him reading it. I wish you a safe trip back home."

After completing the tour, bubbling with excitement over the great amount of knowledge and information they had received, the Galileans returned to the lodge for a few days of rest and relaxation before the next journey.

**** **** ****

Mary seemed gloomy and had barely spoken at all for the past two days, but Zilinos was exuberant. He could not express to Joshua enough the joy he had experienced in their visit to Babylon.

"Honestly, I had read quite a bit about Babylon," he said, "but only now can I put my reading into perspective. The people of Babylon were ingenious." He turned to Joshua. "Now, have you learned all that you have been looking for?"

"This trip is fascinating. I certainly have solidified some of my learning and clarified most of my doubts. But . . ."

"But what? Do you now think that the Torah has copied . . .?"

"Zilinos, I have no problem accepting that the Torah in principle is a Babylonian document with several modifications. But there are many that are left out, and far too many that are vague – the oral Torah."

"Like what, Joshua? Come on, let us have a discussion. Remember, the author or authors of the Torah had to make some significant concessions to the rebellious men folks to pacify them."

"Zilinos, have you read the Babylonian *Book of Wisdom*."

"No. Have you?"

"Yes, I have"

"Tell me about it."

"Yes, of course; this evening."

**** **** ****

In another two days Zilinos, Cassandra and Mary planned to return to Galilee accompanying a caravan heading to Damascus. Joshua planned to stay back in Ctesiphon in preparation to go to India. Mary looked pale and disinterested in food in the morning, but by noon she would have returned to normal. Joshua spent his time entirely with Mary, but after the evening meal they all sat together and talked late into the night.

"So, tell me, Joshua. What got you so interested in the *Book of Wisdom?*" asked Zilinos.

"Teacher, have you read our book the *Proverbs*? It was claimed to be the wise words of King Solomon, but was written much later during or after the Greek occupation of Palestine."

"I don't think I have read it. Even if I did, I have forgotten it all," Zilinos said. "You think they are also a copy of the Babylonian *Book of Wisdom*?"

"Well, almost word by word."

"They have started again, Mary; the boring discussions. Come on; you need some rest," said Cassandra. They went to rest their heads.

"Let them take some rest. Come on; tell me something about your *Book of Wisdom*." Zilinos collected a bottle of wine, two flagons and they went up to the terrace.

Joshua started, "The Babylonian document was written around or before the time of Khammurabi. It is written like a speech from a god of ethics and righteousness to the newly created man, emphasizing his obligations to God, his treatment of the neighbors, and a woman's responsibility to her husband."

"Joshua, I remember you mentioning something about a similar document from Egypt."

"Yes, but honestly, the Egyptian is a much smaller document, and in all probabilities, the Babylonian must be much older, as far as I know. The Babylonian document is very discrete and unequivocal; I love the way it is written. I had known about this in Alexandria, but quite a few pages were missing. After reading these scrolls, I have a very clear view of the *Book of Wisdom*.

"Interesting. Now, the girls have gone to sleep, the night is young, and here the breeze is great; let me open a flask of vine. I would like to hear more."

Joshua started turning the pages of the Babylonian document. "Here again, the first few adages are about the words and behavior of a man. Listen, it says: 'Wise and discrete men must not belittle their knowledge; watch your words; do not speak before you think; words exited from your mouth cannot be retrieved; audacity for wickedness is an abomination.'"

"Excellent; well said. Come to think of it, I have heard those, but was not able to place them. Read more."

"About gods, they say: 'Worship your god with prayers, offerings and incense; fear of God is the beginning of wisdom; begets prosperity and prolongs life.'"

Zilinos took another drag. "Excellent."

"About your enemies: 'Harm not, in any way, your adversary; do good, to the man who does evil to you; oppose your enemy with righteous deeds; always seek after the truth; nourish and respect your parents.'"

"I understand what you say. There are sharp contrasts. Joshua, who do you think wrote your Jewish document, and when?"

"There is no author attached to the Jewish *Book of Wisdom*, except Solomon. The document is written in Greek and not in Hebrew."

"What's your best bet?"

After a moment of thought, Joshua replied, "I believe that during the Babylonian captivity the elite Jewish people came across these documents, and the scribes copied them with little modification, and put Solomon's name to gain popularity and authenticity to the writings."

"Ha . . . ha . . . poor Solomon; he neither knew Babylonia nor learned Greek."

"Now, this will interest you, Zilinos. This is about Ishtar and the temple women. It reads: 'the dedication of a woman of the temple is to her goddess Ishtar. Their talents are abundant; they will never support you in your misfortunes; in conflict she will work against you; if she enters your house, lead her out; the house she enters will be defiled.'"

"I see. It sounds like harlots," reflected Zilinos. "Were they really harlots? What is your take on it, Joshua?"

Joshua thought for a moment, "Harlots. Who are they, after all, Zilinos? I feel very strongly about them. Are they not poor, hungry, self-deprecated, destitute, plagued by hunger, incensed by rejection, ridiculed by the hypocrites, lifting their skirts for a meager meal of the day? Are there not ten hypocrites for each harlot for every night? It's not sticks or stones that a lamb in the ditch deserves, but a rope, some compassion and an unclenched fist."

"Very profound, Joshua. You have strong words. I will tell you this: you don't belong to the land of Israel," Zilinos said. "I promise you, you will be in trouble sooner or later. But I know you are a man who will speak your mind, no matter what."

Joshua casually smiled and wrote some words on the floor with his index finger.

"I get the feeling that you have traveled a lot, read a lot, and seen it all. Then why do you want to go India? Do you think that you will gain anything more with such an arduous undertaking? Haven't you read Herodotus?" asked Zilinos dryly.

Joshua nodded, "Yes."

"I know you fairly well. You cannot be dissuaded from your plans. But I beg you to reconsider your trip to India."

It appeared that discussion rang a familiar note in the room where Cassandra and Mary had gone to sleep. Presently, they both came up to the terrace, Mary wiping her eyes with the back of her hands,

"Zilinos, that is a good suggestion," joined Cassandra to the conversation.

"What is there in Herodotus, you are talking about?" Mary asked.

"You never told me anything about Herodotus."

"Yes, I have read Herodotus, Strabo and Megasthenes, too," Joshua said, "but I am not sure about the truth in their writings about India; particularly Herodotus."

"Why is that?" Cassandra asked.

Neither Joshua nor Zilinos offered an answer. Mary was becoming more and more anxious. She had heard some stories about India from Joshua; nothing ominous, but the tone of the talk about India in the room casted some doubts in her mind. Will Joshua be safe; unknown land; strange people; far away from home – her mind was clouded. Squeezing her fingers, she waited for any one of the men to talk.

"I have read Herodotus and the chronicles of Ctesias many, many years ago, but, Joshua, just refresh my memory," Zilinos said. "Mary, I will tell you the things I remember."

After a deep sigh, Zilinos cleared his throat, took a fresh sip of wine, and started: "There are many horrible things that Ctesias and Herodotus have written about India."

"But I don't think that they are correct," Joshua said.

"Let the teacher talk, Joshua," said Mary. She sat cross-legged with her chin buried in the cup of her palms.

"They have reported that India is located at the farthest end of world where the sun rises and the land is all sand, where there are many tribes in constant conflict with each other, people who speak a multitude of languages. People dwelling by the swamps of the Indus River live on a diet of raw fish and weeds, some others live on vegetables, yet others on human flesh."

"Adonai!" screamed Mary, gazing at Joshua. She was shivering, "Human flesh?"

"Mary, come on over here," said Joshua. He held her by the hand and had her sit near him.

"Mary, these are all stories. Don't you worry; I will be safe and fine."

Zilinos turned to Mary and Cassandra, and said, soberly, "I couldn't agree more. However, these things are written by none other than the greatest historian of all times, Herodotus himself. But Joshua will tell you the whole truth when he comes back. But for now, for our own entertainment, tell us, Joshua, what did he write?"

"So, he wrote that when a man falls ill, the men of the village congregate around him and make plans to make a feast out of him. Even if the man strongly denies that he is ill, they kill him anyway and feast upon his flesh. The women of the village do likewise with the women who fall ill." Joshua turned to the women, spreading his palms, pleading, "These are all just stupid."

"Not only that, Zilinos," added Joshua with a humorous tone, "that is why the Indians have few elders in their society, as the men approaching older age are routinely killed and eaten."

Cassandra was quiet, listening with her palm cupping her half-open mouth. She couldn't keep silent any more. "This is the most outrageous story that I have ever heard. However, this is written by a great man; I studied some of his writings in my school. There must be some truth to it, unless you people are telling all these grotesque stories to scare us. You must certainly reconsider your travel. It is not even fair to your young bride."

Mary did not comment; her face said it all.

"I shall Cassandra, I will," said Joshua. "But listen; Alexander of Macedonia was there. It is said that he wanted to go back to India and hoped to establish the capital of his eastern empire in India. Alexander had brought many scrolls to Alexandria, but they were all lost during the fire."

Presently, Zilinos cheered up, as if awake from a sleep, shouting, "Correct! Correct! Now I remember; my memory door is open. Those Indians, their sexual intercourse is all out in the open like cattle, and their skin color is dark like the Ethiopians, Herodotus wrote. Even their semen is not white like the other races, but dark like their skin."

"Chei!" grunted Cassandra, covering her face and looking down to the ground, shaking her head.

Mary stared at Joshua without blinking.

"Are all these things documented by your great Greek historian, Herodotus?" Cassandra asked.

"Certainly," Zilinos said. "Joshua, can you imagine the comfort of his armchair, where from he wrote all these great eye-witness stories?"

Joshua returned Mary's face with a flirtatious wink, and continued in a light tone.

"Mary, listen to the stories of gold hunters in India."

"Is this also said by your Herod . . .?"

"Yes. Herodotus, he also writes of other Indians – warriors, who are like the Bactrians in the north, the gold hunters. There, in the sand dunes of India, they have ants larger than foxes."

Mary laughed. "Ants larger than foxes?"

"Yes, Mary, ants," Joshua stretched his hand to the level of his knees and said jovially, "about this height. A bit larger than a fox, but smaller than a dog. That is what he has written." At this time they all broke out into a gaily laughter as Mary pounded aggressively on Joshua's shoulders for trying to scare her.

"Joshua, tell me, let us hear the rest," requested Zilinos.

"These ants live under the sand during the high sun, and when they emerge at sundown, they bring forth yellow sand that contains gold. In order to collect this gold, the Indians travel to the desert on a cart pulled by three camels yoked together, two he camels on both sides and one larger she camel at the middle. The rider sits on the she camel. These camels are enormous beasts, with four thighs and three knees on each leg . . ."

The listeners laughed again. Zilinos poured one more drink for himself, took a drag, and held his hand high up in the air signaling Joshua to stop talking. He swallowed the mouth full with a noise and said in a hurry." Hold. Hold. I will tell you the rest. My memory tree is sprouting."

"Herodotus wrote that the camels have huge phallus, as long as this," he spread out this right hand.

This time he only laughed.

"Zilinos, be ashamed of yourselves; stop talking like that," Cassandra said.

"Cassandra, this is history! Written by none other than . . . Herodotus himself . . . but there is more. Well, this thing I talked about, that hangs on the belly, is pointing back, sticking between the hind legs of the camels. Ha, ha." Zilinos covered his face with both hands and sat down.

"Joshua, is it all true? Or is Zilinos just making it up?" Cassandra asked.

Joshua grinned. "Yes, Cassandra, all these are truly written by Herodotus, and more."

"The evening is still young, Joshua," Zilinos said. "These are great stories to listen to; tell us some more."

"Yes, just one more. Then there is another strange genre of Indians with ears so large and flat like elephants', with which they can cover their face and body, and there are others with flat feet, which they can turn up and use as umbrellas."

"Have you heard anything good about India?" Mary asked. "If it was such a terrible place, then why did King Alexander travel there? Why are you eager to go there?"

"Correct. Now you are talking, Mary," said Joshua.

"He had a great imagination about India, this Herodotus", Zilinos said. "But what he wrote about Babylon and Egypt, I believe has some merit."

Joshua replied, "We know very little about India from Alexander's expeditions, but the Greek traveler Megasthenes, who actually had traveled to India, recorded some interesting, believable information about India. In one of the books I've read, Megasthenes explains that the Indians have many scrolls about their religious beliefs, interpretations of God, and all. However, there are some Chinese writers and Persian travelers who have written about India, particularly about a sage called Buddha."

The name Buddha sparked a flash of memories in Zilinos' mind. "Buddha. Buddha." He talked to himself, pressing his thumb against his nose. "I have heard some Greek travelers speaking that name. I cannot remember the details. There are some Indian sages who have the power to control their minds and conquer their bodies. I've heard that they can walk on water and fire. and stay alive in deep meditation for several months without food or water. They are even able to control their breathing and stay under water for up to a day."

"Joshua, is it all another set of stories, or is it all true; tell us," Mary said.

Joshua laughed. "Mary, I am hoping to explore these subjects in more depth. I will tell you all the true stories when I come back."

The last evening, after the dinner, the couples retreated to their rooms without the usual after-dinner chats. Joshua lay on his bed with his arms locked behind his head staring at the sky, watching the gray clouds flying past the shy half-moon that had risen high in the east. Mary sobbed quietly, sitting beside him smoothing his beard and staring at his face. The fine tremor on her lips was difficult to perceive. Joshua folded her in his arms and held her teary face against his chest.

"Mary, I know it is very difficult for you now. The next few years – four, maybe five – will be even harder. I appreciate your willingness to let me go. The stories we described about India were all ridiculous. Herodotus did it all for name or fame. Hypocrite!"

Mary said: "I will pray every day for your safe return. I hope you will be safe and taken care of by the people there. Try not to be alone all the time. You think too much, forget to eat, and forget to sleep. You are a very honest man. I thought about the story you told me with that Egyptian girl. I fully understand."

They talked long into the night.

At first light the Galileans were all up and ready to depart. The bags were all packed and the camels were ready. The mood was somber and there were not many words amongst them. Both Zilinos and Cassandra promised that they would treat Mary like their own daughter, bring her home safely to Nazareth, and visit her frequently.

After Mary and Cassandra, Zilinos embraced Joshua for a long minute with their heads resting over their shoulders. As they unlocked, the old man was weeping like a baby. He couldn't even speak. With much stammering he said, "There is . . . is something for me to look forward to . . . in this old age . . . your return, Joshua."

Zilinos rode on one camel, Mary and Cassandra on the other. When they had proceeded a bit further, Cassandra asked Mary, "Does Joshua know?"

Mary said, "No."

"Why didn't you tell him?" Cassandra asked. "I'm afraid that if he knew, he might not go. I wanted him to go and complete his mission. That is his calling."

Joshua stayed in Ctesiphon a few more days, finalizing his plans to travel east. Ever since Alexander had conquered India, there had been at least two land routes and many guides available to go east. Often he unfolded and studied the papyrus copy of the world map he had collected from Alexandria that Strabo had drawn about two hundred years back.

BOOK VII
Joshua in Taxila

Joshua in Taxila, India

Joshua watched the camels, one carrying Mary and Cassandra, the other, Zilinos, plodding away into the distance and then disappearing over the horizon. He sat on the stone steps of the library at Ctesiphon, lonely, his mind wandering. *Is it fair that I leave Mary behind and set out for a journey into the unknown?* The voice from inside empowered him. "Joshua, I fully understand your passion; you must go, and I want you to go."

He found lodging near the Chinese embassy in Ctesiphon and explored ways to travel east. He pulled out a sheet of papyrus – a world map etched by Strabo from Alexandria – and ran his fingers on it from west to east through the dotted lines. He studied the notes on Alexander's expedition to India and the descriptions of Megasthenes and Strabo.

Joshua knew little of the Chinese, except that over the past two hundred years they had established trading posts in cities such as Ctesiphon and Dura-Europas. But his visit to the Chinese embassy was a learning moment for the young traveler from Galilee.

Joshua presented himself at the brightly decorated pagoda at the entrance to the Chinese embassy. Located about a mile east of the city of Ctesiphon by way of the Silk Road, it was a modest brick building, guarded by men at arms. The guards most politely welcomed Joshua with clasped hands, bowed their heads and asked him, "What can we do for you, sire?" Amazingly, they could understand and speak some Greek; the rest they communicated with facial expressions, gesticulations and drawing figures on the floor or in the air.

Joshua was let into the office of Huang Wu, the senior official at that outpost. Huang Wu, a short man with slanted eyes, was clad in a bright-red kimono. "Welcome," he said when Joshua walked in. They both sat down face to face in dialogue.

"What can we do for you, sire? What do you like to purchase?"

"Sire, I am a traveler from Palestine. I am seeking your assistance and guidance to go east."

"Ah, where in the east?" Huang Wu asked.

"I want to go to India," Joshua said.

"India! That's too vast a territory. Sire, what is your mission? Maybe I can be of assistance if I know better."

Joshua mentioned his previous travels, then said, "I am going to India to learn more about the culture, religion and philosophy."

Huang Wu laughed gaily. "Joshua, China has the greatest civilization of the world. India had a great philosopher, Buddha, who only has a little following in India now. Confucius is the philosopher from whom you need to learn." Then he pointed to a wall-hanging painted in strong red and yellow, depicting the scene of a sunrise and verses from Confucius.

Do unto others that you like to be done to yourself.

Numerous thoughts, scenes and people flashed through Joshua's mind. Do unto others that you wish to be done to yourself, he said to himself. He asked, "Confucius, is he alive now?

"No. Confucius died over five hundred years ago."

When Huang Wu learned that this man from Palestine had traveled to places such as Egypt, Rome, Athens and Babylon, his narrow eyes widened. He said that a caravan returning from Damascus was scheduled to arrive in Ctesiphon in another seven days and would be leaving from Ctesiphon to Kashgar within about a week. It appeared that Huang Wu had some interest in the matter. "I'd like to talk to you further about your travels and experiences. I don't have time now. I am about to receive a delegation from Gedrosia by noon today. I will make arrangements for you to travel with us, but in the meantime you are welcome to come here and go through some of the books and charts we have in our small library."

Joshua visited the library on each of the next six days that followed. The library had several wall paintings depicting portraits of the Han kings, and a large embroidered hanging showing the territories of the majestic kingdom, and its major highways and ports. They had established a network of roads from Ctesiphon to the Chinese territory of Kashgar, which the travelers called the "silk route." Indian merchants traveled at times with the caravans too, but the trade was monopolized by the Chinese traders heavily protected by the present Han Dynasty. When the Selucas reigned in this territory, they had even created a royal courier service through the Silk Road that could take a letter from Ctesiphon all the way to Pataliputhra in India in thirty-five days, but that service no longer existed.

Joshua's attention returned to a colorful painting of Confucius that was prominently displayed at the entrance with the following words:

Righteousness in the heart means grace in your character.

If there is grace in your character, there is harmony in the house.

335

Harmony in the house means, order in the nation.

If there is order in the nation, there will be peace in the world.

Joshua stood wonderstruck as he read those words. He read them again and again and copied them in his papyrus and praised the moment when he had made the decision to travel to the east.

In addition, there were several paintings of flowers, Chinese landscapes, sunsets, sunrises and farmers working in the fields. On each painting was at least one verse from Confucius inscribed like a maxim.

"Remove the vile in you first, before you attack trivial evil in others."

Joshua wrote down the verses on his papyrus: *"Remove the beam in your eyes, before you blame the mot in your brother's."*

The embassy had also created a code of conduct for the civil service employees based on the teaching of Confucius. The civil service employees were required to study Confucius and pass an examination before they began a government job. After obtaining permission from Huang Wu, Joshua copied the whole book line by line within the next few days. Many times Huang Wu had come and watched over him with admiration.

The day before the travel to the east, Huang Wu invited Joshua for a drink of tea. "Joshua, we have been observing your behavior and interest in Confucius. Ah, I was thinking, in my wagon, I will find a place for you, not because I can teach you a whole lot about Confucius or our beliefs in Zen. I haven't traveled much: the farthest I have traveled is up to Damascus. That, too, for business deals. I am interested to hear about the places you mentioned. You don't have to pay anything for trip. We will provide for you. It's a long ride; plenty of time."

Joshua was elated at the proposal and thanked Huang Wu with folded hands and a humble bow. *Finally, I am getting a payment for my studies*, thought Joshua. Then, there became a new thought in his mind, *Beliefs in Zen*, he thought.

On the morning of his departure, Joshua arrived at the embassy before sunrise with his belongings. There were thirty other men in the caravan with twenty-two camels. Two of the men, Varadaraja and

Pushyaraja, were Indians from Pataliputhra. They were Hindus and had connection to the royalty in Pataliputhra.

Huang Wu traveled in a heavily armed, four-wheeled carriage drawn by four horses covered in chain mail. There were four light cavalry bodyguards who rode on camels in the front, and four heavy cavalry – the *cataphrat* – where the horsemen wore iron helmets, chain mail, and armors with swords and lances, and rode behind the carriage. The horses, majestic Palomino and Appaloosa breeds, were strong and fast.

"The Parthian government provided the cataphrat. The price is steep, but it is worth the money. It allows us to travel safely," said Huang Wu.

Joshua noticed that the carriage contained several bags of gold coins, the revenue collected from the trades. As soon as the caravan started moving, they started talking. Joshua narrated his travel stories from Babylon onwards, one nation a day, for the next four days. Amongst the many things Joshua said, his story of the Egyptians taming the flood in the Nile, intrigued Huang Wu. "We have heavy calamities from flood in our Yellow river, year after year . . . I was wondering . . ."

"The Greeks are a genre by itself, always questioned, always needed answers, and always needed an explanation to the answer, Atoms . . . Cosmos . . . Pythagoras . . . Socrates . . . Aristotle . . . Olympics . . . Democracy," Joshua explained.

"Like Socrates, Confucius also asked lots of questions of people," Huang Wu said. "He also wanted to elicit answers from the common man . . ."

At end of the fourth day, after listening to all those immense narrations, Huang Wu looked at Joshua and said, "You have seen it all, probably much more than anybody that I know. What did you make out from those journeys? What were you trying to find?"

Joshua kept quit for a long moment, looking at a distance, cracking the knuckles of his fingers. "All those civilizations have accomplished great things on this earth; looked at the stars, studied the cosmos and practiced democracy. But what is the purpose of our being on this earth? What are our obligations to God and to our fellow humans? There is some wonderful philosophy in our Torah and in the Babylonian texts, but equally, they are also filled with meaningless rituals and pitfalls; punishment for crime is the emphasis rather than forgiveness, absolution or redemption. There must be a better way for humans to live together on this earth."

"Interesting; very interesting," Huang Wu said. "It appears that you have a firm mission. What made you travel to the east? Have you learned about Buddha or Confucius?"

"No sire, I began to learn about Confucius only when I came to your embassy at Ctesiphon. Buddha, I have heard some from Palestine and Rome. There is a tradition that some Buddhist monks have visited Qumran in Judea. But I know not anything about his philosophy."

"Joshua," said Huang Wu, "you will find all the answers you are looking for if you follow the teachings of two sages: Buddha and Confucius. But it might take a long time."

"Certainly, I appreciate all your help. First let me show you a map . . ." Joshua pulled out Strabo's world map from his bag.

Huang Wu glanced at the map Joshua was unfolding, and then he pulled out an elaborate Chinese map embroidered on yellow silk, showing the trading routes, the great cities, rivers, mountains and the boundaries of the Chinese empire. "You should have a copy of this map for your travels from now on. See all these routes, that is, outside of China, from Alexandria to Taxila. These began after Alexander invaded India. There are four Alexandria's within this route."

"Ah, when you check in tonight at the inn in Hecatompylos, make sure that they don't charge you for a companion," Huang Wu said. "You don't appear to be someone who would desire the company of a harlot. As the master has said, 'Spoken words make the character of a man,'" he concluded, smiling.

The caravansary at Hecatompylos was a full-service facility with large restaurants and shops. Young, thin-waisted Persian prostitutes with curly hair and blue eyes, solicited for a short stay or for an entire night. The innkeepers charged guests for a companion for the night, unless notified otherwise.

As days went by, Joshua was more at ease with Huang Wu. "With reference to your going to Taxila," Huang Wu said, "our caravan will take you all the way to Kashgar. We will halt for two nights in all of the major cities, just like here in Hecatompylos. We expect to reach Bactria in about eighty days, and from there you may proceed to Taxila via Begram, which will take another twenty-five to thirty days."

This was the longest trip I have taken so far, but it's worth the effort. This sage Confucius came to me like a golden egg found in the sand. He is a man about whom I should know in full. His words are like timeless maxims.

Huang Wu appeared happy to have conversation and companionship with Joshua. "Ah, usually when I travel long distances like this, my men will provide a Persian girl to travel in my coach to sing, tell stories and provide pleasures. After I saw you at the embassy, I thought for a while and decided to have you instead. You impressed me as a man of substance . . . and I was right."

"Sire, I am humbled by your words. You know my mission now; anything you can tell me about the Chinese beliefs, particularly your philosophy about life, religion, God . . . I will be thankful."

"You see, Confucius has said, *for a man to be effective, he has to be at the right place at the right time,* and it appears that you certainly are. Well, you should know something about our Han Dynasty as a must. Since the Han Dynasty began to rule China about two hundred and thirty years ago, there has been a new order of national consciences and code of conduct in our land, based on the teachings of Confucius, the most widely talked about philosopher of all time. In fact, we have a renaissance of Confucianism, because it is so much a part of our culture. His teachings cover virtually every aspect of human life and relationships."

"First, tell me sire, who was Confucius; a king, priest, philosopher or what?"

"Ah, Confucius was a man of humble means, born to a farmer's family about five hundred and seventy-five years ago, at a time when there was widespread famine in the land and people were dying of starvation and afflictions, while the rulers lived galore with no care or concern for the poor. Confucius was well read on the history of the land. He fell in love with the philosophy of humanism that was practiced by the Chou Dynasty about five hundred years before him."

"Wait a minute; I have something here in my notes about the Duke of Chou . . . mandate of heaven . . ." Joshua searched through his notes.

"Yes, I will tell you, it's a belief: in ancient times the land of China was ruled by Divine spirits who ruled the earth for peace, prosperity, harmony and equality. The kings executed: *The mandate of heaven, the Tao, and the will of heaven on earth.*"

"Did you say, the will of heaven on earth, The Kingdom of Heaven on Earth, really?"

"Yes. The Duke of Chou was the personification of all divine sages in China. Worship of heaven was the central religious belief of the dynasty."

"It appears to me that you are cunningly avoiding the mention of God; tell me what exactly is meant by Heaven?"

"Very smart observation. We will get to that later."

"Well, what made the Duke the most righteous of all, for Confucius to emulate."

"Many things. First, he was against nepotism. During the Chou Dynasty, the kingship was not automatically transferred from the father to the son as an inheritance, but it had to be earned. A righteous man who was found to be most ideal was selected from among the subjects to be the next king. The dynasty believed that this selection process was a mandate from heaven."

"How wonderful. Would that mean that an ordinary man can in fact become the king? Equal opportunity for every citizen in the land?"

"Yes. But, it didn't last for long. After about two hundred years, the administration turned corrupt, which was followed by tribal wars, disarray and anarchy, unfortunately."

"Tell me about Heaven, God . . . the mandate," asked Joshua.

"We have no creation stories in China, Joshua. Nobody talked about the shape of God or a manner in which he created the earth. We believe in Heaven, the guiding and controlling force of the universe." He broke out into a grin and said, "Listen to what Confucius once said, 'We don't know enough about man; how are we to know about the gods?''

Joshua was silent for a long moment. "Thank you. I think I understand. So, what was Confucius trying to achieve?"

"His goal was to restore the order of those golden days. His personal ambition was to be an influential governor, an advisor to the emperor. His attempts failed. He had to leave the village. He said that no man of vision is respected in his own village, and so he traveled from state to state, speaking with people and teaching them. He earned a set of followers who called him 'Master,' and they recorded his spoken words, of which there are very many volumes now. The verses you noted in your papyri from Ctesiphon are all from those records."

No prophet is with honor in his own town, Joshua reminisced, and asked, "Sire, as Confucius traveled from village to village, what was the emphasis of his discourses? Was he received well in the other villages?"

"He talked on very many subjects, except god. He was not received well in all the other villages," Huang Wu explained patiently. "One time, in a village called Kwang, a group of people attacked him. Confucius was bold and resolute in his convictions. He cried out: "Heaven has appointed me to teach this mandate, for which you attack me? He who offends the gods has no one to pray to . . .""

"Sire," Joshua said. "Just now, you said that Confucius never talked about gods, but now . . ."

"You are a very bright listener Joshua," Huang Wu laughed as his belly fluttered and his eyes narrowed. "That was the only occasion he even passively mentioned god. Though he never postulated the theory of an omniscient and omnipotent god, he did speak often about heaven and heaven's will."

"That's where I have some confusion. What did he mean by heaven?" asked Joshua.

"In China, heaven means the eternal guiding force of the universe. Heaven is up above the sky, probably in the firmaments where the ancestral spirits dwelled, that's all."

"So, there is a belief of life after death, the life of the sprits in Heaven. What did Confucius teach about it?"

"Confucius was more interested in this real world which we know, see, touch and feel. His emphasis was about the righteous duties of a man to another man. He refused to discuss miracles, shamanism, life after death or any such things. He was studying life. He said that until we know about life, we cannot hope to understand death."

"I find disconnect here. If Confucius didn't believe in a soul or life after death, why was he a great proponent of rituals and sacrifices?" Joshua asked.

"Joshua. As I told you, he never elaborated on that issue. He was a great believer of ancestral worship for their well-being and continued blessings. He was fond of rituals and sacrifices in the traditional way. He has revered the smoke rising up into the sky from the sacrificial mound as homage to the ancestors. For him, rituals are the means by which mortal beings communicate with the heavens, and auger is the way with which the heavens talk back to us."

"That's strange. So, he believed in augers?" Joshua took a long breath. "What kind of Rituals? Animal sacrifices or . . ."

"Rituals? Simple and elaborates alike. A young man standing up and offering his seat to an older man is a ritual; using the proper gesture of greeting between friends is a ritual; bowing their heads and clasping the hands and welcoming, or even prostrating in front of a king, wearing the right type of garments for appropriate positions and occasions were all simple rituals that he revered. More elaborate rituals such as sacrifices of animals for occasions like a birth, a wedding or a funeral, or even a coronation, were all integral parts of a ritualistic tradition designed to cement the morality of a community. However, calamities like droughts, floods and earthquakes were considered auger of the heavens, and a punishment for failing to properly perform the rituals."

Joshua's thoughts momentarily flew back to the great flood of Noah's times and the destructions of Sodom and Gomorrah.

"He believed that maintaining ideal relationships was the key to the harmony of society – 'love and respect your neighbor,' he taught. 'Family as the center and the finite social unit of the society,' he used to say – the legend of the man who invented 'family.'"

"Invented family?"

"By doing so, the man separated humans from the rest of the beasts."

Joshua laughed delightedly, shaking his head.

From Hecatompylos, as the caravan traveled further east, the landscape turned more arid, and the vegetations more sparse. Aside the caravan route, camels leisurely plodded the loose red soil, herded by men with bulky turbans and crooked staffs. Mud houses in distant villages looked like a cluster of ripe melons half buried in the sand, unpicked. Heavily clad women balancing water pots on their heads walked in rows. The Chinese caravan reached the city of Merv on the fortieth day of their journey for a rest for two nights.

"Joshua, be very careful about all your belongings. Here, the people in general are bandits. They are fierce fighters; very efficient to fight from a charging horse."

"I know a bit about them."

"How? I thought you were here for the first time."

"That's true, but when I traveled from Palestine to Egypt, I traveled with a man from Damascus. Abhi . . ."

"Ah! Abhi . . ." Huang Wu laughed gaily as his slanted eyes narrowed to a line. "He is a very interesting person. He had been transporting our merchandises to Alexandria for the last many years, until he retired."

The caravan started moving east again on the way to the city of Bactria. The Galilean and the Chinese official returned to smattering fun and facts. Huang Wu noted the heavy burden of brochures and hand-written materials with Joshua, which he was referring frequently.

"Joshua, all those brochures, we, the civil servants of the Hans Dynasty, are supposed to know by heart – the teachings of Confucius, and we do, as a matter of our code of conduct. He was a man with remarkable fecundity, very many parables and very many maxims," said Huang Wu.

"I agree, Master; his parables are most remarkable, the best tools to teach . . . " Joshua said.

"His parable about filial piety," Huang Wu said, "virtually every child was taught in China: 'In the middle of a bad winter when all the waters were frozen, a young woman's grandmother, old and frail, was hungry and craved for fish. The devout granddaughter went out in that freezing cold, stood over the frozen lake, and prostrated herself on the ice for two days and two nights, until the warmth from her bosom melted the ice and created two holes in the ice sheet. Through the holes she caught some fish and took them home for her grandmother. The grandmother was delighted. She fried the fish, ate it and rewarded her granddaughter with her blessings and all the wealth she had, and died peacefully."

"That is a beautiful story, really."

"People loved the story so much that later on they added that on the funeral day for the grandmother, the Heavens shone high with heat and light in the middle of the deep winter."

"That indeed is a great parable that sticks," Joshua said. "But some others are questionable,"

Huang Wu's forehead knitted. "Ah, Like what Joshua? I have never heard anybody questioning a parable said by Confucius," he asked.

Joshua read a passage from his notes: "Once, when Confucius was traveling in another state, he came across a court of law where a son was testifying against his father, who had stolen some money. The master became very upset and said, 'In the place that I come from, a son will not testify against his father. When your father is alive, obey by rituals, and when dead, bury by rituals.'"

"Hum . . . what's your objection with that parable?"

"Clearly, there is a moral dilemma here. The father has stolen from another," Joshua said. "If Confucius states that children must defend parents, even when they have been immoral, I disagree. Also, is there any point where he draws the line? What if the father has committed murder or incest; should the child cover up his crime?"

"What would you have done, given those circumstances?" challenged Huang Wu.

"I would certainly have disowned that man; I would have told the truth in the court," declared Joshua.

"Honestly, I have to agree with you, too."

"However, sire, of the many philosophers that I have read, the one I like to take home is Confucius. He stands taller than all the others, and his words stick in my mind as commandments."

"I am glad you took this very long trip; it should be worth the efforts. Now, tell me which is the very best of his teaching parables that taught you the most?"

"Well, there are quite a few, but the one about the tyrants is remarkable."

"There are a few about tyrants; tell me which."

"The story of the fugitive woman who was running away from home," Joshua said.

Huang Wu shook his head. "Oh yes. That one is quite poignant."

It was a story said to have happened once in an early winter when the master was traveling through the valley of Mount Tai. He heard the wailing of a woman from a distance in the woods. He approached the woman. She was sobbing and wailing endlessly in tattered clothes, cold and shivering. When he asked why she was doing so, she replied, 'My husband's father was killed by a tiger here in these woods. My husband was also killed by a tiger here, and now my son has met the same fate." "Then why are you dwelling in such a dreadful place," he asked? "Because," the woman replied, "there are no tyrant kings here.'"

"How is it any different for you, asked Confucius? You lost all your dear ones here?"

"Is there not a difference, Master? The king is supposed to protect us; instead, he persecutes, tortures, kills and lays the body to rot in the streets. Here, the lions kill and, at least, they eat the body out of hunger. Tell me, Master; which is better for me?" asked the woman.

"Sire, at the time of Confucius, there was a group of people called the Realists. Who were they?" He asked. "Were they trying to ridicule the master?"

"Yes, they believed in the strict enforcement of punishment to keep law and order. Another group, the Mohists, believed that universal love could maintain order and harmony in the community. Let me ask you, Joshua, are you a realist or a Mohist?" Huang Wu asked.

"I will be a bit of both – a pragmatist. But, of course, different circumstances will require different kinds of responses. Over all, I believe love and compassion can win more than rules and laws."

"Joshua, in that context, let me ask you what you would say about a man who is liked by all in the country?"

"Liked by all? Even Solomon was not liked by everybody in the country?"

"You are right. But see what Confucius answered, 'To be liked is not sufficient. If a man is truly good, then the good among the townsmen will love him, but the evil will hate him.'"

"How true, Sire. Those words cannot be put in a better way. I have made a note on many of them."

"Let me see," Huang Wu glanced through the notes that Joshua had made: "'First, correct your adultery before you attempt to rectify the slip in others.' What did you make out of that," he asked.

"This is an admonition to a hypocrite, 'remove the beam from your eyes before you whine about the mot in others.'"

"Very good, student," Huang Wu tapped on his shoulders. "From now on, I won't ask you any more questions. You have enough wisdom to critique even Confucius. You are a true gentleman. Everything the master said about a gentleman is truly applicable to you."

"Sire, I am humbled; however, tell me what the master said about a gentleman."

"A true gentleman, he said 'is the one who practices what he preaches, is never afraid to speak his mind, and never wishes something to be done to others which he would not wish to be done to himself. He is never unhappy, afraid or perplexed; does not grieve, nor accuse the Heavens nor blame men for his misfortunes."

"Sire, I beg to disagree. It sounds more like he's speaking of someone who is somehow enlightened and has transcended. Sadness and fear are human emotions, as are joy and courage. Why must a person be devoid of human emotions to be a gentleman?" Joshua asked.

"Indeed, I don't disagree with you, Joshua; you are wise enough even to correct Confucius. I have no doubts. His next statement will justify what you just said."

"Please tell me, sire."

"A gentleman is always under scrutiny and any fault in him will be like a solar eclipse; everybody will see it when it happens, and when corrected, everybody gazes towards him, as well."

Joshua said, "Sire. Sex, lust and strife are all compelling parts of human life. I'd like to hear what the master said about it."

"Of course." the master said. "A gentleman is constantly on guard against himself, against *lust* in his youth when the blood and humors are boiling, against *strife* in his prime when the blood and humors have hardened, and against *avarice* in his old age when his blood and humors are fading. At the same time, he says, sexual desire is extremely compelling, and that he has never seen a man whose moral powers can contain his sexual desire. Do you agree to that, Joshua?" Huang Wu asked.

Joshua thought for a while and finally said soberly, "I agree, Sire, that they are extremely compelling forces. I have fought with them many times, and I have to say that I was not always successful."

"Understood. Listen to this adage from Confucius: 'Man's greatest glory is not in never falling, but in getting up each time after the fall.'"

"I couldn't agree with you more."

Joshua saw a role model in Confucius; a practical philosopher who was different from any he had encountered in the past. Confucius stood in the middle of people and talked about real and tangible ideas, without fear or favor. He didn't envision an ideal republic that resembled Plato's. In fact, he didn't conceive of any republic at all. His idol was the benevolent ancestral king of the Chou Dynasty who would treat men and women equally and rule with fairness and generosity. No eye for an eye; no stoning; no burning; no crucifixions.

It was only three more nights before the caravan was to reach the city of Bactria, yet another one of those cities Alexander wanted to make Alexandria out of. They halted for the night near a red, rocky hill. The servants were busy setting up tents and cooking burnt goat meat for dinner. On a carpet spread on the ground, Huang Wu sat cross-legged for the dinner and invited Joshua to eat with him. For the first time in eighty-two days, Huang Wu ordered a flask of wine, and the two of them shared the drink. When Joshua took the first sip of the Chinese wine, it burned in his mouth and went down like a fireball. However, Huang Wu swallowed the full cup, downed with a gurgling noise, and wiped his mouth with the back of his hand. The yellow on his face turned to crimson, his eyes tightened, and his voice turned gale and jovial.

"Joshua, you are too young in looks, but mature in manners and venerable in wisdom." He took another gulp. "What is the real mission in your . . . this arduous undertaking. I remember your earlier answer. But are you writing a book or planning to teach back in Alexandria?"

"Sire, my people in Palestine are good natured and hardworking folks. Our traditions teach that we are a people chosen by God to rule over other nations of the world. We are commanded to remain unadulterated with the blood of other tribes. Our religious laws, the given truths, are harsh, and their interpretations are brutal, particularly to women."

"Ah, so you are taught to believe that you are a superior tribe . . . to rule over all the other nations of the world. Ha!" Huang Wu paused. "For how long is your nation in existence? How many nations you have ruled over so far?"

"Sire, this is not a matter of joke." Joshua's face turned even more serious. He burned down the cup full of wine, intuitively wiped his lips, and resumed. "I left my land many years ago in search of finding the truth about the religious beliefs, social orders and manner of governance of possibly all the nations of the world."

"Joshua, honestly, this is the most incredible undertaking anybody have ever done. What are you going to do with all this information? Go back and a start a revolution?"

"I don't know yet, sire, but soon I will figure it out."

"Well, to learn something about the very best form of government, you go to China and learn from the present Hans Dynasty about a righteous ruler governing the nation with love and benevolence."

"I agree. I have already learned a lot, but I have decided to continue to explore your model in detail. But, let me ask you a few more questions for my own understanding?"

"Of course, of course, you may ask," Huang Wu pleasantly rubbed his tummy.

"Sire, do you have a death penalty – executions – in China for any kinds of crimes?"

"Ah. Yes, but very seldom; limited to treason and murder. I have never seen one or heard one in my town. But during the times of the tyrants, executions were common for all kinds of offences. In this context, you might want to listen to this story. Once a king asked Confucius, 'Should the lawless be executed?' He replied, 'what need is there for execution, my Lord? If you show goodness and benevolence, your subjects likewise shall be good. Your virtues are like a wind, and that of your subjects like blades of grass. It is the nature of the grass to bend when the wind blows upon it."

Joshua nodded, smiling. "I admire the courage of that man Confucius. But, sire, why did Confucius have to travel from one village to another? Why was he not appointed advisor to a king? Moreover, he challenged the tyrant kings in public. Why was he not silenced by the kings?"

"They could have. But Confucius was very famous and was revered by the public in his own times. If they took the life of Confucius, his *Parable of the Ship and the Sea* would have been fulfilled. The kings were afraid of him."

Joshua was well aware of that parable, which was a nightmare to the tyrant kings.

Confucius said, "The king is the ship riding on the waves, the shoulders of the people. The king can ride the ship in anyway he wants and enjoy the luxury. Dig the oars deep into the water, sail the ship fast or slow, catch the fish to feed, or whatever. But beware! Pay attention to the little tides in the waters and navigate the ship accordingly. Sometimes a gentle tide can transform into a killer squall and sink the ship to the bottom of the sea such that it will never come back."

"That's why in China we say, the power of words is mightier than the sharpness of swords."

"I see that very clearly here," said Joshua. He unrolled a papyri scroll and started reading from it, ' . . . No government will stand without the full confidence of the people.'"

"Yes, the king must get the mandate from the people, too, to rule over them," Huang Wu said. "That was a very important part of his messages."

Joshua smiled. Huang Wu's eyes tightened, and he demanded, "Why?"

"It appears that Confucius had visited Palestine at the time of King Solomon, who ruled our land exactly like Confucius would have wished." Joshua explained.

"Then what happened?"

"We certainly had a few kings who ruled the nation with a mandate from Heaven. But later on the Pharisees – the gate keepers of heaven – made it worse with their own selfish interpretations of the laws."

They talked for a long while. It was late in the night. The next morning the caravan moved to the city of Bactria.

**** **** ****

Owing to the magnanimity of Huang Wu, Joshua had a comfortable and safe journey. He spent the better part of the days with Huang Wu learning all he could about China, Taoism and Confucianism.

"How long are you planning to stay in India?" Huang Wu asked.

"Not more than one year, maybe two . . ."

"How are you planning to go back?"

"At the mercy of strangers. All throughout my travels, I am always dependent on the charity of people, people I have never met before."

Huang Wu took a small piece of blue silk and drew some letters and gave it to Joshua, saying, "Well then, keep this note, just in case you need some help. Present this to our embassies anywhere; they will assist you without a question."

Joshua received the silk piece with both hands. "Thank you sire. I will always remember this charity of yours."

"Well, you certainly are a man of substance. I can only imagine what will become of you. Joshua, if you do decide to travel to China, please come and visit with me in Xian, the original capital of the Chou Dynasty. My office is within the city wall. In India, study the teachings of Buddha in detail. Remember, no foreign religion or philosophy has ever thrived in China but Buddhism, the only exception."

"Why is that?" Joshua asked.

"The Buddhist philosophy is practical, benevolent and non-threatening. You will find many similarities between the teachings of Buddha and the Chinese philosophers, particularly Confucius. I do not think you will find the same similarities in the Hindu culture that dominates India, but, of course, I don't know much about it. You might very well find some surprises. What parts of India do you plan to visit?"

"Taxila," Joshua answered. "Based on my studies, I believe everything I want to know will be in Taxila.

On the eighty-first day of his journey, Joshua exited the caravan in the city of Bactria. Huang Wu's caravan continued to Xian. But the kind man Huang Wu had instructed his embassy scribe Ling Ong to provide boarding and travel assistance for the Galilean for as long as he needed it.

The thin, short Ling Ong with sunken cheeks spoke with a slight stammering: "we-welcome, sire," he said, and took Joshua to his office at the rear end of the embassy building.

"When you travel to the east, you must know Pali, the language they speak in all the northern cities in India. Gr-Greek is known to the people of high co-colors, and Sanskrit to the Bh-Bhrahmins only."

"That thought was in my mind for long. How could I get some help in that matter; some introduction to Pali," inquired Joshua.

"All the st-staff in our embassy know the m-minimum necessary Pali. I ce-certainly will ga-give you some assistance, too."

Joshua stayed at the Chinese embassy in Bactria for three weeks. Each of those days Ling had inquired about a trade group traveling east, but there had been none. During the interim, Ling Ong taught him a bit of the history of the land, some introduction to Pali, and drew for him a detailed road map from Bactria up till Taxila in India.

"When you go-go to a new land, you must have some kn-knowledge about their hi-history and cultures, besides a land like India, where the na-nations of the world have already been mi-mixed."

It indeed was a very complex mix of people, languages and civilizations. In the streets of Bactria, one could hear people speaking Greek, Persian, Bactrian, Parthian, Chinese and Pali. Joshua would soon learn that after Alexander's death the Seleucids controlled all of the territories from the Tigris River to the Indus Valley of India. A very la-large number of Greeks – Alexander's soldiers – had defected. The territories of Parthia and Bactria declared independence from Antiochus II. The Greco-Parthians ruled the south and the Greco-Bactrian, the north. They constantly fought amongst themselves, but both these dynasties had one thing in common: the wish to conquer and rule over India; and conquer they did. The Bactrian Kingdom gradually moved east, invading and occupying large territories in northwest India, including the great cities of Taxila and Mathura, while the Parthian kings carved out large areas of the lower Indus Valley in Punjab, all the way to Jinni, south of Mathura.

In the interim, a savage tribe called the Huns had been gaining power in the farther northern frontiers of China. The Huns advanced south-west, and defeated and evicted the powerful Yeuh-Chi tribe from that area. Now the Yeuh-Chies wandered south looking for another place to settle. They arrived on the banks of River Syre, which was the homeland of the Saka tribe. The Yuen-Chi tribe confiscated the Sakas and took over the land. The newly homeless Sakas traveled further south, conquered the Bactrian state and established their kingdom in Bactria. They grew further east towards India and established the Saka Dynasty in the lower Indus Valley. Another major tribe of the Yeuh-Chies, the Kushans, crossed the Hindu Kush Mountain ranges under the leadership of Kujula Kadphises – their first king – and established their kingdom in northern India.

Most everyday, Joshua would wander through the city, looking for a means to go east. There were mounted police with conical hats and gilded armors patrolling the streets day and night. There were two large marketplaces, one in the northern quarter of the city where the traders from China rested and traded, and another even bigger market in the east which concentrated on trade between India and the west. The highway to Taxila originated from the gates of this market. The central treasury at the marketplace was the busiest building in this city, as traders and foreigners were clamoring to buy and exchange the newly minted gold and silver coins carrying the image of Kujula Kadphises fashioned like the Roman Emperor Augustus. Law and order was maintained perfectly in the whole city, particularly in and around the treasury, lest armed bandits invade – the Huns.

Joshua stood in line and exchanged his twelve gold coins. He received equivalent coins in gold, silver, bronze, and copper drachma. He even successfully communicated with the money changers in his newly learned Pali.

"Master, do you require any assistance to travel to the east?" a man asked from behind.

Joshua was surprised to see a bent old Indian, with a long gray beard and a huge mustache turned upward like a bull's horn, smiling widely and showing his only remaining tooth in the lower gum, tugging on his shoulder bag. He was wearing a turban, and spoke in a mixture of broken Greek and Pali.

"Where to the east, elder?" asked Joshua.

"Wherever you want to go, Master"

"Taxila, are you going that way?"

"I will take you, Master. My horse is strong, only three years old, and my chariot, like king's palace. Outside . . . market . . . come, please. Come with me, Master, if you go that way, please." The old man couldn't stop smiling. Before Joshua said a word, he grabbed Joshua's large bag and guided the way to the outer gate of the market, elbowing his way through the crowds.

"What's your name, sire," Joshua asked.

"Please call me Krishna, Master . . . Krishna. They won't let me ride in the carriage inside the market anymore. They whip us," said Krishna.

It was true. Joshua noted the mounted police officers with large daggers slung on their waist belts, lashing their leather whips in the air frequently and shouting, "Move! Move!" while laughing gaily when people tripped one over the other while trying to escape the whip lashes.

Outside of the market, there were hundreds of carriage coaches pulled by mules and horses. Krishna's chariot was an old carriage coach, and his three-year-old horse was more like a ten-year-old mule. Krishnan assisted Joshua into the carriage by pulling up his hands.

It was a very old carriage, but decorated with paintings, frills and flags. Inside, Joshua sat beside a deep-blue terracotta statue of a man with a woman's face playing a flute, wearing a gold crown and garlands of marigold. The space was filled with smoke from two slowly burning incense wickers.

Krishna stood in front of the carriage and called out with his palms funneled around his mouth. "Is there anybody going to Drapsaca, Nicaea, Taxila, or any place on the way?" When nobody responded, even after several shouts, he returned to the carriage, whipped the mule and started Joshua on his long journey to Taxila.

Krishna appeared thin and frail, but it was difficult to tell as he was clad in several layers of clothes.

Joshua sat comfortably, elbowed on the round cushion studying the blue statue, and asked the driver, "Krishna, whose is this statue?"

"Oh, Master, that is lord Krishna. I am a devotee of Lord Krishna. His blessing . . . everyday . . . always . . . every morning. I pooja Lord Krishna every morning . . ."

"You bear the same name as the Lord?" Joshua asked.

"Hang, Master. Krishna. Many, many Indian people bear the names of the gods. Krishna; Rama; Gopala; Madhava – there are many names like that, my son, little Krishna, but Lord Krishna is the best, the ultimate God . . . the Great Avathar. The ninth Avathar."

Joshua found it interesting to talk to this man who was trying his best to convey the message with a mixture of languages, great intonations, gestures, and even drawing pictures in the air, not only to practice his newly learned dialect Pali, but also to learn from him.

"Krishna, how many Avatars had been so far?"

"Our beliefs . . . nine . . . nine avatars up until now. The first avatar, a fish, Matsya; then Koorma, a turtle; then Varaaha, a boar; the next one Narasimha, half-lion, half-man; then a dwarf, Vamana; then, Parasuraman, Balaraman, Sreeraman, and Lord Krishna. The next, the tenth avatar, will be Kalki." He turned around, nodding to see how his new client appreciated the lecture. "Each incarnation is for saving the world, except Kalki. Kalki destroy. That's all."

Joshua didn't have to ask any question. Krishnan continued engaging his client. "Lord Krishna, he was very naughty boy. Steal butter and eat. He grew up handsome. Plays flute. Aha, seduced girls – he best to seduce girls. Once, the girls all went down to river. Bathe. They kept all their clothes on the shore. Lord Krishna took all their clothes and climbed on top of a mango tree. Ha-ha-ha! You know what happens to the girls; no clothes? But Lord Krishna, good. Love, great love. Lord Krishna, I am devotee. Devotee, get blessed. Bless me. Bless my family," Krishna concluded.

Slowly the land became more arid with orange-colored sand and rocky formations. One village separated from another by several miles. Krishnan knew the places for rest and food. After two weeks of travel with Krishna, listening to his stories, and after crossing four shallow tributaries of the Oxus River, they reached the city of Drapsaca on the western plateau of the Hindu Kush Mountain range.

**** **** ****

The caravansary at the city of Drapsaca was very active with traders from India, China, Persia and Babylon in addition to the Parthians and the Bactrians. "We stay here in Drapsaca for three nights. From now on, we only travel as caravan. The roads, not safe. Afridi tribes. Bandits, many bandits," said Krishnan.

Each one of the three days Krishnan went to the gate of the caravansary and shouted, calling for people to travel to Taxila. Two Chinese, Luangi and Lao Zugi, joined them to ride to Taxila. From their saffron cloaks and shaven heads, it was not difficult to make out that they were Buddhist monks.

They both spoke fluent Pali. They were from the city of Xian on their way for a pilgrimage to the holy places of Gaya, Sarnath, and Kapilavasthu. Luangi, the taller muscular man with a deep voice, had traveled the route once before, while Zugi, the slim one with feminine features, was traveling for the first time. The monks were extremely delighted to meet a man who had traveled the many countries in the west and had endless questions for Joshua. In China, these monks were part of the class of Shi, the administrative elite scribes, and were Taoists before becoming Buddhist.

From Drapsaca, the caravan to the east started off with thirteen coaches drawn by horses, mules and seven camels on the way to the next hill station, Alexandria at Caucasum, about sixty miles uphill on the western Hindu Kush mountain ranges.

By afternoon, the landscapes had started to change further. The road inclined. Rolling hills with deep-green vegetation were in sight, and the sky was deep blue with no specks of cloud. The temperature began to drop as well.

The road from Drapsaca to Caucasum was narrow, winding, and at times deeply eroded with gutters and potholes. In some places they had to get out of the carriage and push the vehicle to get out of the deep waterways on the road, yet in other places mud slide from the high hills on one side had made mud-dunes on the road, so that one wheel of the coach could run out of the road towards the deep abyss where the depth was seen only as fog. The problem was even more treacherous when a caravan arriving from the opposite side had to crossover.

After a week of arduous journey through the rutted, rocky, winding roads, climbing the hills, they reached the hill station of Alexandria at Caucasum, the city built by Alexander as a strategic location when he subdued the tribes and nations of the land during his invasion of India.

From there, through hills and valleys, they traveled south for three days and reached the city of Nicaea, a city bustling with business of wool, textiles, leather, honey and handicrafts, a very important business hub connecting Alexandria at Caucasum in the north and Alexandria at Ghazni in the south, and Nyssa in the east. The men here wore bulky rolled turbans, and the women wore long frilled skirts and jingling tinklets in their ears, and had noses pierced with lapis lazuli stones.

They stayed in the city for three nights for rest and preparations for the most arduous and dangerous stretch of the journey – entering India through the Khyber Pass.

In the meantime, Joshua got to know the Buddhist monks a lot closer. Luangi was more spontaneous and loquacious, "Last time I traveled to Taxila with a group of fur traders from Ctesiphon. In fact, all the men that I have met going to India have been business men, but I have seen men from Babylon in Taxila . . ." Lao Zugi, the silent listener of the two, said something in the ears of Luangi with tender gestures and eyelashes fluttering. Luangi smiled and said, "Zugi would like to know whether you are a monk or not."

"No, I am a student." As Joshua explained, the two of them listened attentively, holding hands. Their journey to the Hindu Kush and the Khyber Pass had started.

From the city of Nicaea, the caravan started riding east through the northern steep banks of the Cophen river, the river that flowed quietly through the deep gorges on their right to the east. Soon, the road turned mostly uphill and winding, with steep rocky mountains on the left and steep valleys and abysses to the right.

On the fourth day of their journey by mid-afternoon, as they were climbing uphill, suddenly the air was filled with very thick fog, such that they couldn't even see the coach immediately in front of them. It was about a mile before the hilltop inn.

Joshua suggested, "Maybe we can walk to the inn."

"No," Luangi warned, "The tigers; they can see in fog and dark. We will stay together until the fog clears."

The fog did not clear until high noon the next day. Joshua stayed covered under the blanket, and the monks stayed under one blanket hugging each other, but without making any noise, eating or drinking. The next day, as the sun rose high and the fog melted, they resumed the journey further high to the hill station of Nyssa. "From here, we will climb up nearly a thousand feet to reach the mountain pass," Luangi told Joshua. "There can be snow there at any time of the year."

Joshua was listening, changing gazes from the map spread in his hands and the steep blue mountain ranges on either side. "This road was much better long ago when emperor Chandragupta Maurya ruled India. They say the young Chandra Gupta had met Alexander, but I am not sure."

"You are from a faraway city in Xian; how come you are aware of all these histories in detail?" Joshua asked.

"In Xian we have lots of travel documents about India. Besides, about four years back I went through these roads to Sarnath. Many of our own people have traveled to India, like us, to visit Buddhist holy places."

That evening the weather changed for the worse. Freezing, whistling winds continuously blew from the west, and the mountain peaks were shrouded with thick fog. Joshua covered his head with woolen shawls and leaned back in the carriage.

Krishnan said, "Master, cover mouth too. No much talk . . . much cold."

"He is a very bright man," said Luangi, "in high cold we lose heat as fog through the mouth when we talk."

After another three days of uphill travel, in the far distance a void was seen in the high Hindu Kush Mountains like a giant footstep that flattened a mud hill, a crack in the armor of the mountain – a gorge. The land was rocky and winding, but uphill no more. As they approached the mountain pass, on either side rocky peaks rose up high into the skies, green at the foot and fog at the head.

Pointing to the mountain pass, Luangi announced, "It's through this pass that thousands of Buddhist monks fled India, finding solace in China. It's through the same pass that Darius of Persia, Alexander of Macedonia and all the Parthians, Bactrians and Kushans entered and conquered India, one after the other."

Conquerors entered; philosophers exited! And now me, a poor carpenter from Nazareth, also joining the elite group . . . Joshua thought.

The caravan rested for a day, paid toll to the javelin-carrying Afridi tribes, and resumed through the winding narrow pass for another three days. On the fourth day morning, bright light from the rising sun fell on their faces. The road quickly descended and a vast landscape opened before their eyes like a green bowl. The farthest end their eyes could not reach, and at the very bottom silver streaks were visible – the plains of Peshawar, the Indus River and its tributaries.

"Now good road . . . India!. . . India!" shouted Krishnan amidst hacking and spitting.

"How far away is Taxila from here?" Joshua asked.

"About one hundred and eighty miles," replied Luangi. "but from here on, the ride will be much smoother and faster. Emperor Ashoka, the grandson of Chandra Gupta, has improved the highways greatly."

Indeed, the roads were wider, well paved with several wayside rest houses, gardens, mango groves, drinking water facilities, porters' rest, and all. Mounted Kushan soldiers with glittering brasses and conical hats were also seen by the roadside.

The caravan halted for three days of rest and relaxation by the banks of one of the upper tributaries of the Indus. The water was very cold, as it was drained down from the upper plains of Tibet, from the snow-capped mountains of the Himalayas. The land itself was robust, with green trees and endless acres of paddy fields.

Why the Chinese, blessed with such wonderful traditions of the Mandate of Heaven, the Hans dynasty that is nurtured by the teachings of Confucius, were turning to be Buddhist monks was mind boggling to Joshua.

Luangi answered: "Ha, Buddhism in China; first of all, the teachings of Buddha were known to us before Confucius was even born. But its spread is a different matter altogether. From the very ancient time onwards in China, people believed in Taoism, the supreme power that existed in nature – the formless, the undifferentiated power – the Way, the Tao. You know about the Shamans, don't you?"

"Yes, the Shamans, the people with superhuman powers, capable of traveling through the sky or under the earth, claimed to possess the ability to generate a hurricane or a rainstorm . . ."

"Yes, yes, such people – the Shamans. They considered themselves equal to God." said Luangi with a sideward smile.

Joshua nodded.

"Certainly not. But such a philosophy cultivated a feeling in people's minds, a sense of confidence that the mind can, in fact, control the body and nature."

"But how does it answer my question? Joshua asked.

"I will come to that in a moment. At this juncture two philosophical thoughts dominated the Chinese minds: Lao-tzu and Confucius. They were contemporaries almost. Lao-tzu was a learned man who believed that there is a certain natural order to life, and humans are expected to conform to that order. He taught that each person had the capacity to understand his own nature and the ways in which he behaved appropriately and inappropriately. We may call it existentialism."

"Was he trying to say that each person has an inner voice, the conscience guiding him?" asked Joshua.

"Exactly, you said it much better than I ever could. He did not believe that it was even possible or to be expected that people would ever know and understand all the realities and truths about nature. 'By doing nothing, nothing is left undone,' Lao-tzu preached, 'when you start doing things, some are left undone, some imperfectly.'"

"But is it not loath?" Joshua said. "Is there not a purpose for our being on this earth?"

"I believe you are right, but there is much more in his teachings," Luangi resumed. "He preached for a quiet and non-interfering life. A village is an ideal place for a quiet, humble, rustic life; minimal needs, minimal desires. Why the dogs in one village bark for the roosters crocking in the other village?"

"Did Lao-tzu have lots of followers?" Joshua asked.

360

"Once upon a time there were. However, Taoism was unsuccessful to influence or govern a population. Ironically, Lao-tzu, the founder of Taoism, traveled to India and became a follower of Buddha later in his life, That significantly increased the luster of Buddhism in China."

"Now I get it. Taoism and Lao-tzu cultivated the Chinese minds for Buddhism to grow and flourish,'" Joshua said.

"You are right. But Confucius had learned Buddhism very thoroughly and incorporated many of the Buddhist principles into his teaching, such that at present the philosophy of Confucius towers high above all other philosophical thoughts in China."

How ignorant is the rest of the world about China and her philosophers. *Why had Alexander decided to go to India rather than China? Why did all those Buddhist monks flee India?* Joshua had wondered.

"There is one thing more you should know." Luangi resumed, "The most famous emperor of the Han Dynasty was Wudi, who ruled over China some two hundred years ago. He was a benevolent ruler who synthesized a national philosophy combining Buddhism, Confucianism, Taoism and legalistic rules. His forty years of rule was the most peaceful and prosperous time of our country."

"Friends, forgive me. Why did you decide to become followers of Buddha?" Joshua asked.

Luangi became quiet for a moment. He looked into the eyes of his companion passionately, and then fixed his eyes in the distance, resting his chin on his fist. "Joshua, this question cannot be answered easily. My reason may not be yours. Buddhism is not a set of rules or regulations. You train your own mind and find the answers to your questions within yourself. Some people feel it, some don't. First of all, it is almost impossible to emulate Buddha. You have to reject all your worldly desires and follow a rigorous path, which is not possible for most people. For me, the teachings of Buddha empowered me to truly understand who I am." Luangi gazed at Zugi then threw his arms around his neck.

Such was the nature of the dialogue between the Chinese monks and Joshua for the following two weeks as they continued their carriage ride to Taxila.

How many new places, faces, beliefs, customs and traditions can there possibly be? Joshua wondered. What's right; what's wrong? Will I ever be able understand it all? And now, this Buddhist idea . . . I cannot empty all the thoughts from my mind. I have a people, a family, a woman, a mission. There must be a reason why I am here on earth. I must do what is meant for me. Only I will know it. For that knowledge, that wisdom, I pray to my Father up in the Heaven. If you don't do anything, nothing will be left undone, says Lao-tzu. Then he goes in search for Buddha. Who is Buddha? Megasthenes says there are seven classes in India based on colors, but let me ask Krishnan. The man, who comes out of the waters wet, must know the temperature of the water best.

"Krishnan, tell me; in your society, what color do you belong to?" Joshua asked.

"Master, in India . . . men born in four classes . . . and the Chandallas . . . no class. Bhrahmins are top." He flailed his hand high up above his head. "All wealth . . . knowledge to Bhrahmins. Next Kshathrya . . . kings . . . fighters. They rule . . . defend . . . country. The third class . . . Visas. I am Visas. We do farming . . . raising cattle . . . merchants, trading, buying, and selling. Then the Shudra . . . servant class. You do that, they do that . . . no do that, they no do that." Krishnan, looking back at the tourists, laughed with satisfaction as he was able to teach something to them.

"Joshua, the origin and growth of Buddhism has a lot to do with that system." Luangi said. "Buddha spoke against this heinous system most forcefully. Apart from the four colors, there is this group, the Chandallas, the untouchables; they are considered subhuman. Nobody speaks to them, touches them, or walks on the land they tread. You won't see any of them on these highways. They have no kings, laws, rules or rulers. They are different."

"Sire, this is the most horrible system of which I have ever heard," Joshua said. "Is it all true, still?"

"All true, Joshua. When you go to Taxila, try to visit one of their alleys; you have to see it to believe."

**** **** ****

From Ctesiphon, after traveling well more than fifteen hundred miles over a period of 180 days, Joshua reached the city of Taxila. The large fortified city of Taxila was under the control of the Kushan king, Kujula Kadphises. Mounted police with conical hats strolled on its mighty embankments, and on its turrets fluttered the yellow standards of Kadphises, with two lions on hind legs holding the globe.

The Buddhist monks continued their journey east. Krishnan helped Joshua find lodging in a servant's quarters – the servants who cooked and cleaned for the wealthy princes who came to Taxila from faraway places – near the east gate of the city. Within the first week of his arrival in the city, Joshua met a southern prince named Ramavarma, a short man with brown skin clad in gold and silk, in the campus of the learning complex. When Rama Varma learned that Joshua was from Israel, suddenly his face lit up. "We have a large population of Jews at the Malabar coast in my kingdom; good people," said Rama Varma gaily. His shapely mustache that was turned up danced in unison when he talked. Joshua was equally excited to hear that his own people were settled in India, too. Rama Varma was the crown prince of the royal family in Muziris, on the southwestern coastal region of Malabar. The prince offered Joshua to move in with him in his private quarters. Joshua accepted the invitation with gratitude and moved in with Sivan and Gopalan, in the adjacent room of the prince. Sivan and Gopalan were the king's assistants, body guards, as well as physician trainees.

The lodging complex at the east gate of the University of Taxila had a large contingent of students from the southern kingdoms of Chera, Chola and the Pandya territories. Those students in general had darker skin, were shorter in stature, and spoke languages that had a musical quality to it. They all seemed to have great musical talents, too. Usually, they gathered in the evenings for discussions and singing songs, playing drums. Walking to the stream early in the morning, exercise, and taking a wet bath were among the Ayurvedic routines of the prince. Joshua joined him every day.

How could there be a Jewish population at the Malabar cost, so far away from Israel. One of those lost tribes? Joshua wondered.

"They came as refugees – some five hundred families – when Jerusalem was sacked, and your temple was destroyed by a certain Nebuchadnezzar from Babylon," Rama Varma said.

"Do they have a synagogue there? What kind of business are they involved in?"

"Yes, they do have a synagogue at fort Cochin," Rama Varma said. "They are mostly in business – exports. There are ships in our port at Muziris from Persia, Babylon and Egypt."

"Tell me, Raja; from your land, how do the boats reach, say, Alexandria by the great seas?"

"From the Malabar Coast, the ships sailed around the coastal areas of northwest India and go west to the cost of Gedrosia, Arabia and to the Red Sea. The ships enter Egypt through the great canals built by the pharaohs, connecting the Red Sea to the Pelusiac Branch of the Nile and finally to the Mediterranean Sea and beyond. The ancient seafarers understood and took full advantage of the direction of the monsoon winds to and fro. For about six months, the southwest monsoon aids travel in the direction of India, and for the remaining six months, the northeast winds will take them west."

The world is getting smaller, Joshua thought. He remembered traveling to Egypt by the side of the Pelusiac branch of the Nile with Abhi Faroosh.

"So, the Jews at Muziris were not slaves, and they were not persecuted?"

"No, they were not persecuted. Joshua, the Hindu culture has a philosophy with wide-open gates. From Rama Varma Joshua would soon realize that virtually anybody can practice Hinduism pretty much anyway they like. There is even room for an atheist. There are some Devi cults who drink alcohol, eat meat, participate in sexual orgies and human sacrifices, and even strangle people to death to fulfill Devi's pleasure.

Joshua's face turned pale hearing such naked truths about some religious sects committing human sacrifices. *Then again, look what Yahweh had ordered Abraham to do to test his faith*, he thought.

"But, Raja, in your kingdom in Muziris, do you practice the color system?" Joshua asked.

"Yes," the prince said. "The color system is fundamental to our culture. But, of course, ours is a culture of great diversity. For example, in many other cultures harlots are stoned, but in our system they, too, have a place."

"I am most interested to hear that," Joshua said.

"Our temple damsels, the Davadasis, may look like prostitutes in your eyes, having sex with several men, but in our society they are just Davadasis, servants of Krishna performing their duty of satisfying others with sexual favors. For the same matter, prostitutes occupied prominent and considerable position in the society. They were invited to the king's courts as preferred guests for ceremonial occasions, including the coronation of a king. I am sure you have seen similar things in your travels?"

"Of course I have," said Joshua. "In the ancient Babylonian civilization, temple damsels were respected and protected as well."

The flowers started blooming, and the days started getting longer. It was spring in Taxila, and they started walking in the evenings, visiting places of interest. Rama Varma had a particular passion to visit Buddhist shrines.

In Rama Varma, Joshua saw a kind and compassionate man, a prince well groomed to be the king, and educated from age five onwards in history, Vedas, the Upanishadts, the *Bhagavath Geetha*, and now in Taxila to study the art of governance and politics from the Chanakya school. *His subjects are blessed,* he thought. In addition to Rama Varma, there were a few other princes also registered at the Chanakya school in Taxila.

"Is it a must that all princes have to come here in Taxila for training before they are crowned?" Joshua asked.

"Not at all," the king said. "Some come, most don't. This city had already been a great learning center for Indian philosophy and advanced learning for about six hundred years. From the Vedic time onwards, Indian kings had established their capitals in Taxila."

"Sorry to interrupt, Raja, but what are Vedic times?" Joshua asked.

"That's the time when the original philosophical principles of India evolved, as an oral tradition, say some two thousand years back," the Prince said.

"Raja, until I came here and saw this great university, I had no idea of such places of grandeur and excellence. Who actually founded the university?"

"All these majestic buildings and departments came into being at the time of Chandra Gupta Maurya. That's a few years after the invasion of Alexander. But Taxila became the greatest intellectual and learning center in the world in the times of Ashoka – the grandson of Chandra Gupta."

"But Ashoka was a Buddhist, was he not?"

"Of course," the king said. "It was the classical times of the Buddhist free thinking and expression. Here in Taxila, mathematics, philosophy, medicine, economics and such other disciplines were freely discussed and taught. Students from India, China, Bactria and even Greece and Rome have traveled here to study at the learning center. It was here in Taxila that the Mahayana movement in Buddhism evolved as a practical philosophy for the entire population."

"Is that the time when pretty much the whole of India became Buddhists?"

"Yes, pretty much."

"Then what happened. Why did the Buddhists have to flee to China?" Joshua asked.

"It's a long story. Asoka's legacy of Buddhism had lasted only for one hundred and thirty-six years when Pushya Mithra Sunga assassinated the last Mauyran emperor and established a Hindu Dynasty with Pataliputhra as its capital. But it's a lot more than that."

"Were the Buddhists persecuted?"

"You know it all, Joshua." Rama Varma laughed gaily.

**** **** ****

Joshua registered for Vedic studies at the learning center of Taxila, but it would be another four months before the school started. The company of the prince was a big solace. As a routine, the prince ate his royal meal early in the evening, all vegetarian, cooked by his servants deliciously with coconut milk and oil. Then he went for a long walk in and around the city and watched the sunset, weather permitting. Joshua was a part of that routine, shadowing the prince for sightseeing and conversation.

The city center had a great square, where religious conventions were held and students usually hung out. It was here in this square that the Dharmarajika Stupa built by Ashoka stood tall. It was a large cylindrical column hewn in red stone, reminiscent of the great obelisks of Egypt, standing on a three-layered pedestal, with Ashoka's inscriptions written for everyone to study and practice, akin to the Stella of Khammurabi in Babylon.

One day, while they tarried along the paved and colonnaded walkways of the university complex, Rama Varma paused for a moment and pointed towards a temple-like stone building with a pagoda at the entrance, and said: "That's where all the original writings of Manu are kept. The Manu's temple of Vedic Studies was established exclusively for Bhrahmins. You or I will not be admitted there."

"Why not you, Raja?" he asked. "After all, you are the king to be. If anybody has to learn the Manu's edicts, it must be you."

"That's all correct." Rama Varma smiled. "But I am a Kshathrya prince. I cannot sit shoulder to shoulder with a Bhrahmin and discuss the edicts of Manu. Only a Bhrahmin priest can interpret the edicts for me. I have done that already."

"But then how am I . . ."

"Don't you worry Joshua; your Vedic studies are not conducted here. Those are up in the teaching halls. Besides, when you go to Mathura, which I very strongly advise, you can gain further depths in his edicts there."

"Joshua, I want to show you something unique." He pointed to an old, stand-alone small stone building on the eastern wing of the university complex, and said, "That is the school of atheism."

"Atheism?" shouted Joshua.

"Yes, atheism. Don't get surprised. Hinduism is a very complex philosophy."

The summer heat and the hot winds of June were at times difficult to bear. The School of Vedic Studies and Buddhism was closed for the summer and would open again in September after the monsoon season. Joshua had a desire to travel to China, too, but Rama Varma advised: "I don't find a reason for you to travel to China to study Buddhism. Here in Taxila you can learn the general principles, and there are many Vihara's in and around the city where you can go to observe or even practice, if that's what you wish."

As if an idea caught on suddenly, the king said, "Joshua, I was thinking. Until September you may come for some lectures with me to the School of Arthashastra, don't you worry about the little tuition fees, keep company to me. If you don't find it interesting, you can stop coming."

"That would be great," Joshua said.

The School of Arthashastra where Rama Varma had registered had been established three hundred years back by Chanakya, the political advisor to the great Mauryan king, Chandragupta. The main topics were the general principles and trainings in state craft, economic policies and military strategies – the skills necessary for the grooming of a king, a benevolent monarch. Chanakya believed that a king should acquire technical understanding and be knowledgeable in many subjects.

For Joshua, it was a time-killing endeavor initially. He was not surprised when he heard the code of conduct of the kings as Chanakya had taught: *The king should model virtue, charity and righteousness by his own example. The king should continually strive for excellence by acquiring broad amounts of knowledge and endear himself to the people by enriching them and treating them fairly. He should practice nonviolence, and avoid capriciousness, daydreaming, falsehood, extravaganzas, indulgences, and associations with harmful people,* nor did he expect anything less.

Joshua could not but marvel at the cardinal differences in outlook of the Indian statesman in comparison to the Egyptian, Roman, Greek or Babylonians and his own, with rare exceptions such as Solomon and Khammurabi. Plato only envisioned a republic that was never realized; Confucius preached about it, but he was rejected from state to state; but here in Taxila, they had already groomed young kings in the real world for hundreds of years!

At the height of the summer in June, Taxila was hot and arid. The dry summer had sucked out the last drops of moisture from the trees. People say that in some years trees go up in flames due to the fiery heat from the sun.

One very humid day in late June, under the dull sky, the students, as usual, were all sitting, chatting and strolling in the university campus. The sun was high, the air was still and the heat was intense. Presently, the winds started blowing heavily, snapping tree limbs and tearing shingles from rooftops. The winds settled for some time only to beat down even heavier. The south winds blew through the buildings and trees with an intense whistling noise. Within a moment, out of nowhere, rain started pouring down; sheets of water, pounding on the roofs like a thousand horse hooves hitting the cobblestones. Soon there were thunderbolts, lightning and even heavier rain which pummeled the land. Water; it was water everywhere like an ocean, all within about an hour. A great tumult broke out, and the people of the city all ran out into the rain cheering, singing and dancing. Men, women, old, young, rich, poor, the prince, Gopalan, Sivan – everybody celebrated the rain. It was monsoon in Taxila.

The rain came at a much-needed time. But now there was water everywhere. The ground swelled. The small puddles rapidly turned into lakes, and then, just as suddenly as it had started, the rain stopped. The sun lit the sky, and the water on the ground drained somewhat. Another bout of torrential rain followed that night, and the next day, and the day after. This was a new experience for Joshua; continuous rain for weeks, and intermittently for three weeks.

**** **** ****

In early August, students from far and near had started arriving. The campus at Taxila turned busy and vibrant with discussions and exchange of ideas between scholars of many nations. In the evenings, students gathered in groups in the vast esplanade of the university to debate and discuss the various pros and cons of their studies and curriculum.

Joshua started his classes with sixty students, eight of them Chinese, two Persian and one Greek from Damascus, and the rest from different parts of India. Bhruga, the man behind a large dark frizzy beard clad in large flowing saffron gown, was their guru. The man, who talked with half-closed eyes, did not like any interruptions, but he was available in the school from sunrise to sunset for clarification of any questions.

Joshua would soon learn that the sage Vyassa the First had classified the ancient Vedic treatise in four massive volumes, the Rig, Yajur, Sama, and Atharva Vedas. At the very outset, Bhruga said, "I will not recite any of those hymns, but I will give you a summary of all of them in the upcoming months. The Holy Vedas are the given truths said by enlightened Sages of ancient times, truths that dawned in their souls at the height of their meditations. We will go through some of the ten thousand five hundred hymns of the Rig-Veda, then a fair portion of the one hundred and eight volumes of the Upanishadts, which are the interpretations of the Vedic principles, and finally a summary of the ethical and religious codes of conduct of the Sage, Manu."

First, Bhruga narrated the Hindu creation story: "In the beginning, the whole universe was a mass of darkness and confusion;" Bhruga's voice resonated, "in which the universal elements were all dissolved, from which large masses of water and dry land evolved, followed by light and glowing bodies in the sky. In that mass of universal power and confusion, Bhrahman," when he said "Bhrahman," the room shook, "created Himself by depositing the glowing seed of life in a shell, from which He came about. From the upper and lower halves of the shell, heaven and earth came about." The guru stopped the lecture and the students were expected to close their eyes and meditate.

Interesting, Joshua thought. *God created himself!* Many such thunderous lectures ensued detailing the creation of the universe. "Bhrahman Himself was both a man and a woman. Thereafter, He created a series of Devas – demigods – Indra, Agni, Varuna . . ."

Then there was the lecture of the creation of man – the Purusha – the fundamental secret of the God-given color system. "Bhrahman created the primordial human – Purusha – when He chanted 'Ohm.'

Then all the sub-gods, the Devas, assembled around the new creation. Purusha was then sacrificed to create the four classes of mankind. From the head the Bhrahmins came about, the priestly class; from the torso, the Kshathrya, the warrior class; from the limbs, the Visas, the class of merchants, artisans, and farmers; and finally, from the feet, the Shudra, the servant class. Of these, the first three classes have colors, and the Shudra are inferior and colorless. Thus, the color-class system of Hinduism is fundamental and God given."

Such segments of lectures with interim meditations, human tales, fairy tales and mythical stories continued six days a week for three months. Soon, he got into the substance of the Vedas. It indeed was the largest compendium of hymns – the central piece amongst the whole Veda literature.

The Vedic hymns were all meant for rituals and sacrifices. All of them invariably started with the lighting of a fire, with chanting of a hymn; invocation of the appropriate God, with another hymn; burning incenses and ghee, with another hymn; then the prayer to the Gods – the request – with several hymns; then sacrifices of animals, birds or whatnot with another set of hymns; then concluding the rituals with a few other hymns; then hymns for putting out the fire, disposing of the remains, blessing to the crowd . . . hymns . . . hymns. There was a ritual and a hymn for everything: to obtain blessings, to enhance pleasures, to gain a child, a good marriage, destruction of enemies, to avoid floods or droughts, sexual pleasures, etc.

But, the rituals could be conducted by the Bhrahmin priests only; and, the hymns were chanted in Sanskrit only; and the hymns were chanted only in a certain precise manner, with a certain tune and rhythm only, with exquisite attention to pronunciations and intonations; which, only the Bhrahmins were divinely authorized to do; and, the script of these hymns came in only by an oral tradition for which no other colors had access; and for each of these rituals the Bhrahmin priests must receive a gift – gifts they were entitled to receive.

However, Joshua found several pearls of wisdom in many of those hymns – the Gayathri Hymn in particular – reminiscent of the Babylonian prayer to the Father in heaven and the Egyptian prayer to Aten. The Vedas did mention a universal god, a universal father, in which everything is included and excluded. In metaphors, Bhrahman is described as the cosmic father; the sun and moon are his eyes, and the air his breath, the earth his body, etc.

The Vedic course itself was intense and tiring, but the discussions that were conducted in the evenings were active, informal, and unrestricted. Anybody in the group could offer an opinion under no duress; even to state that all these stories were hallucinations of the ancient sages under the influence of herbs; that was also acceptable. Students were encouraged to ask questions.

"Guru, from the sacrifice of the Purusha, it appears that the Chandallas were not part of the creation of humans. What are they? Humans or subhumans?"

Bhruga answered calmly, "The untouchables are not humans by the Vedic order. They are definitely subhuman, more like two-legged animals that speak, for which no Vedic traditions are applicable. They live way outside the villages in shanty places, feeding on dead animals and rotten meat, doing menial jobs – toilet cleaning, scavenging, body burning, leather handling . . . ."

"So, they are pretty much employed to absorb the, filth and the pollution of the society?" Joshua asked.

"You may consider it so," said Bhruga.

At that moment, with that question, the attention of the class had turned to Joshua, particularly from the Chinese students.

"Guru, what makes a person to be born to a particular color?" asked a Chinese student.

"It is neither a chance nor an accident; it is determined by the actions or Karma of that person in the previous life, as simple as that," replied Bhruga.

"What is meant by stating that it is the Dharma of Bhrahmins to receive gifts; they wouldn't give away any?" asked another student from China.

"That is correct. Their presence on this earth is the gift to all the others. It's dharma that the Bhrahmins accept gifts. Gifts encompass a very wide array of privileges, including the right to the first night of a virgin, the initiation ceremony," said Bhruga proudly.

"Why is that?" asked another student.

"Because, the Rishis, the people who have seen the truth face to face with God, have said so. The knowledge is with the Bhrahmins. Everything belongs to the Bhrahmins. That is the Vedic tradition."

It was getting more and more clear to Joshua that the Vedic traditions are not much different from the oral traditions of the Pharisees – they knew it all.

Later on one evening, Rama Varma gave a realistic explanation; he said: "Joshua, what they say in the classes is all true; but over a period of time, the Vedic culture deteriorated into just a ritualistic tradition, with numerous, extravagant, mythical stories and mystical spells."

"I reckon," said Joshua. "Let me ask you. The priests claim that with the right rituals and sacrifices, they can bring down any god on the spot, to the fire and make them do whatever they want."

"Yes, honestly, that's the common belief: They are the custodians of the gods. With the high-handed activities of the Bhrahmin priests through several centuries, the whole Vedas became a tool in their hands which they used quite elegantly to their advantage."

The Chinese students were repulsed about the explanations of the spirituality of these rituals. One student from Xian asked, "Teacher, does it mean that a man of means can invite a Bhrahmin to conduct a Vedic ritual ceremony, and the gods are willing to bless their wish, even if the purpose of the ritual is to hurt or destroy others. What is the ethics behind such pretences? Are Gods receptive to bribery?"

Bhruga particularly did not like that question. He gave many different answers, none which made sense to Joshua.

Soon, the discussions turned to major sacrifices. Joshua had smelled blood and violence in all those sacrifices, even stronger than in his own traditions.

The description even nauseated him when Bhruga described the Maha Yaga conducted by some rich kings for their name and fame, sacrifices that lasted for months on end, particularly the medha of the sacrificial horse, something that was unique to the Hindu traditions. A decorated sacrificial horse is let loose by a king as a challenge to the neighboring kings, as a proclamation of his invincible might. The horse gallops around from village to village and country to country, closely followed by an army ready to avenge the challengers. The whole land circumvented by the horse shall be the property of the king who initiated the yaga. Any man or king obstructing the free roaming of the sacrificial horse is considered a declaration of war against the king. After the yaga tour, the horse is ritually sacrificed along with a very large number of animals such as one hundred elephants, five hundred horses or cows, thousands of lambs, etc. as a mega-slaughter followed by a big feast. The Bhrahmin priests who conduct these rituals are equally glorified and rewarded very heavily. To be the chief priest for such a yaga is considered a glory by itself and wealth for generations.

In the open discussions that followed, the students, particularly from China, did not find wisdom, justice or spirituality in these sacrifices. The students who had learned Confucianism and Buddhism even found these practices offensive. Joshua said: "The Vedic rituals is a Bhrahmin-created, Bhrahmin-conducted and Bhrahmin-benefited system."

"Your feelings are all well founded," Bhruga said. "There was significant objection to such practices, even in ancient times."

"Is it around this time that Buddha started his teachings about a new social order?" Joshua asked.

"Yes, of course, but that is another discussion by itself. But, what happened was that later the Rishis, who understood the Vedas better and who disagreed with the Bhrahminic practices, separated out the pearls from the Vedas dealing with God, wisdom, spirituality, and Dharma; and expanded, classified and wrote down as vast treaties, the Upanishadts, which is considered the central piece of Hindu spirituality and our vision of God at present," Bhruga said.

"Do you mean to say that the Upanishadts were a deliberate attempt to filter out the atrocities of the Vedic traditions and to give a new face of wisdom and spirituality that existed in shadows and shrouds in the Vedas," asked Joshua again.

"Yes, well said, you are correct. The Upanishadts were the product of a very active movement to bring the people back to the Hindu wisdom. There are stories in the Upanishadts that even ridicule the Vedic ritual sacrifices, comparing such violent acts to hungry dogs fighting for the carcass of animals. In some Upanishadts there is even mention that the Kshathrya may even be nobler than the Bhrahmins." Bhruga shook his head.

"Unlike the Vedas, the Upanishadts are composed like a teacher calling aside the students to hear the words of wisdom, righteousness, and spirituality."

Joshua took a deep breath.

"The Upanishadts are focused on two principal trajectories of life," Bhruga said. "What is the essence of life and what is the essence of reality? Soul is immortal, beyond comprehension by human senses. Soul is Bhrahman Himself, consubstantial, inseparable, same and indestructible."

He says: "The Upanishadts teach us the ultimate truth that man is the temple and the God is the light within himself. Therefore, one will renounce attachments that are incompatible to such a concept of inseparable association between God and man. To feel God, don't search elsewhere, but within you, the Upanishadts declares unequivocally."

Finally it makes sense, Joshua thought. He meditated on the teachings of the Upanishadts. God is within me, he talked to himself. I am the son of God. My body is the temple where God resides. There is nothing to fear; God is there within me. He liked it.

Joshua wrote down the gems of the Upanishadts in his papyri:

There is only one God, Bhrahman. His spirit, the Atman is the soul.

The Atman controls all the senses. The senses cannot define the Atman

It fills the whole universe. And the entire universe is filled in it.

Towards the last month of the classes, Bhruga was found much more accessible, and he even encouraged the students to ask more questions.

"How did the Upanishadts address the color system?" Joshua asked.

"Not any different; the color system is a given truth of our beliefs. But Joshua, you are raising an important point, which deserves discussion." Bhruga said. "From our earlier discussions, was it not evident that the Vedic ritual civilization had alienated a very large number of thinkers and spiritualists in this nation? Maha Rishi Buddha and Maha Rishi Jain were the first and foremost amongst them. The great Hindu pundits who understood the principles of the Vedas and had already started explaining our philosophy in direct and human terms; the result, of course, was the Upanishadts. But the color system prevailed."

"What was the impact of the Upanishadts in that philosophical revolt led by Buddha and Jain?" asked Lungi, a Chinese student.

"The Upanishadts did not get attention of the population for a very long time. First of all, the writings were all in Sanskrit, which most people didn't know, but more importantly, the vast majority of the great explanations that are said in the Upanishadts were retold by Buddha in much more understandable human terms in the popular tongue of Pali. People understood them better and thought that they were all the words of Buddha."

"It is my understanding that Buddha revolted against the Vedic rituals and the reprehensible brutalities of the color system," Joshua said.

"You are correct. But many of the theological statements that Buddha made are based on the Upanishadts with subtle differences. For example: the relationship between man and God; the Atman is neither born nor dead; the perishable body is only temporary raiment for the soul; the soul migrates from one life to the next."

"Guru," Lungi questioned, "Buddha never talked about God, as such, or Karma the way you put it."

"I do understand that," Bhruga said. "Why? Why didn't he say anything about God? Maybe he didn't have anything better to say. Look at the Buddhists now. Are they not building temples and worshiping him as an incarnation of God?"

The students were either genuinely silent, or they did not want to end the session with more arguments.

"Based on your good or bad Karma, the soul can reincarnate in a noble person or even in a scorpion, in the next life; that is fundamental to the Hindu beliefs. That invisible world where the souls wander after death awaiting another reincarnation is the Samsara. The Hindus consider this Samsara, this wandering of the spirit with no end in sight, as the principal problem of life, that of misery, sorrow and suffering. The ultimate goal of a Hindu is to attain the heaven and totally get rid of the Samsara."

"How does sacrificing the animals and chanting Mantras save the soul to attain God?" Lungi asked.

"As I had explained before, the Vedic style of Mantras and sacrifices to attain God is a bygone era of Hinduism. You students please don't leave Taxila with the impression that sacrifices and rituals are the door to heaven in Hinduism." His voice rose. "In order to obtain heaven, one has to make several sacrifices. Leading a life of Dharma by conforming to the duties of the class are only a good beginning. You have to reject all your possessions and submit yourselves to God unconditionally; then only you are eligible for Moksha, the Upanishadts affirms. Next to Moksha, one has to hope for the best reincarnation, for which one must conform to the duties of the class you belong by doing the right Karma."

For the next ten weeks, Bhruga lectured on ten of the most important Upanishadts in great detail, starting with Eesham. Joshua was moved at the wisdom of the ancient Sages. The Upanishadts in no uncertain terms taught the concepts of non-duality; that 'the human soul is not a separate entity from God; and, in fact, your soul is a piece of god itself'. With a pure soul, acquire the knowledge of Dharma. Through the practice of Dharma, you escape from the cycle of reincarnations and attain Bhrahman.

Joshua's mind percolated with the profundity of the messages from the Upanishadts. *Are there not people who are so evil and corrupt-evil souls? If the soul is part of the God, how is God corruptible? Then again, what is mind? What is that force within you that tells you what to do and what not to do — the conscience. Does not the mind constantly work for you, even while one is asleep — ideas, dreams? Can we control the mind always? How is the mind connected to the divine Atman? Is there not a soul, a mind, a conscience and a life all interconnected in one body? Is God incomplete for want of the souls that he has distributed amongst the humans? But from fullness, if fullness is removed, the remaining is also fullness. Maybe God loves all souls, good and bad, and wants all of them to return to Him as pure as they originally were. Maybe the human mind cannot and need not know all these complex philosophical riddles like the Chinese philosophers believed.*

When such thoughts came into his mind, and a clear answer was not found, Joshua read more of Confucius and tried to sleep.

Not many days passed without the king asking: "Joshua, how were your classes on the Vedas" or "Upanishadts."

"Somewhat mind boggling; unexpected," Joshua would say. It was a big relief that Joshua had Ramavarma whenever he needed a break.

"Well, Joshua, what you have heard for the last several months is only a drop in the ocean of the whole philosophy of Hinduism. The studies are never ending. Wait until you start the classes of Manu and the Vedic laws. I warn you. It will all change; it will really go hard core on you."

"So, how do you practice the religion?" Joshua asked.

"Hinduism is not a religion; it's a way of life. You study and learn as much as you can, then you conceptualize your own god and live accordingly. There is a place for everybody in Hinduism. But in Manu's edicts, there will be a law, a commandment, a guideline, for everything, every aspect of Hindu behavior and life."

"Wait a minute. After much effort, I have come to terms with the philosophy of the Upanishadts. I like them. Who is Manu, and what are these edicts you are talking about?" Joshua asked.

"Look, Joshua, this is very important. When Buddhism was spreading like a storm, and millions of Hindus rejected the Vedic ways of life and embraced the Buddhist ways, the bastions of the ancient religion shook. The movement was so profound and reached its zenith during Ashoka's time. There was a fair chance that the whole of India would have become Buddhist forever. The Bhrahminic sects were losing their hold and became panicky. They mounted a great effort to re-emphasize the greatness of the Vedic ways of life, a renaissance of the old fundamental Hinduism. There was violence, a lot of violence against the Buddhists. In ancient India, there was a sage named Manu who had a code of conduct for fundamental Hindu ways of life. About two hundred years back, another sage named Bhruga, in the same family tree of Manu, refurbished the edicts and created a very large compendium of laws – the Laws of Manu. Their efforts were successful. At present, the Laws of Manu are fundamental to Hindu ways of life."

"Ha, Buddha was defeated; Manu won! How did that come about? The Upanishadts were popularized to rectify the Vedic atrocities, was they not?" Joshua asked.

"Yes, the truth is that there were some fundamental flaws in Buddhism pertaining to politics and governance of a nation," said the king. "Ashoka conquered India not by the might of the sword, but by the power of words. After his time, India became very weak, militarily and politically, creating a power vacuum, such that all foreign invasions started – the Greco-Bactrians, the Parthians, Scythians and now the Kushans."

"I see; religion and politics does not mix. Buddhism turned India weak politically," Joshua said.

"Not necessarily Buddhism, but the governance of a nation based on Buddhist principles was a failure, undoubtedly. Remember, Alexander did not win, nor could have won anything in India when Hindu kings like Chandragupta Maurya ruled India. Hinduism has great flexibility and resiliency. It can accept ideas and adopt changes and conform to new situations."

"I agree," Joshua said. There are some ideas that are great, but unfit to rule a nation. Like the democracy in Athens, good for a city state without any threat of enemies."

"So, now Joshua, there is a great renaissance already on the move in Hinduism, a refined Hindu philosophy, incorporating some of the principles of Buddhism, Jainism and all other Indian philosophical thoughts. *Ramayana* and the *Bhagavath Geetha* are read in all Hindu houses now on a daily basis."

"Are they not Vedic? Can anybody read it?"

"No, they are not Vedic literature. They are popular literature. Anybody can read it, and they read it as well. My feeling is that Hinduism is a philosophy that fits the Indian psyche well, and it is here to stay forever. If you stay here for a long time, you also will turn a Hindu, I promise you – a good one; I can see it."

Joshua gathered his thoughts.

"It appears to me that you are overburdened with too many philosophical thoughts," the king said. "You need a little break. Come with me next Monday to the Shushrutha School of medicine. I will show you something interesting. Take a break."

"Raja, I am a simple carpenter from Galilee. What am I going to see in a school of Medicine? And what is your interest in medicine and surgery? You are being trained as a king."

"Yes, Joshua, but a king should know a little bit of everything. We have a few Ayurvedic physicians in Malabar, but no hospitals. My goal is to establish a hospital at Muziris."

Another day, after the morning bath and prayers, Joshua and Rama Varma presented themselves at the front lobby of the Shushrutha hospital in the Taxila, awaiting the call to go inside. Kesavan and Gopalan were already there as students. There were a few people in the front lobby, relatives of the patients, some seated on the granite floor and some standing in silence.

Within a few minutes, they heard the click-clack sounds of the wooden sandals, the chief physician arriving, followed by a train of assistants, students and other accessories. The physician, a thin tall man with a sparse gray beard, wearing a white cloth wrapped around his waist, was conducted inside, the train following.

Then came two young men; each, likewise wearing white loin cloths. "Raja, now you can come in," one of them said, and the other took the king's wooden sandals and kept them on one corner of the foyer.

In a large room, deadly silent, students stood back straight, close to the walls but not leaning. In the center of the hall on a reed-carpet lay a thin old man, eyes covered. An oil lamp burned at his side with smokeless flames. Beside the patient sat two young physicians, cross-legged, holding his hands, and there were two others at the foot end. There were two silver trays with thin, shiny, sharp, pointed instruments. Just like the rest of them, Joshua also waited for the arrival of the physician, feet close, breathing shallowly.

A sishya with a thread across the chest said into the king's ears, "Seventy-year-old farmer; blind due to cataract. He is given a drink of wine with poppy syrup and powdered marijuana to help him sleep."

Presently, the chief physician entered the hall bare footed. He sat down on the carpet cross-legged with the patient's head extended to his lap. The students formed a circle around the carpet, resting on their knees, no one even whispering. The assistants prepared the hair-thin silver needles in open flames. The physician gently took off the bandages, opened the patient's eyes, and meticulously instilled one drop each in eye. Then he inserted the hair-thin needle into the eye at the junction of the black and white. The patient flinched slightly and then relaxed. The physician then methodically punctured the white bean of the cataract inside the eye, twisted, turned and pushed it down into the bottom of the eyeball. He repeated the same step in the other eye as well. After placing a few drops of medicine in the patient's eyes, he applied new bandages.

"Remove the bandages in five days," said the guru in a low husky voice. "He will see again."

On the way back they visited the post-operative ward, where Kesavan was caring for a patient with a heavy head bandage, whose nose was chopped as a punishment and now operated.

Kesavan whispered to Joshua. "Nose reconstructed . . . release skin from the forehead . . . rotate the graft to cover the nose . . . pedicle grafts. Sire, here some crimes were punished by cutting off noses, lips and ears. There is always a steady supply of patients."

"Shushrutha was the first to describe this procedure; reconstructive surgery," Rama Varma said in a low tone.

These Indians, Joshua thought . Amazing!

**** **** ***

Joshua entered for the classes – Man's Knowledge of Dharma – under the tutelage of Bhruga, also in the family tradition of the ancient sage Manu.

The Edicts of Manu – Man's Knowledge of Dharma – for the Hindus in India in many ways resembled what the Torah was to the Hebrews at the Sinai mountain; 2,694 hymns in twelve chapters, touching on every aspect of Hindu life from birth to death – the statutes and commandments. Manu, no less, received these commandments directly from God, like Khammurabi in Babylon and Moses in Sinai.

Bhruga laid the ground rules for the edicts. Remindful of the first commandment, "Thou shall not have another God . . . " the edicts of Manu states upfront: "Everything on earth belongs to the Bhrahmins, the only people who have seen God eyes to eye. It's only dharma for a Bhrahmin to assume any wealth from the other classes, and it's only dharma for the others to submit them to the Bhrahmin." Unlike the Hebrew commandments it clearly says: "The Holy writings of the Vedas, only the Bhrahmins are entitled to read. But if a Shudra knowingly or unknowingly listens to the holy chants, his ears will be sealed with molten lead."

The students turned their eyes to the lone questioner from Galilee when Joshua stood up with a red face and arm raised. "But there won't be any punishments to you people," Bhruga said.

Manu's edicts didn't leave even a single stone unturned: the rituals to be followed before, during and after a couple copulate, including how to cleanse the genitals; details like how to eat and how much to eat; how to cut the hair or even how to use a cane. The four stages – houses – in a man's life were unbreachable; as a boy he lives in the house of a guru under his tutelage; then he enters the second phase, creating a household, marrying a woman from his own class, and practicing his profession. The day he gets a grandson he should detach from family life, relinquish his possessions and wander away, making pilgrimages and preparing for the final stage of an aesthetic life, renouncing everything, including his possessions, clothes if possible, even his name, and live on alms with prayers and meditations.

"In no uncertain terms, Maha Rishi admonishes, 'Women do not deserve freedom.'" Bhruga said. There was a tumult of "Hi" from the students. Then it was silent.

Freedom of women is plague to the society, Manu admonished. Their sexual desires are intense, and by their innate nature, they will indiscriminately breed with young, old and of different classes with no discretions. Excessive sexual urge, easy vulnerability, and phony love are all innate abhorrent qualities of a woman. Alcohol, any contact with other men, sleeping during daytime, time away from husbands, travel, and staying in another's house, are major incentives for women to cheat on their husbands and seek sexual pleasures with others. They must be under the disciplinary umbrella of a man at all times; in childhood under the watchful eyes of her father; in marriage, under the strict guidance of her husband; and when widowed . . ." Bhruga paused for a moment. "A woman is the shadow of the man. Is there a shadow when the object is gone?" he asked.

Nobody responded. Bhruga's lecture on "Sathi" was horrid.

Many a times Joshua's face had turned red, and he even broke out into cold sweats and was ready to quit; the oppressive rule of the Bhrahmins, the brutality of the color system, and the reprehensible treatment towards women. He thought he had enough of it. The husband is destined to enjoy the pleasures of life, and the wife is in total servitude, even if the man is immoral or illicit. Worst, such was the only way a woman could attain good Karma. But, most importantly, the husband's life is the wife's responsibility. It is her virtuous Karma that keeps him going. The woman may get a slight uplift if she bears a baby boy, but generally it is the man's good Karma that he got a son. If the wife gives birth to a girl or far worse, girls, then she will be ridiculed, if not persecuted. Her life will be the hottest hell from there on.

But the king was always a consolation. "Joshua, what you heard is entirely true to life; everyday practice in our culture," he said. There is no point in you getting upset and leaving the classes. You are here for a reason, a mission. You keep your calm; it's only for one more month."

Back in the class, the edicts of Manu went into some finite details of everyday life. For example, if a boy ejaculates in a dream, he has to undergo atonements: standing on one leg in the middle of a ring of fire, meditating for three days. When a man is choosing a bride, he must avoid blonds, women with large busts or buttocks, too much or too little hair, too tall or too short, cross eyes or crooked teeth . . . so goes that list. Men must not procreate with a woman who is drunk or sleeping. A man must sleep with his wife no more than ten nights per month, and avoid the first four days after the bleeding, a new moon, and the eleventh and thirteenth days of the month. A man shall never spend a night alone with his mother, sister or daughter in an empty house.

The Laws of Manu for hygiene were specific, finite and irrevocable; shall not defecate or pass urine in open spaces, cow sheds, plowed or cultivated fields, near a temple or water. For such purposes they should make an enclosed space, cover the head with clothes and go quietly.

Manu had an edict regarding every imaginable aspect of social, economic and civil life that even the great Khammurabi of Babylon did not have. For example, regarding the units of weights and measures, Manu instructs that the minute mote that is visible moving around on a beam of light is the most basic unit of weight. Eight such motes will make a lisha, and likewise the units went up.

Unlike Moses or Khammurabi, the Laws of Manu were color coded, and there were different punishments for different classes for the same crime. "If a Shudra foul-mouths a Kshathrya, his tongue will be cut off, but if he address a Bhrahmin disrespectfully, then a foot long, red-hot iron bar is to be thrust into his throat."

Manu left no stone unturned in his elaborate and complete edicts on morality. "If a married woman engages in a sexual act with another man, she will be mauled with hound dogs while her lover is charbroiled in an iron cot and the executioners continuously feed firewood under the cot until he is converted into ashes. If a man of lower caste engages in any relationship with a woman of higher class, he will be killed. If a man seduces a woman of higher class, his nose, ears, and penis shall be sliced off. If he provides masturbation to an upper-class woman, even if it is at her behest, he shall be killed. But, if he does the same within his class, his two fingers shall be cut. If a woman engages in a vaginal finger massage with another woman, she will be fined two hundred coins. But if a woman does it on a virgin, then her hair will be shaved off, two fingers will be cut, and she will be put on a donkey and marched through the thoroughfare of the city to be ridiculed by other people.

Joshua was getting more and more disgusted the more he thought of Manu's Laws of Dharma. *Everything belongs to the Bhrahmins! They needed the Kshathrya to keep them protected, to spill the blood; so, it is written: the Kshathrya, who dies in a war, shall immediately be relieved of the cycles of Samsara. They needed the Vaisya to cultivate the land and to feed the nation; and they needed the Shudra for all menial works. They even needed the Chandallas to absorb the filth of the society. Nobody can upgrade the social class, even if brilliant and capable. The Shudra cannot even earn money. In case one does so, it is the Bhrahmin's Dharma to take it away from him! How more ridiculous can it ever be? Buddha failed. Jain failed. The brilliant Bhrahmins prevailed.*

Manu lives, and he must be a sadist, Joshua thought.

"Joshua," the king said, "some people protested against it. There have been movements against it. But the vast belief is that these laws are God given, akin to your Torah. That's the way the Bhrahmins taught our people from the beginning. A man cannot change a God-given rule. If Buddha was accepted as an Avathar – now a few people do – then things would have been different."

"Raja, I reckon, slowly though, it's impossible for any man to fight a god, even if the man is more of flesh and soul and the god is a piece of rock. Man fears the unknown most."

"You are correct. Imagine when you get back to Israel, and if you challenge the writings of the Torah. Do you think you ever stand a chance?"

"Raja, you are a king. Regarding your dharma, a king Manu insists: 'Every day the king should worship the Bhrahmins with ceremonial offerings and rule the nation based on their advice. Protection of the subjects and service to the Bhrahmins is the fundamental duty of the king.' When you get back to Muziris, will you challenge them or abide?"

"A bit of both. See, I am from the south. We have a different attitude about all these beliefs and convictions. I disagree with many of the edicts. But the people at large are still with the Bhrahmins. Say, the view on widows, treating them as walking corpses, even if there is a willing man to marry a widow, Manu ridicules that it is the 'Dharma of cattle to marry a widow.' Manu wins. Maybe in man's psyche, there is an inner soul always wanting violence and more violence," said the king.

**** **** ****

Another uneventful Monson came and went. Joshua was now twenty-eight.

In another three months Rama Varma would conclude his classes and get ready to go south. He had a special liking towards Buddhism, and he believed that Ashoka was the ideal ruler, the one that he wanted to emulate. Many evenings they sat on the stone benches laid around the giant granite column erected in the front courtyard of the Shushrutha Hospital. The imposing column, containing some of the famous edicts of Ashoka, had an exquisitely carved lotus at the capital on which stood four lions facing all four directions of the world. The inscriptions on the column that had specific mention about Rama Varma's home land were his main fascination. Ramavarma pointed to the inscription "Keralaputhra", and said with pride, "Joshua, that's about my land – Kerala. Ashoka is talking about my land and my subjects."

Joshua was astonished to see writings on the column about animal and human treatment centers. The edict read: "King Piyadasi made provisions for two types of medical treatments: those for humans and those for animals. Wherever medical herbs suitable for humans and animals were not available, I have had them imported and grown. Along roads, I have had wells dug and trees planted for the benefits of humans and animals." something which Joshua had never seen in all his travels.

"Was Ashoka your king, too?" Joshua asked.

"Not really. His kingdom included of all of India, with the exception of the three dynasties in the south: the Cheras, to which I belong; the Cholas; and the Pandyas."

"When you become the king, will you make an animal hospital in Muziris?" Joshua asked.

"It's not written that I would be the next king. If I become . . ."

"I thought the son becomes king when his father dies."

"Not necessarily. But most likely, yes. My father is a devout Hindu. He has already made plans to renounce his kingdom and go to Kashi." Rama Varma paused.

"Is it again based on Manu's Laws?" Joshua asked. "He will renounce possessions, live on alms and all?"

"Yes, he will change his name, transform as a Sadhu, and travel by foot all the way from Muziris to Kashi on the banks of the holy River Ganga. For the rest of his life, he will visit the holy places of Kashi, Sarnath, Prayag, and all, and when the time comes, he will pass on to the next life, peacefully."

"Will you see him again after he leaves Malabar?"

"I plan to. He objected to anybody accompanying him. He wanted to do it all by himself, but I will send two of my men with him. When the time comes, they will undertake the cremation ceremony and part of the ashes will be brought back to Malabar where we will dispense the ashes in the rivers and the great ocean such that he will dissolve and assimilate into the land where it all originated," said the king somberly. "Anyways, how was your course overall, Joshua?"

"It was intense, at times repulsive. With the Upanishadts, I was so happy, but then, when I finished Manu, my respect for Confucius has increased a thousand fold. This color system! And this violence against women. I don't understand it. Most ancient religions have got it, of course, mine included, but this Manu, he really is matchless. The state of the Shudras is deplorable and the untouchables, unthinkable."

"Your concerns are all correct," The king tapped on Joshua's shoulders consolingly. "When you get into the teachings of Buddha, you will get some relief, so also Mahaveer Jain. Tomorrow, I will take you to a wonderful place. We will start early in the morning."

The king's carriage was ready with Gopalan and Kesavan. The Dharmarajika stupa commissioned by Emperor Ashoka was the most splendid Buddhist shrine in Taxila, built in shining granite. "The day you told me about the stele of Khammurabi, I was planning to bring you here. This is nothing to do with laws or edicts; it's all about the love and compassion of a king for his subjects. Rama Varma translated the inscriptions for Joshua:

" . . . My ministry will continue to work in the pathway of Dharma so that you all will be happy and free from harassment. They will work among the prisoners for their unfettering, identify people who are ill and need assistance, and pinpoint people who have nobody else to support their families, that are very old, bewitched or ill, to be released from prisons and resettled, to rehabilitate in the outlying towns.

387

Women's quarters belonging to my brother, sister and other relatives will be open for them . . ."

"Raja, is it truly so that the edict is promising rehabilitation of the sick prisoners and protection to women and other family members of the incarcerated prisoners?" Joshua asked.

With a proud grin, the king said, "Yes, Joshua, you better believe it."

Is it the same India, Joshua wondered, *that those hypocrites, Herodotus and Megasthenes wrote about? Ashoka, thy name is compassion,* Joshua thought.

"Joshua, you took the troubles to come here, all the way from Galilee; I insist you go to Mathura and meet Maha Rishi Vyassa. I will take you there. I promise."

"Who is Vyassa? The Maha Rishi?"

"He is the last living member of a very long tradition of sages. He has composed a phenomenal work, the *Bhagawad Geetha*, considered to be the very last words on all the questions concerning Hindu beliefs."

"That's where you have been before you came to Taxila?"

"Yes, I spent eighteen months there. He has a boarding school, but if he likes you in his first interview, he will even accommodate you in his house as a sishya – live in student – which would be great."

Before sunset they reached the Ashoka gardens on the northern outskirts of Taxila, where the much smaller but well-kept Stupa were erected in the middle of the garden. There were many people strolling in the garden catching the evening breeze when they reached there. The writings were very clearly written in Pali. Joshua read: "All men are my children. What I desire for my own children is their welfare and happiness, both in this world and the next. My only intention is that they live without fear of me, that they may trust me, and that I may give them happiness, not sorrow. They should understand that the king will forgive those who can be forgiven, and that he wishes to encourage practicing Dharma so that they may obtain happiness in this world and the next."

"Profound, very profound. I suspect, I am beginning to believe in reincarnations. This is Solomon revisited," Joshua said.

Time passed quickly, and before Joshua knew, it was October. The weather was pleasantly cool in Taxila. The scholars and tourists increased substantially, and the streets and shops bustled with their collective energy.

**** **** ****

Joshua entered the last phase of his stay in Taxila. There were thirty-eight students for the Buddhist classes. Thirty-three of them were from China, including one girl, Swan Hwa, the girl with bright round eyes, two from India and two from Greece. The format of learning was like ancient times; discussions and debates on any subjects on earth, the way Buddha had conducted his discourses many centuries ago. The concept of a group – Sangha – and group discussions were fundamental in the learning process of Buddhism. Sachidananda – the teacher – was an aspirant Bodhisattva, a thin man with sunken cheeks and half-closed eyes. Students met twice a week for twelve weeks with the teacher, and for the remaining days they did their own research and learning.

Gradually, the image of a prince called Siddhartha, and his life and teachings unfolded. It was the story of a man who threw out the shrouds of royal comforts and layers of religious and Vedic edicts covered in silk, and woke up to see the world with a new perspective.

Young Siddhartha saw the world outside the palace walls one day when he was pleasure riding a chariot. He was dejected with the naked realities of the world in the form of diseases, destitution and dilapidations. Amidst, there was a frail sage; the loin clothes his only possessions, happy and contented. He was disturbed by the wide disparities amongst his subjects, awakened by the discordance between wealth, poverty and happiness. Changes happened inside the palace; Siddhartha evaded the dinner wines, concubines and such other pleasures. And, on one night, at the age of twenty-nine, he left the palace for the wilderness of the forest as a lone monk, leaving behind his wife and a child. The discussions began at this point.

"To the best of our knowledge, Siddhartha never came back to the palace to claim his wife and children. Is that right?" asked Swan.

"That is correct," Sachidananda said. "You could make the point that he ran away from the traditional Hindu family responsibilities."

"He probably was a confused person at that juncture. His immediate actions will attest to that," said Tao Chang from Tibet. "Even though he was well trained in the Vedas and traditions, he sought out two Vedic Pundits and challenged the Dharma of kings. The pundits fervently argued to strictly maintain the class system. Siddhartha decided that it was enough of learning about the Hindu traditions."

"Not exactly, he was unsure," said Tao Chang. "What did he do next? Conducting an aesthetic life – like a Hindu tradition – drinking and eating minimally. He almost killed himself. Then he decided that all extremes are evil."

"That's the time he went into a soul-searching meditation under the shades of banyan tree that probably lasted for about six to seven weeks," Sachidananda said. "We don't know what happened there. He came out a different man. We believe that during this time he received enlightenment. There after he challenged the atrocities of the Bhrahminic Vedic class system and presented a new concept to the meaning of life and his thoughts on life after death."

"What exactly is meant by enlightenment?" Joshua asked.

"Joshua, you may have your own definition, but for the time being, I would say Buddha realized the truth."

"Or, more like, it was a retreat. He consolidated his ideas and made a plan to talk about it," Swan said.

"Yes, Buddha had an increasing set of followers, the Sangha. For the next forty-five years, until his last day in the Vaisya family, where he ate boar meat and died of dysentery; we have this huge collection of his teachings. That text is for you to analyze," Sachidananda said.

"Right, all that we have is the uninterrupted oral tradition, of course, written down later on – the hundreds of books – by his disciples," stated Tai Shan.

"Is it truly our understanding that Buddha never said anything about God?" Joshua asked.

"No, he didn't." Sachidananda said.

"Can we pinpoint one message, that, as what everybody says, 'caught up like a wildfire,' that burned the bastions of Hinduism?" Joshua asked.

Swan raised her hand. Her gaze focused on Joshua: "It was not one point. It was a combination. Buddha's mystic charisma was about a man who came down from royalty to the meager, his extreme compassion to the poor, and his instant capability to size up a problem in a systematic fashion, instantly analyze the cause and effect of the problem, and propose a solution. That led others to believe that he really was the enlightened one who knew and saw the universe and truth, face to face. He also said what the others feared to say."

In the silence that followed, everybody understood what she had said.

This Chinese girl . . . Joshua thought, *is as cute as a button and as bright as Aristotle. We need a lot more such women in this world.*

Jian Shu added: "Buddha drew the power of his arguments from Hinduism and created the perfect antidote to fight and kill the Bhrahminic atrocities and the edicts of Manu. He first broke the mystery of the mythological gods that were carved stones, those that neither talked nor acted."

"I am a little confused," Joshua said. "When I visited a Vihara here in Taxila, I saw idols of Buddha made in bronze, and people around appeared chanting and worshipping. How would you explain that?"

Swan cleared her throat. "I believe that in India the concept of an idol is so much in their blood, Buddhist or not, people need an idol to visualize God in their mind."

Many of the Indian students did not like that comment. There were some hushed noises of disapproval . . . "But his most emphatic attack, I understand, was on the rituals and sacrifices, the bribery to the Gods, was it not?" Joshua asked. He thought about the many thousands of animals and birds that were sacrificed at the temple of Jerusalem every day.

"Of course," Hu Jining joined. "The rituals and libations were fundamentally a Bhrahminic domain, trickery to bluff the others. These rituals provide no answers to the real problems of life, Buddha had said categorically."

"At any point, did the teachings of Buddha evolve as a new religion?" Joshua asked.

"In a sense, the teachings of Buddha evolved into a new religion," Swan said. "A new philosophy of life, a religion without a god figure, rituals or sacrifices, a society with no class or class barriers. All men were considered equal and the untouchables were as touchable as everybody else."

"He resiliently preached to discard the close-fisted Bhrahminic version of God. He implied many times that gods do not hide in stones, clay or wood. One has to live a life of their own and diligently search within oneself to find answers of life and salvation," Lue Tan said.

In many ways, Buddha's teachings are reflected in Confucius, Joshua thought. "What exactly did Buddha say about life after death?" Joshua asked.

Swan again started the discussion. "Buddha kept his silence about God, soul, eternity of the universe, and all such hardcore esoteric principles. However, just like anybody else who drank the waters of the Ganga, Buddha also could not but think outside the concept of transmigration of the soul."

"What did Buddha say about the never-ending cycle of reincarnations based on karma?" Joshua asked.

"Mostly nothing. Let us make it very clear. What he said about the transmigration of souls and karma-based reincarnation are two entirely different concepts. One thing I know for sure is that Buddha never talked about the concept of karma. Swan said: "One must walk through his own life to end the sufferings for which no gods or goddesses could be counted on. Don't live a life fearing gods. One has to find a solution to one's problems by one's own soul-searching."

"How differently, if at all, did Buddha consider women in all these discussions?" Joshua asked.

"He found no difference. Women are equally capable of attaining enlightenment," affirmed Swan. "In fact, in Sangha, there are as many women as there are men."

**** **** ****

Sachidananda started the final set of lectures. "Buddha spoke a lot about human sufferings and insecurity. For example, our records from Sarnath written by his scribes, were to explain the fundamental root cause of human sufferings, which he summarized as the noble truths of life. Who would like to go first?"

Swan raised her hand. "The first reality of life he said was 'sufferings' or 'dukkhas', such as the trauma of birth. Then sufferings from diseases, aging, fear of one's own death, bondage to dislikes and, finally, separation from loved ones. An impressive list from birth to death. But I do have some concerns. What is meant by the suffering of birth," she asked resolutely. "I know the woman who gives birth to a child – albeit painful – would consider it as the most rapturous moment in her life, and certainly the child's cry could be an expression of happiness upon entering this world of light."

"Well said, Swan; we are not arguing that at all. Sufferings are all realities of life. How we tackle them, or what he suggested for how to tackle them is the question," Joshua said. "I think his point about selfishness and self-centered behavior as the cardinal cause of unhappiness is the crux of the point – the bondage. Tackling this truth is by introspection and disowning earthly possessions – detachment."

"Good point," Sachidananda said. "Such introspections occur to many a people in the days or hours before their death, Buddha taught. Seldom, if at all does a person before his death regret that he had amassed more wealth or enjoyed more sex or wine. Instead, they regret that they should have done something more to help others at some point in their life."

"Which must be the reason why the confession of a dying man is often the real truth? That is to say, the truth was there in him always. His selfishness prevented him from accepting that." Joshua said.

Joshua felt very much at ease with the Buddhist studies as the course advanced. Many of the comments about the "dos and don'ts" sounded like directly taken out of the Ten Commandments: thou shall not kill, steal, covet thy neighbor's wife, etc. But what he said about a righteous livelihood was particularly appealing, admonishing against prostitution, slave trading, butchery, warring, brewing, executions, and the like.

Is Nirvana death; if not, what is it? Joshua pondered.

"Anybody can die, but only a few, if any at all, can attain Nirvana," Swan said.

"Nirvana is the end of life in this world," Han Bien said. "But it's like a flame that goes out when the fuel ceases; the life ceases to exist; it does not die out. That is probably Nirvana,"

"Yes, cease to exist, that is extinction? Extinction of what?" Joshua asked.

"Buddha must have thought about extinction of self and not the spirit. At other times, he has painted the imagery of the flame passing on from one candle to the other, so also the spirit passes from one life to the other. The flame on the second candle was the same flame that was there on the first candle; the first candle flamed out, but the flame did not die out. The flame on the second candle, for all intents and purposes, is a different flame on a different candle. Depending on the conditions, it may give a different shade of light and heat," Swan said.

It took a very long moment for the group to assimilate what was just said.

"I have been teaching this subject for the last ten years, and this is the best explanation I have heard so far. The self is extinguished, and the flame passes on, which is what he described as bliss – total ongoing, ageless, bliss."

"So, how does this differ from the Bhrahminic transmigration of soul?" Tic Wong asked.

"That is so very easy to answer," Swan Hwa said. "In the Bhrahminic transmigration, the soul is a piece of God itself. But, of course, based on Karma, the soul is engraved with all kinds of imprints, good and bad. With these imprints, the soul goes to the pool of Samsara. From there, the soul goes to another self, man or beast, in the next generation. But in Buddha's bliss concept, there is no imprint on the spirit, pure and simple. It just passes on from one life to the other, like a flame lit from one candle to the next. Moreover, time and again, Buddha has emphasized the impermanence of existence, spirit or self. Things continuously change, he said, such that what we see or feel now did not exist the same way a moment before."

Joshua could not take his eyes off that Chinese girl, appreciating her smartness, presence of mind and in-depth knowledge on subjects.

"Is this spirit, this flame is God himself, or can it be?" Joshua asked.

Another debate followed. It was resolved that Buddha did not acknowledge a creator, a protector or a destroyer god. Buddha did not envision a spirit that is God. Moreover, it was the consensus of the group that Buddhism is atheistic. In many instances, Buddha has stated that human self has no soul. He called it an 'Anatta'.

A short, dark-skinned man, Narayanan, one among the many Indian students from the Chola Empire, stood up with a red face. "Most respected lady, fellow scholars. First, let me tell you a story. In my village, a girl named Sarada was born in a peasant family. From the age of nine onwards, she wanted to go back and see her home from before in another village, some fifty miles away. She named the village, Shivakaram; she said her father was Sukuram, and mother, Devaki. She had two elder siblings, a brother, Muran, and a sister, Sruthi. Sarada kept on pestering her parents to go to Shivakaram. Finally, they obliged. In Shivakaram, in her previous house, she correctly identified her brother, Muran, who was now sixty-two, who was still grieving his sister who died when he accidently pushed her into a well when she was nine years old. Her parents were dead and gone, but she correctly identified the layout of the village, landmarks and several members of the village from fifty years back. Dear scholars, there are many, many instances like this I know of. There is definitely reincarnation, except people who can remember their past are only very few. Moreover, Buddha did not deny reincarnation completely. He believed in a destiny that we can modify. Each life has a causal relation to the previous life that led to it; that's what he said. He stated categorically that our personality has lineage to some previous life. Our attitudes, mental habits, tastes, dispositions, and aversions are all transmitted by a certain lineage."

"Buddha certainly did not condone a concept of Karma, but on many occasions he has mentioned a connection between the present life and a previous one," Tai Shan said. "The present state of our mind is a continuation of the previous moment and the moment before, such that it can be traced back to our mother's womb. Buddha believed that in our subconscious mind, a certain subtle consciousness existed, even before the conception, linked to another body before, somewhere."

"In effect, he is condoning the concept of reincarnation as a law of nature, but not influenced by Karma as affirmed in the Hindu Vedic literature. He talked about this flame, this spirit that passes on without a beginning or end. Is that your understanding?"

The issue was discussed at length by the scholars and it was concluded that Buddha did not have answers to all the questions. The discussions went on and on, and all the scholars widely applauded the one man who so fervently fought the inequities and the atrocities of the society. His concepts about a classless social system based on love, compassion and equality had great popular appeal, and people joined the Sangha, in multitudes, rattling the bastions of the Vedic Hinduism.

"Were there any attempts on Buddha's life? Particularly by the Vedic fundamentalists?" Joshua asked, remembering the many prophets killed in Jerusalem.

"No, there were not. In his times people were joining the Sangha in great multitudes, and Buddhism was spreading like wildfire. Even if somebody wanted to, they couldn't have," Jian Shu said.

Swan Hwa was not ready for the discussion to slip off from the fundamental issue of reincarnation. "For the sake of an argument, let me ask: If you don't believe in reincarnation based on Karma, then there is nothing to be worried about the perils of the Samsara, then, what is wrong in enjoying all the earthly pleasures like food, alcohol, sex and all such other wild things and live for the moment?"

Most of them agreed that it was a very pessimistic view, but Buddha was not a pessimist, they all agreed.

"The concept of reincarnation based on Karma is so Hinduistic that Buddha wanted to stay clear of it," Swan said. "Unfortunately, he was not very successful."

Joshua stared at her with a half-smile, which he couldn't have helped.

Swan turned to Joshua, her eyelashes fluttering, "Joshua, you are so quiet when we are all stating our views without reservations. That is not fair. We need to hear your views as well."

"What I see is a highly purpose-driven life in Buddha. He certainly was a great rationalist. His life as a rebel sage, single handily challenging the Bhrahminic atrocities, is the most glaring one. He brought the awareness that all we humans are created equal, although he never mentioned the word *creation*. He brought dignity and respect to all segments of the society. He was most convinced in his convictions and went forth to face it. In that process he had to make several sacrifices; his kingdom, family and comforts in life. I cannot entirely agree with his contentions about the causes of misery, God, creation, etc. But one thing is commendable; Buddha was not baffled to talk about his convictions."

"Joshua, do you believe in a creator god," Swan asked.

"I believe in a Heavenly Father, the seat of eternal love, compassion, and that we are all his children. Therefore, God is within us always. We are his representatives on earth. Each one of us has a purpose in life. It is up to us to find it out. I believe that is what Buddha did in his meditations; a divine order of the universe"

"Do you believe in Buddha's view that the soul precedes the conception?" Tai Shan asked.

"Certainly, yes," Joshua said. "But it is no subtle consciousness. It is the central piece of our self. It just doesn't flame out. The soul is a part of God, and He wants it back. In my belief, there is no reincarnation of the soul; therefore, it will go back to the Creator."

Such discussions where no stones were left unturned were the most exciting part of the Buddhist studies in Taxila, which continued for another four weeks.

His mind flew back to many different centers of learning that he had visited. What a stark distinction. With the possible exception of the Agora during the times of Socrates, was there any place like Taxila? *Here, scholars learn and talk about religion, philosophy, science, medicine and related faculties. They study, they think, they write and they live in an entirely different academic atmosphere. Of the little I have seen, India has enough intellectual wealth to teach the entire world many times over*, he thought.

**** **** ****

Another December came, and Joshua turned twenty-nine. It was cold, as usual, and people walked around bundled under covers of blankets. They were celebrating Joshua's birthday with the friends from Malabar in their lodge. It was a bit after sunset. The fire in the grate had built up well, and the students sat around chatting gaily. They felt a slight shake in the room, and a few books fell to the ground from the shelf, and the dinnerware made some chattering noises. People at the School of Astrology had predicted that a major earthquake was quite possible within the next few days, Rama Varma said. They were wrong. Nothing happened for the next few days, or even months.

But on an early spring day, in the first week of March around midnight, while Joshua was lying down, awake and debating whether he should go to Mathura, he felt a tremor. He rose on his elbows, looking around. All were sleeping, and it was quiet. But a few moments later, he felt a stronger tremor and some chattering of the kitchen utensils, and a shelf came tumbling down to the floor. "Raja," he called, as he sprung up on his feet. Presently, Rama Varma shuffled out of the bed with a subtle swaying. From the flickering reflections of the light from the grate, Joshua noticed his face tense as he walked towards the door. Then there was another tremor and prattling of the vessels, and a piece of the roof came down. Rama Varma screamed, "Friends, earthquake! Get out! Out you go to the east gate." He quickly got out and looked around. Nothing had changed. The narrow streets were empty, and the oil lamps on the posts were still flickering. Then, there was a prolonged trembling and noises of roofs collapsing. Rama Varma screamed, "Collect your things! Get out quick, to the east gate."

In no time, they collected the bags and got out. It was dark, and the street lamps had all fallen down, spilling oil and spreading flames on the turf. People talked loud and soon the narrow streets were filled with people.

"Stay together. Call out your names when I shout," he ordered.

Heavy winds whistled through the rooftops, rattling the shingles and downing trees and tree branches. Soon the air was filled with one of those most peculiar sounds, as if a thousand lions were roaring from deep under, from the womb of the earth. The whole ground rattled violently, which lasted for well over ten minutes. Large rooftops, city walls, and the smaller residential buildings, all tumbled down to the ground. A tumult of violent cries erupted from all over, people calling out names, screaming for help, wailing and cursing. Instantly, the wind started blowing violently with twisters loaded with sand, soot and moats piercing into the eyes, ears and mouth. Breathing and seeing became difficult. The soil was unsteady, moving to and fro. The lions' roar continued. The cacophony of people screaming, crying, shouting, all continued. Joshua was on all his fours, but still could not maintain his balance with arm or leg forward; he fell down, at times to the front, to the back or sideways. The whole land was filled with tree limbs, rubble, and all kinds of objects flown away from houses. The violent tremors ceased for a moment, only to restart with a vengeance. The wind picked up speed, but this time bringing on balls of fire, embers, burnt pieces of wood, shingles, and kitchen utensils, all floating in the air.

Amidst the endless screaming and wailing, Joshua identified the voice of Rama Varma ahead of him, like a king in the battlefield, continuously calling out the names Joshua, Gopalan, and Sivan. They all screamed back from distances, "Raja . . . Raja."

While avoiding a flying fireball, Joshua fell into a pit and his legs caught in between the rubble. He instantly lost the feeling in his left leg below the knee now buried under the debris. He cried out. "Raja, help! Raja, help!" The numbness in the leg presently turned into a throbbing ache. He was sweated profusely.

The earth tremors continued intermittently. Through the lightning, Joshua could see the whole surrounding covered with dust and debris. As if looking into a deep fog, he could recognize the three men crawling towards him. They cleared the rubble and released his leg. His ankle was twisted outwards and was swelling fast.

"There is a fracture of the ankle. I think there is a dislocation at the hip too," cried Gopalan.

"We must put the joints right. Come on, Raja; hold him by the waist and pull back," commanded Sivan. The king sat behind Joshua and held his hips strongly, holding back. The two physicians pulled his leg forward, flexed at the knee joint and twisted inwardly. With a cracking noise the hip joint fell in place. Then they stabilized the ankle with an immobilizing wrap.

"It will be painful. But first, let us get out from here."

Gopalan and Sivan worked on massaging his legs for a few moments. The violent shaking settled and their feet were more stable on the ground, but the winds still blew powerfully. The east gate was now visible, the bastions of the gates still standing strong. Soon there was intense heat from behind and shadows in front of them. A giant inferno had developed. The quarters were all on fire and the flames soon spread out, engulfing the whole building complex. The wind still carried fireballs through the air, above their head and beyond, and over the gates.

Rama Varma wrapped Joshua's hand over his shoulders and helped him walk; the two of them walked on three legs. In another ten minutes they reached the east gate. They were all covered in thick, dark dust and soot, such that their features were all totally indistinguishable, dotted with holes. One could identify Joshua by his height, and the rest by their voices. Gopalan was limping too. Sivan carried his bags, and the group finally reached beyond the thresholds of the gates, and they were now on the grand highway and slowly walking towards the horses' stable. They saw the silhouette of a carriage in the dark fast approaching them. With no time wasted, they helped Joshua into the coach first and the group rolled east, towards Mathura.

Kesavan gave Joshua two herbal balls to swallow with some water. Joshua's pain quickly eased up, and soon he went to sleep. Next morning he was unable to walk, but was able to move his toes, which was a good sign, Sivan had said. By noon, they halted at a wayside rest house for cleaning and recuperation.

They all knew it was the intuition and prompt action of the king that had saved their lives.

For the next couple of days, they were all somewhat somber and spoke very little. They imagined a lot of people must have lost their lives. What else could they have done? Probably nothing. It was a natural calamity, the wrath of the gods. Later they would learn that the earthquake of Taxila had taken the lives of twenty thousand people and flattened nearly everything. "It is a good thing that we have a physician and a surgeon with us for your services Joshua," said the king.

"Did I break any bones in my leg?"

"No, you had a dislocation of the hip joint and a sprain at the ankle. You need rest for three weeks, then you will be able to walk without problems," said Gopalan.

"Yes, that will be about the time we reach Mathura," the king said.

"Friends, if you were not there, surely I would have been buried in the rubble with fire on top."

"A burial and cremation at the same time," the king said.

They all fell into much needed laughter.

BOOK VIII

Joshua in Mathura

Joshua with Maha Rishi Vyassa

On the south bank of the River Yamuna, the ancient city of Mathura still stood tall, like an old man, weathered yet resilient, who had witnessed the revelations of generations; the city where Lord Krishna – the most revered of all Hindu incarnations – was born.

Escaping from the tumult of the city, the king's coach traveled east through the rutted carriage pathway, skirting the knolls and crossing the creeks. The road, like a long arbor, had a thick canopy allowing only shadowy light to reach the ground. Deer frequently crossed the passage, and moose, startled by the intrusion, gazed suspiciously at the visitors, heads up, ears cocked and ready to leap. The peacocks, unruffled, pecked the grounds in the middle of the path, as if declaring ownership. Mynahs that sang, parrots that talked, and the enticing profusion of flora, the purple ivies, deep-red apples, burgundy cherries and oranges, growing wild and sharing the scent of citrus, made these forests refreshing and magical.

"Joshua, how many years back was that when Moses led the Exodus from Egypt?" asked the king, waking up from a long period of silence.

"About twelve hundred years; maybe a bit more," Joshua said.

"The first Vyassa, who compiled the Holy Vedas, the revered scriptures of the Indian civilization, lived here in Mathura during the same period."

Presently, the carriage climbed the crest of a knoll, and Rama Varma beckoned to Joshua. In the distance they could see a large clearing in the middle of the forest. To the north end stood an enormous banyan tree, thick with foliage, like an old Babylonian temple standing on a thousand pillars. "That's where the Vyassa Muni lives." Rama Varma pointed to the house in the tree.

A narrow road soon connected with the clearing. At the south end stood a small L-shaped thatched house facing the setting sun. "That's where Sukannya lives," the king said. The clearing was kept in good repair, bordered by a wooden fence that cascaded with wild ivy's bearing thick boughs of white flowers – the jasmines.

I have trudged many nations, but have never seen a living sage, Joshua thought, his heart pounding. He was anxious to see the legendary Vyassa as the carriage fast approached at the threshold of the banyan tree.

A tall man came out to the yard, watching the approaching carriage, shading his eyes.

"Sukannya, Sukannya," he called.

Sukannya, a young woman in her late twenties, came out of the house and stood behind the old man.

"Look, it is Rama Varma. He said that he would come this way on going back to Muziris," Vyassa said.

The two servants of the hermitage, Kishan and Vishal, waited behind the banyan tree with their arms across their chests. The carriage coach arrived, and the Raja came forward, closely followed by Joshua. The king prostrated himself at the feet of his guru, touched his feet and then his forehead in sequence three times. Then he pulled out a splendid brown shawl made of silk and wool, and reverently garlanded the guru. Maha Rishi Vyassa, in turn, extended his palms on the king's forehead and blessed him. Likewise, Joshua also came forward, bent down and began prostrating on his feet, but the guru quickly lifted him up by his shoulders intensely reading his face and blessing him.

Joshua's eyes flickered between the two figures in front of him, the sage and his niece, and finally fixed on the man – a man in his early seventies, thin, tall and strong in build. His silvery white hair was braided and put up above his head with a knot, while his white flowing beard grew wild to either side. With bright eyes, a strong nose and graceful alertness, he appeared distinguished. He wore a simple cotton loin cloth, and around his neck hung a garland of rudraksha beads. His large forehead lined with deep furrows of age and wisdom was decorated with three horizontal lines of sandalwood paste extending from one temple to the other that identified him as a Vaishnavite Hindu.

Then his eyes intuitively turned to the tall, thin girl, with her light-brown hair pulled to the top and tied around with a bunch of jasmine flowers, and the long bundle of hair tumbled down like a waterfall past her buttocks. She wore a white loin cloth wrapped around her waist, and her small apple like breasts were covered over with a red brassiere.

Joshua glanced at Sukannya in passing: their eyes locked for a moment, but she quickly turned and went ahead to greet the king. Joshua, taken by surprise, stood in awe for a moment. He had never expected to see such a beautiful girl in the middle of a forest. With sparkling eyes, a smooth nose that gently curved up, rose-petal-like red lips, thin waist, strong hips with a slight flare, and smooth, long legs; she looked like a Greek goddess, a woman of sublime ethereal countenance.

405

In a deep yet soft voice, the Vyassa said, "Many people come and go. They all say that they will come back, but only a very few actually do."

Very soon, Vishal and Kishan brought two earthen amphora's full of water and washed the king's feet first, and then Joshua's.

The king turned to Sukannya and said, "Sukannya, I hope you are keeping well."

"Of course, Rajan, all is well. I hope your studies went well and the mission is accomplished," she replied in a silky voice.

"Yes, and I am very happy to travel back home now." Then, he turned around and held Joshua by the shoulder and brought him to the forefront as if presenting a trophy to the Guru.

"Rajan, tell me who is this respected guest," Vyassa asked, his eyes fixed on Joshua.

"Guru, this is Joshua from Galilee, a scholar par in excellence and a philosopher in the making. I met him in Taxila, and already I have learned a great deal from him. It is my pleasure to introduce him to you."

Joshua bowed his head. The Guru nodded. Sukannya glanced at the visitor casually, and their gazes locked for a brief moment for a second time. "This man has traveled the world extensively; he is noble, wise and righteous. I warmly recommend him and request you to accept him as one of your sishyas. You will be delighted, I promise."

The Guru raised his eyebrows and gestured towards Sukannya. She smiled passively and nodded.

Joshua began his first day as a sishya at the hermitage; it was an entirely different atmosphere – serene, rustic and peaceful.

That evening, Vyassa Muni invited Joshua to his abode, a commodious wooden house built on the first large trifurcation of the banyan tree. The thick foliage and lush boughs of the banyan tree resembled a thatched house. The foliage was so strong, it could endure the monsoon rains, and water seldom reached the ground. Joshua sat with the Muni under the shades of the tree engaged in dialogues as they got to know each other.

"Joshua, I am very happy to have you here, and I hope your stay will be comfortable," Vyassa said.

"I thank you, Maha Rishi, for letting me stay here," the Galilean said.

Within calling distance of the banyan tree, on the south end of the clearing, facing the setting sun, stood the ancestral home of the Vyassa, a modest house made from timber and canes, its roof thatched with palm leaves, where his niece, Sukannya, stayed. Adjacent to the house, on the south paw, was a small guest house reserved for special guests.

As the evening fell, the mynahs from the banyan tree started their evening songs, calling their little ones gliding in the skies to come home to roost. Even after the evening gray had shrouded the air and the faces were difficult to read, the Guru and Sishya continued with their discussions. Then they heard a sweet voice, "deepam . . . deepam," from the hermitage, followed by a light, and then the beautiful face of Sukannya emerging from the front door to the courtyard. Sukannya held a single wicker lamp in the cup of her hands. She reverently placed it in front of a flower bush, the thulassi, that yields bunches of the bright-red flowers and leaves that were used for the guru's daily prayer rituals.

At dusk they all sat cross-legged in the foyer under the dim light of an oil lamp. Sukannya served them hot tea. A short while later, she served them rice cakes, toasted jack nuts, yogurt and spiced mango pickles – the humble dinner of the hermitage. For quite a while after the dinner, the men sat sharing stories of their studies in Taxila, and particularly the earthquake.

Vyassa had already sized up the young man from Galilee and was impressed with his soft words, gentle countenance and knowledge. "You certainly have all the attributes of a Bhrahmin; I am glad to have you here," Vyassa said.

What are the attributes of a Bhrahmin, Joshua wondered. He recollected his lessons from Taxila – Bhrahmin the representative of Bhrahman on earth. *That is quite a huge compliment,* Joshua thought. A subtle smile curled his lips, which only Sukannya noted.

Vyassa had already accepted Joshua to his tutelage and offered him lodging in the guest house after seeking Sukannya's permission. She was surprised that Pitha Maha had permitted a virtual stranger to stay at the house. *The king's words really counted,* she thought.

Immediately after the dinner, the Rishi retired to his tree house; the king went to his carriage, and Joshua, to the guest room.

Joshua felt strange and detached the first night at the hermitage. He lay on the floor mattress, sleepless, tossed about by the thoughts clamoring for attention in his head. No matter how far his thoughts traveled, they inevitably flew back to a small house in Galilee guarded by the tall cypress and the poplars. *My search . . . me? . . .* the men, scenes and events milled around in his mind: Confucius, Buddha, the Babylonian praying at Esaglia, the little family in Amarna making papyri, these Vedas, these Upanishadts, Manu – all mind boggling. What was post-Vedic Hindu philosophy? What was this greatest work they all talk about, this Song of God? *Bhagavath Geetha?* Maya, Karma, incarnation, reincarnation, samsara, endless unremitting, birth and rebirths. . . . soon he fell into a deep sleep.

Before the break of the next day, Rama Varma and his carriage coach took off for Muziris. That morning, Vyassa sat down with Joshua in the foyer of the house for extensive discussions. The foyer itself was adorned with a red carpet, several seat cushions and a round pillow, a book stand with a thick voluminous book opened and bookmarked. Behind, stood a tripod on which three earthen pots were set up one top of the other for drinking water to be filtered and cooled. An impressive painting hung on the wall, depicting Lord Krishna seated on a decorated chariot and a handsome warrior aiming arrows at the enemy.

"You have a solid understanding about the things you have learned. I am really impressed," said the Muni. "First you get used to the life here at the hermitage for a few days, then we will make a plan for your learning," he said.

They continued such meetings for the first ten days.

The daily routines in the hermitage were predictable. The sage awoke two hours before the first light in the east, prayed and chanted for about one hour, then took a long walk to the nearby stream for a morning bath, ignoring rain or snow. Deep in the woods, the stream was a tributary of the River Yamuna, with a small rapid and a pond-like expanse where he swam and meditated, standing on one leg immersed in water, neck-deep, and with his hands folded above his head. Well before sunrise, one could hear the clank of his wooden sandals and the sounds of sand crunching beneath his feet near the thulassi bed. He would stop and pick up a few leaves or flower petals and stick them behind both earlobes, adorn his forehead with the three horizontal lines of sandalwood paste and return to the tree house for his daily work. By mid-afternoon, he would come out to the house for his dinner of cooked dhal, boiled rice, vegetables, nuts, and yogurt. After his meal, he would go for a long walk in the woods – most of the times accompanied by Sukannya. He talked to the animals, birds and trees, particularly the two peacocks that followed him in the woods every day. The spotted deer usually ran to him, and sometimes he sat down with them. They licked him and scratched his back gently with their sharp horns. The sage then went for his evening prayer, bathed in the stream, sat down with Sukannya, talked for a while and then dictated some verses or sermons which she would scribe. Sometimes, he shared just a few lines, other times several pages. A bit after sunset he would drink a bowl of soma juice and then he retire to the tree house. This was the daily routine of the sage and all the others lived around it.

The next morning, Joshua awoke to the noise of an unfamiliar bird, something with a squawking crow-like voice. It was early in the morning. He went out and sat in the foyer, and there she was, with a wicker basket delicately balanced on her head, wiggling smoothly from one foot to the other – Sukannya was feeding a group of peacocks, scattering nuts and grains on the ground, the birds pecking at them as soon as they reached the ground only if they failed to catch the grain in the air. The peacocks danced around Sukannya, their iridescent, green, blue and golden tail feathers fanned out, reflecting the morning sunlight, surely one of the most colorful and rare sights he had ever seen. *A piece of the simple and humble rustic life of the hermitage*, Joshua thought.

"Arya, did you sleep well?" asked Sukannya without losing the balance of the basket on her head.

"Yes, Sukannya," Joshua said, "and you?"

"Of course. Have you seen peacocks before?"

"From a distance, yes; this close, for the first time," he said.

The next day, Sukannya took Joshua for a walk in the woods, showing him the various types of birds and plants in the surroundings woods, accompanying him down the walkway to the stream and sharing with him her flower gardens, Pitha Maha's herbal garden, and the simple routines of the hermitage.

"Pitha Maha has told me to take care of you," she said.

Slowly they started talking, and she put him at ease, and the "stranger" feeling soon evaporated.

Gradually, Joshua began to move to the slow rhythm of life in the secluded dwelling of the hermitage. Joshua learned that Sukannya's mother was a sister to the Maha Rishi, and that she had lost her father to a snake bite when she was only eight years old. She talked to him as if they had known each other for years.

"One day, my father went out to the forest to collect sandalwood. He was brought home dead by four Chandallas," she said. "He was all blue and motionless. There were two tiny bite marks on his feet. Soon all the family and relatives assembled. There were many ceremonies prior to the cremation." Her voice trembled. "My mother was utterly devastated. Immediately, she took off all of her ornaments and clad herself in white." Sukannya stared into the distance for a long moment before continuing.

"Soon, the elderly women of our family and the neighborhood all converged to our house. They started pointing fingers at my mother, blaming that she had brought bad luck to the family."

"Let us sit down for a moment," he suggested. They sat on a stone by the stream dipping their feet in the running waters.

Again a woman is at fault! He ground his teeth with indignation. Women, what have thou done to yourself for this type of treatment? Blames – whatever that would be, misfortunes – whichever that may be, calamities – wherever that could be, disasters – whenever it might be; it's all due to the fault of women! India is no different from Galilee.

He gently patted her shoulders, "I am so sad to hear this Sukannya. Continue, if you can."

"But grandmother, Malliamma, was the worst. She took my mother to a nook and started screaming at her, pointing fingers right into her eyes. My mother slumped to the ground and covered her face in the cup of her palms. The old women of the village then sat around her and started praising her blessings, "Sathimatha had blessed upon you. I can see the glow in your face. It is glory to our house, so on and on . . ."

"What blessings are they talking about? A young woman losing her husband?" Joshua asked.

Sukannya's face clouded again. She had no answer to that question. She bit the inside of her lips to clear her head and continued. "My poor mother was trembling and crying wildly as she held me tight to her body. I remember her face pale and petrified. My brother was also crying bitterly, hanging on to my mother's clothes. The women of the village kept on saying, 'This is a happy occasion for her, and that she must not cry. You now start preparing,' they said."

"A happy occasion!" That's also what the priest said before Rachel was sacrificed.

"They tore me away from my mother. I grabbed my brother, and the both of us sat silent at the nook of the room, me cupping his mouth. The poor boy was trembling and sobbing with an occasional big sigh. While, all the men were sitting around my father's body, clad in white and lying on the floor, chanting and praying in the front foyer, the women continued to shower my mother with insults and abuses in the back room. It was horrible, Joshua; it was terrible."

This is even worse than what happened to Rachel. The priest's voice echoed in his mind: "this is a happy occasion."

"Sukannya, they are blaming and abusing her on the one hand and saying that it is a blessed occasion on the other. How is that?"

"Yes, the death of my father was my mother's fault, worse than the snake itself. Now that he is dead, Sathi is a blessed occasion and the goddess of Sathi has blessed the house; that's what they are saying."

She paused a moment. "They took my mother to the backyard, shaved her head, bathed her and painted her with ashes and sandalwood paste. They squeezed open her mouth and forced her to drink this terrible drink. I think it was soma with bitter opium. They drugged her. She was drowsy and disoriented, and she never recovered, and they wouldn't let me near her again. My mother looked so scared, so helpless and miserable. She was so drowsy and just sat there on the floor, trying to hold her balance, eyes closed, trembling. The women gathered around her and started singing and chanting out loud, clapping their hands, praying to the Goddess Sathimatha."

Joshua noted with surprise that Sukannya didn't have any noticeable burden in telling this horrific story of her mother. "Sukannya, I know this story is emotionally draining on you, I can understand. But why didn't the women try to dissuade . . ."

"No, Joshua, I have no more emotional burdens in me. I am way beyond that. You are asking why the women persuaded my mother for the Sathi?"

"Yes."

"Well, the women were more interested in the Sathi. Don't ask me why; maybe it's the passage of the rights; I don't know," she paused. "You want me to continue?"

"Of course, Sukannya, if you can."

"The songs and prayers continued the whole evening, and they wouldn't let my mother move from that spot. The men prepared the funeral pyre in the ground south to the house. They put my father on the wood and covered him with layers of wood. They soaked the pyre with oil and ghee. The men circled the pyre numerous times, chanting Vedic songs and sprinkling holy waters. Maha Pita lit a small wicker flame, put it in my brother's hand, and guided him to the pyre. The small wick of fire ignited the heap of wood, and the fire grew large and wild in no time. My mother was still slumped to the ground, stunned, unable to even cry. My grandmother and two other women dragged her up and led her close to the fire. She writhed and resisted, trying to take steps back. She screamed, thrashed, while her legs kicked in the air as they lifted her up. That struggle continued for some time. Nobody came forward to save my mother," Sukannya said.

"The chorus of praise to Sathimatha grew louder. Four men with long poles in their hands raked the woods and embers, keeping it burning hot and bright. It was so hot, I could feel the heat from where I was crouched behind layers of people around the pyre. I wanted to hug my mother; I wanted to kiss her. I snuggled between the feet of people and somehow reached near her. They tossed me out to the custody of two women. I saw the four men with burning poles in their hands coming to my mother's side and ordered the other women to move out. The men pushed my mother with the burning poles towards the giant pyre. My mother shrieked, begging for help, but there was no help to come for her. The men impaled my mother with the burnt end of the poles and held her steady in the pit of the pyre, until the flames fully consumed her and her cries dissolved with the voices of the crowd shouting with exuberance.

"'Jaiho Sathimatha. Jaiho Sathimatha,' The men chanted. When the celebrations ended, everybody went from there for a grand feast. On the third day, they collected the ashes and floated it in the River Yamuna."

Looking at the distant skies, Sukannya pursed her lips and nodded to herself, as Joshua extended an arm of comfort over her shoulders.

"The next day, Maha Pita brought me here, and since then he has given me everything I wanted and taught me everything I know," she said.

"What happened to your brother?"

"He was picked up by my father's brother."

Joshua was dismayed to see that Sukannya had not even a drop of tear in her eyes. She seemed to be holding back emotion and composing herself throughout. It's hard to believe that she had no grief – she was a little girl who had just lost her father and who had then had to watch as they burned her mother alive. Joshua held her palms in the cup of his hands, gently pulled her close to him, and patted on the small of her back.

Most of the next week Joshua spent with the Rishi, speaking to him about the wonders of the places he had visited, the people he had met, and, most of all, the philosophies he had studied, in particular

Akhenaton, Aristotle and Khammurabi. The sage had a very good understanding of the Chinese philosophers, but the splendors of Egypt, the wonders of Rome and the profundity of Alexandria raised great curiosity in him. He was interested in the Hebrew religion and was so impressed with Joshua that at a certain point he repeated his previous observation, "You have the attributes of a good Bhrahmin, Joshua."

**** **** ****

Vyassa outlined the plans regarding Joshua's study at the hermitage. He met with Joshua and Sukannya in front of the Krishna painting in the foyer of the house.

"I know you have a good understanding of the Vedas and the Upanishadts. Your studies in Taxila certainly helped you a great deal in that regard," Vyassa said.

"Therefore," he turned to Sukannya, "You start teaching him the story and characters of *Ramayana*. It's the story of the most ideal king, like your Solomon; I hope you like it." The guru left for his evening routines.

"Sukannya, I am surprised to learn that you are a teacher to the legendary work of *Ramayana*. How did that come about?" Joshua asked.

"I don't claim to be an expert on the book, but I have copied the whole work of *Ramayana* and *Mahabharata* four times, my job for the past seventeen years. Pitha Maha has taught me a lot, and, of course, I am two years older than you, so I can be your teacher." She laughed.

The tutelage began. They started reading from early in the morning and continued until the afternoon. She recited the poem as a beautiful melodious song, explaining the sub-plots and allied stories. *Ramayana*, the illustrious account of Lord Raman, the eighth Avathar of the Hindu divine incarnations, had been composed by Maha Rishi Vathmeeki about three hundred years back.

Sukannya began reading: "Dassarathan, the king of Ayodhya was turning old and frail and had decided to anoint his eldest son Raman by his first wife Kawsallya as the crown prince. This news evoked a seizure of wrath from his second wife, who insisted that her son Bharathan should be the next king, reminding Dassarathan about two boons she had been promised by the king earlier on. She claimed the boons. She demanded that Raman should be exiled to the forest for fourteen years, and that her son Bharathan would be anointed as the crown prince. The king, who believed in truth and Dharma, had to agree to the demands.

Raman, with his beloved wife, Sitha, and his brother, Laxmanan, left to the forest and lived quietly in exile in a hermitage deep in the woods. In the meantime, the old king died, but the righteous Bharathan refused to be crowned as the next king while Raman was alive, and he proceeded to the forest and pleaded with Raman to be crowned as the next king. "No." Raman declared, "My father's will should prevail. You go back and rule the nation righteously." Bharathan returned to the palace with Raman's wooden sandals. He placed the sandals on the throne and ruled the nation on behalf Raman.

Four weeks were past, and the guru and sishya turned more like friends. The rains and dark clouds of the skies had left Mathura, and spring announced itself with the white and yellow blooming musk roses, chick weeds and sun flowers. In the afternoons, Sukannya took Joshua for a walk through the woods, to visit the small stream and the pond. The footpath to the stream was covered with a canopy of the lush foliage from the trees on either side. On the sidewalks, jasmines grew abundantly and cascaded over the hedges, their shimmering white flowers scenting the air.

"I love jasmine," she said. "The shrub blooms throughout the year except in winter." She plucked a bunch of flowers and held them to Joshua's nose. "See, this fragrance is so sweet," she said, smiling radiantly. It was obvious that she loved jasmine, as she always wore the lovely white flowers in her long, dark curls.

As they sat near the stream, dipping their feet in the running waters, she inquired: "Arya, last evening you didn't eat much at all. Did you not like the food? Our cooking is very simple, as Pitha Maha will not eat meat, fish or any kind of roots. But, if you like, I can arrange to have some game meat cooked by Kishan or Visal. They go for hunting frequently."

"Have you ever eaten fish or meat?" Joshua asked.

She smiled, a small secret smile, and looked deeply into his eyes. That was the first time Joshua really observed her face up close, a large, well-shaped forehead, intelligent eyes like sparking bluefish, and full, rosy lips. Her jaw was square and prominent, her teeth like well-set pearls, perfect but for one tooth too many on the right upper row. But in Joshua's eyes, that slight imperfection only added to the character of her smile in that perfect face.

"Sukannya, I would like you to call me Joshua. After all, I am younger than you."

She smiled to herself, or rather, it was a giggling. Her chest heaved, "Joshua, Joshua," she repeated the name to herself. She couldn't contain the laughter, her rosebud mouth parted wide, with her chin pointed down. She looked up at him and said softly, "This is first time I see a Joshua. It is a nice name. Alright, I will call you Joshua, Joshua. But when Pitha Maha is around, I will call you Arya."

Back in the foyer at the hermitage, the story of Raman continued. In the forest, Raman fought and destroyed many demonic, man-eating Rakshasas, who came to devour them. Some of the demons were also the envoys of King Ravana of Lanka – the most ruthless, powerful, gifted, and handsome Rakshasas of all.

"Ravanan had coveted Sitha. He had a ship that flies in the sky faster than thought," Sukannya narrated.

"How interesting, a ship flying faster than thought?"

"Of course, you will hear many such imaginative creations in our stories. In any case listen, Joshua: Ravanan abducted Sitha from their house, took off in his ship and disappeared in the skies."

"So, Raman lost his kingdom and now his wife, too?'

"Yes. Now it's the mission to rescue Sitha. The grieving Raman, his younger brother Laxmanan, and his servants trudged through the southern terrains of India and encountered the monkey god Hanuman near the banks of the river Pamba."

"You mean Hanuman was god of the monkeys?"

416

"Oh no, the clairvoyant Hanuman is a high god in the pantheon of our house of gods. He took Raman to Sugreevan – the aged and supreme god of the monkey dynasty – with whom they made an agreement that the millions of monkeys would search and find Sitha. In return, Raman would annihilate a monkey demon called Bali who was the arch enemy of the Sugreevan dynasty. Bali was killed, and the monkey army engaged to find Sitha.

"One evening, Sugreevan, recovering from a memory lapse, recalled that a few days earlier, when he was sitting down with his ministers in the palace gardens, a low-flying airship passed over them, and they remembered seeing a woman screaming inside the airship. She had dropped a set of ornaments, including earrings and anklets, packed in a shawl. Naturally . . ." Sukannya said with a grin.

"Naturally, Raman quickly identified those items as belonging to his wife Sitha, didn't he?" Joshua smiled.

Sukannya answered that note with an enticing pouting of her mouth and continued with the poem. "Raman gave his signet ring to Hanuman as a proof of his confidence, before leaving for the mission."

"In the meantime, Hanuman made plans to crossover the ocean to the beautiful island in the Indian Ocean. The divine Hanuman grew in mighty proportions; he anchored his giant feet on Mount Mahodra – and, leaning forward, he pressed all of his weight against the mountain. The rocks crumbled, the trees withered, the earth trembled, the mountain compressed, the rivers broke open and giant snakes squeezed out of their holes, hung loosely like ornaments from the mountain side. Hanuman flew up into the sky like a rock catapulted from a launcher. Giant trees, boulders, soil, dust and debris swirled behind him, caught in the cloud of his cyclone as Hanuman continued his flight to Lanka."

"In Lanka, Hanuman disguised himself as he searched the island for Sitha, even including the bedroom of Ravanan. In the dim light he saw Ravanan asleep on a bed amidst fully naked women lying crisscross on the bed. One woman, frozen in sleep, still had her hands on the breasts of one woman and her face nestled in the groin of another, but Sitha was still nowhere to be found."

"Sounds disgusting," Said Joshua. "Where was Sitha after all?"

"Finally, Hanuman discovered Sitha in the Ashoka Gardens crouched under a tree in tattered clothes, weeping and rocking with arms around her legs, surrounded by demonic women imposing themselves upon her and coercing her to succumb to Ravanan. When the guards were away, Hanuman met with Sitha with the signet ring. 'Devi, I came to rescue you. I will carry you safely on my shoulders back to your husband.'

'Ravanan has threatened to kill me if I don't submit to him soon,' Sitha said. 'I am exhausted from this torture. Now I am preparing for my death.' Sitha's face turned red. 'No!' she screamed. 'Ravanan violated the queen of Ayodhya! He hugged me and brought his demonic lips close to mine to kiss. It is only Dharma for my husband, the king himself, to come here and destroy this enemy and take me home in glory. It would be cowardly if I escape with you, and totally unfitting for the pride of my kingdom. I will not go with you.'

"Then Sitha took out a diamond from the package and gave it to Hanuman saying, 'the king will recognize this; he knows; I always wore this in my crown.' Hanuman took the diamond from Sitha as proof of their meeting and left the garden."

Sukannya narrated the book with remarkable exuberance and enthusiasm. It took nearly thirty days to reach this point. In the meantime, the teacher and student became closer and spent time exploring the woods and sharing stories after dinner until late into the night. Sukannya had an insatiable passion to hear the Babylonian, Egyptian, Greek and Roman stories from Joshua, a passion Joshua tried to fulfill by making his stories come alive, but he was no match for the musical storytelling skills of Sukannya. Listening to her, Joshua felt as if he was watching a great theater show.

One evening, as they were strolling to the stream, Joshua wondered, "Sukannya, this is a very long and exhaustive story, I am not getting the religious or ethical message of the story so far, and I am at a loss. How could a great sage like Vathmeeki elaborate scenes of orgies in such explicit terms in a revered book like the *Ramayana*?"

"Joshua, the sages have full knowledge of all the pleasures on earth. They are not celibate at all. In fact, most of the sages described in *Ramayana* or *Mahabharata* had great sexual desires and needed instant gratification as well. They would concoct any excuse to justify their needs to penetrate a woman," Sukannya said, smiling seductively.

"Sages and their sexual urgencies," she continued, "Joshua, there are many, many, stories that you may not even want to know! I will tell you something that happened to me right here in this hermitage – not today, maybe tomorrow."

Joshua was a bit perplexed. He looked at her intensely, his curiosity roused. *What could have happened to her at this hermitage?* he wondered.

The next day after the morning classes they took a walk in the woods, Sukannya collecting herbs. A few deer crossed the pathway, leaping over, springing, their hoofs barely touching the ground. Instantly, Sukannya clapped her hands and called out. "Alli . . . Alli." Joshua was frozen still as he saw the group of five deer coming back and buzzing around her feet, some licking her feet and some tenderly caressing the horns on her legs.

"You know these animals by their names, and they answer your call?" Joshua asked.

"You saw that," she said.

"You are one of a kind, Sukannya. You amaze me every day. Well tell me the rest of the story from yesterday. What happened to you at the hermitage?"

They sat under a lush mango tree which was yielding bunches of very tender olive size green fruits. She paused for a moment. "Yes, Joshua. This is not a story I like to tell at all. But somehow I feel confident in you, and I like you a lot, and, therefore I tell you this much. I was only thirteen years old when Pitha Maha completed composing the *Bhagavath Geetha* – which you will study later. Already a great many of the sages knew of his work. Once, a famous Rishi and Astrologer, Partha-Suthan, visited here from Pataliputhra to discuss some of the philosophical disagreements he had with Pitha Maha."

"On one hot summer night, the full moon was up in the sky, well lit amidst innumerable stars glittering. Pitha Maha had gone to sleep. I saw Partha-Suthan pacing to and fro in the front yard, at times dallying with his phallus and watching the stars. He had a wicked look that I had noted from the very beginning, and I had always felt uncomfortable in his presence. I watched his movements closely, then, earlier that evening, I overhead him telling Pitha Maha that that night on the third watch the moon and the stars would have some special alignment, and that if he procreated a child after midnight, the child would be a boy and that the boy would grow up as a great philosopher, a great philosopher for generations to come. I believe he then requested permission to marry me in a Gandharva style that night."

"Marry you?"

"Yes. Me."

"What is a Gandharva style wedding? Did Maha Rishi grant permission for such a thing, even without asking you," Joshua asked. He felt his anger growing as if it was something that dearly mattered to him.

"He did tell me the Rishi's wish. It is one of the many varieties of Hindu weddings where the man and the woman join in procreation first, and thereafter sanctify the yoga of wedding," she explained.

"So, are you wed now?" Joshua asked.

Sukannya grasped his hands and continued. "No, but listen. I wanted to run away because Pitha Maha granted such a request. Then I thought of another plan. I made a cut on my yonni and stayed outside on the veranda with a bloodstained loincloth pretending that I was unclean. At the prescribed time after midnight, the man came and told me about the dialogue he had had with Pitha Maha. When I told him about my situation, that fox of a sage, that old wrought, insisted on looking between my thighs. I wanted to scream. I wanted to kill him. In fact, he pulled off my cloth, looked at my groin, pronounced that the bleeding was very minimal, and started trying to separate my thighs. I hit him hard, kicked him, and ran into the woods. He was still dallying with his phallus." Sukannya said. Her face had turned pink.

"What did Pitha Maha say the next day?" Joshua asked.

"Nothing! He left the next day."

Ramavarma was right – any man would covet her to be his wife, Joshua thought.

As the days went by, they became even closer, going out together to draw water from the brook, swimming in the river, washing clothes, collecting twigs and nurturing the flower plants together.

In a short time, the landscape became filled with the flowers of spring. The white shimmering jasmines that cascaded over the hedges and shrubs grew in abundance. The fragrances of roses, lilies and sun flowers carried in the morning breeze blessed them with the fragrance of spring and swept over their faces. Spring in Mathura was at its peak.

Sukannya's love for flowers was obvious. "Joshua, you know, jasmine are flowers of the night," she said, "Dressed in white like brides, they bloom in bunches at night, spilling the fragrance all around. They all look up, smiling at the stars, and the stars return their love by twinkling and winking their eyes. They spend the whole night together in silent conversation, but it is short-lived. In the morning when the sun comes up, the stars fade and the flowers bow down."

They walked up to a high land filled with bright yellow sun flowers. "But the sunflower has a different story. She is in love with the sun. As the first light of the mornings shine on her face, the sunflower wakes up smiling and gazes at the rising bridegroom with great reverence. She follows the path of the groom all the way from east to west until he dips down between the great mountains. The disappointed bride bows down her head and spends the night weeping: then again she blooms fresh in the morning, looking at the rising sun – another day of hope."

"Sukannya, you have such beautiful poetic images in your mind. It's fun listening to you."

"Well, let me ask you something else. Do you have kurinji flowers in your land?"

"Probably not. What are they?"

"If you stay here another two years, you will see them for sure. They are small flowery shrubs, deep blue in color. When they bloom, they cover the whole land like a blue carpet, but they bloom only once every twelve years."

"Two more years; no, I don't think I will be here that long."

Sukannya's face clouded.

**** **** ****

The next day they resumed the story of *Ramayana*.

"Joshua, where did we stop last time? Do you remember?"

"Yes. Sitha is imprisoned in Lanka, and King Raman was on his way to the island with several million monkey fighters to kill Ravanan and rescuing Sitha."

"Good. Very good." She playfully pounded on his back and laughed. "Yes, in Lanka, Raman's army annihilated several million of the enemy forces until finally Raman met Ravanan on the battlefield."

Sukannya described the war scenes in great detail. "Both of them possessed the most destructive weapons in their quivers, which they used one after the other. Some arrows carried fireballs, others split into a thousand arrows and then further split into ten thousand arrows. Some arrows fired spitting snakes, others fired disks that flew through the sky, severed the neck of the enemy, and returned to the quiver faster than thought."

"It was a fierce fight: a fight between good and evil, a war between God and demon, a struggle between the just and the wicked. It was the mother of all fights."

"Finally, Raman strung his bow with the ultimate arrow – the Bharahmasthram – and triggered it off against Ravanan's chest. The mighty arrow split his chest, felling the demon king, and returned safely to Raman's quiver."

"Interesting! But this story is nothing special, there are many such stories in the Greek epics of Homer and Hesiod," Joshua said.

"Maybe, Joshua, but wait. From this event onwards, *Ramayana* tells the story of Sitha. Wait and see, Sukannya said, "Then we can see if you still think it is nothing special."

"Sitha was not only the most beautiful queen," Sukannya said. "She was also the epitome of the most ideal wife. She worshiped her husband, never even looking at the face of another man. She abandoned all the royal comforts of the palace to follow her husband to the forest, in the most adverse conditions, and she accepted all that with grace, patience and endurance. Except for when the demon king Ravanan forcefully hugged her during her captivity, no man other than her husband had ever touched her. She was pure, honest and ethereal."

Why does a woman have to worship her husband; we worship only God, Joshua thought.

"After his victory, Hanuman liberated Sitha from the prison. The maids bathed, perfumed and dressed her up in all gold and jeweled ornaments, placed a tiara on her head, seated her on a royal palanquin, and carried her to Raman in a ceremonial procession fit for a reunion between a king and his queen. Sitha was ecstatic, shedding tears of bliss, her face glowing like the rising sun.

"Amidst an ocean of cheering subjects, seated on a high throne, ceremonially crowned, an impatient Raman awaited Sitha. The crowd parted way for the procession to pass, and Hanuman conducted the queen's palanquin to the king's court as the crowd cheered with exuberance.

"But, as Raman sat on the throne, his face grew stone-like. A rage of mixed feelings, anger, happiness and revenge boiled in his mind. His face turned dark purple with emotions, his eyes burned like embers, and his face quivered. He rose to his feet and cried: 'Put down the palanquin. Let Sitha walk! Let all my subjects see her well.' A terrible silence ensued. No one moved. The crowd stood paralyzed."

"Sitha, her breath frozen, slumped to the seat with her face aghast, all color drained from her lovely cheeks. After a long frightening moment, she climbed down from the palanquin and walked towards to the king, her head down, her shoulders slumped."

Many a flashback passed through Joshua's mind: the Hannaniahs house, Mary crouched behind the bed weeping, the trial at the temple, Jeduthun admonitions, and many more.

"The king's forehead was knit with an angry frown and he gritted his teeth."

"What a woman needs the most is morality and not this type of pomp and extravaganza," the king's words echoed loudly from wall to wall.

"All eyes turned to Sitha. She gently walked towards Raman, her head veiled and face down. She stood in front of Raman at a lower step of the balustrade, lifted up her eyes, and very softly addressed the king, 'Arya.'

"Raman ignored her. He looked to the crowd and made a speech emphasizing the great deeds he had undertaken to avenge the enemies and to rescue Sitha, his valor, his voice high and shrill and hands flailing.

"Raman put one foot down on the lower step, bent forward and pointed his finger into Sitha's face. He growled. 'I can bear all that, but you must understand that I fought this war not to save you, but to erase the notoriety that has tainted my family due to this kidnapping of yours by Ravanan.' Then the king raised his voice further and screamed, 'I doubt your chastity! Your presence here makes me uncomfortable, like a bright light flashing into my sore eye. Therefore, I grant you permission to leave this kingdom immediately, depart from my sight, now.'

"Sitha slumped to the ground as the crowd stood spellbound. Nobody offered any show of compassion or moved to lift her up from where she cowered on the ground.

"Raman continued to berate her. 'You lived in Ravanan's bedroom,' he yelled. 'You sat in his bosom. You are defiled. How on earth can a proud and honorable man accept such a profane wife? My mission in this war is all over. I have neither love nor passion for you. Of course, you are very beautiful and sensuous. Who would believe that you are still pure after living with the most vulgar libertine and sexually infatuated demon king for over ten months?'"

"Strange, is there any proof that Sitha was defiled?" Joshua asked.

"No. It's up to the woman to prove her innocence."

Well, Israel revisited, Joshua thought. He was anxious to hear the rest.

"Sitha rapidly regained her brave composure, rose up to her feet and addressed the king boldly, with her chin up.

"'Honorable King, you talk like a heinous man, addressing me like a festering woman – a whore. But listen, I am no infidel, certainly spiritual, I am not despicable, but most definitely respectable. I am not promiscuous, but chaste to the core, I am a queen. The demon king was mighty and monstrous; he hugged me against my will, but I fought off any further advances. My mind is untainted, and it has always been submitted to you. I believe you are under pressure now, and I beseech you not to let your anger turn you into a cheap, silly man. I am the daughter of the most honorable emperor – Janaka. I was born divine from the womb of Mother Earth, not from a sinner's yonni as you knew from my childhood.'

"Having said this, she turned to his loving brother and said, 'Laxmanan, let a pyre be prepared. Now.'"

"A pyre? What for? Is it another Sathi?" Joshua asked.

"Joshua, this story is alive and well in the minds of all the women in India. It's true to life. The mistake is always for the woman. She has to prove her innocence."

"But the king is so irrational . . . and I would say incompetent."

"Why incompetent, Joshua?"

"He is the legal heir to the crown; when his father died, he had the obligation to go back to the kingdom and rule the nation righteously. He went to the forest; he was careless. He didn't protect his wife, and now he is talking about Dharma and righteousness! I would say he is an inept king," Joshua said.

"But he is a man," said Sukannya. "The man makes the rules. Let me tell you, Joshua. I am a Bhrahmin; I learned all the Vedas and Upanishadts from none other than Maha Rishi Vyassa himself. Say I have to bear arms and go to war with my husband to avenge the enemy. Say, we won the war, but my husband died in the battle. No matter what you think, his death is my mistake. I will have to jump into his pyre."

Joshua was speechless. He rested his face in the cup of his arms and waited for the rest of the story.

Sukannya continued: "A large pyre was brought into life and the flame grew up into the sky. A bold Sitha turned to the flames, clasped her hands, looked up to the Heavens, and proclaimed:

'Oh Heavens, the god of fire, if I am chaste, save me unscathed.

'If my mind had been deviated, even for a moment, from my king

'Oh God of Fire, do consume me.

'If by thoughts, words or deeds, I have not sinned,

'The great gods of the universe spare me from this inferno.'

"Having said that, she bowed her head, folded her hands, circled the pyre seven times, and entered the fire boldly with a calm face. The whole crowd was sobbing and screaming, tears running down their faces."

Joshua took a deep breath and searched for the words to say something.

"Then everybody witnessed a miracle in the making," Sukannya resumed. "All the gods of the universe appeared there in person around and above the pyre. They all testified the chastity of Sitha to Raman and to the public. Soon they all saw a glowing fire god coming out of the pyre carrying a totally unharmed Sitha, and, the god took her to Raman and ordered him to accept her, as she was as pure as the fire itself."

Then Raman replied, "Oh my God. I always knew that Sitha was pure . . ."

"Oh no. He is a hypocrite," Joshua said.

"'If I had accepted her without a test, my people would have branded me an idiot of a king. I did it to convincingly prove to the universe that Sitha is chaste, even after staying in Ravanan's house all these days.'"

Sukannya stopped the reading for the day. She asked her student, "What do you make out of this story so far?"

"I am a bit surprised by the king's behavior," Joshua said.

"Correct. That is the genius of the writings of Vathmeeki. He wrote it cunningly."

"Sukannya, I see a curious and unfortunate resemblance in how women are treated in my culture as well as in yours. Is it always the duty of the woman to prove her innocence rather than the accuser to prove her guilt?"

"Yes, Joshua, if the flower got struck on the thorn or the thorn got struck on the flower, it's always the flower that's damaged."

"Well said, Sukannya, well said."

"You wait for the end. Pitha Maha will quiz you on all these issues. You prepare your answers well."

**** **** ****

It was late spring in Mathura, and the Ashoka trees were in full bloom. Thick bunches of deep-yellow flowers came out of the tree, even masking the branches and choking the tender leaves. The entire tree became a bouquet and the ground was covered with a yellow carpet of blossoms.

It was also the mating season for peacocks, and large numbers had begun to venture out of the woods in search of mates. They always came very close to the house to get hand-fed by Sukannya, and it appeared that she knew each and every one of them by name.

"Joshua, I think the peacocks are the most beautiful birds in the whole world," she said.

"Have you been to the whole world?"

"Of course not, but you have been. Tell me, have you seen a more gorgeous bird than this one." She picked up one bird and folded it under her arms close to her chest, gently smoothing its feathers, and asked, "Aren't they gorgeous Joshua? I love these glistening iridescent plumes, ornate with this gorgeous eye at the center." She turned towards Joshua with her winning smile.

"See. You can hold them, too." She handed the bird to Joshua, tenderly, cautiously, like a mother handing over her newborn baby to her husband for the first time.

"Surely, this is quite a beautiful bird, but . . ."

Suddenly the sky was overcast with dark clouds, a single thunderbolt rattled the earth, and winds started blowing heavily form the south, the tree leaves fluttering and their heads bowing to the north – the first thunderstorm, the predecessor of the early monsoon. The peacocks began to squeak and craw, and then, as if directed by a choreographer, began to flap their wings, spread out their tail feathers like a fan, and dance. Before long, the peacocks began to dance around, sometimes hopping on one leg and chasing after the peahens. The peahens faithfully bent down, lifting and spreading their little tail feathers – the monsoon mating season was in progress.

"Look at them. These birds – do they worry about anything?" Sukannya asked.

How sweet are this woman's demeanor and observations? Each day I learn something more about this lovely, lovable woman, he thought.

"No, Sukannya, they don't. They are some of the happiest of God's creations – free birds."

The monsoon rains were very heavy in Mathura, with strong winds and heavy downpours as usual. The little pathways and grounds swelled like streams and ponds. Joshua and Sukannya sat in the foyer watching the rains, the drizzle spraying their faces and giving them goose bumps. They frolicked, touching the goose bumps on the other's faces, laughing and splashing the waters in the rain. Like a symphony of tiny drums, the rain beat on the thatched roof, playing music over their heads.

As time went on, Joshua and Sukannya had grown into intimate friends. Joshua felt as if they had always lived in that house and played in its foyer. Some nights they shared stories of their childhood experiences, but most times, Sukannya made him tell the stories of the Greek dramas.

"Joshua, you are a very lucky man, able to travel all the lands, to see and learn about the world, and finally you are now sitting here with me in this little hut in the middle of a forest. I am so lucky that I got to know you and hear all of your stories. By the way, Pitha Maha talked to me again about you. He is really impressed with you; he told me that you have all the noble traits of a Bhrahmin; he thinks you are a philosopher, already." She smiled.

"What did you normally do when you were alone in this house before you were teaching me?"

"I meditate a lot. In fact, I have been meditating three hours a day for over twelve years now. Some days when I am alone, I do more."

Joshua confessed, "I have tried to meditate, but my mind is not always focused; it wanders from one thought to the other. At some point can you teach me how you are able to meditate for three hours in a row?"

"Of course, I was planning to talk to you about that, but I warn you. When you decide to commit to meditation, it will demand a lot of time and dedication."

**** **** ****

Sukannya resumed reading the story of *Ramayana*. "So, Raman returned with Sitha to his kingdom in Ayodhya on the flying ship Pushpaka. He held Sitha in his lap throughout the journey.

"The people of Ayodhya watched the Pushpaka airship, a distant speck up in the horizon, rapidly approaching and landing on the ground amidst the thunderous cheers of the subjects of Ayodhya. Up closer, the Pushpaka was an enormous flying city. Bharathan put the wooden sandals on Raman's feet, and the transfer of power was symbolically completed.

"A jubilant Ayodhya welcomed Sitha and Raman's return with an extravagant reception, decorations, drums, bugles, thousands of soldiers marching with swords drawn out, and the city exploded with music, dance, and all kinds of celebrations.

"With the return of the king and the queen, peace, prosperity and tranquility returned to Ayodhya – no tears, no wailing, no poverty, no pestilence, no accidents, no acts of thievery, and not one single child death. The fruit trees bore fruit in all the seasons, plants brought forth flowers through all the year, and there was neither flood nor drought – the Kingdom of Heaven came upon Ayodhya, the Rama-Rajya."

"So, this is what the Maha Rishi was talking about: the Rama-Rajya – the heaven on earth?"

"Yes."

"So, what did the king do to achieve this – kill the demon king Ravanan?"

"That's only part of the reason. He maintained the structure of the four colors of the society perfectly in order, each class engaged in the jobs assigned to them only, without unrest, protest or the gnashing of teeth."

"And that was the reason, God incarnated as the king – to maintain the colors in order?" Joshua asked.

"But wait, Joshua. There is more to it. A few weeks later, the king held an assembly attended by pundits, poets, musicians and political experts. As they were telling jokes and casually chatting among themselves, the king posed a question to his assembly: 'What is the mood of the villagers and city dwellers? What do they say about the new order of my kingdom?'

"The courtiers mostly praised the king for destroying the evil kingdom of Lanka, but some questioned why the king had accepted his wife, Sitha. She had lived with Ravana for a good long time, and the demon king was known to have raped every woman he set his eyes upon. Therefore, Sitha must have been defiled, they contented. The king had set an atrocious example in accepting a wife who had slept with other men, they thought."

"Sukannya, only yesterday we learned that Raman's kingdom was the heaven on earth," Joshua said. "Now, there is gossip and bad mouthing about the queen, even after her miraculous escape from the pyre. Why would her chastity once again be called into question? I don't get it. What is this; some kind of a game on Sitha? Is Raman a normal man or easily gullible to meaningless gossips?"

"You decide it by yourself, Joshua, and tell Pitha Maha what you think about it. Let me read the book."

"Raman became very gloomy and dissolute. He summoned his brother Laxmanan.

"'Dear brother,' Raman said, 'now these stories are making me uncomfortable, and I fear they will bring dishonor upon me. I am resolved to do everything possible to quell the ill-fame that is threatening our dynasty.'"

"Sukannya, stop for a moment," Joshua said. "Is that the only goal of an ideal king – fame and glory? How about serving his people with honor, protecting them, respecting his wife, being fair and righteous?"

"Once again, Joshua, you are the one to answer those questions," she said.

"Laxmanan was stunned and didn't speak. The king made the final declaration, 'Therefore, Laxmanan, tomorrow you will take Sitha to the banks of the River Thamassa where our father's friend Vathmeeki has a hermitage. You will leave her there and return quickly to the kingdom. Do not question my orders; do not speak of it again,' Raman said.

"When Laxmanan reached the hermitage, he broke down in front of Sitha and wept like a baby. He informed Sitha of Raman's decision to abandon her and the reasons thereof.

"The story read, Sitha fainted but quickly recovered. She advised Laxmanan to go back and serve the king faithfully. She said, 'The king must rule the nation without scandal. I would kill myself to spare him this embarrassment, but look at me – I am very much pregnant. If I die now, Raman's kingdom will not have any proper inheritance.'"

In Sukannya's teachings, Sitha's story gradually unfolded. "Sitha stayed with the Rishi at the hermitage and in due course she gave birth to two beautiful healthy boys, Lavan and Kushan. The boys grew up as Kshathrya. They learned all the Vedas and Dharma's and gained expertise in all the tactics of war particularly archery.

"Around this time in Ayodhya, a major incident occurred. One day a Bhrahmin came to the king's court, wailing that his twelve-year-old sons had died. Children's death was not to be in Raman's Kingdom of Heaven. The king immediately convened a conference of Rishis and pundits of the nation. The clairvoyant Rishis arrived at a conclusion quickly.

"'There is a Shudra somewhere in your kingdom,' the Rishi's said, 'engaged in the yoga of meditation to gain wisdom and Heaven.'"

"Sukannya, I am getting it," Joshua said. "It's all in the Laws of Manu right?"

"You are right."

"What did Raman do? The story is getting really cunning."

"As you can imagine, Raman was devastated. 'A Shudra meditating! That too, in my country?' He stood up and screamed."

Joshua couldn't hold laughing, but Sukannya stared at him, implying it was no laughing matter.

"Raman ordered his ministers to keep the Bhrahmin boy's body in a bath of oil. He immediately took off in his Pushpaka plane in search of the Shudra, and after a thorough search of the land, deep in the southern territories, the king found the Shudra indeed meditating in a pond, standing on his head immersed in the water. The airship landed by the pond. The king pulled the Shudra out of the water and demanded a reason why he disobeyed the Dharma of colors and engaged in the yoga of meditation.

"The Shudra replied, 'My Lord, the king, I committed this violation with the desire of going to heaven.'

"Raman's eyes turned red, and the muscles of his face contorted in fury. 'How on earth in my kingdom could you, a low-class Shudra, engage in meditation? Why would you expect this would admit you to Heaven, even if your intentions are pure? Did you forget you are a Shudra? This is a blatant violation of the principles of Dharma,' he said.

"Raman pulled his sword and severed the Shudra's head. As the head rolled into the water, the gods in the heavens rejoiced, restoring peace and stability to the heavenly kingdom of Raman."

"And the Bhrahmin boy came back to life?"

"Of course."

Joshua didn't really know how to respond to this story. What was appropriate – to cry or to laugh? Was it a satire or a serious drama? He was unsure, but Sukannya reminded him that the holy *Ramayana* was not a subject for laughter. "The Holy Ramanya is akin to the stories in your Torah – it's holy, it's revered, and it's the word of the Lord."

Absurd! Joshua thought.

Sukannya entered the last part of the story. "At the peak of his glory, Raman decided to conduct the extreme yoga of the 'horse sacrifice' to purify the nation from all defilement and scandal."

"Oh yes, I know about the great Maha-yoga sacrifices of the Vedic times."

"From your studies at Taxila?"

"Yes. I am familiar with that. Let me ask you, did Raman's children Lavan and Kushan stop the horses."

"No, the yoga was successfully completed later. But about this time the two boys Lavan and Kushan came to Ayodhya as musicians and storytellers. Maha Rishi Vathmeeki had taught the two sons of Sitha how to recite stories in the classic melodious style. In fact, the story was actually the story of their parents, Raman and Sitha. The boys' performances in the streets of Ayodhya caught the attention of the palace guards. Raman invited the boys to recite the songs in his assembly of ministers and invited guests."

"Did the boys know who their father was?"

"No, not yet. As the boys began to sing, the crowd was enthralled by the genius of the story and the style of recital, but even more so by the unmistakable physical similarities that the boys shared with the king. As the story progressed, it was obvious to everybody in the court that Sitha was the mother of these two boys. The king soon realized that the boys were his children. He began to repent. He sent two of his ministers to the hermitage to spy on Sitha, and, if they found her to be chaste, they were to bring her to the court the next day to take a final oath in front of the whole assembly before accepting her as the queen."

"Is this not the third time Sitha had been tested for the same unfounded charges?" inquired Joshua.

"Yes, Joshua, Sitha is a woman: a woman can be tested as often as it pleases the man. That's their prerogative, and here in India, the God-given right of men. It has always been this way and always will be."

"Sukannya, you don't talk like a girl in a hermitage. Do I know you at all?"

She smiled and whispered "No, probably not. A few days later, Raman's ostentatious court convened with the ministers, dignitaries, Rishi's, prostitutes and invited guests. All patiently waited for Sitha's arrival.

"Then, a tumult of cheers erupted at the entrance gate of the hall; all heads turned towards the entrance door, and a luminous figure appeared at the threshold of the majestic golden arch. There it appeared, Vathmeeki conducting Sitha towards the court, Sitha following the Maha Rishi with her head bowed and hands folded like a lotus bud. As they approached the rostrum, the palace orchestra played a vibrant song and the crowd erupted into cheers, even some of them who had questioned Sitha's faithfulness.

"'Most honorable King Raman, here Sitha has come obeying your commands, standing in front of you, and now it is clear to you that the two boys reciting your story are, in fact, your children through Sitha. But most honestly, with all the divine powers that I possess, let it be known that Sitha is faithful, pure and divine, and I believe that you rejected her in fear of a scandal,' Vathmeeki said.

"Raman rose to his heels politely, 'Maha Rishi,' he said, 'I have no reason to disbelieve your words, and I realize these boys are my sons. But I demand, in witness of this assembly, let Sitha make a final oath that she is pure and unspoiled.'"

"Not again," Joshua said.

"There was a long tense moment in the hall. Sitha took off the veil. She glanced around the crowd. Her sparkling eyes beamed with resolve. She paused, spread her hands up to the heavens, looked down to the earth, and affirmatively prayed in a voice that sounded like a declamation.

"'Mother Earth,' she screamed. 'Show me the way if my chastity is pure and untainted. Mother Earth, consume me if I have submitted to anybody other than my husband.' Sitha's voice filled in the air, oscillating from wall to wall. She slowly slumped to her knees, put one hand on the ground, and with the other she pounded on Mother Earth and screamed again, 'My mother, you know I am telling the truth. Open thy womb and take me away from this hell.'

"The crowd remained spellbound as Sitha rested her crown to the ground hitting and sobbing.

"Presently, the earth rattled violently, Raman's throne collapsed, and his crown fell off, rolling and clanging down the steps. An unsteady Raman struggled to rise to his feet, a pang of anxiety and fear gripping his stomach as if some mighty forces were descending upon him. The earth rattled again, and with a thunder the earth split open right at the rostrum. A shimmering throne emitting a bright light ascended to the rostrum from underground, on which was seated Mother God Earth, smiling. She fondly embraced and kissed Sitha – her daughter – and folded her in her lap. Soon, the throne descended and the split on the earth was healed, thick clouds covered the face of the sun, and Raman's court was in darkness.

"But Bhrahman himself came to the scene to console Raman. Raman successfully concluded all his yoga and erected a life-sized gold statue of Sitha on the yoga rostrum. Raman continued to rule the country, the Kingdom of Heaven on Earth again."

After forty and one days of reading, "That is how the story ended," Sukannya said.

**** **** ****

Joshua was ready to join the discourses on *Ramayana* with Vyassa, who sat on a wicker sofa under the banyan tree surrounded by Joshua and seven other new students, students in their forties and fifties, all clad in saffron-colored loin clothes, with long hair and cotton threads across their necks to the waist, who had come to the hermitage under tutelage with the Maha Rishi to argue and discuss the philosophical and transcendental aspects of the work.

Vyassa introduced Joshua to the group as a man of wit and wisdom. "Joshua, all these men here are from different parts of India. They are all pundits in our religion and holy writings, but you are new to us, and this story is new to you. We will be much interested to hear your views and assessments of the work. You'll be free to critique in any manner you like; we would like to hear."

Joshua bowed to the group and sat down on the mattress cross-legged.

The pundits analyzed all the events of the story step by step and gave a philosophical explanation based on the fundamentals of Hinduism and Dharma.

"Beyond any doubt," said Sanathanan a student from Gandhara, "the stability of a nation depends on the solid foundation of the color system. The safety of the nation relies on the chivalry of the warrior class; peace and prosperity of the nation is from the blessings of the Bhrahmins of the nation."

Another student, Chokaraman from the land of Pandya, said, "so long as the classes are behaving as they are supposed to, things will be in order and the country will be blessed by the gods."

Another one, Dharman from Bodha-Gaya, leaned forward. "A person was born to a specific color entirely as a result of the positive or negative karma from their previous life."

The guru gestured and lifted his hands towards Joshua, inviting him to comment.

Joshua took a breath. *All these saffron-clads are color blind*, he thought. But he started slowly and soberly, "Maha Rishi, when I listen to you talking about the glory of the color system, I am reminded of a Greek philosopher, his name Plato. Plato also extolled the glories of a strong class system as the backbone of a solid Republic. But he did not invoke any gods or incarnations to push his ideas. He didn't say it was God given, but you do. With apologies, I would like to put it you that the color system is fabricated by the Bhrahmins to serve their own purpose, to push their agenda."

"*Santham . . . Papam: Santham . . . Papam,*" chanted two of the older Bhrahmins in the group. Their faces contorted and they looked away.

Joshua's face turned white.

Maha Rishi intervened. "Don't be concerned Joshua; there is nothing new in your views. We have heard worse from the Buddhists. There is always room for free thinking and exchange of views in Hinduism. Each view has its own merits. Please continue."

"But let me tell you something about the work itself," he tried to pacify. "In terms of rhymes, rhythms, allegories and metaphors – in poetic composition – Vathmeeki is superior to Homer. However, in terms of character development, depth and novelty, he should be a student to Homer. Let me ask you, gentlemen, *Ramayana* is a prefabricated story, is it not?"

When most of the men with white threads across their chests scowled, the Maha Rishi answered: "Result-oriented story, written for a purpose? Yes, it is."

"Deeply extolling the fundamentals of the Manu edicts, is it not?" asked Joshua.

"Joshua, as I told you earlier on, the Edicts of Manu are fundamental to our beliefs, akin to Moses in yours," replied Vyassa.

"Sitha is nothing more than a scheme to destroy the bad guys of Lanka, a ploy to invoke a war, is it not," Joshua persisted.

"Just like in any story, each character has a purpose – Sitha, too."

"And to exploit the theme of woman's Dharma?"

"Yes."

Soon the dialogue turned out to be between the Maha Rishi and the Galilean. The other Bhrahmins didn't care much about Joshua or his arguments. Questions and answers in a like manner continued for several hours. The Bhrahmins were turning restless, and some even yawned loudly with wide-open mouths.

"I have to say that Vathmeeki belittled Sitha to the core, insulted, abused and tortured for a reason. Why a woman has to be treated that poorly, again I believe it's the Manu edict, 'woman do not deserve freedom', is that it?" Joshua asked.

Vyassa smiled widely. "What's that 'reason,' Joshua?"

"In no uncertain terms, Vathmeeki is saying that for a woman, it's much better to return to her mother's womb or even be buried alive than to live in such a fundamentally abusive Manu's world!" Joshua said.

Vyassa smiled at the young man without blinking for the rest of the session.

At this juncture, the two Bhrahmins who had shouted before stood up cursing, "*Santham . . . Papam, Santham . . . Papam,*" and walked out of the scene, talking to themselves and flailing their arms.

This time Joshua didn't mind the protest. "The Shudra story," he swallowed heavily. Presently, bile rose to his temples, "The Shudra story! That story is inserted there to cement and justify the atrocities of the class system, is it not?" Joshua said. "How strange that the Bhrahmin's child dies because a Shudra meditates – despicable!"

Vyassa did not contest any of his arguments; instead, he encouraged Joshua to speak more. "Go on, Joshua, you have some valid arguments, go on." Vyassa sat deep back in his sofa, rocking and holding his knitted arms behind his neck.

"Maha Rishi, the Shudra, is he not a creation of God? Hasn't he got a soul? In your Upanishadts it is elegantly stated that we are all creations of God, that our soul is a part of God, and that the soul has to finally attain God? And above all, why did the gods in heaven rejoice when Raman committed such a heinous act?"

Joshua's commentary was sharp, to the point, and inconsiderate. Vyassa listened attentively to his critique, pleasantly, patiently and with a gracious grin, while rolling his thumbs one over the other.

"Joshua, now you are practicing Hinduism exactly as it is supposed to be. You can define the beliefs based on your convictions. You can criticize the philosophy in any which way you like. Nobody will object. Our beliefs are eternal; the self in you is ultimately responsible for your beliefs and convictions. But let me ask you this: in your temple, can you freely express your objections and criticisms with impunity, in a manner that you express here?"

Joshua was silent for a moment, serious and absorbed. "I never stated that my religious traditions are without faults."

"All right, give me your take on the work of *Ramayana*."

"Yes, I can. It is a great work of literature – I have learned a lot. But when it comes to the main theme, Raman is a weak character; he is gullible to silly gossips, never took the efforts to find the truth of an allegation about his wife, and his demeanor and actions don't fit that of an ideal king, let alone an incarnation. He is preoccupied with the notion of his name, fame and glory, even if it is to destroy the personality of his wife. It is clear to me that the story is written with the preconceived idea that the whole problem of the nation is rooted in the freedom of women and the equality of the Shudras: the idea that woman is a shadow of man, and the Shudra is something less than a man!"

The Maha Rishi smiled graciously as the intensity of the questions sharpened, and the crow's feet at the corners of his eyes came to life as he convincingly argued in favor of the writings.

"Rama's kingdom was heaven on earth. He ruled the country for the satisfaction and prosperity of the people; that is his Dharma, his Karma, his tribute," he said. "To achieve that status, some sacrifices are necessary; in this case, he had to sacrifice Sitha." After a pause, he resumed, "Joshua, I am very glad to see that you took the efforts to think about the work and were bold enough to speak your mind. But remember, good and bad the way you perceive it may not be the same way in the view of another. Ruling a nation, keeping discipline, and observing the well-being of the people is far from an ideal situation. Remember, in your stories of Exodus, when the crowd turned unruly, Moses had to go to the mountain top and to come down with a certain set of rules and commandments. Honestly, even for a moment, can you say that he met with God at the mountain top? In your writings, did not Yahweh demand the life of Jacob?"

Joshua's silence was a concurrence to the statement. Vyassa continued soberly, "Hinduism is sanathana, like an ever-growing banyan tree; some branches may die and fall off, but more and more roots will grow down to earth, sprouting more branches and strength."

"But I have to add this, too. When the story is finally smelted down, the glittering story is that of Sitha, her righteousness, beliefs and the unwavering faith in her husband, and, above all, the story extols the universal fact that only a divine intervention can liberate the women of the world from the insults abuses and tortures of men," the Maha Rishi concluded.

Joshua was inspired to hear those words from the Maha Rishi. *Finally, the Rishi is getting my point*, he thought.

The discussion went on and on for the whole day. Finally, the Maha Rishi said, "Very good. It took only four months for you to study this work. You have come all the way from Galilee and spent all these years going from one nation to the other. You have spent another six more months studying the *Mahabharatha* and the *Bhagavath Geetha*. I hope to have an even more lively discussion.

**** **** ****

Summer had come to Mathura. The sweltering heat was oppressive, at times unbearable. Maha Rishi spent most of his days under the shadowy umbrage of the banyan tree relaxing on a wicker rocking chair. Joshua and Sukannya spent a lot of times plunging in the stream. Sukannya had mastered the yoga of breath control and could stay underwater for a long time, her hair floating on the surface like a medusa with a thousand tentacles.

As the days went by, thoughts of Sukannya began to take root in Joshua's mind, first as a silent curiosity, but growing into a preoccupation in his solitudes. One evening, while they were walking shoulder to shoulder from the stream to the hermitage, Joshua impulsively put his arm around her shoulder, and she grasped it against her chest as if it was the right thing to do.

It was a late night in September, and Joshua woke up to the tumult of a thousand drums playing on the roof as the downpour beat against the thatched roof, and a chilly wind whistled through the treetops – the latter-day rains of the season were in full force. He came out to the foyer to watch the rain. In between the lightning he enjoyed watching the fluttering silhouette of the forest and the millions of droplets coming down from the heavens, and the oblique draft blowing into the foyer and beyond into Sukannya's room through the half-open door.

Then, he was startled by a noise, a hushed murmur, chattering of the teeth and an occasional cough that came from behind the kitchen from the back foyer. *Sukannya must be sleeping*, he thought. *But why is the door is half open?* He crossed the kitchen to the foyer behind and saw a woman crouched on a wet mattress, head buried between her knees, covered in a shawl, shaking and shivering. It reminded him of Rachel hiding behind the head board in Hannaniahs house. He pulled her up to her feet and removed the shawl from her face.

"Sukannya, what is this? What's the matter with you? What are you doing here?"

She didn't respond, even as he gently shook her shoulders. She tried to loosen his grip and move away, but he was holding her too tightly. She continued to try to back away, "No, Arya, don't touch me, I am unclean, I cannot come inside the house," she said.

"What's the matter Sukannya? I don't understand. Tell me what are you doing here on this wretched night?"

"Joshua, I am unclean, please don't touch me."

"Sukannya, this is not fair, really it is not. Traditions must not be perilous. I can't let you sleep outside in the rain; you could meet death with it."

Joshua carried her into his room, her body ice cold with goose bumps on her face, breasts and all over, still her teeth clinking with chatter. Joshua dried her, and dressed her in some of his clothing, and clasped her in his arms against his warm chest. He whispered into her ear, "Sukannya, today you consider this room – my room – not a part of your hermitage. You will lie down here and sleep tonight. You are not unclean, it's just one of the mysteries of your creation. Be proud; you are a woman."

He put her on his bed, her face resting on his chest and his lips tightly glued to her forehead, and he softly caressed her back, down to her smooth thighs, while she, still shivering, snuggled her face in the safety of his chest and slept peacefully.

The sun had risen high in the sky. Sukannya had already been to the streams for her cleansing bath, but Joshua was still asleep. She sat down by his bedside and watched him for some moments, ran her fingers over his lips and patted his shoulders to rouse him. He opened his eyes, and their gazes locked. They acknowledged that something had changed.

"I am clean," she said. "I hate to wake you, but Pitha Maha is looking for you."

Joshua found her smile endearing, her presence charming and her countenance serene. *Joshua, you are crossing the line. You are deviating from your mission,* he thought.

Joshua's final project was the study of *Mahabharatha* and the analysis of *Bhagavath Geetha* – the *God's song*. The book is more than double the length of Homer's *Iliad* and *Odyssey* combined.

Sukannya began teaching. Teacher and student sat cross-legged on a mattress facing each other. "The great king Vasu of the Cedi kingdom once went into the forest for a hunting expedition. But the burden of refraining from sexual intercourse for too long tormented him. Up in the woods, the ambience of the spring, the lush flowers, succulent fruits, the singing birds and the music of the running stream evoked a mighty sexual urge in the king, and he had a great ejaculation. Unwilling to waste the drink of the life in the forest, he collected his seeds in the cup of a leaf and sent it to his dear wife through a messenger bird. While the bird was flying under the clouds, another bird fought with the carrier and the fluid dropped into a river below. A fish drank the semen, impregnated, and in time gave birth to a gorgeous girl, who carried the stench of a fish. The girl grew into a woman, and she took up the job of navigating a boat in the river, taking passengers from one shore to the other for a fee."

"One day, the great sage Parasaran was a lone passenger on the boat. Enticed by the beauty of the girl, he requested the girl to submit to him for sex. The girl was reluctant to spread her legs in broad daylight while people were watching on both the shores of the river. The sage, who had superhuman powers, immediately shrouded the boat with a thick cloud, but the girl had additional demands."

She said. "Yes, I will do it, only if you change my smell to that of a pleasant perfume, and I remain a virgin after childbirth. The impatient and already aroused sage, eager to penetrate, readily agreed to all the conditions. The boy born to the girl grew up as the greatest Rishis of all, Veda-Vyassa, the author of the great story of *Mahabharatha*."

Later in the story, the Kuru dynasty of Hasthinapuri was without a heir when crown prince Vichithravirya died young, widowing two wives, Ambika and Ambalika, without any children. The queen mother, Sathyavathi, summoned her eldest son, Vyassa – a sage by the time, with long knotted hair, unkempt tattered clothes and brazen scarred face – and advised him to father children with the two young widows.

The so far celibate sage entered the bedroom of Ambika, but she couldn't stand the look of the sage and closed her eyes, and the boy born consequently, Dhrutharastar, was born blind, too. Next, Vyassa entered the room of Ambalika, but she was petrified with the looks of the sage and instantly became pale and blotched. Consequently, the boy born was with blotches – named Pandu.

Although the Dhrutharastar was the elder of the two, because of his blindness and apparent inability to rule the nation properly, Pandu was declared as the crown prince, which created tension between the brothers.

"In due course, Dhrutharastar married Gandhari and fathered a hundred children – the Kauravas. Pandu married two women, Kundhi and Mardi. However, he had a curse from before that he would instantly die if ever he sexually attained a woman and, therefore, was unable to father any children. But Kundhi had received special boons from before, utilizing which she was able to conceive children from gods, even without sleeping with them and remain a virgin."

"So, the tradition of a woman bearing a child from heaven and still remaining virgin was popular in your stories, too?" said Joshua.

"Yes, I don't know why, but the story is repeated many times," she laughed.

"However, even before this marriage, Kundhi had exercised one of her boons and had obtained a child named Karnan from the sun god. But to avoid a scandal, she floated the boy in a river covered in a reed basket."

Upon hearing this floating story Joshua smiled.

Sukannya stopped reading and gazed at him searching his eyes.

"Yes, Sukannya, as I had told you before, the story of a boy floated in a river and later growing up as a hero is seen in the old Babylonian epics as well as in the Torah," he said.

"But Joshua, who described the story for the first time?"

"I believe it was the Babylonians, then the Moses story. Anyway, keep on reading; I'd like to see how it compares," Joshua said.

"The child was miraculously saved by a Shudra. This boy – Karnan – grew up as a mighty warrior and joined the Kauravas, not knowing Kundhi was his mother. While living with Pandu, Kundhi conceived three more children from the gods, Udhistiran, Bhima, and the invincible Arjuna. Her sister-wife, Madri, also had two children fathered by Devas, named Nakulan and Sahadevan. These five children of Pandu are the Pandavas.

"The Kauravas and Pandavas grew up under the tutelage of the great sage Bheeshmar and were schooled in war tactics, archery, yoga, Vedas and Upanishadts. In spite of their identical training, the two clans were distinctly different in ethics, morality and character. The Kauravas were more self-centered, cruel and spiteful. But the Pandavas were righteous, ethical and forgiving, with the exception of Pandu's second son, Bhima, who had superhuman physical powers and a bullying personality even though good at heart. He would taunt the Kauravas, lifting them all with one grip, pulling their hair or trying to drown them in the river. This added oil to the fire of rivalry between the cousins, and the Kauravas were making plans to annihilate the Pandavas for their own survival. They even tried to poison Bhima and drown him in the river, but Bhima escaped all their attempts."

So goes the story that all the boys were mighty warriors, but Arjuna – the third Pandava, fathered by the god Devendra – was the most special and the mightiest archer of all. A sharp flying disc launched from his quiver could slice off a thousand or more heads in a second and return safely to him faster than thought. He also had special arrows that once shot would instantly cleave into tens, hundreds, thousands and millions and wreak devastating damage to his enemies. Likewise, each and every Pandava had great skills and destructive powers, and it is no wonder fear grew in the Kauravas circle day by day.

"One day, while Pandu was hunting in the woods, he felt an overpowering sexual urge, and in the heat of his desire forgot about the curse from the Rishis. He had passionate sex with his second wife, Madri, and instantly died. Madri voluntarily entered the pyre of her husband and joined him in heaven." Sukannya looked up.

"So, the practice of the wife jumping in the funeral pyre of her husband is a very old practice?" Joshua asked.

"Yes." Now, there is crisis. Pandu died, and his eldest son Dharmaputhra was crowned as the king of the Kuru dynasty, even with the objection of Dhrutharastar who wanted to crown his eldest son Duryodhana to the crown, and the family feud worsens."

"One day, the Kauravas invited the Pandavas to one of the beautiful hill stations for rest and relaxation and to participate in the festival of Lord Shiva. The Kauravas made a special, majestic, glittering palace in the middle of the forest for the Pandavas to stay in during this time of festivities. The Pandavas soon discovered the plot and the motive behind the sudden hospitality of their cousins and escaped by way of an underground route into the depths of the forest. As planned, at midnight the palace went up in flames, the palace walls filled with wax and fat. The Kauravas rejoiced and the Pandavas laughed, now living disguised as Bhrahmins. Back at Hasthinapuri, the Pandavas were all presumed dead, and the Kauravas assumed the guardianship of the kingdom."

"Around the same time, in the neighboring kingdom of Panchala, the king had invited princes from neighboring countries for a ceremony to give away his daughter Draupathi in marriage to the winner of a series of arduous competitions."

Sukannya stopped reading and asked, "why are you smiling, Joshua – tell me, what's the fun that I missed?"

"I was thinking, this story reads like a typical Homeric story, and you read them so melodiously. It's very nice to rest here and listen to your reading."

"Well, then listen, but listen carefully. The Pandavas, who had just escaped an assassination attempt by their cousins, attended the bridal marriage in disguise as Bhrahmins. The qualifying game: up on the top of a tall tree was hung a revolving cage with one door, in which there was placed a wooden parrot. The archer could see the head and neck of the parrot through the door only for fraction of a second. During that time, he would be required to shoot five arrows simultaneously, and every arrow had to strike the neck of the bird. The winner would be eligible to take the hand of the bride, Draupathi, in marriage."

"Naturally, Arjuna will win and claim the princess, right?"

"Right," she said. "After the marriage ceremony, Arjuna took her home to his mother."

"In those days, the Pandavas – disguised as Bhrahmins – would wander around villages taking alms for their sustenance, and in the evening they would go home and share the food with their mother. But on that night when Arjuna married Draupathi, they reached home late. Mother Kundhi had already gone to bed and the doors were locked. With great excitement, the Pandavas shouted, "Mother! Mother! We have something special to share with you today." The half-asleep Kundhi replied, "You all equally share the same between yourselves," and thereby Draupathi became the wife to all the Pandavas."

Joshua smiled again, which Sukannya ignored with a sharp pinch on his ear.

"As the brothers all took turns with Draupathi in the bedroom to avoid any confusion in sharing the bed with her, it was agreed amongst all participants that when one brother goes to bed with Draupathi, he will keep his footwear outside the door. The system worked out very well. It was also stipulated that if anyone was to violate the agreement, he would have to do penance for twelve years in full celibacy as a sage.

"In the meantime, Arjuna saw a Bhrahmin being attacked by bandits in the neighborhood. He needed to enter the bed chamber to grab his bow and arrows to kill the robbers. However, Arjuna found one pair of shoes outside the door. Arjuna was tormented. Between sexual interruption and saving the life of a Bhrahmin, Arjuna chose the latter. Respecting the agreement, he went into the woods to do the twelve years of penance of celibacy."

"However, the virile Arjuna was not celibate at all. Sauntering through the villages, he reached the land of Prabhasam, where he met Lord Krishna, who introduced to Arjuna his radiantly beautiful sister, Subhadra. Krishna urged Subhadra to oblige Arjuna even with sexual favors. Later, Subhadra was wedded to Arjuna and the son born to them – Abhimanue – became a great master of archery. But above all, with this new alliance, the Pandavas established an even closer relation with Lord Krishna. The Kauravas were getting more and more scared. They now knew the Pandavas had survived the inferno."

**** **** ****

It was late in summer in Mathura; nights were getting shorter and the days, longer. The thick foliage in the trees and shrubs turned the whole land all green accented with white jasmine. The waterfall by the stream also turned thinner, and the pond was only knee deep.

While on the way to the falls, Sukannya looked at Joshua, "I heard your arguments were sharp and inconsiderate during your discussions about our king Raman."

"You should be proud, Sukannya; the student reflects the teacher," Joshua said.

"Pitha Maha was greatly impressed; he is planning to ask you to consider staying back. Joshua, if he asked you so, will you consider staying back?"

"For how long?"

"For very long. He has the great idea to start a learning center here in Mathura, where all religions of the world would be taught and critiqued."

"No, Sukannya, I am anxious to get back to Israel. I have lots of work left undone. I think from now on we will start reading a few hours in the evening as well, if you can."

The idea was agreeable to her, and thus they started to read the great book at night as well.

"The Kauravas decided they'd better make a truce with their cousins. They went to the forest, invited the Pandavas and announced that they would like to divide the kingdom between them and live in harmony. The Pandavas accepted the truce and went back to Indraprasta and established their kingdom. The Pandavas ruled their half of the country righteously, and they grew in peace, prosperity and fame that fueled an ever-growing jealousy among the Kauravas. 'The Pandavas must be annihilated at any cost,' they decided. Shakunni, a conniving and shrewd political advisor to the Kauravas, had contrived a plan: engage the Pandavas in a high-stakes gambling game. Shakunni was the master bluffer in the game of dice. Challenge them. Refusal would be cowardly.

"It was a great gambling game that lasted for several days and was witnessed by many invited kings and dignitaries. Shakuni's cheating worked. The Pandavas lost their stakes one after the other: the gold, the jewels, the cows, the horses, the elephants, the land, and then the four younger brothers, all of them became possessions and slaves to the Kauravas. At that stage, the Kauravas demanded that the Pandavas place Draupathi, as the next stake. They lost her, too!

"Infatuated with pride, arrogance and insolence, Duryodhana – the Kauravas king – screamed, 'Draupathi is now our slave. She will stay in my palace, clean my house, cook in the kitchen, and oblige to whatever we desire ha . . . ha . . . ha . . .' He danced around the floor in jubilation.

"Indignant with anger and insult, Draupathi stood up to leave. Then Dushassana – the second Kaurava brother – grabbed her by the hair and started stripping her clothes in public. With her hair tumbled down and bathed in shame, Draupathi remained frozen, head down, with her arms folded across her naked breasts. The Pandava brothers, their mighty hands tied, stood still, angry, shamed, and mortified. The mighty Bhima stood like a smoking mountain ready to erupt.

"Draupathi cried out to Lord Krishna, who was among the dignitaries in the court: but Krishna kept a grin on his face, taking no notice of the events on the floor, casually brushing off the motes from his clothes. Dushassana was busy stripping Draupathi, but the more clothes he removed, the more clad she appeared. He was getting frustrated.

"The building rattled – a great roar. Bhima cried out, 'Dushassana! One day, I will rip open your heart and drink of it, and anoint Draupathi's hair with your blood. Until then, she will not put up her hair!' Lord Krishna still smiled serenely.

"Then the grand patriarch – Dhrutharaster – stood up and declared a truce. 'The game is all over. Let the Pandavas go. Wish them well.' His blind face could not hide the fear. The Pandavas left.

"The Kauravas could not settle. They designed a new plan – another gambling game. But this time the defeated parties must relinquish all their belongings and live in the forest for twelve years, and then one additional year in exile, during which they must not be seen by anyone at all, or they would have to repeat the punishment all over again.

"The pride and dharma of the Pandavas did not allow them to decline the challenge. The final result was the same as the prior, and, stripped of all processions, the Pandavas left for the forest for twelve years of disgrace in exile.

"Amidst all adverse circumstances, facing innumerable human and superhuman enemies, the Pandavas successfully completed the thirteen years of exile and came back to reclaim their kingdom. Not surprisingly, the Kauravas refused to share half of the kingdom with the Pandavas, and the two sides prepared for a final showdown.

"To avoid a war between the two brother clans, Lord Krishna went to the Kauravas to mediate a truce, but the insolent Kauravas rebuked Lord Krishna. 'The Pandavas do not deserve any land at all, not even turf to pin a needle,' they said.

"The Kaurava mother Gandhari and even Bheeshmar pleaded with the Kauravas not to go to war with the Pandavas. 'No. No land for the Pandavas,' they affirmed.

"On the contrary, the Pandava mother, Kundhi, ferociously insisted that her children go to war and annihilate the Kauravas: 'What grace is there in living like this; what pride is there surviving like a slow burning grate of damp husk? Live like a glowing torch, a torch of frankincense, emitting fragrance and glittering light. A truce? A truce is an insult to Draupathi. Draupathi shall not, will not, must not put up her hair until it is doused with Dushassanan's blood. And that's your mother's wish.'

"And so, the stage was set for the ultimate war. Kurukshethra the holiest of holy places was the chosen site."

Sukannya continued the story with remarkable exuberance and enthusiasm. "The neighboring kingdoms aligned with either one of the clans. The Kauravas forces consisted of a massive force of eleven battalions, each consisting of several hundred war chariots, warring elephants, archers, sword fighters, baton fighters and foot soldiers. The Pandavas had only seven battalions of soldiers, the composition similar to that of the Kauravas.

"Lord Krishna gave the impression that he was impartial; he gave the choice to both parties either to choose him or his massive warring forces – one or the other. The greedy Kauravas took his warring forces and Lord Krishna gladly joined the Pandavas and became the charioteer and field advisor to Arjuna.

"The rules of engagement were clearly established. Amongst many other stipulations, it was agreed that the elephants fight only the elephants, the cavalry fight the cavalry, and the infantry fight only infantry. No one was permitted to interfere in a duel. All retreating and wounded soldiers, those who lost weapons in the battle field, drummers, buglers, standard bearers, or cup bearers, servants, and any others who were not fighting, must not be harmed.

"The field marshals, Bheeshmar for the Kauravas and Dhrusta-Dhumnan for the Pandavas, were ceremoniously ordained and ritually decorated with a drop of blood from their own fingers, pasted on their foreheads. The greatest war ever to be fought in the universe, as prophesied by Manu, was about to begin."

"Sukannya, come to think of it, Duryodhana – the elder Kauravas son – is the legal heir to the kingdom when Pandu died. You agree?"

"Yes."

"Dhrutharastrar was denied the crown because he was born blind, right?"

"Yes."

"So, he was discriminated against because of a birth defect. Pandu also had a birth defect. I see some reasoning in the indignation of the Kauravas. Don't you?"

"Good point, Joshua. You wait to the end of the story; hopefully, all your questions will be answered," she said. "The war is about to start."

The moment of Bhagavath Geetha. (Indian epic)

"With multicolored standards fluttering, drums beating like thunder, soldiers screaming war cries, bugles blowing, elephants roaring and horses stomping, the earth rattled, as the Pandava army marched first to the battlefield and arrayed facing the glow of the rising sun. The roar of the army reverberated to the four corners of the earth. Gold, silver and iron chest shields and swords reflected the rays of the rising sun like a blinding fire.

"A much larger Kauravas force marched in with even louder fanfare and settled opposite to the Pandavas facing the setting sun. The breadth and depth of the two armies reached far across the battlefield, a frightening scene, like two raging oceans about to meet and crash. The field marshals from either side met face to face in the middle and restated the codes of conduct of the war once again.

"When the war was about to begin, Arjuna requested: 'Lord, take me to the middle of the two armies'. Lord Krishna did likewise. Arjuna stood up on the chariot, took a lingering glance at his enemies, his elders, gurus, brothers, relatives, and the vast ocean of people that

451

he had to sacrifice. Arjuna, deeply saddened at the sight, erupted into a heavy sweat, his mouth dry, his face drained of color. Nervous and frightened, he slumped to the chariot floor.

"Lord Krishna turned calmly to face him. At that moment, time stood still; the entire universe, except the archer and the charioteer, were frozen. Here, at the epitome of the most dramatic scene, Lord Krishna recited the *Bhagavath Geetha*, the ultimate dialogue between man and God began. The rest, Pitha Maha will teach you," Sukannya closed the book.

**** **** ****

Two days later, on a warm and windless summer night, Joshua was lounging under the banyan tree after the dinner, cooling himself, relaxing. The stars glittered low in the sky; the moon lit the forest milky white, except when the clouds intermittently cast a shroud over the sky. Joshua looked up and saw two men coming through the carriage pathway towards the hut. They stopped and remained silent at a distance under the shade of the bushes. A bit later, a tall figure, head covered with a shawl, stole out of the house, walking like a cat towards the men. The men moved slowly to the side, and the figure continued walking as the men trailed behind.

Joshua returned to the hermitage looking for Sukannya, but, as he had suspected, she was nowhere to be found. Disturbed by her disappearance, perturbed by the heat and humidity of the season, and unable to sleep, Joshua turned and tossed on his bed anxiously, at times bolting up for a noise, thinking that it would be her footsteps, and then being disappointed because it was not. Well after midnight, he heard gentle footsteps approaching the house, and then Sukannya's door opened and closed. His heart pounded. *Why?* He wondered. In that darkness there were no shining answers. Joshua had noticed that Sukannya seemed gloomy and often preoccupied. She had grown thinner, but had not lost the color on her face or the smile on her rosebud lips. However, he had a feeling that there was a lot more to know about Sukannya. She remained as a growing curiosity in his mind, and he struggled not to ruminate about her, but often it was impossible.

The next day they went for their morning walk as usual and swam in the stream, but there was a certain restraint for both of them to open a dialogue. Upon returning from the stream, Sukannya asked Joshua, "Joshua, how long are you planning to stay in Mathura?"

Joshua didn't have a quick answer. "Sukannya, my mission is coming to an end. Early next spring I am planning to leave; I have much work left undone at home."

Her face clouded momentarily. Their pace quickened. She appeared concerned for his well-being. She reached out and held his hand companionably and said, "Joshua, I have noticed that you are turning weaker, at times gloomy, is there anything I can do for you?"

"No, dear, nothing. I feel quite good. You have done more than enough," he said.

Feeling fatigued, that evening Joshua went to bed early and did not get up for his usual dinner with Pitha Maha. When the guru came, he inquired about Joshua. Sukannya said that Joshua had not been feeling well, and that he had gone to bed early. Joshua overheard the conversation from his room. *I never told her that I am not feeling well; is she a mind reader?* he mused with eyes closed.

A while later, Joshua woke up to a tapping noise on his door. As he looked up from his bed, he saw her standing at the threshold, her silhouette filling the gray of the squire door, her face highlighted by the pale rays of the oil lamp that fell obliquely on her face.

"Arya," she called in a soft, loving tone. "I want to bring something for you. Can I come in?"

"Yes, come in," he said, trying to sit up on his elbows. She brought a wooden tray covered with a wicker basket, and as she lifted the cover of the tray, the aroma of the roasted meat filled the room. "What a pleasant surprise," he said. He sat up, crossed his legs, and rubbed his palms in anticipation of tasting the freshly roasted rabbit meat. "Why, Sukannya? I thought meat was not permitted here? Who cooked this?"

"Shhh . . ." she whispered and pressed her palm against his lips. "Visal made it. Visal and Kishan, they are hunters. I asked them to make this for you."

"No, this was not necessary. Aren't you violating the rules of the hermitage?"

"Rules? I will talk about the rules at another time. Now please eat this," she shrugged. She set up the meal on the floor mattress around the oil lamp. "You definitely have become weaker since you came here. You have lost weight." Joshua couldn't disguise the smile on his face as she helped him eat the dinner.

"Do you eat meat?" he asked.

"Not usually. But I have, once or twice."

The meal, roasted rabbit meat, cornbread, boiled zucchini and vegetables, tasted like manna from heaven. He invited Sukannya to eat with him, but she refused. Instead, she sat by his side and watched him eat. When he was finally finished, she brought a cupful of warm herbal broth.

"What is this drink?" he asked, sniffing at the cup.

"This is just herbal broth – shiva-mooli. It is very good for fatigue; sound sleep, too. You will feel fresh and stronger tomorrow. Pitha Maha drinks this broth every night. It may taste bitter on your tongue, but they say it is sweet on your heart."

Joshua lay in his bed thinking about Sukannya. He had just eaten the most delicious meal since Babylon. *There are so many things I don't know about this girl. Never in a lifetime would I have thought I would be eating rabbit meat in this hermitage. Who is she? Why do I care? Who is she to me? A teacher, of course – she knows all those texts, but does she believe in any of the things she reads to me? In these writings, women do not deserve freedom. Is she free? Maybe she is . . . must be . . . craving for it – everybody does. Where did she go the other night? To some secret places, caves deep in the woods? Maybe she is escorted to them . . . for love . . . universal love . . . love that is everywhere . . . in the vineyards, cornfields, temples, streets, homes . . . everywhere.* His eyes gradually closed. He felt calm, light on his head, like floating. A thousand images milled around in his mind. Love, like pure jasmine . . . white bunches of jasmine cascading over the fences, spilling fragrance all over, the smell of the hermitage, fragrance of Galilee, Japha, Carmel, Capernaum, all blooming with flowers, flowers of all colors, like rainbows, large rainbows of flowers up in the sky, like a bridge from Galilee to Babylon, sky bridges from Rome to Alexandria, from Athens to Taxila, all connected with rainbows of flowers . . . children walking through the rainbows from one nation to the other, all dressed in colors of rainbows with glittering tiaras on their crows, all hand in hand, singing songs, songs of love, one class of men – one scent of woman . . . all workers in the vineyards, cornfields, orchards of olives, pomegranates, dates and figs . . . all peaceful all under one God, one nation . . . the Kingdom of Heaven on Earth, no anger, no spite, jealousy or selfishness, no statutes nor commandments, no eye for an eye, all for one and one for all . . . you share everything, if you may have two, give one to the other who have not, share your love . . . no, wait . . . all waves and waves and colors . . . colors mixed like red, yellow, blue, like the peacock feathers . . . iridescent blues and greens, all waves of colors, like the rainbow, deep red and glowing, floating, flying and dancing over the mountains, one step on the waves of the ocean, another on the shell of the sky, everywhere, colors filling the air. . .bright glowing bodies floating in the sky, large white balls dancing in the air, a moon, a thousand moons, undulating in this ocean of colors. Sukannya, floating in the air, not one, not a hundred, not a thousand, a million Sukannya's all floating in the sky, floating forever, ever and ever and ever and ever . . .

It was difficult to open his eyes in the morning, he rubbed them with the back of his hands, lay down again, lazily, looking at the wicker-lathed ceiling with slit eyes. The door was open, the shadow of the thulassi plant had shortened, and the sun had risen up in the sky. *Did I sleep with the door open?* He got up and looked for Sukannya; she was nowhere to be seen. Rising on his elbows, he lounged on the foyer, indolent, empty of thoughts, as if something was missing, though he was not sure what it was. At the top branch of the banyan tree, two mynah birds were feeding their young ones. For each berry the mother bird offered, three little beaks opened crying meekly. The male bird flew over the tree in a circle, twice, and came back perching on the branch singing, "soo . . . nya, soo . . . nya, soo . . . nya."

Joshua walked to the stream: there she was, all wet, moist clothes wrapped over her breasts, and the wet clothes stuck to her waist, carrying two pots of water, one on either hip, as if carrying two children. As usual she was smiling and shifting her eyes between Joshua and the mynah birds.

The bird called her again, "Soo . . . nya, soonya, soo . . . nya." Joshua soon realized who the birds were calling. With a wide smile and great excitement, still looking at the birds, he asked, "Sukannya, are the birds calling you by your name?"

"Of course, Joshua. They cannot pronounce 'ka'; therefore, they call me soo . . . nya. Wait, let me give them some bites. I can teach them your name, too."

She went inside the house and came out with a handful of grains in the cup of her hands. With her lips pointed like a rosebud, she whistled a tune; the bird glided down from the tree top, even without flapping its wings, and hung in the air pecking the grains from her hands, then flew back to the nest. She sprayed the rest of the grain on the ground; the birds were still calling 'soonya, soonya.' Enjoying that delicious moment, she came back and sat on the foyer besides him.

"Joshua, I didn't want to wake you up; I hope you had nice comfortable sleep. Do you feel refreshed?" she asked.

"Good, Sukannya, I feel very good. Thank you for that drink. I saw many colors and scenes last night," he said.

"You were also calling some names, I heard." She said.

"Like what; what names?"

"I heard names like Mary, then there was a Cassandra, and then something about rainbows."

"I am sorry. That drink was really something else. Did I call your name, too?"

"Many times. Many, many times," she said with a delicious smile on her lips.

Joshua tried to hide his own smile, but he couldn't.

When Joshua came back from his own plunge in the stream, Sukannya had already prepared dinner. It was early.

"Arya, tonight at the temple, there is the Krishna Jayanthi festival. If you like, I can take you there."

"That would be nice, but instead, I would like to see the dwellings of the Shudra and Chandallas, if possible."

"Why, what's your interest there?"

"I have heard a lot about them, and I would really like to see their dwellings, their life, if you can take me there once."

"Arya, no problem. Visal and Kishan are from there. I can arrange for you to go to the village of the Shudras. But going to the Chandallas dwelling is risky. They live in the mountains. Nobody goes there. If you insist, perhaps Visal can help you."

It was mid-October, and there had not been a drop of rain for the past two months. The monsoon did not show up that year in Mathura, and the land was baked brown and cracked; the dry heat was intense and unbearable. The wind had turned turbid with heavy dust and dry leaves, and sand swirled up in the sky like pillars. As the sun beat down intensely, the air near the ground simmered and sizzled up with dazzling undulations like wind caught up on a placid lake. All of the little ponds and wells were dried up, and the mountain brook was nothing but a narrow channel of water. Even the great River Yamuna was dry, reduced to a sandy, rocky riverbed, except with tiny trickles of water.

A few days later, news came to the hermitage that many people were dying in the Shudra villages. Kali was angry; she had sowed the seeds of pestilence, the epidemic of vassuri!

"Joshua, people are dying in the villages from vassuri; you must not go this time," Sukannya said.

Joshua looked into her eyes with confidence. "I am not worried. What is this pestilence you are talking about, tell me."

"Vassuri, you may not have seen it. In some families, the illness affects virtually every member. It starts with high fevers, severe headaches and extreme weakness. The mouth and throat swells. Breathing and speech become difficult. Within a day or two, pink vesicles appear all over the face, mouth, and sometimes even in the eyes. In another week, the pocks become dark and bloody with pus. Some people are buried alive at this point. However, most die within a few days."

"Sukannya, I think I know what you are talking about. Such pestilences are everywhere, even in Israel. We also have elders who say that it is a curse from the heavens. I think you must not go."

"Don't you worry, Joshua." Pointing to an imperceptible pock mark near to the dimple on her right cheek, she said, "See, when I was seven, I had the illness. Once you have had vassuri, you will never get it again. I think you must not go."

Joshua was anxious to go to the Shudra village, even though Sukannya was not at all in favor. With much insistence from Joshua, she agreed to take him. In the afternoon they left for the Shudra village.

The two men, short, darker in complexion, with deep, dark pock scars on their faces – Kishan and Visal – waited in attendance far behind the house. At the sight of Joshua, the men cupped their hands, bowed in obeisance, and took a few steps back. Sukannya led the way with Joshua, and the two men followed behind.

"Joshua, you should know, vassuri comes from Kali's curse. She is angry, they say," Sukannya said.

"Tell me why."

"They say she needs her share of blood every day. When the sacrifices are low and when she is thirsty for blood, she curses."

Sacrifices . . . sacrifices, he thought. *Gods thirsty for blood . . . blood . . . blood . . . is it all they want?*

"They have started Kali pooja and sacrifices, three days now, Kishan told me."

The air stood still; the heat was intense, but no sweating. At times Sukannya blew air to her breasts, pressing her chin on her chest.

The Shudra village was a series of small mud huts deep in the woods on the valley of a hill with a temple on top. People cooked outside the hut, under the trees or out in the streets. Both Joshua and Sukannya had covered their heads and faces as suggested by Kishan, yet somebody in the village recognized Sukannya and made a shouting noise. Those who heard the shouts virtually ran backwards as if when dry leaves are blown away by a heavy wind. Then Vishal and Kishan shouted back to them. Some stopped, others kept on retreating.

They first went to Kishan's house. He had two children who were severely ill with pocks all over. They lay on a ragged mattress, motionless except for the guttural sounds of their labored breathing. After giving them some presents and kind words, Sukannya asked Vishal to take them to Kittu's hut.

"Do you know all these people, Sukannya?" asked Joshua.

"Not all, but many."

"Obviously, you have been here before?"

"Many times. I will tell you the story of Kittu later, but first let us visit him."

Kittu's hut was nearby. On a reed mattress lay a man of about thirty years of age. The right side of his face and cheek were hollowed by a gaping wound. His left arm and left legs were wasted and motionless. He attempted to smile, but the muscles on the left side of his face quivered and his eyes opened and closed convulsively. Sukannya gave him a package with some food and clothes. Kittu made some happy guttural sounds and waved with his right hand. Joshua sat by his side holding his hand with closed eyes for a moment before they left the house.

At the Kali temple on top of the hill, the festival was in its fourth day. The sun was about to set, the evening gray turned dark, and people were climbing the hill with their torches lit.

"You may not want to go there, to the temple," Sukannya warned again.

"I would like to," Joshua said. He climbed towards the temple, pulling Sukannya by her hand.

Up on the hill the temple was a capacious mud-walled building, with about two hundred people in it. A fearsome statue of a female figure in dark stone with red painting over its face, long curved fangs emerging from the corners of the mouth, large pendulous breasts, enormous protruding buttocks, and a pendulous yonni, stood high on an altar against the rear wall of the temple. This stone statue of Kali –

ornate with a garland made of children's skulls, a sword in one hand, a severed head in the other, appeared dancing on Sivas dead body. In front of the statue stood a large, yonni-shaped ritual stone, stained with old and fresh blood. Numerous torches were burning on holders bracketed to the mud wall, emitting yellow light and dark smoke that billowed up to the roof, swirling.

The crowd chanted:

"Ohm, Kali, Bhadra Kali.

"Maha Kali, Karim Kali.

"Kodum Kali, Amma Kali."

While this thunderous chanting was going on, a man with large matted hair, unkempt beard, a red loin cloth, face painted with blood, brandishing and fluttering a long-handled sickle, screaming, moving with a jittery tremor, and neither walking nor running – the oracle – entered the scene. The sacrifices were about to start.

"Drink our blood, Kodum Kali,

"Give rain, Bhadra Kali,

"Blood for rain, Amma Kali,

"Blood for rain, Divya Kali."

The crowd erupted, shouting even louder and moving around aimlessly in circles.

Joshua and Sukannya stood motionless, leaning against the rear wall, their heads covered in disguise. The oracle started shaking and flicking his sword much more violently. This chanting and shaking continued for quite some time.

Then a thin, dark woman covered in tattered clothes stepped forward holding a shrieking child in the cradle of her extended hands. She placed the child on the yonni-shaped sacrificial stone. The oracle lifted the child by its foot and spun the sacrifice like a fan several times in the air above his head. The intensity of the chanting reached a climax until no one could shout any higher, and no one could hear any louder. The oracle continued spinning the child more violently until he himself was unsteady and then he smashed the child on the yonni stone.

"Hhoo!" cried Joshua, but nobody heard him, as the chanting was at its deafening climax. The child went limp, the head hanging loose. The chanting continued violently, and they all started dancing and jumping as if possessed. Joshua, aghast and dizzy, made an incoherent noise, but Sukannya quickly pulled him out of the temple, covering his mouth with the palm of her hand.

It was pitch dark out. They didn't know where Visal and Kishan were, nor did they wait to collect them. Joshua felt weak and unsteady, short of breath, wheezing and his heart pounding. Sukannya circled her arms around his waist, as he threw his arms around her shoulders firmly and the two of them descended hill, speechless, their minds full of screaming children, shattering heads and chanting crowds. They reached home fatigued and totally devastated. Joshua felt sick in the stomach, vomited once, and he was put to bed soon, as Sukannya stood by his side, holding his hand and caressing his forehead.

"Would you like anything to drink," she asked.

"Anything will be fine," he said.

Sukannya quickly made some herbal soup. She lifted the steaming bowl to his lips, gently blowing. He took a gulp and swallowed noisily and quickly; the color came back his cheeks.

Quite softly, she said, "This is the third day. They will sacrifice three children today, four tomorrow, and so on. There are some years when they have sacrificed up to thirty-one days until the rain fell." Joshua covered her lips with his palm, saying, "Enough, enough." He searched her eyes vacantly as if looking through her. Sukannya hugged him as if consoling a child. She involuntarily lifted his face and kissed on his lips tenderly. He didn't resist. She felt intensely desirous to him, feeling near to faint, he clasped her impetuously in the folds of his arms, caging his passive desires, which at times boiled hot. Her face slowly descended and rested on his chest for the remainder of the night.

Joshua was breathing heavily and at times sobbing. "When I saw Kittu," he murmured, "I thought I had seen the worst of all, but Sukannya . . . this is the most obnoxious scene anybody can ever witness. I am sorry; I wish I had never seen it. I can't believe it. Is this the land of the Upanishadts and Buddha?"

The next day, Joshua once again woke up late. Sukannya had already returned from her morning routine with wet clothes and bottles full of water. The day was gloomy, overcast. They could hear the peacocks singing in the nearby woods.

The sacrifices at the hill top might come to a stop today or tomorrow, he hoped. It felt like a lazy day. That afternoon Joshua asked Sukannya, "What happened to Kittu?"

"Kittu's story is connected with my brother Chandra-Sennan." Sukannya was hesitant to talk. "Joshua, you had a very bad experience yesterday. Your mind is disturbed; your sleep was very light last night. Should I . . ."

"Yes Sukannya, please tell me. Nothing can be worse than what I saw in the temple."

Finally, with Joshua's insistence, she opened up. Sukannya sat down beside him, her face clouded and her voice trembling.

"Chandra-Sennan is a year older than me. He is well-versed in the sacrifices and rituals as a young practicing priest. He was very much interested in conducting the initiation rituals of young girls."

Joshua looked into her eyes, asking what the ceremonies were. With further hesitancy, she continued, "When a Kshathrya girl comes of age, she is given a cleansing bath, dressed up ceremoniously, often with new clothes, garlanded with flowers, and her forehead is decorated by sandalwood. An elderly woman of the village teaches her the art and principles of sexual engagement. The girl is then isolated and kept alone in a room meditating. Other family members chant songs of Rathi Devi."

"That's the goddess of love?" Joshua asked.

"Rather the goddess of love making," she said.

"By tradition, the Kshathrya girls are initiated by a Bhrahmin – a priest. The priest is invited into the girl's room; however, most priests perform the ritual by simply touching the girl's yonni with his phallus, or just penetrate namesake and finally sprinkle some holy water. But my brother performed the full course of sex with every girl, as it was his pleasure and privilege. Some days he initiated as many as ten girls:

he also chewed a lot of Yohimbine to empower him. He is a wicked priest, my brother," her face contorted in disgust.

"How is this story connected with Kittu?" Joshua asked.

"Kittu was a servant boy in a Kshathrya home where a girl was initiated. This boy knew and liked the girl from childhood. But remember, he was a Shudra. He painfully hung around the house when the ritual chanting was going on. When my brother came in, he saw the Shudra boy hanging about the house listening to the Vedic chanting. He became furious. Shudras are not permitted to hear the Vedic chanting or even be around the places where such rituals are conducted. Kittu was summoned. My brother, seized with anger, ordered the girl's father to fill the boy's ear with molten lead. The Kshathrya family had no choice other than to obey. They forced the boy down, poured the molten lead in his ears and further severed his tongue, too."

"They severed his tongue, too?" Joshua asked.

"Yes"

"Why?"

"He shall never recite a word from what he heard, at all!"

"Sukannya, another gruesome ritual. I remember; this is also from Manu, isn't it?"

"Of course, you saw Kittu – a living reminder to all Shudras of what will be to them if they happened to be somewhere they are not supposed to be. To make matters worse, the young girl witnessed all of these punishments. She fainted to the floor, motionless, yet my brother initiated her anyway. The girl never spoke a word thereafter. Three days later, her body was found downstream in the Yamuna River."

"This man is your brother?" Joshua asked.

"Arya, my brother never comes here. I hope I will never see him again."

"Is he still continuing the initiation ceremonies?"

Sukannya shook her head vertically, looking down with a somber face.

Different from any other woman he had ever known, Sukannya remained a silent curiosity for him. There was something incomprehensible about the girl: endearing, compassionate, erudite and even critical of her own upbringing!

**** **** ****

Maha Rishi Vyassa began his discourses on *Bhagavath Geetha*. Although Joshua was only one among the seven students, it was obvious that the Rishi was focusing on the young man from Galilee whom he considered a Bhrahmin.

"So, you have seen that Lord Krishna took the chariot to the center of the battlefield." The guru started the discourse. "Arjuna, lost of his will, petrified at the thought of avenging his own gurus, uncles and brothers, slumped to the chariot floor unable to move."

With a gentle smile, Vyassa turned to Joshua, "Joshua, I want you to read the rest of the story." the guru said. Joshua was a bit baffled. He was fairly fluent in Pali, but Sanskrit he could only read with difficulty.

"Don't you worry, Joshua, I will help you," the guru encouraged.

Joshua read: "Arjuna, this weakness of yours is a disgrace for a Kshathrya prince; your enemies will mock you for the rest of your life; wise men do not grieve the dead or rejoice the living. These lives you see here ahead of you neither existed nor ceased to exist. These embodiments are all transient. Arjuna, wake up. You must not be bothered by these silly sentiments. It's not befitting to your Kshathrya blood."

Joshua was to read only Lord Krishna's lines. Following each reading, the guru gave a detailed explanation of the scene. "Unable to move, resting his chin . . . " explained the guru.

But Joshua's mind wandered. *Similar to the invasion of the Promised Land – Yahweh invigorating the children of Israel to avenge the enemies,* he thought.

Joshua read: "Arjuna, rise up to the call of duty. What you see, touch and feel are all impermanent. You are neither slaying anyone, nor is anyone slain. That which is embodied cannot be slain. It's

464

indestructible, eternal and ever present. It's only the mortal decaying bodies that are slain, but slay you must."

"Arjuna was numb and speechless, unable to move, unable to speak," the guru said.

"Grieve not, Arjuna. Just like we abandon worn-out garments, the spirit shall abandon the worn-out bodies and enter new ones."

Frightened and struck by grief, Arjuna remained motionless; the guru acted out the scenes.

"Fear not, Arjuna. Look at those bodies; the spirit in them cannot be pierced by an arrow, burned by fire or drowned by flood. Arjuna act now; string your bows and annihilate the enemies."

Arjuna sat like a stone, still, did not blink, and did not breathe.

"Arjuna, thou shall not grieve for living beings. Death is certain for the one who is born, and rebirth is sure for the one who is dead. Waste not a moment, Arjuna. String your bows and be assured that you are not slaying the embodied, nor are you capable of it."

Arjuna tuned his head to the enemy line for a long moment, and his gaze returned to the charioteer again, was not convinced, even if convinced not fully resolved to act.

"Rise up, Arjuna. You are wavering in discharging your duties as a king. Is there anything more benevolent, more honorable, than carrying out your dharma of fighting this holy war?"

While reading, more than anything else, Joshua was moved by the strong convictions of the man who wrote these verses, who believed that karma is more important than dharma. He was elated by the fortune to sit beside the very person who wrote it, gazing at his constantly rolling the beads on his neck. Many a times, Vyassa rose to his feet and stretched his hand to the far distance, pointing to the enemy lines as if he himself was lord Krishna.

"Oh, Arjuna," Joshua continued, "Is there anything for you to lose in this war? In victory, you have destroyed the evil and saved the country; in death, the doors of heaven are open for you.

"Arjuna, can you imagine surrendering here without a fight? The undying infamy you shall endure; the dharma you abandoned; the misfortune you shall bring upon your people; is death any worse than that? Arjuna, open your eyes," Joshua read.

After each chapter, Maha Rishi Vyassa gave a prolonged discourse, citing different sides of the stories and examples from the grand epics opposing or justifying either view. He sat deep in the wicker chair, at times holding his folded hands back on the nape of his neck and turning his head left and right to alleviate the tension from prolonged sitting and talking. In spite of this, his voice was strong with no wavering or fatigue, and his eyes were still bright. Of the eighteen chapters of the Great Song of God, he reviewed one chapter in-depth each day from the first light of day to dusk.

The next day, the students again assembled under the shadows of the banyan tree beside the Rishi's hermitage.

Joshua read the portions of Krishna. "Arjuna, the same people who praised you and honored you as the most invincible warrior will say that you are a coward amongst cowards. Arjuna, your dharma is to do the right thing in happiness or suffering, victory or defeat, gain or loss, without fear of favor. You must rise up now."

The Lord bent down holding the warriors shoulders lifted his face to him and spoke to him slowly and convincingly.

"Arjuna, at this moment you must become absorbed into me as one, in the yoga of supreme meditation, to be detached from all earthly bondages. Free yourself to do your duty. You shall be free from all desires, passion, fear, or anger, and you shall be established in thought and in peace with me. Listen to me, Arjuna." Most of the times when Joshua was reading, the students from the lands of Kandahar, Vindhya, Chola and Pandya were seen motionless with closed eyes.

Joshua's mind was filled with conflicting thoughts pulling in antipodal directions – words of wisdom versus the call for vengeance. *But why can't they resolve; why fight; why the bloodshed?* he wondered again and again without reaching an answer.

"Arjuna, like a tortoise withdrawing all its limbs into its shell, recall all your senses of sight, sound, taste and pleasures. When all those sentimentalities of 'I' and 'mine' are totally severed, then only can you really do your dharma. Now, rise up and string your bow and destroy those enemies," Joshua read.

Vyassa kneeled on the floor like Arjuna explaining the scene. "There was a deep silence between the Lord and Arjuna. Then there was a slight movement in the warrior's face, and he asked, 'Oh, Krishna. You speak in all high-sounding words. I am confused. If total detachment is what I have to do, tell me why do you drag me into this dreadful war?'"

There was silence. Vyassa turned to the students, "Students, tonight I want you to meditate on discernment; imagine yourself in the position of Arjuna; what would you have thought and done? We will see you the day after tomorrow."

**** **** ****

Vyassa continued with his story. Joshua read the part of the Lord.

"Oh, Arjuna. I am the taste of the water, the radiance of the sun and the moon, sound in space, and the sacred utterances of the Vedas. There is none beyond me. Arjuna, I am the fragrance of the universe, the sound of music, the brilliance of fire, and the force of the universe."

"Still unable to speak, Arjuna gazed at the Lord in amazement," Vyassa acted out.

"I am power devoid of desires and passion. I am the path, the truth and the life of all beings."

Step by step, Krishna revealed to Arjuna the secrets of the universe, to cast off all elements of fear and doubt from his mind and to empower him in the ways of Dharma, yet Arjuna remained reluctant to act. But he finally realized that the ultimate knowledge is the knowledge of Bhrahman – God.

"Arjuna woke up, color rose high on his face, he regained some confidence, and requested of Krishna, 'Lord, define Bhrahman – God,'" said the guru.

"'*I AM*,' the Lord replied." Read Joshua.

Joshua read the passages slowly and thoughtfully. At times, he felt that he was reading the Holy Torah itself. "*I AM* the spirit, the supreme knowledge, the guiding principle that should rule souls like kings rule their people. I send them out, and finally all will return to me as the life cycle of the universe. I am the sacrifice itself, the ritual, the sacred mantras . . . the mortality, the immortality, the being and the non-being."

While reciting this portion, the Maha Rishi appeared to be in a trance and uttered the scriptures silently.

"Arjuna," Joshua read, "Know it forever. I am the beginning, the middle and the end; the un-beginning and the endless; among radiance I am the sun; among the luminaries I am the moon."

"His bewilderment partially dispelled, Arjuna prayed," Vyassa rose to his feet: "Krishna, I beg you out of my ignorance, reveal to me thy supreme self."

"The Lord was pleased. He put his arm on Arjuna's forehead and blessed him." The guru put his hand on Joshua's brow. "Son, with your perishable eyes, however brilliant you are, you shall not visualize my universal self. But now you shall see me."

"At that moment a divine third eye opened on Arjuna's brow," the guru explained with gestures. "With the divine third eye, Arjuna watched the cosmic transfiguration of the mighty Lord. Krishna grew in proportions beyond the world, beyond the sky, beyond everything in unspeakable form, emitting blinding radiant light as if a million suns were rising in the sky at one time and place. The sun and moon were his eyes. An explosive fire erupted in his mouth. A violent thunderstorm broke out. Arjuna witnessed the most horrific sights in the Lord's mouth: the Kauravas, his teachers, uncles, brothers, and the army as a whole were flying fast into the Lord's mouth like moths fly into a blazing fire to their destruction. The Lord devoured them, skulls crushed, blood spilling, arms and limbs hanging between his teeth."

"Watching this horrible sight, Arjuna cried out, 'Who are you my Lord, with such a terrifying form. Who are you? I wish to know you better.'"

"A thunderous voice came out of the Lord's bloody mouth," Joshua read. 'I AM TIME,' the Lord replied. Those warriors arrayed on the opposite side are all dead, even without you slaying them. Fear not, Arjuna. Destroy your enemies and prosper your glorious kingship. You are a Kshathrya, and your duty is to fight. You are a part of me as you

468

just now saw in my cosmic figure. You are doing your Dharma for no glory or rewards. You are not at all the doer of these actions. Arjuna, as I am the truth so also are you. The waves are not different from the ocean. You are in me; I am in you. Now you know: to destroy the enemy is not a choice but the only choice. Sin is the deeds of the sinners. You are no sinner. You thought that you would be able to change the course of the events in this war, but Arjuna, please be advised, it has already been decided. The natural events of the universe are not controlled by creations, but only by the Creator. You have no control over anything, and believing that you did was your mistake. Arjuna, I am the truth. I am the life. I am the path. I am your only solace.'"

After a long pause, Joshua resumed.

"I have told you everything to erase the clouds of doubt from your mind. But a blind believer you must not be. You think about it, examine and analyze all the points carefully, and arrive at your own decision to fight or not to fight."

Vyassa sat deep back on the sofa with satisfaction, flipping back the red shawl.

"Arjuna gradually rose up," Vyassa resumed, standing up, "grasping the Gandivam firmly in his hands, his face calm and tranquil. Arjuna took a final lingering glance at the enemy line. This time he did not see Bheeshmar, Droner, Karnan, or any of his uncles or brothers. What he saw was a huge line-up of evildoers, condemned to death or already dying, waiting for the final strike . . . He pulled the first arrow from his quiver, and as he stretched his bow, the final war between the forces of evil and the fighters of Dharma began."

At this point, Vyassa's illuminating discourse on the *Bhagavath Geetha* came to an end. Joshua was moved by the powerful writings of Vyassa, and the war scene was played over several times in his mind.

That November, the nights were particularly cold, and frost was not uncommon in the morning. At night, Sukannya would make a small bonfire on the brazier in the kitchen and meditate beside the fire. One very cold night, as the winds were gusting and the dry leaves on trees fluttered and whistled, Sukannya invited Joshua to sit by the fireside as she was making preparations for her meditations.

"What do you meditate on?" Joshua asked.

It appeared that the question was difficult for her to answer. After a long pause, she said somberly, "On sunnyatha – emptiness."

Joshua was a bit confused. He asked, "Emptiness? Emptiness of what? How can one meditate on emptiness?"

"Joshua, you had a preliminary introduction to Buddhism, but there is a lot more about Buddhism that is not taught in Taxila. Emptiness is a Buddhist concept," she explained.

The answer caught him by surprise. He thought, Buddhism? The granddaughter of Maha Rishi Vyassa – the sage who composed *Bhagavath Geetha* – is meditating on Buddhist principles?

"I thought you are an expert on *Bhagavath Geetha*. How do you know a 'lot more' about Buddhism? Who are you?" Joshua asked.

"Joshua, I am what I am as you see," she said, smiling pleasantly. "As I have told you before, you have qualities that are innate to a Buddhist and not that of a Bhrahmin as Pitha Maha contends."

The charcoal fire had picked up on the brazier, and the reflections of the flames undulated on her face. Joshua stood rubbing his cold palms together.

She motioned him to sit by her side, patting on the mattress to her left. Beside the fire, they sat cross-legged with knees touching.

"What qualities do you think I have that are innate to Buddhism, Sukannya?" Joshua asked.

"Joshua, the day you arrived, after your meeting with Pitha Maha, he called me to tell his impression about you. Pitha Maha is a brilliant astrologer, as well as a face and mind reader. He told me that you will turn out to be a great philosopher and a leader that the world will come to know. That's why he was trying to persuade you to consider staying here in Mathura."

Joshua was speechless.

"Sukannya, I am no prophet or a leader. I am nothing more than a carpenter from Galilee, with all the innate weaknesses of men. I was shocked when Pitha Maha permitted me to stay here under his roof, stranger that I am. But please, tell me how the innate qualities of a Buddhist vary from that of a Bhrahmin."

Sukannya poked the embers with a splinter, and the fire crackled with long tongues and sparks. "Look at my brother and Pitha Maha, Joshua. Both are Bhrahmins. Are there any similarities between the two?"

Joshua laughed, "So, what kind of a Bhrahmin do you think I am? Not like your brother, I hope."

A big smile lit her face. "Never. You will never be like my brother. You are a loving, caring and compassionate man. You are without anger, greed or selfishness. Your love, concern and compassion are written on your face, in your kind words, and in your deeds. Those qualities are what I call the innate qualities of a Buddhist."

A soothing silence filled the room.

Sukannya broke the silence. "I know you are the right person to understand and practice meditation. But before I continue, let me ask you," she turned to him, searching his face intensely and asked firmly, "Who are you, traveler? You are no ordinary carpenter boy; you have come a long way here to learn the Hindu philosophy and wisdom, but who are you? What is your goal? I have been meaning to ask this question for a long time, but the moment was not right."

They had lived in that hermitage for nine months, but never before had they spoken so intimately. It was evident that each wanted to know the other better. Joshua took a deep breath and looked deep into her eyes.

"Sukannya, I was born to a carpenter's family in Galilee. My mother was a fifteen-year-old, unmarried Jewish girl when she conceived me. I know not my father on earth...but in heaven. A very kind man stepped in and saved my mother from stoning. Quite intensely, I studied the holy scriptures of my faith. But there were some daunting issues that troubled me deeply. My belief system taught that justice was an eye for an eye and a tooth for a tooth, and to hate and destroy people of other beliefs. I was taught that I was part of a people chosen by God to rule over the others, but my land has been ruled by foreign forces for the last six hundred years. In our holy scriptures, certainly there are words of wisdom akin to what lord Krishna is advising Arjuna, but the words are twisted and interpreted quit differently by the men of cloth."

Joshua sat silently, gazing at the embers slowly dying out, but Sukannya was not willing to let it go for long.

"Come on, speak, Joshua. What made you travel the whole world? It's no easy undertaking . . . speak," she pressed.

"One day, when I was thirteen years old . . . my cousin . . ." Joshua told his travels up till Mathura.

A cold wind whistled over the house. Joshua threw another peat onto the fire, and the flames surged, crackled and flickered. Sukannya unlocked her crossed legs, held the sole of her feet against the fire with arms held across her knees, and asked.

"Joshua, you have traveled so far and learned so much. Did you get the answer you're seeking?"

"Not entirely," he said.

"A simple girl in a hermitage in a forest is no person to advise you, but I believe the answer to your question is within yourself. You have to find it."

Joshua was pleasantly surprised by her advice. He knew that there were many mysteries surrounding Sukannya.

"Tell me more, Sukannya." Joshua sat with his chin rested on his knees, staring into her eyes. He could clearly see himself and the reflection of the flickering flames in her eyes.

She said calmly, "Sunnyatha; emptiness. You have to meditate on emptiness. You will realize what you are seeking."

"Tell me more, Sukannya. I am not sure I understand what you are saying."

"It is an entirely different way of looking at the universe," she explained. "A totally different way of looking at yourself, and at some point you will become enlightened with the answers to your questions. The answer is definitely within you. You have to dig for it and find it for yourself."

Sometime later that night, a revelation about Sukannya came upon him.

"Joshua, I have been learning and practicing Buddhism from a very early age."

"Practicing?"

She nodded. "When I was nineteen, I decided to follow Shree Buddha's path. I learned meditation from the guru Gunananda, and I have been practicing it for eleven years now. You may have noticed me in my yoga, although I do it as privately as possible."

"Sukannya, before long, tell me what made you follow Buddha? Does Pitha Maha know that?"

"Yes, Joshua. He knows."

"I am not surprised at all; your mother's experience, the story of Kittu, and your own experience are all fresh in my mind. But still, being the niece of Maha Rishi Vyassa . . ."

"Yes, being the niece of the Maha Rishi is what permitted me to do what I wanted. You are yet to know him; in his mind all beliefs are the same when it comes to God. But when it comes to traditions, he is a proponent of the color system; that's the way he is; he is convinced about it. But he is an open-minded man; you can speak your mind, and he will listen."

In the long silence that followed both of them stared at the embers, motionless.

"So, you have been meditating for over eleven years? At some point, I would like to learn how to meditate?"

"Yes, Joshua, I am a yogini. It would be my pleasure to teach you the yoga of meditation. You would be a perfect student."

That night Joshua tossed and turned in the solitude of darkness, finding it hard to sleep. The picture of the yogini sitting by the fire side, fully composed, calm, and tranquil, stuck in his mind. There was a certain sublime quality to her presence, a soothing effect. *What a brilliant artist is God to have created a woman like that? Her form and manner is so ethereal that it makes every atom in me crave with passion, a passion, that makes the pleasures of my soul and flesh one and the same,* Joshua mused.

Why did the Maha Rishi allow me to share the same roof with this lovely girl? Does he like me that much? What is he thinking of? Did he imagine that we would live together here, forever?

**** **** ****

As the days grew shorter and the nights colder, the fire in the brazier turned into an essential comfort. The conversations between them had become more personal and more philosophical. It was very clear to Joshua that Sukannya was a practicing Buddhist with profound knowledge in the ways of meditations.

Sukannya started teaching Joshua the fundamentals of Buddhist meditation. They sat down by the fireside cross-legged again.

"I will teach you how to meditate on emptiness; I will tell you what emptiness means, but first you have to cultivate your mind," she said.

She placed her hands on Joshua's forehead as an initiation, while Joshua sat down, eyes closed, chest up and arms spread over his knees. Sukannya spoke the instructions into his ears, calmly, smoothly, and serenely.

"This is just preparation of your mind for meditation," she said. "You breathe very gently and slowly all the way in until your chest is full, and then breathe out slowly, very slowly, calmly and peacefully. You focus only on the process of breathing, nothing else. Focus on the rising and falling of your chest. Think it's quiet and dark, and you are alone here. Weed out the little thoughts and images that grow in your mind; you feel light – very, very light – as if your weight had disappeared; you feel like floating; it's silent and dark; it's you and you alone; that space you reached is empty entirely to yourself."

Joshua sat meditating with closed eyes, motionless, his breathing shallow.

"Many thoughts and images will attempt to invade that space and distract you. Weed them out, cast off all thoughts, focus, and concentrate on that empty space; no worries, no concern, no anger, no possessions, nothing. It's all empty; it's nice; you are in union with yourself, peaceful; it's nice; it's peaceful."

Sukannya's voice grew softer, and Joshua's breathing became slower. Sukannya sat quietly beside him, and it appeared Joshua was motionless and in a trance for a long while. Peaceful for a long time.

The next several nights they practiced the meditation in front of the bonfire. "What you practice now is the first step in meditation. You will learn how to empty your mind of all thoughts and visions, and prepare your mind for real meditation on sunnyatha – emptiness," she reassured him.

"Sukannya, explain to me what is sunnyatha."

"Joshua, in *Bhagavath Geetha* you heard the Lord Krishna talking about Maya. The concept comes from the Vedas. It is stated that this life and this universe is not real, but an illusion – Maya. In a sense, Krishna is saying that the true reality is the ultimate consciousness, God. The rest is all Maya, a kind of illusion. Some people may also say hallucination. Emptiness in Buddhism is Buddha's answer to Maya, in Hinduism."

"Sukannya, this appears confusing and profound all at the same time. "Can you explain this more clearly?"

"Sunnyatha fundamentally means that our existence is inherently empty and without an independent self. Just imagine that you are alone in the universe all by yourself. You can have no independent existence without the deep interaction of the universe. That is, everything in the universe is connected to everything else."

Sukannya picked up a twig and poked at the embers; the twig burned with flame and crackled. "It is a piece of wood that came from a tree. The tree existed because of the earth, rain and the sun, and the wood is burning because it was lit. But in order for the twig to burn, it would need air, but if the air is taken away by covering this flame with a pot, the flame will disappear. A moment ago there was a flame, now there is not. The flame is empty. It has no inherent existence separate from the other things that made its existence possible."

After she had finished, they sat in a sweet silence for a long moment. By midnight they had gone to sleep.

The next day, Joshua was in deep contemplation: "We are all flames," he said to himself, "at one moment it's here, yet other moment it's not here. I am a part of the universe, connected and interdependent; therefore, what sense is there in pride, selfishness, anger, and possessions, or thoughts of, I, mine, or myself separate from others? Love, affection and compassion for all elements of the universe are the right pathway as Buddha teaches. How can we exist without our neighbors? What is a king without his subjects, what is a rich man without his laborers, what is a man without a woman?" Sukannya's words circled in his mind again and again. "You are without a separate self. Once you understand this and meditate on it with a clean mind, you will become enlightened. You will develop your own philosophy; that is the way to nirvana, the eternal bliss."

**** **** ****

The next day, the students – thirty men from different parts of India – assembled with Maha Rishi Vyassa for the concluding remarks on *Bhagavath Geetha*. Joshua remembered what Sukannya had said about the work. "*Bhagavath Geetha* was composed as the final answer to any and all negative criticisms the Buddhists have raised about the Vedas and the Upanishadts. Above all it was written to give a true credibility and justification of the Hindu philosophy of life, death and life after death, once and for all."

The Rishi came out and sat on a pillow surrounded by his students with the never-fading smile on his face. He was now covered with a thick woolen shawl, and kept a burning charcoal brazier close to his feet.

Guru Vyassa welcomed the students. "I am glad to tell you that teaching and learning is a dual process; I have always learned from my students. This time we have a young scholar, Joshua from Galilee. He has already taught me very many things from different civilizations of the world. I will encourage you to be bold and ask any and all questions in your mind. They need not be from *Bhagavath Geetha*, but whatever you would like to ask."

Joshua very briefly shared what he had observed at the Temple of Kali and asked, "Maha Rishi, tell us what could possibly justify such an action of child sacrifice."

Vyassa leaned back deep into the wicker chair with his hands held against the nape of his neck, squeezing.

"Joshua, the issue of child sacrifice appears brutal and totally unjustified, and I am not a proponent of such practices. Remember, it was a Chandallas temple. They are not part of the true Vedic traditions. The experience and tragedy of the child in this life is certainly the result of destructive karma of the previous life, resulting in the rebirth in a cursed womb. That point must be understood very well. In this endless chain of rebirths, some lives will be despicable and miserable, while others may be glorious. Death is also one of the many manifestations of God."

"Will that child attain Moksha?" Joshua asked.

"Certainly not," answered the Rishi. "To attain Heaven, one has to abandon wealth, sexual pleasures, completely detach from all the bonds of this world, and fully submit to God and join Him, or die in the line of duty, as Krishna has implied in the story we are talking about. The child was sacrificed by the Chandallas priest and did not have a chance to follow the pathways that are needed to attain Moksha. However, for the child, a better rebirth is possible."

Joshua's questions were many, "Is salvation possible for the poojari who sacrifice those children? How can you believe that sacrificing a child will bring forth rain? Is it Devi's anger that is truly the cause of the drought?"

The Rishi smiled and replied calmly, "Again, this child sacrifice was not a Vedic sacrifice, not performed by a Bhrahmin. If the poojari sacrificed the child with no malicious intentions or thought of gain, which I doubt, with full devotion and faith in God, submitting himself to God, with the feeling that it is his karma to do it, and that his true self is not performing the action, then the sacrifice could be pure. Joshua, you have learned in *Bhagavath Geetha* that even the karma of bad actions can be absolved, provided those actions were taken in full devotion to God. Though some of the sacrifices may look heinous, they are made necessary by the needs of the situation of this world."

The remaining parts of the question about Devi and her intentions are difficult to explain and are subject to interpretation and beyond the scope of this study, the Guru agreed. Is Devi part of Bhrahman? Of course, yes. Everything is Bhrahman, good and bad, he affirmed.

Joshua next asked the question that bothered him intensely. "Maha Rishi, why is the color system so fundamental to your beliefs, as you have very heavily emphasized implicitly and explicitly in the *Bhagavath Geetha*? Is it not true that all men are created equal?"

Maha Rishi smiled widely, stretched his back, and answered, "This is an excellent question that I have been asked many times, mostly by students from outside India. Joshua, the four colors are fundamental and God given, starting from the creation of man by the sacrifice of Purusha. Why the Bhrahmins are Bhrahmins and the Shudras are Shudras in one life is determined by their karma of the previous life. Some of the Bhrahmins of this life may have been Shudras in a previous life; likewise, some of the Bhrahmins of this life could very well be reborn as Shudras in the next life."

The Rishi paused for a while and glanced at Joshua with a grin.

"Joshua, tell us for the benefit of all, what you told me about Plato's vision of the ideal Republic, and how a similar class system was envisioned by him in Athens?"

Joshua gave a detailed description of the Gold, Silver and Iron class system as proposed by Plato in his vision of an ideal republic, although he did not condone it. The Maha Rishi was amazed at the depth of Joshua's knowledge and the profundity of his discourses, and warmly congratulated him for an enlightening presentation.

"In Athens, Plato spoke of an ideal republic that never came to be. But in India, we had the most ideal and benevolent vision under the rule of Raman, the 'Heaven on Earth' described in *Ramayana*."

"Forgive me, Guru, Joshua interrupted, "Heaven on earth for men of color, yes. But Rama's kingdom is fiction, is it not?"

"Joshua, Raman is a concept. God is a concept, as you should know," the Guru concluded.

But Joshua was not ready to let it go. He continued. "With due respect, Guru, I will put it to you that the color system is the most despicable treatment of people that I have seen."

"Joshua, I can understand your emotions," the guru replied calmly. "The class and color distinction is unquestionably a creation of God, no matter where it is. To fully answer your question, I need to explain the fundamental innate qualities of human types. This will be applicable anywhere in the world; you are a scholar, you must know it. There are three types of fundamental human types: first, the Sathuas – the noble men – as we find in Bhrahmins, the purest of all, calm, restrained, kind, compassionate, and sincere, with inborn and realized knowledge of purity.

"Next, are the Rajas – the princely class – as we find in Kshathrya, blessed with valor, heroism and lordship? And finally, we have the Thamas. Likewise, the Shudras are blessed with the innate skills of performing all kinds of services to others."

Vyassa continued with emphasis and reiterated: "Every human being must belong to one of these inborn primordial natures, colors."

Joshua's face turned cloudy, his voice combative, yet rational, "Guru, even if I accept your classifications, why would a Shudra trying to get closer to God through meditations and arduous karmas be unacceptable and deserving of death?"

Vyassa replied smoothly, yet firmly, "I understand, you have read of a similar situation in *Ramayana*. Joshua, for the well-being, safety and prosperity of a nation, there *must* be a division of God-given responsibilities, to be accomplished in an orderly manner. In a sense, all of these classes are equal in that they each have their karmas and duties to perform. How could a Shudra rule a nation or perform the rituals and sacrifices of a Bhrahmin? The net result would be chaos, hell. Therefore, this discipline of color is God given, and absolutely fundamental to Hinduism," he answered emphatically.

Joshua raised his hand to ask another question. The Guru raised his hand to hold it, crossed his right leg over the other, and continued uninterrupted.

"Dear students, all of the creation has purpose. You look at any creation of God, a tree for example; it has roots, a trunk, leaves and flowers or fruits. Each part of the tree serves a purpose and has a duty to fulfill. Likewise, each person has a purpose and a duty to fulfill. When a person faithfully discharges his karma, he will enjoy pleasure and satisfaction in his creation, the fulfillment of the essence of his soul, the essence of his creation. The Bhrahmin enjoys performing a sacrifice. The king derives pleasure in ruling his kingdom and destroying his enemies. The Vaisya takes pleasure in growing corn, and the Shudra in cleaning the toilet. They are all essentially the same. Each one is fulfilling his own karma."

Joshua interposed, "Maha Rishi, I am sorry to state this; it is your contention – just contention – that a Shudra enjoys doing menial jobs for the rest of their life. But for sure you don't know that. Moreover, you cannot compare humans to trees and fruits. We are a special creation of God."

Vyassa countered, "Once again, Joshua, I see your frustrations. But you are seeing only a very small segment of the endless chain of life. Innate qualities are different from acquired skills. A rose flower does not bloom on a jasmine. A man coming out of a cursed yonni can never become equal to the one who came out of a blessed yonni."

Joshua resolutely framed his next question.

"Maha Rishi, in your view, what are Chandallas, the untouchables – the beings that are not even counted among the four colors? Do they have any place in humanity? Do you consider them human or subhuman?"

"Among God's creations on earth, however, mankind consists only of four colors. The chandelles are not created as humans. They don't have any of the innate qualities of humans, and their qualities are that of an animal, although some look like humans and walk on two legs. They are dwellers of the forest, living like animals, feeding on animals. None of the Vedic rules are applicable to them. They can have their own life in any which way they want."

"Maha Rishi, I am saddened to hear this answer to my question." Joshua decided that there was no point in asking any more questions. *The Maha Rishi is not unlike any of the Pharisee in Israel,* he thought. *They have an answer for all the questions supported by the Holy Scriptures. It's like pouring water on a pot turned upside down; it can never be filled.*

"Let me ask one more question, Maha Rishi. Sage Manu teaches that women do not deserve freedom. What is your view on that?"

Rishi replied, "I do not fully agree with the teaching of Manu; there must be exceptions. But in general, a woman's role is to be an abiding cohort of a man, to please him and to worship him. The well-being of a man is the righteousness of the woman. She is to receive the seeds of life from him and generate children. A woman should not have an existence independent from man. A holy Sathi is a respectable and advisable end to her life. Time and again you have seen in our life and writings the woman gracefully entering the funeral pyre of her husband. How can there be a real existence for a shadow when the object is gone?"

For every question, Vyassa had an answer consistent with his beliefs and writings in the *Vedas* and *Upanishadts*. He maintained that "Buddhism is not new or different from Hinduism, and Buddha has not presented any ideas that are not already contained in the Hindu writings. Buddhism is merely a different interpretation, a way of individual thinking. The Sangha is only a commune of similar thinkers, but Hinduism is a way of life, encompassing every aspect of human life and every class of humans. It is like an ocean vast and deep. Any number of rivers may join the ocean carrying their dirty, muddy, or colored waters, but the mighty ocean will absorb all of them and still be blue and salty, powerful and raging. Hinduism is sanathana – immortal and eternal."

On the final day of the discourses the Maha Rishi was relaxed and gay. He had decided to ask his students a few questions.

"Now, I want to ask you a question or two. Who is Lord Krishna in the story of *Bhagavath Geetha?*"

The students presented many different answers, saying that Krishna was the ultimate lord, he was the creator, he was the destroyer, etc., but Maha Rishi didn't accept any of these answers. He glanced at Joshua with a confident half smile, jutting his bearded chin towards him.

"Joshua, tell me. Who do you think Krishna is?"

Joshua replied, "Maha Rishi, I believe Krishna is a thought in Arjuna's mind. Krishna is his consciousness."

For the first time the Maha Rishi smiled and laughed loudly. "Excellent, excellent. Now, tell me who won the war?"

"Maha Rishi I have a bit more to say," Joshua said. "Honestly, I cannot say that what Krishna advised Arjuna is right or even wise."

"Why would you say that, Joshua?" asked the Rishi.

"The good destroying the evil through war and violence is not anything new. We have seen such stories time and again. Krishnan's advice to Arjuna is all about the glory of the color system. Because you are a Kshathrya, you do this; it is your duty to do that; you alone are not doing it; instead, I am doing the other, and so on. But I give you credit for the power of your writing. Krishna's speech is convincing and is a good example of perseverance, an excellent example of cleansing the mind of a confused man."

The group was silent. Maha Rishi was thinking with his forehead knitted and his thumb rolling one over the other.

"War is never the means to peace; war is not even a temporary fix to a problem, it is an abhorrent gore with no winners or losers. There is nothing that war has achieved that peace could not. In war you strive for death; in peace we strive for life. War is evil; man must not indulge in it and gods must not provoke it."

"Very well said, Joshua. Now, let me ask you all another question. Who won the war?"

Again the opinions were numerous and varied. Some said Arjuna, others said Krishna, but obviously most of them said it was a victory for the Pandavas. But Joshua disagreed. "In this war there were no winners," he said.

Maha Rishi was elated listening to that answer. Tapping on the mattress on his right, the guru called Joshua to sit by his side. Joshua did so, and sat cross-legged. The Maha Rishi encouraged Joshua to answer the rest of the questions posed by the other students. Towards the end of the discussions the Guru said, "Joshua, I invite you to stay at this hermitage as much as you want; you are the best student I have ever had."

"Thank you, Maha Rishi," Joshua said." I haven't seen my home land in many years, and need to return."

**** **** ****

"Pitha Maha told me all about your discussions and your answers to his questions. I have never seen him this happy in all these years," Sukannya said, beaming with joy as the young Galilean successfully completed the discourses on the *Song of God* and spoke his mind boldly.

"What else did he say," Joshua asked. "What else."

Sukannya blushed, as that question was unexpected. She searched his eyes and struggled for an answer, yet smiled endearingly.

"You probably know already, Joshua. He asked whether you liked me or not," she said lowering her eyes.

"What did you tell him?"

"I am not a mind reader. You certainly didn't come here to settle down in this poor hermitage. I know that, I said."

There was a moment of silence.

"Anyway, you must read the remaining portion of the story before you go," Sukannya said. "It is probably the most intriguing part of the book. And, it's very brief," she said quickly.

That night they discussed the rest of the story.

"Joshua, when the war was all over, when the Kauravas army was all annihilated, Gandhari came to the battlefield."

"She lost all her sons, right?"

"Yes. It was a heartbreaking scene that she saw. Littered with the dead, body parts floating in pools of blood, freshly killed men still bleeding, foxes and dogs ripping apart the stinking corpses, and the skies above dark with vultures circling for their share of the sacrifice, the Kurukshethra – the war field – was the most gruesome scene."

"In the beginning, it was said that Bheeshmar wouldn't die without his consent. What happened to him?"

"In the middle of the war field, barely breathing, his entire body struck and suspended on a bed of arrows, lay Bheeshmar, the ultimate guru, awaiting his death."

"What did Lord Krishna think or say about this massacre?"

483

"Nothing. He orchestrated it all. But wait. I will tell you. Staggering amongst the dead bodies, looking for her beloved children, Gandhari – the queen mother of the Kauravas – wailed loudly, cursing Lord Krishna. At a certain point, she called Lord Krishna to her side, 'Krishna, you are the overseer of all. Why did you let this disaster befall the Kauravas? Why did you not stop this war and establish peace? You must suffer the consequences of this heinous act. Therefore, I curse you. Soon, all your tribe will be killed, and you shall suffer a very painful death," the mother said heart brokenly."

"Did the curse strike?"

"Yes, of course. In due course, Krishna's kingdom was taken over by other tribes, and the land was totally devastated. Knowing that the end was near, Krishna sat down under the shadow of a tree in the forest and meditated. Thinking he was a wild animal, a hunter launched an arrow that struck deeply in the feet of Krishna. With intense pain and suffering, Krishna died in the woods and then ascended to heaven."

"Interesting. The incarnation of God, who came to earth to teach Dharma and wisdom, suffers a painful death and then goes back to heaven?" Joshua smiled.

"Why you are smiling, Joshua" asked Sukannya.

"I have heard this story before; the story is the same for all prophets. Did all his wives commit Sathi, too?"

"Again, how did you know that?"

"It's totally expected. In his last gathering, the guru had endorsed Manu's teachings that a woman is nothing more than a shadow of the man," Joshua said.

"Well, you guessed so many things correctly. Tell me what had happened to the Pandavas and Kauravas after the war?" Sukannya asked.

"As would be expected, the righteous Pandavas will ascend to heaven and the others . . ."

"Ha-ha, you can be wrong, too," Sukannya said. "That may be the way the Greeks wrote their stories, but remember, this is written by Maha Rishi Vyassa. Now listen. Upon hearing the news that Lord

Krishna had been mortally wounded, pain and despair fell upon the Pandavas. They finally realized that all victories were meaningless and decided to go away from their land to the unknown, forever."

"So, Vyassa is saying that there are no winners in this war? Now it all makes sense to me."

"Maybe, but listen. In the presence of a very large crowd of weeping subjects, the eldest Pandava, Udhistiran, began walking to the north, not once looking back. He was followed by his brothers, Draupathi and an orphan dog wagging its tail. After many long days and nights, as they passed beyond the Himalayas, their wife, Draupathi, collapsed and died. Thereafter, the brothers each collapsed and died, one after the other, but Udhistiran kept on walking, refusing to look back."

"This is a most strange ending to the story. Why did all the Pandava brothers die one after the other, particularly Arjuna?" Joshua asked.

"Each one of them had committed a sin or deviated from dharma and was unworthy of heaven. Draupathi loved Arjuna, way more than her other husbands. Sahadevan boasted about his profundity. Nakulan was a narcissist. Arjuna's self-esteem was boundless. Bhima bragged about his might, and was a glutton. So, they all died."

"Brilliant. I can't wait to get to the end of the story. Keep on reading," Joshua said.

"Well, it is quite a captivating story, Joshua. After all, who do you think will go to the heavens? Can you guess?"

"This story is not like any others I have read. I don't want to guess," Joshua said.

"Then listen," Sukannya went to the last part of the story. "After a while, when Udhistiran was alone with the dog, Lord Indra came down from heaven and took the elder brother to heaven and offered him a throne."

"Is it because he was the only righteous Pandava?"

"Yes, but having not found any of his brothers or Draupathi in heaven, and seeing his arch enemy Duryodhana glowing, seated on a golden throne amidst the Gods, he refused to accept this throne and demanded to be taken to the place where his family was, even if it was hell."

"With some reluctance, Lord Indra took Udhistiran to his family."

"Plodding through a dark pathway, stumbling over dead and decaying bodies, waddling through puddles of pus, blood and debris, unable to breathe due to the horrific pungent stench, they reached a place of shadowy darkness. The air was dense with smoke, soot, and suffocating fumes. Mud, blood, feces, and vomit covered the decaying bodies teeming with fleas and maggots. The cries of people were deafening, wailing and screaming in their pain and anger. This was a place where people were wiggling like worms in a large heap of rotten corpses, some devouring meat pulled out from limbs, some others sucking up the eye balls or drinking of the body cavities, all at the same time warding off vultures, dogs, and hyenas fighting for the same food."

"Hell," Joshua murmured.

"Yes, the hell. Amidst the cacophony of the noises, Udhistiran recognized the voices of his brothers and his wife. For a moment he thought that he had gone mad. Then he turned to Lord Indra, demanding, "Why are my brothers in this hell? What is their crime?""

"Indra explained the pitfalls of his family at some time or another and justified their punishment in the purgatory, but promised him that one day they would all finally ascend to heaven."

"Sukannya, why was Duryodhana the evil king ascended to heaven?" Joshua asked.

"He lived as a Kshathrya king and died valiantly on the battlefield. He fulfilled his Kshathrya dharma; so also all the Kauravas."

"I understand, what ultimately matters is the dharma of the classes. Everything else is secondary. So, finally, both the Pandavas and Kauravas attained heaven?"

"Yes, Joshua. Everything finally dissolves in God. The world itself is an illusion, a Maya, a game of God. That's what Pitha Maha extols in this work."

"But for him, the maintenance of the colors is the most important aspect. I believe this work is to establish that fact." Joshua said.

Sukannya stared into his eyes. "Yes, Joshua. You got the point right."

**** **** ****

It was a rare warm and humid October afternoon, and thick, gray clouds had already invaded the skies above. The sun was descending in the west, the leaves on the trees infused with colors still hung heavy with moisture, and the air was thick and sweltering without a breath of breeze. Joshua was lying under the banyan tree, deeply preoccupied and gloomy, for the concept of meditation had caught on in his mind.

As the first drops of rain began to fall, Sukannya came out running to the front yard, her face flushed red with heat, her clothes wet with sweat, and her hair tumbling down beyond the shoulders. She turned her face to the sky with lips wide apart, trying to catch the rain directly into her mouth. She called out to Joshua, "Let's go for a dip in the pond." The idea provided a needed break for Joshua. They started through the footpath to the stream hand in hand and plunged into the pond until it was dark.

There was rain off and on for several days, but in mid-November the weather suddenly turned cool, and the north winds had begun, ushering in a brutal winter. There was heavy snow in Mathura, which was unusual. The intense wind and the chilling cold were difficult to bear. Joshua was making plans to return to Galilee, but the caravan would not be available until April.

Joshua found it difficult to master the yoga of meditation on emptiness, although the concept attracted him immensely. Many nights he practiced yoga with Sukannya.

"When you enter the deeper phase of the meditation," Sukannya said, "there won't be any perception of senses. You will not hear any sounds, feel any touch, or smell any odors. Your inner eyes will be opened, and your vision will be clear. That phase is akin to Nirvana, at least temporarily. When you practice it many, many times, you will reach that zone without difficulty, and at some point you will realize that we have no intrinsic existence, and that we are all empty. You will be liberated from all bondages."

Joshua tried his best, but was not always successful.

It was a very cold evening. The fire in the grate went up again, and the two of them sat besides, cross-legged again. There was a firm determination on her face when Sukannya said, "Joshua, amongst all people, you must not find it difficult to learn the concept of emptiness. Let me ask you a few simple questions first. You have a certain concept about your god, haven't you?"

"Yes."

"What does your god look like?"

"God created man in his own likeness; that's our belief."

"A belief it is, all right."

"What is your god's color?"

He contemplated for a moment and said, "All colors."

"That's the same as no colors, or no one color to distinguish. Don't even think that I am trying to belittle your God, but what is his height?"

"I can't answer," he pursed his lips.

What is his weight?

"His height?"

"His smell?"

Joshua was unable to define any of those questions.

"But you agree that your god is the most powerful of all, don't you?"

"Yes."

"The most powerful force you can imagine?"

"Yes."

"Joshua, let me rephrase your answers: God is a colorless, odorless, formless, weightless force, the ultimate force, a force that is empty, an empty force capable of creating anything and everything your little mind can imagine. That unimaginably large potential force contained in that emptiness is the thing you call God. Buddha never invoked God; for him, this emptiness was the ultimate being of all beings. Now you can start to meditate on emptiness."

After that mind-boggling discourse on emptiness, neither of them had anything further to talk about that evening. As the embers died out and covered with ashes, they both went to sleep, but Joshua had a sleepless night again.

I have no idea who this woman is, his curiosity about her heightened, and his passion about her strained, fighting to break the cage.

One cold winter evening in early December, Sukannya invited Joshua. "Will you be interested to visit a Sangha near the city in Mathura. I am going to visit a dying man," and he accepted.

Trudging through the winding pathways in the woods, Kishan and Visal guided them to the Vihara, the same pathway through which Joshua rode to the hermitage the first time.

On the way, Sukannya explained the mission. "The man who is dying is named Gunananda. Pitha Maha knew him very well. He used to come here frequently to discuss and argue out their beliefs and views for days on end. I was very eager to hear their heated discussions, and Pitha Maha let me listen to them. At times, Pitha Maha would instruct me to take down a point or two. But Gunananda is probably in eternal bliss by the time we reach there."

"I am sorry to hear that, Sukannya."

"Joshua! There is nothing to be sorry about that. He is in eternal bliss now. That's what he worked for, hoped for, his whole life. We are all striving for that eternal bliss at some point, aren't we?"

"Does Maha Rishi know that you have been a follower of a Buddha?"

"He knows everything. He even once said that Buddha is an avatar."

On the eastern outskirts of the city of Mathura, amidst a village of several hundred orange-roofed brick houses, stood the Buddhist Vihara, an imposing, domed building with a carved pagoda at the entrance.

"This is where Gunananda had lived and taught Buddhism to the monks and nuns for many years," Sukannya said . . ."What happened? Was he ill for some time?"

"No. He was not ill at all. Seven days ago, he called his disciples to his side and informed them that his time had come to meditate and pass on to eternal bliss. That evening, on an empty stomach and a mind filled with peace and satisfaction, he entered the meditation, and now is in the bliss."

Crossing the dimly lit foyer, they noticed some of the monks and nuns sitting cross-legged in rest and meditation. Passing through a large, stone arched doorway, they entered the central hall. There, in the shadowy darkness, they saw Gunananda lying on a stone bed covered in bright red and yellow sheets. The room was dark and still except for the faint flicker of the slow-burning candles placed on the foot of the bed and the soft guttural music that filtered into the room from an adjacent hall.

Joshua breathed deeply. He had never experienced an environment of such absolute calm and peace. There were a few monks quietly meditating by Gunananda's bedside. Sukannya sat down by the bedside for some time, and Joshua joined her in meditation. After a long while, she quietly got up and stood behind the head of the man lying down, placed her index finger on his forehead for a few moments, and then put it on her forehead and quietly walked out.

The monks told her in quiet, hushed tones that the guru had entered the nirvana the previous night. They will keep his body like that for three more days before burial, they had said.

After about two hours, Sukannya and Joshua braced themselves for the walk back to the hermitage on that cold, windy night. Snowflakes, dense and relentless, fell like a heavy curtain to the ground. The rising moon painted a milky sheen over the forest. Sukannya shared her thick shawl with Joshua, locked his hand in the nook of her elbow, and hunched her shoulders against his, as they slowly traversed the woods, the two Shudras following closely behind.

Sukannya whispered into his ears, "The guru is in eternal bliss now, but we believe he still has a subtle consciousness in him. He can hear the things we say."

"Sukannya, this is beginning to confuse me. Is he alive or dead now?" Joshua asked.

"Joshua, beliefs cannot be delineated clearly as black and white, as in your faith or in Hinduism. In our belief, death is a slow process. After about three or four days, his soul will enter the brad – the intermediate stage. Within forty nine days, his soul will enter another body. During those days, there will be prayers and song in the Vihara, and they will keep food and drinks for him outside in the open air."

"For what purpose, Sukannya?"

"People provide food and drink for the subtle consciousness of the dead. It is believed that it feeds on the odor of the food."

"You really believe that? I didn't think Buddha ever talked about feeding this subtle . . ."

"Joshua, so much more changed in Buddhism after Buddha."

The wind blew heavier. Joshua's hands and feet became numb with cold. He held on to Sukannya, his arms around her neck, and murmured in her ear, "Sukannya what is this subtle consciousness. Tell me the difference between the concept of the soul and your subtle consciousness."

"Oh yes, you ignorant student, I will tell you the differences," she said with a laugh, as she pinched Joshua playfully on his belly.

"In Buddhism, the soul as such does not exist. The subtle consciousness does not carry the karmic imprints to the next rebirth. Buddha's belief is that the mind is immortal. It is a stream, a continuation from your previous birth, whether you recollect it or not."

"You have read a great deal; what is your belief about the notion of reincarnation?" Joshua asked.

"It's only an idea, Joshua. This life is too good to end with no consequence, at least for some; the idea of a rebirth is another life, derived out of our desperation to end our life once and for all. I personally do not believe in reincarnation. This life is a gift from some unknown power; you might call it God; I might consider it emptiness – all the same. It's an illusion – Maya. A hundred years back, nobody could have envisioned you and me walking through these woods, and a hundred years from now, it will be like we never existed. Life is an illusion. Believe in your convictions, teach what you believe, and do what you teach."

"Sukannya, for me life is no illusion, it is real, designed and for a purpose."

It was nearly midnight when they arrived back at the hermitage. The howling winds whistled through the brushes and the roof of the hermitage. They made a fire in the brazier and sat next to each other, holding their palms against the blazing fire. It was too cold to separate and to go to their own rooms; instead, they lay down beside the fire and huddled together, Sukannya pillowing her head on his shoulder and holding his hand held close to her chest.

They both tossed and turned for a while, unable to sleep. The exhilarating woman's scent on the nape of her neck, the fragrance of jasmine from her locks, the feel of an ethereal woman within his folds, a craving mind, and a yielding body was irresistible to Joshua. His heart pounded, and his groin swelled with the pleasures of the flesh at that delicious moment of lassitude. Joshua felt her bosom in his palms. At that moment, the passion of his heart and the pleasures of the flesh found a common ground in coexistence. Neither of them wanted to break the silence of the night. The wind blew stronger with the whistling music. At a certain point, Sukannya turned to face him, her lips nearly touching his. The warmth of her breath was right on his face. She was the bold one to speak first.

"Joshua, you can't get to sleep, right?

"Right."

"What are you thinking now?"

That question was very much familiar to him, he mused. Mary.

"It's a wandering mind, Sukannya," he murmured.

"I can understand, Joshua. The mind never rests. It's always working for us, sometimes against us."

In that darkness, she gently ran her fingers through his brows, nose and lips, and then gently rested her palm on his chest. Her breathing turned heavier and her grip stronger. She slumped to his chest with passionate desire, ready to cleave. "I can't get to sleep either Joshua," she murmured.

Presently, the image of a white, flat-roofed house guarded by a tall dark cypress and sheltered by a few poplars showed in his mind. In the front porch of that house was sitting a frail, middle-aged woman stitching a blue boarder for a long, white cloak, and a young lady with curly hair playing with a child. Joshua closed his eyes tightly and prayed that those images would never fade.

The previous night, Maha Rishi was debilitated with a fever and severe headache and difficulty opening the eyes to bright light. In the morning, he woke up with no feeling on the right side of his face. His eyes were watery, and his right eyeball rolled up as he tried to close the eyes.

Except for boiled barley water, he couldn't tolerate any food at all for two days. Then he was able to swallow pulverized shiva-mooli in goat milk in the morning, and warm soma broth in the evening. At times, he held on to Joshua, calling him "son" and "my son," and babbling incoherently. Still, this evoked affectionate memories for Joshua of his father, Joseph. On the fourth day, the Rishi recovered well and took a walk to the stream with his arms thrown around the shoulders of Sukannya and Joshua. Sukannya was a bit shaken by this event, as it was the first time she had ever seen the Rishi losing his mind, even if briefly. On the fifth day, the Rishi recovered well, ate boiled rice with yogurt, and went to sleep early. There was a combined relief at the hermitage.

Joshua lit the fire as the evening fell and lay propped on his elbows on a reed mattress, and Sukannya sat at his feet facing the fire, gently caressing his feet. That night she talked incessantly about her grandfather – the banyan tree in her life, the man who resurrected her, protected her and gave her the freedom to pursue whatever she liked.

"Joshua, you are a man of few words who has traveled a quite large area. It is very difficult to read what is in your mind. Can you tell me what is 'mind'? Tell me, if you can. How did a man like Pitha Maha lose his mind? What is the mind, and who controls it?"

"The mind?" Joshua asked.

"Yes, Joshua. What is your understanding of mind?"

What is in your mind? he wondered. "Sukannya, this is a very tough question, nearly impossible for me to answer correctly or fully."

"But try," she said. "It's a very simple Buddhist mental exercise."

"Well . . . the mind is where all your knowledge is stored, where your knowledge and experience is worked into reasoning and wisdom."

"More. Tell me more. You can tell me more," she said.

Never have I been in such a situation. Yet on this cold wintery day, amidst a forest in a hermitage holding the wisest and most beautiful woman I have ever seen. What am I to say? he thought.

"The mind," Joshua said, measuring his words, "the mind is without form, color, odor, taste, shape, or weight, yet we can feel it. In a physical sense, it is empty, yet it can control all your activities. The mind decides what the body does."

"Joshua, now the real question. Are the soul and mind the same thing?"

"No, I believe not. The mind is the shadow of the soul. This is something I have already thought about."

"How correct, Joshua. I will tell you once again, you are a Buddhist in your heart. With so little knowledge of Buddhism, you already have more perception about the Buddhist concepts than anybody I have ever seen. For a Buddhist, it is really important to differentiate between mind and soul."

Only when the cock crowed did they both realize how late it was. They closed their eyes to get some sleep. Sukannya drifted off quickly, but Joshua's mind was like the unsettled weather outside, tormented, his thoughts of soul, mind and flesh.

Raised up on his elbow, in the dim red light from the grate, he studied the sleeping beauty lying beside him. *God*, he thought, *what a great artist is He, to create woman like this, in a form and manner that would stimulate every atom in a man yearning for love, nurture and ecstasy.*

**** **** ****

Another December had come and gone, and Joshua had turned thirty. In another three months he was to take the journey back to his home in Israel.

Joshua now felt comfortable with the techniques of meditating to cleanse the mind, to meditate on emptiness. He found that practicing meditation made him feel calm, peaceful and refreshed.

Many times Joshua thought about Sukannya, a wild flower, radiant and fragrant. *I know she has strong desires, passion of pleasure. I have done wrong, he said to himself. Certainly I have flamed her passion. Is she totally detached? She said she likes to talk to me. Likes my company. After all, it has been about two years that we have been sleeping under the same roof.*

Sukannya approached from behind and sat beside him, asking, "Joshua, how much longer will you be here?" She didn't appear particularly sad or concerned – she just wanted to know. "Just three months more," he replied.

She sighed deeply, and then remained silent for a while, until saying, "I have been here since the age of seven. The farthest I have gone is the Vihara. I haven't even gone to the city of Mathura." It was followed by a long minute of silence.

Then she lifted her head and looked straight into his eyes with an endearing smile. "Joshua, may I travel with you for a while?"

"What do you mean, Sukannya? You would like to go with me to Galilee?"

"Oh, no. I would just like to travel with you for a little while. I am not sure, Joshua," she interrupted with a sigh, "but just leave it for the time being. Let me ask you something else. Is there anything else you wanted to ask me or ask of me?"

"Not really, Sukannya. My visit to India was the most fruitful of all my travels. But most of all, I have a feeling that I have learned all that I can from you. I was thinking – you may please clarify – how Gunananda remained in a state of bliss for five days. For me he died the evening we saw his body; for you he attained nirvana? Which is it, really . . .?"

"I will. I am glad you asked that question. Nirvana. For Hindus and most others like you, death is the end of physical life, when the soul discards the body like a snake casts off its outer skin and moves on, it can be a frightening or a miserable experience for many. But for a Buddhist, if you have discarded all your attachments and meditated on emptiness, you will enter the eternal bliss with pleasure; it's a period of rejoice and not torment; it can continue for a few days," she explained.

Joshua was curious and still struggling to understand this concept. "What exactly do you mean by bliss?" he asked.

Sukannya moved closer to him, stretched out her legs and pillowed his head in her bosom. As she stroked his hair softly, she answered. "Bliss is the ultimate ecstasy in yoga with God. Joshua, I believe you are fully mature to understand the yoga of bliss. If you were to stay longer, I would gladly train you in the meditation leading to bliss, but for now, just know this."

A long minute of anxious silence followed.

"Buddha has taught us that the end of life need not be painful or with misery. It can be an eternal bliss, a phase of extreme ecstasy, but we don't have to wait until death to enjoy that feeling of blissful consciousness."

"Wait a moment, Sukannya. Are you saying that one can attain the bliss in his lifetime without dying?" Joshua asked.

"Indeed, with proper practice and meditation, we can achieve blissful enlightenment in one lifetime, any number of times, but this yoga has to be taught with extreme caution and supervision, preferably by a teacher with whom you are yoked in spirit, mind and body," she said.

"Really?" Joshua looked up at her face, tightening his eyes in serious thoughts. "I read something like this from the writings of Cicero of Rome who borrowed the ideas from an ancient Greek philosopher – Pythagoras. But I thought it was not practical, although you sound confident and convincing. Sukannya, I would like to try the meditation you spoke about, if you think that you can do it within the next three months?"

I can try," said Sukannya looking through the flames and wringing her fingers intuitively, and she beamed as if she was awaiting just such a request.

"But before you finally make up your mind, think it over for a day, and let us talk about it tomorrow."

The next day, Maha Rishi felt a lot better. He came out for a walk with a cane. The right side of his face had drooped and looked lifeless, and his mouth was pulled to the left. Visal and Kishan made some warm water and gave him a bath. After the dinner, they helped him up to the house on the tree.

Sukannya appeared somewhat sad. A gloomy silence hung in the house. That was a night of rest for all. Nobody talked anything further. Joshua fasted for the night and went to sleep.

As soon as he lay down, a pang of sudden excitement gripped his mind. His heart pounded heavily, and he felt that his mind was losing control over his body. He struggled to get to sleep. Attachments . . . attachments . . . that night he meditated on his own life, his calling, the purpose of his being on this earth, the terrible impulses inside him, his passion for Sukannya, his obligations to his wife and his nation. At times, he doubted whether the mind can always control the body. He remembered what Confucius had said.

The next morning Sukannya knocked on his door and came in beaming, almost shouting, "It's almost noon, Joshua. Get up. Pitha Maha is almost normal. We went for a walk to the stream. I am so very happy."

"I am happy, too, Sukannya. I will go and see him soon."

It was a cold, gray day. Joshua visited with the Rishi, who had recovered well form the recent affliction but still looked weak, and the bright sparkle in his eyes had disappeared.

Amidst discussions, the Maha Rishi suddenly snapped, "Joshua, there is something bothering you, I know, some bewilderment. Your mind is churning, I see that." The old man was reading his face intensely.

Joshua was held on a half-breath. He swallowed heavily and met the eyes of the guru, and said, "You are right, Maha Rishi; advise me how to get out of it."

The Rishi leaned forward on the sofa, knitted his fingers behind his neck, squeezing, and said calmly. "Bewilderment is failure to identify the priority; you remember Arjuna at the wedding ceremony of Draupathi? When he strung the bow and aimed at the neck of the bird in the cage, he couldn't see anything else, the tree, the rotating cage, the tiny door, the cheering crowd, nothing. There was no thought in his mind of the reward or the consequences, let alone the glory or the humiliation. What he saw was the eye of the bird, nothing else; what he thought about was the shooting of the arrow, nothing else."

After a long, enlightening dialogue, Joshua left the tree house for a lone walk. *Yes I have lost my focus,* he thought. *I have deviated from my path; I have sinned. I did let it go this far; I have mislead her, or did I? Temptations . . . temptations . . . my mind is weak . . . unable to hold my body . . . I can't define what exactly is that force, that force constantly pulling me towards her . . . why can't I meditate without distractions . . . I should be able to . . . just like Arjuna . . . focus . . . focus on the eye of the bird . . . nothing, nothing else.*

As the evening turned dark, he returned to the hermitage. It was biting cold in early February.

After the sunset, embers glowed on the brazier again. The guru and her student sat cross-legged facing each other. The final phase of the meditations.

The undulating flames reflected as golden waves on their faces, and they saw each other's reflections in their eyes. Sukannya's face was aglow with an endearing smile, and when she spoke, her voice was sweet and tender.

"Joshua, when I teach you this guru yoga, I will function as your karmamudra, your consort, your partner in yoga."

"There are certain times when your mind achieves a state of deep absorption, almost like a trance. We experience this state in sexual ecstasy, in dreams, and even in death. With proper meditation, we can navigate our mind stream to that state of bliss. There are multiple ways to achieve this state, including sexual yoga, although some people believe that is the only way."

She closed her eyes in meditation for a few minutes, the embers in the brazier at times cracked as the peat and spindles caught on with fire.

She spoke very softly. "This yoga is to be practiced only by those who have mastered the concept of meditating on emptiness. The practice of guru yoga has its roots in the Kundalini meditation practices of the Hindu yoga."

"What?"

"You close your eyes and focus on what I say. I will explain the words step by step." Joshua closed his eyes, resting his chin on his clasped hands.

"Kundalini is the cosmic energy lying dormant, compressed and curled up in the lower backbone. By proper meditation, we can arouse this dormant Kundalini to rise up in force through the sushumnas to the brain. That's what we are trying to achieve."

Sukannya paused.

Joshua sat by the fireside, listening to her teaching. His heart raced, and his face flushed as she spoke. Sukannya looked so beautiful that his concentration at times slipped. Her ebullient energy, confidence and depth of knowledge made him wonder who she really was. *I have traveled the world for fifteen long years searching for truth, knowledge, wisdom and God. This angel, who has never gone far beyond this simple hermitage, knows it all. Who is she?* He wondered.

"In this yoga," Sukannya resumed, her eyes closed, "you learn to meditate by visualizing an object as the focus. To make it easier and more practical, you can meditate and visualize me as the guru. Likewise, the guru meditates on the consort, as they both are yoked together. To attain this meditation, going through a group in a Vihara observing a variety of images – mandalas – are useful, which is the common practice. But you can do it without any of those."

The flames in the brazier were slowly fading, yet the embers glowed. "You look at me for a moment, get the full image in your mind, and then close your eyes," she said.

They gazed at each other with eyes locked. But for the gentle sounds of their breathing, there was silence.

"Now, I will ask you to begin breathing gently. Breathe in deeply, and breathe out very slowly through the nose. You prepare for purification of your mind, and empty all thoughts of guilt, fear, concern and bad karma."

Sitting cross-legged, eyes closed chest and chin up, and his stretched arms resting on his knees, Joshua was positioned quite like a Buddha statue, barely moving. Sukannya also sat like a frozen statue, commanding with subtle lip movements. There was a sheen of peace and tranquility over their faces, and the words from her lips reached his ears gently, gliding through the air, while the reflections from the golden, yellow flames from the grate danced with undulations on their faces.

"Now you have entered a space where you alone exist, detached from all exterior senses. Into that space you evoke your guru. Open your inner eyes and visualize her, and see that she is the only glowing body in that space. Millions of brilliant light rays are emitting from her. You will see everything you wanted to see in her. Unlock your inhibitions. Look at her closely, very closely – her hair, eyes, lips, breasts, waist, yonni, legs and feet, again and again. You raise your arms and clasp her close to you and caress her – her face, her hair, her lips, neck, her breasts and waist and all the nooks and deep seated curves of her body, over and over again. You gently stroke her and keep her at ease. You do it over and over again with both your hands, and now you will feel and touch her. Likewise, she also comes to you, touching and feeling you all over, time and again. You feel that she is within your folds."

Like in a trance, Joshua's hands slowly went up in the air and stood frozen and his breathings strengthened.

"Her radiant images are now penetrating into your crown chakra. This will evoke and release energies that will travel down through the sushumna, stimulating lower chakras, releasing warmth, palpitation and excitement. The positive vibrations from the chakras are now stimulating further down, dormant chakras, one after the other. Now the vibrations are finally knocking on the doors of the Kundalini chakra in the vicinity of your backbone."

Sukannya, with her eyes closed and hands folded, continued in a slow monotone.

"The Kundalini awakens with a deep-seated throb, releasing heavy vibrations that spread around the waist and further stimulate the structures, including the phallus."

Joshua appeared to be in deep sleep. His body tightened with a reflexive flutter and an uncontrollable jerky movement.

"You are in total control. Do not release. Let it go on for long. After a few such cycles, the Kundalini will rise, and you will feel like a volcanic eruption that rises up to the brain like a lightning glow, stimulating everything in your body. You continue to hold on to her. Now you are entering the zone of bliss. If your mind is strong, you can stay in the bliss for a long, long time. You are in union with God."

After a long while, Sukannya opened her eyes, Joshua, still in deep meditation. She shook him to life again.

"To get to that stage," she continued softly, "you need years of training and practice. It will be quite arduous to begin with, but as you mature in meditation, you can achieve that stage of enlightenment and bliss much more quickly and with ease, particularly if your object of visualization is familiar and pleasing." She closed her eyes again in meditation.

They sat, suspended in their silence. The embers had died out. It was dark. It was solitude. It was bliss. They did not speak any further that night, and went to bed.

That night Joshua heard Sukannya coughing, more than usual with a moist sound. The cold was intense, and the winds continued to whistle. *Union with God in eternal bliss,* Joshua reflected. *The philosophy of the East, the endless chain of thoughts, love without attachment, subtle consciousness, the soul, hungry ghosts, rebirths, karma, yoga, yogini, mandala – maybe it's all Maya. Maybe, I have seen it all. But, for how many springs have I missed almonds blooming in Galilee? Are the Romans still crucifying my people, and the Pharisees still slaughtering the animals and waxed with tithes? Sure, violence is not the answer to oppression; aggression is not the answer to suppression. Challenge them with no anger, with no pride, with no attachment; resist them passively, lovingly and convincingly. I have to fulfill my karma. That I will; I will.*

**** **** ****

It was the beginning of March. The weather was much better than expected. The days were getting longer and the afternoon sky was lit by the bright sunshine.

One morning, Sukannya asked, "Joshua, I am going to the Vihara this evening. Would you like to come with me?"

"I would love to."

Once again guided by Kishan and Visal, they tramped the wild road to the Vihara. It was the same place where Guru Yogananda had attained nirvana a few weeks ago. "Joshua, I know you are an inquisitive traveler," Sukannya said. "But don't be surprised; at the Vihara, you will find some people following a different path of yoga, but remember, in yoga all are meditating to yolk with the supreme consciousness. They are all attempting to reach enlightenment in one way or the other."

"Tell me more; different ways to attain enlightenment?"

"First, let me tell you a parable taught by Buddha. We are all mortal beings – travelers – on the shores of a vast, raging river. Your shore is that of poverty, ignorance, pride, anger and selfishness, all desperately wanting to cross over to the shore of love and eternal bliss. It doesn't make any difference what kind of raft you use to travel, provided you arrive safely on the other shore. You agree. Don't you?"

"Yes."

"In that journey, once you are in the middle of the water, you are not on your own, and your only solace is your fellow passengers and the raft. Those fellow passengers in Buddhism are the Sangha, and the raft is the pathway."

"So, this Vihara is your Sangha, your support group?"

"Yes, and Vajrayana Buddhism is my raft to take me to the other side of this raging river. I come here every week, for spiritual empowerment and reinforcement."

"Sukannya, what's Vajrayana Buddhism? There was no mention of such a branch in my classes at Taxila. I know somewhat about Theravada and the Mahayana pathways."

"Well, Vajrayana Buddhism is the only path where we can attain the luminous compassion of Buddha, the bliss, the ecstasy, in our lifetime, many times."

Many thoughts momentarily crossed his mind, Eros of Hesiod, Phaedrus of Plato, but above all, a lack of clarity. "Sukannya, could you make it more clear," he asked.

"It's Tantric Buddhism," she confirmed.

The epiphany struck him, a pang of anxiety, sex and God, Kundalini yoga, the way to nirvana. He stood still for a moment. She took his hands and moved forward.

The Vihara was dimly lit. They crossed the ante room to the main hall. Leaning against the wall were two rows of musicians clad in maroon cassocks with tall glittering hats, making guttural, and low-toned humming sounds. All the words they sang sounded like *ohm*, which gently vibrated the still air. More than eighty people were meditating in that room, all of them in pairs. At the center of the hall on a high platform, was a shining metallic statue of Lord Buddha sitting crouched with his legs apart, and a female deity lay on his lap facing him – her yonni and the Lords phallus in full engagement, as in deep sexual union. The platform was decorated with several painted images of women and men in various styles of sexual union– the Mandalas.

At the very entrance of the room, Joshua stood in shock, barely breathing. He quickly glanced around and closed his eyes, but the images in his mind did not disappear. They only shone brighter, the tighter he closed his eyes. Virtually nobody looked at anyone else. They all have closed eyes, except for one or two calmly looking at their partners.

Sukannya whispered in his ears, "You can do whatever you please." Then she left the grip on him and moved to the thicket of the crowd.

Several minutes passed. Joshua failed; he was not able to keep his eyes closed. He felt warm and sweaty. Sukannya had drifted away from him by a few feet, closer to the mandala. She was meditating alone. Presently, there was a subtle movements on her body. She appeared to be swaying a bit, but with good balance. After a while, she clasped her hands in front and began making some subtle gestures that resembled the dancing of a snake.

In a short while, a woman in one corner started breathing very heavily and soon her breathing broke into screaming. Her body began to contort and convulse, and, arching backwards, she stood on all fours, fully cleaved, while her cohort thrust deeply, nearly violently, into her sacrificial yonni, as she herself bleated with pleasure – the yoga of bliss.

It appeared that nobody else in the hall heard or noticed them. Joshua stood watching Sukannya – who was still meditating deeply in a trance. But soon he felt dizzy, and darkness crept into his eyes. He could see nothing but fog, felt like he was losing his weight, his power to hold on, and was afraid of falling down. He reached out to Sukannya, pulling her towards to him. But she was already in a trance and didn't know a thing. He breathed heavily, but the feeling was that the air was not getting in; it stuck in the chest with a knot. He wanted to run away, but the legs wouldn't move. He cursed the moment, but then again there was a supreme sense of peace in the room, nobody against anybody, all in peace, all in harmony, all in yoga. He stood, still holding on to her. Suddenly in his mind, he saw the skies were lit like fire, fire that was coming down to earth, blazing balls of sulfur, falling down like rain. The meditators all froze still, like pillars of salt.

Some time had passed, and Joshua was brought to the surroundings by the shriek cry of another woman from next to him. Her body twitched as if possessed with clonic movements, and she fell to the ground, landing on her elbows and knees. She pushed her buttocks as high as she could, shaking and twittering. Her consort immediately complimented her with the yoga of bliss. The screaming and convulsions slowly settled.

Joshua was nearly ready to leave. Sukannya, still dazed, made some gestures, spreading out her hand in the air as if she was reaching out to touch him. She was. She had a visible tremor, unsteady and nearly fell to the ground before Joshua caught her. She was spastic and warm, and her face deeply flushed red. Then she barely opened her eyes and looked at him – a vacant look – and her eyeballs soon rolled back. Her mouth was parted wide with honey dripping. She clawed his hands, and soon relapsed into a vigorous spasm with her buttocks fluttering like the wings of a butterfly. She fell onto his chest, red, hot and spastic. With a sudden rush of passionate desire, Joshua's face sank to her breasts intuitively, holding her tight and strong. His lips parted and neared to her ready to kiss, his heart pounded, bile boiled, groin swelled, then again a sudden rush of guilt and fear held him back. The spasm and flutter in her, lasted for a long time as she clung tightly to him, sweating. After a while, he unclenched her fists, but she stayed still for some more time, in total bliss. Then, slowly, her grip loosened. She regained consciousness, and came to life with a shuddering sigh, looking into his eyes, her eyes still vacant, a countenance of total detachment.

They walked home together hand in hand, her head hunched over to his, and he holding her by the waist, without saying a word.

Joshua went to his bed, and Sukannya to her room. He buried his face in the pillow, but struggled to sleep. The images at the Vihara erupted in his mind, one after the other. The ultimate bliss, in union with God, the ecstasy of yoga. The more he tried to erase the images, the more it illuminated vividly in his mind. He tried to divert his mind to many places, to Nazareth, to Alexandria, but all the same his mind spun back to her, the slim ethereal woman swaying in trance with her lips parted, honey dripping. This is a very long night he cursed, vow to the moment when he decided to go. After a while, he woke up to the crow of the rooster. *Oh, I had dosed off,* he thought. He felt tired, and his eyes closed effortlessly, and he drifted to a half sleep.

It was at the end of March in Mathura, and Joshua had two bags packed, making preparations for the return journey. The evening before, covered in a woolen shawl, the Maha Rishi had come to the house, wished him well, and invited him to return anytime he desired. Sukannya showed no emotions as she prepared for his departure. She arranged a delicious last supper for him – roasted rabbit meat cooked by Vishal. She sat by his side as they ate, but neither of them said much. She coughed intermittently during the meal – a dry, hacking cough. Joshua noticed that she looked tired, and the color was gone from her cheeks.

After dinner they sat on the carpet by the foyer, under the dim light of the oil lamp. A cold wind blew over them. The undulating flame of the lamp fluttered to die, but Sukannya shaded the flame with her palm against the wind, while her palm glowed red, like a colored lampshade. That's the moment Joshua noted a pearl in her eye ready to fall.

Joshua took her by the hand. His voice quivered, and he said, "It's nearly two years now. I have never seen you this much down. I thought I will never see tears in your eyes . . ."

"Joshua," her eyes flooded for the first time. Her voice vibrated as she said, "I believed that I had truly conquered myself. I convinced myself that I would not be engulfed with grief and sentiment and believed that I had lost all attachments through my beliefs and meditations, but now I realize that no woman is capable of that. There were many nights that I haven't slept. I wished you would come over to me. I have come to your closed door many times, but then again I felt that I haven't truly known you at all. I fathom that you will be a man remembered throughout the ages, the finest of all creations. I fear I will be a distraction to you; after all, you are also a man of flesh and blood. Therefore, you go and fulfill your karma, Joshua. You will always be here in my meditations; you are my meditation. It was my bliss to know you, but now I shall remain here."

Joshua was speechless for a long time, but he regained strength and said softly, "Sukannya, there is no other person in my life about whom I have thought or meditated more than you. I have been attracted to you intensely. Ever since you taught me the yoga of meditation, you have shined as a mandala in my mind, unable to escape. I have tried hard to tie myself down to my bed and not walk to your room intuitively . . ." He paused for a minute. Sukannya was reading the undulating flame of the oil lamp shaking her head horizontally.

"You are the most unusual and interesting woman I have ever come across. I have learned a lot form you, mostly learning about you. You will always be there in my thoughts and prayers," he added.

"You are a very kind man, Joshua," Sukannya said slowly and softly, still looking at the flame, "your words are healing and I admire your courage, your convictions. You came as a big surprise and curiosity in my burned-out life. For long, I had determined not to think about any man in my life at all. You shattered it all. I fell down to the ground as a broken glass. But it was none of your doing, all mine, but now I am well over it."

They both sat for several minutes as if they were all talked out. Presently, Sukannya sat erect, rubbed her eyes gently with the back of her hands, pulled her hair back and tied it tight, and looked at him as if it was a new day and a new beginning. She made an effort to smile and asked, "Joshua, you will be leaving tomorrow, and do you think we will meet again, ever, in this life or another? What do you think?"

"Sukannya," said Joshua, "this life on earth is definitely not the end of anything; it's only the beginning of our eternal life, life in heaven. Yes, I believe we will certainly meet." Then he turned to her and asked, "What do you think?"

She smiled innocently and said, "I think never. This life of us in this world is a one-time deal. I don't even believe what the other Buddhists believe. There is no wandering of the spirits or reincarnations. This is it. The moment the spirit leaves my body, I die, and my subtle conscience, which you may call soul, will dissolve in the emptiness of the universe where it came from. I will have no awareness of myself, as I do not exist anymore."

"I respect your view, but I tell you this: man is the supreme creation of God; there must be a purpose in our creation; it cannot just flame out like that and end up uneventfully in the emptiness you are talking about. There must be another life awaiting us. Otherwise, this life does not make any sense."

"Then, Joshua, you look for me there; we will catch up with our unfinished business at this hermitage." Her face glowed when she said this, but for him it was difficult to fathom whether it was agony or ecstasy.

Early the next morning she went to bathe as Joshua was getting ready to leave. She came back to the kitchen quickly, prepared a flour cake, and warmed up a cup of goat milk for his breakfast, and sat by his side as he ate it. "You are going to be in Mathura for a few days, right?"

"Yes, at least for a week, until I get a caravan or horse cart to go with."

"I wish you reach home safe, you traveler," she said with a husky voice, as she swallowed heavily. Then she turned her face away from him, unnoticeably opened a small cotton purse tied to her loin, took out the two gold coins that she had sheltered for long, and grabbed his hand. She opened his fist, placed the two coins in his palm, and folded it firmly, holding over it, and begged, "Please don't say 'no,' Joshua. This is all the wealth I have . . . got it from my mother . . . I have no need for it . . . you might need it on the way." She pulled his hands closer to her face and kissed on it for a long minute as tears poured down from her eyes into the cup of his hands.

Joshua stood frozen, unable to speak.

Then he turned around and pulled her close to him, and he held her for a long while, both of them silent. Finally, he ended their embrace, saying, "I will keep these gold coins for long, Sukannya. I know I will see you again." He kissed on both her eyes, gripped on her shoulders firmly, and shook her to awake, pursing his lips and looking deep into her eyes. She woke up, and their eyes met again for the last time. This time there was a subtle smile on both of them.

Visal was waiting near the banyan tree carrying one of his bags as ordered by the Maha Rishi. Joshua adjusted the sling of his bag across his chest and started off to Mathura. Sukannya slowly came down to the front yard; she walked behind him for a few steps up to the threshold of the compound fence and stood there looking at the slowly disappearing traveler.

In the early spring, the city of Mathura woke to life with the clatter of the wares and the shrill cry of the hawkers, with the usual trade, commerce and tourists. Joshua stayed at a wayside inn, awaiting the first caravan going west, which was scheduled to leave within two weeks. Visal was instructed to stay with him until he departed – a special instruction from Maha Rishi.

Narayan, the inn keeper, was a man in his fifties, a Vaisya by color, and an interesting conversationalist. He was very interested to hear that Joshua had escaped the earthquake in Taxila.

The next day or so, Joshua was walking the neighborhood clad in a saffron gown with Visal. Joshua didn't let Visal walk behind him; instead, they walked together. Narayan was unhappy and concerned about his gust. He came running behind him and said, "Mater please go back to the inn now . . . please now." Joshua obliged, and asked what the matter was.

"People will think you are Buddhist . . . not safe . . . many are killed . . . not safe," he said humbly.

Later it was revealed that there was much hostility and brutal attacks against the Buddhists by fundamentalist Hindus in many parts of the northern cities of India. At a Vihara in Indra-Prastha, nearly five hundred monks and nuns were murdered in the middle of the night. Many Buddhists were abandoning their houses and escaping to China and to the lands of the east and the islands of the south.

Why is it so that the Buddhists are attacked, Joshua wondered. Narayan knew the answer.

"The upper-class Hindus are very upset," he said. "Many people . . . converted to Buddhism. Master, I am also Buddhist, but I don't show it. The Bhrahmins fear; they lose the power. The country may go back to Buddhist . . . like Ashoka."

Violence in the name of beliefs, Joshua contemplated, *my God is better than yours; my God is stronger than yours. What is the end for this human madness? Who can stop these atrocities?* He once again remembered what the Greeks had said: 'Are the Gods blind?'

It was few more days before he could catch a caravan going west. He spent the days and nights thinking about and preaching about a world, a world of love and harmony, the Kingdom of Heaven on Earth.

But for the occasional early spring rains, the land was mostly shrouded with a fog so thick that it seemed as if the clouds had fainted and fallen from the sky. On the seventh day of his stay at the inn, Joshua was lounging outside on the porch, wrapped in the thick woolen shawl that Sukannya had made for him, making notes on his papyrus from Amarna, the pearls of wisdom he had learned from his travels.

He saw Kishan emerging out of the fog, approaching the lodge and Vishal going out to meet him, and both of them conversed for a few seconds near the gate. Presently, Visal crumpled to the ground wailing with the sounds of grief and sadness, a wailing so deep that

Joshua was alarmed and he sprung to his feet. Kishan clasped Visal, attempting to console him. Did something happen to the Maha Rishi? he wondered.

Both of them walked slowly towards Joshua, their eyes red, tears rolling down. "What's the matter, Kishan," Joshua inquired.

Kishan replied, his shoulders heaving from his sobs, "Yogini Sukannya attained nirvana the night before."

Joshua stood transfixed. After a while Kishan continued. "Yogini went into meditation almost immediately after you left. She continued meditating for six nights and six days without even a sip of water. Six days and six nights, Arya," he said, supporting himself with the column on the veranda.

"What did Maha Rishi do with that kind of extreme fasting?"

"The first evening, he didn't come to the hut as he was fasting. On the second evening when he came, Yogini was in deep meditation. She had written a note to Pitha Maha that she was offering a Maha-yoga and was not to be disturbed. On the third day onwards, Maha Rishi spent the whole time with her in the house, speaking to her slowly, gently and continuously. She didn't move. She didn't reply. All the relatives were summoned yesterday."

Joshua sank to his seat with his hands folded over his heart and gazed up to the heavens.

"The night before last she fully attained nirvana . . . sitting. This morning she was cremated near the hermitage. Today at sunset her ashes will be sprinkled in the holy Yamuna." Still sobbing and weeping, Kishan sat down, hugging his knees.

Joshua sat on the chair the whole night, praying and meditating. The yogini who lifted the subtle conscience in his soul, the woman who loved him dearly, the teacher who had taught him for two years, did she sacrifice her life for him? He wondered. Her words rang in his mind again and again, "Joshua, will we meet again ever?

Visal remained with Joshua until the caravan moved west. The traveler was finally on his way back home.

BOOK IX
Joshua in Israel

On the highway from Damascus to Ptolemais, in the heat of a late summer evening in the month of Elul, a caravan crawled to a stop at the crossroads on the hilltop in Sepphoris near the old Temple. A lone traveler emerged with two bags, one slung across his chest and the other held in his right hand. His journey had come full circle. Joshua kneeled to the ground, kissed the soil and rested his brow on the soil for a long minute. As he stood up, the sun behind him descended, and his shadow, twice as long as him, seemed to gaze at him, asking, "Where have you been all these years? Did you abandon the land of your forefathers?"

"No. No," he said to himself, "I was born a Jew, I was raised a Jew, and I will die a Jew." He stepped on his shadow and began the descent to the verdant orchards of Galilee through the rough, rutted road leading to Nazareth.

The evening air was warm and dry. His throat was parched, his lips hard and cracked, but as the evening breeze brought the fragrance of the orchards of Galilee, he forgot the fatigue of his long journey from Taxila. The boughs of the apple trees hung low with heavy clusters of red and green fruits. As the winds continued to blow, the leaves rustled with the music of the orchard. Succulent bunches of grapes swung on their vines, collided, and spilled their purple juice. He could hear the hum of the bees as they hopped from one grape to another.

Joshua entered the orchard, pulled his bag from his shoulders, and sat under a vine arbor. He reached into his bag for a knife, cut down a large bunch of grapes, and devoured them, the sweet purple juice squirting from the corners of his mouth to his tattered tunic. The nectar of the grapes moistened his lips, and pacified both his thirst and his hunger. He reveled in the sweet familiarity of his homeland, and though he had been away for nearly half of his days, it still felt like home.

A great bunch of fruit flies hovered around his face like a faint hallow, while a little lizard hanging upside down as if holding up a large bunch of pomegranates stared at him, jerking its head from one side to the other. Joshua smiled as he got up, positioned his bag slung across his shoulders, and started down towards home. He tasted with delight the sweet smell of the air swept away from the grapes, olives, figs and almonds.

As evening fell, the golden rays of the setting sun reflected on the silver-green leaves of the olive branches dancing in the breeze. They shimmered like a million tiny candles lit for the welcome reception of the son of Israel. The birds flew low to their nests to roost, the little birds from the tree tops sang their songs, and the crickets chirped in harmony.

As he approached the low-lying farmer's hamlet, the evening noises of the villages came to life, dogs barking in the distant villages, the donkeys braying, children laughing, and the women chanting the melodies of the evening prayers as they set their tables for the family meals.

As the sky turned gray, the first lights of the villages by the roadside began to shimmer on top of the bushels. Joshua moved to side quietly, watching as the men goaded their herds home. The aromas of roasting lamb and spices swirled up from the flues of the little white flat-roofed houses, and Joshua inhaled so deeply that he could almost taste them. "Yes, I am finally home."

He could barely contain his desire to see his little house where the poplars and the old cypress stood guard, to bite into a morsel of bread and share a cup of wine with his aching woman. Or do I have the right? A sudden sense of foreboding gripped him. His heart raced and he broke into a sweat. Joshua breathed heavily, feeling an odd combination of guilt and apprehension like Arjuna in the battlefield. Presently, he heard a strong voice from inside, like Lord Krishna advising Arjuna in *Bhagavath Geetha*, "Joshua do not be bewildered; do your karma; move forward unfettered. Sacrifices you will have to make, but be true to the purpose of your creation; be strong and do your karma."

Thinking back on fifteen years of traveling the world and studying the works of so many philosophers and religious sages, he realized that he emerged with an unshakeable confidence. "I shall not be intimidated. I shall speak my mind," the thirty-year-old Joshua said to himself. Both embittered and emboldened, he turned to the final stretch of the country road towards Nazareth.

His body was fatigued and his face showed the years, but his mind remained tranquil and serene. He had reached a place of peace and calm. His vision was clear, his path well lit. He picked up his pace and walked with long, confident strides towards home. *Too many times these almonds have bloomed in Galilee, and I have not been here to see it,* he mused.

As Joshua neared the village gate of Nazareth, lightning pierced the pitch-dark skies, and for a flickering moment Joshua could see the giant cypress and poplars standing over the little flat-topped house.

Dogs barking at distances, some howling like wild foxes, like satanic voices piercing the night, echoed from one village to the other. The rain that began with a few drops became a waterfall as sheets of water poured down from the sky, one of those early rains of Elul destined to kill the heat of the night and the thirst of the earth. Joshua was drenched, and as he walked, his leather sandals splashing into the rapidly forming puddles.

The lightning further cleaved the skies as he stood at the threshold of the front yard of his house under the poplar. After a moment, a six-year-old boy came out running into the rain. Then the boy hesitated for a moment, looked into the stranger's eyes and cried boldly, "Are you Joshua, my father?"

Joshua threw his bags to the ground and hugged the boy. "Yes my son, I am."

This time Joshua's mother, now frail and looking much older than her age, lifted the lamp to his face. He looked at her, soaking in her smile, the one thing about her that remained unchanged.

Mary, who had been washing the dishes, nearly dropped them as she ran to the threshold of the foyer, her hands still dripping wet. She stopped for a moment, staring at his face with an expression of disbelief coupled with ecstasy. She then took a half step back reflexively and passively. Her lips were painted red, her hair perfumed. She stared at the man without a wink. Her once young husband looked a lot older than his thirty years. His once golden hair had darkened to a deep brown; the beard had grown long and was highlighted with silver streaks. The years that had passed were carved into his forehead as three shallow, long lines, the skin around his eyes crinkled, and the once blue eyes now hazel with rings at the rim. Though he looked weary, she noted that his voice resonated more deeply. *Yes, this is my Joshua*, she thought, *but not the one that left me so long ago.*

That night they talked for hours on end, and it was Mary who finally said, "Joshua, I realize the passion and the calling in you. Your path ahead is perilous and littered with danger. I will not ask you to stay back for my sake or our son's. All the things you told me tonight make a lot of sense. I want you to go. So long as I know that you are safe and well; that is all I care about."

"So, you heard about the earthquake in Taxila?"

"Yes, from the caravan riders we heard that the whole city was in ruins and nobody survived."

"Maybe it's like I am born again," Joshua said.

"I don't doubt it a bit, Joshua. You are a new man; you are certainly born again for a new life, a new purpose."

Mary was resolved. Joshua started his public mission in Galilee.

It was the time of hot winds, dry air and grape harvesting in Galilee. Absorbed in deep thought and contemplating the next step in his life, Joshua sauntered through the villages of Galilee talking to people and listening to them, observing their lives, and discerning their hopes and fears, feeling compassion for their plights.

In the vineyards, women with covered heads and children with bare chests stood in rows, carefully clipping and collecting the grapes in their bushels tied to their backs. The men, walking in line, carried heavy baskets filled to the brim with freshly picked grapes to the wine presses. There were scantily clad skinny men stomping the grapes in wooden vats, and yoked mules rotating the millstones, pressing out the last drops of purple juice. They all worked for pittance, as if resigned to their lot. In their midst, were gaily dressed rich men carried on a litters finding fault and screaming admonitions.

Porters with sunken eyes and bony chests kneaded clay on their wheels. Older women spun threads and knitted mittens. The younger women drew water from the village wells, and shepherds tended their herds, fed the sheep, and sheared the fleeces. Joshua watched the fishermen patiently waiting for the fish to bite, while old, black-robed Rabbis with long white beards seemed to float down the country roads carrying their leather-bound holy books. Then there were the crying babies and consoling mothers; such were the people of Galilee.

Many shared with him their beliefs that tomorrow would be no better than the day before. They would wake up weary, still ruled by the Romans, and with no opinion, voice or land of their own. Joshua saw a nation choked with desperation, poverty and hopelessness.

One morning, Joshua found four men sitting tight on the old carpenter's work bench under the poplar tree in front of his house. Perched like ravens in a tree on a rainy day, they waited patiently for him to wake up, knowing not that Joshua had already left before the first light of day to take his daily contemplation walk.

The men stood as they saw Joshua approaching from a distance. The men, in their late twenties or early thirties, were all thin, but of good substance and solidly built. Two of them wore daggers about their waist belts. Joshua saw them and quickened his pace as he approached them, shifting his gazing from one face to the other. The sudden flash of recognition pleased him, and he cried with a smile, "Ah! You are Benjamin, son of Amalak?"

"Yes, Joshua. I am glad that you remembered me, but you are difficult to recognize. The young golden boy – Joshua, you have changed a lot!" cried Benjamin. The two of them hugged each other and kissed on either side of their cheeks. The men, Benjamin, Barnabas, Daniel and David, were all from the Turan valley, northeast of Sepphoris.

The old friends settled down on the work bench. "Joshua, for quite some time, in fact, for several years, we have been searching for you. Where have you been?" demanded David, a stocky man with brown eyes and a dark bushy beard.

Daniel said, "You seem to have come back out of nowhere and the timing is perfect. We need your help. Tomorrow evening there will be a meeting of our brothers in the house of Simon."

"Simon is my brother," said Barnabas, one of the men with the daggers by his belt.

They continued speaking in hushed voices, flailing their arms and gesturing with conviction. Joshua finally shook his head in acceptance and the four men quickly left.

Joshua would soon discover that he had returned to a Galilee quite different from the one he had left. Beneath the simple tranquility, he would discover that the land of Israel was roused with frightful convulsions of rebellion and violent cries for liberty. There was tension in the air and fear in the minds of a people who had been crushed by Roman brutality. Israel had become a nation weak and paranoid. Most hesitated to speak their minds for fear of Roman retribution. Others feared the stones of the Pharisees and distrusted the groveling of the Sadducees to enslave them.

The country had become a cauldron, boiling with conflicting camps. Recalcitrant zealots determined to slit every Roman throat, resolved to win their freedom, and were willing to choose death over enslavement. In contrast were the Sadducees, who cowered and licked the boots of their oppressors and the complacent Pharisees felicitous with their convenient tithes. The meek Essenes wailed aloud about the last days of Solomon and met secretly in caves. The once proud Zion was now crushed under the yoke of oppression. Then there were the squatters, the anarchists and situationalists amidst the vast ocean of poor slaves, farmers and fisherman – a house divided against itself, speaking in many tongues, like at the tower of Babel. It was, indeed, a different Israel that Joshua walked into this time, a population ripe with violence, helpless and hopeless, and ready for harvest with the sickle of hope.

**** **** ****

About a mile northeast of the city of Sepphoris in the Turan Valley, the lone house of Simon stood on a small rise facing the setting sun amidst a wooded area with no houses nearby. About an hour before sunset, when Joshua reached the house, there were already some thirty men assembled under the shady trees in the backyard of his house, some sitting, some stretching on the ground, some raised up on their elbows, some leaning against the tree trunks, and some idling here and there, but all were engaged in whispering dialogues. Most of them were armed with swords and daggers, not so concealed under their long gowns. Shortly after Joshua arrived, Barnabas got on with the business of the evening.

"Dear brothers," he addressed the crowd, "we have added three more members today." He introduced a bronze-skinned, bearded man with a shallow nose bridge and thick lips as Judas from Kerioth.

Another man, a fair-skinned and tall Shaashgse from Rumah. Lastly, he introduced Joshua from Nazareth. He continued, "I know Barabbas was in Sepphoris last night. He will arrive here after the sun sets, but we can begin now," he said with an official-sounding tone.

From about the middle of the crowd, a middle-aged man with a gray beard and low set eyes stood up. He grinned and began to speak.

"Last week in the town of Sogane," he said, "at the betrothal of Phoebe, daughter of that rascal Heroidian Methuselah, there was a great crowd of Pharisees, wine merchants and rich people, all celebrating with meat, wine and cakes. As the sun went down and as the wine got into their heads, I slipped in." He hushed the others, holding his palm about his mouth. "I did not drink any of their wine or eat the burnt calves. I stayed close to that bootlicker Blastus." He looked around. "When the noise was high and the knife went into the betrothal cake, mine went straight into his heart like . . . through a skinned goat." He pulled out a short, double-edged dagger from under his gown and waggled it around like a trophy. At this point, many of the others also pulled out their own daggers, waved them in solidarity, and cheered in hushed voices. "But I wailed for that bastard I killed." He attempted a smile by twisting the corner of his mouth and continued, "I even hugged his wife and gave a great cry while hot blood was gushing out of his chest like a gap in the Roman aqueduct." The crowd rejoiced with delight.

Joshua's face turned purple as he listened to the story and the cheers of the other men. He bit his lips and squeezed his hands together with indignation, but nobody noticed him in the fast darkening dusk.

Four men also shared stories that were even more brutal – stories retelling the cold-blooded murders of rich Jews and Pharisees.

In each case, a man or two from the group would sneak into a crowd of rich Jews and Pharisees at some kind of celebration. They mingled with them, posing as guests or participants, and at an opportune time, usually as the sun was going down and the wine had gone to their heads, they chose their victim, pulled out the hidden dagger and plunged it into his back or chest. Once the victim fell and the ensuing tumult began, the murderer pretended to be horrified, actively participating in the sobbing, wailing and other displays of false grief.

They were all members of an underground Jewish group named Sicarii. The group was founded eighty years earlier to protest the heavy poll tax introduced by the Roman governor Quirinias. The Sicarii believed that the Jews who supported Herod were even more contemptuous than the Romans themselves.

As the night fell, the backyard was pitch dark except for a foggy square of light peeking out of the rear door of the house lighting a small portion of the crowd. A streak of light lit the left side of Joshua's face as well as a few additional men.

A young man with a thin face and luxuriant beard, who had been sitting next to Joshua, began to speak.

"I have learned," he said, "that four days from now at the Roman Theater in Sapporo, they are staging a Greek play. A great crowd is expected – Romans and their Jewish stooges. It will be a great opportunity; easy to enter; easy to exit. Are there two men amongst you who will go with me?" Joshua watched as ten daggers going up in the sky reflected in the slice of light.

Joshua rose.

"Brothers," he cried. The crowd grew quiet as all eyes turned to the carpenter from Nazareth.

"My dear brothers. Just like all of you, I also feel the pain and desperation of our people. I am with you. I am one among you. But tell me, how can we achieve a real and meaningful peace? This is the question that needs to be answered."

There was a commotion of whispering voices in the crowd as Joshua paused.

"Slaughter them! Slaughter the Romans like goats," one growled. The crowd echoed, "Amen. Slaughter the Romans like goats."

"Burn the Pharisees on the stakes," yelled another. The crowd repeated, "Amen. Burn the Pharisees on the stakes."

"Nail the scribes to the cross."

"Stone them."

"Burn them."

"Bury them."

As the grumbling grew up with heat, Barnabas stood up, spreading out his hands over the heads of the men. "Let him speak," he said.

"Who is he?" demanded another.

Joshua lifted his right hand and asked permission to speak. "I am Joshua from Nazareth," he stated soberly.

"Who is your father?" shouted another.

There was no reply.

"Who is your father?"

"Are you a bastard?" cried one.

"I was born to Joseph of Nazareth. But I am the son of the Almighty Father in heaven."

This time the crowd broke into disdainful laughter.

"Ha! What does that mean? You think you are the Messiah, the promised one of the house of King David?" one of the men asked.

Some of the men began to laugh; others spat on the ground in disgust.

Joshua remained calm.

"No, he must be the Prophet Daniel, born again," another man yelled.

"Is your father the Prophet Ezekiel?" asked another one scornfully, showing all his almond-colored teeth.

"Do you think you're the Prophet Elijah?" asked another man. "His Father in heaven. Phoo . . . hmm."

"Please, please, hear me out," Joshua yelled.

The crowd slowly turned silent, and Joshua began to speak.

"Brothers, do you really believe that this violence is going to bring us peace? Has any meaningful peace ever been achieved by violent means? Is it not written that 'thou shalt not kill'?" Joshua paused briefly and continued in a deeper, more resonating and commanding voice, "I tell you this, my brothers: violence only breeds more violence.

A sword against a sword shall keep the blood spilling, limbs falling, and heads rolling. Remember, we ran over the Canaanites with our mighty swords. We felled cities and cut them to waste, kings and kingdoms, one after the other, all thirty and one of them. Did we achieve peace?"

There was a brief silence.

The place was filled with overwrought men, burning with anger and indignation, fatigued faces, hollowed cheeks, hungry bowels, grinding teeth, clamoring for revenge. These men had no patience for such nonsense. "You are a false prophet." One man yelled. Then the entire assembly took up the chant screaming, "False prophet."

"Have you not read the Torah?"

"Did we not establish the kingdom of Zion?"

"Did Solomon not build the Temple of Jerusalem?"

"Yes," Joshua replied, "but did we achieve perpetual peace? We fought amongst ourselves, divided the Promised Land. Israel became easy prey to the Assyrians. Then a nation with a sharper sword came upon us, raised our temple to the ground, killed our people, raped our women, enslaved the rest, and exiled to Babylon."

Again there was a brief moment of silence. "Did Nebuchadnezzar achieve perpetual peace? Another nation with a bigger sword, the Persians, ran over them, ransacked their cities, and the Jews were freed. But did we achieve freedom? The slaves remained the same, only the slave masters changed."

The crowd settled a bit. Some seemed willing to at least hear him out. Others nodded their heads when he spoke.

"Did the Persians enjoy lasting peace?"

One meek voice from the crowd answered, "No." Joshua looked to that corner and continued, "Then a much bigger tyrant came upon us – Alexander. We were again slaves under a different slave master. The Greeks started rituals to Apollo at the Temple of Jerusalem."

At this moment, Judas of Kerioth stood up face to face with Joshua, "But Rabbi, Judas Maccabeus and our heroic Jews slaughtered them and we established a nation. Did you forget . . . your prophet?" He uttered the words with contempt and spat.

"Brother," Joshua replied, "A much bigger nation descended upon us – the Romans. We are again slaves. Now you fight them with daggers and knives as we did for thousands of years without any success. They respond with stoning, burning, and nailing on wooden crosses. Do you ever think this will end? Do you truly believe that the Romans are the final occupants of this Promised Land? I say to you, no."

"The way to achieve peace is not with a sword against a sword. *They, who taketh the sword shall ultimately perish by the sword.* Blood against blood shall flood the world stinking red. Therefore, I beseech you, put away your swords. Learn to love your enemy."

The voices of disapproval rose as a tumult. Some murmured with anger, some guffawed with disgust, and some spat on the ground.

From the back corner, a rough voice charged with anger and hostility shouted, "Rabbi, tell me of one war that has been won without a sword?" The man, Barabbas from Judea, was two heads taller than the rest. He began moving towards Joshua, his eyes bulging, his chin jutting forward over his thick bull neck. Waving a double-edged dagger and carrying a short thick sword, he continued to guffaw in disgust. Getting close enough to touch Joshua's nose, he thrust forward his large red beard and pointed his finger, shouting, "It won't be long before there shall be vestal virgins in the Temple of Jerusalem. Remember, we are slaves of Romans. The Romans dictate the rules, the Pharisees execute them, and the Jews suffer them. Fool. We need to smite them, smite them now, smite them hard." There were cheers and applause for Barabbas.

In a loud voice, Joshua responded, "Tell me, brother. What is the victory in a war after all? Is it not the count of heads without a shoulder and tallying the numbers on either side? War!" cried Joshua, "war only brings forth misery for people, suffering on men and destruction to the people. War shall never yield peace. It has but only one outcome – destruction. It is merely the degree of destruction that separates the winner from the loser, and in war there is no true peace and no real winner, only losses and losers. We all lose. If you kill one Roman, they will crucify seven Jews and torture seventy. Therefore, I tell you, fight your enemy with a weapon that he cannot resist. Fight your enemy with the weapon that pierces not the heart, but his soul. Fight your enemy with love, courage and resiliency. Caesar is mighty in hand, but empty in soul. We shall conquer Rome, conquer we will, not with the might of the sword that spills the blood, but with the strength of love that fills their minds. Conquer we will, I assure you. The throne on which Caesar sits now, shall be occupied by the ministers of my Father in heaven. If they slap you on your right cheek, show him the left." His eyes beamed with radiance as he turned around observing the crowd.

Amidst the tumult of disgust that followed, Barabbas guffawed from behind, "What will you do, carpenter boy, if the Romans stab you in your chest? Will you simply turn around and show them your back, too?"

The crowd broke out into rapacious laughter.

"Spilling blood is our destiny, brethren. Blood spilled for a just cause is never a drop wasted for a noble cause. Death is nothing to fear. Like birth, death is just a manifestation of God. If you have lived your life justly, I assure you, you have secured a place in the Kingdom of Heaven, the kingdom of my loving Father."

"Joshua, are you an agent of Caiaphas?" a man asked.

"Caiaphas is a Jewish rogue with a Roman heart," Barabbas yelled. "This carpenter boy does not know how to cut the wood or slice the throats," he said disdainfully, and spat in the air.

"Rabbi, you know not what is happening. My own brother was crucified last week. He was not openly accused of anything, no known offence," he said. Blood rose to his face, and his muscles twitched. "There are no more virgin Jewish girls since the Romans took over. They take our women and do whatever they want."

"We must kill all the rich. The poor may have their morsels of bread," said another.

"Sacrifices are offered to Caesar in the Temple of Jerusalem."

"They have brought a golden idol of Tiberius for the Temple."

"Where is the Promised Land?"

"Where is the milk? Where is the honey?"

"You are a paid pacifier, an agent of Caesar. Show the left cheek. Phoo." Barabbas moved to the light at the door and faced the crowd.

"Israel can never be saved by love or clasped hands like this carpenter boy prays," he said. "This nation was built by the sword. It shall sustain by the sword. It shall be victorious by the sword." He took out his short, thick sword and brandished it around in the air with its gray metal reflections. "It is about time to rewrite the words. An eye for an eye – I say a hundred eyes for one eye." The crowd became reinvigorated after the dull somber talk of Joshua.

Barabbas continued as he threw his heavy arms around Joshua's shoulders, "We are the citizens of Israel, but slaves of Rome. Slaves forever! We work only to pay taxes to Caesar. The Romans wish it, Caiaphas executes it, and we suffer it, I told you. We have only one thing to do." He raised his sword high up in the air. "Slice their throats. Our Promised Land has turned into a whore, fornicated by civilizations of all kinds. Let us spread out her legs. Let the Roman blood fill her womb, not their rotten seeds. That is our duty, our destiny."

Barabbas stomped into the darkness.

An older man with a gray beard and thinning hair came to Joshua and in a relatively calm voice said, "Joshua, you are young. I have seen many more Sabbaths and Hanukkahs than you. The primary duty of a Jew is to observe the Torah and preserve this Promised Land. It is the inheritance of our people from the Lord of Abraham, Isaac and Jacob. Obeying the laws and commandments as told to us by Moses is our duty. The Jews that disobey the holy Torah: stone them. Infidels who invaded our land: slay them. The Jew who plays host to the Romans: nail them. I am ready to kill. I am ready to die for the deliverance of Israel." Then he silently walked to the rear of the crowd.

Barnabas approached Joshua with a firm face, flailing his hands, and shouted sarcastically, "Joshua, what is this Kingdom of Heaven of which you speak? Of whose 'father's house' you are talking? You are confusing the issue here. For me life is here today, now in my wretchedness, in my slavery, and in my humiliation. What good is it to suffer like this now, and hope for peace in another life that I do not know? For me this is heaven, the land of milk and honey, this land, my Israel. Tomorrow is unborn, uncertain." Then Barnabas walked out into the rear of the crowd.

Joshua raised both of his hands again for attention. "Brothers, please hear me out. We have been warring with our enemies all along. Now, we are warring amongst ourselves as well. What have we become as a people? Jews murdering Jews. Jews enslaving Jews. Jews turned against Jews. We have become a house divided against itself. We have become a nation of different people talking different languages. First, we have to unite, not with war and not with vengeance, but with love and compassion. So long as our minds are filled with anger and vengeance, we are at war with ourselves. Let us go back to the essence of our beings. Eliminate the feelings of anger and possession from our minds. Love our enemy, respect our neighbor. Let us live in peace."

"Will your love bring peace to this land? Will your love liberate us from bondage?" demanded Nathan, a thin man with a pointed mouth and slanted eyes.

"I tell you yes," Joshua said. "Violence is not the means to bring peace; peace is the means to end violence. A dagger against a dagger is the death of both. Anger is our enemy. Vengeance is our downfall. When anger and vengeance is within you, the enemy is within you."

A tumult rose in the crowd, a thunder of disgust and disapproval. Then an old man, his head and shoulders covered with a tallit, his long nose stuck out, rose to his feet and said calmly: "The Romans are strong in their arms. They are merciless killers. How are you, young man, going to fight them with your love? How do you calm a raging bull with your words of love?" Then he sat down quietly.

"Yes, the Romans are mighty with weapons, but empty in their hearts. We will reward their anger with love. We will fill their hearts with compassion. When you are slapped on the right cheek, show them the left. But first, let us, the people of Israel and Judea, be together, be peaceful and united, speaking with one voice."

The crowd laughed disdainfully against murmurs of disapproval.

"Rabbi," Nathan raised his hand for his attention, "You heard Barabbas. When they dig you in the chest . . .?" Again there was noise of ridicule.

"There is no metal that will not melt in the heat of love," Joshua said. "There are no stones hard enough that cannot be shaped with a chisel into a delicate form. Winning the heart of your enemy is the real victory, not counting the dead ones. No honorable warrior or valiant soldier will want to slay an unarmed man asking for peace and love."

"Rabbi, you are not speaking as a devout Jew. We are a people to rule over the world. We speak to our enemy with swords, not words," Simon said.

Jacob, a balding man with a puffy face and large bags below his eyes, stood up and asked soberly, "Rabbi, suppose the Romans break into my house, murder my son and rape my wife. Am I to show the other cheek to him, and give him my daughter as well?"

"Brother." There was a sense of authority in his voice. "Do not misjudge apathy to duty, indifference to responsibility, or negligence to justice. Closing your eyes to violence is to promote it, not speaking against it is to encourage it, and not acting against it is to justify it. Violating children and desecrating women are the most horrific abominations of all. You are justified to tie millstones on their necks and send them to the deepest fathom of the ocean, those violators."

There was a long silence after that dialogue. People looked at each other, raising their eyebrows and with half-open mouths. As time went on, they interrupted far less frequently. There were very many questions, but his calm approach, unantagonizing answers, his soft and deep captivating voice and endearing smile had a calming effect on the crowd. Though most of them did not agree with his views, and some of them violently opposed to his thoughts, all of them wanted to hear more from him. More answers about the very many questions they had in mind. By midnight, the meeting had ended, but this time there were no solemn oaths holding onto their short daggers to kill more like the times before.

Some people in the corners whispered to the others in their ears.

"Look at him. He speaks with such authority. Could he be the Messiah?" Yet others muttered under their breath, "He speaks of things that Daniel or Elijah failed to mention, about hope." The man with the puffy eyes even doubted that he was the one that they expected for long.

After the others had left, Judas, Simon, Labbaeus, Benjamin and David remained at the house of Barnabas. But Judas was the only one who openly said, "Joshua I liked the way you talked. Your words make a lot of sense to me. You speak in such a way that your words stick in the mind. I believe you are correct. There must be some other way to our salvation other than killing the Romans."

Simon, deep in his thoughts, remained silent throughout the evening, and looked repeatedly at Joshua, trying to read his face. He said, "We have sunset meetings in virtually every village in Galilee, in Saab, in Sogane, in Garis, and in Ramah. We speak of things that are entirely different from what you say. Would you come with us and speak to our people in those meetings?"

Joshua smiled. "Brother," he said, "I will go anywhere, everywhere. I will speak to people willing to listen, and I will speak even more to people unwilling to listen."

Joshua ate and slept under the roof of Barnabas that night. He was deep in thoughts that night, happy that he was able to address the people and saddened to see the violent mood of the crowd. *Do they really know these Romans?* he wondered. They will all hang on crosses in no time. All the men of Israel, all with any size and substance, will all be annihilated. I have to speak up more. I shall not permit that. I have to fulfill my karma. I have to. The picture of Krishna advising Arjuna came to his mind. He drifted into a short sleep.

Over the next few months Joshua traveled to many villages in Galilee. He attended meetings by night and walked the places by day, speaking to people in the villages, on the streets, in the vineyards, cornfields, orchards, on the corners of the streets, and by the village wells. Some began to follow him, some simply liked him, but most didn't pay any attention. He found the most listening ears amongst men working in the fields and women by the well drawing water.

One dreary afternoon, late in the month of Tishrei after the early rains had begun, two men of the village hurried to the carpenter's house, one sobbing and panting. "Rabbi, rabbi," the elder one cried out from the front yard." Joshua came asking, "What is the matter?"

"Rabbi, they are about to stone a woman at the village gate. Please come. The elders of the village have just released her to the crowd. Please come, quickly. A poor simple girl, the locksmith's daughter; please save her," said the one who was sobbing.

Who am I to go there and save the woman? he thought. Still I must voice against injustice, my karma, my call. Joshua ran with them to the village gate, which was only five houses and some bare land away, memories of Rachel returning once again. Outside the east end gates of Nazareth, a large crowd had formed.

From a distance Joshua heard the roar of a crowd. There were at least fifty men wielding stones in their hands. The men had formed two tight circles around a woman crouched on the ground, sobbing and wailing. Her eyes darted back and forth, like an animal surrounded by hunters. Even as she sobbed and wailed, she knew her fate had already been determined.

As Joshua approached the scene, one among the crowd shouted, "Look who is coming." A few turned around and saw Joshua walking towards them. The men parted as Joshua walked to the center of the crowd.

The woman, her face swollen with grief, stretched out her arms pleading, "Have mercy on me." Her voice was hoarse and weak, her clothing, dirty, nearly shredded. The men shouted, "Harlot . . . harlot . . . slut . . . adulteress, filth of the village . . ." Joshua looked at the crowd and took another step into the circle; the woman slumped to the ground, placid and listless.

Joshua raised his hands, grasped the woman by her hands, and lifted her up. The trembling woman crumpled against him, attempting to cover her breasts. For a few moments all was silent, but the sobs of the condemned woman. The men seemed confused and stood with stones in their hands, awaiting the final signal to begin.

Joshua, still holding the hand of the condemned woman, turned slowly, his eyes scanning the circle, staring at the men one face at a time. Joshua, a head taller than the rest of the men surrounding him, stood calm at the epicenter of the scene. His face was calm, but his eyes glowed like burning charcoal. Joshua lifted the woman's hand up to the sky and declared, "This woman is a daughter of Abraham. Imagine that she is your wife, your sister, your mother, your daughter. She may have come to her desperation – hunger, poverty and ignorance. Perhaps she was a victim, violated by men for their lust, wretched pleasures of the flesh. Tell me," Joshua asked, pointing to the faces in the crowd, "Who has defiled this daughter of Israel? Where is the man or the men who have defiled and violated her? Should he not be stoned, too? Yes, a coward . . . a brute . . . now hiding in shame . . . a man, perhaps even one amongst you now . . . you hypocrites!"

His penetrating eyes bore through the crowd. He issued his invitation in a voice simple and strong. "Come forward, if there is one amongst you who is without sin and cast the first stone upon this woman." Joshua slowly turned around with the woman, again searching their faces one after the other. Each man, as his eyes met Joshua's, dropped his gaze to the ground. There was a long minute of strained silence. A few stones dropped to the ground. A thin man with a pockmarked face and dark bushy beard raised the stone in his hand and waved it at Joshua, and guffawed contemptuously, "Are you without sin, prophet?"

Joshua turned to him calmly and said, "I too am a sinner, brother." The man angrily hurled the stone to the ground and walked away. Others who had raised their hands stopped mid-way. More stones dropped to the ground, and several men turned and walked away, their heads down, but a few remained.

Finally, a frail old man with thin hair and sunken eyes began to weep uncontrollably. He kneeled before Joshua and began to kiss his feet. A young boy of eleven with a bony bear chest, with snot dribbling, flung his arms around the weeping woman and began to comfort her. Joshua lifted the man to his feet. The man raised his hands to the heavens and proclaimed, "Rabbi, rabbi. You are an angel from heaven. You saved the life of my daughter."

Joshua turned to the woman, looking into her eyes. "Go home now," he said softly. Repent of your sins and live a better life." The three of them slowly disappeared.

The story of the 'un-stoning the harlot' spread like wildfire in the villages of the Galilee. When the news reached the Pharisees, they were outraged.

But something new was happening.

Poor and working families around the dinner tables, women around the village wells, workers in their farms, and men in their wine presses began to talk about the carpenter Rabbi, his courage, conviction, and the message he was sharing.

"Look at him. His face shines like the lights of a hundred lamps," said the people.

"He speaks with such calm and authority," commented some elderly men.

"His voice is powerful, yet he does not shout," said many.

"His presence is comforting," said the destitutes.

"His words are healing," said the ill and the meek.

"The words come from his mouth like rose petals," said the women.

"He is brave. He is a savior, a Messiah for us," many said.

It was not long before every woman in Galilee had heard the story of how Joshua had saved the condemned woman. This story, with its unlikely outcome, created hope where there had been no hope, and they privately rejoiced.

Thereafter, wherever Joshua walked the streets, heads turned to look at him. The women particularly made an effort to get even a glimpse of him. They peered from behind the gates, tiptoed from behind the hedges, through half-open windows, from rooftops shading their eyes and some even made excuses to go to the street when Joshua was passing by.

Whenever Joshua went out to the streets or to the little synagogues in Nazareth, people would gather around to ask questions – not only about the stoning incident, but also of the many laws and statutes in the Torah. Very soon the people around him swelled mostly to listen and learn from him, but some, including the Pharisees, tried to discredit him with tricky questions.

On a Sabbath day in the month of Tevet, the elders asked Joshua to read the Scriptures and speak to the people at the synagogue in Nazareth. Joshua was thirty years then. He was not unknown to the crowd, but people had known that he had been for many years from the land of Israel. Young Mary also had accompanied him to the synagogue.

It was a small synagogue fashioned like a humble Greek temple, open to the sunset and facing Jerusalem. It stood on four large Doric columns, had a spacious open hall, a small platform at the rear, and a stone enclosure with a single door behind where the scrolls were kept.

Joshua sat cross-legged on the platform, with about thirty men and children sitting at his feet, and about fifteen women at a distance to the right on the threshold of the square, standing, faces down, with their heads covered.

First, Joshua waved the women to come to the floor and to sit by his left, which raised some eyebrows in the crowd at the very outset.

"Brothers and sisters, children of Israel," he said. First, he read a passage from Deuteronomy. "And you shall overthrow their altars and break their pillars and burn their groves and fire . . ." It was a passage known to the crowd, and there was nothing new about it.

Then he paused, put the scroll back in the box, and faced the group. A few years ago, I learned a parable from a gentile sage from the far east." The elder of the synagogue who had invited Joshua was a bit puzzled with that introduction, but he, men, and women gazed at him attentively.

"The sage said our life on this earth is a journey, a journey to cross a raging river from one shore to the other, from the shore of pain, suffering and mortality to the shore of peace, hope and immortality. We are all passengers on that boat riding the same waters, breathing the same air, drinking the same water, eating the same food, and eager to reach the other shore safely. On that ship, is it not wise to live in peace and harmony, rather than revolt and fight, lest the boat sink. On that ship, is there any sense in saying I, me or mine. On that ship, is it not foolish to hate your neighbor and fight your enemy? In fact, is there an enemy on that boat at all?" Joshua paused for a moment for his words to sink in. His voice rose.

"Brothers and sisters, we are all passengers on the same boat. We all want to reach the other shore safely. In the scriptures it is written, love thy neighbor and hate your enemy." The crowd shook heads vertically and said, "Amen."

Presently, four men were seen approaching the synagogue from a distance. They appeared to be in a hurry. One man, tall and heavyset, dressed in silk robes, was a Pharisee. Following him were three black-bearded scribes dressed in white robes and carrying long staffs with shepherd's crooks. They came to the threshold of the hall and arrayed themselves, scowling at Joshua. Joshua nodded his head as a sign of welcome, and continued.

"But I say to you;" Joshua said, "Love thy enemy, too. Any man harboring hate in his mind, building up anger in his soul, is on the way to Satan.

"What good is it if you bring offerings to the temple when you harbor anger against your brother, hate for your neighbor, or lustful thoughts about your neighbor's wife? Repent. Repent on your sins, and cast off your anger, greed and lust from your mind."

The carpenter's speech was that of a different tone, a different tempo. Some didn't understand his message well – most did – but all liked his style. One or two old men turned their heads around, gently nodding, studying other faces and making sure that all were getting what the rabbi was saying.

"We are all transient in this world. Your body will wither away when the soul departs from you. You are only a caretaker of your soul for a short finite period of time. You came from dust; alas, with your last breath, you shall return to the dust again."

Joshua's voice rose: "Brethren, whatever wealth you have amassed on this earth, the many silos filled with grains, the many slaves you own, the treasure chests you have filled with gold, think for a moment . . . can you take any of them with you when you are dead and buried?"

Joshua paused for a long minute. It was obvious that his comments were not meant for the poor people sitting on the floor.

"Gold and silver are not the measures of wealth. If you have two, give one to the other who has none. Power and positions are all transitory. Purity of your soul is the wealth that is eternal. You are precious. You are the creation of Yahweh, created in his own image. Your body is the temple that holds the spirit in you, the heavenly spirit."

Those words struck a new uplifting chord in the hearts of his listeners. The lowly people of Nazareth, who had never heard such teaching, were transfixed, barely blinked, and breathed noiselessly. They looked around in unbelievable awe. "I am something; I am worthy of heaven?" they talked to themselves.

The four men began to ridicule Joshua, hissing and mocking him with laughter.

"Ha . . . ha . . . who is he talking? Carpenter prophet?" said the Pharisee standing tall with legs apart and his clenched fists fixed on his hips.

"Therefore, keep your temple pure," Joshua said, taking no notice of the antics of the visitors. "The moment your mind is invaded by greed, your temple is defiled, and becomes the seat of mammon. Greed: greed is the root cause of all abominations, cravings for pleasures, pleasures of wealth, flesh and power. Therefore, I say to you, cast out evil thoughts from your mind. Let your heart be pure so that you shall enter the Kingdom of Heaven."

That sharp statement form Joshua created a little tumult amongst the Pharisee and the scribes. One scribe even took a step forward, while another stomped the ground with his staff, but the Pharisee held them by the hand and pulled back.

"We are all travelers in this inn for a finite period of time," Joshua said. "We are all passengers on the same boat. Why this anger? Why this strife? Therefore, I say to you, love yourself first, the temple that houses the spirit of Heaven. Love thy neighbor. Love your enemy."

"Enough said," shouted the Pharisee. He pointed his staff to Joshua above the heads of the crowd.

Joshua rose and spread out his long hands over the people. "Fear not! We have everything to hope for. All of your worries and sufferings are temporary. All our hopes are eternal and immortal. Brothers and sisters, the Kingdom of Heaven is here and now. Discard your possessions and follow me to the villages of Israel and Judea. Let us spread the words of hope, words of peace, words of the Kingdom of Heaven. Once again I tell you I have come amongst you, my loving people, not to speak against Rome and not to raise my fist against Caesar."

The four visitors now pushed towards the platform where Joshua was speaking. Soon the Pharisee had placed his foot on the platform, preparing to climb.

Joshua continued as if he hadn't seen him, "Look at us. Are we not a house divided? Yes, we had family feuds all along. Yet under King David we were one nation, strong and prosperous. Under Solomon we were one people, peaceful and loving. But look at us now; a Jew against a Jew. The rich Sadducees dancing to the Roman tunes are governing our temple like the Pagans of Rome and Athens. Peace and righteousness is gone from the Promised Land. We are plagued with sufferings and hopelessness, but I say to you, this will not be the end of our story. There is hope. There is hope of salvation. There is hope of the Kingdom of Heaven on earth."

The Pharisee, the tall hefty man with a husky voice, stretched out his hand against Joshua's face and cried, "Enough said. Answer me; are you the man who released Sarah from the judgment of the elders?"

Joshua gazed at him with no answer.

"Sarah, the harlot," shouted another.

"I am," Joshua said.

"On whose authority did you disobey the judgment of the elders and release the harlot?"

Joshua looked around to the crowd, his mouth pursed and eyes tightened. The men moved closer to Joshua with fire in their eyes. The women sobbed noiselessly. But then some ten men from the crowd got up and arrayed behind Joshua, like a stone wall. There was one man in particular, with strong shoulders and muscular arms, clenching and unclenching his fists ready to charge.

"You hypocrites," Joshua said. "Was there a man amongst those stoners who had not sinned against God? I ask of you, who violated that woman? What right do you have? What authority do you have to sacrifice that woman in the name of righteousness, you brood of vipers?"

Two of the scribes raised their staffs ready to swing, but then again sensing the mood of the men behind Joshua, their hands slowly fell.

"First," Joshua commanded, "before you complain about the speck in your brother's eye, first, remove the beam from your own eye."

"Enough said, you false prophet," screamed the Pharisee, "under the authority of the elders of the city of Nazareth, we forbid you to teach in any of the synagogues of Galilee. Out, out you go, you scum of a prophet." Soon, the four of them put their hands on Joshua.

The men behind moved forward, searching Joshua's eyes seeking for permission.

"Don't," he admonished, raising his hand.

The men poked him with their staffs, pointing to the distant roads. As Joshua bent down to collect his belongings, the Pharisee put his hand on Joshua's face and pushed him out, smothering. Joshua fell back into the arms of the men behind, saying, "don't . . . don't."

Humiliated, drenched in cold sweat and weeping in his heart, Joshua left the Synagogue, wiping his brow with the palm of his hand and talking to himself, "No prophet is honored in his own village." The men followed him. One among them was a man named Simon from Cana, a reformed Zealot. Another one was Judas from Kerioth, who had been following Joshua since the meeting at the Turan valley.

Word quickly spread in the towns and villages of lower Galilee that Joshua, the false prophet, was forbidden from entering or teaching in the synagogues.

Two days later, Joshua and the two of his followers were evicted from the synagogue of Baser.

Joshua and four of his followers were also cast out of the Synagogue of Sogane.

Joshua and six of his disciples were thrown out from the synagogue of Saab, as well.

Likewise, he was not received well in the synagogues of many other cities of lower Galilee. This seemed only to increase his popularity, and the numbers of his followers grew.

Word of his teaching spread and seemed to resonate with the oppressed and the downtrodden. They were moved by his message of hope. Women wept under their veils, and farmers, harlots and the landless praised, "the first man to ever talk about us." The Sadducees did not much care, but the Pharisees rejoiced as they got rid of the man of some consequences, and the scribes justified the evictions based on the books of law.

**** **** ****

Joshua continued to travel from village to village, talking to people at the four corners of the village, under the shade of trees, at the village well, and at times as an invited guest in houses of publicans or farm workers. Now he walked, not alone, but always surrounded by a small crowd, Judas and Simon always by his side.

Among the rich, around the dinner tables, wedding celebrations and revelries, he was a thorny subject of conversation. A few choked and yet others scowled at the mention of his name.

But among the poor Jews, he was the subject of conversation in the alleys of the wretched, market places, harvest fields, as the one who had saved the harlot from stoning, the one who addressed women as daughters of Jerusalem, daughters of Abraham, the man who talked about hope for eternal life in the Kingdom of Heaven. Women particularly longed to see him and to hear his soothing words. "With what authority he speaks," the women acknowledged.

"He is a savior," some said.

"He is a prophet," said some others.

"Certainly he is the Messiah," a few others said.

Wherever he traveled, Joshua first sought out the sinners, harlots and publicans, those were rejected and scorned.

"I have not come to call the righteous, but the sinners to repentance," he said. He talked to them with words of comfort, dissuading them from the ways of sin. He gave them something to hope for.

But the Galilean increasingly preoccupied the minds of a few free-thinking rich people, too. "Never before had a rabbi touched a harlot, let alone saved her from stoning." And they wondered what kind of man could this be?

"Never before had a rabbi said he is the Son of God. Maybe he is a prophet," a few wondered.

"Never before has a man said to the Pharisees that the publicans and harlots will enter the Kingdom of Heaven, way before them," said others praising his uplifting words.

"Never before has a Rabbi promised that the Kingdom of Heaven is at hand and now," said others hopefully.

A few of them were ready to follow him. He even made some scribes curious enough to once again search the books of law and examine their own beliefs. At least a few Pharisees thought that there was some sense to his words, but all agreed that the Galilean was a trouble maker.

Scorned in Nazareth, evicted from many synagogues of Lower Galilee, and ridiculed by the scribes, a dispirited Joshua sat under the shades of a roadside poplar tree with his disciples one evening on the way to Capernaum. He appeared sad and absorbed in thought. The sun had gone down, and the night had fallen. "Where shall we rest our heads tonight, and what shall we feed on?" The bread basket was empty, and what were left for drink were just two skins of wine. The disciples talked around.

Looking to the distant gray sky, he said, "The foxes have holes, the birds have nests, but the son of man has nowhere to rest his head. Woe to Nazareth. Woe to Bethesda. If only we had done the same work in Sodom and Gomorrah, the heavens would have saved the rains of sulfur and salt, and we would have saved a lot more souls."

That night, his stomach empty and his lips dry, Joshua rested his head on a rock and drifted off to sleep. It was also a night the followers talked amongst themselves dispiritedly. There was a certain disappointment in the air; a few of them even wondered whether it was a mistake to leave their homes and belongings to follow this man.

A few days later, Joshua and the eight of his followers were traveling from the town of Garis to Ruma, when a rich publican named James, the son of Alphaeus, came to him. He bowed before Joshua, and with open arms said, "Master, bless my house with your footsteps. I have heard much about you. Rest in my house, break bread with us, and drink of our skins."

James was a gruff-looking, middle-aged man, short with a bull neck, and bushy brows that met in the middle, but his eyes were kind and his voice gentle. He had become wealthy supervising the public works and keeping back a big portion of the taxes, but he was always good to his workers. The pebbled road that led to his stone house upon a rise facing the setting sun was studded with the tiny huts of his workers. As Joshua approached the house, men, women, and little children from the nearby houses came out and followed behind him to the flagstone-paved courtyard of James's house.

As soon as Joshua passed through the arched gate, the women of the house brought water in long-necked clay pots and washed his feet.

Joshua sat on the hearth, and the men and women sat cross-legged at his feet. Russia, the first woman of the house with fleshy face and gray hair, brought perfumed oil in an alabaster jar and anointed his head. Joanna, the second woman of the house, with wide eyes and large bosoms, brought glass chalices and fresh skins of wine to celebrate the guest. The servants out in the back yard were busy slaughtering a young waxed calf to serve to the guest of honor for a burnt-meat dinner.

Presently, the setting sun lit the shining marble floor, and the reflected rays fell obliquely on the rabbi. James brought out the seven-wicker lamp, lit and placed it on a marble table facing Joshua.

As they sat in the light of the lamp, Sophia, a thin woman with a narrow face, began to sing in a soft melodious voice: "Rejoice and exalt the daughters of Zion," the words of the prophet Zachariah. Soon, all of the women in the group joined in the chorus:

"Shout for joy the daughters of Jerusalem.

"Your king has come to find you."

The waves of the song floated through the air like a solemn procession. There hung in the air the aura of a king being anointed. The women, who had known only to weep in their lives, smiled. Some who knew how to smile, laughed.

"Master," said James humbly, "The men are preparing the dinner. Please speak to us." Joshua searched James's face intensely, calmly and pleasantly.

"James," he said.

"Master," James replied.

"Come and sit by my side."

"I shall. I will," James replied, and sat next to Joshua. The woman with the narrow face continued to perfume Joshua's feet, at times kissing them.

"Rabbi," she implored. "Teach us about the Kingdom of Heaven."

Joshua looked at Sophia compassionately, placed his hand upon her head in blessing, and said, "I shall." He took a draw of wine from the skin, swallowed it slowly, and began. Against the shimmering flames of the seven-wicker lamp, his face shone like the rising sun.

"The Kingdom of Heaven is eternal life," he began, "life with our Heavenly Father. Our sojourn on this earth is nothing but preparation for that eternal life. Remember, we are but made of clay, given life by the breath of God. That breath, your soul, is a part of God within you. You are the custodian of that soul, throughout your life. You are a walking temple. Once your body withers and returns to the dust, your soul goes back to its creator. The Kingdom of Heaven is your place after your death. That, nobody can take away from you. You have hope."

There was silence and a sense of peace and tranquility in the house of James as he spoke.

"Dear brethren," Joshua resumed. "Men are greedy for the pleasures of today." Then he turned towards James, searching his eyes passionately, and asked him, "But James, can you definitely say that you will wake up to see the first light of tomorrow?"

James never expected that question. He had never thought of that. No words came out of his mouth. Joshua didn't press for an answer. He continued: "Only your spirit can claim the morrow."

One man said "Amen," soon to be followed by all the others.

"James, I know you were not prepared for that question. But be prepared. Nobody knows where or when that call will come. A watchman on duty will not sleep. It doesn't make any difference how much wealth you have or positions you hold, you must relinquish them all at the end. The only possession you can carry to my Father's kingdom is your immortal soul. So, why bother to accumulate wealth in this world? I say to you, hoard wealth that is not washed away by rain, blown away by wind, eaten away by moth, or stolen away by thieves. Give away your wealth to the poor and the needy. Open your door to the one who knocks. If a man takes away your coat, give him your cloak, too. If somebody compels you to walk one mile, travel two miles with him. But verily I tell you, James, you are a blessed man. I didn't have a place to rest my head tonight. You opened your doors to me. You washed my feet and anointed my head. I was thirsty, and you gave me drink. I am hungry and you are roasting meat for me. You are a blessed man. On the day of the judgment, the Kingdom of Heaven will be there for you. For you, James, I tell you. Follow me, the harvest is truly plentiful, but the laborers are few. Follow me to the villages of Galilee and Judea."

James sighed deeply, his face lit as if a heavy burden had been taken from him. "Rabbi, I shall. I will," he said.

A comfortable silence followed. Russia announced that dinner was ready.

"But rabbi, tell us more . . . more; how shall we prepare?" begged Sophia without letting go her hold on his feet. The call to dinner had only little response; it appeared that his words filled their hungry stomach.

"Talk to us more, rabbi. How will we be judged; will you be there at the judgment?" begged some others, too.

Joshua explained. "No man knows what is in the waiting for tomorrow, but on the Day of Judgment you will be judged, your good deeds against your bad. To the righteous, my Father would say, 'you obeyed my commandments and you loved and respected your neighbors. Your soul is pure. Therefore, I will open the door of heaven for you.' To all the others who disobeyed and misinterpreted the commandments, who burned and stoned women in the name of righteousness, the door of Hades will be open for them."

The small crowd sat inspired and transfixed. The women prayed, "Rabbi talk to us more; such words of comfort we have never heard before. We know you are a prophet. Please teach us more."

"Therefore, I tell you, your sufferings and pains are short-lived. Your miseries and worries about tomorrow are meaningless. The eternal tomorrow, the Kingdom of Heaven, is at hand for you. Build up your treasures in the Kingdom of Heaven. Accept pain with pleasure. Accept suffering with hope of relief. Accept suppression without protestation."

Joshua looked around. The evening was getting ripe, and dinner was getting late. In a concluding tone, he said: "My Father in heaven is neither stiff-necked nor angry. He is a loving and forgiving God. Ask Him, and it shall be given to you. Seek, and you shall find it. Knock, and it shall be open for you. Open your heart, repent your sins, and pray to almighty God. You have hope. The Kingdom of Heaven is near. The Kingdom of Heaven is at hand."

There were deep sighs of relief in the crowd. Some wept, but soon a dirge like heart-wrenching weeping erupted from near his feet. It was Salome sobbing and breathing in short brakes. "Rabbi, I am a sinner, a prostitute . . . do I have any chance to enter the Kingdom of Heaven?"

Joshua looked at her with compassion. He called her near to him, put his hand over her brow as a blessing, and continued very softly, "Daughter, you have now repented. You are now whole. You shall certainly enter the Kingdom of Heaven, way before those Pharisees and scribes, those who sit on Moses' seat."

Joshua answered many such questions that evening. After dinner the crowd dispersed to their abodes. James had been so moved by Joshua's message, that he decided to leave behind his home and wealth to his children and the workers who worked in his fields. He told Joshua, "Rabbi, I am blessed that you came to my house today. The words you spoke are beyond any of those our prophets said. Those words must not be left unwritten. I shall follow you wherever you go, and I shall be your scribe."

The next day, Joshua left for Capernaum. The group that followed him included Labbaeus; Judas from Kerioth; Bartholomew; James, the son of Alphaeus; and Simon from Jerusalem.

On the way to Capernaum in the town of Magdella, there lived a rich scribe named Philip, a Jew with Greek blood, a man who owned many orchards of figs, walnuts, dates palms, and who was known to Simon from Galilee. Philip invited the men to stay in his house for a night, not necessarily because he liked Joshua or his teachings, but he wanted to meet him and ask him some questions that were close to his heart.

Philip was a well-groomed man clad in silk robes. He was married to Jezebel and had two daughters, Leah and Lydia. They received the men cordially on the front porch of his white marble house overlooking the blue waters of Lake Ganezareth. The feast they had prepared seemed more like a wedding celebration than an evening meal.

After the dinner they seated Joshua on a chair, and his disciples sat at his feet. Likewise, Philip was seated facing the guests, and his wife and children sat by his feet.

Amidst the conversations, Philip asked somewhat dryly, "Rabbi, many a story we have heard of you, talking about love and compassion towards women and children. My wife, Jezebel, was most anxious to listen to you." Jezebel moved closer to her husband, hand on his shoulders and reading Joshua's face. "Thank you for being a guest in my house, but I would like to ask you this. Our nation has gone through turmoil and slavery, but now we are at a juncture of peace, and certainly there are signs of prosperity across the land. The Romans do not interfere in our religion. The Temple services are uninterrupted. Rome is splendor, Rome is power. We are part of the Empire. Rome builds bridges, roads, tunnels and aqueducts. They conduct sports festivals and feasts. They keep law and order in our nation. Israel's enemies are laid to waste. Why bother to disrupt this peace with your sermons and movements. People are speaking about you and against you. They say you are an adulterer, a corrupter. You lure away the workers from the farms, and fisherman from the sea coast, giving false promises about a certain Kingdom of Heaven. You are against Caesar, against Caiaphas, and you even speak blasphemy against Moses. You don't look like or speak like a troublemaker, but I see you are a troublemaker.

Joshua was quiet for a long moment. Simon was becoming agitated by the long silence and opened his mouth calling. "Philip, can you . . ."

Joshua signaled him to stop. Calling back his thoughts of Buddha's teachings, he turned to Phillip softly.

"I admire the honesty with which you speak. There might be people or false prophets coming in my name and saying what I said not. I am not against Caesar. I say to you, give Caesar what is due to Caesar, and give God what is due to God. The kingdom I talk about is the Kingdom of Heaven. The God I talk about is my Heavenly Father."

Phillip nodded. He sat deep on the chair, his eyes fixed on his guest, with his arms folded across his chest.

"But what I said about the Pharisees are not for sale. Those who sit in Moses' seat do not practice what they preach. They are only concerned about the outward glitter of the cup, and not the filth that is contained in it. They lay heavy burdens on the poor, sit on the highest honored seats in celebrations, eat the best cut of meat, drink from the best skins of wine, talk loudly about the copper coins they donated, and demand respect – salutations – and insist on others calling them Rabbi, Rabbi. Yes, I've spoken about rich men like you. Philip, tell me, what are your biggest worries? What are you afraid of? You have enough wealth, a house built of marble, many servants, and abundant orchards, yet in your mind are you at peace? Or, do you worry about the protection of your wealth?"

"Yes," said Philip obligingly, "I do worry."

"You worry about robbers coming at night."

"Yes."

"You worry about tomorrow."

"Yes."

"You worry about the prosperity of your children and your children's children."

"Yes."

"You are terrified about death?"

"Yes."

"Are you disturbed about leaving all of those things you earned that are dear to your heart, and not being able to take them with you?"

543

"Yes."

"And you would pay anything if you could live forever."

"Anything," Philip said, looking at Joshua.

"Certainly, I tell you, Philip, you are not alone," Joshua said. "You suffer amidst plenty. On your neck is tied a millstone of possessions. Until and unless you shed that burden, you shall sink to the deepest fathoms of despair."

After a long silence, Philip muttered, "Yes." Jezebel wept. Lydia and Leah gazed at Joshua with amazement.

"Philip, the moment you reckon the weight of your burdens and the moment you decide to unload them, peace shall shine upon you. You wanted to live forever, you said. To attain that immortality and to be in heaven with my Father, first, you have to die in this world," Joshua said.

"But I tell you, it will be much easier for a camel to pass through a needle hole than for a rich man like you to enter the Kingdom of Heaven. Until your good deeds and righteousness exceeds that of the Pharisees and scribes, you shall not enter the Kingdom of Heaven. Therefore, I tell you, take no heed of what you eat or what you dress tomorrow. Tomorrow will take care of itself. Look at the ravens in the sky, they neither sow nor reap or store in the barns. God feeds them and protects them. How much better are you from them?"

Philip remained silent, gently shaking his head.

"Philip, we are all created for a purpose. That purpose is to prepare our soul to enter the eternal Kingdom of Heaven, to be eternal. You are immensely rich, I agree, but see how limited you are. You can neither add an inch to your height, nor prevent one hair from turning gray. This life is given to you for a purpose. Unload your burdens. Sell all that you have, give alms to the poor, and follow me. What good is there for you if you shall gain the whole world and lose your soul?"

Philip was greatly moved. He got up from the high chair and said somberly, "Rabbi, I am not worthy of sitting on the high chair at your level." He sat down by his feet. "You showed light into the darkness of my soul. Permit me to follow you." Judas and Phillip wrote down the words Joshua said. There was an air of peace and comfort in the house.

The next day, the men left for Capernaum, with Philip leading the way.

On the northern coast of the sea of Ganezareth next to the Via Maris – the great Roman highway connecting Damascus to Alexandria – sat the cities of upper Galilee, Magdella, Capernaum and Bethesda. It was here in Magdella – the promiscuous city of all where sparsely clad women invited the pleasure-seeking men of the world – that Naomi was raised in a shack near the caravansary.

The coastal city of Capernaum areas was dotted with rows of small dilapidated fisherman's huts arrayed on the waterfront one behind the other. In the highlands above resided the rich Pharisees and scribes in houses of white marble with Doric columns. Most young women conveniently escaped to Magdella for more profitable jobs – serving the rich businessmen crisscrossing the city. Many people were afflicted with wasting diseases of consumption, non-healing ulcers, sudden seizures, and demon afflictions.

Joshua and his disciples entered Capernaum on a Sabbath day and first, they went to the synagogue. It was an old, white limestone building, overlooking the blue tranquil waters of the Sea of Galilee. The exterior of the synagogue was adorned with carvings of palm trees, a menorah, and a scene depicting the procession of the Holy Ark.

The synagogue was only half full. Close to the dais remained two empty pews, behind which sat a few men in tattered garments, their sunken eyes focused on the flagstone-paved floor. At the rear end of the hall sat a small crowd of women dressed in dark shapeless clothes and black veils. In contrast to the others, stood a tall, bald man, who leaned against the rear wall, his jaw strong, and beard dark and luxuriant. Two younger men that stood by him also looked healthy and well fed.

Absalom, the minister of the synagogue, was a well-fed man with jowls and a gray beard. Adorned in a black robe, he was already sitting on a stone bench on the platform studying the people as they entered and positioned themselves in the various places.

Presently, an elderly man with a fleshy face, clad in flowing silk garments, entered the synagogue with his wife and two young men. Absalom almost stood up and bowed his head. The man looked around in slow motion and occupied one of the two long benches. The two well-groomed young men were of light complexion, and the younger of the two bore a perfect female face with rosebud lips and curly hair. Joshua and disciples moved to one corner of the hall, some stood with feet close, and some leaning against the columns.

An assistant brought over a wooden chest with several scrolls to Absalom. He picked up one and quickly spread it with jerky movements of his fingers. He read the scroll silently, then looked to the crowd, noticed a stranger in the crowd – Joshua – and nodded for him to come over to the dais.

Joshua gladly walked up to the dais, took the scroll with head bowed. He sat on the stone bench and glanced over the crowd as his bright hazel eyes took in the assembly. He unrolled the scroll and read the first sentence.

"The spirit of God is upon me." Then he devoutly folded the scroll and held it in his arm against his chest and continued to recite the passage.

" . . . because the Lord has ordained me to preach his message to you. He has sent me to mend the broken heart . . ."

That was a new voice in the synagogue, a voice smooth, convincing and endearing with precise modulations of voice, pause and emphasis. Then he put the scroll back in the box, took a step forward, stretched out his hands, and called out to them.

"Brothers and sisters, the spirit of the Lord has always been with us, but we have been too blind to see him. The voice of the Lord has always been with us, but we were deaf to hear it. He came to us in the form of . . . but we walked away from him holding our noses. He came to us, to our doorsteps and village wells destitute and thirsty, but we did not pour water in the cup of his hands. He came to us finding no place to rest his head, but we closed the doors on his face. The spirit of the Lord was always with us."

The crowd was spellbound. They held their collective breath, cocked their ears and held their palms against their chests as the words pierced straight into their hearts.

"Brothers and sisters," Joshua's voice rose. "The custodians of our Holy Scriptures, the men who sit on Moses' seat, only saw the letters of the law, not the spirit of the law. They saw only a hard-hearted, stiff-necked God. The commandments say to love your neighbor, but we practiced annihilating our neighbors. But I ask of you, who is your neighbor?"

By this time the synagogue was full. More people had arrived and joined noiselessly, and most of them stood leaning against the walls. His words felt like fresh water to those who had been thirsting in the desert. Absalom stood transfixed, at times stroking his beard and wondering whether he made a mistake, to invite this stranger to read the scriptures.

"A certain man went down from Jerusalem to Jericho, and by chance he fell amongst thieves who robbed him, mutilated him and left him by the wayside to waste," Joshua said." There came up a priest on the way, but he left the scene quietly. Then a Levite came, and likewise he escaped the scene. Then there came a Samaritan. He saw the man, felt compassion for him, nursed his wounds with oil and vinegar, gave him a drink, took him on his donkey to an inn in Jericho, and entrusted the innkeeper to look after him, paying money and then went on his way."

"Brothers and sisters, let me ask you again, who is your neighbor? Is he not the one to console you when you are sick, pour water on your rooftop when the house is on fire, protect your boundaries from the invaders, and bury you when you are dead? Joshua looked around. "How did the Amorites and the Hittites treat Abraham while he was wandering in the land of Hebron?"

"Amen." A very loud lone voice cracked in the back. Nobody moved. Some thought it came from the man with the strong jaw leaning against the rear wall. A few men nodded, some cupped their hands and looked up to the ceiling of the synagogue.

"Brethren, the land of Israel is a blessed land, with rich soil which brings forth the best of the Lord's creations. There is enough for everybody. Why then is there poverty in this land? Is it not the greed of those rich Sadducees, Pharisees and scribes that own and control everything? Exploitation of a poor Jew by a rich Jew! They are putting heavy yokes on our shoulders. They rob the temples, and they tax; they tithe and tithe again."

Presently, a young lady making a loud scream fell to the ground with convulsions; eyes rolled up and tongue bitten, spilling blood.

"She is possessed with a demon," the other woman shouted. Immediately, two men ran to her and began to lift her off the ground.

"Where do you plan to take her," Joshua asked.

"To the thistle bush," the men replied, as it was the practice to leave the women possessed with demons in the thorny bushes to be pricked by the thorns and bitten by the wasps until the devil departed.

"Leave the daughter right there." Joshua said. The men left her on the floor and withdrew.

Joshua came to the woman, lifted the veil from her face, wiped the blood and the froth out of the corners of her mouth, put his hands on her brow and pronounced in a tone of authority, "Come off the woman, thou unclean spirit. Come off the woman, thou unclean spirit." Then he shook the woman and shouted, "Woman I command you to get up."

Nothing happened for the next several minutes. Slowly the clonic shakings of her limbs settled, her spasms eased and she woke up foggy, confused and stupefied. The crowd in the synagogue held their breath in disbelief, their mouths agape as they stared at the new Rabbi and wondered what kind of man this was?

"Has he got powers over the devil?"

"Is he the Messiah?"

"Is he the prophet that Isaiah and Micah prophesized?"

The woman looked around, wondering why people were gazing at her. She pulled over the veil and sat there as if nothing had happened.

Joshua concluded the sermon, emphasizing the power of faith and belief. "Have faith in God," he declared, "absolute faith. When you stand up to pray, forgive anyone against whom you have grievances."

When he had finished the crowd gathered around him in rings, wanting to see him more, wanting to hear him more, wanting simply to touch him.

Zebedee was the rich man in the silk cloak. He often came to the temple to sit in the first seat and show off his silk cloak and ornaments. But his younger son, John, was strongly drawn to Joshua and the elder one, James, wanted to speak Joshua.

As he walked out of the synagogue, the tall, bald man who stood against the rear wall, Peter, and his brother, Andrew, came and stood near Joshua, their reverence evident as well.

"Rabbi, bless my house. Come and break bread with us," Peter asked. "Our mother is laid to bed with high fever. Please come and heal her."

Joshua followed Peter to his house, which was near the gate of the synagogue. A great crowd followed him.

As soon as the bedridden mother saw lots of people coming to her home, she got up cheerfully and came to the door. This is truly a miracle, even before the prophet entered my house my mother is made whole, Peter thought. Peter and his younger brother Andrew instantly became followers of the Galilean.

Peter served dinner to the Rabbi and his disciples. It was a humble dinner with bitter barley bread and a pottage with small portions of fish from his catch, some vegetables, and simple herbs. Joshua and the six disciples with him were strangers in Capernaum, but no more, they accepted Peter's invitation and decided to remain with him in Capernaum.

The news of the arrival of a new Rabbi in the town spread quickly in the streets, villages and towns of upper Galilee. The Sadducees did not care much about him, they just disregarded him. The Pharisees despised him, and the scribes abhorred him, but they were afraid to lay hands on him, as he was always surrounded by multitudes worshiping him.

But the men and women of the poor class adored him. They were astonished at his teachings, as he taught them as one having authority, as one with grace, love and compassion, not like the Pharisees who did it for a job and collected the revenues beforehand.

In the villages, the people shared their wonder.

"You have to hear to believe it. I have never heard such powerful words," said some with excitement.

"Even the unclean spirits obey him," some marveled.

"Fever disappears even before he enters the house," some observed.

"His face shines like the rising sun," said many with admiration.

"He is the Messiah," a few were convinced.

"He talks to women just like he talks to men," said many women.

There were others who resented his presence and questioned his authority.

"He is a blasphemer!" screamed a few who heard of him.

"He speaks against Moses and the Torah," the Pharisees were convinced.

"He was evicted from the synagogue in Sepphoris," some brought it up.

"He is corrupting the people," the scribes lamented.

In his name there were divisions within houses. The women adored him and spoke of him above their husbands' voices. Zebedee's wife sang unabatedly her admiration of the new Rabi and was an inspiration for many women in the neighborhood. Her two children, John and James, left home to follow Joshua in his travels.

Soon Joshua became a major presence in the social and religious life of the people in and around the city. Like in lower Galilee, he spoke to people under the shade of the trees, in the synagogues, and at the four corners of the town. He frequently traveled by boat between the coastal cities of Capernaum, Magdella, Bethesda and Tiberius.

One day in the city of Magdella, Joshua met the tax collector named Matthew, a clever and learned man of great composure. Matthew had heard about Joshua's words and deeds. He discerned that Joshua was not an ordinary man, probably a prophet or more. He abandoned his position to follow Joshua along with the other disciples. He was determined to create a written record of his words and deeds as precisely as he could.

It was also in Magdella that Joshua met another man named Thomas, a man known to be a skeptic. Like Joshua, he too had studied Greek and Latin, and he wanted the opportunity to meet Joshua and to decide if he was authentic. At Magdella in his house, Matthew had the opportunity he sought. One night, late into the evening, a group of twenty-one men sat around Joshua.

Thomas asked the first question: "Rabbi, you were away from the land of Israel for many years. People say that you have traveled the world and seen all the lands that Alexander conquered and beyond. Some say you learned sorcery. In any case, you speak with authority. Tell us the truth. Are you a prophet?"

Joshua looked into the searching eyes of his disciples, one after the other. "I know I am the son of my Father in Heaven," he replied.

"Why are you here? What is your mission?" Thomas persisted.

"I am here for the salvation of our people."

"Strange. Are the Israelites corrupt and doomed to fail without a savior?" asked Thomas dryly.

"Certainly, we need introspection. Yes, I have traveled a bit, as you said. In a land called India – a land tarnished by the color system – everything belonged to the Bhrahmins, I learned. Ours is not far different. The Sadducees, the Pharisees and the scribes do not make even two out of ten in our land. Yet they control everything. The vast majority of our people are poor, nothing but slaves in our own land, speechless, powerless and bewildered. The rich are too comfortable and blinded by greed, power and selfishness. This is a nation divided: yes, it's doomed to fail."

"You yourself have countered and disagreed with the writings of the Torah many times, haven't you?" Thomas asked.

"I have. Many of the things written in the Torah were to appease the stone-headed rebels in the Sinai desert, and it is high time that we corrected it," Joshua said.

"This Kingdom of Heaven you are talking about is never preached in the synagogues or temples," Thomas said. "You speak that it's for us to claim. What's your authority?"

"Is it not written in the scriptures that Yahweh created heaven first and then the earth, the dream of Jacob and the vision of Isaiah? And the lamentations of Job?

"But when Samuel appeared to Saul, did he not come out of the womb of the earth?" Matthew asked.

"Indeed, heaven and hell exist," Joshua said. "Those are the very subjects we need to talk about, to teach about. Matthew, Thomas; could you please be with me."

Thomas persisted, "Master . . . this nation divided, disarrayed."

"Yes. Help others. Part with our possessions, give to the poor, do not take even spare raiment, and follow me in full detachment. We can save Israel."

"What do you mean, full detachment? Celibacy?" asked Thomas dryly.

"A man must not remain celibate unless God destines him to be a eunuch. Fertility is the blessing of God. The mystery of the creation of man is the glory of God. A child born to a woman is the celebration of God. Celibacy isn't anything that I demand from you; full faith and dedication is what I demand," Joshua said.

That evening Joshua answered many questions of his disciples about the beginning of a new era, a new vision. The disciples themselves were convinced that the man at the apex of their mission was no ordinary man.

Finally, Matthew stated to the others: "The more I see him and the more I listen to him, the more I am convinced that he is a prophet."

"He is a miracle by himself," said Peter. "The other day until sunset we cast the nets in the sea only to see weeds and tiny fry. I had spread the net and dozed with fatigue. In my dream I saw Joshua walking on the waters towards me, and he instructed me to cast the net where he pointed to. I woke up and did the same. Behold I had the greatest catch. I am sure I saw him walking on the waters," Peter said.

There were also stories spreading around the villages of Ganezareth that the new Rabbi had healing powers. Some gave testimonies of how he had cast evil spirits; an old man who had been unable to walk got up and went to the crowd to hear him; in Gergesa, a girl dumb from birth spoke for the first time after touching the hem of his robe.

But besides all of these miracles, there was a general awakening of the spirit in that sullen atmosphere of the Jewish alleys. His doctrine gained acceptance and gathered momentum. The destitute of Galilee had been given the courage to face their oppression and suffering with fortitude. They became convinced that death was not the end of life. They believed that they could fight a war without a sword. They believed the Kingdom of Heaven was upon them. The words he spoke about love and compassion, freedom, equality and hope melted the frozen, brazen hearts of the fisherman. The good words the Galilean spoke gave them something to hope for, something to live for, and something to die for.

It was on a Sabbath day in the first week of Sivan that Joshua and the disciples crossed the sea on a boat from Capernaum to Magdella. The west wind was considerable and the waves tall. The ship was tossed from one wave to the other. They landed at the west coast of Magdella in the high sun of the afternoon. All of the shops were closed, and they walked towards the synagogue near Mount Arbel as they became increasingly hungry, hot and thirsty. The disciples spotted a grain field. They nipped some ears of wheat, rubbed the kernels between their palms, and started eating the grains sitting by the side of the field.

A group of Pharisees and scribes who had been following Joshua came to confront him. They had sticks and stones in their hands. They closed in on him.

A poor farm worker who lived in a hut at the threshold of the wheat field noticed the unusual movement of the Pharisees and the scribes. The workers quickly recognized the tall man with flowing beard and white cloak. From rooftop to rooftop they called out: "He's coming! Joshua is coming! And the Pharisees are going after him!"

A multitude of men, women and children converged upon the site and clustered in several circles around Joshua and his followers.

"Is it not against the law that you work on the Sabbath? Eating even without washing your hands?" a scribe named Nathanial said in a husky voice, pointing his staff so close to Joshua that it nearly touched his nose.

"Take away the staff from my master's face," said Peter, taking a step forward. Nathaniel's face crimped like a dried fig. He lowered the staff to the ground leaning on it.

"The Law of Moses is long gone. The Babylonians dumped it in the mud of the Euphrates," cried a strong voice – a voice of rebellion – that resonated from behind the crowd. All eyes turned to see who it was. It was a young farm worker with mud on his hands. It was not difficult to observe a flash of fear on the faces of the Pharisees and the scribes. Joshua turned to them, his face serious and absorbed.

"You hypocrites," he said in a strong voice. "In your books, is it against the law if a mother opens her bosom to feed a child on a Sabbath day?"

"Is it written that it is unlawful to do a good deed on a Sabbath day?"

Nobody answered.

"Did you question David when he entered the temple of Jerusalem on a Sabbath day, drank wine and ate the shewbread, or did you forget yourself blaspheming the temple on a Sabbath day? You hypocrites! You brood of vipers."

There was a tumult of noise from the crowd; noises of ridicule, but all subsided as Joshua turned around raising his hand.

"You never understood what is written in the Scriptures. You saw only the alphabets of the law, but the meanness of your spirit and the coldness of your heart did not comprehend it. You read out loud in the synagogue, but you never truly understood the writings on the scroll or the writings on the wall."

"You've transgressed the traditions of the elders," cried a man named Adelphus.

"Indeed, you have transgressed the Commandments of God with your own interpretations," Joshua said. "You, men sitting on Moses' seat, demand seat of honor at weddings and festivals and enjoy the best cuts of meat and the finest skins of wine. You frequent widow's houses and then make long pious speeches in public."

There was laughter of ridicule from the workers.

"On the day of Sabbath," Joshua said, "I ask of you to give rest to your mean spirit. Take stock of your deeds for the past six days, count your transgressions, and repent."

The Pharisees and scribes turned around and looked at each other's faces, searching for a way to extricate themselves from the crowd.

"Your hands are stained with the blood of prophets, yet you make tombs in their names . . ."

Then Peter came forward and signaled to the people. The people parted ways. The Pharisees and the scribes quietly left.

What kind of people are they? The farmers were upset with the harsh approach of the Pharisee finding fault with the hungry men eating an ear of wheat on Sabbath. However, they were overjoyed when the Pharisees left with their faces down, flushed and red hot. They ran to their homes and brought bread, wine and whatever, to celebrate. They all assembled under the shades of a tree, ate the bread and drank the wine. They beseeched the master to speak to them more.

"This is a rare event in their life," Joshua said. "They enjoy the attentions of men addressing them respectfully as Rabbi, Rabbi. They are only concerned about the glitter of the outside of the cup, but not the substance in the cup. Woe to these hypocrites, woe to them, these gatekeepers of heaven. They will neither enter heaven, nor let anybody else to go in there either. They are concerned more for the tithes of Minas, Anise and Cummings, and not for the weighty matters of justice, judgment or righteousness."

Joshua explained to them: "Brethren, wearily I tell you: that which defines a man is not what goes into his mouth; instead it's what comes out of it. Certainly, I tell you, overseers of the law, their minds are defiled with evil thoughts, fornications, murder, adultery and wickedness. Those men, why do they bother to come to the temple to offer sacrifices? I say go back to your home, reconcile with your brother, neighbor and everybody around. Be clean in your mind, then come to the temple. My father's house is no place for exchange of indulgences. He talked to the people at length until late in the afternoon.

The news of the Galilean and his followers harassed by the Pharisee reached the ears of an old Sadducee – Nicodemus – who lived near the coast. That night Joshua and his disciples were invited to break bread in the house of Nicodemus. Joshua gladly accepted the invitation, not wanting to waste an opportunity to talk to the man – a big fish.

On the way to the house of Nicodemus, a group of young children from the neighborhood gathered around Joshua making noises and frolicking. The short-tempered Peter was annoyed with the children and pushed them away. One young boy of about eight fell down, skinned his knees and began to sob. Joshua was annoyed. He turned around, staring at Peter. He hoisted the child in the cradle of his arms and walked to the house of his guest, a large mansion on a rise made in white stones overlooking the blue waters of the Sea of Galilee. The other children followed jovially. Nicodemus came to the front gate and took the child, and advised his servants to clean the wound with vinegar and oil.

Nicodemus, his three wives, and eleven children warmly welcomed Joshua and conducted him to the high seat at the head of the table. In the elaborate dining hall, a feast was arranged in honor of Joshua and his disciples. While fresh wine and aged cheese were being served, the children, encouraged by Joshua's kind treatment, slowly gathered around the man on the honor seat, some asking him inconsequential questions, some sitting in his lap, some pulling on his beard and kissing his cheeks. All of the disciples, even the learned Thomas, became annoyed with the children, feeling that they were wasting the valuable time of their master. Thomas began to chase the children away.

"Stop," said the master. The disciples were a bit perturbed, and they stood still knowing not what to do next. They couldn't grasp why Joshua did not want the children to be sent away when the adults were discussing mature matters.

"Prevent them not to come to me," Joshua said.

There was an uncomfortable silence in the room.

"Children, the gifts of Heaven, pure at heart," he said. "But certainly I tell you, until you become like those little children, you shall not enter the Kingdom of Heaven. He who offends one of those little children and those who corrupt and defile one of those little ones, certainly I tell you it is better that a millstone be tied around their neck and send them to the depth of the sea."

There was a distinct difference in the tone of his words, Thomas and others noted. What had happened here, after all, for him to make such profound statements, they wondered.

"Beware, and I tell you, those false prophets! Woe to them, and their disciples with long flowing robes; they are the very first who would violate our children. Pedophiles! Those are the very first who should be turned to the stakes." At this statement Joshua's face had turned red and there was command in his voice. The disciples, who had been with him for long, had never seen him so, never heard him so.

But Nicodemus found the rabbi interesting. After the dinner, Nicodemus talked to Joshua privately for an extended hour, asking many questions about his mission and future plans. At the end, Nicodemus said, "Joshua, I am amazed by the way you speak and the matters you talk. I need some time to think about what you are saying. Certainly, another time I will come to you and talk with you."

Joshua and the group rested that night in the house of Nicodemus, and the next morning they left for Capernaum.

**** **** ****

The stories of the Galilean preaching to people with seething denunciations of the Pharisees, and news that his ministry was rapidly gaining followers all over Galilee, and the humiliation of the Pharisees and the scribes who confronted him, all reached the highest echelons of the temple administration in Jerusalem. The Pharisees and the scribes had counseled amongst themselves to discuss the carpenter prophet, who spoke against the very existence of their being, the man whose followers were swelling up by the day, the man who could mobilize the crowd with the power of his words, the man who was always surrounded by throngs of followers, the one who was afraid of nobody, and the one who could not be tricked or outwitted by anybody.

The Pharisees talked amongst themselves in conclaves.

"He is a clever and crafty man," said one.

"Why is he not talking against Rome and Caesar?" wondered another.

"Get rid of him." they decided.

It was a Sabbath day, and Joshua was teaching in the fisherman's wharf in Capernaum. The Pharisees sent their agents to Joshua, asking, "Master, you are an honest man preaching God's words, but tell us: is it lawful to pay taxes to Caesar or not?"

"You hypocrites. Why are you testing me? Show me the coin that pays the census tax." They handed him a Roman coin. He kept the coin in the spread of his palm and demanded, "Whose image is this? Whose inscriptions are these?"

"Caesar's," they replied.

"Then pay to Caesar what belongs to Caesar, and to God what belongs to God."

The agents were tongue tied, but refused to leave. The crowd made some gestures of ridicule to the agents of Pharisees.

They came up with another tricky riddle: "Rabbi, a woman is married to the eldest of seven brothers. The husband soon dies. According to the Law of Moses, the next eldest brother married her. He also died. Likewise, she married all seven brothers, and all seven died. Tell us Rabbi, in your heaven, whose wife shall she be?"

"Oh, you ignorant men, you never understood the Scriptures. Beware: at the resurrection, they neither marry nor are given in marriage."

The agents retreated, ashamed and abashed. They left the scene through the back alleys with their heads covered.

As days went by, Joshua seemed to become more and more absorbed, serious and preoccupied like a placid ocean before the hurricane. It appeared that at times he was getting frustrated and tense. There were people around him and about him constantly and incessantly, so much so that even basic daily routines were difficult. At times, he spoke to the multitudes on the shores from the deck of the fishing boats, and yet other times he rode the waves from one shore to the other with his disciples escaping the tumult for some quiet and tranquility.

Then Thomas came up to him with a plan. "Joshua, from now on, you must talk to the large crowds only, in prearranged large sessions." Joshua was immediately resolved to the idea. Amongst the disciples, there was also a growing feeling that they had done all they could in Capernaum and that it was time to move on to Jerusalem.

"I shall go to the hills and talk to many," he agreed. "Let those who have ears hear it, and let those who have eyes see it. No one lights a lamp and hides it under the bushel, but keeps it on the lamppost."

The disciples identified the place for him to speak. They announced that Joshua would preach on a mountainous terrain in the middle of a large expanse of pastoral land overlooking the Sea of Galilee, west of Capernaum and north of Magdella.

The news of the meeting was spread from one mouth to the other, shouted from one housetop to the other in the villages, and from the fishing boats to the others in the coastal areas. It was in the first week of Nisan; the almonds were in full bloom, and wild daisies and the violet and orange lilies virtually filled the lands of Galilee. For seven days prior to the meeting Joshua detached himself from his disciples. At times, he took a boat, anchored it far beyond the shores and spent hours in quiet contemplation. Other times, he went to the deserts and meditated by himself days on end. He went through the very many little scrolls on which he had made notes from the teachings from Akhenaton, Cicero, Aristotle, Confucius, Buddha, Ashoka, Vyassa and many others. He ate little, and looked more aged. And though his hair and beard were streaked with silver, he was energetic with determined sharp eyes.

On the day of the preaching, from morning onwards people started moving towards the hill in small and large groups. Many blew the shofar and the women sang songs, but all carried a few branches of olives or flowers in their hands. The large movement of men and women alarmed the Pharisees and the scribes, and raised concern in the Roman barracks. Joseph of Arimathea – an elderly man of power and prestige who was also a member of the Sanhedrin in Jerusalem – who had been studying Joshua for quite some time, supported the meeting and even spoke to the centurions in Capernaum, reassuring them that the group was assembling for a prayer meeting and not for a violent uprising. In spite of his assurances, the Romans placed a good number of mounted soldiers in the area.

The spring sky was light blue, and shattered firmaments slowly moved from west to east, and the sun beat down descending to the west. A great multitude, more than five thousand, had assembled around the hill and sat in circles from the bottom up leaving a pathway to go up and down. At the top of the hill the disciples had created a carpet of green leaves spread for the master to sit.

Joshua appeared, clad in his loose white robes and the bag slung across his shoulders, and flagged by about twenty others, gradually ascended the mountain. Matthew carried several scrolls and writing materials in a bundle at the tail of the train.

At the sight of Joshua the crowd erupted in cheers, waving the flowers and the branches up in the air. As he ascended the hill, the people began to sing and showered him with petals of flowers. It took some time for the master and the disciples to reach the top, and as he reached the carpet of leaves, a shofar sounded that brought silence to the crowd.

He looked around, his face deeply absorbed, and he certainly knew what was in the making. As he spread his arms, the soft wind from the west fluttered the loose sleeves of his gown like the wings of a white dove. The cheers and chants erupted again and continued for several minutes, and when they finally settled down, he sat down cross-legged facing southwest. The glinting yellow rays of the spring sun shone on him, and he appeared to glow. The whole mount with the multitude of people in layers, looked like a decorated cake with a candle lit at the top.

"Children of Israel," he announced, "I have come amongst you not to destroy the laws of prophets, but to fulfill them. I have come to you not to raise my fist against Caesar, but to tell you, render to Caesar that which is due to Caesar, and to God that which is due to God. I have come to remind you that the purpose of our creation in this mortal world is to prepare for our salvation to the immortal world. This sojourn, this tour of duty, is finite and for a definite purpose. Children of Israel, the Law of Moses and the prophets were only until John. Today it's a new dawn, a new beginning, the Kingdom of Heaven."

His words rang high, confidently and emphatically, and the crowd was spellbound, so quiet that one could hear a breath. The opening remarks set well for the crowd, and the Roman soldiers nodded; they were at ease.

"It is written in the Scriptures that thou shall love your neighbor and fight your enemy. It is in written in the Scriptures that your God will put curses on your enemies, and that he will deliver them to you, and that we smite them and waste them. But certainly I tell you, live in peace with your neighbors and love your enemies. Do not unto others that which you don't want to be done to yourself. Israel never shall have peace until we live in harmony with our neighbors. Therefore, I tell you, love your enemy: do good, to those who hate you. Pray for them that curse on you. Bless them that despise you.

"It is written in the Scriptures 'an eye for an eye and a tooth for a tooth', but I say to you even an eye for an eye will turn the whole world blind. Face anger with compassion, hatred with love, violence with nonviolence, and suppression with passive resistance. If someone strikes you on one cheek, show him the other, too.

"It is written in the Scriptures that thou shall not murder, but I say to you, whoever breeds anger and vengeance in their mind has committed sin and shall be subject to judgment.

"In the Scriptures it is written that thou shall tithe and offer burnet sacrifices for your sins, transgressions and trespasses. But I tell you certainly, it is neither the life of lambs nor the gore of the goats that will save you from the judgment. Repent and pray to God for forgiveness with full devotion. It shall be given to you."

Matthew and Thomas were busy writing down the words of the rabbi, as quickly as they could. Peter slowly turned around and watched the crowd; his face was lit with satisfaction. *The Rabi is cutting through the pages of the Torah, even I know it. They are all receiving the message well,* he breathed with satisfaction. *Even the Roman soldiers are listening with cocked ears,* he saw.

"Who is our enemy? Look at the enemies we fought against, the Midianites: are they not the descendants of Abraham? The Hivites and the Jebusites: are they not descendants of Ham, son of Cain. The Moabites and the Amorites: are they not descendants of Lot? We are all brothers and sisters – children of God. Do not swing the sword against anybody. I tell you, a sword against a sword will keep the heads rolling and limbs falling. It will never solve a problem. Remember, a sword can only pierce the flesh, but it can never slice the spirit, that makes man a man . . ."

"Children of Israel, those days of fiction, the days when people were hoisted to heaven through the clouds, are all over. But certainly I tell you: nobody, nobody, shall escape the final judgment to enter the Kingdom of Heaven. Narrow is the gate and arduous is the road that leads to eternity, but wide is the gate and well-paved is the path that leads to destruction and Hell."

"Blessed are the poor in spirit, for theirs is the Kingdom of Heaven," he declared. "Blessed are the meek, for they shall inherit the earth," he emphasized. "Blessed are those who mourn and suffer, for they shall be comforted," he proclaimed. "Blessed are those who hunger and thirst for righteousness, for they shall be filled," he predicted. "Blessed are the merciful, for they shall receive mercy," he affirmed. "Blessed are the peacemakers, for they are the sons of God," he confirmed. "Blessed are the persecuted in virtue's sake, for theirs is the Kingdom of Heaven," he said.

Presently, the speech entered the second hour. Nobody moved or made a noise except an occasional *Amen.* Upon finishing his message, Joshua rose to his feet. The sun descending on the western horizon had turned golden yellow, and its dazzling rays fell on him obliquely. As the evening wind had picked up, the loose sleeves of his gown fluttered. He spread his hands over the crowd. The moment of anticipation gradually grew.

"Sisters of Israel, Daughters of Abraham," he cried: "From the very beginning, the transgressions about you and against you are countless. You carry the seeds of Israel in your womb for ten months – behold at the time of birth, if it is a girl, you are unclean for fourteen weeks. Why for a boy, it's only seven weeks. Why is a girl more of a pollution than a boy? Why is a baby boy worth five shekels, and a girl only three? If a father sells his boy as a slave, the boy gains freedom after six years, but for a girl, she is branded a slave forever. Why is she – the woman – worthless?" His speech gained a new tone, a new momentum.

"Sisters of Israel, the abominations against you are beyond narration. If a man rapes you, destroys your virginity, pride and honor, you are expected to marry the rapist. That's what the law says. Your father may gain compensation – bride money – from the rapist for damage of properties. In the law it says that if a pregnant woman is assaulted by an aggressor and upon losing the baby in miscarriage, the woman will not even receive an apology. The husband gets some shekels for property damage. If your husband is seen beaten up by an aggressor, and if you decide to save your husband by clutching on the aggressor's balls, alas, your hands will be cut off, that's what the statutes say.

"Adultery! A man having sexual intercourse with his neighbor's wife is adultery, but if he is having an affair with his daughter, there is no law against it.

"Men are free to visit a prostitute in spite of the commandments, but it is she, the prostitute, who is always the adulteress. A woman shall not talk to a stranger, it is commanded. She shall not walk in the streets without a man, must cover her head in public – it's a man's law, made for the stone-headed rebels in Sinai. If they cannot find the token of virginity or, even worse, if the husband has a jealousy about you, there is a law to take you to the village of your father and the men of the village shall stone you to death. Stoning to death, they do.

"A man can marry as many damsels as he pleases and divorce them at his whim – you have no pride, no honor, and no rights. In the law you are nothing but a piece of property.

"Daughters of Abraham, in the land of Israel, women are not even worth counting in the census. A vow taken by a man is binding, but that by a woman, can be nullified by a man, her father, or her husband. A woman has no voice in the witness stand, no inheritance in her father's property until there are no male heirs. How much more demeaning can it be?"

Presently, some women said, "Amen, Amen," but every woman in the crowd had teary eyes.

"Behold, Lot is still an honorable man. He offered to throw out his maiden daughters to be raped by the hooligans to save the honor of a man, a Levite, a visitor in his house. Lot still is an honorable man. Behold, daughters of Israel, I weep for you; my heart bleeds for you. Therefore, I say the law and the prophets are only up to John. This is the dawn of a new morning in Israel, where all humans are regarded equally. Everybody counts. The Kingdom of Heaven is upon us."

He paused for one short moment.

"Now, I shall stand with you in prayer to my Almighty Father."

The people stood up with their arms spread and waving, and their gazes fixed on the Galilean carpenter.

"Our Father who art in Heaven," Joshua cried out.

Five thousand voices chorused:

"Our Father, who art in heaven,

"Hallowed be thy Name, thy kingdom come . . ."

Joshua had spoken until after the sun had gone down. The multitudes started crowding around him, chanting, "Blessed is the son of God. Hail to our Messiah." The disciples made a strong circle around him to avoid stampede and suffocation. Men lit torches and made signs and announcements for people to disperse, but all in vain.

Joseph of Arimathea had been standing at the threshold of the crowd right from the beginning to hear his speech without missing one word. Elbowing through the crowd, the frail old man struggled to reach the place where Joshua was still standing. Joseph finally reached Joshua, collapsing onto his feet, weeping and pounding his chest. The old man said to Joshua, "I never thought, I would live to see this day. You are the Messiah. The one we were waiting for." Joshua lifted him up, kissed both of his cheeks, and held him closer to his chest. The old man sobbed with pleasure.

Another tall man, his head covered with a black shawl, also struggled to reach Joshua by stretching his hand from behind the rows of men. Joshua recognized him – Nicodemus. He reached out and pulled him close. "Rabbi," said Nicodemus, "I heard about your meeting here today. I am glad that I came. I will tell you, people will remember this speech until the end of times." He descended the hill, still his head covered with the shawl.

The night had fallen, but the mount glowed with the lights of hundreds of torches, and the air reverberated with the jubilation of the people who did not want to return to their homes. It was time past for dinner. Most everybody had brought dinner baskets, but they were reluctant to sit down and eat fearing that it would spoil the transcendental joy of the moment. Some came empty handed with no meals to eat or share.

Thomas suggested, "Let's all sit together and eat our meals, sharing with each other."

Peter liked the idea, "We all eat together with the rabbi," he was thrilled.

"Come on, I have wine to fill a thousand in my cellars, and some bread, too; maybe a few baskets of smoked fish," offered Joseph of Arimathea. Peter, Andrew and four other men followed the old man to pick up wine jars, bread, and fish from his house.

The disciples made announcements for dinner. Joshua's words still echoed on their minds, and they felt they were full; they all wanted to share their meal with the others, even if they didn't eat – more people to share, less people to eat. Wine, bread and fish were brought over. People were seated in rows of two facing each other, and they pulled out their food baskets and spread it out for others also to eat – a giant feast was in progress. All shared their food and drank with others until they were all filled, and still there was excess bread and fish.

That night, Thomas and Matthew were busy writing down the words Joshua had spoken. The words spoken were many, but that which were recorded were only a few.

**** **** ****

The news of the great *Sermon on the Mount* near Capernaum spread with lightning speed to the high circles of the Sanhedrin in Jerusalem. As usual, the Sadducees ignored it as "nonsense" spoken by the carpenter sage, but the Pharisees and scribes took it as a serious threat to their power.

It was the fifteenth year of the reign of Tiberius Caesar. The waves of unrest were felt in the highest echelon of the Roman government. Several detachments of soldiers were deployed to quell even the slightest revolt amongst the Jews with the most severe punishment of crucifixion. In public markets and hill tops, the decaying bodies of patriotic Jews being pecked at by vultures was not an uncommon sight.

Jerusalem was tense during the first week of Nisan. The nation of Israel was getting ready for the Passover celebrations. On the first night of the Passover celebration, the high priest Caiaphas called an extraordinary meeting of the Sanhedrin to be held on the second floor of the Hanna bazaar on the Mount of Olives at the private residence of Annas. Calling such a meeting was contrary to the tradition of holding any meetings of the Sanhedrin during Passover celebration, or on Sabbath for that matter, that too at night. They believed the matters to be discussed were of supreme importance to the prestige and survival of the Pharisees and the scribes, to the maintenance of peace and order in the nation, and to avoid even greater Roman wrath.

As the evening set in, the palace was guarded by temple police consisting of Jews only. All seventy-one members, including Joseph of Arimathea, Nicodemus from Bethany, Gamaliel from Sepphoris, Portha from Cana, Annas, Caiaphas, Rubin and Pediah from Jerusalem – members of the governing tribunal – were all present in the main hall of Annas' mansion. They all sat facing each other with Caiaphas presiding on the Moses seat.

The tall dark-skinned and gray-bearded Caiaphas, with the long, pointed nose wearing the ceremonial purple robe and the breast plate, called the meeting to order with a gesture of respect to his father-in-law, Annas.

"Many stories I have heard about this man called Joshua from Nazareth. I request to you, respected members of the Sanhedrin, to tell us what you know and what you have heard regarding the blasphemy spoken by this man," stated Caiaphas without an introduction. The members spoke one after the other in an orderly manner.

Meshelemiah from Capernaum spoke first, "This man's transgressions are many. The other day, amidst a gathering of over five thousand people, he convincingly stated that, "'The Law of Moses and the prophets are only up to John."

"John who?" Annas snared.

"The madman beheaded by Herod."

"Oh, yes," Annas agreed, "What exactly did this . . . this carpenter mean by that statement?"

Meshelemiah rejoined, "That the time of Moses and his laws are all over. He stated that the people of Israel are yearning for a new beginning."

There was a tumult of disgust in the group. "He cursed the Pharisees and scribes; called us a brood of vipers, hypocrites, clean on the outside and corrupt on the inside, filled with extortion and self-indulgences," stated Jehael from Accaron.

"He claims that he is the son of God," stated Joachim from Jerusalem. Many members shouted, "Blasphemy! blasphemy!"

Caiaphas raised his hands to bring the meeting to order.

Othniel from Bethel said, "Let my tongue not cleave to its roof. What he said about women . . ." Caiaphas covered his ears half way through his narrations.

"He called us 'whitewashed tombs,'" shrieked Sosthenes from Bethpage. Caiaphas rose to his feet with anger, his face contorted and his eyes red hot.

"Is it true that he also obstructed judgment by the elders?"

"Yes, Rabbi," answered Zabdiel from Nazareth. "He took out a harlot from the execution of the law."

"What else? Is it true that he showed miracles?" There was a tumult of noises but no clear answer. Caiaphas shivered with anger. He balanced his weight from one foot to the other, hitting his fist on the palm of his hand as if he was just about to throw a punch.

"Yes Rabbi," answered Mizzah from Cana. "His followers say that he cured the blind and took out evil spirits from people."

"Some say he even walked on water," added Maadia from Jerusalem.

"Followers! Followers for a carpenter?" screamed Caiaphas. "How many?"

Many in the group responded, "Yes, followers. Many followers. In one sermon in Capernaum there were over five thousand people in attendance," lamented Nathaniel.

"If this continues, soon most of Israel will be following him."

Enough said," shouted Caiaphas. "What do you think the prefect and Caesar are going to do? They will declare war on us, and thousands will die. We need peace. We need Romans. We need this mass dispersed." He pressed his shivering lips. Nobody spoke; there was silence.

Caiaphas declared, "It is better that one man die lest the Romans kill us all."

Nicodemus stood up and looked around graciously. "This man, Joshua, is no threat to us at all. He claims he is the son of God"

A few members snickered.

"He preaches about his Father in heaven, peace, hope, and some general things of that nature." Nathaniel scoffed it off.

"He says that his kingdom is not of this world. Instead, it is in heaven." Nicodemus said.

"Rabbi," cried Cosane from Bethlehem, pointing a finger to Nicodemus, "Are you a follower of the false prophet?"

"I am not a follower of Joshua, but there are many thousands who believe that he is the prophet."

"He is dangerous," bellowed Annas.

A few heads nodded in agreement.

Caiaphas' face clouded with doubt for a moment. He turned to Annas for clarification, *Prophet*, he thought to himself. "Remind me of what is written in the scrolls about the coming of the Messiah."

"The prophecy is that the Messiah would be born in Bethlehem of the house of David, and not in Nazareth as the son of a carpenter," Annas explained,

Most people laughed in ridicule. Joseph of Arimathea arose to his feet gently. "There are many who believe that he is the Messiah."

"You, too, are a believer in him?" demanded Caiaphas. Joseph did not answer the question but continued. "Respected members, let me ask you. Does our law judge a man before he has the opportunity to defend himself?"

Caiaphas rose to his feet majestically. His body convulsed. He swept to the center of the council, tore off his purple cloak and started screaming as if he was possessed. "I will not let this go any further. What other proof do you need? He is a blasphemer. He spoke against Moses, against the law. He is a trouble maker. He should die. Judgment he deserves, and judgment he will get."

They made plans to arrest Joshua and to bring him before Pontius Pilate at the earliest possible time.

**** **** ****

After the *sermon on the mount*, Joshua spent much of his time alone, meditating in the shade during the day and on the desert sands at night. There was a very clear and visible change in his countenance. He spoke little and ate only enough to sustain. Yet at other times, he spoke as if he had prepared his words and intended to deliver a specific message. At times, it appeared that he went into a trance, and at other times, as if a superior force was speaking through his lips, a transformation his disciples couldn't miss.

The disciples continued to talk amongst themselves. Thomas was convinced that the mission in Capernaum had come to a successful conclusion. *We need to know clearly what is in his mind – the next step,* Thomas thought. They called for a meeting. They all sat around for dinner that night. Joshua appeared gloomy and unusually downcast. His face appeared heavy and his eyelids swollen.

"Master, you haven't spoken to us in three days. It seems to me that you are avoiding us. "Tell us, please, what are you thinking. What is the next step?" said Thomas.

"We all did great works here in Capernaum," said Peter. "But it appears to me that we are at a standstill."

"The next step," Thomas said, "would be going to Jerusalem," bringing the subject to the forefront.

"But I would warn all of you, Jerusalem is no Capernaum," said Matthew. "That's where the prophets are lynched, men are crucified, and it's also where Pontius Pilate lives, and the Roman soldiers roam the city."

"We will not be received the way we were here," said Matthew soberly, "Jerusalem is all about power, soldiers, trade, wine and prostitutes. But it's also where the temple is."

After a moment of silence, the disciples looked to Joshua for an answer.

"Matthew," he said. "I know Jerusalem; I will go to Jerusalem, and I intent to speak at the temple. But I ask you: are you all ready to stay with me?" asked Joshua searching the faces of his disciples.

"Yes, I will," said Peter.

"Think it over; I will not compel any one of you to go with me. The road to Jerusalem is littered with thorns. This time the travel will be uphill and treacherous."

"I will go, too," declared Judas.

"I will . . . I will . . . ." said each of them until they had all committed.

In Galilee it was well known that Joshua had incited the wrath of the Sanhedrin, and the high priest wanted him alive rather than dead. The evening before they planned to leave for Jerusalem, Joshua sat alone on a rise, meditating behind the Synagogue.

Matthew had come with a message.

Matthew stood right in front of Joshua patiently, but the rabbi was in deep meditation, at times subtly moving his lips. Finally, Matthew broke the silence, "Master, Master," he called.

Joshua awoke as if from a deep sleep. He had never been interrupted during his meditation time. Matthew was uneasy, but soon Joshua put him at ease and asked, "What's the matter Matthew?"

"You have visitors from Nazareth. They want to see you."

"Who are they?" Joshua asked.

"Your mother and four others: The boy . . ." Matthew smiled, "he is a great kid, with never-ending questions."

Joshua spread out his palm and looked at the lines for a long minute without an answer.

Matthew was not sure what to make out of this silence, and he demanded uncomfortably, "What should I tell them, Master?"

"Matthew, please send in the boy?"

"Only the boy?"

"Yes, only the boy."

The boy ran to his father, jumped into his extended arms, sat in the laps hugging his chest and holding on to his beard. Joshua kissed the child many times and talked to him for a very long time. The boy came back rubbing his eyes with the back of his hands, and the rabbi went back to his prayers. Matthew watched the scene from a distance but he was not sure as to what they had talked about.

The boy who had run to his father with a red face returned to his mother with a bright face.

Within two days, Joshua and the disciples discreetly moved on to Judah and settled in the village of Ephraim to plan their next steps. A few days later, they came to Bethany, to the house of Mary and Martha, two sisters in their early thirties who lived in the house with their young brother Lazarus, a cripple with seizures.

Martha, the elder of the two, a woman with grace and good manners, immediately began preparing dinner for the guests. She baked bread, cut the meat, and stirred the pottage, while Mary, the younger, more beautiful sister with sparkling eyes and long curly hair, was seized with pleasure at the first site of the Galilean; she sat by his feet the entire evening. Soon Mary was moved with passion. Her face flushed, and her hands began to tremor ever so slightly. Her bosom throbbed, tensing the brassieres to break, and the nipples sprouted.

"Oh, my lord . . . Oh, my lord . . ." she said as she held Joshua's feet, washing them with her tears of joy and drying them with her hair. She opened a Lebanese alabaster jar that was filled with the precious perfume spikenard, anointed his hair and massaged his neck, limbs and feet. She sat by his feet again, holding onto his legs while listening intently to his every word. Martha was annoyed, the disciples were indignant, but Joshua was pleased.

Soon Martha's great uncle, old man Azarisch, smelled the boiling meat in the house next door and walked over to her home, limping and leaning on his tall shepherd's staff. The old man with weeping eyes, large, beaked, wrinkled nose and sparse white beard, was angry that he had not been invited to the feast.

He soon realized that the guest of honor, the Nazarene about whom he had heard many stories, was feasting in his dead brother's house.

"I want to see the impersonator, the false prophet," he demanded abruptly, pounding his staff on the floor. Martha welcomed him and offered him a drink and a seat.

The man tore off a large piece of bread and served a plate full of meat for himself in a hurry. He soaked the bread and meat in the mouth with wine, yapped it a few times, and swallowed with noise, closing his eyes. After a few cups of wine, the old man was more settled but still upset, and he began to interrupt Joshua's teaching.

"Hey, you," he said, pointing his finger at Joshua, "I heard that you preach about God and heaven to harlots, sinners, tax collectors, and all. Now, you are sitting on my dead brother's seat, drinking and merrymaking with women, tell me . . ."

Joshua answered him respectfully. "Elder, that is correct. I have not come to comfort the fit, but to console the sick."

"Hum," he said. It looked like the old man liked the answer. He smiled, showing the one remaining almond-shaped tooth. He drank a few more cups of wine, tried to get up from the seat, but fell to the floor. He made some meek noises. A while later he slowly crawled out of the house on all fours.

During and after the dinner, Joshua told many parables, but he was significantly preoccupied, and there was a hint of sorrow on his face. More than anyone else, Peter noted it.

After dinner, Joshua went alone to the backyard and sat deep in contemplation under a pear tree. Many scenes flashed back through his mind. The deserted palace of Akhenaton in Amarna; the last days of Cicero, the man who preached preparation of death yet fled at the moment of truth; the cup of hemlock near the lips of Socrates; the escape of Plato; the man Confucius treading from one village to the other; the experiences of Buddha; the teachings of Vyassa; and the last meditation of Sukannya.

That night he was restless and counted the watches of the night, heard the first rooster crow, the first birds sing, and watched the first gray in the east. He talked to himself, "I must travel to Jerusalem. I will speak to the Pharisees. They don't have to search for me; I will seek for them. It cannot be that a prophet should perish outside of Jerusalem." Fatigue caught up with him. He fell asleep against a rock, resting his face on his arms. The sun was high in the horizon when he finally awoke, still fatigued, and the crescent bags under his eyes swollen. He saw Peter and John sitting crouched, leaning against the tree, awaiting the master to rise. Joshua stood up, steadying himself on their shoulders. It was the second day of the festival in Jerusalem, and people were heading west towards the city to celebrate the Passover.

Judas was growing impatient. He had criticized Mary the previous night for wasting a full jar of expensive perfumed oil to anoint his master. The words his master spoke rang in his ears, "She is preparing for my burial." He regretted his choice to follow Joshua, who had angered all of the authorities, and was now distant and moody and speaking about his death and burial. He made a quick trip to the local Synagogue in Bethany and had some words with the Pharisees that evening.

As the day ripened, Joshua appeared detached and gloomy, but he instructed Peter to prepare a dinner for all twelve men and the seven women, his disciples, including Mary and Martha. Miraculously, Lazarus had not seized for the last two days, and even sat and ate some pottage that morning.

As the night fell, a cold wind swept from the west, followed by thunder, some lightning, and a quick downpour, one of the latter-day rains of early spring. Martha made a fire at the hearth. Mary lit the seven-wicker candle, and the disciples set the table for the dinner – fresh unleavened bread, goat meat, wine and almonds.

Joshua sat in the middle of the dinner carpet, leaning on a pillow, the others surrounding him also sat likewise. The normal aura of jubilation of a Passover dinner was not felt; instead, the air in the house was tense and foreboding. As the dinner progressed, Joshua looked around and addressed them. "Friends," the very first time he addressed them "friends" ever. All eyes were fixed on Joshua. The sad countenance of his face belied the pain in his heart. "My days are numbered. My hour is fast approaching," he said.

Everybody remained silent, barely breathing. Joshua's face turned tranquil. His voice was deep and soft. The words came out slowly, one by one.

"I shall suffer many things, condemned by the Pharisees, rejected by the elders, and ridiculed by the scribes. I am prepared for the scourging and persecution awaiting me." He closed his eyes for a moment. Nobody had ever seen him that tense.

"Friends, I am not bothered by the thought of torture, pain or fear of death. They can only mutilate my body, but cannot kill my spirit or touch my soul. I have known the joy of my life in this world; now I am ready to go to my Father's house. Death is the gateway to heaven, the eternal bliss."

"My going to Jerusalem is neither incidental nor not well thought of. It is my destiny. I shall carry the cross for all of your sakes. I warn you: all those who stay with me will also be chastised, ridiculed, and may even be crucified. You have listened to me for the past three years, I have said many things, but certainly I tell you, heaven and earth may pass. My voice could be silenced, but my words shall continue until the end of this earth."

The disciples were visibly shaken without exception, and Joshua could see the fear in their eyes. He could also hear the muffled sobs of the women.

"Because I do nothing for myself . . . " he paused for a while, and then his face glowed with delight and started talking as if he was in a trance. The words that followed were strong and powerful, said with absolute authority.

"You have heard my words, but they were the words of my Father in heaven speaking through me. You shall know the truth, and the truth shall make you free." Then he closed his eyes and went into a long minute of meditation. The disciples were confused. The women were weeping silently, and a few were even scared. Peter thought that his master had undergone some transfiguration in mind, and truly thought that God was speaking through him. The resolution and determination of his voice was beyond that of a man.

"I spoke many words, but I give you only one command – you love one another as I have loved you. Do not unto others that which you don't want to be done to yourself. Those are my final commands. I will not leave you orphans. I will remain with you in spirit. I will live in you, with you, and guide you."

The disciples reached out to each other and locked their hands together for combined strength.

"You shall go to every village," Joshua told them, "every house in Israel, knock on their doors and spread the words of the Kingdom of Heaven. Nurse the sick, assist the lame to walk, speak for the mute, see for the blind, and hear for the deaf. There shall be doors shut in your face, ablution waters poured on your head, and you will be spat on and beaten. You shall be hated because of my name. You shall be apprehended and chastised in my name. You shall be scourged. You shall be mutilated. You shall be killed. But remember, they cannot touch your spirit. But those who endure this treatment shall rise up to heaven and sit on the right side of my Father in heaven. Fear not those who kill your body, but fear those who kill your soul. Beware of those men in long cloaks holding the law in their hands, posing to be the agents of God, the hypocrites, the vipers that are able to kill your soul, corrupt your daughters and defile your children; beware of them."

Joshua paused for a while. His eyes beamed with light. His voice boomed with power.

"Friends, I have preached peace throughout my life. But think not that there would peace all over the world. The evil forces will rise most certainly. In my name there will be violence, there will be wars – son against father, daughter against mother, husband against wife. There will be division in the house, house against house, village against village, nation against nation. But remember my words: the reason for your creation is the preparation for the permanent salvation. Do your karma without fear or favor. Spread my words. He who loves his father or mother more than me is not worthy of me. Whosoever will follow after me, let him deny himself, take up the cross of your sufferings, your desperations and follow me. The Kingdom of Heaven is at hand." He again went into a long minute of silence and closed his eyes.

The disciples were confused and tearful. They had many questions to ask, but the words got stuck in their throats. Thomas, the skeptic amongst them, had the courage to break the silence. He believed that their master was getting ready to offer himself as a sacrifice. His voice trembled. but he managed to say, "Rabbi, I am saddened by your words. When I took the first step with you, I dreamt of a place where we all lived together in harmony, loving each other and supporting each other. For generations the nation of Israel has been waiting to see the Messiah. They missed it again. They keep on waiting. I believe I saw the Kingdom of Heaven before closing my eyes. Rabbi, tell me truly, is this the end of ages? The temple of Jerusalem . . ."

"Jerusalem," Joshua said, "is the hideout of thieves and marketers. They are blind to see the light of Heaven. They are deaf to hear the voice of wisdom. Those things you see in Jerusalem – the days will come in which not one stone shall remain on top of the other that shall not be smashed down," he declared with conviction.

"Rabbi, tell us when will these things all be, and what signs will there be?" Thomas asked.

Joshua's face turned sad. "The end will not come immediately, but it will be foretold. Nation will rise against nation, race against race, tribe against tribe: that will be the sign of the times. False prophets will spring like mushrooms, showing magic and miracles in my name. Son killing father, husband killing wife, parents killing babies: that will be the sign of times. Men and women eating maddening herbs, binging on alcohol, marauding around and killing people for pleasure – that will be the signs of times. As you have never seen before, the earth will shake, mountains will spew fire, oceans will rage, floods and droughts will follow one after the other – that is the sign of times. There will be famines, petulance and fearful sites, gluttony and lassitude will reign, men and women will swell like maggots – that is the sign of times. The just shall be suppressed, the unjust shall be exalted, and you will certainly be persecuted in my name – those are the signs of the beginning of the end."

After the prolonged discourses, Joshua went out again to sit in the moonlight away from the others.

Peter, Matthew and Thomas followed their master to the backyard. Thomas pleaded: "You must not travel to Jerusalem. Your life is in danger."

"Brothers, why didn't you listen to my preaching? Or was that like water poured on a bottle turned upside?"

Thomas was dissatisfied with the answer, "The light of your life is what we need. You are the torch to lead us the way. If you die . . ."

The scene of the Kurukshethra war, Krishna advising Arjuna quickly visited his mind: "I will tell you again. Death is a manifestation of God, just like birth."

Joshua continued staying out in the darkness leaning on the stone under the fig tree.

Much later in the night, the disciples assembled near the hearth in Mary's house. Joshua's words lingered in their minds. They all knew the end was near for them and for their master.

"He has made up his mind to go to Jerusalem," said Thomas ruefully.

"He is the Prince of Peace, and the government shall be upon his shoulders as Isaiah prophesized," said Peter.

"Brothers," addressed Matthew, who knew the scriptures much more than all the other disciples, "there cannot be any doubt in the prophecies. What we are witnessing now is what the nation of Israel has been waiting for all these years."

"Yes, like the prophets Micah, Jeremiah, Isaiah, and Daniel have said. Let the scriptures be fulfilled. Let our master enter Jerusalem tomorrow, riding a colt, in triumph, just as foretold by the great prophets," Thomas said.

It was the day of Sabbath. Well before sunrise, the disciples knocked on all the doors in Bethany, calling men and women to go to Jerusalem as a procession by the side of the Messiah. The men and women of Bethany, who had heard a great many things about Joshua, were enthralled to see the Prince of Peace and to walk with him by his side. Peter and Matthew were convinced that going to Jerusalem in small numbers would be dangerous, because the Pharisees were plotting to kill him. They believed, a great multitude must enter the city triumphantly, and their shouts should shake down the walls of the city like their great forefathers did in the city of Jericho. They themselves were ready with swords hidden under their gowns, accompanying the men who taught them to show the other cheek.

At the break of day, John and James brought a colt to the house. James threw his red cloak on the back of the young beast and made a saddle. Men and women who had traveled from and around Bethany began to arrive at Mary's house by the hundreds, waving branches of olives, their faces shining with joy and their eyes fearless and bright. Against the rising sun, the silvery olive leaves glinted like knife blades. Many of them carried palm leaves that looked like green spears shaking in the air. It seemed a parade worthy of a king.

From early morning onwards, Martha and Mary were busy by the feet of their master, preparing him for the procession. They clothed him in a new white robe with blue borders, anointed and perfumed his hair, and placed leather sandals on his feet.

As Joshua appeared at the threshold of the door, his face was calm and majestic, yet profound and unpredictable like the placid ocean before a storm. As he exited the house, the crowd rose to cheer him, fluttering the olive branches and palm leaves. They greeted him with tumultuous applause and stomped the ground with thunderous cheers. They cried out:

"Messiah, Messiah!"

"Savior of Israel! Savior of Israel!"

Men parted ways in front of the house. The colt was brought over and Joshua was seated on the saddle. Two men walked ahead of the procession, shouting:

"The king is coming!"

"The prince of peace!"

"The Messiah is coming!"

The twelve men walked immediately in front of the colt. A mass of humanity marched behind him, jubilant, shouting slogans, "Hosanna to the king."

But there was a group of young men, not more than six, already high on wine in a carnival spirit. Above the voice of the others they screamed, "Death to the Romans, death to the Pharisees."

Joshua was seen disturbed; he turned, looking to the direction where the shouting came from.

Thomas, in turn, approached the boisterous few men and admonished them and brought them under control quickly. The procession moved on in an orderly fashion.

Men and women joined the procession from the side roads and the alleys with the army of the Kingdom of Heaven.

A woman from a rooftop by the roadside cried, "Blessed is the womb that bore you." Another holding her breast shouted, "Blessed are the breasts that nursed you." Some women beat their breasts and cried with tears saying, "Prophet."

"You are the prophet."

"Save us to the Kingdom of Heaven."

Then an older man with heavy bones and hair as coarse as bristle ran towards Joshua holding his hands up towards the sky and prostrated himself in front of the colt. Then he rose with mud on his face, "I never thought I would live to see this day. You are the Messiah on the colt."

"Oh, Abraham, Isaac, Jacob; I can die today a happy man, for I have seen what the prophets foretold."

"I can die today." He ran to the wilderness like a man possessed.

The group swelled by the minute. A great multitude followed him: women with their heads covered, men with sunken bony faces, prostitutes in tattered clothes, blind men and women lead by the others, the paralyzed carried on litters, and the lepers in wicker baskets, old bent disheveled men shading their eyes with trembling hands, children shouting with joy of a celebration, all climbing up to Jerusalem with renewed enthusiasm.

Presently, Peter walked past the crowd and turned around to get a look at the crowd as a whole. He liked what he saw and breathed a sigh of satisfaction thinking, *this is what I hoped for. I can die today.*

After two hours of uphill trudging, as the sun was high and beating down, the shimmering temple on the hill was in view with many figures moving and many voices colliding. Joshua rode forward, his eyes fixed on the temple amidst the many towers within the mighty city gate. The large Roman standard with the double-headed eagle fluttered high from the turrets of the Antonio's tower on the right, way above the small white temple flag on the apex of the temple dome.

"See the Roman flags; Pontius Pilate is in town," one mother murmured in her child's ears.

The city where God tested Abraham, Joshua ruminated, *the city where temples were built, destroyed and rebuilt, the city where prophets are born are killed.* It was into that city that the man with a white tunic and leather sandals rode with his words as the sole weapon, to challenge all those that existed and to declare a new commandment of the Kingdom of Heaven.

The suburban hills and the temple premises were jammed with the caravans from afar who had come with wares and merchandise hoping for a great season. The temple grounds were filled with small little shops and stalls selling wine and broiled meat. Men and women who had gone far in wine were sauntering, swaying and at times falling to the ground. The area surrounding the Hulda Gate was crowded with doves, lambs and oxen in the thousands. The sacrificial animals and birds were ready to spill their blood for the pleasure of Yahweh.

The temple grounds had been transformed into a flea market, filled with noisy vendors yelling and bargaining, and money changers giving out temple coins for a killing profit, amidst the scantily clad, red-lipped harlots sprawling their way.

The procession of a thousand or more people entered the eastern grounds of the temple facing the Solomon's gate. The temple sacrifices were in progress. Dark smoke rose up in great swirls above the temple, and the smell of burnt meat sank to the ground. The people from Bethel were greatly energized and much animated at the very sight of the temple, the temple for which Jews lived their lives, fought their wars and shed their blood. They shouted their slogans even louder.

"Hosanna to the Prince of Peace. Hosanna to the Messiah. Hosanna to the Savior," the people chanted.

Presently, there was a great crowd and commotion at the north end of the temple. The high priest Caiaphas had just arrived, and he was conducting the ritual ablution at the Israeli pool. Roman police as well as Jewish temple police parted ways in the crowd for the high priest to pass.

Joshua and the crowd watched the scene from a distance. Eight men carried Caiaphas on a litter gilded in gold and surrounded with silk curtains to the golden gate. Inside the litter sat the tall, dark-skinned man with his head shaved like an ostrich egg. Two young ladies with red lips sat beside him looking after his well-being. The litter gently tilted side-to-side with the ups and downs of the footsteps of the soldiers. As the litter was laid on the ground, the temple soldiers conducted the scarlet-clad high priest with silken cassock and emerald-laden crown to go up the steps to the temple.

Roman soldiers waited around the temple grounds in pairs, showing off their red-feather, flowing helmets, and glittering brasses, impressing visitors, disciplining traders and picking up girls, and having a wonderful time. A few frail, black-robed men plodded the upper grounds of the temple, going from one place to the other, wailing aloud and prattling about the lost glories of Jerusalem, not even noticing the little copper coins thrown at them by the tourists.

Joshua stood there for several minutes, gazing at the tumult of the temple; his lips moved as he talked to himself. "When God's house is protected by armies, then you know its dissolution is near. Matthew and Phillip noted the subtle whispers on their master's lips. They put their ears close up to his lips to hear him amidst the noises."

"This will not last forever. God's fire is coming up on Jerusalem. It will be ashes to ashes," Joshua said, pointing at the temple on the high grounds.

Suddenly, Joshua's mood turned serious, his face darkened, and his eyes burned like charcoal. The voices in his mind clashed: *be calm, don't be angered*, echoed Buddha; *don't be afraid, do your karma*, admonished Krishna. He came to a resolve. He dismounted the colt, separated from the disciples, and moved rapidly towards the golden gate, in long steps, now speaking quietly to himself. "The day will come when not even one stone shall be left upon another." The disciples became frantic. To avoid the fanfare of a commotion, they also followed the rabbi to the upper grounds of the temple.

Joshua raced to the marble stairs two steps at a pace to the Court of Gentiles. What he found there was even worse. Very close to the altar where sacrifices were going on, it was nothing but a boisterous marketplace, throngs of people who were drunk, shouting and shoving each other, while harlots negotiating prizes, wiggling their pointed breasts and parting the ways through the crowd.

From the moment the procession from Bethel had entered the temple grounds, a husky Roman soldier, wielding a spear, had been closing, watching and following the movements of Joshua.

Joshua elbowed his way into the most crowded Royal Stoa where the money changers were converting gold, silver and copper into the temple coins. "Yes, at this point, this is my karma," he said to himself.

"Out! Out!" he cried, as he lifted and overturned the tables of the money changers with one hand. He chased out the moneylenders and the vendors with his cane swinging crisscross in the air. He cast out those who bought and sold doves and lambs, kicking off their seats. Silver and copper coins jingled and spilled on the ground. Doves flew into the skies, lambs brayed, running in circles, and some ran off into other shops.

A whistle blew. The temple police converged onto him like ants to a piece of fresh meat.

"On whose authority are you doing these things?" a Pharisees shouted, accompanied by two policemen.

Joshua turned around majestically. "This is my Father's house, a house of prayer," he said. "You have turned it into a den of thieves."

"On whose authority are you . . .?" A Roman soldier kicked him in the groin.

Joshua fell to ground writhing in agony.

Soon, Andrew, James, John and Phillip and others enveloped him from the police attacks, but the hefty soldier had pinned Joshua to the floor face down, holding onto his hair, and his boots pressed against his neck like a sacrificial animal was held before cut. Then a bugle sounded an alarm note. The noises of Roman boots from distance were converging to the spot in a hurry. Mighty Peter, who was in the lower grounds at that moment, pushed his way up through the Hulda Gate three steps at a pace shouting, "Master, get out! The big army is on the way."

Joshua was not even able to breathe. His mouth filled with blood. Soon the disciples came to life. Eleven of them overcame the soldiers, lifted Joshua from the ground and flung him to the big man. Peter, who caught him in the air, covered him with his clock, swept down the Hulda Gate, and disappeared into the ground. The disciples ran, but the Roman centurion seized Judas by his leg and dragged him on his face to the Court of Gentiles. They held him to the ground, wringing his neck with cracks. Judas's skinned face was weeping blood.

"Who is your leader?" the centurion shouted. Judas was unable to speak. "Is he the carpenter from Galilee?" inquired Caiaphas, who came to the scene momentarily.

"Yes," replied Judas.

"Can you identify him?"

"Yes."

"Take him in," commanded Caiaphas.

It was about two hours after the sunset; the silhouette of the temple buildings had long dissolved in the darkness of the night sky, the tumult of the Passover revelry had settled, and the crowd had disappeared. To the east of the temple beyond the Kildron Valley, on the southern slope of the Mount of Olives, in the Garden of Gethsemane, some twelve men had assembled, covertly, noiselessly with a heavy feeling of foreboding.

Eleven of them, alarmed and mystified, swathed in heavy cloaks, sat crouched in gloomy silence under an old, bent olive tree, while Joshua, detached from the crowd, was in deep meditation leaning against a rock. The men were all hungry and fatigued, as they had not taken a drink since the early morning procession from Bethel.

By the second watch of the night, a few of the men had slumped to the ground in sleep, but the rest were vigilantly watching for noises or people approaching them? Defying notice by the temple police, they had not even made a fire for the night.

"What happened to Judas?" Peter whispered to Thomas?

"They took him in and must be interrogating now," he said.

With a panic Peter rose to his feet, holding on to a low-lying tree branch. In the distance he saw three specks of light – shaded lamps – moving towards them. Matthew and Peter also rose to their feet, keenly watching the specks of light. Soon, in the dim yellow light that fell to the ground in circles, leg movements of men were discerned. After a few minutes the lamp and men disappeared in the Kildron Valley.

Several tense moments passed by. "They are not Roman soldiers. I did not see any high boots," said Thomas with relief.

"Right, I did not hear the crunching of the sand either," said Philip.

"What is next," Thomas asked.

"Let the Rabbi wake up. We have listened to him so far. Let him say what is next," said Peter.

The gloomy silence continued and they once again sank to the ground.

What have I come about after following this man, thought Thomas to himself. *I had a good enough life, a family and a job. Now I am a fugitive on the run, but then again I believe in what he says.'* Such thoughts debated in the minds of the men like the protagonist and antagonist of a Greek drama.

Some time passed. Peter again rose to his feet, cocking his ears and listening to the approaching crunching noises.

"I hear footsteps," he murmured. He gasped for breath and intuitively felt for the hilt of the sword under his mantles. Thomas knew that Caiaphas' police would be there at any moment. He squeezed his pounding temple between his hands. A cold sweat poured over his body. His cloak stuck to his body with the wet of his sweat. With his heart in his mouth, Thomas whispered through his teeth into the ears of Peter, "They will be here any minute. What shall we do?"

Joshua noticed a subdued commotion amongst his men. He rose and was on his way to the rest of the men when Peter went to summon him.

In the dim lantern light, they soon saw men walking up the mount towards them, emerging from the valley in close proximity.

In no time the men from the temple were on their faces, arrayed in a semi-circle, legs apart, chins thrusting and lanterns held high searching their faces. From their attire it was obvious that one of them, a man of about sixty with a beard, skullcap and long gown, was a Pharisee. The other six were temple police. But there was another man a few paces behind, his head covered with a black cloak.

Searching the faces of all, one after the other, the Pharisee finally rested his gaze on Peter, who was standing tall and broad, almost shielding Joshua.

"Who amongst you is the carpenter from Nazareth?" he asked calmly.

Joshua made a slight movement to take a half step forward, but Peter's hand came across him.

"The troublemaker, the carpenter," shouted the head of the police.

Presently, a wailing, incoherent guttural noise was heard from the man behind with his head covered. He quickly leapt forward, grasped Joshua by the shoulder and cried in a shrieking voice of high lamentation, "Rabbi, Rabbi." He kissed him on both cheeks and quickly withdrew to the darkness behind. Instantly, the two policemen laid their hands on Joshua. Peter instantly drew the sword and swung, aiming for the neck of a policeman. The man reflexively jolted out of the blade's path, but the saber sliced his ear.

Joshua came to the forefront. He turned calmly towards the Pharisee, stretching his arms in submission he said, "I AM. I'm the one you are looking for."

The policemen were still trying to subdue Peter, but the big fisherman just slid them off. The Pharisee cried, "Leave him. We have the man." Then they laid their hands on Joshua.

-The End-

Dr. Theckedath Mathew

Born to an Orthodox Christian family in a Hindu culture, Dr. Theckedath Mathew secured several postdoctoral diplomas in Western Medicine and a doctorate in Eastern Philosophy. As a cardiologist, he has lived and practiced in four continents of the world, which gave him the unique privilege of mending the hearts and touching the souls of several thousand fellow human beings. Author of the "Treasures of the Heart", a nonfiction medical book. He is also a teacher, historian, public speaker, and television commentator. Although his profession involves fixing the broken heart, it was his passion to comfort the soul that inspired him to write "Joshua: The Odyssey of an Ordinary Man".

www.ingramcontent.com/pod-product-compliance
Lightning Source LLC
Chambersburg PA
CBHW020454020726
47493CB00001B/29